Ingo Schulze

NEW LIVES

Ingo Schulze, born in Dresden in 1962, studied classical philology at the University of Jena. His first book, *33 Moments of Happiness*, won two German literary awards, the prestigious Alfred Döblin Prize and the Ernst Willner Prize for Literature. He lives in Berlin.

ALSO BY INGO SCHULZE

33 Moments of Happiness

Simple Stories

NEW LIVES

The Youth of Enrico Türmer
in Letters and Prose
Edited and with Commentary
and Foreword by

Ingo Schulze

Translated from the German by John E. Woods

VINTAGE BOOKS
A Division of Random House, Inc.
New York

FIRST VINTAGE BOOKS EDITION, OCTOBER 2009

Translation copyright © 2008 by Alfred A. Knopf,
a division of Random House, Inc.

The Library of Congress has cataloged the Knopf edition as follows:
Schulze, Ingo.
[Neue Leben. English]
New lives : the youth of Enrico Türmer in letters and prose /
edited and with commentary and foreword by Ingo Schulze ; translated from the
German by John E. Woods.—1st American ed.
p. cm.
Originally published: Berlin: Berlin Verlag, 2005.
I. Title.
PT2680.U453N4813 2008
833'.92—dc22
2008019615

Vintage ISBN: 978-0-307-27798-5

www.vintagebooks.com

Printed in the United States of America
10 9 8 7 6 5 4 3 2 1

For Christa

For Natalia

For Clara

For Franziska

Contents

Foreword

SOME SEVEN YEARS AGO, while casting about for the stuff of a novel, I began to collect material on German entrepreneurs. Heinrich Türmer aroused my interest because within just a few years, he turned a newspaper into a small empire and brought the entire region along the border between Thuringia and Saxony under his influence. The collapse of his widely diversified enterprise was both unforeseen and sensational. As 1997 turned into 1998, debtors and tax collectors found themselves gazing at open doors and empty coffers. Türmer had fled to avoid prosecution. Others were left to pay the price of his speculations. The consequences are still being felt throughout the region.

During my research I stumbled on many extraordinary and unusual occurrences. One modest detail, however, led me to a discovery that could not have astonished me more.

Türmer's first name was originally Enrico, and it was not until midyear 1990 that he began using the German form, Heinrich. The fact is, however, that I knew an Enrico Türmer who had been born and raised in Dresden. He was the brother of Vera Türmer—a friend with whom I had lost all contact after she left for the West—and also a schoolmate, although in a different class. I found it hard to believe that the overweight, elegantly dressed executive in newspaper photos could be the unremarkable Enrico with whom I had played soccer and sung in the choir.

I was even more surprised when my search under the keyword Türmer turned up a handsomely bound edition of short stories (Göttingen, 1998). I presume its publication could not have been possible without financial backing from the author. The scattered reviews were without exception derogatory. Rightly so. Were it not for the bitter aftertaste of his flight, one might respect Türmer's attempt to give a literary hue to the workaday world of the entrepreneur, with all its worries, pressures, and joys. In his foreword Türmer praises the world of work as "the promised land of tomorrow's literature."

My attempts to establish contact with Heinrich Türmer through his publisher met with no success. I did, however, receive a reply from Vera Barakat-Türmer. She even encouraged me in my intention of using her brother's life as the basis for a novel. In a selfless and generous gesture, Vera Barakat-Türmer placed at my disposal all the papers her brother had already transferred to her care in 1990, thereby preventing the court from seizing them. And now, or so I hoped, I would be able to trace Türmer's career to at least the initial phase of his entrepreneurship.

There were five dusty shoeboxes stuffed with diaries, letters, memos, and fragments of fictional prose—along with receipts, train tickets, shopping lists, and the like. Most of what Türmer had put to paper between 1978 and 1990—as a schoolboy in Dresden, a soldier in Oranienburg, a student in Jena, and a man of the theater in Altenburg—proved, however, to be of no use for my purposes. The juvenile tone was barely tolerable. Every sentence Türmer wrote, even in his letters—or so it seemed to me—kept one eye cast on an imaginary audience. Of telltale significance is the fact that he always made carbon copies of his own letters, but only very rarely kept those addressed to him.

A growing aversion to the figure of Türmer now threatened to jeopardize my plans, when I finally struck it rich.

Before me lay the letters to Nicoletta Hansen. Their quality led me to doubt Türmer's authorship, but I sought in vain for any validation of my suspicions in the handwriting.

Among the letters to Nicoletta—at irregular intervals but from the same period, the first six months of 1990—were others addressed to Johann Ziehlke, a friend since boyhood. As in his correspondence with Nicoletta, here too Türmer appeared to have succeeded in ways that escaped him in his attempts at literary prose.

In response to my request, Vera Barakat-Türmer managed to persuade both Nicoletta Hansen and Johann Ziehlke to hand over the entire original correspondence for my personal inspection. In addition to this, Vera Barakat-Türmer provided me with thirteen of her brother's letters addressed to her.

Once I had put the letters to all three addressees in chronological order (from January 6 to July 11, 1990) and read them as a whole, there unfolded before me a panorama of a period when everything in Türmer's life—and not just his—stood in the balance.

I read about a man of the theater who becomes a newspaper editor, about a failed writer who becomes a lucky entrepreneur. I read about a schoolboy whose longing for fame proves to be a curse; about a soldier who manages to avoid an attack on Poland, but not an attack by his comrades; about a student who falls in love with an actress; about a fence-straddler who becomes a hero against his will. I read about demonstrations and the first steps westward; I read about a brother who cannot live without his sister; I read about illness and exorcism—in a word, I read a novel.

And I decided to set aside my own plans for a novel and devote all my energies to publishing these letters.

To anticipate the question: Both the search for a publisher and discussions with the interested parties lasted several years.

It was not always possible to obtain the consent of all parties or to comply with their provisos. Almost everyone who came under Türmer's gaze has learned how biased, indeed how false and malicious, his representations can sometimes be. Nor was the author of these remarks spared the experience of finding his image distorted in Türmer's funhouse mirror.

My special thanks go to the actress Michaela von Barrista-Fürst and her son, Robert Fürst, with whom Türmer lived at the time. Without their understanding and magnanimity the project would have been doomed to failure. Elisabeth Türmer hesitated for some time to give her consent—after all, publication will not cast her son in the most favorable light. That she finally did agree merits acknowledgment. Likewise his schoolchum Johann Ziehlke, who later studied theology, had to jump over his own shadow to give his consent. Türmer's flight was for him—as his confidant and chief executive—not merely a betrayal of friendship, it also brought with it major legal and financial difficulties for him and his family. What few deletions he requested were perfectly acceptable and insignificant in terms of the larger context.

At times consent was obtained only on the condition that a counterposition be included. I am very pleased that Marion and Jörg Schröder, his former newspaper colleagues, agreed to such a compromise. Last but not least, I would like to thank Nicoletta Hansen, who had severed her relationship with Türmer by 1995. In some instances such consent is lacking—as, for example, in the case of Dr. Clemens von Barrista—when people's whereabouts could not be established.

As to the appendix and notes, I would like to state the following:

Twenty of the letters to Nicoletta Hansen were written on the reverse side of old manuscripts. These manuscripts are—and Türmer himself was the first to recognize this—mediocre at best, as well as fragmentary and incomplete. They are included in an appendix in order here and there to explicate matters excluded from or merely implied in the letters.

The footnotes are meant to facilitate the reading experience. What may seem superfluous to some will be greeted with thanks by other, particularly younger, readers. I have refrained from comment whenever circumstances are explained in some later context.

The attentive reader will not fail to notice that in writing his letters Türmer describes the same incident in very different versions depending on his addressee. It is not the editor's task to assess the implications of this.

In response to my astonishment at Türmer's almost manic obsession for self-revelation, Vera Barakat-Türmer offered the following explanation: "I always wondered why Enrico had such a great need to attach himself to people and open his heart to them. In every phase of his life there was someone whom he admired unconditionally and to whom he was almost slavishly devoted."

Ingo Schulze
Berlin, July 2005

Foreword to the American Edition

To both my astonishment and delight, I have become aware that Enrico Türmer's story in letters and prose has met with lively interest outside of Germany, a testimony to the fact that a book can be addressed to national, indeed regional, concerns and still speak to the core of human experience.

Over the last year speculation about Türmer has run riot, and has remained speculation.

There is nothing more to be said now about Türmer's whereabouts than was the case when *New Lives* was first published in October 2005. We know no more about it than we do about his state of health.

In the meantime, however, Türmer has become an author of literary interest to German readers and, with uncustomary swiftness, his slight volume a topic of academic research. This has brought me praise and recognition as a publisher, and also criticism that in my foreword I ranked Türmer's prose as "mediocre at best." Certainly that evaluation can now no longer be advanced. Nonetheless I prefer to maintain a critical skepticism in regard to the author of the letters and prose works presented here.

The American edition has been supplemented with a few additional notes.

I would like to express my heartfelt thanks to John E. Woods, my friend and excellent translator, for what has been an especially stimulating cooperative effort. Last and not least, my thanks to my American publisher for a generous and conscientious reception of this book.

I.S.
New Year's Day 2008

Editorial Note

Most of the letters are handwritten, a smaller number were typed, the last ones on a computer.

With few exceptions T. always kept a carbon copy or printout. Wherever there was both an original and a copy, only significant changes are noted, scratch-outs for instance. Words underlined by T. are set here in italics.

Matters are somewhat less transparent with regard to the small body of thirteen letters to Vera Türmer. Only three of the letters sent to Beirut have survived, all in the form of copies. The two faxed letters no longer exist as received letters. The final letter was never sent.

Errors in grammar and spelling have been corrected without remark, although both regionalisms and Türmer's own idiosyncrasies were taken into consideration.

I.S.

THE LETTERS OF

Enrico Türmer

[To Vera][1]

. . . like that?" Instead of trotting along behind us as usual so that he could demand a reward for every step he took, Robert bounded ahead like a puppy. We had to cross a hollow, the snow had a bluish sparkle and came up to our calves. Suddenly Robert gave a yell and started up the opposite slope. The moldy soil beneath the snow had not frozen. Michaela and I were running now too. When we stopped there was only the white field up ahead and grayish pink sky above us. We kept climbing, crossed a dirt road, and made straight for the woods. The wind swept the snow from the winter planting. I had to work hard not to be left behind. But the two of them didn't turn back at the edge of the woods as we had agreed, but entered it. And so I also followed the sign pointing to Silver Lake.

The pond was frozen over. Before I could say anything Robert was skidding across the ice, with Michaela right behind. Robert, who is very proud that his voice is breaking, crowed something that I didn't understand. Michaela shouted that I was chicken. But I didn't want to risk it and stayed onshore. The snow hid most of the trash lying around, but there was a toy horse jutting up out of it. I was just bending down when I heard my name, turned around—and something struck me in the eye. It burned like hell.

I couldn't see anything. Michaela thought I was putting on a show. It was snow, she shouted, just snow, a snowball!

It took me a couple of seconds to pull myself together. I was happy to feel Robert take my hand and begin to lead me. Not until that moment did I finally seem to realize that your letter wasn't a dream, but that I had

1. Two pages are missing; this page is numbered "3" at the top. It was possible to reconstruct the date.

actually received it and that it was in my breast pocket. Yes, it was as if I had started to breathe again only now.

Plodding along behind us, Michaela told me not to carry on so. She probably thought I was going to cry. She thinks I'm a hypochondriac, even a malingerer, and was afraid I was just looking for some new excuse for calling in sick again.

She panicked in the middle of the field when a mutt from the village came racing toward us. He was barking and jumping around like crazy, but I was able to quickly quiet him down. Then I couldn't get rid of him. The mangy animal escorted us all the way to the road leading downhill into town. Robert waved, and right away a car stopped. The woman sat ramrod straight behind the wheel and gave me a nod in the rearview mirror. The throbbing pain in my eye felt like my heart pounding inside my head. But the pain, or so it seemed to me, was something external, not anything that could hurt me, anything that could upset me, no matter what happened with my eye—because I have you!

At the entrance to the polyclinic I ran right into Dr. Weiss, the physician who usually attests that I'm too sick to work. "You don't lose an eye that easily," he said, grabbing me by the shoulder. He told me that I normally wouldn't find anyone here at this time on a Friday, and that I should hold still—a doctor's a doctor. "Let's have a look," he ordered, and turned me to the light. People going in and out shoved past us, I blinked into the fluorescent fixture. "Just a little vein," he muttered, "just a burst vein. Nothing more than that!" Weiss left me standing there on the threshold as if he regretted he had even bothered with me. And called back that there was no need to be a crybaby, handing Michaela her triumph. By then it didn't even hurt anymore.

The snow has already thawed again. The grass under the clotheslines looks like muck garnished with spinach. I have to drive Michaela to her performance. How easy everything is when I can think of you.

Love,
Your Heinrich[1]

---

1. Enrico always called himself Heinrich when dealing with his sister.

Dearest Verotchka,

I've been going out every day, never for less than an hour. Besides which I'm responsible for shopping and cooking and now outshine Robert's school cafeteria food, which is no great feat. Every evening Robert is granted his wish for the next day's noon meal. Today I gave pancakes a try. And what do you know, Michaela ate up all the leftovers. Her cookbooks are the only thing I read these days.

I've already had to write Mamus[1] twice this week. The second letter was necessary because Michaela had phoned[2] her to ask whether she'd heard about my decision.[3]

We are not dealing here with trivialities, this is about the betrayal of art—betrayal of it, which means of Michaela, of our friends, of life itself, so that my response to her is always that I'm not the deserter, art is. Of course, she doesn't accept that.[4]

I was in the "editorial office" for the first time yesterday afternoon. The building, which belongs to Georg, who is one of the two founders of the paper, is on Frauen Gasse, about three hundred yards behind the post office. You think you've arrived at the end of the world. But once you've passed through the eye of the needle—the ruins of a one-story building and a tilted wall—the world turns more hospitable again. Georg's house is in the middle of a garden, a country home *en miniature*. The garden gate is arched over by a rotting wooden structure, a rose lattice. The bell could wake the dead.

"You've actually come," he said. The vestibule was filled with all sorts of garden tools and quite a few bicycles.

Turning left, opposite the stairs, you first enter a windowless antechamber and then a small room with a floor of wide planks and a beamed ceiling that I can touch with my outstretched arm. A table and chairs take up almost the whole room. It smelled of furniture polish and coffee. When seated I'm taller than Georg, whose short, skewed upper

---

1. The nickname both brother and sister called their mother.

2. There was no phone either in T.'s and Michaela's apartment or at his mother's home in Dresden. His mother could be reached only at Friedrichstadt Hospital, where she worked as a surgical nurse.

3. T. had quit his job at the theater in early January.

4. This same cryptic statement is repeated in later letters in different versions and in greater detail.

body squats atop endlessly long legs. The whole time he talked about plans for the newspaper he stared at his folded hands. Whenever he paused, his mouth vanished into his beard. Then he would glance up at me as if checking the effect of his words. I was uncertain how to address him—at our first meeting we had used formal pronouns with each other.

There are various postal scales on the windowsills. The glass of the panes is old, distorting the view to the garden. You only have to move your head a little and trees shrink to bushes or shoot up sky high.

Later we climbed up behind the house, the garden rises in several terraces. When I thought we would have to turn back, Georg made an opening in the thicket and began walking up a steep footpath. I had trouble following him. Then a marvelous view: the town lay at our feet under a lilac sky, the hill with its castle to our right, Barbarossa's Red Tips to our left.[1] There was something agreeably unfamiliar about it all, it even felt like I was looking at the theater for the first time.

I inhaled the cold air and the smell of moldy soil and felt very glad that from now on I'll be able to enjoy the view whenever I want.

Jörg, my other boss, had arrived in the meantime and made tea. He's that same little bit shorter than Georg is taller than I. Jörg formulates his sentences so that they're ready to be set in print. He seems to have his doubts about me. He never let me out of his sight and responded to everything I said with a slightly mocking smile. But I won't let that scare me.

Georg and Jörg want to pay me the same salary they make, which means I'd earn two thousand net a month, almost three times my wages as a dramaturge. They've given up trying to get money out of the New Forum.[2] The main thing is that I don't have to go to the theater anymore. I was falling apart there. There's no place more boring!

A little before six o'clock Georg invited us to a light supper. His wife, Franka, and his three sons had already gathered round the table. As we sat down there was a sudden silence, I automatically expected someone to say grace. But it didn't happen.

I'm now reading newspapers. On the first page of the *ND*[3] is a photo-

---

1. Altenburg's hallmark. All that is left of the convent founded during the reign of Kaiser Friedrich Barbarossa are two brick steeples that are said to symbolize the tips of the kaiser's red beard.

2. Their original idea was for the paper to be the New Forum's weekly and for it to be financed by the Citizens' Movement.

3. *Neues Deutschland.*

graph of Havel.[1] He changed professions just in time. Whereas Noriega's picture looks like a mug shot.[2] Some soldiers in Gleina went on strike for a few days.[3] They demanded a new military code. Even an army prosecutor was sent in. But they refused to be cowed. And now, so I read, there actually is a new military code.

I think about you all the time.

Your Heinrich

[Sunday, Jan. 14, '90]

Verotchka,

Your letter has been lying here in the kitchen, on top of the fridge, since yesterday. Michaela brought the mail in, so the mailbox was empty when I took a look. Just now, right after breakfast, I suddenly recognized your handwriting on an envelope.

Now that the date is set and you've booked your flight . . . for the last few days I've been feeling stronger than I have for a long time. I was even a match for Jörg, who's like a fox lying in ambush. But it won't be long now and you'll be so far away . . . oh my, I'm sounding like Mamus. Does she even know anything about it?

I have no idea what Beirut is like, but I can't understand why Nicola[4] doesn't want to bring his mother to Berlin instead? And how much business can there be amid all that rubble and desolation?

I'm frightened for you—which is also egoistic of me. I won't be able to help you. I've got two thousand marks in my account. Do you need it? How much is that? Three hundred West marks?

I've got plenty of time to give you, however. I'm living under some kind of spell, I'm awake at four or five at the latest. Even though I rarely

1. Václav Havel's first foreign trip as president of Czechoslovakia took him to the GDR, then to Munich.

2. U.S. troops took over Panama on Dec. 24, 1989. President Noriega, a former CIA agent, sought asylum in the Vatican embassy, which he then left on Jan. 3, 1990. He was later tried on charges of drug smuggling.

3. Gleina, south of Altenburg, had a large radar station for the National People's Army.

4. Nicola Barakat, Vera Türmer's husband since January 1989, a Lebanese. He ran a fabric shop in West Berlin where V. T. worked part-time. Toward the end of 1989 he visited his mother in Beirut. He came up with the idea of reopening his parents' business in Beirut. V. T. followed him then in late January.

go to bed before midnight. And yet I'm not the least bit tired, not even in the afternoon. When I get bored with brooding, I thumb through the dictionary. It's amazing how many verbs and adjectives we know without ever using them.

I called Johann in the middle of the week to tell him I had quit the theater and am joining the crew of a start-up newspaper. He was extremely distant and brusque. And now I get a letter that could have been dictated by Michaela. I never used to read newspapers, so why was I trying to avoid these new artistic challenges (and he used that very phrase!). And went on like that for four pages. What a stranger he's become.

What you wrote about this nobleman sounds really promising. If in fact he does want to come to Altenburg, you can give him my address, and our editorial office will soon have a telephone.

Verotchka, if I'm not going to be able to see you, at least write and tell me about what you're doing, about taking care of final details, anything! There is no one else who I can count on.

Your Heinrich

Thursday, Jan. 18, '90

Dear Jo,

I got your letter and read it, but I simply don't have the desire or the energy to argue with you. I would just repeat myself anyway. Wait a few months, and then we won't even need to talk about all this anymore.

I take short walks, read newspapers, and cook our noon meal. I suddenly have so much time that I don't know what to do with myself.

Yesterday I even attended a meeting of the New Forum, I must admit not quite voluntarily. Rudolph Franck, who's called the "Prophet" because of his gray cotton-candy beard, asked me to come along. I owe my job at the paper to him, he initiated things and put in a good word for me. It's still a mystery to me what he thought my attendance would contribute. I probably disappointed him.

Jörg thinks there's a rumor—no, rumor is too strong, more like a whisper—that something is not quite kosher about people (like me) who couldn't stop spouting off last fall, but then vanished from one day to the next. I'm afraid it's Jörg himself who's spreading this stuff. It would be just like him.

There were a few hundred people in the hall. I was about to take a seat when I heard my name from behind me. I didn't know the man—brown eyes, average height, dark thinning hair. He said he was glad to see me here again. His wife assured me that her Ralf had told her so much about my speech in the church that day. I ended up joining her and Ralf at one of the tables up front. Georg and Jörg were already seated with the steering committee. And then things started rolling.

First came a steady stream of votes confirming all sorts of previous actions. I've never had to sit through anything like it in all my life. I felt robbed of my freedom, I was suddenly a prisoner.

Ralf, on the other hand, seemed happy and excited. He rolled his shopping bag back like a sleeve to reveal a piece of cardboard backing and a letter-size notebook. His hopes, his pride, yes, his fundamental convictions were invested in the care with which he slipped in the carbon paper, lowered his head just above the page, and began to write. Whenever Jörg's speech was interrupted by applause, he would stop and clap soundlessly, ballpoint clasped in his right hand.

Georg sat almost motionless at the front table the whole evening, staring straight ahead. Whenever there was a vote, however, his arm was usually the first thrust into the air. Jörg, as acting chairman, was all smiles as he kept greeting acquaintances he spotted in the hall. I recognized, way over on the left, the loudmouth who had saved the November 4th demonstration. His eyes were glistening.

Maybe there have to be meetings like these. But this one left me downright sick with boredom.[1]

After about an hour a woman two tables away stood up. Her glasses were so big and her mass of hair so wiglike that it was hard to tell her age. Whatever she had to say, it was incomprehensible. When ordered to speak louder, she shouted, "I am prepared to assume leadership of the New Forum." Asked to give her name, she cried out enthusiastically, "My name is—" but then broke off abruptly and repeated her offer to take over the leadership. Egged on by applause and catcalls, she greeted us with a raised left fist.

Out of consideration for Georg and Jörg, and especially for Ralf, I didn't join in the applause. Even my smile appeared to offend him.

---

1. T. apparently failed to realize that within the foreseeable future he would have to report on such events as this.

9

After her, the loudmouth on the steering committee grabbed the mic. He stressed every second or third word and bounced up and down, flexing his knees. He laughed as he spoke, as if every word were practical proof of just how undeniably right he was. He then pointed his pencil at who ever he decided to give the floor to. Shouted insults—he was a stewie[1] and a bungler. "There's a solution to everything," he shouted, "once basic issues of power are resolved and democratic structures are put in place."

Whole groups were now deserting the hall. Suddenly Ralf was speaking. With one hand on his belt, as if to keep his trousers from drooping, he held both the mike and his manuscript in the other. He was also gesticulating, making him barely comprehensible, and didn't understand what all the shouts of "Mike! mike!" were about. Finally he stated his demands, point by point, but got out of sync with himself because he turned around to get a look at his hecklers, while his wife kept hissing, "Keep going!"

"No establishment of West German parties, partnership with other democratic forces in the East, a halt to full-scale demolition in the old city, investigation into the sale of the Council Library, punishment for Schalck-Golodkowski,[2] free elections, brown coal mines to be kept open, continuation of Wismut[3] for peaceful purposes, dismissal of agitators from school faculties, withdrawal from the Warsaw Pact, alternative service . . ."

"Keep going! Keep going!" his wife whispered.

After a good three hours, the meeting was declared adjourned. A few voices took up the German national anthem, but were drowned out by general noise. Most of the items on the agenda had to be eliminated, including the announcement of our newspaper.

Ralf fell silent. I tried to smile. His wife lowered her gaze as if in embarrassment—for herself, for me, for Ralf, for the whole assembly. As we left, Ralf asked my opinion. "And be honest, Enrico, really honest."

Outside the coatroom I ran right into the Prophet. "No! No! Terrible!" he shouted at me, and a moment later blocked someone else's path

---

1. Drunkard, "stewbum."

2. Colonel in the State Security, after 1966 head of "KoKo" (Commercial Coordination), which was supposed to keep the GDR solvent by means of covert business transactions.

3. Soviet-German joint-stock company that mined uranium at various sites in Thuringia and Saxony.

with his "No! No! Terrible!" He could still be heard until we were out of the building.

Georg invited me to join them at the Wenzel,[1] where people were expecting us.

A hulk of a man was propped against the front desk, but he spread his arms wide once he saw us. There were sweat stains in the armpits of his gray jacket. He pressed me to his chest and greeted me by murmuring my first name in my ear. He had already been a guest at my home, he said. Then he instructed us to address Jan Staan, whom we would meet shortly, by his name, to say not just "Good evening" but "Good evening, Herr Staan" (I could have sworn he said "Staan"), and to use phrases like "A pleasure to make your acquaintance," or "Very happy to meet you." A waitress was just closing up the restaurant, and since Wolfgang the Hulk had fallen silent, we could hear in the intervening moments her footfall, purring lamps, and distant music. Suddenly screams, laughter, shouts, a deafening racket. A woman staggered past, bumping my shoulder, blond, plump, a wart on her chin. She dabbed at her damp décolletage, her white blouse clung to her belly and breasts, and her mascara was running. Faces in the doorway vanished again. The blonde threw her shoulders back and displayed herself as if before a mirror.

Wolfgang the Hulk brushed against her as he made his way toward the bar, she lurched as if he had given her a push. We followed him into the shadows. I stayed close behind Jörg. "Does anyone want to dance a polonaise?" a woman shouted, thrusting her hot hands against my back. Someone patted my rear end. The most I could make out as I looked around were bright articles of clothing. The spotlight above the dance floor, with bare arms writhing under the cone of its beam, was my sole orientation point.

The farther we pressed forward, the better progress we made and the brighter the light. We steered for a group of men standing in a circle. They stepped back, revealing a clutch of women who had squeezed themselves by twos and threes into the few armchairs.

We halted in front of a man sitting in the midst of these women. Groaning, he pushed himself to the edge of his armchair, but stood up with surprisingly little effort considering his massive belly. As he fumbled at the buttons of his sport coat, dots of light from the disco ball danced

1. The only hotel in town at the time.

11

across his forehead. I was the last to receive a handshake and a business card: Jan Steen. His gaze slid down over me, he smiled and fell back into his chair.

"It's time to do some business," one of the men shouted in a commanding voice, and clapped his hands. One after the other the women reluctantly stood up, and we sat down on chair cushions still warm from their bodies.

Jörg and Georg had sat down on each side of Steen. Because they had to shout to be heard over the noise and music, it looked as if they were telling him off. Steen, however, obviously soon lost interest in my bosses, and his glance skittered about the room. But when he held out his glass to the waitress—a bleached-blond Bulgarian who, had the contest been on the up-and-up, should have been last year's Miss Altenburg—he smiled and raised it in a toast to the women. They pretended not to notice. They were sulking. One was so insulted that she dismissed us by turning her bare pudgy back on us.

To make up for Jörg's total abstinence and Georg's restraint, Wolfgang and I drank every brandy Steen ordered. Wolfgang lined up his empty glasses next to the ashtray between his feet and kneaded his hands. He said he worked for Air Research Technologies, whose abbreviation was the same as the Altenburg Regional Theater—ART. I told him the story of how the staff of the Wenzel thought they had caught a swindler when Air Research Technologies refused to pay my bill. Wolfgang smiled to himself. Even those few sentences had left me hoarse. We spent our time toasting in various directions and drinking. I was soon aglow with a surge of goodwill.

A very tall woman—a good match for Wolfgang the Hulk—was now standing beside him. She pulled rimless glasses out of her purse. I was about to offer her my seat when Wolfgang gave my thigh a slap and stood up. Without so much as inviting her to stay, Jan Steen kissed the woman's hand in farewell. Jörg and Georg now departed with the two giants. And suddenly I was alone with Jan Steen, who was tapping his knee with his right hand to some inscrutable rhythm. When I raised a glass to him he responded to my greeting with a broad wave of his arm. Slowly the women returned and gathered around him again. I shouted to him how wonderful it was to drink and at the same time watch drunks dance. And then I burst into laughter because I suddenly found it very funny that he and I expected nothing more of each other than to sit here side by side and watch these women down their drinks and teeter around the dance floor with wilder and wilder wriggling motions. If only it doesn't stop now, I thought, if only this can go on and on.

Beneath his narrow face Jan Steen's double chin led a remarkable life of its own. The more I gazed at it, the more clearly I could make out a second, perfectly independent physiognomy. In every other respect Steen's body was all of a piece and surely preordained to carry his bulk. We kept smiling and toasting each other, relishing our side-by-side existence.

The moment I spotted her face, I was instantly filled with desire and melancholy. Her dance partner's long, lean back kept interfering with our exchanged glances. But she never stopped looking my way. Evidently she wasn't sure just what roles Steen and I had assigned each other. I didn't know myself what I was doing here. She was no great beauty, but I was infatuated with the earnestness of her face.

In the few seconds between songs I asked her for the next dance. Her escort shouted that I could go to hell. We began to dance. Unwilling to yield the floor, he stepped between us. One twirl was enough to leave him standing alone again. Anticipating his next move, I took her in my arms, not even thinking whether it was the right or wrong thing to do. But when she acquiesced, as good as fleeing to me, I felt nothing but pure happiness. The skinny man's voice quavered with outrage as he stared at his beloved. With rolled-up sleeves and hands half raised, he appeared on the verge of separating us by force. She could only have sensed what was happening from my reaction, from the motions of my body. She tossed her head to one side and, as if spitting at his feet, let loose with a cascade of what I took to be Romanian curses.

I have never seen anyone capitulate so submissively just by lowering his eyes. I didn't catch his stammered words. Finally he steered for a table at the edge of the dance floor, where he literally collapsed as he sat down.

She kissed me on the neck, and I was drunk enough to respond with lust so tempestuous that just by diving into it I could forget my own sense of forlornness. All I needed was to feel this woman next to me and everything seemed simple and clear.

I asked whether I could get her a drink. With an almost pleading look, she shook her head. A little later, however, I took her by the hand and led her to the table where Steen and the women were now waiting for us.

No sooner had we sat down, a tray of full glasses in front of us, than her friend walked over and demanded in a very serious voice that she dance with him. Without looking up, she shook her head. "Dance with me," he said again. It was an order, but his trembling chin betrayed his fear.

"Say something," he suddenly thundered down at her, "tell me to go! Say something, and you'll be rid of me."

"I beg you," I said as I got to my feet, "please go."

"One word from that beautiful mouth suffices," he said in suppressed fury. "I obey orders from this woman, not from a gasbag!" As he pointed at her, a tattoo emerged on his wrist—faded letters, a D and an F.

The women began arguing with him. The men in the background had stood up at the same time I had. I was ready to hurl myself at him, I wanted to put an end to this farce.

I can't say whether it was a cry of fear or some hasty movement that made me look at Steen. He had never taken his eye off my beautiful companion, but now he was staring at her. His smile had frozen at the corners of his mouth. A woman behind him gave a shriek. In horror, people averted their eyes from my lovely dance partner. I was the last one to whom she revealed herself. Have you ever seen a mouth filled with black stumps? She laughed, well aware of how it only increased her ugliness.

The skinny man sighed, turned, and shuffled away. Before I could say or do anything, she had jumped up to follow him. It was easy to make out her path to the exit, because the crowd parted before her and closed again only hesitantly in her wake.

That's it for today!

Your E.

Friday, Jan. 19, '90

Dear Jo,

This is the same manuscript paper that all articles have to be written on, thirty lines to a page, sixty strokes to the line. So I'm practicing now.[1]

This morning I sent off a letter telling you about my late-night adventures. Our next test was lying in wait for us at noon today. Georg, Jörg,

---

1. The paper was set in linotype.

and I had to use surprise tactics to obtain our business license. The printer in Leipzig finally demanded an official seal. No registration, no contract. Our application has been lying around in the district council office since mid-December.

The reception room was empty. We knocked on the door of the councilman for trade and commerce, and a moment later we were inside his cave. Believe me, for the first time in my life I saw light *ooze away*. Every ray met its end in a mesh of miasma, of cigar smoke that had hung there for decades and lay like volcanic ash on potted plants that still managed some green. The unwashed windows and the yellowed white curtains did their part too, but the murky seepage came from the man himself. It was a miracle that when he stood up from his desk we even spotted him amid the colorlessness and lack of any shading—*his* colorlessness, *his* lack of any shading. What I noticed above all—beyond big teeth, a badly trimmed yellowish beard, and stringy hair—was his laugh. By the glow of the match he used to light his cigar, scorn and fear flickered across his face.

There was no way, he said with a laugh, that he could grant us a printing license. Pause. He ponderously took his seat again. Georg bent toward him and said that he was deliberately delaying publication of our paper, yes, was trying to prevent it by exceeding the limits of his authority, making it a case for the Commission Against Corruption and Abuse of Office. Vulcan laughed and asked Georg to repeat the long title. So far as he knew, no such commission existed yet. It didn't matter what he knew or thought, Georg shouted, his brow now dark with rage, because such decisions were no longer in his hands. His job was to stamp our application, he wasn't being paid to do anything else.

"Hohoho!" Vulcan cried, baring his horse teeth and exhaling more smoke with each "ho!" Georg kept right on leaning forward, staring straight at him from one side as if the man belonged to some as-yet-unnamed species.

"Hoho, haha, your application, hoha, your application, ha, doesn't even exist, it's never been presented, hoha, your application, ho, at least not to me, hoha, you've come to the wrong man, really the wrong man, hoho, who can't do a thing for you, hoho." Then he took another puff of his cigar and blew wordless smoke. I could already see us on our way to some other department.

"Doesn't matter!" cried Jörg, who so far had kept strangely silent and now doffed his beret as if giving some prearranged signal. "Then we're presenting it here and now, orally. You hand us the application form and stamp it." The councilman's laugh first ran up the scale as if trying to melt into the thin air of mockery, then faded away in a long sigh.

Unfortunately, he was all out of application forms, he said. There were too many people wanting to apply, far too many, "can't end well, nope, it can't." Vulcan hastily puffed several more clouds that dissipated into the twilight of his cave. "New regulations are required," he added worriedly, looking from Georg to Jörg, then to me and back to Jörg, "yes indeed, new regulations. Just ask the cabdrivers . . ." A gesture of his free hand suggested an attempt to fan away the fumes, then he laid his cigar in the ashtray.

Neither Georg, who had taken up a position at the door, nor I budged. Vulcan thrust his spine against the back of his chair and splayed his fingers across his potbelly as if holding a pillow against it.

"I'm not even responsible for newspapers," he said in a flat voice. Those decisions had to be made in Leipzig.

"You see!" Jörg shouted. "Just takes a little goodwill." Vulcan had no cause whatever to worry, worries weren't part of his job. Jörg paused, took a step back, grabbed my arm, and presented me as an artist, a master of touch-typing, all ten fingers. "Enrico Türmer!"

I sat down at the typewriter, rolled three sheets of the official district council paper into it, and typed the date and place. Not just the "a" and the "o," but all the letters were so clogged with gunk as to be almost indecipherable. Besides which the left caps shift was missing. There was, however, plenty of carbon paper.

After a few puffs on his cigar, Vulcan grumbled again about how it was long past time for his noon break. Georg tossed me his pocketknife so I could give the letters a crude cleaning.

"So?" Vulcan asked ten minutes later. As if judging the quality of a work of graphic art, he inspected the page and then laid it down in front of him. "So? What am I supposed to do with this?"

"Number, stamp, receipt," Jörg replied.

"Whatever you want, whatever you want," he said, "but it won't do you any good." Jörg demanded both stamp and signature on the copies too, and left one of them on the blotter.

Without another word, we left Vulcan behind. Out on the street we clapped each other's clothes, dusting off volcano ashes. Jörg took off for Leipzig right away.

I tour the countryside passing out flyers printed in red. The announcement and subscription form for the paper looks like a warning against rabies.

Michaela asked me to send her greetings too.

Enrico

Friday, Jan. 19, '90

Verotchka,

I can't stop thinking about you and I count the days that you're still in Berlin, as if we're living together and will soon be separating.

The newspaper's telephone number is 6999. Do you think maybe you can call from Beirut? Mornings I'm almost always alone, but that will soon change. Have you heard anything more from your nobleman?

Sometimes I'm afraid of myself, no, not of myself, but of where things are headed. It's all happening so inexorably and logically, and I suddenly see myself right in the middle of it all, as if in a dream. I'm afraid I'll wake up one morning and not know what to do next, what to do period.

Yesterday and today I wrote Johann and told him a couple of stories. He's always impressed by stories. He'll envy me my job yet.

Mamus is determined to give us a bus trip to Paris. I hope I can talk her out of it. She claims it's because of the bet, that I won the bet, and she's going to keep her word.[1] Michaela and Robert are all excited. Michaela's schedule of performances will probably prevent us from going, at least I hope so.

Michaela has started accusing me of being cold. She gets just as aggravated when I'm around as when I'm not. To keep her from getting any more upset, I even try to avoid abrupt movements and gestures when I'm around her.

The last few days we've fallen into a morning ritual that makes the first hour feel deceptively like our old routine. (Except we don't eat eggs anymore, they're unhealthy, she says.) The moment Michaela is done in the bathroom I pour coffee so that she can drink hers right away. Every peaceable minute is a godsend. On the way to the car we usually talk

1. T. had bet his mother that he would see Paris before his thirtieth birthday—information provided by Elisabeth Türmer.

17

about Robert and school, an inexhaustible topic. As long as we keep talking, we stay clear of danger.

But as soon as we drive off, the tone of voice changes. By the time we're even with the train station we're not talking—that is, Michaela has fallen silent and I can't bring myself to say another word either. As we pass the museum, our silence turns icy. Once we're at the theater parking lot, at the latest, Michaela explodes. The eeriest part is the predictability, the way the whole thing repeats itself, as if every morning Michaela realizes for the first time that I'll not be getting out of the car with her, that she has to go into the theater alone—and she seems all the more surprised because up to that point everything has been just like it used to be.

I turn off the engine, so she won't feel I'm trying to push her, and listen to my lesson on how there are theaters in the West too, how there always has been, always will be theater, and how both man and society come to self-realization in the theater. Once she's flung her words at the windshield, she sinks back into silence. But in a state of intense concentration, like right before an entrance. The worst thing now would be to remind her of the time. I sit beside her as if waiting for the rain to end and make sure I don't touch the steering wheel, avoiding any kind of gesture that could be held against me as impatience.

Suddenly she flings the door open and runs off, without a good-bye, head thrown back, purse pressed to her chest, coat fluttering behind her.

Bent over the steering wheel, I watch her go, ready to wave in case she might turn around. After Michaela has vanished I start the car and catch myself smiling in the rearview mirror.

Three minutes later I'm in the office—add some coal, put water on, and wait with my back to the stove until the coffee's ready. Georg comes down shortly afterward, taps the barometer, winds the grandfather clock, and checks the thermometers outside the window and next to the coatrack. Captain Nemo couldn't keep closer watch on his instruments.

Afternoons I usually drive around the area, dropping in on town halls. At first they're frightened when they hear "newspaper." The secretaries generally catch on more quickly than their bosses that I'm not a threat, and are extremely friendly. Robert comes along sometimes. During the drive we talk about all sorts of things. He has a clear understanding of what my job is. How a newspaper uncovers things and tries to see justice done on all sides. I really enjoy the time with him.

Our first edition is supposed to appear on Friday, February 16th. It all sounds like a fairy tale. You come up with an idea, carry it out, and make a living from it. As if we're returning to some long-forgotten custom, to a way of life familiar to everybody except us.

On Tuesday we'll be driving to Offenburg for three days, but not as part of the official Altenburg delegation. A well-wisher[1] will be paying our hotel bill. Let's hope our Jimmy holds up.[2]

Verotchka, my dearest! Hugs!

Your Heinrich

Thursday, Jan. 25, '90

Verotchka,

Just imagine how much money that would be if we exchanged it! Maybe a hundred forty, a hundred sixty thousand? What madness! But the best part was still the telephone booths.[3] Am I asking too much to be able to hear your voice once a day?

At times I thought it really still existed, the West. A constant flood of old daydreams and reflexes. People like Gläsle—the man at the town hall, who couldn't understand why so many Altenburgers keep sending decks of skat cards[4]—must have taken us all for barbarians.

Georg, who had spoken with Gläsle on the phone, got the impression that we were being invited to plunder their store of office supplies to our hearts' delight. Gläsle led us to a stockroom in an attic not far from the town hall. We immediately pounced upon the treasures. No sooner had we stuffed shopping bags full of felt pens, Scotch tape, erasers, and colorful paper clips than we emptied them again and stuffed them with file folders and transparent covers, with ring notebooks and tubes of glue. We even laid claim to a white magnet board. We ransacked it all as if in a

---

1. Jan Steen.

2. He means his car, a Wartburg Deluxe.

3. This letter presumes that some information about the trip to Offenburg, including T.'s impressions, had already been shared with his sister, evidently in phone calls from there.

4. Skat and a factory for skat playing cards has been Altenburg's claim to fame. During this same period the Offenburg town hall was inundated with packages filled with decks of skat cards. The backs were often female nudes. Most senders wanted to establish contact with families in their new sister city.

frenzy. Within a few minutes I didn't even recognize myself. How could we have done this without asking even once? We had to unpack it all again, taking inventory, counting, figuring prices, and putting more and more items back. Gläsle had turned paler than we were. Thank God Georg had the envelope of money with him. It turned out that this was Gläsle's attempt to do us a favor by giving us the same discount the town got for office supplies. He was acting against regulations. He warned us not to say a word to anyone. All the same Gläsle performed a rabbit-out-of-a-hat trick, lifting the cover from a huge electric typewriter. He called it the "green monster," and asked if we might want it, with a bag of ribbons included. That, he said, was a gift he could give us. Gläsle looked downright relieved and wondered out loud what else he could send along with us—although the typewriter was problem enough. We finally fit it—fat and green like a giant toad—between Georg and Jörg on the backseat.

We first have to be civilized. Our blunder came not necessarily from a lack of character—no, our entire sensory system was out of whack.

With two hundred D-marks in my pocket, store windows suddenly took on real interest. Stopping or moving on no longer meant the same thing they once did. I can't explain how it was that we ended up in a shop for pots and pans. All I had to do was lift one of those heavy lids and I was fascination's plaything. I assumed the edge of the pot had to be magnetic, for it seemed to attract the lid and automatically provide that perfect fit.

We were still lidding our way through the shop when Wolfgang the Hulk came in. He joined in our game, while the saleswoman tried to offer the salient points of each, waxing enthusiastic about stews, soups, vegetable casseroles, Swabian spätzle, roasts, and just about every other sort of fare that had ever been prepared on a stove in her town.

We listened. Wolfgang rapped his knuckles on pots as if checking a bell for purity of tone.

At some point it became clear that our money would be left behind in this shop. We had already agreed on two unlidded pots when Wolfgang slipped us another fifty. Now we had enough for the sale item: three pots for 249 D-marks, lids included. The saleswoman—we would never regret our choice—escorted us to the door. Only then did she hand over the third plastic shopping bag to Michaela.

I was searching for my car keys when Michaela was greeted by a woman that I had to look at twice before I recognized her, and then only from her coat. The newspaper czarina had a totally different hairdo. She asked how we were doing, and all I could think of in response was to hold out our shopping bags. "What pretty pots!" she exclaimed with the kind of fervor you show little children, took out the pot, and turned it around and around. I was afraid her rings might scratch the metal.

"What a pretty pot!" she cried loudly, handing it back to me and vanishing with the regional farewell—an *"Ade!"* accented on the first syllable.

Ah, Verotchka! As if there were nothing more important to write about. If only your Herr von B. would finally make his appearance here. Does he have a real name? I'm off to the post office now, so your letter can be on its way today yet.

I have such a longing for you!

Your Heinrich

Friday, Jan. 26, '90

Dear Jo,

Jan Steen has decided our fate. It was scary like a fairy tale, but in the end stupid Ivanushka[1] got his treasure.

Had we known prior to the trip just what was at stake, we probably wouldn't have waited for Michaela to make up her mind, which she didn't do until the night before and first had to ring Aunt Trockel's doorbell the next morning and ask her to look after Robert.

We had only a little under six hours left for a seven-and-a-half-hour drive—just one more than Jan Steen needs to travel the same distance in his sports job. Michaela claimed the navigator's position and, laying Robert's school atlas across her knees, acted as if Jörg and Georg weren't in the backseat and Jan Steen hadn't given us directions. All the same I was glad she had come along.

I had to open the trunk at the border in Schleiz. The customs agent reached for the shoebox full of flyers and issues of *klartext*[2]—Michaela had insisted we bring them along. The agent held the "printed matter"

---

1. Figure in a Russian fairy tale in which the youngest, and presumed dumbest, carries the day.
2. The newsletter of the Altenburg New Forum, published by Michaela Fürst. Its five issues were considered the precursor of the *Altenburg Weekly*.

between his gloved hands and read, or at least pretended to, while car after car rolled past us. What was this stuff? he asked. "What it says it is," I replied, "a call for a demo once the State Security's villa is taken over."

When he went to put it back, the stack of flyers had shifted and no longer fit in the shoebox. He crammed the papers back in, gave me a wave of his hand that could have meant anything, and shuffled off—the morning sun reflected softly in the shine of his boots. I drove very slowly across the bridge so that we could see the clear-cut path through the woods.

My three passengers soon nodded off, but I was savoring it all—the pink winter morning, the odd fluttery sound of tires against pavement, the expansive curves, the speed, the music, the traffic bulletins, the semis and the cars hurtling past, the fields and villages and hills. To my eyes even the snow had a Western look that morning.

Our only stop was just after Nuremberg. The gas station and rest stop were bustling with our fellow countrymen, some of whom were picnicking on bagged sandwiches and thermos coffee behind rolled-down windows. You could have spotted them just from their restless eyes and the eager way they chewed. Once I had found a parking place and opened the trunk, Michaela rebelled. There was a restaurant here, and no way was she going to be the dog left outside the door. She offered to pay.

While Georg, Jörg, and I slowly dithered past the glass cases with their displays of food, Michaela's tray was already stacked high with fruit salad on top of sandwiches, rote grütze and vanilla sauce on top of apple strudel. She ordered scrambled eggs for us all and told us we only needed to bother about our coffee and tea.

Even Jörg, who as I first noticed when we sat down had brought his own sandwich in, capitulated before this magic banquet, smearing butter on his D-mark kaiser roll and piling it high with scrambled eggs and ham.

Georg went back for a plate of white sausages with sweet mustard. Michaela discovered cucumber salad—cucumber salad in winter!

We filled our tank from one of our gas cans, and drove downhill in the passing lane. The names that began to pop up on signs delighted me: Heilbronn, Karlsruhe, Strasbourg, Freiburg, Basel, Milan. It wouldn't have amazed me to find ourselves suddenly whizzing along under palm trees.

We pulled into Offenburg a little before noon, found the Ratskeller—and right on time, there we stood opposite Steen, who was sitting having a beer with Wolfgang the Hulk. Michaela was the center of attention. Steen invited her to ride with him, Georg and Jörg were packed into the backseat, and I put-putted along behind with Wolfgang.

He had greeted me with a hug and silence, but was now chatting my ear off about how important it had been for us to show up on time. We'd pulled it off with pizzazz, real pizzazz. Steen thought a great deal of us, finally somebody he could depend on, people who knew what they wanted, went for it, and didn't expect to be handed anything on a silver platter. Steen had reassigned his entire advertising campaign for the Leipzig Fair to us, now didn't that show pizzazz on his part too? He gave my thigh a slap. We were moving up into the Black Forest now. A few serpentine curves and we had lost Steen. Only after we started back downhill did we link up again. "Demand a thousand marks, a thousand dee ems per page," Wolfgang said without turning his head. "A thousand D-marks per page," I replied.

Georg and Jörg were standing in the Hotel Sonne parking lot, each off to himself, like two eavesdroppers. It was the air! It was so delicate and cold that it hurt to breathe.

Michaela, more recumbent than sitting, played with the darkened windows, sending them up and down with a hum, and didn't get out until a hotel employee asked about our luggage. She followed him, while Steen steered us toward the restaurant. Steen was carrying on several conversations at once, and we listened with bated breath. "A thousand D-marks," I whispered to Jörg.

The restaurant seemed to be closed; we were the only guests. Steen headed for a corner table and slid along the bench until he was seated under the stuffed head of a stag. I went to the restroom. I wasn't sure whether Jörg had understood me or not, and so I took my time, but neither Georg nor Jörg followed me.

Jörg was talking about our planned first printing, the distribution structure, the number of pages, etc. "And you two are the owners?" Steen interrupted, nodding at Jörg and Georg. He intended to "shift his advertising" to us. About how much would that cost?

Georg and Jörg said nothing. But at least Georg knew enough to ask just what sort of advertising was involved. Steen's double chin went back into action, but then quickly settled down. "Air Research Technologies," he exclaimed, "what else? Full page!" Georg began one sentence, then another, then the next and one more without finishing any of them.

"Twelve pages to start with, need every column, an ad no one will understand, just twelve pages, sub-tabloid format, isn't much, and if you, and Air Research Technologies, just getting a handle on it, in the Altenburg area, a whole page, why a whole page?"

"What's he talking about?" Steen cried, turning to Wolfgang.

"That you have to consider . . ." Jörg said, but then broke off midsentence and cast a glance Steen's way, but he had vanished behind his menu—we all had one now. Wolfgang took a deep breath . . .

"A full page costs one thousand two hundred D-marks," I burst out, as if I had finally calculated costs. Steen's head reappeared and looked from one of us to another. "One thousand two hundred," I repeated, and attempted a smile.

"Ahhh," Steen groaned and threw himself back in his seat. He eyeballed me, which evidently he enjoyed doing.

Jörg gave me a broad wink, as if I were sitting several tables away. Georg stared at his hands. Wolfgang took another audible deep breath. And I had already begun working up my monologue of apology.

Steen said something that sounded like "whaddaya know" or maybe it was "I dunno," braced himself against the edge of the table, and said these exact words: "I'll advance you *twenty* thousand for now, and then we'll see, agreed?" He stood up halfway and extended a hand first to Georg, then Jörg, then finally me. His tie dangled into an empty wineglass and was still draped over his plate as he sat down. "How do you want it, check or *hard currency*?"—the last two words in English. The waitress presented us each a glass half-filled with champagne.

"Well, which is it?" Steen asked.

"Check doesn't work for us," Jörg said.

"*Hard currency!*" Steen stated, and reached for his glass, but stopped short because no one else had budged.

"Cash," Wolfgang cried, lifting his glass, "hard currency means cash."

Silence. Jörg said cash was good, very good. At which point Steen's body raised up a little, his mouth flew open and let loose with a laugh, a laugh that ricocheted off the walls, a laugh unlike any I've ever heard in my life. "Cash!" Steen howled when he was finally capable of getting a word out, but now catapulted into another volley of laughter, gasped for breath, swallowed wrong, coughed. *"Hard currency!"* His double chin shook angrily. By now the laughter had grabbed hold of Wolfgang too.

The longer the outburst lasted, the more tactless I found it. Wolfgang's laughter began to wane now, and finally he just clamped his eyes tight, as if all the laughter was pressed out of him.

"Cash is very good!" Steen shouted. He swiped a folded handkerchief across his mouth, got up, and walked toward Michaela. She took his arm and he escorted her to the table. They were as incongruous here as a couple dressed for the opera is on a streetcar.

We noticed too late that Steen simply raised his glass to toast, whereas we all touched glasses soundlessly. I emptied my glass in one chug. My life force was gradually returning. Contrary to my initial impression, the flowers on the table were real.

The venison was served with spätzle and an incredible sauce. Steen also topped off each forkful with some kind of marmalade. The starter was broccoli soup (they showed us a raw stalk, sort of like cauliflower, but dark green). As if everything else had now been settled, Steen spent the whole time instructing us about food, but then disappeared with a hasty good-bye shortly before dessert—a dark Italian cake, soft and moist and creamy.[1]

I don't know when I last saw Michaela look as beautiful and at ease as she did during the meal. When we got up from the table she asked what Herr Steen had been laughing so hard about, and Georg replied that he wasn't certain of the reason himself. But Herr Steen had every intention of handing over twenty thousand D-marks to us. Twenty thousand D-marks, Michaela responded, bought a lot of uncertainty.

We were supposed to be in Offenburg by five. We had lain down for a little nap, but when we arrived the delegation from Altenburg was just climbing off the bus. The Offenburgers were annoyed that they couldn't spot anyone in charge of the expectant throng. Their tall, well-tanned mayor shook every hand, and despite his height kept standing on tiptoe as if afraid he had overlooked someone. Just as Steen had done, he offered Michaela his arm and led her into the town hall, where he took us on a kind of tour. He made a point of always letting Michaela precede him into each room.

We admired the cream-colored carpets, the computers, the desks, the push-button phones, and we took turns lounging in the mayor's plush

1. Tiramisu.

desk chair. The finale was marked by toasts with champagne, the snacks disappeared quickly.

A small elegant man in a yellow sweater sidled up to me as if just by chance, and after a while asked me whether *I* could explain something to him. Thanking me for my help, he described his problem. Every day ten to twenty little packages arrived for him from Altenburg, each containing a deck of skat cards with a nude female color photo on the back. These people wanted him to provide them other addresses in Offenburg. He stared at me. And what exactly was his question, I wanted to know. He hooked a finger inside his the collar of his sweater, gazed at me a moment longer, thanked me, and then departed as inconspicuously as he had arrived.

Receptions had been planned for those of us in the press to meet with the various political parties, with the exception of the Free Democrats (which has only five members, but does have a seat on the town council).

Michaela wanted to visit the Greens, Jörg was already assigned to the Socialists, and that left the Christian Democrats for Georg.

None of us had any idea what a mistake we were making.

Michaela and I proved a disappointment for the Greens in any case. After we had introduced ourselves and asked for an ashtray, they began to go around the room with their introductions. Whoever had the floor looked directly at us, while the others chatted and giggled. Michaela started off jotting down their names and various activities, but she stopped when someone asked her why she needed to do that. I asked what CI meant, because they were constantly talking about CIs (citizens' initiatives), and about "collecting toads." Most of them said, "I'm in the CI for airport noise and collect toads." I asked the woman beside me what toads meant. She didn't understand. Suddenly, however, she shrieked, "Guess what Enrico thinks toad collecting is?"

In the minor uproar that followed one very beautiful woman who spoke in the singsong cadence of her native Swabia stood out above all the rest. "They've blown their cover now! They've blown their cover now."

Michaela bravely came to my aid. She had made the same association— toads was a common enough slang term for money. She herself had used it often.

But in fact they did collect these animals and carried them across highways. Toad tunnels were already being constructed.

The beautiful woman wanted to know why no one from the Library on the Environment or the civil rights movement had come with us, but before we could answer, she declared, "Those guys are all just the old bigwigs." Michaela spoke about her *klartext,* and I could sense how much she would have liked to talk about Leipzig and all the rest, if only someone had asked her. "We're not part of the official delegation," she exclaimed. "We're not part of them!" The environment would be given a lot of attention in our new newspaper, I said. It somehow sounded feeble, and hardly anyone was listening anyway. At the end we sat drinking mineral water with a married couple who told us all about their trip to Weisswasser and Karl-Marx-Stadt. We were hungry.

I got lost on the way back, and it was almost eleven before we found the Hotel Sonne. Jörg came storming toward us.

"What a screwup!" he shouted. "A total screwup!"

Dressed in suit and tie, Wolfgang sat enthroned in the lobby. Like a drunken Bacchus, he dangled limp arms over the armrests of his chair, his crown of hair stood straight up.

"And where were you?" he barked at us, and his arms took on life again, paddled at the air, found their way to the armrests. It looked as if he might stand up, his eyes bugged out—then he sank back again. As he closed his eyes I was afraid he was going to cry.

"They didn't even offer us anything to eat," Michaela protested. Jörg kept rubbing his eyes and forehead. Georg paced back and forth on his long legs, his upper body as lopsided as a jockey's.

Jan Steen had spent the whole evening waiting for us in a "fancy restaurant" up in the Black Forest. Wolfgang had tried every twenty minutes to phone us. Around ten o'clock Steen had angrily tossed his napkin on his plate and driven home. Heaven only knew if we would ever see the man again.

"But how were we supposed to know that?" Michaela asked. "Nobody knew about it!" Jörg shouted. "Nobody, nobody, nobody!" Instead of responding to the question, Wolfgang spoke oracularly about the one that got away, the really big fish that got away. The phrase gave him some kind of grim pleasure, in fact he seemed to console himself with it, because we didn't hear him utter anything but that phrase for the rest of the night.

Jörg and Georg sat on our beds. We peeled our eggs over the cloth on the nightstand. Our one luxury consisted of trading the sandwiches we had fixed the night before. Plus cold tea drunk from the cap of the thermos.

We were now the same people who had climbed into a Wartburg in Altenburg before dawn. What lay between that long-ago morning and our evening repast was merely a strange dream.

Michaela suddenly stopped chewing. "This may well be our breakfast," she said, putting her nibbled sandwich back on the table. "And who's going to pay for our rooms now?" Between us we had just under seventy D-marks. Georg tried to set our minds at ease. But then he was the only one who had eaten. The saddest part, as Michaela saw it, was that Steen had been waiting for us in a *fancy* restaurant.

The next morning we were actually awakened by the crow of a rooster.

Later on, we each double-checked to make sure that the breakfast buffet was included in the price and that two nights had been paid for in advance. We didn't run into Wolfgang in the dining room, and he wasn't in his room either. We were, so to speak, hanging around paradise with pink slips in hand. Michaela arm in arm with the mayor adorned the front page of the local paper.

The second day passed without fanfare and included visits to the hospital and the daily paper that has a monopoly here. We saw nothing of Burda Publishing. Jörg was interviewed on the radio. In the evening the newspaper czarina held a dinner for us. During the two hours of "exchanging views" we took turns stealing off to place a call to the Hotel Sonne, prepared to cut out on a moment's notice.

The czarina—as far as I'm aware, the first millionaire I've ever seen—had, wouldn't you know, grayish blue eyes, black hair, and skin like milk. Over dessert she offered to supply us with printers, computers, and everything else we might need for a newspaper.

"So you want to hire us?" Georg asked. The czarina unfolded her slender hands in a gesture that was intended to say: You heard me right.

Jörg explained to her that our first issue would be coming out in three weeks. The czarina's eyes grew ever narrower, and her smile took on a dreamy look.

"We belong to us, so to speak," Georg summarized in an apologetic voice.

"That's a shame," she said, "really a great shame." For a moment I had the feeling we were making a mistake.

The next morning Wolfgang pounded on our door. "He's downstairs waiting. He doesn't have much time."

Steen was in a splendid mood. His remarks kept Wolfgang in smiles the whole time. I was just launching into my speech about a big misunderstanding, when Steen cried, "Open wide!" He held a fork under my nose, expecting me to take a bite. It was just bacon, but was it ever good! Steen placed an order for me. Jörg and Georg likewise opened wide.

Michaela, who had wriggled into her old jeans, was the last to arrive. Steen obliged by following her every step, but his old enthusiasm had faded. Nevertheless he acted as if we had all spent the last two days together amusing ourselves. He waxed enthusiastic about the Black Forest, about Basel and Strasbourg, only out of the clear blue sky to urge us to buy German cars. For him anything else was out of the question. It was his way of helping the economy circulate. Anyone who wanted to do well had to make sure others did well too. I'm doing a poor job of recapping here. He said it better. Far more important was his tone of voice. Steen is full of self-confidence, confident that he has an honest relationship with the world, ready to render a full account of his deeds at any time.

Once again he kept his good-byes brief. He wished us a good trip, kissed Michaela on both cheeks, and vanished.

We shouldn't make such long faces, Michaela hissed. Wolfgang hadn't budged the whole time, and his good-bye to Steen had been just a nod. He wasn't in any hurry after that either. He pulled up closer to the table, gave his lighter a click, and lit a cigarette. He noisily slurped his coffee. I already suspected he had been assigned to tell us something. No one had dared blame him for yesterday evening's screwup. After all, we had him to thank for booking our hotel rooms. Wolfgang shoved his plate to one side, brushed crumbs from the tablecloth, pulled out a couple of sheets of paper, and laid them out in front of him. "Here," he began without any preliminaries, "are two hundred twenty-six addresses that the newspaper should be sent to. Here are two hundred D-marks for gas and another hundred in expenses for each of you, and here's . . . twenty thousand. In addition," he continued in a monotone, "he left this for you." He now emptied a cloth bag emblazoned with the same advertising as the lighters, ballpoint pens, notepads, and pencils that cascaded across the plates and cups. "You only have to sign *here*." He shoved the gewgaws aside, laid a paper in front of me, and handed me his pen. I thought it had to do with the hundred D-marks and gas money. So I signed and passed the sheet on. Only when Michaela hesitated did I realize I had signed a receipt for the twenty thousand. "One more can't hurt," Jörg said, signed his own name, and passed it on to Georg. In return we received a paper with a series of flourishes that formed the name Jan Steen.

But that still wasn't the end of it. You remember that old German proverb, don't you, about how the devil always shits where the piles are biggest? Well, the Offenburg town hall phoned and said that, if we had time, we could stop by—they would like to put a few things together for us, office supplies and such. (Swabians say office "stores.")

We had a splendid view out over the Rhine valley, all the way to some distant mountains in France. The hills around Offenburg roll gently, most of them unforested on top; the highest peaks of the Black Forest couldn't be seen from here or were hidden by clouds.

Gläsle was waiting for us outside the town hall. It wasn't long before our eyes were welling with tears. When it was all over we even hauled away an electric typewriter that we've baptized the "green monster."

Gläsle drove Georg and Jörg to a used-car lot—we want to buy a VW bus—so Michaela and I strolled through town. And because we suddenly had money in our pockets we went shopping—stainless steel pots, as if for our trophy collection.

That's it for this time. Hugs, Enrico

Monday, Jan. 29, '90

Verotchka,

Mamus sends her greetings. All your postcards are on her kitchen counter. She's a little peeved at us both—because your own children really shouldn't lie to you.[1] I wrote down your address for her. She wants to know how long you'll be staying and if it isn't dangerous and if Nicola's mother is feeling better.

We're supposed to go to Paris this weekend. Mamus sees herself as a

---

1. Until the end of 1989 Elisabeth Türmer had believed that, after V. T.'s departure for West Berlin in the summer of 1987, she had at last begun a career as an actor there.

personal ambassador of happiness. She's plundered her bank account and won't admit it, but drops all kinds of coy hints.

Although we—I took Robert along—were in Dresden only yesterday, our time there is somehow a haunting memory of nowhere in particular, as if I had merely dreamed it. Mamus had baked a cheesecake. But the apartment was so cold and tidy it was almost as if it wasn't lived in.

It's only when you see her there inside her own four walls that you realize how much Mamus has changed. I was happy to spot any gesture I recognized—the way she lights the stove and kneels down to check the flame, the way she stands at the pantry threshold as if it might be easier to reach rather than take another step, the way she pivots on the heel of one foot when she opens the door to the fridge, the way she holds her coffee cup with both hands, elbows planted on the table. Sounding as if she were offering me some condensed milk, she asked if we would also be voting for the Alliance for Germany.[1] Mamus has suddenly begun to spot people toadying everywhere and sees her fellow nurses as "pure opportunists." I asked her why she herself had never thought of leaving. I wouldn't have wanted to, she replied, without looking directly at me.

There's been no change in her situation at the clinic. If she has bad luck and is assigned to a shift with her "tormentors"—and that probably includes most of the nurses in surgery—she sometimes doesn't say a word the whole day.

Robert treats Mamus like a second grandmother, which obviously does her good. And each time Robert agrees to come along, I feel like I've been honored too. Although I'm always afraid I'm boring him. This time I should perhaps have made the trip without him, except that it would have taken on its own special significance, as if I were pressuring her for a heart-to-heart talk. There would hardly have been a chance of that in any case, because the doorbell was constantly ringing. Maybe the change Mamus has undergone has become the rule now. All sorts of people are showing their true colors. Did you know that Herr Rothe is a longtime fan of Franz Josef Strauss? Frau Schubert explained to me what difficulties I would have had as a teacher, and the two Graupner sisters talked about Denmark, where a cousin of theirs lives, and how at last they could write to her. When I asked in amazement why they hadn't

1. A coalition made up of the Christian Democratic Union, the German Social Union, and the "Democratic Awakening."

written to their cousin before now, I was corrected by cries of "Wrong, completely wrong," and then Tilda Graupner proudly proclaimed: "As head of accounting I didn't dare have contacts in the West." You're the star of the building. Your leaving makes you the first to have made the right decision. And some of the glow from your halo illumines your brother. The Schaffners are said to leave their apartment only after dark, or at least the revolutionary (or reactionary?) residents of the building have agreed not to greet those Stasi spies.

Robert wanted to look at photographs again. I had never noticed before that the albums only go up as far as Father's death.[1] The cupboard still has that same old darning-egg, sewing-kit odor.

Suddenly Mamus grabbed a photo and looked at it over the rim of her glasses—a handsome young couple—and cried, "What are they doing here!" She shredded it like a check that she had filled out wrong. "You weren't even born yet," Mamus informed me. "Total strangers!" She kept the scraps in her hand and went on providing commentary for the pictures that Robert held out to her. I secretly pocketed two shots of you. Sometimes I'm afraid I can't bear our being separated any longer. If only I could figure out what your plans are.

We had supper with Johann. His epistles are getting shorter. There were still a dozen of them lying around here, and I had no choice but to read them before the trip. When I did, it occurred to me that he might be gathering materials for a novel about a parish. Ever since he confessed to Franziska about us,[2] he's behaved rather rudely to me, especially in her presence. He could barely bring himself to offer me his hand. He had to "finish something up," he exclaimed, and disappeared. And so Robert and I waited in the kitchen, helping Franziska set the table and gazing out the window at the city. Franziska's charm has entirely deserted her over the past two years. She talks quite openly about her drinking and that she really needs to quit. Listening to her you might think she simply doesn't have time to spare for treatment at a clinic. Johann confided to me a couple of years ago that he sometimes provokes arguments because he needs the tension to be productive. I can't help thinking of that when I see Franziska like this.

1. Herrmann Türmer died in 1968.

2. There are just a few places where a strongly homoerotically tinged relationship between T. and Johann is suggested, and rarely is the implication as overt as it is here. Without knowledge of this fact, however, several passages would be incomprehensible.

She knows about my letters, because Johann reads them to her to prove that "nothing's going on" between him and me.

Gesine will soon be five. At first glance she seems untouched by all this unhappiness. She chose Robert as her knight, led him through the apartment, and played the piano for him. It was something new for her to learn that there are people who don't play some instrument.

When Jo's finished with his theology exams, there's a pastorate with three parishes waiting for him in the Ore Mountains, not far from Annaberg-Buchholz. Franziska and he have already visited it; the parsonage is large and has a huge orchard. It would never have come to this a year ago, Franziska said, because Johann would have looked for a job that left him time for writing and his band. Franziska doesn't want to leave Dresden come hell or high water, or at least not to go to Annaberg. And then came the bombshell! She was sure I already knew that Johann planned to be a candidate in the local elections. And three weeks ago it was he who accused me of betraying art.

When I asked him about it later, he beat around the bush. He had wanted to tell me in person and not write me. He didn't have a chance anyway, was doing it out of sense of responsibility, people had pushed him into it, maybe he could make a little difference. He sounded like someone who had just become a "candidate of the Party."[1] I told him there was no need for a bad conscience or for him to justify himself and that I thought he had made the right decision.

He also mentioned a bit too offhandedly that he hopes to publish a book about the events in Dresden last October.[2] Jo resents his own fate, because he was denied the privilege of being arrested, interrogated, and beaten. Believe me, I know him.

Jo had no questions for me. His aloofness, if not to say coldness left me paralyzed. If it hadn't been for Franziska, who was constantly passing me something, filling my teacup, and fussing over Robert, it would have felt like being shown the door.

But when I talked about you, he slowly thawed, and suddenly smiled at me with a heartfelt warmth that left me more helpless than his silence

---

1. Candidate of the Socialist Unity Party.

2. Between October 2nd and 8th there was a massive police deployment in Dresden. The initial cause was a fracas outside the Central Station, where trains carrying refugees from the German embassy in Prague had been passing through. Hundreds of people hoped to find a place on one of the trains. Cf. also the letter of May 25, '90.

had. He jumped up and presented me with a book, a duplicate he had found in a rare bookstore—a first edition of Eisler's *Faustus*[1]—and said that we definitely had to see each other more often, especially now. In the end we are all left with only a few friends anyway. He insisted, absurdly enough, on fixing sandwiches for our trip back; there might be a traffic jam. Robert and I took turns pointing to what we wanted and watched our sandwiches being prepared. Like a mason working plaster, Jo pushed the butter to the outer edge, spreading it around again several times as if to make certain everything was well greased. Then he looked up as if to say, this is something I'd do only for you.

Hugs, your Heinrich

PS: I'm sitting at the "green monster" and feel a draft at my back. I think Jörg or Georg has just come in. I turn around—and have to sneeze. "Gesundheit," a woman's voice says. I hear the door close. I sneeze two more times, and each time the same composed female voice blesses me. —"Who are you?" I ask, and walk toward her. She is crouched next to the stove, massaging her toes. A smile skitters across her face, briefly easing the tenseness in her features. Then she makes a hissing sound as she draws air in through her mouth and breathes it out again audibly through her nose. Her stockings have holes in the heels. "Don't look," she says. "I thought," she continues, and presses her lips together for a second, "I thought you asked me to come in. I knocked." With her back to the tile stove she slowly pushes herself to her feet. She tries to slip into her shoes. "Ouch! Ouch!" she whines. "That hurts!"

"For heaven's sake," I exclaim. She is looking up now, and what I had taken for a strand of hair stuck in the corner of her mouth turns out to be a scar. I realize that she's a noblewoman.

"It no longer keeps me warm," I say apologetically, pointing to my coat hanging beside the door. I am angry at myself because I've been planning for days to take it to the cleaners so they can restore its old qualities. "Would you like to come along?" I ask. "If we leave now we can make it to the cleaners by six."

"How can I possibly do that?" she cries. Her voice is clogged with

---

1. Hanns Eisler, *Johann Faustus* (Berlin, 1952).

tears. Didn't I have eyes in my head, even a blind man could that see she was in no condition to take so much as a single step.

"May I carry you?" I ask, unable to suppress the expectation in my voice. Her blouse has come open at the waist, and I see a triangle of her stomach, her navel at its center—just like the eye of God, I think. The comparison pleases me. The most wonderful opportunities often arise out of minor inconveniences, I say. She bursts into laughter. She lets her eyes wander openly over me. Evidently everything about me makes her laugh, I appear to provoke it. Finally, putting both hands over her mouth, she is overcome by a seizure of laughter she cannot control. She struggles for air, buckles over. Her hair, the tips bright red, falls down over her face, hiding it completely.

By now I was sitting on the edge of the bed and listening intently, I was that certain I had heard laughter. It was four in the morning. My day had begun.

Tuesday, Feb. 6, '90

Verotchka,

I don't like leaving the office here because I'm afraid I'll miss your call. Each time I come in it's all I can do to keep from asking about you. I get testy if Jörg or Georg stays on the telephone too long. I tried reaching you from Paris, but I was doing something wrong and couldn't understand the recording either.

Yes, we were in Paris, at least we claim we were. We were back by nine on Sunday. "We've just come from Paris," Robert announced to a neighbor in the stairwell. Instead of being amazed or asking questions, she gave Michaela and me a nasty look, as if we tolerated lying. Then what Michaela told her about the procedure with our papers made her all the more suspicious. Truth is no help when you're trying to convince someone.

I'm glad it's behind us. I finally let myself be talked into going along for Robert's sake—it was a family outing. Michaela was sure we'd have a fine time even without money. The official title was "Three-Day Trip." The first day was Friday. We were scheduled to leave Eisenach at 5 p.m.

Hundreds of people were waiting on a muddy square surrounded by buildings waiting to be demolished and a couple of murky streetlamps. If it hadn't been for the bags and plastic sacks, it would have looked like the start of a demonstration. Mamus had been waiting for us in Eisenach since two in the afternoon. She was all on edge because we didn't arrive until around four thirty. As the armada of buses pulled in, we were shooed from one end of the square to the other. When the bus doors opened the drivers appeared and called out their destinations, then sat down behind the wheel again.

There were two for Paris. We were afraid they were going to pull out without us, but then found seats in the third and fourth rows, far enough forward to see out the windshield. Next to us was the ferry to Amsterdam, on our left one for Venice. The procedure was the same for everyone. First we were given West German papers that—except for name and address—had all the details right, down to height and eye color. At the French border, so we were instructed, we were to hold the papers up[1] and look inconspicuous—whatever that meant. In the Venice bus they were busy practicing holding their documents up. They waved as they drove off.

Robert chose me to sit next to him; the seats were very comfortable and you could barely hear the motor. Not one loud word disrupted our gentle flight along the dark autobahn. As if it were a familiar routine, I left the bus at each stop with everyone else, joined the dash for the restroom, and while we waited stuffed my mouth with a hard-boiled egg from Mamus's picnic box.

Just before midnight we reached Frankfurt Airport, the trip's first sightseeing stop. We wandered the deserted departure halls, reading the names of airlines, and greeting the dark-skinned cleaning ladies, who responded by turning away.

The French had no interest in our bus, and we were first aware of France at our next pit stop. Mamus was snoring softly. It was dawn before I began to feel tired. I saw dark gray hanging over the Paris suburbs, and the next thing I knew we were driving through the city. It was drizzling, and the sky looked even darker. It wasn't until the Place de Bastille that I figured out where we were. From there on my sense of orientation worked without hitch or flaw. I displayed my brilliance for Robert and Michaela, but even I was amazed to be driving along the Boulevard Henri IV and see the islands emerge on our right and, yes indeed, Notre-

1. A standard procedure at the time, as the editor himself learned firsthand.

Dame.[1] I prayed the mantra of our yearnings: Quai de la Tournette, Quai de Montebello, Quai St-Michel, Quai des Grands Augustins, and gazed at the old familiar booths of the *bouquinistes*.

Even as I was prophesying the Louvre right on time, I felt uneasy. I was shooting off the fireworks of our knowledge of a faraway world without feeling a thing. Maybe it was simply that you weren't there, or maybe I suspected that within an hour it would sound as profane as a taxi driver's chatter. Ah, at that same moment it degenerated into the know-it-all lectures of a paterfamilias who has conscientiously done his vacation homework.

We drove north across the Pont de la Concorde, past the Madeleine and St-Lazare, and up the Rue d' Amsterdam. I presumed Sacré-Cœur would be our next goal and was hoping that with the first ray of sun and some coffee things would improve somewhat, when the driver announced that we were on our way to the most famous "mousetrap" in the world. We made two turns, taking them very slowly, while our bus rocked back and forth and was lifted up as if on a wave before we were rolling again.

Then I saw the women lining the sidewalks—whores at eight in the morning. Conversation in the bus died; the driver blustered on about love for sale. In the middle of his babbling there was a thump underneath us as if we hadn't cleared something. The driver cursed, and with a crackle the loudspeakers went silent. We drove on slowly. Everyone stared out the window in a kind of devotional silence. The monstrosity of being able to select a woman for a bit of cash! Robert turned to me with a crazy grin, hesitated as if about to ask a question, but then gazed straight ahead again, his forehead pressed to the glass.

Suddenly one of the women stepped away from the facade—her skintight pants opened from the calves down to wide bell-bottoms—and ran along beside us. Her hair was covered by a bright scarf wrapped around her head pirate-style. She approached our window, moved closer—she was very young—kissed her hand, and pressed the fingertips to the window right where Robert sat. Even though she had to run to stay even with us, she gazed earnestly inside, but the women behind her had burst into laughter, buckled over with laughter, and we could hear

1. As children the two had had a Hungarian street map of Paris that they had tried to learn by heart.—Information provided by V. T.

their catcalls and yowls—a cordon of women laughing at us. She rapped on the window three times, then the whole scene vanished.

Patches of red emerged on Robert's neck. "She just liked you," Michaela said, trying to put him at ease.

We set foot on Paris soil at the base of Sacré-Cœur. The air was milder than I had expected. The sea of buildings gave off a serenity that even the few cars and mopeds glistening through the streets like minnows could not disrupt. We climbed the steps. "How often, ever since we had seen fall arrive on the Boulevard St-Germain, had we come up here, our work done, chilled, looking out at the rain on the Seine," I recited.[1] Robert wanted to know what the large roof off to the left was, and was surprised I didn't know for sure which train station it might be, or if it even was a train station at all. I was amazed at how few prominent features there were—the Madeleine, the Louvre, the Eiffel Tower far to the right, all the rest was a blur, which was fine by me. What I wanted to do most was to stretch out on one of the benches and sleep. The white stone reminded me of the Fisherman's Bastion.[2] The pigeons scared off by the street sweeper came from Neustadt Station.[3]

Suddenly a man was kneeling in front of me in the middle of the sidewalk. He was like a stone that had fallen out of the sky. He was looking at the ground as if praying and offered us a view of a wreath of sweaty strands of hair. The shapeless thing in his hands turned out to be a cap that held a single coin. I didn't have any francs and yet didn't dare move on. Mamus came to my aid, stuffed a bill into his cap, and whispered in perfect German: "From the whole family." A woman who we later learned was a German teacher from Erfurt said it was unacceptable for one person to grovel before another like that. As she went on speaking and a semicircle formed around her, poor Lazarus—probably thinking she was speaking to him—slowly raised his head. When the group saw his badly scraped forehead and nose and gazed into dead-tired eyes and a toothless half-opened mouth, they fell silent. We regrouped and fled.

After that time took flight. As if every spot deserved a special sniff, we were let out near the Centre Pompidou, the Arc de Triomphe, the Place de la Concorde, and Les Invalides, although with the exception of the Centre we would have had a better view from the bus.

1. Ernest Hemingway, *A Moveable Feast*.
2. Built in Budapest at the end of the nineteenth century, it offers a view of the Danube and of all of Pest across the river.
3. Train station in Dresden.

When we stopped at the Eiffel Tower, at the far end of the field, we set off, *en familie,* in search of a restroom. On the way back we saw our travel group gather within a matter of seconds at the middle door of the bus and then just as quickly form a queue. Our female copilot was spooning soup into white plastic bowls with an oversize ladle. Robert and I got in line. At last it was our turn, but since neither of us could produce either bowl or spoon, we were told to be patient and wait until some fast eaters, as our copilot put it, could hand over an empty bowl that we could rinse out.

In the course of all this I missed the announcement that, having now been "fortified," we were supposed to "climb" the tower. The first group was already on its way when I attempted to persuade Mamus and Michaela to join me in a walk. I succeeded only to the extent that Mamus slipped me a few francs—and with that we went our separate ways.

I thought of running after them, even took a few steps—suddenly I was on the verge of tears. The realization that for two hours I would now be freer than I had ever been in my whole life robbed me of my will. I went back to the café where we had made use of the restroom and decided that, protected against all eventualities, I would wait there. Probably because he recognized me, the garçon hurried over to prevent me from entering; he didn't even make the effort to wave me off with his whole hand, but just flexed his extended fingers in disgust a few times. I pointed to the empty barstools and went for one.

I pronounced coffee with the accent on the second syllable and also ordered a *mineralnaya voda,* as if it were less embarrassing to speak Russian than German. I then just pointed at one of the two bottles that the woman behind the bar held up under my nose, and noticed too late that it was the other one I wanted, the carbonated one.

Oh, how I wanted to talk with somebody. I watched the waitress fiddle with a huge espresso machine, stared at the clasp of her bra shimmering through her white blouse, and felt totally superfluous.

I was served coffee with foaming milk, made good use of the large sugar shaker, and watched the sugar sink beneath the foam and cling to the rim of the cup.

I had already drunk two or three sips when my nose suddenly picked up the scent of burnt milk. I stirred in another spoonful of sugar, and went on sipping, but the second I set the cup down again, I smelled burnt milk again.

The waitress was peeling a lemon right in front of me. My first thought was that a coworker had taken her place—the hands were so alarmingly old, so wrinkled. I pulled out my wallet, stood there waiting to pay the bill, and forfeited half my francs because I didn't want to look cheap by leaving only coins behind.

And I hadn't even finished my coffee. The memory had been too overwhelming, the memory of plastic cups—those green, red, or brown plastic cups[1]—brimful with scalded milk, the skin floating on top, which would reappear no matter how often I fished it out and wiped it on my pants or the edge of my plate, then would stick to my lips, leaving me gasping in disgust for air. I left.

Although it was windy and cold, spring seemed to have suddenly arrived on earth. Everything was bathed in a different light. I walked on, as if I could find you in Paris, as if it were possible that at any moment you could be walking toward me. I wanted you here beside me—and with you everything that we knew, that we had seen, that belonged to us, our streets, our world. The concentration, amusement, and delight in all the things we honored and embraced, all the things we craved as brother and sister. The white décolletage of the woman selling cigarettes against the shadows of her little booth. I had to bend at the knee to see into her face. A twenty-five-year-old, who, wrapped in her scarf, turned fifty-two yesterday. I say what I want, she greets me, she repeats my request, she hands me the pack, I pay, she thanks me, I thank her, we say our good-byes.

Like a man gambling, I let my route be decided by each new stoplight. I didn't know what I should be looking for, the only thing I knew for certain was that I would find you. My first steps of freedom, it kept going through my mind, my first steps of freedom. I wanted to forget my age, my name, my birthplace. All I wanted was to see and to set one foot in front of the other and have you beside me.

Two North Africans asked me something in voices as costly as some heavy glistening fabric. I shrugged and walked on. Awakened to bray its market wares, Paris was offering a sale on spring in early February. I touched fruit crates, metal railings, house walls, door handles. I knew you were near. I didn't see you, that would have been too much, but I was certain that we were breathing the same air, I could hear you.

1. For T. plastic cups were the symbol of the official world, from kindergarten to the army—information provided by V. T.

I pointed at a portal and said: "The gate for the riders, madame," and you said, pointing to the next door: "The gate for the pedestrians, monsieur."[1] You were constantly seeing something I did not see, that I didn't notice until you pointed it out to me: the sign DANGER DE MORT on a blue box wrapped in transparent foil, DANGER DE MORT. I am afraid of losing you. But I dare not let anyone notice. I must decide, I must board the train in two hours—back, back behind the wall, they've only let me out for a short time because my book has been published here, because it lies in every bookstore display, and we stroll from window to window. It is still too early, the shops are closed.

At an intersection the letters on the canopies above the Dome and Rotonde and Toscana[2] line up in a row. No, I say, no. I don't want to be without you. I want to see Dresden with you, when the sun has not yet risen above the roofs and the morning star is shining in the pastel pink air, the fog above the Elbe, the various reds that encircle cigarette filters before they are tossed over the curb at a bus stop, the bright lady's glove on the sidewalk, that everyone avoids, no one picks up, no one steps on, that I take to be a lily that has fallen from your bouquet, DANGER DE MORT.

Suddenly Mamus and Robert were standing right in front of me, Michaela was listening to an older gentleman explain something to her, looked up, and gave me a wave. "Punctual to the minute," Mamus said, praising me. On my return from the world beyond I was punctual to the minute. It was drizzling.

Michaela gave me a handkerchief, telling me to wipe the sweat off my face. Mamus made me put on her scarf. The wind had wrecked her umbrella.

We followed Robert, walked passed the nearest cafés, and quickly lost our orientation. I was shivering, and at one corner, just as we were walking by, a huge omelet was being served, and I almost died of hunger. Mamus held up her wallet and nodded. Of course we had now landed where no one wants to land. The waiter laid a garish red place mat of washable plastic in front of each of us, as if we were children. Michaela put her school French to use to order and blushed as the waiter departed with a *"merci, madame."*

The waiter brought a can of beer and poured it for me while we

1. Quote from André Breton's *Nadja*.
2. Café in Dresden.

watched in devotion. No sooner had we whispered our *"merci"* than Michaela said she had actually just ordered water. I drank the bitter Scandinavian import and in my weariness would have loved to lay my head on the table. I had to squeeze past barrels and sacks lining the narrow hallway to the restroom. From the depths of the building someone was coming toward me and going through the exact same motions. Just before we met we both dodged simultaneously to one side. So then, my doppelgänger dwells here. My beer proved to be as expensive as my omelet. We wrote a few postcards, one to you.

The whole time we heard music outside, a band that must have been playing nearby. Aware of how much his curiosity pleased Mamus, Robert insisted that we had to move on. He was all the more disappointed then when there was no stage, no audience to be found anywhere, as if the Beatles, Neil Young, and Elton John were just hanging in the Paris air.

A Japanese man was sitting at a corner in the midst of some instruments, with a frame attached to his shoulders to hold his harmonica and a guitar across his knees. It took a moment for me to realize that we were standing before the answer to our riddle. This Japanese fellow was the real thing, the true Orpheus of Paris. During "Heart of Gold," when he wasn't playing his harmonica, a little white cloud of breath formed in the cold air as if he were literally singing his soul out.

We listened in admiration for a while. I gave him what francs I had left, which felt very satisfying. Happiness and indifference seemed interchangeable. We could stay here or leave on the bus, it was all good.

During the final "tour of Paris lights," which was really just part of the return trip, I fell asleep. I had the feeling I kept waking up every few minutes but without ever letting go of my dream. At one point I have to get back as fast as possible, suddenly my pass reads SL instead of EL.[1] I can't find my uniform anywhere in the apartment. I'm angry because I really didn't want this leave in the first place and am now sitting without my uniform on a train that stays longer and longer at each station in order to keep to its schedule of arrivals and departures. The sunlight is so dazzling outside that the names of the stations are illegible. No one at the base gate will believe I'm a soldier. Then I remember my short-clipped haircut. I keep tugging at it, practicing how I'll use it as proof.

Instead of my ticket I pull out currency and hold it as if I'm looking at

1. Military abbreviations: Short Leave of two days; Extended Leave of three days.

a pocket watch. It's a ten-franc bill. Which means I have ten minutes to get back. Although one franc after the other goes by, I'm not worried. I know that I'm dreaming and that I only have to wait a bit and I'll be able to wake myself up and be in Paris. Once in Paris I'll sell my watch in order to pay for my stay there. I reach into my pocket. Instead of a watch I keep pulling out ten-franc bills. I calculate how many times I'll have to do this to be able to stay for a day, a week, a year.

Even though the travelers with whom I share the compartment are behaving more and more like schoolkids on an outing and dazzle one another's eyes with West German passes, which they hold in the palms of their hands like pocket mirrors, I remain calm because, after all, I have my stuff. I am convinced that I can present my things at least as fast as they can show their passes, because my yo-yo hand is becoming increasingly deft now at catching and tossing brightly colored pieces of fruit as if they were tennis balls. And not just that. I give each piece of fruit a name. How easy French is, I am reading it from a little blackboard that appears with each piece of fruit—I don't even have to learn vocabulary. Not until I catch the same piece of fruit twice in a row—it shimmers a dull orange and has five syllables—do I realize that my voice changes with each piece of fruit and that for some time now I've been singing a melody. To catch the attention of my fellow travelers I have to keep fruit moving in sequence at juggler's speed, otherwise the music that accompanies my movements will go unnoticed. But in the next moment I regret this new tempo. It is impossible to pronounce polysyllabic words at anything close to full length. The *merci* fruit flies toward me twice, but both times all I manage is just a *mers. Mers,* I croak, *mers.* My voice is gone. No matter in what rich colors the fruit glistens, all I can croak each time is *mers, mers,* just *mers.* My fellow travelers make a joke of trying to snatch my fruit away. I am outraged by this. Mamus encourages them, in fact, because she thinks she's doing precisely what I want. I scream at Mamus, but before I can see her face, the compartment door is flung open. In the same moment all the hand mirrors are flashed in sync at the badge on the border guard's cap. He nods and is about to close the door again when his glance falls on me. I raise my hand, but only as if to greet him, because even I no longer believe that any fruit will be flying toward me. Everyone groans. Because of me we are being shunted to a sidetrack.

Your Heinrich

Dear Jo,

At some point you will get a postcard proving that we were in Paris.

On Monday, the day after our return, we learned purely by chance that Aunt Trockel, the woman who looked after Robert, had died. Just three weeks ago, while we were in Offenburg, she cooked for him and looked after him. She was no longer among the living when we wrote her from Paris. Our last visit with her at New Year's had been such fun.[1]

Aunt Trockel was Michaela's first friend in Altenburg (and maybe her only one too). Michaela claims that Aunt Trockel resembled Virginia Woolf a bit. I disagree. To me it always looked as if she had far too many long, crooked teeth in her mouth. Aunt Trockel avoided smiling or even laughing because then her ivories were bared to the gums. If she laughed anyway, she automatically put a hand to her mouth, which looked like an affectation. Her invitations always terrified me a little, for ever since she stopped working in the variety store, what we were treated to was all the stuff that had run through her mind over the last week. Michaela always showed a patience that often left me flabbergasted, or even angry. But in Michaela's eyes Aunt Trockel enjoyed total diplomatic immunity. For without Aunt Trockel's support she might have had to throw in the towel as an actor.

What should I tell you about Paris? It was too late. For me it was like someone who upon his arrival—having longed for the day a thousand times over—learns that the person for whom he has eaten his heart out all his life has just left town.

During the two hours that the family was romping on the Eiffel Tower and I could do whatever I wanted, the wall-demon took possession of me. I panicked, as if I had to decide whether to stay or leave, even though I was in control of my senses the whole time.

Why should articles be an agony for me? In principle they're just stories. Concrete lead, everyday situation, focus, then pack it full of all the facts you know, maybe a couple of similar cases, finally the closing surprise pirouette that leads you back to the beginning—that at least is how Jörg the engineer describes it. He reads newspapers all day to expand his

---

1. At the end of this volume of letters the reader may perhaps see the occasion differently.

repertoire of tricks and twists. Jörg has managed to smuggle his way onto the Commission Against Corruption and Abuse of Office as the representative of the New Forum. That will supply him with our future headline stories, free delivery included.

I'm awake between four and five every morning. I'm slowly getting used to it. I listen to the radio or study grammar books. I'm a diligent *élève* in the office—make coffee, sort what little mail there is, deal with the telephone and the stove, edit as I type, and practice writing news articles. My concluding initials, however, betray me. If I don't capitalize them, the alien becomes a classical *et*.[1]

I'm afraid above all of careless mistakes and the unknown—of some miscalculation or the printer's vagaries or what will be in the mail. I live here in an oasis. Michaela tells herself that everything's fine at the theater, but it's a disaster. My mother gulps down tranquilizers before going to the clinic. And what Robert has to say about school isn't exactly amusing either. I'm amazed these kids aren't turning into cynics. You have to love them just for that.

I spent the afternoon today with Larschen, an old farmer who has assured us several times that he's waited to have a paper like ours to read for more than half his life. He ignored my objection that it doesn't exist yet. The whole revolution, he claims, would be nothing without people like us, who do something with possibilities. He mumbled the first two syllables of "revolution," turned the third into a trumpet blast, and swallowed the last. "Do something!" is his battle cry.

He wrote his memoirs for his family, for his three granddaughters, but without any hope of ever being published. When I asked him to take over the "Tips for Garden and Field" column, he just asked about length and deadlines and offered to deliver his text on our manuscript paper—he owns a typewriter.

Fred, who's supposed to organize sales and always looks as serious as an elector prince painted by Cranach calls Larschen "Snowcap," because of his towering mass of thick white hair.

Our family is slowly expanding. We'll have a secretary starting in March, Ilona, who currently helps out only part-time. Her glasses are way too big for her little head, a grandmother who flirts with the line

---

1. The E.T. in Spielberg's film of the same name becomes a lower-case Latin *et,* meaning "and."

"and I ain't even forty." For Ilona men like Jörg and Georg have a purpose in life, the newspaper, whereas Fred and I, the born peons, should be happy just to lend a hand. Mention a name, and you can be certain Ilona knows the person and has an opinion of them, usually a poor one. No sooner has she made her disparaging remark than she takes a frightened look around and whispers, "Oh m'god, did I really say that?"

For Marion, Jörg's wife, the pecking order is unclear. She is the only one who addresses me with the formal pronoun, and likes to talk about the sacrifice I'm making. She thinks I abandoned the theater for the sake of the general welfare, says I've given up what is best and most beautiful, and then gazes at me very fondly. She's already been given notice as the librarian at some branch mine of the Brown Coal Combinat, and says she can well understand what it means to turn your back on art. Then she nods and raises her already raised eyebrows even higher as if waiting for me to agree. Ilona thinks Marion looks like Mireille Matheiu. She reminds me more of a silent-film actress whose photo I ran across in a book from Reclam, landscape format as I recall.[1] Marion will be working for us half days starting in March. Georg bestowed on her the title of editorial secretary.

Robert, who is on vacation, stops by the office around one o'clock. Then we go together to innkeeper Gallus, who recently granted us the privilege of a reserved table. Of course everyone is welcome, but they won't find a seat. We have a table for four set aside for us at one p.m. Soup, main course, and dessert cost between two fifty and four marks. The accompanying status, however, can hardly be overestimated. Our innkeeper is in his early sixties, but smooth cheeks and observant eyes constantly darting back and forth lend his face a youthful look. He takes special delight in asking questions like: "Have you protested yet?" None of us knows what he means. "And you call yourselves a newspaper?" We look contrite. "They're opening the market up to anyone who wants to jump in, that shouldn't be, should it?" His usual conclusion then is the assertion that the new market economy is going to destroy old estab-

---

1. Anna Seghers, *The Trial of Jeanne d'Arc in Rouen, 1431,* radio play (Leipzig, 1975); T. evidently means still photographs included in the book and taken from the silent film *La passion de Jeanne d'Arc* (1928), directed by C. T. Dreyer.

lished local businesses. "They're ruining their own people! Am I right, or not?"

By "their own people" he means in particular the illustrious circle with tables reserved for noon. The nooners can choose among three dishes; we have to take whatever's left. The nooners are Altenburg's senators, its noblemen of commerce and crafts. These good dozen quaint old gentlemen have apparently chosen a lady to preside over each table—all elderly ladies, who betray their nobility by their stiff posture at table.

In their eyes we're parvenus who bear keeping an eye on. Thus far they've only approached us in writing, although they've been very frugal about it. Our innkeeper is forever handing us the torn-off margins of newspapers or receipts ripped in half, on which there's often only a name and address, along with an added: "Knows something."

On days when these notes are passed along, we're treated with special attention. Instead of plying us with questions, he gives the shiny table several extra swipes. While he serves, his belly bumps against a shoulder. When we pay the bill he rummages through his change, pulls up short, fully perplexed—even after our second "That's fine!"—and with wide eyes lets the coins drop back into his change purse. Just as we're about to stand up, he braces one hand against the table, lowers his head conspiratorially, and slips the note out on the table. "Lend an ear," he says, "this is quite a case, famous man, Dippel, doesn't mean anything to you? Dippel! Ran a nursery, major operation. The Botanical Garden, that's his work, did all the landscaping for Dietrich, sewing machine Dietrich, and around the train station, all Dippel, famous man actually, it was all taken away, had never been a Nazi, all confiscated, totally unfair, put out, tossed out of his own house, pay a visit, be worth your time, definitely." We promise to follow the lead first thing and thank him for the tip. At which point our innkeeper's eyes close, his lips pucker with satisfaction. "Knew I could depend on you," he says, extending his big soft hand as if it were a gift for each of us, including Robert.

Hugs, Enrico

PS: Yesterday morning a smiling man in a dark blue dederon smock stopped in. He wanted to place an ad, asked for pen and paper, drew a square box, and began to write. At one point he had to make a call to ask the price of wooden ladders. There was joy in his every word, his every movement. I made a mental note of even his most casual gestures—like the way he shoved the page at me and then rapped it with his pudgy fingers ending in short, black-rimmed nails.

When I told him the price of the ad (one mark eighty per column millimeter), he whistled through his teeth, then angled to one side to reach under his smock and pull out his wallet, from which several hundreds spilled out over the desk. He would take care of that now, he said, and thumbed four Karl Marxes out onto the desk.

I said thank you, but he didn't budge. I said that his ad would appear on February 16th in twenty thousand copies, at ninety pfennigs a copy. When he still showed no signs of departing, I listed our various columns: news, local politics, business, history, art, and sports, and also promised crossword puzzles, a horoscope, and caricatures. He nodded his approval. Unfortunately he didn't have much time, was going to have to leave. I said that I didn't want to keep him. "But now," he said, "I need the receipt."

A receipt. I knew nothing about receipts. I began searching and tried to make my motions look purposeful. He said he'd be satisfied with just a normal sheet of paper as long as it was "banged with a seal." At just that moment I found our Offenburg bag of gewgaws and among them was, in fact, a receipt book, incredibly practical, including carbon paper, and cardboard backing, so that even without instructions I might have managed to fill the thing out.

Without his amiability flagging in the least, our customer apologized and said it had to be stamped, otherwise that lovely West-style receipt was of no use to him. He asked me to send him a stamped version, he trusted us. He rapped the table once more in farewell.

Monday, Feb. 12, '90

Dear Jo,

(Maybe what life is about is finding an appropriate layout for yourself.) I never realized what layout actually means. It wasn't until after I saw how easy it is to calculate the size of an article so that it can be transferred to the page proof that I once again believed we were going to make it. Layout is our map, our constitution, our Lord's Prayer. Layout (Jörg accents it on the first syllable, Georg on the second) prevents you from being unfair and yielding to your own biases, there's no showing favor or disfavor, there's no forgetting. Layout is civilization and law, it's courtesy and decorum, a taskmaster who grants you your freedom.

The work itself was an orgy. The fiat to complete the job was larger than our wills, than our energies, and immunized us against exhaustion. It grabbed hold of us like a demon, a three-headed, six-handed monster. A surgery team probably knows something of the same frenzy. Only now can I appreciate what a miracle a newspaper without blank spaces really is.

The days leading up to it, however, were a nightmare, as if our ship were capsizing at launching. We were drowning in material, but whole pages were still empty. The worst was Georg, who wouldn't sign off on anything, not even his own articles. The first issue was supposed to be something special.

When Fred likewise put his two cents in—as head of sales he'd be the one that readers would first vent their anger on—Jörg threw him out of the room.

Sunday morning the only page in the folder was Jan Steen's. The other eleven still lay ahead of us. Georg's wife, Franka, took her boys to church so that Georg could polish his gas-station article in the living room, Jörg did yet another rewrite of his lead article, I paged through dictionaries (I now know how to spell *mise en scène*) and tended the stove. Fred went to Offenburg to pick up the VW bus. On the evening before he had laid linoleum in the room opposite. It's to be our second office.

Around eleven o'clock the doorbell rang. Three men wanted to see Georg and Fred, claimed that they had an appointment, had made his acquaintance at the public market. They hung their long coats on the coatrack, three in a row. The short fellow in charge wrinkled his nose and began snooping about the room, he had to touch everything, pick up everything. His fingers set the postal scales into stormy motion. He patted the stove tiles and the table, gave the wood on the chair arms a once-over with a thumbnail, and told his adjutants to rap the ceiling beams. "Incredible," was his diagnosis, "truly incredible."

His outfit—brown corduroy pants, dark green sport coat, yellow westover[1]—had a refined look compared to those of his lackeys, whose

1. Sweater vest.

taste ran to lilac and burgundy. Once their undersize boss had shaken our hands and taken a seat, he couldn't hold back, he had to share his impressions of this "legacy of Communism."

Jörg went right on hammering away at the "green monster," snorting like Sviatoslav Richter. Each time their boss paused to catch his breath, the colorful guys jumped in to announce their own observations, calling us enthusiasts, men who were rolling up their sleeves at last.

When I asked their leader what *his* profession was, he stood up and with profuse apologies snapped business cards onto the table, as if playing a jack of trumps. Followed instantly by two aces. I was dealing with the "managing director" of the newspaper in Giessen, plus two of his editors.

While we talked and talked, I fetched our page proofs from their cubbyhole and spread them out over the table. As if decorating a table with gifts, I laid the photographs and articles on my side. To cap it off I picked up our layout design and gazed upon it with the certainty of a magician who has pulled off his trick.

The managing director bent forward, spread his arms, and exclaimed, "Hot type! You're working with hot type?" For a moment I mistook the little tufts of hair on his fingers for flies. "You don't even know what that is," he barked at his lackeys, smiled at me, passed a hand over the white sheets of paper, and pointed his chin at the layout design. "That's how it's going to look?"

I nodded.

"Fine, fine," the managing director said, and began asking me enigmatic questions—for instance, how many points the headlines and the subhead had—but fortunately each time provided the answer himself: twenty-two, or eighteen, and twelve for the subhead. And the text? Right, eight. And the font? We gazed out over the wide, white sea that lay placidly before us. "I haven't even asked you," he said, suddenly spinning around, "for your permission."

"But of course," I said, casting my eyes back to the horizon. Jörg hammered away incessantly at his keyboard.

The managing director, who had his jacket off by now, stretched imperious arms. His boys hurried over and eagerly undid his cuff links. He meticulously rolled up his sleeves. Suddenly his hands were hovering over the proofs, darting here and there like dragonflies above water, halting briefly, only to begin tracing their invisible pattern.

He demanded a pencil, typometer, and pocket calculator—"A slip of paper will do too"—stepped back briefly, then set to work.

What followed was an hour during which for the first time I learned something that might prove useful for earning my daily bread—that is, a craft. And for the first time since leaving school, I solved an equation with an unknown.

The managing director was not interested in getting rid of nouns and increasing the number of verbs, or in varying sentence structure, while keeping the meaning clear; the managing director asked about the number of characters and lines, about which photo belonged with which article, about what was intended for two or three columns. His hands had now become mice scurrying across the paper.

My article on Dippel the landscape gardener was six lines too long in both columns. I deleted and was terrified by how easy it was. The managing editor presented me with my next cutting job.

Life came coursing back into me. The page was finished. The managing director was already planning the next when Georg appeared and invited us all—including our guests from Giessen—to a midday meal. In their hunger the adjutants forgot the purpose of their boss's outstretched arms. "Cuff links," he hissed, and both began rummaging in their jacket pockets.

At first I assumed we would finish by eight that evening. All we had to do was calculate and cut. Ten o'clock came, midnight, then one, then three. Around four we slipped the pages into their folder. The best part was tidying up. Georg cleaned the stove, Jörg his electric typewriter. Finally we found ourselves sitting next to the folder lying there ready to be handed on—as if waiting for our baby to fall asleep.

Tomorrow we'll drive over to proofread.

Hugs, E.

PS: Vera sends her greetings. She called from Beirut. Her mother-in-law (who bears the lovely name Athena) is ill and is resisting any idea of traveling to Berlin. Nicola is toying with the notion of giving up his shop in Berlin and taking over his dead father's. The building is in ruins, not one stone left on top of another. But the more expensive fabrics were in the cellar and survived both bombing and plundering. Mother and son see this as a sign and wonder. Apparently no one has any idea what role Vera is to play in these plans, or at least she doesn't.

And since my sister is famous for taking offense if she doesn't feel as if she's the center of attention, I try to offer every conceivable declaration of my love. It's questionable, however, if my letters even reach her. If you want to give it a try—Madame Vera Barakat, Beirut—Starco area—Wadi aboujmil, the building next to Alliance College—4th floor.

Tuesday, Feb. 13, '90

Dear Jo,

This past week I have had more new, and strange, encounters than ever I used to in a year. The day before yesterday[1] I was working over a couple of lines about the new animal shelter (it has yet to become an animal shelter, more like a wild zoo, previously the dog division of the VP).[2] I had enough material, and the headline too, but was getting nowhere writing it. Either it sounded too sentimental or too aloof. I needed a thousand five hundred characters, but no more. An hour into it and I still hadn't put together one reasonable sentence. It was as if I had been bewitched. When I went to add coal to the stove, it had gone out. And I couldn't get rid of the odor of "wet dog." I washed my hands, sniffed at the wastepaper basket, checked behind the typewriter, cursed. The moment I put my fingers to the keyboard, there was the "wet dog" again.

I dreamed the whole night through and felt befuddled all morning. I had appointments the next day in Meuselwitz and Lucka, and in between I collected news in nearby villages and had the secretary in Wintersdorf make me some chamomile tea.

Back at the office I found some photos in my cubbyhole, including the ones I had made at the animal shelter. There were still hot embers in

---

1. The dating of this letter is problematic. There is hardly any way to make the details dovetail. T. is evidently mistaken about the date. "The day before yesterday" was Sunday, that is the same day on which they worked late into the night. An earlier date is likewise hardly possible. And yet discrepancies also arise for Wednesday and Thursday. The most probable time for the letter to have been written is Thursday morning, although it seems odd that there is no mention of the day on which the first issue was published.

2. Volkspolizei, the People's Police.

the stove. This time I stuffed it with briquettes, as if planning to work the night, and sat myself down at the typewriter.

My eyes hurt. From time to time a shiver went up my back. The cold is leaving my bones, I told myself. The idea comforted me. But then—it sounds more mysterious than it was—I had the vague sense that someone behind me had just carefully set a hat on my head.

A man was seated at the table—if we haven't locked the door, no one pays much attention to our hours in any case—someone whom I knew from somewhere, someone I associated with good news of some sort, not some local folklorist.

"Don't let me disturb you," he said very amiably, and by way of greeting offered a hint of a bow. "I shall wait with all due respect, it is solely my fault that we have failed to meet, please, do continue." That's more or less how he put it, as if it would be perfectly all right if I ignored him and went on typing. His whole demeanor matched what one imagines a proper older gentleman should be—though he's forty at most. His choice of words and pronunciation reminded me of Hungarian students studying at Jena, who have learned their German from Rilke and Hoffmannsthal—his rolled "r" fit nicely as well.

"We had an appointment at twelve," he said, trying to jog my memory. "I hope that my failure to keep it has not given rise to any difficulties for you. I am at your service, whenever it suits your conveniency." Conveniency! He used words that he evidently dared to utter only with a bow. I was just about to say that I didn't recall an appointment, when a sound arose from his direction, a decorous yowl—or how do you describe a dog yawning? So *that* was it. The dog in the animal shelter photos. And him next to it, clearly in focus, although his glasses had reflected the flash. He had spelled his name for me, but I had forgotten to ask for his address and profession, had been angry at myself for not doing it. So I could make up for it now.

I had wanted to characterize the dog as "a little wolflike," above all the muzzle, its build not as powerful as that of a German shepherd, the pelt blackish gray. It's blind in one eye. Its fate was to be the framework for my article.

"Everyone will read about your good deed," I said, walking over and handing him the photos. He looked through them, but before I could sit down again or had time to learn his name, there they were in front of me again, on the edge of the table. What I really wanted was to ask him to repeat the trick—he had tossed the little stack so casually with a flick of the wrist. There was nothing arrogant about it, more an expression of his keeping a sympathetic distance toward himself.

He bent down to the dog at his side—a singsong, no, a calming lullaby, and in English!

"I hope I need fear no indiscretions," he exclaimed with what I discovered was an English accent. "I understand nothing of literature and eternity," he continued. "My visions are of another sort!" I had no idea why he had said this, and assumed I had missed something.

He merely wanted to remark, he said, coming to my aid, that it would be better if people who were the subject of an article did not read it in print themselves. He could not help being aware of one thing or another that was publicly reported about him. Often it was the journalists themselves—few who called themselves that deserved the proud title—who compelled him to read such things and then were amazed . . . he waved me off, and in the next moment was holding a business card between his fingers—"better one too many than none at all"—and slipped it across the table to me.

Clemens von Barrista—white lettering on black. Nothing else. But that wasn't how he had spelled it for me. But it seemed familiar all the same.

You would of course have no real picture of Barrista were I to leave out a description of his eyes—compared to his glasses, yours are a windowpane. Huge google-eyes, as if he's peering through a peephole. A dark mustache provides makeshift cover for his harelip and, together with his black hair, makes his acne-scarred face look even more pallid. Evidently he has come to terms with his looks—not a trace of insecurity. He pushed back from the table a little, his white shirt spread taut across his little potbelly.

The more I lost myself in gazing at him, the less I knew what I was supposed to do. At which point Clemens von Barrista stood up and said something like, "There's nothing to be done," and offered his hand in farewell. Where had my mind been?

"Please do sit down," I said quickly. "Make yourself comfortable." He thanked me, looked about the office, and, once he was seated again, fell back into his peculiar German that I can barely reproduce, if at all. He made fun of our hard chairs, or better, he praised a good armchair as the "hallmark" of reason, of reason thirsting for deeds, hungry for deeds, and sang a hymn in praise of luxury, of humankind's rebirth in a spirit of luxury. His patois culminated in the aphorism: "The beautiful would appear beautiful, the good may be good, but better is better!"

I found his insinuations tactless, removed the pillow from my swivel chair, and offered it to him. "There's not a lot of luxury here," I said.

That wasn't what he meant, not for the world! It had been a quote, intended as a compliment, a quote from the treasure chest of a relative, of a true friend of animals, an adage that had become dear to his heart.

"What is it you would have of me? How may I be of service?" I asked, sensing how his stilted phrasing was already rubbing off on me.

Clemens von Barrista looked up from the bottom of the sea, bowed slightly, and said without any accent whatever, "You hoped to have reached your decision by today."

After a bow that imitated his I replied we had first met each other on Tuesday,[1] at the Volkspolizei kennel, where, much to my regret, we had barely spoken and had departed without arranging any further meeting . . .

"I banged my left knee at your place yesterday," he said, flaring up, "because the light wasn't working, and still isn't." With each word he gained better control over his exasperation. "We sat here and I offered suggestions. Your newspaper"—he took off his glasses and massaged his eyes with thumb and forefinger—"was recommended to me!" I expressed my regret that I knew nothing of this.

"Then you are not Herr Schröder?" His google-eyes were now peering through his glasses again.

I introduced myself, mentioned again our meeting at the VP kennel, and was about to step out and turn on the vestibule light, when he halted me with a vigorous motion of his upper body.

"My concern is the visit of the hereditary prince!"

Finally the coin dropped. Of course I knew about the prince's ambassador. Barrista is an acquaintance, if not to say admirer, of Vera's. Except that I had pictured him quite differently.

"We've been notified of your visit, accompanied, of course, by the loveliest expectations on all sides," I offered by way of apology. I had

---

1. Presumably he means on Tuesday of the previous week.

jumped up, but then, as if this knowledge had robbed me of my energies, I realized that I was having trouble speaking. I was suddenly afraid I might spoil things, very important things. Hadn't a smile meandered across his lips at my mention of "loveliest expectations on all sides"? It can't have been just my fault that I caught only some words, a few fragments of a sermon, like an AM broadcast after nine at night. ". . . excellent reputation! . . . accomplishments, commitment, will . . . substantial . . . can well imagine . . . new energy, new energies . . . waiting for this . . . resurrected out of . . . trust . . . impeccable . . . times such as these . . . speculating . . . congratulations, yes, my congratulations."

He was doling out compliments. That much I understood. His turns of phrase had me on the verge of laughter. "We bid you the warmest of welcomes. We do indeed," I managed to say, but was afraid it may have sounded like a parody. I weighed words in my mouth as if they were fillings that had fallen out, and it wouldn't have taken much and I would have bowed and scraped like a lackey.

Barrista had warmed to his topic, spoke, if I rightly recall, without accent now and rubbed his hands as if under a tap. With total determination he cried, "Not I! I am not one of those for whom speech is silver and silence gold. Balderdash, no, no, my good man," he said with a smile, "special considerations not even on behalf of those involved, even a child knows that, truly, even a child. Moaning and groaning, the sooner the better, wean themselves, aware of that myself, does no good, no training, can't fail to be noticed, no one left, nowhere, no father confessor, unoccupied position, second-rank, third-rank, an enormous transformation, absolute void, on this side and that, unique chance!"

I was no longer trying to follow his leaps and bounds from one thought to another, and assembled a few sentences about myself instead. Sprawled now on his chair, Barrista gave me exaggerated nods as I started to speak, raised his eyebrows, and with a flood of ahs and ohs urged me on—his shy pupil, who kept to short statements in order to maintain his footing. It was all so terribly simpleminded, but his encouragement calmed me. When I fell silent, Barrista look disconcerted. What did he expect? I shrugged.

"Well, he'll probably not be stopping by now," he sighed, and rummaged in his pants pocket. Before I could ask whom he meant, he apologized. "Oh, beg your pardon. It really is late." He scrutinized a wristwatch without its strap. "Ten till twelve," he said, suppressing a yawn.

"Ten till twelve?"

"My first thought," he said, ignoring my astonishment, "was that your eyes were shining with enthusiasm. But, my dear Herr Türmer, you need to look after yourself. May I give you a ride, may I take you home?"

I pointed to the window. "I have my own—" was all I managed. I meant my car.

"Then perhaps I may escort you?" He extracted two slightly used red candles from an attaché case that I had not noticed until then, held the wicks together, and lit them both at the same time with a lighter. A candle in each hand, the attaché case under his left arm, he stood there like a Saxon Christmas ornament, his deep-sea eyes directed at me. You know my weakness for courteous people, but I had to smile all the same. He waited until I had gathered up my things. The wolf scraped with its front paws. Before I turned off the light, I noticed wax running down over Barrista's hands and dripping on the floorboards in front of the wolf's muzzle. I edged past the two of them, opened the door to the small antechamber, then the one to the vestibule, where I groped for the switch.

"Why do you mistrust me?" he asked. His eyes swam toward me. The switch clicked, but nothing happened. "No problem, no problem," he cried, raising the candles higher. I was embarrassed and angry, and especially the latter because I could hear Fred's excuses.

"I have made it my firm custom to be prepared for anything here in the East." He again gave a hint of an apologetic bow, because he would not let me precede him. "Dealing with people is a fine art, truly a fine art." Undaunted, he hobbled ahead of me, holding the burning candles as far away from his body as circumstances allowed. "Work must be learned as well, and never make any exceptions to that!" He anticipated my move and opened the front door with his elbow. The draft blew out the candles. Clemens von Barrista, however, strode ahead by the streetlamp's murky glow as if he himself were still lighting the way. Then the bell of Martin Luther Church began to toll. The next moment the streetlamps went out. A brief flicker, and night had swallowed Barrista and his wolf. For a while I still heard footsteps and his English singsong. I called out my good-byes twice in his wake, and waited for the lights of his car to come on at any moment. But it stayed dark, and after the last toll of the bell there was universal silence.

I slept like a stone.

Enrico

PS: When I got to the office today, Jörg was already fully informed and asked what I thought of Barrista. "A special case," I said, and immediately wanted to correct myself. I don't like the term. But Jörg agreed with me at once. "A special case" was probably the best way to put it. "But whatever the case," he said, turning to Georg, "Barrista wants us! Us and nobody else."

Jörg had dropped by the Wenzel at eight o'clock, where he had in fact found Barrista eating breakfast and joined him in "beheading a soft-boiled egg," as he put it. Barrista had not only filled him in on his fellow guests, but was also able to mimic their gestures and speech. It had struck Jörg as "funny as hell!"

What Barrista had to say about the hereditary prince had, despite requisite caution, pricked his—Jörg's—interest and curiosity about the old gentleman's upcoming visit. Barrista's sole proviso had been a "reasonable outcome of the election."

When Fred showed up, I took him to task. But he just turned on his heels, leaving both doors wide open behind him—and switched on the light. The vestibule was bathed in previously unknown radiance. Fred claimed he had put in new bulbs yesterday, something everyone but me had noticed . . .

Here's hoping you at least believe me,

Your E.

Saturday, Feb. 17, '90

Dear Jo,

And now I've typed your name once again, but the man who wrote you that previous letter, the very same man who two and a half days ago walked out on Market Square with bundles of newspapers, seems so strange and childlike to me. Don't expect any epiphanies! It was all terribly secular and ordinary. As I paged through the newspaper that had seemed so faraway and mysterious during proofreading, I was relieved just to find no white spots. It all had to go so fast. The drivers had been sitting around on their hands since Wednesday. The volunteers from *klartext* days had divvied up the Konsum Markets among themselves. The telephone never stopped ringing. I didn't even finish the champagne that Jörg treated us to. Georg gave Robert a conductor's satchel, plus a supply of small change. I slung an old pouch of crackled patent leather around my shoulder, the strap across my chest. Then we hustled off through the drizzle, each with two bundles of 250 copies.

Once at Market Square, near Sporen Strasse, we set down our bundles and massaged our fingers—they were numb and scarred purple from the cords. Five booths were huddled together as if afraid of the expanse of Market Square. A fruit and vegetable vendor took up residence closest to us. The D-MARKS ONLY sign hung above these splendors of paradise was as large as it was unnecessary. He called out the names of exotic fruits, but they might just as well have been oriental spices. The truly fabled wares, however, were the tomatoes and cucumbers, the pears and grapes. The few people scattered across Market Square could hardly have been the reason for his ballyhoos. His highly trained voice was the icing on the artificiality of the cake. He could have been trumpeting arias.

I worked at undoing the knots on my bundle, but never let anyone heading our way out of my eye. I expected every one of them to stop and ask whether we were selling that new newspaper, the *Altenburg Weekly*. Robert was staring at my hands. He was already so unsure of himself that it never occurred to him to hand me his pocketknife. But he readily let me drape a sheaf of papers over his forearm. I stood next to him and unfolded the front page with the masthead at eye level.

After several people had walked past us without asking about the paper, I suggested Robert speak to people. He needed to tell them what he had here. But as soon as anyone approached, instead of opening his mouth he stuck his newspaper arm out a little farther like a clumsy waiter. Michaela had told me it was irresponsible to "corrupt him with child labor." It was too late now to send him away, he would just have to hold out.

I finally had no choice but to show him how it should be done. I left no one out. I fixed my eye on people, smiled, and spoke to them, even those who passed a little farther away did not escape. "Do you know about the new *Altenburg Weekly*?" I shouted. No one stopped, no one bought. They didn't even look at me. That very morning a large article about us had appeared on the regional page of the *LVZ*.[1] Even they thought we were important.

Now and then someone bought a fish sandwich. I don't know how I would have felt if I had been alone. Robert's presence was agony for me.

Suddenly an elderly woman came up, her shopping bag swaying back and forth, and asked us what we had to offer.

"Well now," she said, eyeing the front page. Her coat was buttoned wrong and hung askew. "Then give me one." Her arm plunged up to the elbow into her shopping bag. I asked for ninety pfennigs and handed her a newspaper from the middle of the stack. Her index finger poked around in her change until she found a one-mark piece. I dropped a ten-pfennig piece into her outstretched hand. After she had folded the paper and crammed it into her bag, she gazed at me as if trying to make sure just whom she had been dealing with, and then with a loud "good-bye" moved on.

It works, I thought. Just one success had turned me into an addict. I needed more. I handed the mark to Robert.

It wasn't long before I hit the jackpot again. A slim man with smooth black hair held out a mark to me, waved me off as I held out his change, and smiled so affably that his eyes vanished into a tomcat's little angled slits.

With that I lost all inhibition, walked over to two women, and asked them whether they already had their copy of the *Altenburg Weekly*, the new newspaper for the whole region. I fixed my attention on the younger one. Not until I was standing directly in front of her did I notice the countless wrinkles that blurred the traits of her girlish face. She reached for her wallet, when her companion, a woman dressed all in black, barked at me, asking what all this was about. "It's not important!" the woman in black said, interrupting my reply. "Not important!" She slapped the back of her hand against the newspaper and shouted, "Ninety pfennigs? Ninety pfennigs!"

"Ninety pfennigs," I insisted, and all I had to do in that moment was take the mark from the open palm of the gentler soul.

"It's not important at all. Not important!"

---

1. *Leipziger Volkszeitung* [Leipzig National Newspaper].

The hand closed slowly, and I stared at the little fist, delicate enough to be porcelain.

Rage and desperation welled up in me. *"Altenburg Weekly!"* I yelled after them. *"Altenburg Weekly!"* I must have been heard as far away as Martin Luther Church.[1]

Ah, Jo, you won't understand how I could carry on like that over something so trivial. But suddenly it was all there again—the last six months, the fear, the desperation, the accusations, the theater and its horrors, the horror of my sickroom, my mother, Michaela, Vera, the whole bottomless pit. And Robert standing beside me, who had set his heart on those bundles, all one thousand copies.

Every bit of reticence left me. I don't even know where the rhythm came from that I adopted to proclaim my AL-TEN-BURG-WEEK-LY! I hammered, banged, punched hard each time, aiming at the black core of my dactylic syllables. AL-TEN-BURG-WEEK-LY. I did it for Robert, for myself, for Michaela, for Georg und Jörg, for my mother and Vera, for the town, for the whole region. And after each verse, I breathed more easily. Someone held a two-mark piece under my nose, he actually demanded two copies and no change. And Robert likewise got rid of his first copy. The two of us quickly sold five papers, one after the other. As if trying to make up for what I had failed to do last autumn, I shouted my AL-TEN-BURG-WEEK-LY to the hammer strokes of SANC-TION-NEW-FO-RUM! This was my revolution now.

The fruit vendor evidently took it as a challenge and responded with a sirenlike yowl.

Ten minutes later I picked up two bundles and took up my post across from the Rathaus. From there the market booths looked like the coastline of home. I don't know why—was I exhausted, had I taken a chill, did I miss Robert—at any rate my cries lost their power. After each verse I stopped to watch what was happening.

I changed positions again, this time farther up Market Square, at the corner leading to the Weiber Market. There were more people there. And I could watch Robert extending his arm to hold out newspapers to passersby. I was responsible for this tragedy. It wasn't hard to imagine how his pride at seeing my name in the imprint, his admiration for the

1. Martin Luther Church is at the opposite end of Market Square, a distance of about eight hundred feet..

art of making a newspaper, how all that was suddenly collapsing. I had always been afraid the whole thing might fail—because of a lack of authorization, poor delivery, or our incompetence. I had never given sales a thought. If I was wrong about something like that, why shouldn't I doubt everything, our entire strategy? What I wanted more than anything was to tell the whole world that we would be bringing the hereditary prince to Altenburg. Yes, suddenly I wanted that strange man, Clemens von Barrista, beside me. I found thinking about him somehow comforting. But I said nothing and let people pass by as if I were invisible. And then . . .

I had already grown so used to the fruit siren that I didn't even notice at first. But something at any rate was different. It was now shouting *"Weekly!"* No, shouting isn't even close. *"Weeeekly, Weeeekly, Aaaltenburg Weeeekly!"*—it stressed the first syllable, swallowed the second, then ascended from the depths and like a siren blared the A of Altenburg, his mouth stretched wide. And then came the unmistakable imperative: "Buy it, folks, buy it!" followed at once by the equally urgent "Only ninety pfennigs! Ninety pfennigs for the *Aaaltenburg Weeeekly . . .*" The beginning and end, the A-E, A-E rose into the air above Altenburg Market.

The town began slowly to come alive, as if the cry of the fruit vendor had found its way to both Altenburg North and Southeast.[1]

A group of women surrounded me—they all bought and no one wanted change. To lend support, as they put it. One of them recognized me as the Herr Türmer from the theater, who had given that speech in the church.

My luck held. In a few minutes I had disposed of thirty copies. And it just kept up. I only had to hold up the newspaper and, once the fruit siren's *"Weeeekly"* had died away, to repeat the idea, as if explaining to everyone around: Weekly, he means our *Weekly*. And then—at first I thought it was a woman's voice—I realized that a new *"Weeekly! Weeekly!"* was Robert's.

I didn't need to say anything more, from then on people bought all on their own.

By day's end it was so dark that I could barely make out faces. I could give change with my eyes closed, and I stuffed bills into my pants pock-

1. Two new residential developments, one with fifteen, the other with five thousand inhabitants.

ets. My feet were ice cold, I couldn't even feel my toes now. The patent-leather pouch hung heavy at my neck. And whom do you suppose I sold my last copy to? Yes, to Clemens von Barrista. But he and his wolf didn't seem to recognize me in the darkness. Or might I have been mistaken about that?

Robert was still busy, and it was only by his irrepressible smile that I could tell he could see me. Erwin, the fruit siren, didn't want to hear anything about thanks. He handed me a sheet of paper, an ad—we're to publish it every week—and gave me a hundred-D-mark bill! We left the rest of Robert's copies with him; he planned to distribute them in his hometown of Fürth, in Franconia.

We started the walk home empty-handed, but our satchels were stuffed full and banged against our hips with every step. A record—one thousand, one-twentieth of the printing. In four hours Robert had made ninety marks (twenty pfennigs a copy), plus tips.

Jo, my dear friend. What a delight it is to sell something you've made yourself. My laurel wreath is woven from the oak leaves on every coin.

Your E.

PS: Your copy is being sent in a wrapper. Unfortunately the photographs are very dark.

Tuesday, Feb. 20, '90

Dear Jo,

We've been working like the devil. And I still didn't get home until after midnight.[1] But four hours of sleep are enough, and since I pass the time writing letters, I'm gradually learning to love these long mornings.[2]

I won't bore you with newspaper stuff, but I do have to tell you something I wouldn't have mentioned if it hadn't been the cause of our first crisis.[3]

---

1. They had been preparing the second issue.
2. T. wrote the majority of his letters, especially those to N. H., between five and nine a.m.
3. The first two paragraphs of this letter reflect contradictory intentions. On the one hand T. describes letter writing as a pastime; on the other, the idea that he "has" to say something suggests that he regards it as his duty to report about his work. This ambivalence, despite whatever embellishments accompany it, is always present.

Have I ever told you about the Prophet? He's an odd duck. Everyone notices that right off. The Prophet's mouth is constantly in motion, as if he has just sampled something and is about to announce what it tastes like. He keeps his chin jutted out, so that his beard, which appears to have the consistency of cotton candy, is thrust menacingly forward.

During the demonstration after the wall came down, he demanded the creation of a soviet republic. He's always full of surprises.[1]

The Prophet arrived early to honor our first-issue celebration[2] with his presence, but quickly retreated into a corner. As we've since come to know, he didn't like the look of our guests. Jörg's and Georg's invitations had gone out—as is only proper for a newspaper—to the town council, to the district council, to all political parties (with the exception of the comrades), to the museums and the theater, to Guelphs and Ghibellenes. The only guests to arrive on time, however, were members of the old officialdom, because all the rest, those who felt they naturally belonged at our side (the reception was held in the office of the New Forum), were slow to make an appearance since they had been out selling and delivering our newspaper.

Even the "bigwigs," as the Prophet later called them, seemed out of sorts. Either they didn't want to talk with one another but with "fresh faces" instead, or they were very skittish. When I suggested to the mayor that I wanted to interview him soon, he removed his glasses, rubbed his eyes for a good while, and then asked, "What is it you want from me?" Before I could reply, he exclaimed, "Do you know what I'm going to do? Not one thing. I've done far too much already!" And sad to say Jörg and Georg weren't exactly at the top of their form, either. Jörg kept pumping the mayor's hand and had hardly been able to unlock his jaw to thank him for a monstrous pot of cyclamens. Georg gazed down on his well-wishers with all the earnestness of a Don Quixote, amazed that the same people he wanted to take on were smiling and squirming at his feet. But all this just in passing.

By the time Dr. Schumacher, the mayor of Offenburg, entered the room surrounded by his minions—with roses for the ladies and a Dicta-phone for us—the bigwigs had fled the scene. Once the citizens of Offen-

1. One month previous, on Jan. 18th, T. had written that he owed his job at the paper to the "Prophet," Rudolf Franck. "He initiated things and put in a good word for me."
2. The launching celebration was held on Feb. 2nd, the first day of sales.

burg had vanished and just our sort, as Michaela might have put it, were still amusing themselves, the Prophet tapped his glass with a spoon, jutted out his beard, and asked in a loud voice, "What's in the *Altenburg Weekly?*"

He gave a table of contents, page by page. It sounded more than just a bit too droll, but I laughed along—certain that kudos would follow. But by the time he got to Jan Steen's ad, which he called a mockery of our customers and readers, the effrontery of his speech began to dawn on me. "What was it we wanted?" the Prophet thundered, paused—while his mouth began the search for some new taste—and asked in a tone of bitterest accusation, "No, what was it you wanted?" And it was not a rhetorical question. But to make a scene? Because of this crazy man?

He laid into each of us, even nitpicked at my gardener Dippel article. There hadn't been one thing in our paper he couldn't read these days in the *Leipziger Volkszeitung.*

And finally, alluding to our launching celebration, he added, "Are you once again the lackeys of authority, the lackeys of the same bigwigs who harassed us for forty years?"

Naturally I hoped that one of our guests would defend us. They had been listening to the Prophet somewhat too eagerly while they sipped at our wine and champagne. Only Wolfgang the Hulk and his wife bravely shook their heads, but even they did not risk protesting aloud.

Presumably they considered any disagreement superfluous, that a response would lend this farce too much significance. "What do you plan to do?" the Prophet boomed in conclusion and, after shooting a glance around the room, marched straight out the open door.

Now people began to mimic and make fun of him. The mood grew more relaxed, and there was even some dancing after Fred discovered a piano in an adjoining room and "cracked" the fallboard. Although I was glad that Barrista had been spared the crazy man's theatrics, I also regretted that our invitation had evidently not reached him in time.

On Friday Georg confessed that it never would have occurred to him in the old days to drink champagne with bigwigs, and I didn't realize at first just what he was getting at. But Marion now joined in the self-flagellation. Suddenly once again none of our articles was good enough for them. It was totally absurd. Even Jörg strewed ashes on his head and no longer understood why we had invited erstwhile officialdom. When I asked him what harm the invitations had done, a hush first fell over the room. "They harmed our reputation," Georg said finally, and Marion added, "Our dignity."

"Not mine," I replied, which initiated a great silence that didn't lift until yesterday.

Hugs, Enrico

PS: We've heard that we were rebuked as idolaters from a Protestant pulpit last Sunday—because of the horoscope on the next-to-last page.

Tuesday, Feb. 20, '90

Dear Frau Hansen,

If you knew what it had cost me to bring myself to ask Frau *** for your address. I puffed myself up like a fourteen-year-old and claimed you had promised to show me Rome.[1]

I'm sorry I was of so little help to you and that it was on our account that you missed meeting the museum staff. To make up for it, I'm enclosing the little Reclam volume[2] and a few other items about the pavilion. I've prepared a list of a dozen people for Frau *** to interview and have already sent it to her. I think that ultimately it doesn't really matter with whom she talks. The best choices are left to chance.[3]

When do you plan to or when will you be able to come back again? I would love to know for all sorts of reasons.

With warmest regards, Your Enrico T.

---

1. As a photographer Nicoletta Hansen had accompanied a journalist who was doing a story about the countless number of newly founded newspapers, especially in Thuringia and Saxony. When the article finally appeared there was no mention of the *Altenburg Weekly*. T. had asked the reporter for N. H.'s address.

2. Apparently this was a bilingual edition of Apuleius's *Cupid and Psyche* (Leipzig, 1981), in which there were color photographs of the nine frescoes executed in 1838 by Moritz von Schwind for the music pavilion in Rüdigsdorf near Kohren-Sahlis.

3. These additional plans evidently led nowhere.

Dear Jo,

Yesterday, as if meeting me for an appointment, Barrista came bounding down the long stairway of the Catholic rectory. The man at the front door with whom he'd been talking watched us without budging from the spot. Which was why I thought Barrista would be returning to him. Instead, he asked if he could join me, and was soon sitting in the passenger seat with the wolf in the middle behind us. He had made a find. "A Madonna," Barrista said, "a Madonna, Herr Türmer, a Madonna . . . And no one knows where she comes from." I barely recognized him, his speech was so lively—without accent or stilted bombast.

He said he didn't care where I was going, that I should make no special allowances for him, if need be he'd simply wait and walk the dog. When I stopped at the gate of Larschen's farm, I interrupted Barrista's gushings about the Madonna. He ignored what I had said and followed me with his wolf. I had to express myself more clearly and ask him to excuse me for a few minutes. He stopped in his tracks in the middle of the courtyard, muttered something, and only now seemed to notice where he had landed. A couple of chickens beat a retreat and a farm dog was barking close by. Anton Larschen appeared before I had even found the doorbell. He grabbed me by the elbow and led me to a low doorway, commanded Barrista to follow us, and insisted on treating us as his guests. "Ten minutes!" he exclaimed, and preceded us up a steep set of stairs that I wouldn't have ventured on my own. Barrista hesitated as well. The low room was very overheated, the bed, the only object of normal size, looked huge. Anton Larschen hurried to set another place at the table, buttoned the top button of his jacket, and plucked at both trouser legs. He wasn't wearing socks, so his naked heels were visible with every step of his felt slippers. The top of his tower of white hair brushed the ceiling beams. "Please!" he cried. We sat down at the table, he vanished back downstairs.

"Splendiferous!" Barrista whispered, holding his cup up to the light. I no longer remember the name, but evidently Larschen's porcelain is Chinese. The room looked like a museum, everything in perfect order. The only chaos was a hodgepodge of items that lay or stood atop the radio: a battered convention mascot, a mug from Karlsbad, a ship in a bottle, a darning egg, a straw doll, a pair of framed photographs, and other stuff. The wolf had stretched out in front of the dark blue upholstered armchair and now blinked up into the narrow boxes of light—the windows were barely larger than roof scuttles. I was about to tell Barrista a little about Larschen when he came climbing back up the stairs, teapot in hand. He passed us a plate of licorice cookies and ginger pastries. (No novelties to Barrista!) These, as well as the tea and the lump sugar, came from relatives in Bremen, Larschen explained.

Barrista apologized for his barging in like this, but he spoke so softly that he was interrupted by Larschen, who announced how glad he was to be able to welcome two guests into his modest home. Yes, it was an honor, and now he began a speech he had evidently prepared for the occasion. As he spoke he held a folder clamped under his arm, stroking it constantly, as if to dust it off and press its corners flat. With downright frightening candor he described what he called the dramatic high point of his "little opus"—that is, his failed attempt at flight to the West. Not only would it have provided him with a farm to match his wishes, it also would have meant the fulfillment of his love for a married woman. The woman had not been willing to get a divorce, but was prepared to flee with him. They were betrayed, arrested, interrogated. He didn't recognize his lover in the courtroom. Her hair had turned white as snow. He knew the people who had betrayed them—but that knowledge would never give him back those lost years. For him, the knowledge was an additional punishment. Larschen used the phrase "a nobody like me" several times, and in conclusion asked if I would be willing to cast a brief glance at his "memoirs." I reminded him that that was, after all, why I had come. Barrista's wolf, which had at first been startled by Larschen's rhetoric—there's barely a sentence he doesn't speak with added emphasis—was now dreaming and shuffling its paws.

As we were climbing back down the stairs, the grandfather clock struck eleven. Exactly twenty minutes had passed since our arrival.

Barrista had again spoken too softly for Larschen, who therefore didn't hear the answer to his question about whether Barrista would also like to read the manuscript. "If it's only half as good as what he told us," he said, "you should print it." He even suggested that we turn it into a book. Barrista thanked me profusely. I couldn't imagine, he told me, how much this meeting had meant to him. And had I seen the darning egg? He had been genuinely touched. He himself always carried a darning kit with him, not because he couldn't afford new socks, but because darning had a calming effect on him, took him back to the evenings of childhood, and inspired his best ideas. He described for me at length his vain attempt to find a darning egg. No one had been able to help him—not in department stores, variety shops, not even in secondhand stores, until finally a salesclerk had taken pity on him and brought him a darning egg from home.

As I was about to drop Barrista off in Altenburg, he asked if there was any reason why he could not accompany me farther. It was so interesting to him, he said, all the things I had to do, all of it without exception. And so I turned up everywhere with my little companion—the council hall in the village of Rositz, the town hall of Meuselwitz. I introduced Barrista to secretaries and in Wintersdorf even to the mayor. The wolf remained in the car, and I enjoyed the freedom—at Barrista's encouragement—of leaving the keys in the ignition. He's right. It is a different way of living.

On the return trip Barrista urged me to turn right on the far side of Rositz, he wanted to show me a discovery.

The scene presented to me was desolate: a soccer field overgrown with weeds, next to it a barracks with a sign reading REFEREES' RETREAT and white grating at the windows and doors. Not a soul far and wide. Barrista strode ahead in his old-fashioned pointed boots, and although his left knee was still giving him trouble, he nimbly took the few steps of the small porch, opened the grated door, and stepped inside. I couldn't believe my eyes. The interior was furnished as a hunting tavern, neither the wainscoting nor the numerous guests matched the wretched exterior. Barrista took off his coat, rapped each table affably, greeted those behind the bar, and slipped into the corner bench set aside for regulars. I was barely seated before a beer was placed in front of me. The most remarkable thing was that the innkeeper, a bald-headed man, called the wolf "Astrid"—and Astrid came trotting over, looking neither left nor right, and vanished through the open kitchen door. Barrista rubbed his hands. "Isn't it wonderful here?"

We had mutz roast.[1] It was so tender and so well seasoned that I would have loved to place a second order.

Barrista was in his element. I told him how we had all gathered to

1. A specialty in Altenburg and Schmölln: pork roast (either rib or shoulder) marinated in marjoram and roasted on a spit over a birchwood fire.

count the take from our first issue, had rolled the coins, and been halfway satisfied with the results—until it occurred to Georg that the currency was still in the safe. Barrista couldn't get enough of such stories.

I kept my eye on the innkeeper the whole time. There was something unusual about him. It came as something of a relief to realize that it was just that he had no eyelashes.

Let me hear from you! E.

Wednesday, Feb. 28, '90

Dear Frau Hansen,

Here is a little scene on the topic of art that might interest you: I was on the telephone this morning, when a man with fire in his eyes entered the office, doffed his seaman's cap, pulled over a chair, and slipped a well-worn wallet from his hip pocket. My hunch told me he wanted to buy an ad.

"May I speak?" the man asked, even though he saw that I still hadn't hung up.

"Does this mean anything to you?" he asked, thrusting both arms up high and tucking his head between his shoulders. "Doesn't this mean anything to you?" He repeated the gesture. "We've got to get rid of them—our monuments to the cult of the proles!" We as the "new media" had to take up the issue. "Communist art belongs on the junk heap!" He offered to write a letter to the editor.

You would probably have grasped more quickly than I what he wanted, and been quicker at showing him the door. He wants to tear down your favorite statue[1] outside the museum. He crammed his wallet back into his hip pocket and departed with a promise to finally bring the West German tabloid *Bild* to Altenburg.

We're still waiting for our Golden Age of art. But as for what lies hidden in our desk drawers, which is the hot topic at the moment—you can forget it. Who's still interested in that? Our experiences are as much use to us now as a medical education from the last century.

All the mistrust with which people such as ourselves[2] have been

---

1. *Large Neeberg Figure,* by Wieland Förster.
2. This is the first time that T. describes himself, however indirectly, as an artist / writer.

regarded for thousands of years was far more justified than any respect or admiration.[1] No, I no longer have any part in it, thank God that's behind me. It wasn't easy. You think you have talent, and then you screw up your life with it.

It's a new experience to be living without a future, in a world where a D-mark will get you anything you want, but with no prospect of redemption. But I far prefer this present state of affairs to that of the past. Even the loveliest memories seem obscene now.[2]

I'd like to tell you about Johann, a friend of mine. He is too clever not to realize that not one stone will be left on another, but too in love with himself not to keep on going just as before all the same. Johann studied—although not quite voluntarily—theology in Naumburg and this summer will have to report as a pastor to a village in the Ore Mountains. In Dresden, however, he's known as an underground poet and musician. Besides which, his wife has a last name that counts for something even outside of Weisser Hirsch (the neighborhood for bigwigs that looks down over the city) and the city of Dresden. He's trying to save himself by going into politics. Even if he should get elected, he will quickly sense that as an ersatz drug it's too weak.[3]

I don't know whether this is of any interest to you at all. I simply wanted to send you greetings that, even if they may not quite read that way, are sent with the warmest intentions.

Your Enrico T.

Thursday, March 1, '90

Dear Frau Hansen,

Had the letter not been in your handwriting, I wouldn't have believed it could possibly have come from you. Please don't let this be your final word.

I shall never forget how you came bounding down the broad stairs of

---

1. Strangely enough, T. has chosen the least appropriate place here for his confessions, since he is advocating much the same thing as the lowbrow that he just threw out of the office a few hours before.

2. This passage sounds the central motif of his letters to N. H. for the first time.

3. If one applies this mode of thought to T. himself, one might well conclude that he has found a strong "drug" for himself.

the museum and did not look up until I greeted you. And your confusion, because you thought we knew each other, and hesitated to go on your way. You didn't belong in Altenburg, anyone could see that. But in that moment what I lacked was more than courage—I had no notion what to ask you, how to address you.

I had decided during the press conference in the museum to invite you to join me somewhere—if good fortune should give me a second chance.

And that is why I regarded our second meeting as a special dispensation. I don't want to make excuses by appealing to unlucky chance, but your friend, your colleague, was directly blocking our line of sight. And to be quite honest, I noticed your reaction and had no objection, because I was afraid that I would betray myself too soon otherwise. You can accuse me of that. But only of that!

The way you leaned against the windowsill, camera in hand—I was happy to be in the same room with you, and tried hard not to stare too often, forced myself, that is, to look only rarely in *your* direction. But my looks could not have been taken wrong [. . .]

Why did you follow me into the garden? And why these accusations now? Why didn't Frau *** complain to you then and there? I don't understand any of it.[1]

To be candid, when you both had gone, I said: This woman is dangerous, and of course everyone knew whom I had in mind. I meant it in a general, impersonal sense—I can't help thinking of that now.

Hadn't the interview turned into a cross-examination long before that? Without your remark to rescue him, Georg would have ended up accused of being lost forever in "the good old days." We aren't children. I won't even mention the microphone insistently shoved under his nose. And I won't carp about the sharp tone of voice in which he was presented with one well-formulated written question after the other. And unless you're given time to think things over, how can you ever reply at that same level?

What Georg called "real life" became "existential" for her. She quoted him as saying the end of the wall was "secondary," when he had called it a "logical consequence." She left him no choice but constantly to justify himself.

1. Despite various attempts to learn the nature of these accusations and what had preceded them, I am still in the dark as to the meaning of this passage.

Your interjection: "But after all, a person has to see the Mediterranean!" is the most beautiful sentence I've ever heard. It was a kind of redemption. Yes, I do want to see the Mediterranean.

I haven't forgotten one word of everything you said. The way you spoke about how lucky we are to live in a place like this, a home to such splendor, and how every road to Italy has to lead through Altenburg—yes, I know, you were talking about the museum's collection . . . But for me it was a metaphor, a promise, and to be able to stand that close to you was already its fulfillment.

I can still see those bright pale blue streaks along the horizon, and towering into them the cones[1] at Ronneburg, which you called pyramids, and above us the heavy blackish gray blanket of clouds that had already brought the streetlamps on, so that we looked out over the town as if gazing out of a window. And then how we broke off in midconversation because the streaks of cloud had turned bright orange [. . .] I want to remind you of nothing more than that.

Your Enrico Türmer

Monday, March 5, '90

Dear Jo!

What do you think of our newspaper? Robert and I got rid of another thousand copies last Thursday. Michaela, however, is beside herself. She had convinced the general manager to remount *Julie*,[2] after almost a year and a half. Flieder[3] was here only very briefly. He has a brain tumor and is to be operated on in Berlin this week. So even without Sluminski[4] interfering, there is no way he'll be considered for new head director. Yesterday's performance, the second premiere so to speak—which Michaela had such hopes for—was a disaster, only 32 tickets sold. Despite our having promoted it well, thanks to Marion.

As I walked over to the theater around eleven—I had a "newspaper to

---

1. The piles of tailings at the Wismut mine.
2. *Miss Julie*, by August Strindberg.
3. Franz Flieder, director.
4. General manager.

get out"[1]—it was already dark and there wasn't a single car in the parking lot. The doorkeeper refused to let me in yet again. First, I didn't belong here anymore and second, there was no premiere party, because this hadn't been a premiere, and there was certainly nothing to celebrate, either. "Thirty-two in the audience! Thirty-two! Just imagine!"

As I entered the canteen, Michaela was declaiming, "Oh, I am so tired. I cannot do anything more. Oh, I'm so tired—I'm incapable of feeling, not able to be sorry, not able to flee, not able to stay, not able to live—not able to die. Help me now. Command me—I will obey like a dog."

So you see, I still know it by heart.[2]

Four of them were sitting there, the new girl from props with handsome Charlie from costumes, and at the corner table Michaela and Claudia, her friend and colleague. Claudia declared she was going to last till morning. I asked how they planned to do that with just half a bottle of vodka.

"Go on," Michaela exclaimed.

"That was before," Claudia began, and clamped the cap of a felt pen between her upper lip and nose. "Now we have other things to think about." With these words she threw herself across the table and burst out laughing. Handsome Charlie applauded and tried to join in the laughter.

"If you would ask me how it was, assuming, that is, that you would ask me," Michaela replied, "then I would respond on the spot—well? What would I say?—I would say . . ."—and after a brief puff of laughter—"thrilling!" With a grand gesture she presented the deserted canteen to me.

And it went on like that. You can call what the two were up to absurd or witty, but I was slowly starting to feel anxious. It's my suspicion that Claudia was enjoying the flop. She had been humiliated at not being cast as Julie the first time.

"Aren't you my friend?" Michaela asked, looking at the girl from props. There was a long pause, during which Michaela stared at the poor woman, until she blushed and peeped, "Yes, of course I want to be your friend." Claudia couldn't suppress her giggles.

1. The first performance of the remounted production took place on Sunday, March 4th.
2. All quotes agree verbatim with the text, which may indicate that T. had a copy in front of him when writing this letter.

"Flee? Yes—we shall flee!" Michaela went on. "But I am so tired. Give me a glass of wine." Charlie got up to pour her what was left of the wine. Michaela appeared to be on the track of some realization, as if she had noticed something that had escaped her until now. The sentence "Where did you learn to speak like that?" truly moved her. After another pause, in which she sat up ramrod straight, Michaela announced mournfully, "You must have spent a good deal of time in the theater."

No one laughed. It was eerie.

"Excellent! You should have been an actor."

The silence was breathless, like after the last note of a requiem.

Michaela let me lead her outside without resistance. I told her to call in sick, but she won't do it, says it's not her way.

I can't console her. The theater has become an alien world to me.

In our latest issue we have an interview with Rau.[1] Jörg was given the chance, and not the *Leipziger Volkszeitung*. Rau gave a speech on Market Square praising the "more private" style of life in the East, and said that his only worry was that "a passion for the D-mark will turn everyone here into what we already are." He too seems to be searching for his soul in the East. Let him. Then he just chatted, like another skat player, so to speak, and told us how to cast our votes right, and presented Altenburg Transit with six buses from North Rhine-Westphalia—they still have the old ads on the sides. Michaela was peeved because Rau handed over the keys to, of all people, Karmeka, a dentist who had kept nice and quiet all last fall, but is now a representative at the opposition Round Table. Tomorrow Otto von Habsburg will be here at the invitation of the German Social Union. At one point they distributed flyers reading: "If we had hanged them, we would have been no better than those who ruled over us with their Stasi and 'shoot to kill.'"

Clemens von Barrista and his wolf are everywhere and nowhere. Last Friday he climbed out of a big black American cruiser and asked for water for Astrid, the wolf. When I asked if he wanted some coffee, Barrista responded exuberantly, as if some secret wish had come true. We left the office together. I had to go to Lucka. He wanted to know if he could come along. "Yes," I said, "of course!" And with that he opened the

---

1. At the time Johannes Rau was the prime minister of North Rhine-Westphalia, had been nominated as the Social Democratic candidate for chancellor in 1986, and was later elected president of the Federal Republic of Germany, 2000–2004.

door of his black vehicle and tossed me the keys. The wolf jumped in. I said I'd rather not. It was a mystery to me how he had ever negotiated Frauen Gasse with the monster. "Give it a try," he said, "it's child's play, you'll see."

How right he was. We rolled gently through town and then zoomed off. I could feel the wolf's breath at my right ear. Every fear had vanished. Suddenly everything turned bright and loud—Barrista had put down the top.

Twenty minutes later we pulled up to the town hall in Lucka. I left the keys in the ignition, the wolf jumped up front.

During my first visit in January Robert had come along, and we had found Frau Schorba, the mayor's secretary, crumpled up in her chair, weeping. I had finally offered her a handkerchief. Even now I don't know what it had all been about, but at my next visit she returned my handkerchief, freshly washed and ironed, and asked whether there was anything she could do for me. And now Frau Schorba takes in ads for the *Weekly*.

Standing at the door, Barrista observed our weekly ritual: While I skim reports in the *Weekly* file, Frau Schorba sways back and forth, playing her typewriter as expressively as a pianist. After watching her for a while, I always say, "I do admire you, Frau Schorba."

Then her hands sink into her lap. I ignore her pregnant silence, express my thanks, and call out as I depart, "See you next week."

"You've forgotten something," she then replies, casting me a wicked smile. In one hand Frau Schorba holds out the ads, in the other the envelope with the money.

"That's a record!" I exclaimed loudly this time. Three of the six ads were for two columns, one of them eighty millimeters long.

Suddenly Barrista was standing right there. He grabbed her hand and said, "Someone like you really should be taken under my protection." I was no less flummoxed than Frau Schorba. "Whenever you need me," he promised, laying his business card next to the typewriter. Bowing and spinning elegantly around, he said his farewell and was out the door.

"He's the hereditary prince's ambassador," I whispered to her, and followed him out.

We again drove out to Referees' Retreat for "lunch," as Barrista called our noonday meal. After Barrista had asked me what year I was born, he then invited us—Jörg, Georg, and me—to be his guests at the Wenzel on Tuesday. I'll tell you all about it.

Hugs, Enrico

Dear Jo,

Vera keeps calling from Beirut. She sits in a cramped little booth; last time the connection was relayed via New York. I'm always standing in the middle of the office, the receiver pressed to my ear, and seldom alone. The stories that Vera has heard, the misery she sees around her, the cripples, the blown-up buildings and palm trees, the barricades, and then at home there's her headstrong mother-in-law and dithering Nicola, the whole dreary scene—I don't know what I'm supposed to say to it all. My letters don't get through because the post office isn't functioning. But there's no problem buying French cheese, cognac, or other delicacies. I hope Vera comes home soon.

Michaela has gone to Berlin to visit Thea, her famous friend. She also wants to see Flieder in the hospital. It's strangely quiet here. Even the crime rate dwindles from week to week.

There's only the occasional office argument about ads. There's no talking to Georg about it. The ads bring in about the same amount we lose on returned copies. But according to Georg we're losing readers precisely because we print ads. He talks himself into a rage—we're not keeping to our agreements and without a second thought are throwing our real cause overboard.

All the same, after each of us had said his piece, we put the argument behind us. But then Ilona stuck her head in at the door and reminded us that Herr von Barrista had called several times now and wanted to know what year each of us was born.

"I've never set eyes on the fellow," Georg shouted, "and yet all I hear is Barrista, on every side, Barrista, Barrista. Well, I know where he can shove my year of birth!" Jörg quickly calmed him down, reminding him of the possibilities that a visit by the prince could open up for us. Besides which he'd get to know Barrista come evening.

At eight on the dot we were at the Wenzel. The restaurant was full, and Herr von Barrista hadn't reserved a table, which he did every evening, but not today, no, sorry, not today. The bar was closed. Our only choice was armchairs in the lobby.

Fifteen minutes passed and we agreed to give him another ten. At which point the elevator opened and Barrista stepped over to us. He sighed with a shake of his head; his upraised hands expressed both regret and reproach. Everything was ready and waiting. And here we were just sitting around!

Barrista confided to us in the elevator that he had hoped "we might have found quarters for *him* here—in the Prince's Suite. That really has a nice ring. But it is out of the question. *He* cannot stay here." To my eyes, however, the suite to which Barrista now opened the door was splendid. An armada of three-branched candelabra cast the room in a honey gold light. The furniture shimmered honey gold, the place settings sparkled honey gold, the very air seemed bathed in the hue. "Beeswax?" Georg asked. "Excellent!" Barrista replied. "And do you know where I get these candles? From Italy, from an ecclesiastical supply house."

The stereo system was stupendous; we were standing in the middle of an orchestra, it was playing Handel.

"Damn it all!" the waitress said, who had evidently been standing the whole time in front of the mirror puttering in vain at her hairdo, but now, tossing her head back and forth a few times, sent hair cascading down over her shoulders. She extended a hand to each of us; her smile squeezed her cheeks into little hillocks behind which her eyes twinkled. Her white blouse hung loose, but this could not disguise how deeply her skirt's waistband was cutting into her flesh. I recognized her from some-where, but couldn't place her.

Barrista admonished us not to just stand around—there was so much to do yet. And so we sidled along the old-fashioned chairs as if playing musical fright[1] and tried to decode the names scribbled on place cards.

"Let us drink, drink; champagne must be enjoyed ice cold." After a brief toast to our common future and a successful outcome to our plans, he lifted his glass to each of us. When it came my turn, we gazed into each other's eyes longer than normal—that is, I gazed into a vast dark-ness floating behind his thick lenses.

My dear Jo, if only you could have been there. Just that first sip of champagne—how ridiculous to call it effervescent or bubbly. Oh no, no sooner had this liquid touched the palate and tongue than it evaporated into something lighter still. What a shame, I thought, that was it—and only then did I feel an unfathomable coolness deep within, yes, for a moment I myself was nothing but an icy pleasure. As if examining myself under a microscope I perceived with perfect clarity how this elixir diffused from cell to cell.

---

1. A local term for musical chairs.

It was as quiet as a prayer meeting. A raised eyebrow, a connoisseur's smacking of the lips, even a word of praise would have been silly, would have been a sacrilege. Barrista likewise surrendered to the mysteries and hearkened to some inner voice. And for the first time I understood why someone would smash a wineglass. Forgive me the pathos—but already the second sip had a soupçon of the mundane.

I used to want to be able to describe pleasure in all its nuances and hues. I am now content to have experienced it.

The waitress placed a silver bowl in our midst, and from its center a glittering dolphin leapt up out of a sea of ice, on which—or so I thought—lay twelve black wrinkled mussels, plus lemon slices and another smaller bowl of sauce. The waitress gave my shoulder a pat, as if she were the hostess.

The baron began his lecture, using an open hand in lieu of a pointer. At first there was something touching, if not almost absurd, about the earnestness with which he provided us the names of different kinds of oysters, their origins and characteristics. But that impression quickly vanished. There were various species—Pacific oysters, Atlantic oysters, Antarctic oysters, oysters from the north of France.

"And now proceed as follows." Barrista brandished a curious little fork. "Separate—lemon—sauce, not too much—slurp!" And he actually slurped. The liquid in which it floated was, he claimed, still seawater.

No sooner did I have the slippery stuff in my mouth than he cried, "Chew! You have to chew, chew, and do you perceive it?" It had the odd taste of something that isn't really food and yet has a flavor, a little like nuts. I paid no attention to the others—Jörg later admitted he would have loved to spit his out—and reached for a second. The oyster experience was the opposite of that of the champagne. I truly enjoyed the second one.

Barrista raised his glass again. White wine, he said, clarified and enhanced the taste. I slurped a third.

"Evidently they've lighted a fire!" Barrista clinked glasses with me and divided the rest of the oysters between us.

He had driven to West Berlin at six o'clock that morning and shopped "in certain specialty establishments." This was a treat for him more than anything else. He had refrained far too long and was happy to be able once again to enjoy himself in our company. We should not imagine that first-class quality was easily obtained, one often had to journey far to find it. One could depend only on one's nose. Which was why he traveled with just one small suitcase, and why most of the space in his car's trunk was filled with coolers and his portable infernal machine. The waitress stepped to one side and gestured with both hands toward a two-burner stove.

"Avanti!" Barrista exclaimed. "Steamed scallops!" We were each served just one, garnished with herbs and a dark sauce, a Chinese specialty.

"You will be amazed," Barrista said, announcing the next course. We need not take fright, this was not a dessert, but a mere nothing, as he liked to call it, a nothing that would give our taste buds a chance to recover, a kind of peppermint ice cream. (It had another name and wasn't really ice cream.) He then passed around cigarettes, in a pack that reminded me of our Orient brand.

"The hereditary prince," the baron commenced, "sends his warmest greetings. You should perhaps know that the prince draws only a small pension, the lion's share of which is withheld to defray the cost of his lodgings. The moment you have made his acquaintance you will want him to be your friend."

He went on to say that beyond his chambers, His Highness—that being the correct form of address—had no assets, nor did he lay claim to any, having, it should be noted, no right to do so in any case. And yet it had always been his dream to be allowed to return to the place from which he had to depart more than seventy years previous. He, Barrista, was saying this not so much to allay any possible suspicion, but rather he feared that there might be certain expectations and hopes attached to the person of the hereditary prince that he could in no way satisfy, however much His Highness himself might wish to do so. "We therefore have," Barrista said in summary, "only money to lose." Here his English accent reasserted itself. "You, of course, have nothing to lose," he remarked, raising his glass. "I am responsible for the loss of moneys. Your responsibility is to assist me in that."

He paused and smiled at his aphorism. "You will have exclusive rights. That is all."

"And what does that mean?" asked Georg, who had suddenly grown quite calm and relaxed. Obviously glad that one of us had opened his mouth, Barrista turned slightly to get a better view of Georg and explained in his hyperbolic fashion how it was through us, the *Altenburg*

Weekly, that the city and region of Altenburg would learn of the prince's visit, it was to us that politicians would come if they wanted to know something about it, through us that people would first be informed of the events surrounding the visit—and even be provided with a quick course in proper court etiquette, although the hereditary prince placed no exaggerated value on that. Although people should at least make some effort. At that moment the waitress arrived with four globes of lettuce—iceberg lettuce, Barrista explained. These were accompanied by a plate of sliced gingered duck and two small bowls of a special Chinese sauce. The baron peeled away a leaf of the green iceberg, slathered it with brown sauce—which was, he noted, the very best quality—and, using his fingers, wrapped the leaf around two slices of duck.

"If you knew how long I've waited for this! There's nothing finer," he said, and took a bite. "Absolutely nothing," he whispered as he chewed. The sauce dribbled on his napkin.

Among the loveliest surprises of his expedition was the discovery of decent meats in the East, including mutz roast—he mispronounced "mutz" with a short "u"—which was a first-rate delicacy. And who knew what all might become of it, for what was offered in gourmet temples from Monaco to Las Vegas was in large part simple peasant food ennobled by sophisticated preparation. At which he took his first sip from a new bottle of white wine—drawing it through his teeth with a hiss, pursing his lips, shifting them from side to side like a miniature elephant's trunk—culminating, then, in a brief smacking sound. We toasted home cooking.

I took advantage of the silence as we set our glasses down to finally ask him what his profession was. I had no idea what it was I had done. His entire body recoiled from me. He wasn't joking when he said, "Surely you're not asking to see my tax return?" I assured him that, for God's sake, I wasn't trying to get personal. "Leave God out of it!" he barked at me even more sharply.

"Is it customary," he said, turning to Georg, then to Jörg, and finally back again to me, "for you to ask someone his profession?"

I could only reply with a perplexed yes.

He had never presumed to ask such a thing except when conducting job interviews. Of course it was of interest to him—we shouldn't take him wrong—of burning interest how someone earned his money, since a job was often the only thing that wasn't ridiculous about a person. "Then perhaps I can parry with the same question to you later?"

One could, "simply and cogently," term him a business consultant, which was the simplest euphemism for what he did and did not do. And yet his "interpretation" of his profession differed somewhat from the usual definition. He made investments of his own at times, in this and that, since in his eyes it "made sense" not only to provide his clients the necessary trust in his recommendations but also to supplement their investments with his own capital—for he could never offer anything more than recommendations. To him it seemed immoral to take money from his clients independent of their success or failure—as was the preferred practice of banks or his special friends, lawyers. He did not wish to comment on his own profession, since all too often the results were those of the fox guarding the henhouse. He fell into a study for a few moments, muttered something, and then apologized for his inattention. He would gladly, he continued, subject all professionals, including physicians—them above all—to such a law of success. He could only say that one's own interests were always the best councilor—not only for oneself, but for the community, for mankind. Of that he was profoundly convinced.

We were now offered toothpicks from a shiny golden tray. Barrista took a good many and, leaning back, tipped his chair. As if pitching back and forth in a rocking chair, he went on. If there was one thing he did not understand about this world it was the regrettable fact that there were hardly any people of his stamp. Why did people constantly get involved with crooks? That was the question he put to the world. Several years previous he had written a little book on the subject,[1] in the hope of finding adherents to his method, indeed he had secretly—and he jabbed at his teeth behind a hand held up to his mouth—dreamed of being *called* to a chair at a university. We needed only look at how the Nobel Prize was awarded to the wildest economic theories. Nobel Prizes for theories that when applied plunged entire nations into ruin. One of his few dreams still left unfulfilled was to become a university professor.

"Ah," he exclaimed, "a chair for poetry!"

As if he hadn't noticed our astonishment, he put the screws to us like a real professor.

---

1. Clemens von Barrista, *Living Money—Lebendes Geld* (Heidelberg, 1987).

"What comes to mind at the mention of 1797?" he asked.

"The year of the ballads," I said.

"*Hyperion*,"[1] Georg said.

"Very good," the baron said, "but this is not a literature class."

"Napoleon," Jörg shouted.

"Napoleon is always right. But this is about England, an achievement for which the entire civilized world is indebted to the Empire. On February 24, 1797, a law was passed that allowed the Bank of England to refuse to offer coinage in exchange for paper money."

We stared at him.

"And what, gentlemen, happened next?"

"Inflation?" Jörg inquired.

"No!" Barrista cried. "Just the opposite. Exchange rates rose. One sees what a dubious figure Napoleon is, because besides other mistakes, he believed this would mark the end of British stability. Meanwhile Napoleon, the stupid magpie, was hoarding all the precious metals he could. But by April 1797, French *assignates* were worth only one-half of one percent of their face value. Just imagine! Even though they were backed by all that ecclesiastic property. From which one draws what conclusion?" We were silent.

"Where something is, nothing comes of it!" he gloated. "And where nothing is, something comes of it! If that isn't poetry, then I don't know what poetry is." His final confession, that he loved dealing with money because nothing is more poetic than a hundred-dollar bill, even sounded plausible to me.

The baron[2] tipped his chair back upright at the table and shook his head.

He had grown accustomed, he said, to being a voice crying in the wilderness, and was grateful for other gifts that fate sent his way instead of fame. "Doing good business is so easy. Today, however"—his right hand traced a semicircle, as if he were admonishing us to be silent—"today we have other things to talk about."

The baron called the waitress over. She had been kneeling down beside Astrid the wolf, stroking its coat, which looked almost mangy

---

1. Most of Goethe's and Schiller's ballads were written in 1797; it was also the year in which Hölderlin's *Hyperion* was published.

2. T.'s nickname for Barrista, taken from his "big black American cruiser," a "LeBaron."

against the universal glow of honey gold light. The waitress hurried over and[1] began to clear the table. Tugging his napkin from his shirt collar, the baron stood up, and cast a searching glance around the room. He was handed a basket, the contents of which were hidden under a white cloth.

"Gentlemen," he said, "I have taken the liberty of bringing along a little present for you. It took some effort"—he lifted the basket briefly, as if to imply he was speaking of its weight—"but I hope that my inquiries haven't led me astray." He stepped back a little—I thought I spotted something stir in the basket—and flung the cloth aside. Dust rose. And revealed dark bottles with mottled, tattered labels.

As we could see, the baron instructed, the authentic hallmarks of age had been preserved. His gift came with one modest request—that we invite him to partake of only a half glass of each.

Ah, Jo! His nose almost touched the label. He removed the first bottle from the basket as if it were a newborn being lifted from its bath to be dried and swaddled.

"Let us begin with the youngest, with you, Herr Türmer—a '61 Château Ducru-Beaucaillou."

I had stood up, but he motioned for me to remain seated and pretended he could see me over the rim of his glasses. He noted that he never opened an old bottle without consternation, indeed anxiety, for what was to be revealed in a single moment was the work of decades. The baron scratched the enamel seal on the cork with his fingernails—which are far too short, I think he chews them. "Even I am helpless," he declared, "against the actions of time and chemistry."

Of course every child knows that wine can turn to vinegar. But none of us comprehended the enormity of this admonition.

We heard the baron bark a laugh. Almost soundlessly he pulled the cork from my bottle and gave it an investigative sniff. "My congratulations!" he said, pouring me some—not much, barely more than a finger. We both reached for the glass at the same time, I jerked back. The baron swirled the wine endlessly, just as Jan Steen had with his brandy, and held it up to his nose. "May it be a blessing," he said, filling the glass for me. I felt like a charlatan as with purposeful circumspection I gave the wine in its chalice a swirl, smelled it, and then, following the baron's example, set

---

1. Crossed out: "without having first washed her hands,"

it to my lips. I rinsed my mouth with it properly, but swallowed as I felt the tongue and lining start to turn numb somehow. Well that's that, I thought. The baron fixed me with his eyes, no one said a word.

Gradually something earthy rose up within me—alien and pleasant, the herald of the remembrance of another existence.

Am I boring you? My words awaken no memories within you. It's six o'clock already, it's my turn to read proofs in Leipzig. So I'll cut this a bit short.

What happened next was somehow depressing, although we didn't want to admit it.

The baron passed white bread around before picking up Jörg's bottle and announcing, "Vintage '53!" I wasn't really paying close attention as the baron described this '53 Beaujolais. When I looked up, he was red-faced, struggling with the cork. His cheeks, which had been parentheses for a smile, suddenly went limp. He could tell just from the odor of the cork. We couldn't even persuade him to let us sip at our own risk. Barrista, his face still red, was deaf to our pleas. I was surprised how easily he lost his composure.

Georg muttered something about how *he* was usually the wet blanket on such occasions, Jörg attempted a laugh. He'd never liked the year of his birth anyway, so this hadn't come as much of a surprise. I'm afraid Jörg's remark was closer to the truth than he admitted. But—not that I'm blaming him—it was Barrista's fault. Perhaps Barrista felt he'd been swindled, a wine like that doesn't come cheap.

Georg, our '56 baby, sipped the Barolo dedicated to him. It took a good while, and then he said, "Thanks so much. That was magnificent."

Then came a most extraordinarily noble chateaubriand and for dessert, chocolate pudding and Italian schnapps.[1]

The baron chattered away about the hereditary prince, but he wasn't able to hide his own disappointment. Just one dud had ruined the atmosphere.

We left the honey gold Prince's Suite shortly before midnight. The waitress escorted us downstairs, along with the wolf, who needed to be walked. Out on the street Jörg asked what Barrista really wanted of us. Whereas I, with a glance toward the old familiar train station, asked

---

1. Presumably T. means mousse and grappa.

myself where we had been exactly. What did he suppose Barrista wanted? To find out who he was dealing with. If only everyone would make half the effort he had.

We had gone our separate ways when it came to me where I knew the waitress from. She was the buxom blonde who had stumbled past us leaving the bar back in January.

Your E.

PS: Something I keep forgetting to write: Gesine's musical presentation so impressed Robert that, although we didn't buy Aunt Trockel's piano from her, we did manage to jockey it into Robert's room. Robert's actually taking lessons. What poor Aunt Trockel was never able to accomplish, Gesine did. We'll see what comes of it. At least he's already learned a few notes.

Thursday, March 8, '90

Dear Nicoletta,

Ever since you left, I've thought only of you. I don't have to imagine you. You're present, and I listen to you. Only sleep interrupts our tête-à-tête. When I awoke, the separation was more than made up for by a sense of incredible joy—it was no dream, you really had visited me. Your presence had restored me to consciousness. Don't laugh! It's not easy to write something like that. I was happy to be with you. When I'm with you I find myself in a state of grace—I don't know what else to call it. Nicoletta, I want to tell you everything, everything, and all at once, but I would give up all those words just to see you.

Do you remember—you were telling me about your famous uncle,[1] about the peculiar circumstances surrounding his death—how you said that when it comes to really important things we never know what we should actually think? You said it so offhandedly and went on to something else. No, we don't, I said, still stuck on that remark, and you looked at me in surprise, and I had to control myself to keep from kissing you.

I was in agony the whole hour I knew you were still in Altenburg. You should have waited here, in my room, even if we hadn't said a word. *That*

---

1. In order to protect the rights of privacy, no details can be provided.

would have really helped me to "rest up." I didn't calm down until the moment I could assume you had left town. I hope your train was on time and you made all your connections.

Wasn't the proof room[1] like being in school? You, the *new girl,* looked hesitantly around the classroom, as if not knowing where to sit. Then you decided on me, to share my desk, and stuck out your hand, as if you'd just read in a guidebook that that's how it's done in the East. And while the others were running around during recess, we sat there like model pupils. I watched the calligraphy of your proofreaders' marks grow denser and denser, and my courage failed me. The goose bumps on your arm, clear up to the shoulder, the scar on your left elbow, kept distracting me. There wasn't a single motion of your right hand that I failed to notice. You asked for a dictionary and were so intent on making corrections, it was as if you wanted to give me time to get used to your presence.

It suddenly seems so absurd to be writing you, instead of simply taking off to see you. I can only plead my current condition as my excuse. By now I'm in hardly any pain.[2]

I kiss your hands,
Your Enrico

Friday, March 9, '90

Dear Nicoletta,

The first bus has already gone by, and the next thing I hear will be footsteps above me and the sounds of morning. My window is cracked ajar. How are you doing? I would love to talk with you. And when I think of how you won't get this letter before a few days have passed, these lines seem to lose all meaning. I can't wait that long!

The headaches have become bearable. I convinced the doctor at the polyclinic to remove the neck support. Holding his hands to my temples, he watched me as intently as if he expected my head to fall off. I'm supposed to imagine I'm balancing my "skull" on my neck, then the right

1. The proof room at the printing shop of the *Leipziger Volkszeitung,* where the *Altenburg Weekly* was read for corrections every Wednesday.
2. Cf. the letters that follow.

posture will follow all on its own. I don't think people moved around the Spanish royal court with any more dignity than I do here within my four walls.

I've ordered myself to stay away from the office. I definitely prefer the hope that greetings from you, however cursory, may be waiting for me there to the disappointment of that not being the case.

Maybe I'm lying here in bed so that I can think of you without disruption. How many letters I've already written you—eyes closed, hands folded across my belly. If only we could take up our conversation again where it got broken off! I was so angry and disappointed at the day being ruined and at your having to depart early that I was no longer in any condition to even notice what a stroke of luck your visit has been or, for that matter, how lucky we both are to be alive.

Where did you get the notion that the accident was an intentional attack? The first thing you cried out was: "That was on purpose!"

And so immediately I imagined that I knew the two men in the classy white Lada. I do everything I can to dismiss this as a chimera, but even as a figment of the imagination I don't like the idea. And now, as I write this, it seems totally absurd. And yet those two figures loom up ever more clearly in my mind. It's like in a fairy tale, when the devil demands his tribute at the very instant he's been forgotten.[1]

Dear Nicoletta, it's evening now—and still no letter from you.[2] I know, I shouldn't have said that.

I've been in a strange mood all day. I smell unusual odors, suddenly imagine myself being in another room, and need a couple of seconds to come to myself, as if I were just waking up. On days like this you only have to be inattentive, and you stumble and fall and fall. Is it only our imagination that we feel someone's actual grasp, even though they have long since let go? Should I say that the past is grasping me or, better yet, that I've never been young? Do you think someone like me is capable of

1. The question as to what extent these "susurrations" (cf. below) had anything to do with T.'s real experience is something each reader will have to decide for him- or herself over time. Quite obviously he is searching here for some reason to be writing these letters. A rather poor motivation.

2. T. apparently expected that N. H. had written him before she even left Altenburg. The accident had happened only two days before.

stealing a weapon? Forgive me my susurrations. It all sounds so preposterous. I'm merely afraid I'll fall back into the same state I was in at the end of last year. I was ill and lay here in my room just like now. And that—and I'm not exaggerating—was the worst time of my life.

For several weeks now I've been toying with a question. At first I didn't take it seriously; it seemed too commonplace. But over time I've come to think it's justified. The question is: What were the ways and means by which the West got inside my brain? And what did it do in there?[1]

Of course I might also ask how God got inside my brain. It amounts to the same question, though it's less concerned with the matter of my own particular original sin.

Needless to say, I can't offer any precise answer. I can only try to grope for one.

One of the few rituals observed in our family occurred whenever I tried to revive my earliest memories. I had achieved my goal whenever my mother would exclaim, "Impossible! You were barely two!"—or, "At eighteen months, out of the question!" She would successfully manage a good five such exclamations of astonishment. It gave me deep satisfaction to find my memories confirmed. Each incredulous shake of my mother's head made me feel like some sort of wunderkind. (My sister Vera never failed to offer some corrections; I had no chance against her four-year head start and always had to hear how happy everyone had been before I arrived.)

Here's one of my showpieces. I wake up, the room is still dark, but in the next room there's light and voices. My mother carries me out, my grandmother says, "Sweetie pie." A hat lies on an armchair, two coats with fur collars are draped over its back—strangers! There are strangers in our apartment. I start to cry. The strangers are hiding. Someone gives me a Duplo candy bar that sticks out of its wrapper like a half-peeled banana. My sister has a Duplo too. I can't understand why she's so unconcerned. The Duplo is meant to help me get over these strangers, who are going to move in. I'm given a little red car. A bright rod sticks out between the front wheel and the door on the driver's side. That's for steering it. The headlights are glass beads. "Diamonds," my mother says, "from the West."

1. Here T. addresses the central theme of his letters to N. H.

Present after present is lifted out of suitcases and shown to my mother. My grandpa tickles my palm with an electric razor. It all comes from the golden West. I can see most of the room, but the strangers are hiding. They're whispering with my grandpa.

Back in my bed, I ask whether the strangers are going to stay for a long time. I'm certain they're going to move in with us. I don't believe my mother.

I'm afraid, I'm impressed—toys with diamonds, and they come from a world made of gold. That's also the reason why we're not allowed to go to the West. Of course we'd all rather live in the West. I'm not allowed to play with my car outside, in fact no other kids are supposed to know about my car. Otherwise they'd be jealous because they don't have a red car. The red car is irreplaceable, you can't just buy one. Only a few kids here have Matchbox cars and Lego blocks and tins of Kaba powder. I also had shirts and pants from the West, and in time I would look just as handsome as the boy on that chocolate drink for kids. Actually I was a child of the West myself.

Are you still listening to me? Or do you think by now I'm utterly mad? Let me finish my story. With each passing year I understood better: We had things other families didn't have and couldn't have, no matter how much they longed to have them, even if they earned more than my mother and had more money in the bank than my grandpa. Items from the West were like moonstones, either they were given to you or they remained out of reach. Our relatives in the West were just like God and the Lord Jesus—they loved you, although you didn't know them and never ever saw them face-to-face. And anyone who laughed at me because I believed in God was at least envious of my red car.

There were five special days in the year. St. Nicholas, Easter, my birthday, Christmas—Christmas was the high point, but Christmas was outshone by the day when my grandparents returned from their visit to the West. The evening of their arrival at the Neustadt train station in Dresden was the real, unsurpassable Christmas Eve.

Every year my mother took off work for the day, and we were allowed to come home for our noon meal. After doing our homework, we helped her with chores, which gave us the feeling that by dusting thoroughly and polishing lots of shoes we were adding to the number of presents.

In our best clothes we walked to the streetcar after darkness fell.

What was so splendid, if not to say colossal, about it all was that it was we who had been chosen. How could other people live a life in which there would never be a day, an evening like this? I felt sorry for my schoolmates. I pitied them as I pitied Africans who had no *Sport Aktuell*, no coverage of four ski-jump tournaments to watch on Saturdays.

Once on the streetcar, where all the vacant seats only increased the thrill, we gazed rather haughtily at the other passengers. We were unrecognized royal children, and I was happy to be no one but me.

Then it began—the back-and-forth of deciding which platform the train would arrive on. We listened expectantly to the crackling loudspeakers, trying to sort out the syllables "Be-bra" from the rest of the cacophony. And what would the waiting have been without the train running late, or the autumn air without the steam of the locomotives.

There were no disappointments, there couldn't be any, for every present from the West was a priceless treasure all by itself. The stories our grandparents told went beyond our powers of imagination—for example, escalators, escalators in a department store. You stepped on a carpet, held fast to a richly ornamented railing, and were borne soundlessly upward, floating like an angel on the ladder to heaven.

In the West the streets were heated from below ground, the gas stations never closed, and when people in the West didn't know what else to improve, for the fun of it they tore up streets only recently paved with asphalt. Neon signs flashed above every shop, every door, the nights were bright as day and flooded with more traffic than filled our streets after a May Day parade. All the same, in the West you could always find a seat on a tram, bus, or train. In the West gas smelled like perfume, and train stations were tropical gardens where travelers could buy the most marvelous fruits. In the West people had hair down to their shoulders and wore jeans and chewed gum that let you blow bubbles as big as your head. And what was more, the global market was in the West. I didn't know exactly where, but it was definitely in the West. When you pronounced the word "East," didn't your mouth spread in a simpleton's grimace? Whereas "West" hissed like a Lamborghini Miora speeding off on superfast tires. "East" sounded like cloudy skies and omnibuses and abandoned excavations. "West" like asphalt streets with glass gas stations, terraces where the drinks came with straws, and music drifting across a blue lake. Cities with names like Cottbus, Leipzig, or Eisenhüttenstadt couldn't possible be located in the West. What a different sound places like Lahr, Karlsruhe, Freiburg, or Graching had. Vera and I—despite all our quarrels—were always in agreement when it came to the West.

Just one thing more (please be patient with me): packages were something that by definition came from the West. Their contents weren't immediately put away, but left lying out on the living-room table. It was New Year's before the coffee, soap, stockings vanished into cupboards and drawers, where they never lost the aroma of their origin. They were resistant to all attempts to blend them into the world, were a category of things all to itself. They didn't lose their value when used or eaten. The idea would never have entered our heads to throw away an empty tin of Kaba or Caro. Our cellar storage space was full of such cans and tins.

I would often go down into the cellar just like Willi Schwabe entering his attic—does the name Willi Schwabe mean anything to you?[1] And just as he might find a roll of film or maybe some other object that reminded him of an actor, the Kaba and Caro tins filled with nails or screws spoke to me of happy holidays and the West. Today I'd say that they first had to lose their use-value to become sacred objects.

These treasures also proved that Aunt Camilla and Uncle Peter had always thought about us, had always known our most secret wishes, and wanted only the best for us.

When I prayed, I prayed to God, who knew everything about me, always thought of me, and would always be there for me. And although he didn't look like Aunt Camilla and Uncle Peter, he must in fact have been like Aunt Camilla and Uncle Peter, except more so.

Robert's alarm just went off.[2] I'm going to make breakfast, wait for the mail carrier, and then go to the doctor again this afternoon.

With you in my thoughts, I remain

Your Enrico T.

---

1. *Willi Schwabe's Attic*—an East German television program. At the beginning of each episode Willi Schwabe, with lantern in hand, would climb the stairs to a kind of storage room. The background music was the "Dance of the Sugarplum Fairy" from Tchaikovsky's *Nutcracker.*

2. At the start of the second part of the letter it was still evening. Either T. had slept in the meantime or—though it is hardly likely—it had taken him all night to write it.

PS: It was from Aunt Camilla that I first heard I was a writer, because in my thank-you letter I described what our Christmas was like and how we had barely been able to wait to open her package—which was a lie, since Aunt Camilla always stuffed it with candy (and coffee and, rather absurdly, condensed milk—truly no rarity for us), whereas in Uncle Peter's package you might find Matchbox cars or even a cassette, which always made his package a real event. Aunt Camilla wrote back that my letter was the loveliest letter she had ever received, a real short story, which she often read aloud to other people.

Monday, March 12, '90

Ah, Verotchka, you were two hours early![1] And now you're paying for your mistake with worry. But this message is sure to get lost like all the others. It's so absurd.

If only it had been Georg or Jörg who picked up the phone. But Ilona! An accident! His sister! How marvelous! She told me she calmed you down and provided you all the details. I can just imagine how she calmed you down. By the time she was done you probably thought it was a stroke of good fortune that your brother ended up in a wheelchair instead of in Hades.

There's a rumbling inside my skull—a concussion, but nothing more than that. What did she tell you about Nicoletta? She came away with just some bruises.

We had left Leipzig and were heading for Frohburg by way of Borna. We were on our way to the Schwind pavilion.[2] It was actually nobody's fault. A Lada (a white one, I think) had passed us in a curve to the left, slipped back in between us and the car ahead of us because of oncoming traffic, I braked, and in the same moment the windshield shattered—nothing but ice crystals up ahead.[3] I banged it with my hand, trying to

1. Refers to a phone call that evidently came earlier than had been agreed on. T.'s letters to V. T. never made it to Beirut. Thus the only ones that still exist are those that T. made a carbon copy of, plus two faxed letters.
2. Cf. footnote 2, p. 66.
3. He means the "ice crystals" of the shattered windshield.

93

see something, the car went into a skid, and we plunged headlong down the embankment—I think I heard, and felt, the second loud crash. Sudden silence. We had come to a halt and were staring through a big hole in the windshield. The silence came straight out of a fairy tale.

I wasn't in any pain, but what I wanted most was just to sit there. We had managed to sail right through a gap between trees; on Nicoletta's side the clearance wasn't two feet.

I didn't notice the blood until later. Nicoletta used her handkerchief to dab at it. And then—you know me—I started to feel sick to my stomach. I tipped my seat back, closed my eyes, and left everything to Nicoletta. The people who came to our aid were more of a nuisance. Someone spread a blanket over me and kept trying to tuck it under me on both sides. I pushed the guy away because I thought I was going to throw up. From this position I studied the little piece of ground beside the car for a good while.

By the time the police and ambulance arrived my nausea had given way to a nasty headache.

Everything took forever, the ride to Borna, the X-rays, the neck support, the police again, the endless sitting around, then finally the taxi ride to Altenburg. There are suddenly more taxis than you can shake a stick at. Robert stared in horror at my neck support and turban à la Apollinaire. Nicoletta told the cabdriver to take her to the train station right away.

She lives in Bamberg. People like her can't or don't want to believe that I left the theater voluntarily. She has contributed a lot to our newspaper,[1] and since she's writing about De Chirico and Moritz von Schwind is supposed to have been one of his favorites, I had arranged for her to visit the frescoes in Rüdigsdorf.

I'll write about Barrista some other time. Thanks to his boots and Astrid the wolf he's already become a fixture in town. He's interested in everything and everybody, and he gawks at women's breasts with his google-eyes. But that "von" in front of his name, his mission on behalf of the hereditary prince, and, last but not least, his courtesy and consideration—including a phenomenal memory for names—

---

1. This surely must either be a wish or a fond hope. It is quite unclear what T. meant by this. There is no record of anything by N. H. ever being published in the *Altenburg Weekly*.

have not failed to have an effect. Was he ever one of your unrequited admirers?

Ah, Verotchka, my darling, how long must this waiting last?

Kisses from

Your Heinrich in his neck support[1]

Tuesday, March 13, '90

Dear Nicoletta,

I'm feeling better, much better. I plan to give the office a try on Wednesday, just for a few hours. And what about you? How are you doing? When I catch myself not thinking about you, it scares me, as if I had lost my wallet.

For some strange reason you're the only person with whom I feel free to talk about my past and to explain why I've become the way I am.[2]

There's something I want to mention first, however.

My father was an actor—not even a mediocre actor, otherwise he would have had better roles—employed by various stages in Saxony. He had heart problems and knew that he would probably never make it to forty. Maybe that's why he became such a tyrant. He was obsessed with the notion that my sister Vera was blessed with great talent, was an actress the likes of which appear only once in a generation. Vera was twelve when he died.

Sometimes I'm afraid that even now she still believes the only thing that kept her from a spectacular career was the lack of a father. At sixteen, seventeen, she was still blaming me for his death (he was supposed to pick me up at the afterschool club, was late as usual, and stepped out into the path of an oncoming car). Besides which, he stubbornly insisted that it was because of the long commute that he had rented a room in Radebeul, where the central office for all the state theaters was located.

In fact he lived in that room with a singer from the chorus and slept at

1. T. had already noted in his letter to N. H. that the neck support had been removed.

2. T. and N. H. knew each other for only a few hours, and those were full of misunderstandings and accidents. The fact that N. H. came from the Federal Republic of Germany must have played a major role in T.'s attraction to her. T. is explaining and justifying himself for a Western audience here, a quite typical stance in East Germany at the time.

home only when my mother had the night shift. The singer regarded him with the same awe in which my mother had once held him. He could once again tell her how he hoped to die onstage, and she could console him for having to live with a woman as hardhearted as my mother, who, according to him, once told him that, given the roles he played, no one would notice if he did die onstage, and to finally leave off harping about it.

If it weren't for photographs I probably wouldn't know what my father looked like—or his peculiar smile with just the left corner of his mouth raised. He thought it made him look Mephistophelian. Vera—there's a snapshot of her—dressed like an adult for the funeral, all in black. She didn't cry, or if she did, then only when she was alone, just as she didn't speak to us about it, but confided things only to her diary. No one knows why Vera rejected my mother—well before the accident even, before puberty. Whereas, as long as I can remember, Vera was the favorite, which I felt was perfectly natural, since Vera gave the impression she had lost both parents and was forced to live with us—while I had my mother, after all. Our mother worked hard at fulfilling her husband's prophecy and did all she could to turn Vera Türmer, Dresden's admired "recitation prize winner," into a stage diva, a Dietrich.

Although my mother was and is truly a good surgical nurse and, thank God, had no artistic ambitions, so-called normal professions were considered unimportant in our home. On our walks across the Dresden Heath the conversation was always about Mozart, who had been buried in a pauper's grave, about Hölderlin, who went mad, about Kleist, who committed suicide, about Beethoven, whom his audience would laugh at. Had not every true genius been mocked, hadn't they all—with the exception of Goethe—suffered horribly, and yet despite everything, hadn't they created something for which humankind must be infinitely grateful today? To struggle out of darkness into light!

My mother's experience with my father had changed none of that; on the contrary, she simply ratcheted up her notions of the genius and his work just that much higher. In other words, if my parents had been halfway satisfied with their life, they would have spared us, especially my sister, a lot of problems.

I'm sharing all this with you just to fill in details, they explain everything and nothing.

I'm not trying to tell you my life story, I merely want to trace the path down which I went so miserably astray, but my description of it may ultimately result in a kind of story, a painful story, which might not be without some purpose as a cautionary tale.[1]

Three weeks of my summer vacation after the seventh grade—I started school a year later than other kids my own age, so I was almost fourteen—were spent with my mother in a cottage. It stood in the middle of a pine forest, near a little clear-water lake, in Waldau, southeast of Berlin.

This country place belonged to a childless couple from Jüterbog, friends of my father, who spent their summers in Bulgaria or Hungary, but whose continued loyalty to us was not entirely unselfish. My mother, who paid rent for our stay, was also the one who cleaned the gutters, washed the curtains, beat the carpets, pulled a handcart to the flea market, had the propane bottles refilled, called in the man to clean out the septic tank, and even initiated little improvements like the installment of an outdoor light—she wasn't about to step on a toad a second time.

The cottage didn't have a television, and even before we left I was afraid I'd be bored. Boredom defined my life in general. I was bored every day, although three times a week I took target practice—I was considered to have some talent at Olympic rapid-fire pistol.

There's a snapshot of me in Waldau—I'm wearing shorts and sitting bent over the table, staring straight ahead and massaging my calves. I still know exactly what I was thinking at that moment: I was dreaming of the new soccer season and of Dynamo Dresden winning game after game with a perfectly balanced team, of their becoming league champions and taking the cup.

When I was in kindergarten I thought of reading as something magical, that when you reached a certain age you mastered it without even trying. But when the day came that I realized reading was all about a tedious, monotonous combination of letters and syllables, it turned into just another dreary subject in school.

---

1. These words remind one more of the opening of a novel than of a letter. It remains unclear for whom this "painful story" is intended, for whom it is supposed to serve as a "cautionary tale."

So when my mother asked what books she should pack for me for our vacation, it was a question of almost unsurpassable hypocrisy.

For my sake she played badminton, chess, or battleships. I rode my bike and did the shopping at the village Konsum store, where the *Sport Echo* went on sale after eight in the morning. As an early riser I spent the first hours of the day on a rickety man's bicycle, riding through the woods, listening to my music cassettes played on our landlord's Stern tape recorder that I tied to the basket.

On my third early-morning excursion, I misjudged a puddle. My front wheel got stuck, as if an iron hand had grabbed hold of it—and I went flying. Pain, pain worse than the worst stitch in your side, knocked the air out of me. Sand burned in my eyes. But the awful part was the silence. Half blind, howling with rage and pain, and with a couple of broken ribs, or so I believed, I crawled back to the puddle and pulled the Stern tape recorder out of the muck. I ejected the cassette once, twice, three times, reinserted it again each time—all in vain. Only the radio still worked.

As I knelt there in the sand, trying to scratch the mud out of the cracks in the wooden housing, morning devotions were being broadcast on AM. God's word falls like rain upon the soil, but it may indeed run off to no avail. To catch the rain, we must dig ditches. The pastor spoke at length about digging ditches, which was exactly the same as reading the New Testament in order to be prepared to receive God's word. Moreover, God gave each of us a sign in due season. At the pastor's concluding words, I turned the radio off.

I didn't know what to do. One corner of the housing had broken off. A Stern tape recorder cost more than my mother earned in a month. When I looked up, there was a deer standing in the road about twenty yards away. It turned its head to me. After we had stared at each other for a while, it strode off, vanishing into a copse of young trees.

Had it been a unicorn, I could not have been more profoundly moved. Suddenly I was praying. I thanked God for his sign, that he had led me into the woods and spoken to me. And for the first time it was I who directed my words to the Lord God, not just some child reciting bedtime prayers. No, *I* was praying now. I begged for help, help amid my distress, and included my mother and the radio pastor in my request for eternal life. I promised that henceforth I would dig my ditches, deep ditches, which would collect God's word and from which I would draw water forever and ever. Now strengthened and calmed, I in fact found the broken-off piece of housing and hoped for another miracle.

Had I fallen among thieves, my mother asked.

I rummaged the bookshelf above the night storage heater. Lord, I prayed, give me your New Testament. In my hand was a thick gray book without its dust jacket. I deciphered the red lettering as *Martin Eden*. The name Jack London meant something to me. I sat down in a chaise longue and started to read, and I would normally have given up very quickly, since it wasn't about wolves or gold miners, but about a writer. But the fact that this book had chosen me could not be accidental. The more I read, the more the story spoke to me.

It was one o'clock, well after one, when I was called in for our midday meal—the entire morning had flown by. I had been reading for more than three hours. Then it came to me: I didn't have to be bored anymore. Anyone who was a reader as a child cannot understand what Copernican dimensions that insight had for me.

The day was not over, and you may suspect what happened next. After all, I was reading the story of a starving but determined and undaunted writer who would make it in the end . . .

As I took my shower that evening I asked myself about the meaning of this substitution. I had been looking for the Bible and had found *Martin Eden*. What was God trying to say to me? As warm water ran down over my face, I was struck by my third insight of the day: I was meant to become a writer!

I stood there motionless under the shower for a while. I was meant to turn my experience in the woods into a story about how strange it was that my tape recorder had fallen silent, while the radio had remained intact so that I could hear the voice of God. I would write what others dared not say, that the West was better than the East, for example, that we weren't allowed to travel to the West even though we wanted to. When everyone else went to work, I would stay home and write. When I entered a pub, everyone would turn around to look at me. Because everyone knew about my speech in which I had indicted the state. "One man at least," they'd whisper, "one man at least who's willing to speak out." My family and I would have a difficult time of it, however, because I was a thorn in the government's side.

Cold water wrenched me out of my dream world. My mother called me inconsiderate and selfish for not leaving any warm water—after all, she was the one who had heated the stove and glued the broken corner back on the tape recorder.

Her accusations were a double blow. I had to remain silent, however. But the day would come when I would write about it and my mother would read and finally understand that it had not been selfishness or even a lack of consideration, but just the opposite. She would be proud of me, would laugh and at the same time have to cry a little, because she had had no idea that a writer was being born, although it was happening right before her eyes.

When I awoke the next morning, I smiled when I spotted the gray book beside my pillow. I felt like Martin Eden was my brother. And then I had to smile for having smiled.

I rode my bike to the village bakery and waited until the Konsum opened. I hid my first notebook, a five-by-eight sketchpad, in the shed.

After breakfast I retreated to my chaise longue. But I was too excited to read. I felt compelled to record what I had experienced, was afraid I'd forget things. When my mother wasn't watching, I laid the book aside, slipped the sketchpad under my shirt and a ballpoint into my saddlebag. I would write my first sentence at the place of my conversion. The first sentence of a great writer! For neither at that moment nor later did I ever doubt my talent.

When I finally put pen to paper, the pen didn't work. Which is why my memoirs begin with crazy squiggles above the date and time. At ten on the dot I finally wrote: "Praise be to Jesus Christ!"

What happened then can only be explained as the work of the Holy Spirit. He guided my hand for seven pages, without my hesitating even once, without my having to correct so much as a single word. My turns of phrase thrilled even me. I was giving the world something unlike anything it had known before in this form. Even if I should never put another word to paper, these lines would endure.

When I returned home I discovered something remarkable that—though I was now acquainted with miracles—frightened me. The roof of the cottage was covered with snow. I got off my bike. What I saw, I saw—snow! A field of snow as large as our tin roof. No white anywhere else, and even after walking my bike halfway across the yard, what my eyes saw and what my reason told me were incompatible. Suddenly my mother was standing beside me. "Daydreaming?" she asked. My gaze was fixed on the tin roof. "Snow," I said. "You're right," she said, "it does glisten like snow."

Happy days followed. Mornings, between seven and eight, I would take my seat at a little table in the perfect silence, watching the sun cautiously grope on spidery legs through the pine trees, lie down on the bed of moss that my mother had raked free of needles and cones, turning it lustrous. The sketchpad lay under my opened *Martin Eden,* and no more than the book could hide it, was I now going to make any effort to hide my calling. That wasn't even possible. I switched back and forth between book and sketchpad so often that reading and writing became one and the same. It was the only thing that I took any pleasure in and for which I seemed to have been born. Suddenly I found a hundred thoughts inside me, where before there had not been one.

I remember, however, hardly anything of *Martin Eden* and nothing of what I wrote at the time. It now seems to me as if I pursued the whole thing simply so that the world might be captured inside those pages, so that all its sounds, smells, and colors can fall into my lap whenever I remember those days. Otherwise how could I recall the Igelit[1] tablecloth, a green and white checkerboard that clung to my bare knees whenever I sat down to write? How many times was I just about to shove it aside, which would have been easy as pie, but then never did it, as if afraid I would lose the source of my inspiration.

When from the chaise longue I would gaze up through the crowns of the pine trees—the sunglasses I had found in a kitchen cupboard cast a turquoise hue over everything—I felt as if I were at the bottom of the sea, looking up to the surface. When the sun slipped behind a tree trunk, pinks and reds turned purple. Sunsets were the loveliest part, when the evening light lay almost horizontal over the lake, lending trunks and branches a rusty red glow. When the light vanished at last from the treetops, it drenched the bellies of the clouds in violet—to have looked away would have been a sacrilege. Each morning when I went to fetch our breakfast rolls, the gossamer webs draped among the grasses were the same whitish gray as the morning moon—lingering phantoms and shadows of night.

Every sound was there simply to affirm the silence (a silence that I will get around to talking about later, much later).

Happy that her son had finally come to his senses, my mother thanked me by coddling me and watching as I played with the twenty-six symbols.

1. An oilclothlike material that could be wiped off.

I sat down to my meals as a writer exhausted by his labors. And I wanted to write about that too, about what it's like when you rest from your work. Every thought, every sensation, every observation was precious and transient. I was a collector, a discoverer on a mission to glean all things remarkable and noteworthy, to describe them, to share them with humanity. How had I possibly lived before this? How had I endured this life? How did my mother endure her existence?

Vera visited us for the last few days. She asked no questions. She just looked at the book in my hands and announced, "Oh, Enrico is reading a book with the fascinating title *Father Goriot!*"—or—"Ah, my brother Enrico is familiarizing himself with the works of the great humanist Charles Dickens." I had nothing more to fear from her. Besides which I profited from my mother's conviction that anyone sleeping or reading was never to be disturbed—a rule that until then had worked to my disadvantage.

With almost half a sketchbook filled with the adventures of my soul, I experienced our arrival in Dresden as a triumph. Only three weeks before I had left the city as a foolish boy who had known nothing about himself and the world or his calling in it. I returned as a young writer who would soon be famous.

You will take this for childishness, Nicoletta. For me it was the beginning of the path that led me astray. I shall probably hear what you have to say about all this.

Thinking only of you, Your Enrico T.

Tuesday, March 13, '90

Dear Jo,

I had a car accident, and a madman who as good as forced us off the road was at fault. I have a slight concussion and pulled a couple of muscles in my neck, but that's really all. We[1] were lucky. Suddenly we came to a halt—with a shattered windshield—midway between two trees.

Without a car I feel like an amputee, everything's a mess at the moment, and it's downright depressing too. There was a time when I just had to look at Jimmy[2] and I felt better. The cost of repairs

1. T. doesn't explain who lies concealed behind this *we*.
2. It was quite common for people to give their cars names. One explanation might be that you drove, or better, had to drive, "your car" for ten years or more.

will probably be so high that it's not worth it. It was Michaela's late father's car, that he fussed over and took such good care of—and for her mother it was the chief reminder of better days. Worse still, she's now going to find out that we never took out collision coverage.

I'll be back at the office starting tomorrow and will try to call you from there. I'm glad I'll be back among people. Just lying around here is not living.

I've had plenty of visitors. Old Larschen walked all the way here, his backpack full of homegrown apples—each wrapped individually in rustling tissue paper—that he now placed one by one on the table like precious jewels. The apple, he informed Michaela and me, belonged to the rose family, to which Michaela replied that it had been a long time since she'd received such lovely roses. The two were instant friends. She's even allowed to read his memoirs manuscript. We invited him to share supper with us. When we sat down at the table, Larschen broke off his excurses on the juniper, lowered his chin to his chest, and prayed silently. Robert witnessed this for probably the first time in his life. We looked at each other, but didn't dare smile. Larschen raised his head, saying, "The juniper can grow to be five hundred years old, the broad-leafed linden can reach a thousand." And we were in motion again now too, as if the film had just stuttered briefly. After Larschen left, something of his odor lingered in the apartment. But there was also the fragrance of apples.

Jörg thought he would need to console me, since we're selling only seventeen thousand copies or fewer. The election will help us, and Jörg is still following leads for a couple of stories from his Commission Against Corruption and Abuse of Office. He's the only untainted person on it, and so has an easy time of it.

Today Wolfgang the Hulk appeared at the door, along with his equally hulking wife. He hadn't heard about the accident and they had come to invite us to dinner. When we bought our pots in Offenburg, he had promised to cook for us. (So far we haven't dared use our pots.) He's working for Jan Steen now, drives a company car, and is evidently earning such a pile of D-marks that he's embarrassed to talk about it. Jan Steen, Wolfgang says, reads every word in our paper. He's interested in everything. When I asked what he himself thinks of it, he gave a tentative laugh. A little more pepper wouldn't hurt, he said. I reacted somewhat angrily, after all you can't have a scandal like the Council Library[1] every week (and even there everything is said to have been on the up-and-up) or some incident in the schools.[2] He responded to my question about his old job as if I were giving tit for tat, though I had asked it more out of discomfiture. From his wife's hints, I concluded the decision still bothered him. But as for Jan Steen, he didn't want to hear[3]—"a word said against him," was what I was about to write. It's almost midnight. Barrista was suddenly standing at the door. He's incredible. The bouquet was so big that I couldn't tell who was standing there in front of me. There's no one I'd have been more surprised to see. He, on the other hand, seemed astonished to find me in "such fine fettle."

Robert was greeted with the same bow that I received. Barrista spoke to him as if to an adult and expressed his "appreciation"—he knew what it meant to stand all on your own in the marketplace, and told him how very lucky he was to be so young in these times, to be able to learn everything, to begin everything anew. Barrista's sermon had thwarted Robert's attempt at flight. Without being asked Robert looked after Astrid the wolf while I laid out napkins for our light supper, adding a bottle of cabernet and a serving fork for the cold cuts, which Robert accepted as concessions made for a guest. (Michaela was onstage, she's still having to work as the backup in *Rusalka*.)[4]

Barrista buttered his bread with a meticulousness that I've never seen anyone except you apply and positioned his slices of cold cuts with such precision that the curves of bread and sausage were nearly congruent.

As I was about to pour him some wine, he declined it and stared at me through bulletproof glass. Would I be willing and able to drive him to the train station in half an hour? The situation was as follows—and then he explained in great detail and at great length why it was better for him to take the train, in a sleeping car of course, to Stuttgart (or was it Frankfurt am Main?), and ended by asking if he could leave his LeBaron in my care.

1. Approximately one thousand very valuable volumes were removed from the Altenburg Council Library under the pretext of their needing repair, but were then sold in the West under the aegis of Schalck-Golodkowski's Commercial Coordination.

2. There were a good number of cases in which school principals were either demoted or fired.

3. Presumably broken off because Barrista had appeared.

4. The heroine in *Rusalka* had broken her leg. She continued to sing, but Michaela Fürst had to stand in for her onstage for several performances.

Of course I should drive it, he would very much like that, indeed he took joy in the idea. Laying his hand imploringly to his heart, he repeated how happy it made him to think of me driving his car and that he wished in this fashion to be of some assistance to me in the wake of my accident. Of course he had, as always, selfish motives. He couldn't leave his car here parked in the same spot for several days. "Please don't misunderstand me, my dear Herr Türmer," it wasn't that he'd had any bad experiences here with such things, but one need not provoke an incident, either. If he absolutely could not persuade me, I should at least obey his maxim that one ought never present the state an unnecessary gift—after all the taxes and insurance were paid in full, the car was parked out front with a full tank.

There was just enough time left to make him some coffee. While Barrista excused himself to wash his hands, we slathered a few sandwiches, piling them high with what cold cuts were left, and Robert came up with the idea of sending him off with a thermos of hot coffee. The baron was touched.

I was the one who drove the car to the station. I was afraid that in return we'd be required to take care of the wolf, which sat beside Robert in the backseat. The baron and Robert talked about music, or what Robert calls music. The baron knew most of the bands and even some gossip about Milli Vanilli and their ilk. The source of his knowledge was in the trunk, a stack of *Bravo* magazines that he bequeathed to Robert. He had already read them himself—it's required reading, a way of getting some idea of what young people are up to. Which brought him around to his own two children, whom he's allowed to see far too infrequently. There wasn't time for more questions. At his urging I tested putting the top up and down—since spring is on its way, after all—and was handed the registration. A can of dog food, a big plastic ashtray (a Stuyvesant cigarette promotion) for a bowl, and his attaché case was all the baggage he had.

He lifted the wolf onto the train, said a quick good-bye, and pulled the door closed behind him. Robert and I followed him down the platform, moving from window to window, watched as he took a seat, opened his attaché case, and extracted a pile of papers. As he read he rested his head against the windowpane, as if dozing. In that moment I think I gained some understanding of why he always has the wolf at his side.

Do you know the series with David Hasselhoff and his talking car?[1] This LeBaron looks a lot like it. You steer more from a prone position than sitting upright. And that was how I watched people streaming out of the theater as we drove by. I felt like a reptile gliding quietly through the water. Almost in shock, people turned to watch us pass.

Michaela got in without so much as a comment, that's how despondent she was. She didn't even say anything about Robert, who should have been in bed by eight. "Just get us away from here," she said, which I took as a request for a little jaunt.

All the same she enjoyed the ride and smiled when we hit a hundred and sixty on the long straight stretch on the other side of Rositz. When we got home I thought Michaela and Robert had fallen asleep, but actually they just didn't want to get out of the car.

Once in the living room we pounced on Barrista's box of candy—chocolates that melted on your tongue. Michaela took one of each sort and, sitting down where Barrista had just sat, laid them on his plate, assuming it was clean. I managed three, Robert two, Michaela ate them like cherries, and took the rest with her when she sat down in front of the television—where she still is, listening to oracles about the upcoming election.

Dear Jo, I find it hard to say anything about your latest work.[2] All that seems so far away now. Invented stories no longer interest me. That's no argument, of course, and certainly no criterion for measuring quality. The new literature, if it does come about, will be literature about work, about business deals, about money. Just look around you! People in the West don't do anything but work. It will be no different with us.

Say hello to your wife and daughter for me, hugs, E.

[Thursday, March 15, '90]

Nicoletta, what happened?[3] I'm practically numb. I heard about it just in passing from Jörg. But don't know anything else about it. Why should you care about Barrista? When I think about how I was lying in bed at

---

1. The talking car from the TV series *Knight Rider* was named KITT.

2. No literary work by Johann Ziehlke has been found among T.'s papers.

3. More details of the argument between N. H. and Barrista can be found in later letters to N. H.

precisely the same moment, counting the minutes until your departure—and now I know. I suspected something of the sort, something disastrous. But Barrista? What does he have to do with us? When it comes to us, he doesn't exist. What are you accusing him of? Or me? Why is he important at all? Isn't he a person who ought to arouse our sympathy, or forbearance? As a man who has to compensate for so much? But none of that matters. Why are you making me atone for what he did? How else am I supposed to understand your silence? At first glance B. seems an odd duck. I have no idea where he gets his strange manners and attitudes. Do they have any purpose other than to draw attention away from his looks? People here make fun of his pointy boots with their out-of-whack heels. Ultimately I can't tell you anything about B., other than that he approached the newspaper with his unusual request. The explanations he gave for it are flattering. Is there any reason why we shouldn't cooperate with him?

Where do you know him from? Or was he—I don't dare put it in words—impolite or otherwise crude? Believe me, it would take no more than a hint of something of the sort—and he can go to wherever!

B. has left, no one knows when he'll be back.

Please drop me just a couple of lines, I beg you.

With all my heart,
Your Enrico

Monday, March 19, '90

Dear Nicoletta,

Up until the very last minute I was certain you'd appear at the office, as if there were some natural rhythm that would necessarily bring you back to Altenburg. Sometimes I'm seized with the fear that you might be ill, that something's wrong, maybe in aftermath of the accident. Have you had X-rays taken?

My desire to see you was so strong that I believed it might conjure up your presence. That's also why I came to the office early—and thought I had been rewarded. I ran into Georg in the vestibule, and he promised me a visitor, in fact someone was waiting for me. Georg's smile was so broad I had no doubts whatever.

But I played the innocent—yes, I blame myself for that now, as if my foolishness had driven you away—shrugged, as if I couldn't imagine who it might be, and asked Georg what needed to be done, hoping you would hear my voice. Of course I had nothing against his going right back upstairs. Ah, Nicoletta, those few moments of promise!

Three men from the newspaper in Giessen sat sipping coffee, happy to have new playmates. I recognized one of them from his lilac-colored jacket.

My responses were mechanical. My thoughts were racing here and there, but at some point I calmed myself with the realization that there was lots of time left, that the day had just begun, so everything still lay ahead of me, a day with lots of hours with lots of minutes—and you might arrive at any one of them. With astounding speed the familiar happiness that comes with such an expectation reasserted itself. The soft light of a spring day too warm for this early in the year could only be your harbinger.

The men from Giessen had been out watching polling stations open and had retreated to our office as if to a pub. They didn't believe me when I told them I'd been up for only an hour instead of doing research since the crack of dawn. But after I asked them to pass on their article on the general mood, they set their misgivings aside. I laid out the page proofs and started in. I wanted to earn your appearance, Nicoletta, and be finished early.

Each time the door opened it seemed more and more likely that you would appear.

The fellows from Giessen deployed their forces one by one, but were never gone for long. Their favorite story was about how Hans Schönemann, the former "district secretary for ideology and propaganda," was now a candidate of the German Social Union. Although I told them right off that there were two people who went by that name, the guy with the hedgehog haircut kept telling the story over and over, and left it to me to correct him. Then he would smile as if to say: Are you sure of that?

Around two I stuffed myself with pastries and was afraid you'd catch me with my mouth full. I expected you by five, or five thirty at the latest, at any rate before the polls closed. I was as convinced of that as if you had just told me so over the phone.

Around four I had finished up with everything and would have been done even earlier if I hadn't had to play host the whole time, as well as putting off calculating the last article. I wanted you to find me hard at work.

Franka had some folding chairs that were usually set out halfway up the back garden—the white paint was flaking and stuck to your trouser seat. We had put the newspaper to bed and had shoved the table's extensions back in. There hadn't been that many people in our parlor the day of our first issue. I hadn't seen many of them since last October or November. Georg announced that he had figured out that anyone born after 1912 had never taken part in a genuine election.

When the clock struck the hour, the sixth stroke caught me unawares. I thought I had counted wrong, but the portable radio also announced six p.m. Squeezed in among the crowd, it seemed to me other people were holding their breath too—utter silence. Until Jörg laughed out loud. Others joined in. Suddenly everyone was shouting something—the prognosticators were vilified and mocked.[1] I fought my way outside and climbed up the garden slope.

The fellows from Giessen and a few of our delivery people were still there an hour later. They were sitting around the table where the radio stood—silence reigned. At any given point at least one of them was shaking his head. The fellows from Giessen drew the harshest conclusions, talked about betrayal, betrayal of the ideals of last autumn, and even abandoned their story about Hans Schönemann.

They were also the only ones who really dug in when Franka set out a tray of sandwiches. Georg had crept away somewhere. Staring at the table between his elbows, Jörg shooed away Georg's boys and finally turned off the radio. At that moment the telephone rang. Or maybe the telephone rang first. Jörg was closest to it, but took forever to pick up the receiver. He said "Hello," repeated it more loudly, and finally bellowed that he couldn't understand a word. The guy in lilac nudged me. "The receiver," he whispered. I didn't get it. "Look at the receiver," he hissed. Shouting into the earpiece, Jörg was holding the receiver backward. I sig-

---

1. The Alliance 90 (New Forum, Democracy Now, Initiative for Peace and Human Rights) received only 2.9 percent of the votes. That put the Citizens' Movement out of the running for good. The Alliance for Germany (Christian Democratic Union, German Social Union, and Democratic Awakening) received 48 percent, the CDU taking 40.6 percent of that; German Socialist Party, 21.8 percent; Party of Democratic Socialism, 16.3 percent. Voter participation was 93 percent.

naled the fact to him, which only made him angrier. I took the receiver away from him, but by then there was nobody on the other end.

I said my good-byes, Jörg caught up with me at the front door. He wanted me to write the editorial for the front page—on the right, boxed, a thousand characters, he'd always done it until now. When I got home I gave myself over to the notion that you were watching the same pictures on television.

Those thousand characters were easier than I had expected. Georg will probably accept it, I'm not so sure about Jörg. There's not much time for major changes. After all the hopes I had pinned on this day, I find my fatalism almost heroic.

My thoughts are with you,
Your Enrico

Tuesday, March 20, '90

Dear Jo,

I hope you were able to cope with Sunday better than Michaela (my views on the election will be on the front page). You can hear "two point nine" sung by Michaela in all keys and timbres—today sardonic, yesterday more despairing, toneless, dramatic. Compared to her I felt like a stone. Ever since her *klartext* was consigned to the grave, Michaela hasn't been near the New Forum. She also steadfastly refused any and all nominations, though she was flattered by the offers. Send Michaela Fürst to parliament!

As if knowing what was coming, she had had her hair cut short on Friday. Not even Robert knew about it. The idea came to her at the beauty parlor. And so she's playing Nefertiti, as somber as she is standoffish. Sunday mornings, when I set out at eight thirty, she never fails to ask if I had ever imagined my new life would be like this. Let's hope she doesn't see the line of people at the train station waiting to buy their *Bild* tabloid.

On Sunday Michaela made her appearance in a new dress that Thea had given her—more an outfit for the opera. Our delivery staff and the people from the New Forum who crowded into our office received her as if their legitimate sovereign were making her entrance.

She kept her composure after the first predictions came in. As long as the people around her reacted with despair or, like Marion, broke down in tears, Michaela could even play the consoler. She kept repeating that it's never over until it's over. Some people cursed Bärbel Bohley and her entourage for doing nothing but their Berlin thing, others damned the Greens in the West for having neither a clue nor any money. Marion then remarked that we hadn't been hard enough on the bigwigs. We did ourselves in with our own false notions of fairness—why hadn't we published all the Stasi lists and banned the old parties? What had been the point of reading Lenin in school?

Within a half hour the outrage had exhausted itself. And with each person who slunk away, Michaela lost a piece of her energy. People didn't even bother to say good-bye to one another. The simplest things went awry. Cigarettes refused to be stubbed out, two glasses were tipped over within seconds of one another, we bumped into each other or stepped on people's toes. Michaela admitted to me today that for several minutes she had been unable to recall if Marion's name was Marion. The fellows from Giessen kept jotting down notes, but in the end appeared to take offense at the results and said things like "the ugly side of the East."

Once we got home Michaela couldn't be dragged away from the television. Wrapped in a blanket, she didn't even turn her head when she spoke to us. At every miniscule change in the numbers she would call us in and stretch out an arm, pointing at the screen.

Michaela had promised Robert she'd make fondue. It was all ready to go, the trays in the fridge, the broth in the pot. But even when it was on the table and we two had stuck our forks into the pot, she was still crouched in front of the TV. Robert was on the verge of tears. I asked her twice to join us—she knew how it had turned out.

What did *I* actually have to say about the disaster? I was acting as if it were no concern of mine, as if our provincial rag hadn't also played its part in the catastrophe. I replied that there were few things that could keep me from eating my fondue. I'm sure you know how I meant it. But Michaela turned to stone.

Nothing, nothing had any meaning, she said, if people were going to cast such sick, idiotic votes. She couldn't breathe the air here, could barely look anyone in the eye, and I was just as moronic as everybody else.

As if hurling the question at me from the stage, she suddenly asked: Who are you, who are you really? I had to laugh, not at her question, but at what raced through my mind. A searcher, I said. And what was I searching for? The right kind of life, I said, and surprised myself at how calmly I pronounced those self-evident words. Astonishingly enough, she then sat down with us at the table.

Ah, Jo, what am I supposed to do? I want so much to help her. But she won't listen to the truth, at least not from me.

When I returned from my midday meal today—innkeeper Gallus was "flying the flag," meaning he had laid starched white tablecloths to celebrate the election victory—there at my desk sat Piatkowski, the local CDU vice chairman, sucking on lozenges to cover the alcohol on his breath. And who was he talking with? With Barrista!

When Piatkowski saw me come in, he opened up a dark red document folder and handed me the letterhead of the Altenburg District CDU announcing that it was "deeply moved" and thanking the men and women who had given the party their votes. I said we couldn't accept anything more—nothing more this week.

"Or one could pay the surcharge," the baron said. That's what he'd done recently. For twice the price one could surely buy a half page. Piatkowski's moist lips began to quiver. What, he asked, would a hundred fifty marks get him? Barely two inches, one column wide. Mulling this over, Piatkowski cinched the folder's black-red-and-gold cord tight, then finally agreed—with a sigh at having to forgo his new CDU symbol (their old *ex oriente pax* was evidently no longer valid)—and chose one of the heavy obituary frames. You'll need a magnifying glass to read the text. I gave him a receipt for his cash payment.

Once Piatkowski was gone, I asked the baron whether he knew whom he had just been speaking with. Last October, the day after Altenburg held its first demonstration and Michaela and a couple of others had been invited to the Rathaus by the district secretary of the Socialist Unity Party, Piatkowski had been sitting across from them at the table and had threatened them, saying anyone who tried to block open dialogue should not count on magnanimity—a statement that even earned him the censure of the secretary, who declared how "deeply moved" he had been by the demonstration.

The baron shrugged. What was I upset about? About that poor nobody who had just slid out the door? Piatkowski, I said, was the last man on earth to get my pity. But I was told to consider what I was saying. The fellow wouldn't be watching the next local elections as a Party official, and Piatwhatever knew that better than anyone. He would lose his job for the same reason. Did I know why Piatwhatever had joined the CDU? To salvage his parents' drugstore, because he had been told it was either stick with the Socialists or lose the store. And he had sought refuge with the CDU in order to keep the business afloat for at least as long as his father was still alive.[1] Then he'd been offered an administrative position, in the exchequer—the baron's term for the budget office. (Piatkowski had evidently completely turned his head.) We could finish him off with a snap of the fingers, the baron replied, we only had to place a call and threaten to write an article, that's all it would take, we didn't even have to waste column space on him. And hadn't I just seen proof of how hard they were making things for him, just to get a line or two published, whereas I could write as much as I wanted on any subject. He didn't like to see me wasting my time with people like Piatwhatever, the baron said, quite apart from the fact that it wasn't very chivalrous to kick a man when he's down.

"Especially now that we've reached a critical point," he said, "you have to know what you want to do." His voice was insistent, but so low that even Ilona, whom we'd just heard moving about in the kitchen, could not have heard him. Then Felix, Georg's oldest boy, came back from taking the wolf for a walk, and the baron asked if I'd care to accompany him on a stroll through town. So far he'd just been rushing from appointment to appointment, but now he'd just like to be carried along with the current. I had to turn him down, but was told we can keep the car for a while yet.

Your E.

Wednesday, March 21, '90

Dear Nicoletta,

Even more promising than the Bamberg cancellation on the envelope are the two exclamation marks in the margin and the underlining, which I take is your handwriting.[2]

Barrista is back in town already. He admitted that you had had an argument. Of course he denied my questions at first and refused to

---

1. For self-employed people like Piatkowski a position with the LPDP (German Liberal Democratic Party) would have offered a more likely "refuge" than the CDU.

2. Nicoletta had sent T. some newspaper articles about Clemens von Barrista and marked up several paragraphs.

admit that there was an "argument," but then conceded that he had not understood why he should have any less right to spend time in our office than you. If we didn't want him here, then I should tell him so. Finally he confessed that his reaction had been a bit "defiant," but assured me twice that he had no reason to accuse you of anything, and spoke effusively of your articles in *Stern* magazine, of which I'm sorry to say I was quite unaware. If there needs to be a reconciliation, he's willing to take the first step.

Barrista went on to ask whether I might not be thinking differently about some things today. I asked what he meant. In the West, he told me, considerably more people were disappointed about the results of the election than here. He—that is, Barrista—wasn't interested in any particular political point of view, but rather in democracy. The state at any rate stood in its citizens' way more often than it advanced their progress.

When I showed him the articles you sent me, he raised his arms and then wearily lowered them again. That was precisely what he meant when he had suggested talking things over calmly. Barrista had once expressed a wish that as time went on we ought to discuss things more, so that we could put as many ideas on the table as possible—although that surely is not quite the same thing [. . .]

From his attaché case he pulled out a binder that was much too small for the mass of paper bulging out of it. On top was an almost undecipherable cover letter—I could barely make out my own name—in which he advised who ought to be informed of the contents of this dossier. For the most part it contains copies of newspaper articles and documents by his defense lawyer, plus the final court decision [. . .]

While I thumbed through it—your own material is all there—he worked hard to persuade me. After all, a man doesn't just walk in one day and say, "Hello, fellows, the prosecuting attorney showed up at my front door two years ago."

As I would come to realize myself as soon as I assumed the responsibility of running a business, you always stand with one foot in prison. You have to make decisions that—because of unexpected developments, or somebody else's mistake, or just plain bad luck—can end up taking a wrong turn. All too often he had had to take responsibility for what had been done against his advice, counter to his opinion, counter to his express wishes.

He offered to answer each and every question I might have, although he saw no reason why he should have to justify himself to us.

He urged me to place more stock in the court's final decision than in the charges. The law regarded him as having no criminal record.

His glibness has made me very suspicious, at least for now. But it is only a hunch, a feeling. Will you help me ask him the right questions?

And now the continuation of my efforts, although I don't know whether you even want to hear[1] another chapter.

With warmest regards, Your Enrico

The first weeks of school saw the high-spirited and happy mood of my vacation deteriorate occasionally into one of sanctimonious self-accusation. Not a day went by that I didn't fail in my attempt to obey God's commandments. Keeping a diary meant answering for my conduct. Future generations were supposed to know what their famous author had felt, thought, and done as a young man and learn what high standards he had demanded of himself.

What I'm going to tell you about now isn't in the diary. I'll try to be as brief as possible.

After my arcadian summer I found my classmates—we were eighth graders now—to be a childish bunch. No one with whom I would have been able to talk about my incredible experiences, nothing they might talk about in discotheques, garages, and cellars held any interest for me. Hendrik must have sensed this, it must have emboldened him.

A speech defect and frightening skinniness had made Hendrik a favorite object of bullies since first grade, and I had defended him on many an occasion, although without much real sympathy. He would strut around me like a raven, holding his birdlike head at an angle and pointing an elbow at me, crooking first his left arm, then his right, as if scratching at his armpit, and then lunge closer with a hop to ask me a question. Sometimes he wanted to know if I had gone on an excursion over the weekend, sometimes whether we had a record player, things like that. Each time I would provide an answer, to which he then responded with a wicked smile and slunk away without another word, evidently convinced he had just had a great conversation.

It must have been November already—we had stopped going to the schoolyard for recess—when he whispered to me something about crea-

---

1. Of course the correct verb at this point ought to be "read," not "hear."

tures of a higher intelligence. This was all the more surprising since his mother worked for the police and his father, a stern, tightfisted man, was the school janitor.

From then on, day after day, Hendrik muttered some new infallible proof for our having descended from extraterrestrial creatures and—while intertwining arms and hands as if trying to put himself in shackles—offered his theory about the form of energy he assumed they had used to power their extraterrestrial spaceships. Shortly before Christmas Hendrik asked me if I now believed his theory. It was the first time he had sounded angry. "No," I said, "I believe in Jesus Christ."

The words—I had never spoken them before—shocked even me. It was as if a voice had announced from the clouds during roll call: "Enrico, you are my beloved son, in whom I am well pleased." It took me all weekend to capture this last scene in my diary.

On the morning of December 24th, Hendrik appeared at our door and, without waiting to be asked, stepped inside on his raven legs. He had to talk to me. As if his mother actually did dress him—as everyone claimed—almost nothing of his face was visible between cap and scarf. He admired my strong faith, he said, wanted to be able to believe the way I did, and asked me for help. He announced this in our vestibule. The pair of flat-nose pliers in my hand didn't seem to bother him. My mother—we had been pulling tendons from the turkey's drumsticks—told Hendrik to take off his coat and dismissed me from duty.

What I told him was that there wasn't much I could do, that he had to do it himself, but I offered to read the Bible with him, something from the New Testament, and to pray. Obedient as a sick patient, he cracked open the Bible—and his eye fell on the passage where Jesus asks the children to come unto him. Did I think that was a miracle? he asked. I told him that everything is a sign from God. After we read the whole chapter, first I prayed in a low voice, then he did. Suddenly I opened my eyes as if to assure myself that we were actually doing what we were doing. My gaze fell on the ankle-high work shoes that Hendrik had taken to wearing now that his feet were unfortunately as large as his father's. They hung from him like weights and turned his already stilted gait into a perfect circus act. Although he himself would sigh and try to laugh it off, there wasn't one gym class in which those old boots weren't sent hurtling around the dressing room.

I had credited it to my own influence that after the last gym class before summer vacation his shoes of tribulation had stayed in one spot. Hendrik sat down to put one on, but as he picked it up water gushed out, drenching his stockinged feet—and I likewise found myself standing in the middle of the puddle, which added to the hilarity. And those same shoes had now crept into our house, had made their way to my room, where their heels were scuffing my bed frame.

"Amen," Hendrik said. His hands still lay folded on the open Bible. His head hanging askew, he eyed me as if it were now my turn. "Amen," I said, and stared again at his shoes.

Since I didn't know what else to do and could hardly ask him to repeat his prayer, I suggested we take a walk. He instantly agreed. But first I had to take the pliers back to the kitchen. Have you ever roasted a turkey? My job was to set the pliers to the tendons my mother had cut free and tug them out while my mothers held on to the headless bird. The meat on the drumstick would slip up the bone to form ridiculous knickerbockers. Each drumstick has several such tendons, and although I would pull my mother almost across the table, while she let out little screeches, we never managed to rip them all out. Already repacked like a Christmas *Räuchermännchen,* Hendrik watched us, and then smiled vacantly as he took leave of my mother with a low bow.

Hendrik didn't leave me in peace for a single moment of our walk. He wanted to know how often I prayed, what I did when I felt I couldn't love certain people and instead really detested them, and if the desire for eternal life wasn't selfish. Hendrik elaborated on his own understandings and suggestions, and where before he had talked about "Christians," he now said *we,* which at first I misheard as *ye,* until it became absolutely clear that it was *we* who no longer had to fear death and *we* who were called to conduct ourselves differently from other people. His conversion was obvious, but because I wanted to be totally convinced of it—yet found a direct question inappropriate—I kept extending our walk. It was only as we passed the parish hall on our way back that I was granted certainty. There was a poster pasted in a street-level window: "God's word lives. Through you!" The poster was about a special donation, but it seemed to me that Jesus himself had written this with me in mind. I smiled in some embarrassment and lowered my eyes, expecting Hendrik to break into cries of astonishment, if not admiration. Wasn't it a miracle—this poster, right here, right now? But Hendrik didn't notice the poster or didn't apply it to us, though that did nothing to alter my certainty that I had saved a soul and become a true fisher of men. I said good-bye to Hendrik. His visit, I told him, was my finest Christmas present. We shook hands—his mother had taught him to grip with exaggerated firmness. I was about to turn away, when Hendrik's upper body tipped forward. I assumed he was going to bow—instead his forehead touched my shoulder. And at that moment my entire euphoria vanished. I realized that from now on I'd have Hendrik on my back.

I've described this to you not for its own sake—there are so many other things I could tell you—but because I planned to make the experience the stuff of my first short story.

The broad rib of the fountain pen that had miraculously found its way into Aunt Camilla's package along with the candy gave my handwriting a certain evenness. Writing itself—the motions of my hand, the look of each loop—provided me an unfamiliar satisfaction.

My new pen accelerated my thoughts; after only three pages I had arrived at our joint prayers. When suddenly—and at that moment I was still certain that the flow of my words would lift me imperceptibly across this dangerous reef—my memory was paralyzed by my mind's digression, by the sin of having thought of Hendrik's shoes and my schoolmates' high jinks instead of praying for his conversion. If I couldn't manage to lend assistance to someone struggling toward salvation . . . I screwed the cap back on my pen, holding it in my left hand and turning the pen three times, then laid it, the tool of my trade, across the top edge of my diary. It was as if I had ended each workday with this same gesture for years.

Suddenly I understood: The fact that I had failed as a person, as a creature of God, was precisely what would enable me to be a literary figure. And that was the crucial realization: I was not to keep a diary, but to write a work unlike any other, a work that glorified the deeds of God.

I slipped into the living room, where the fragrance of Western coffee and Fa soap contended against local odors, and pulled my mother's stationery pad from its drawer. I flipped it open, set the lined paper to rights, took out my pen, placed the cap on the other end, and without hesitation wrote the word "Birth," centering it at the top of the page. And beneath it: A Story by—new line—Enrico Türmer. And as content as if I had just completed my opus, I went to bed.

In the light of dawn and with a sweater pulled over my pajamas, I was once again at my desk. I longed to describe my failure in expansive loops that swung above and below the lines, forming as if all on their own great, long sentences. But since this was to be a story, I first needed to describe the terrain and the persons moving across it, so that after my first sentence—"The doorbell rang."—the plot came to a halt for a long while.

My plan for completing my work over the first two days of Christmas, then at least before year's end, and finally before the end of the holiday break, proved illusory.

I was deeply aware of the ambiguity of the situation—meeting Hendrik in the morning and then writing about him in the afternoon. As expected, he had lost all inhibitions and made a beeline straight for me. He would even be sitting in my seat every morning, as if to say: I've been waiting for you. It was almost impossible to talk to anyone else without him at my side. If he tripped over an outstretched leg, or couldn't find his shoes, or saw drawings on the blackboard—the teachers called them smut—bearing his name, he would simply draw himself up, set his head at an angle, and smile, which was his way of saying: I shall turn the other cheek to you. At least I was able to convince him to unbutton the top button of his shirt. I also put up with Hendrik's babblings about positive and negative energies in the cosmos, for who besides Hendrik could tell me what it felt like to be seized by the Holy Spirit—the greater the detail, the better.

One day during winter break as Hendrik and I made our way to Youth Fellowship, I interrupted him in the middle of his theorizing about the creation of the world. Hendrik didn't understand what I meant. I turned angry—so did I need to ask him outright whether he had heard a voice and what it had said to him?

The Christian faith, Hendrik replied at last, brings order into life. And besides—and here came his "turn-the-other-cheek" smile—it certainly couldn't hurt to be a believer. If it isn't true, Hendrik concluded, we'll never be aware it of anyway.

I flinched. I wanted to smack his ugly face, call him a goddamned fraud, hand him over to every torture that the hell of a schoolroom is capable of. "The devil is a logician!"—I later read somewhere in Heine.

"Hendrik slapped the pen from my hand"—for months that remained the last entry in my diary.

I was still wallowing in my suffering in August when we returned to Waldau, where I did nothing but read eight volumes bound in marbled gray and bearing a gold-on-blue mantra on their spines—the name Hermann Hesse. They were a present from Aunt Camilla, which had simply arrived without notice. Hidden in their pages was a fragrance richer and finer than any Intershop[1] perfume. The fragrance filled my hours of reading, it was my incense and blended only very slowly with the scent of the Waldau woods and cottage. But I didn't realize that until I was back home.

    Yours, yours entirely, Enrico

Wednesday, March 21, '90

Dear Jo,

    Yesterday the baron and I made good on our stroll through town, the weather was just right. Leaving the Red Tips behind, we went on to the Great Pond and then down along the hat factory. I suggested he take a walk with Georg, who could tell him all about Barbarossa and the abduction of the princes, about Melanchthon, Bach, Lindenau, Pierer, Brockhaus, Nietzsche's father, and so much more. The island zoo was closed. I wanted to take a little detour past Altenbourg's[2] house, but since the name meant nothing to him, we walked back by way of the movie theater and then up Teich Strasse, which is no more than ruins, with hardly one building occupied. We made slow progress because Barrista was constantly taking photographs. Both his steps and gestures were as cautious as those of an archaeologist or spelunker. We couldn't even get into a good many courtyards; the walls had buckled to create organic shapes, protruding potbellies, sagging rows of windows. Young birches sprouting from the roofs looked like feathers on a hat. I told him what everyone says: Even after the war a man could hardly have drunk a beer in every pub along Teich Strasse—reportedly there were over twenty of them, now just one is left.

---

    1. In Intershop stores Western goods could be purchased with foreign currency. The potpourri of odors from soap, detergent, coffee, chocolate, perfume, etc., created a special fragrance that no longer exists, but that at the time pervaded the immediate vicinity of these stores and was perceived by many as a promise of the "Golden West." At no point, however, does Türmer consider the moral and social implications of such Intershop stores for the populace of the GDR.

    2. The painter Gerhard Ströch, born 1926 in Rödichen-Schnepfenthal, lived in Altenburg and in 1956 adopted the name Altenbourg; he died on Dec. 29, 1989, in a car accident near Meissen.

Every so often Barrista would run his hand along the plaster. It was his show of sympathy—it opened my eyes and shamed me. As we walked along it came to me: the utter coarseness of it all, a coarseness inside me, inside us, a coarseness that meant letting a town like this fall into ruin, yet without going crazy. I had always regarded this deterioration as the natural order of things.

I thought of the frog experiment that the baron mentions on most every occasion—if you raise the temperature one degree per hour, so he claims, the frog ends up boiled, even though it could jump out if it wanted to. And maybe all those who jumped out of this country did the right thing. That's what I was thinking as I watched the baron take shots of the faded lettering and signs above walled-up windows or capture the murky twilight of shops through broken panes.

(Georg is sitting just behind me at the table. I can hear him groan and sigh as I write this. He wanted to know if I could tell him what to say when he's asked why we founded the newspaper. I repeated his own words from those days: Create transparency, accompany the course of democratization, provide the people a forum, tell the bigwigs . . . Yes, he knew all that, Georg interrupted, but could we still write those same words today? His scruples won't let him finish a single article, and instead he constantly nitpicks at ours.)

When Barrista and I finally reached St. Nicholas cemetery, he asked a man of indeterminable age who was leaning against one jamb of the bell-tower doorway whether we were very late. The man shook his broad head, grinned as if he recognized me, set two fingers by way of greeting to the bill of his cap (Robert calls it a "basecap"), and pulled out a cord with a large key, then a safety key, and finally a sturdy wooden weight. I was amazed that it all came from one pants pocket. He gave another salute and sauntered off whistling like a street urchin. He was the same man who had been talking with Barrista on the steps of the Catholic church the day we took our little excursion to visit Larschen.

As the baron turned the safety key in its lock, the sound echoed inside the tower.

I'd probably have no trouble making the climb, Barrista remarked, and waved me on ahead. He followed. I tried to keep some distance between us, but he stayed hard on my heels, meanwhile chatting away about how the tower was closed because the stairs were in need of repair—I should watch my step. He had found Proharsky to be a man who carried out little requests without further ado. Proharsky was actually a Cossack, the child of so-called collaborators, whose adventures had landed them as strangers here among us. He had helped Proharsky's mother apply for a special pension that had long been hers by rights.

"You know," he said as I took the last step and my gaze swept the rooftops, "I've fallen in love with this town. While I was away I felt it more strongly then ever before. All the jabbering and blathering we do over there had me literally longing to get back here."

The baron even had a key for the watchman's room, a cluttered mess with a foul odor.

The baron had fallen in love for a strange reason: The town had as good as no chance, and if it ever could be saved, then only by a miracle. He laughed and massaged his left knee. The name itself, Altenburg: "old" plus "fortress." Old didn't sound all that inviting, a town with that prefix would have a difficult time of it from the start. And people associated fortress—here he laughed more loudly—with awful things, with cold, cramped dungeons. *Nomen est omen*—all he had to do was say "Alten-Burg" and foreign investors would throw up their hands at the thought of some colonial fort abandoned by Charlemagne. That was without even mentioning an autobahn that was as far away as hell and back. One glance at a railway map and it had been clear to him that it wouldn't be long before only milk trains stopped here. Moreover, I could ask anyone I wanted—the local factory behemoths were close to folding, and the D-mark, whenever it did arrive, would finish them off. D-mark wages would put an end to selling vacuum cleaners at dumping prices, and as for industrial sewing machines—that train had left the station long ago. And the vehicles for the Volksarmee, those fully obsolete trucks—for the Western German army maybe?

Then we stepped out onto the encircling balcony. It took me a long time to find Georg's garden and our viewing spot there, but I immediately located the Battle of the Nations Monument on the northern horizon.

Brown coal, the baron went on—and I knew this as well as he—had, according to his information, a water content that made it more profitable to process it as a fire retardant. And environmental agencies would close that muck spinner[1] in Rositz the moment the cancer rates became public knowledge. And as for uranium—we were looking now at the pyramids to the west—that was a matter of pure speculation.

"So what does that leave? Altenburger liqueur? Altenburger mustard and vinegar? A couple of decks of skat cards? The brewery maybe?" And suddenly, turning toward me: "I'm asking you!"

How was I supposed to know? I replied. But he wouldn't let go. Surely I'd given it some thought, ultimately it was all of a piece, and without money in their hands it didn't matter what people were offered. One really ought to be able to expect a prognosis from someone who had founded a newspaper, which itself involved no inconsiderable risk.

"The newspaper doesn't have anything to do with any of this," I replied. These kind of worries, I proposed, had played no role in our founding the paper. Barrista was scaring me. I thought of my grandfather's prophecies: someday I'd find out just how hard it is to earn my daily bread.

So tell me more, was what I really wanted to say—the same way you do when you want to hear how, as improbable as it might seem, the storyteller escapes in the end.

"There isn't much left, in fact," Barrista finally said, "except for these towers, houses, churches, and museums. The theater, if you'll beg my pardon"—he bowed—"surely can't be something you would add to the list. Two years, maybe three, and its glory days are over." And after pausing, he added, "Wonderful view, isn't it?" Then he fell silent, and strolled on. We could see the Vogtland to the south and the ridgeline of the Ore Mountains, and to the east, behind Castle Hill, I thought I could make out the gentle hills of Geithain and Rochlitz.

"But it's all got to be kept going somehow," I exclaimed. He turned around and, after gazing a while in astonishment at me with his deep-sea eyes, raised his right eyebrow in silent-film fashion. "Well, then tell me how . . . !" he cried.

"Why me?" I burst out.

"And why me?" he echoed with a laugh. Yes, he was making fun of me. The matter required some thought, he went on. A good general with only half as many soldiers as his foe needed to come up with something— or seek refuge in retreat. After all, I had studied in Jena and surely hadn't

1. A tar-processing factory in Rositz.

forgotten what had happened there in anno Domini 1806.[1] Hegel's *Welt-geist* wasn't going to come riding into town all on its own.

I shuddered, as if someone had slipped an ice cube under my shirt collar. The baron had turned up the collar of his jacket. "If only the hereditary prince could see this," he said. "What all wouldn't he give for such a view."

The baron laughed and then began rubbing his hands like crazy. "We've got to find something—a vein of silver, gemstones, something's always lying buried somewhere. We just have to find it!" He gave a raucous laugh and showed me the red palms of his hands, as if they had just released something into the air. "Shake on it," he said, and I grasped his hand without knowing what pact I was entering into. But because his hand was warm and his gaze so momentous, I clasped his hand with my left as well—on top of which, obviously moved, he laid his other hand.

We were greeted down below by Proharsky. Without a word he took back the keys and wooden weight, and wandered off.

We walked across town, heading for the office. I slowly began to grasp what he had in mind, that is, the decision he had come to. Approaching by way of Nansen Strasse, with Market Square lying in its full expanse before us, he merrily prophesied that within a short time I would see how everything he touched would turn to gold. He himself had ceased to be amazed that this was so. First he needed an office, a spacious office with a telephone and all the rest. He would be grateful if I could help him find one over the next few days.

Now I had to laugh. Was he just playing stupid, or was he really that out of touch? With everybody wringing their hands these days in search of a few dry square feet of office space, he wants to be able to pick and choose?

He plans to announce the opening of his real-estate office in the *Weekly*. "During the next few weeks of renovations, contact possible only by mail." By the time the ad appeared, he said, he'd have his business license. He asked me to suggest a name. "LeBaron," I replied without a second thought. Not bad, he replied, and asked whether Fürst was my life partner's last name, he had seen it listed next to mine on our door. I nodded. "Well then!" he announced, joy apparently propelling his step.

---

1. In 1806, at the battle of Jena and Auerstadt, Napoleon's troops defeated the armies of Prussia and Saxony. At Jena the French forces were larger, whereas at Auerstadt—to which Barrista was obviously referring—they were only about half as strong as those of their foes.

That was the ticket, but even better in the plural, Fürst & Fürst, Prince & Prince, which would probably present few problems, he added, since there was surely no one else by that name in Altenburg. He would, if I had no objection, ask my partner for her consent, a deal that would provide some ready cash for Michaela—he actually called her Michaela.

What I really wanted to do was invite him to Robert's birthday party, if only because of the wolf, which Georg's boys normally take for an afternoon walk. But there have been enough arguments already, because both grandmothers are arriving tomorrow, and Robert can't be dissuaded from selling newspapers on Market Square. Michaela's mother insisted on at least keeping Jimmy's steering wheel. I'll present it to her tomorrow—the urn of her deceased companion, so to speak. I'm to keep the LeBaron for now.

You really must meet Barrista, if only to taste his wine and to behold a Hero of Contemporary Literature.

Hugs, E.

PS: Georg is still brooding, but breathing calmly and regularly.

Saturday, March 24, '90

Dear Nicoletta,

There are times when I interpret your silence as a test to maintain my trust in you and not to let my emotions drive me crazy. I go over and over the hours we spent together, searching for some clue as to what I might have done wrong. If only I knew that much! Is my task to discover my own failings? Or have they sent you to Hong Kong? Can Barrista really be the reason for your silence? A single word from you—and I'd have no trouble making that decision. Or is my search for reasons itself presumptuous?

If the question weren't so absurd, I'd ask whether you read my letters. Not one has been returned. Which gives me the courage to continue.

The high point of my second summer in Arcadia was our annual visit to Budapest. Instead of whiling away the night on the train, we flew—the ultimate in luxury. Plus the added benefit that we traveled without Vera, who had a job at a vacation camp on the Baltic.

Our landlady, Frau Nádori,[1] whom as always we paid with bed linens,[2] greeted us with an invitation to join her in the kitchen, made us coffee, and puffed away on a Duett from my mother's pack. She inhaled deep and blew the smoke into my face. (She had been a friend of Tibor Déry's mother and had helped Déry's wife out during the difficult days after '56. The name meant nothing to me at the time.)

As always we walked up to the castle. This time, however, I was no longer a child—I had my pencil and notepad with me.[3]

And then I saw it, the tower! It reigned over the street like one of those all-seeing, omnipotent constructions in a Jules Verne novel. A tower like that could strike us with some mysterious ray or send a life-saving message. But if we got too close to it, it would vanish.

"Foreign currency hotel"—Frau Nádori's term for this miraculous tower of golden glass—missed the mark completely. The thing we were staring at was not of this world, and yet stood on solid ground. A UFO—it had inexplicably landed in the here and now and had simultaneously become the crown, the capstone of our own world.

I'll never forget my mother's smile as she entered the Hilton, or her wave to me to follow her. Unmolested by either the police or State Security officers we made it inside—just as we were.

You need to know that prior to that I had never seen the inside of a hotel, not even a fourth-class one. We walked across carpets still wearing our street shoes—no one cared. I heard primarily West German and English and one other language, presumably Italian. Plus there was an inexplicable light, neither bright nor dim, and a general hush, even though people spoke here more loudly than on the street. Mostly older married couples were sprawled in leather armchairs, something I had never seen before in public. Some of them had even pulled up footstools to stretch their legs out across them. No one demanded these Westerners remove their shoes. And to my even greater astonishment I saw one of the uniformed personnel heave suitcases and bags onto a gilt cart and push it toward the elevator. They were police, weren't they? Or were

1. According to information provided by V. T., the children first heard Frau Nádori use the word "Mamus" for Mother/Mama, which they then adopted.

2. This sort of barter was customary inasmuch as citizens of the GDR could exchange their marks for only a limited number of forints.

3. Since the family had previously always taken this trip during spring break, T.'s last trip to Budapest had occurred before his "Awakening."

they servants maybe, real live servants, who carried Westerners' luggage for them? A portal onto the underworld could not have astonished me more than this passageway into the beyond.

My mother, who evidently wanted to confirm the reality of the species, asked a lanky uniformed fellow, whose hair was cut far too short—were they soldiers maybe?—where one could have a cup of coffee here. He directed her with an open hand to our left, circumvented us with a few short steps, and repeated the gesture. My mother thanked him loudly, and in German. German of all languages, she had always drummed into us, should never be spoken loudly in other countries.

I recognized the tall, uncomfortable stools from a milk bar in Dresden. I was both disappointed and relieved to see something for which I had some reference.

My mother closed her purse and shoved it onto the counter. A pack of Duetts crackled in her right hand, the cigarette lay between the forefinger and middle finger of her left, her ring finger and pinkie pressed a brown D-mark bill against the ball of her hand.

So as not to betray us with her box of matches, she asked the woman working the bar for a light. This time my mother had spoken too low. I had to help her, had to protect her. I went over the question in English several times before I risked asking it out loud. "Do you have matches, please?" I repeated it and blushed. I was less in doubt about the correctness of my English than whether it would be understood outside my schoolroom.

The pack of matches not only shimmered white, it also bore a flourish of golden letters and lay on a white porcelain saucer. And then the shock: "You are welcome, sir." The woman had called me "sir" in front of my mother. The phrase instantly suffused my flesh and blood, and I would use it later to the amazement of my English class.

I took a match from the pack, set it ablaze, and cautiously raised it— for the first time ever—in the direction of the cigarette.

My mother looked older. The worries of the last few years, my arrest, and finally my expatriation were deeply traced in her features. Her joy in my worldwide success could not change that either. Her only son had been taken from her. When had we last seen each other? It had taken five years for me finally to be issued a visa by the Hungarians. The whole time we had each thought one of us would be sent back at the border, just as had happened so often before at the last moment. But then, incredible as it seemed, it had happened, and mother and son could embrace. Was it not perfectly understandable that words came slowly, if it all, that we simply took silent delight in each other's presence?

I had no idea what my mother was thinking as we waited for our coffee and orange juice. I had always found her occasional social cigarette something of an embarrassment, because she preferred to squint and cough rather than give up her imitation of whoever it was she was imitating. But here and now it seemed right.

I was so charmed by my new role that I despised these Westerners—children, all of them, young and old. How naive they were! What did they know of the rigors of a divided world—they could reach out and grab anything in their world, not to mention ours.

Gazing through the windows on the other side of the counter, I could see the columns, arches, and fragmented walls of a former grandeur. And above them now rose this tower. From up here the city lay like a gift at your feet, and here I celebrated my triumph. Even Westerners fell silent when they recognized me.

While I had been dreaming, my mother had ordered a fruit pastry. No, that was for her! The pastry was hers to enjoy, I could have it anytime. But of course to her—and I had booked her into the most expensive room—all this had to seem outrageously new and incomprehensible. She didn't dare let all this splendor touch her too closely if she wanted to continue to set one foot in front of the other. And so I ate the pastry.

To show just how at home I felt here, I went to the restroom and sat myself down on the shiny toilet seat—something I normally did only at home. And I have never—ah, Nicoletta, forgive me for such intimate indiscretions—never since taken such a glorious dump. In that same moment, I decided to learn Hungarian.

I luxuriated in washing my hands with warm water and liquid soap, examined myself in the huge mirror—and liked what I saw.

My mother was waiting for me. She took my hands in hers and smelled. "How fragrant," she whispered. And with that we stepped out onto the street.

At least *two* roles were available to me over the next few days. I vacillated between that of the banished writer and that of the precocious, observant poet. Only a couple of years lay between the two.

The next day we made our pilgrimage to Váci utca. Whereas on previous visits I had been on the lookout for devotional trinkets like printed

T-shirts, Formula One posters, or records, this time I was drawn to book displays. As if to mock me, the jackets offered the names of authors—Böll, Salinger, Camus—but all the rest was hidden behind an unpronounceable barrage of letters.

I found myself standing before yet another bookstore, and at first didn't even notice that I was reading and understanding. Once inside the shop I couldn't believe what I actually saw. Even when the clerk, protected by a counter from his numerous customers, took the book down from the shelf and presented it to me, I was slow to grasp the reality. It was in German, had been printed in Frankfurt am Main, bore the logo of three stick-figure fish, and no matter how many times I read the title and the first and last name of the author, they remained the same. Impossible as it was, what I held clenched in my hands was Sigmund Freud's *Interpretation of Dreams*.

The moments stretched out endlessly until I found a chance to ask the price. Slowly seeping into my mind was the certainty that I would never have to let go of this book again.

If this particular work by Freud was what I wanted, my mother said, then she'd gladly buy it for me. More out of a sense of duty than curiosity, I had the clerk hand me one volume of Freud after the other. Although he was evidently supposed to put each book back on the shelf before he could hand over another, one quick glance over the rim of his glasses and he capitulated, stacking the collected works in front of me. It was a hopeless situation. Even if we had stayed out of the bar in the Hilton and had headed home right then, we still would not have had enough for all the volumes. Can you understand what it was like? Suddenly, as if by a miracle, here was a chance to buy something you couldn't buy, and now there wasn't enough money.

I decided in fact on *The Interpretation of Dreams*, because it was the thickest and hardly any more expensive than the others. I watched as it was passed on to the cashier, who wrapped it; but no sooner was I out on the street than I ripped open the brick-shaped package to seize *The Interpretation of Dreams* as my inalienable possession.

It didn't matter to me where my mother went now. All I wanted to do was read.

I began reading on a bench beside the Danube. I read and read and loved my mother for doing nothing but sunning herself and smoking. "Don't gloat too soon," she warned me that evening, "it's not across the border yet." Never, under any circumstances, was I to admit that the

Freud belonged to me—that could, if worse came to worst, cost me high school, my diploma, university, my entire future existence.

Whenever after that Frau Nádori provided me a room for a week, for the first two days I would rummage through secondhand bookstores and visit the shop on Váci utca. Moderation was pure torment. Every book shortened my rations. I had to decide what I could afford to eat and in what quantity—a strange, bewildering feeling, which I mistook for hunger. By the same token, each book left behind unbought in a bookstore was agony. How could I be justified to write anything as long as I had not read all of Freud—or everything else, for that matter?

On the flight back the sky turned red in the dusk of sunset. But it was still bright enough that I spotted our building shortly before we landed. I regarded the fact that I had been able to locate it from such a height as an honor bestowed on the place to which we were returning. And for a moment I thought: This is how God looks down on us.

Enough for now. I have to be on my way. Once again in the hope of receiving a letter today,

Your Enrico

Wednesday, March 28, '90

Dear Jo,

And now Böhme too! It just keeps getting more and more absurd. State Security was the de facto founder of our opposition groups.[1] The local CDU candidate withdrew when it came out that all members of parliament would be subject to a check.[2]

Our most recent issue sold better. There were a few responses to my election editorial.[3] One letter said that the people of the GDR had shamed themselves before the whole world. It ended with the sardonic wish that we wouldn't go bankrupt all too quickly in the capitalist

1. Ibrahim Böhme, the chairman of the East's sister party to the West German SPD. Both he and, prior to him, the lawyer Wolfgang Schnur, one of the cofounders of "Democratic Awakening," which then later became part of the CDU, had been denounced as spies of the former State Security.

2. T. is perhaps too hasty here in insinuating a suspicion.

3. It is difficult to recapture the provocation that T.'s election editorial is said to have represented in March 1990. T. concluded his hardly original commentary: "Certainly more important than the results is the fact that it was possible to hold an election at all."

marketplace we so admired. The Prophet reappeared as well. There he suddenly stood in the office, looking from one of us to the other, but without responding to our greetings. He thrust his chin out in triumph, his cotton-candy beard protruding into the room, and then ripped to shreds a sheet of paper—our subscription form, as it turned out. He tossed the confetti into the air. "That was that," he said, and departed posthaste. The scene proved all the more grotesque, because Fred has assured us that the Prophet's name was nowhere on our subscription list.

We now have four extra pages. We're lucky if we're done before one in the morning.

This morning the baron stopped by to tell us about his latest discoveries. Astrid the wolf always trots straight for her water bowl.

He had more to tell us about the Madonna. Evidently no one knows how it ended up in the parsonage. He has already invited an expert from Hildesheim who is supposed to offer some clarifications. "Shall we pilfer her from the clerics?" Barrista asked. From his attaché case he pulled an illustrated volume,[1] wrapped in the same washable protective jacket as Robert's textbook atlas. He read to us from it—the purport being that in its Sienese and Florentine panels Altenburg possesses a collection in which can be traced the birth of postclassical art in the West. He asked if I could guess his intentions.

"Just picture it—the hereditary prince arrives, and the Madonna enters the museum in triumphal procession."

To be honest I don't understand why that should be so important.

As he spoke Barrista ogled the plate of pancakes Ilona had set dead center in the table. I told him to dig in. Which he did, and with gusto, and forgot all about his Madonna. He pursed his lips, licked at the sugar, and opened wide. Ilona's eyes grew bigger with each new pancake Barrista gobbled down. She was still chewing on her first. Once his plate was empty, Barrista sighed. Lost in thought, he patted his potbelly, slipped down deeper into his chair, and licked the fingers of his right hand, one after the other. He left it to the wolf to clean up his left hand dangling at his side. Ilona chewed and chewed some more.

An older gentleman burst into this idyllic scene. He asked for

---

1. The "illustrated volume" in question is Robert Oertel, *Frühe italienische Malerei in Altenburg* [Early Italian Painting in Altenburg] (Berlin, 1961). "The two centuries whose course we can survey in the Altenburg Collection were decisive not only for the future of Italian art, but also for the artistic spirit of Europe itself," p. 50.

Georg—they had an appointment, and he was right on time. Georg and Jörg had left for Leipzig to read proofs. I hoped that would take care of the matter. "No-o-o," he bleated, this time he was going to insist on speaking with someone in charge, even if evidently only people who pulled up in black limos could get a hearing here. He meant the LeBaron. But a yawn from Astrid the wolf and one glance at its blind eye were enough to disconcert him.

"Pohlmann—from Meuselwitz, Thuringia," the man said, introducing himself, greeting first me, then the baron, with a handshake. Still chewing, Ilona jumped up and ran into the kitchen.

The man was not, as I had feared, a local folklorist, at least not one with the usual photographs of the kaiser. Once we were alone in the next room he seemed calmer, more friendly.

"You should know," he said, and addressed me by name, "that I have waited forty years for this moment." An enlarged passport photo lay on top. "Siegfried Flack," he said, "my ninth-grade German teacher, was arrested on March 27, 1950." Pohlmann listed the names of teachers and students, most of them from Karl Marx High School, who had passed out flyers and painted a large F (for freedom) on building walls—which had cost all of them their lives, except for the few who managed to flee to the West. One of the leaders of the group, a pastor's son, had smuggled flyers in from West Berlin on several occasions. At some point they nabbed him. It wasn't until 1959 that his parents were informed by the Red Cross that he had "passed away" in Moscow's Lubyanka prison in 1951. Pohlmann spoke with deliberate calm, and sometimes his sentences sounded rehearsed. As he handed me the folder, he stood up. "We must break the silence. Truth must see the light of day at last." I assumed these were his parting words and thanked him. But Pohlmann sat down again and gazed at me. I paged through his folder. I flinched each time he thrust his hand between the pages. Again and again I was forced to leaf back and submit to yet another explanation, even if the previous one was far from finished. And all the while I could hear the baron's singsong coming from the editorial office.

Pohlmann had entrusted me with letters and minutes of conversations, all meticulously dated and footnoted. I asked what he wanted done with them, and just as he shouted, "Publish them!" Ilona burst into the room. Ashen pale she stood on the threshold, staring at me as if I were a ghost. "Oh, here you are," she said lamely, and retreated.

Ilona had frequently rescued me from annoying visitors. But this time something really must have happened. Pohlmann had likewise been disconcerted by the sight of her.

I asked him to wait and walked across to the editorial office. The baron was leaning against the table, waving a fan of hundred-D-mark bills. "All you need to know is right here," he said, spreading the money on the table as if showing a winning hand. The wolf shook itself, its collar rattled. "They didn't ask for a receipt," the baron said, tugging at his right lower eyelid with one finger, and was gone.

There were twelve, twelve D-mark hundreds. All I could read was GRAND OPENING, and to each side a rather deftly sketched hand extending an index finger.

Hoping to learn more about what had occurred, I entered the little kitchenette. Ilona cringed. I touched her shoulder; she collapsed onto the low stool.

I crouched down beside her. I was hit with the scent of Ilona, a mixture of perfume and sweat that doesn't usually pervade the office until noon.

"I'm so embarrassed," she whispered. "I'm so embarrassed!" Steering clear of any questions, I took her cold hands between mine, and only then did Ilona start to talk, although it was all so muddled that I constantly had to interrupt.

She had thought she was alone in the office, except for me and Pohlmann, of course. She had cleared the table, but also stacked the platter with more pancakes, and started to wash up. There was a knock and she was about to go to the door, when to her surprise she heard my voice—at least, she thought it was mine. She had felt sorry for me, because once again it was me who had to play receptionist.

But then—and she swore she never eavesdrops—it had been such fun listening to me deal with the two Westerners. They finally came around to admitting that they were interested in getting in on the ground floor of the video business "in a big way."

She had had to chuckle at how good I was at describing the local appetite for videos, particularly special videos—I knew what she meant, right?

I had claimed we couldn't possibly take any more ads for next week, that we already had more than we could use—actually, I had said "over-committed"—and deeply regretted, given present circumstances, that we were in no position to increase the number of pages from one day to the next. She had especially admired this last assertion.

One of them kept asking what it would cost—and it was immediately clear to her what he meant, but I had played dumb. In the end she ventured to step across into the office. At first she had seen only backs—two charcoal gray overcoats bent over the table. And then, yes then, she saw Herr von Barrista in the swivel chair, his sticky hands folded across his stomach. Barrista had spoken in my voice, even grinned at her, and gone right on talking in—yes, she would swear to it—in my voice.

I gave her time to have a good cry, and then tried to get back to basic facts as quickly as possible.

I asked Ilona what was so horrible about all this. She had simply confused the voices coming from the room on her left with those coming from the right—they were both about the same distance from the kitchen. An acoustical illusion, that was all. Why would the baron imitate me?

But Ilona just shook her head. What was that supposed to mean? I asked. She shook her head again; to everything I said she just kept on shaking her head.

Suddenly Pohlmann was standing at the door. He offered to leave his folder here with me for a few days. I thanked him.

"The money," Ilona suddenly exclaimed. "Where's the money?" It was still lying there fanned out on the table. But instead of calming down now, Ilona pointed at the platter and whispered, "He ate every one, all by himself!"

I sent Ilona to the bakery. The fresh air did her good. She kept mum too, since I could hardly tell Georg that it was Barrista who had accepted the ad for us. We got into enough of a squabble as it was, because Steen's full-pager also had to appear in our next issue. Georg says we're digging our own grave for the sake of short-term financial benefits. And I'm offering all the wrong arguments in claiming that the article is yet to be written that would increase sales by twelve hundred D-marks.[1] Jörg said not a word until I offered to return both the money and the ad. Because actually none of it is really any of my business.

Hugs,

Your E.

---

1. At the time, twelve hundred D-marks were worth approximately three to four thousand East-marks. A comparable profit would have required an increase in sales of at least four if not five thousand additional copies.

Dear Nicoletta,

I'm not sure whether all the things I'm allowed to experience these days should be called compensation for those I've missed out on until now. Believe me, I love to wake up and to fall asleep, brushing my teeth is as much a joy as shopping or vacuuming. I love to calculate the price for a half-page ad at 20 percent discount as a standing order plus a 50 percent surcharge for being on the last page. No matter what I do I am suffused with a quiet sense of passion, a contentment that is very difficult to describe. It's not a sense of being lost to the world, like a child at play, although it's probably more that than anything else. It's as if I can now take up in my hand every object that I could only look at before, as if it's only now that I'm able to experience the world as space and myself as a body. As if I've finally been granted permission to participate in life. Each memory, precisely because it brings such misery with it, allows me to judge how wonderful the present is.

I've been trying to describe my fall, my original sin, to you, just the way I remembered it before I began to write my novella. Because now there's hardly a memory left—at least in regard to those days in October—that I can trust. I've toyed with these images too often.

Picture the hiking map outside a country inn and the red dot that says, "You are here," until it's erased by countless fingertips tapping at it day in and day out. Over the years that white spot gobbles up its environs, the local tourist sights and outlook points vanish, then a village, a city—it's all merely a question of scale.

Of course this is no special inadequacy peculiar to me, but rather the standard practice of every writer. Not an experience that isn't trimmed away at and twisted, that doesn't undergo amputation and then get fitted with a more efficient prosthesis. It's really quite simple, but until you realize it, your most important memories have already been bungled. There's truly no lack of examples.

Which is why, for example, I always imagined the autumn of my second summer in Arcadia to have been cradled in the sounds of Schütz motets. Their spiritual tones seemed to have flung open the school windows, they filled late Saturday afternoons in the Church of the Holy Cross,[1] and resounded every day from my record player. Like some comforting prophecy, they accompanied me, enveloped me.

---

1. He is referring to the vespers sung by the choir of the Dresden Kreuzkirche.

Ten years later, as I was working on my novella (I always called it a novella, although its oversize torso had grown to several hundred pages),[1] I only needed to put on *The Seven Last Words* and I would react like one of Pavlov's dogs. In a flash those days of September and October would reappear: the chestnut trees in front of the school, the rusty bicycle stands, the wind—at times a wild ocean gale that would scoop up the wet leaves still lying shimmering yellow on the asphalt, at other times a warm breeze that seemed to hold within it the last days of summer as it swept down across the Elbe from the slopes of Loschwitz with its Italianate villas. My characters emerged out of those voices, and I could see the muted light of trams, see clouds angled against the wind in the bluish pink late-afternoon sky; but I could also hear the rattling key chain of Herr Myslewksi, our homeroom teacher, whenever he led us down to the cellar for one of his "private talks," as he called his interrogations.

After I had given up on my novella—so that *The Seven Last Words* reminded me more of my attempt at writing than of that autumn—I noticed the dedication on the back of the album cover: For Enrico, Christmas '79, from Vera. Which meant I had been given the motets two years afterward. And to this very day I own no other Schütz recording.

In writing to you about all this, I have to pull my memories out from under the opulent scenes of my novella the way a medic pulls bodies out from under a wreck, not knowing whether they are alive or dead.

Holy Cross School,[2] with its looming dark walls, was my Maulbronn.[3] Enmeshed in my Budapest dreams and the freedom of my vacation reading, I could regard this building, which I would enter and leave for the next four years, only as the setting for a novel. At the same time I wanted to take seriously the inscription written above its main portal: "To the glory of God, in honor of its founders, and for the benefit and piety of the young."[4] From the first day after my return from Budapest, when I

1. This is a misleading statement, since one of T.'s manuscript pages contained barely half the number of words found on a standard typed page.

2. A consolidated high school (with grades nine to twelve) whose pupils also included the boys and young men of the Kreuzkirche choir (so-called *Kreuzianer*).

3. The setting for the stories and novels of Hermann Hesse, who in 1892 fled from Maulbronn after only seven months there.

4. Incorrectly quoted. "To the *honor* of God, in *memory* of its founders, and for the benefit and *profit* of the young."

inquired about the shortest route to school, that motto fit nicely into my Hermann Hesse world. As did Schiller Platz with its Café Toscana, the Elbe with its ferries and meadows, the Blue Wonder Bridge, the Elbe Hotel, the Wilhelminien villas and palaces in Blasewitz—they all enlivened my dream world. Farther up the Elbe one could trace the rocky plateaus of Saxon Switzerland, beyond which—after a hike of several days—lay Prague. Just as in Montagnola,[1] a pilgrim in search of the good and the beautiful could stop to sojourn in all these places. Reread *Narcissus and Goldmund* or *Beneath the Wheel* and you'll understand what I saw.

The drama of the weeks that followed, however, was not because of Myslewski, who called us boys, one by one, to the cellar, where in a locked chamber full of oscillographs he began my interrogation with the question of why I thought world peace was unimportant. Nor was the drama a matter of my suddenly getting Cs and Ds instead of As and Bs, plus an F in spelling. I might even have been able to cope with the loss of my free time had it not been for HIM. HE left me in a despair unlike any I had known until then—and would not experience again until last autumn.

Geronimo[2] was a choirboy whose voice was cracking and who sat beside me at our desk. He was the only one who didn't wear a blue shirt, having declared himself a conscientious objector at age fourteen—even though the lenses of his glasses could have been made from the bottom of soda bottles. All the things I had imagined in my boldest summer daydreams, he managed almost offhandedly—like finishing his homework on the walk home, while I brooded over my textbooks on into the evening. He was playing the role that I wanted to claim for myself later. And he played it magnificently. He was not only the head of the class, who spoke only in sentences ready to be set in print and used a slightly old-fashioned vocabulary that coming from anyone else would have made people laugh, but he was also loved by his schoolmates and teachers alike. And those who didn't love Geronimo at least respected him in a way that I had never before seen among boys my age. In Geronimo's

1. The town in the Swiss canton of Tessin where Hesse lived from 1919 until his death in 1962.
2. The nickname given Johann Ziehlke, although it is not quite clear just why. Apparently in the sense of "the last honest man standing." The historical Geronimo (1829–1909) was the chief of the Chiricahua Apaches, who did not surrender until 1886, i.e., very late.

case, the "private talks" were conducted not by Myslewski, but by the principal.

Geronimo was my nightmare—even though I ought to have been grateful to him. He never contradicted me in German class, never inundated me with English or Russian vocabulary words I couldn't possibly know. He slipped me his homework for problems that to me seemed beyond solution. In music class, however, he did cover his ears whenever I finished one of my attempts at singing, amid the laughter of the whole class. He was a total failure only at sports.

Geronimo had chosen me to be his pal, or better perhaps, his attendant. Every week he demanded I supply him a new Hesse. In return I received dog-eared tomes by Franz Werfel jacketed in newspaper. I never touched them, if only because their stained and yellowed pages disgusted me. He, on the other hand, took potshots at Hesse, although he also quoted him often enough. No one suspected that I had read the books too, let alone that I had supplied them to him. I would have accepted that as the price I paid for his forbearance in other matters, but likewise not a week went by that he didn't ask me: Why do you do it? Do what? I would ask in return each time, blushing and breaking into a sweat. He would eye me through his deep-sea glasses and his lips would form a pained smile. What he meant was: If you're a Christian, why aren't you a conscientious objector too, why do you agree with the proposition that existence conditions awareness, why don't you say grace before meals, why does your voice sound high and thin when Myslewski says something to you, why do you waste so much time on this school crap? Geronimo didn't have to ask any more questions. I knew them all by heart.

Every day began with the prospect of my being subjected to a painful examination. I began my walk home each day either relieved that for once I had escaped him, or suffering the torments of hell. For I never had an answer for him, and hoped the school bell would soon end our strange dialogue, which often concluded with his offering me a Bible quote: "Fear not, for I am with you always even unto the end of the world." Once he said, "It's my guess that you'd make a very good catechumen." It was left to me to be content that Geronimo, who planned to study theology, at least found me good for something.

I was no better at keeping up my diary or praying—apart from a fervent Lord's Prayer or two—than I was at providing Geronimo with answers. What was I supposed to write, or pray for? I really did know right from wrong. There were lies, and there was the truth—you could be either a traitor or a man of God. I didn't have to put my self-indictment in writing. I knew as well as anyone that there was not a single argument I could offer that would not have been an admission of my guilt. Cowardice, duplicity, doubt, weakness—why couldn't I act like Geronimo? Why was I living my life like everyone else?

The conflict once again grew more intense at the end of October, in the week after fall break, during which the flu had preserved me from worse torments.

That Monday Myslewski ordered me to join him in yet another cellar conversation. I felt honored, was surprised that I was the only boy to be summoned for a second round. Geronimo made sure everyone heard that he would be waiting for me at the school door—to lend me his aid, to stand by me.

Myslewski was apparently unprepared for my refusal to become an officer in the National People's Army or at least to serve for three years as a noncom with weapon in hand defending the homeland against all enemies. He stammered with outrage, struggling to deal with this from my first "no" on. Suddenly he shoved a book at me, in which he said I would find all the information necessary to deliver a ten-minute report about the aggressor, the West German Bundeswehr, during Friday's physics class. He smiled and patted me twice on the arm, so paternally that I felt a need to thank him, to cheer him up, to tell him that I would reconsider serving in the NPA for three years. Yes, I would not have minded staying there with him a while longer. I left school through the side entrance and, making a wide detour, ran to the bus stop.

I was disgusted with myself, because I had to admit that I would have much preferred to hug Myslewski and win his friendship, and had now run away from Geronimo. And although a greater disgrace was hardly imaginable, my real humiliation still awaited me. The ugliness of what I had just experienced and the ugliness of what lay ahead were so overwhelming that I finally started to take pleasure in my misery—a pleasure that found pubescent release as I ran to catch the streetcar. I swear to you that it took an act of will just to stay on my feet and not sink to my knees, whimpering with delight and shame at the moist spot in my underwear.

My novella, however, revolves solely around the days between my second cellar conversation and the ten minutes of my report. The situation had everything the genre requires, from exposition—by way of a bit of suspense—to a surprising twist at the end.

Although my feelings at the time have long since been exhausted literarily, I still have a sense of reeling back and forth for hours between those two end points, as if bouncing from one wall to another and never finding my footing. How could I, in the presence of my classmates, in the presence of Geronimo, present arguments against him and against myself?

I shall spare you the further agonies of a ninth grader's soul. What I find touching now is my mother's fear and helplessness. In the end it was she who wrote my report and persuaded herself to forbid me from even mentioning conscientious objection—there would be time enough for that later. But her words had no influence over me. On the contrary. It didn't take a Geronimo to remind me of Jesus' words about forsaking father and mother to follow HIM.

In presenting the finale in my novella I oriented myself roughly on the stations of the cross. In fact I was totally at the end of my tether when my name was called ten minutes before the bell marking the end of class. I got up, pushed back my chair, and stepped into the aisle, without any idea of what I would now do.

My knees were shaking—a phenomenon that I registered with both amazement and interest. My upper body remained unaffected, my hands were calm, although moist as always. Out of some sense of tact in regard to my body, I stepped behind the teacher's desk, where I did an about-face like a soldier. Here my knees could shake as much as they wanted. I raised the two letter-size pages a little higher and was ready to begin to read. All the rest would take care of itself.

I kept to my mother's text, word for word—my tongue worked hard at it, but what burbled up were sounds, sounds outside the human realm, gibberish that evidently provoked laughter. Was in fact everyone laughing—except a couple of scaredy-cats—but that Geronimo and Myslewski were glowering at me? Or am I just quoting myself again?

My second attempt failed as well. I gagged on each syllable, my tongue performed wondrous feats—while my vocal cords remained out of control.

The chair at the teacher's desk had been pushed away. I fell back onto it, shoving the teacher's grade book aside. From a seated position, I could manage words for the first time, the first sentence formed slowly. And with that Myslewski's barrage of words drowned out everything else.

The class was hushed. I knew that numbness only too well.

The next moment I watched myself stand up and lean against the desk, bracing myself on one fist, the thumb of my other hand hooked into a belt loop, the report dangling between forefinger and middle finger. Everything about this boy expressed contentment, like the lethargic pleasure you feel while you dress yourself still half-asleep or when you stretch your legs.

But was that boy at the teacher's desk me? Wasn't *I* floating above everything, out of everyone's reach and surveying the whole scene in a way I had never done before? I gazed down, observing what was happening below me, a diorama of school life, nothing unusual. That fellow Enrico Türmer interested me no more or no less than the other students. Enrico Türmer differed from the others only because I could give him instructions. I said: Smile—and he smiled. I said: Don't fight back, just stay on your feet and ask to deliver your short report. I said: Ignore the demand to sit down—and he ignored the demand to sit down. I fell silent. I wanted to see what he would do without me. Enrico Türmer likewise fell silent. A few quick breaths later and he repeated: "I would now like to deliver my short report, I worked very hard on it." After he had paid no attention to yet another demand to sit down, I knew enough. Another brief breathless hesitation—I gave my permission, and Enrico Türmer returned to his seat.

He heard Geronimo clear his throat, heard Myslewski's squeaky shoes scrape the floor. He looked around—no one returned his glance. When the bell rang Enrico Türmer got up from his seat like everyone else and smiled as he watched Myslewski depart. It looked to him as if Geronimo, who scurried out the door next, was following like an attendant, as if he hoped to carry the grade book back to the teachers' lounge.

For the next few minutes I was completely happy—you must believe me. What a grand reversal of affairs it was! Do you have any idea of what had happened? Can you imagine what I suddenly realized, how the experience hit me like a thunderbolt?

I was invincible, I had become a writer!

Although this realization came not as a revelation, but more like something I had always known, but that for various reasons had slipped my mind only just recently.

"It's my guess," I said, mimicking Geronimo as I walked home, "that you'd make a very good catechumen." If it weren't too pathos laden, I'd have to say: I gave an infernal laugh. A fourteen-year-old[1] can manage that better than people generally like to believe.

And do I also need to say that it was only several days later that I first noticed that I had lost God, that He had been expunged without my having even been aware of it? Not a single Lord's Prayer has ever passed my lips since.

I was hovering in the same place from which God had been looking down on humankind. But now it was I who was gazing down on them, at myself as well as at Geronimo or Myslewski, and I could observe what they were doing. I knew that it was of little significance whether they were brave or cowardly, strong or weak, honest or deceitful. The only important thing was that I was observing them.

Geronimo could do or not do whatever he pleased. It would vanish in the universal mishmash. I would determine whatever picture of him was to remain. Yes, no one would even care about Geronimo unless I wrote about him today, tomorrow, or whenever.[2] I was the keeper of the keys to Dante's hell.

My disaster of a report had no repercussions. I didn't speak to anyone about it. The explanation I fed to my mother was that I had been saved by the bell.

I had every reason to keep my experience to myself. For a while I even concealed it from myself and tried to assign some other origin to my carefree state. Needless to say, my novella also took a different and surprising turn.

At the time I had no idea of the price I would pay for being so carefree.

Within a few days my pattern of speech, my voice had changed. I smiled as I spoke. Everything I said had a shade of ambiguity, isolating me from my classmates. What was meant in earnest? What was just a game? For the first time I was living the life of the outsider. Other people no longer interested me. Time spent with other people, at least those my

1. Türmer was born on Nov. 29, 1961, and was fifteen years old that autumn (1977).

2. In publishing this I am, willy-nilly, opening myself to the charge of being the enabler of T.'s conceit. I wholeheartedly reject any such an interpretation of my actions and wish to point out that what I am offering here is a critical account of T.'s life, intended to serve as a cautionary tale.

own age, was time wasted. Could the intensity of a conversation ever match that of reading a book? I needed what little free time I had for reading and writing. Those hours were too precious to piddle[1] them away in the company of others.

Geronimo avoided me, but without attacking me. He was praying for me, he whispered to me at one point when he caught me observing the sharp line of his clenched jaw and the nervous twitching of his lips.

I took delight not just in my triumph but also in my having escaped both him and Myslewski—small revenge.

Whenever there was a game during gym class, usually soccer or volleyball, and Geronimo and I were chosen to be on the same team—he was almost always the last choice—I never missed a chance to pass him the ball and thus include him in the team, just the way our gym teacher demanded.

Nothing frightened Geronimo more than a ball. His body would instinctively flinch. He first had to overcome his urge to flee—but then when he did confront his foe, as he always did, it was too late. I was successful right off. Soon a victory by any team Geronimo was on was considered a sensation. Scorn, mockery, and rage were directed solely at him. The altruism of my playing the ball to him was evidently never questioned.[2]

On the day grades were handed out at the end of our sophomore year, a "farewell" was extended to five of our classmates. Four had to leave because of their unsatisfactory performance (I had found refuge somewhere in the middle), plus Geronimo for still insisting on being a conscientious objector. With the approach of our last day in school together, old anxieties returned. I had the sense that accounts were due to be settled, that for months now Geronimo had been planning some spectacular action that would imprint itself for good on our memories. But I wasn't afraid of that. My insecurity came from feeling so secure, because I couldn't imagine an attack that could really touch me. My carefree state was suddenly full of care.

My memories of that day are bathed in the garish light of July. Geron-

---

1. Crossed out: squander.
2. Since I myself participated in these same gym classes, I can only assert that T.'s descriptions are inaccurate.

imo's long, never really dirt-free fingers trembled above the surface of his desk.

"I must likewise say my farewell to you today," Myslewski remarked, drawing himself up beside our desk. Once Geronimo was standing fully erect—a good head taller than Myslewski—he started shivering, as if suddenly chilled. Glancing at the grade card, Myslewski announced the grade average: a perfect four point, disregarding a two in gym. Somehow Myslewski managed to grab hold of Geronimo's hand and held it for a while.

As he sat down Geronimo bent forward as if he were going to throw up, and then began to weep. He wept as if he had been saving up his tears his whole life long and were trying to shed them all in the space of thirty minutes. To the sound of his weeping, with here a sob and there a whimper, we were all handed our grades.

I laid my hand on his shoulder, on his head. I ran my hand over his hair, which was greasy. Geronimo never looked up until the bell rang.

With that, I left the classroom to wash my hands.

When I returned Geronimo was encircled by our classmates. They stood so close to one another that I couldn't even see him. And so we parted without saying good-bye.

Suddenly I shuddered at the thought of transforming this scene into literature, either immediately or in the future—of turning my greasy hand into a metaphor. Because I have never succeeded in doing so, my recollections of that day are still very clear.[1]

Saturday, March 31, '90

Dear Jo,

Events have come tumbling one after the other over the last few days, and I'd give a pretty penny to know how we come off once you've read this.

Friday we were all sitting together in the office—Georg, Jörg, Marion, and I. We needed to decide whether to publish an article submitted by the local Library on the Environment. It's not about Altenburg, but

---

1. Both the original and the carbon copy of this "letter" end without complimentary close or signature. Caught up in telling his story, T. had evidently completely forgotten N. H.

about Neustadt an der Orla, a town in the loveliest part of the Thuringian Forest, where a farm factory for fattening two hundred thousand hogs was built in the midseventies. Children in the area were having asthma attacks, pollution of well water was ten times above allowable limits, villages were getting water only from tank trucks, and so on. Pipping Windows, which places ads with us, wants to buy into property there. The crucial issue is that they also want to take over management of the hog farm. But the farm belongs to Schalck-Golodkowski. Eighty percent of the hogs were for export. All of which prompted an environmentalist to write an open letter to Herr Pipping, whereupon several of the comrades she mentions in it filed suit against her. You'll get to read about the whole thing.

Georg, who usually keeps meticulous minutes, sat there propped on his elbows, deep creases between his eyebrows, hands covering nose and mouth, while he listened to Jörg read the article. If we publish it we'll lose the account of the Altenburg subsidiary of Pipping Windows—and at two columns / sixty, on a weekly basis (one-year contract), with 50 percent surcharge for the last page, that loss comes to 10,870 marks, more than half of it paid in D-marks. And what's more, we can't check the accuracy of the article, nor can we know the legal ramifications of publishing it. It's a head-on attack, based solely on our confidence in the environmentalists. On the other hand there's no one we trust more than Anna, the Jeanne d'Arc of last fall. Other papers had squirmed out of it. Pro and contra cancel each other out. But there came a point when there was no ignoring Georg's silence.

"I'd like to propose to you," Georg said with a smile, tucking his head between his shoulders, "that we shut down the paper." As he went on talking his forehead shifted swiftly back and forth between a smooth surface and deep furrows. We should hold out until local elections,[1] and with that our job would be done.

There suddenly came a moment when I could no longer endure his smile. I despised him. There was nothing left to mull over. He wanted to rob us of our daily bread and drive us out of the same office into which he had lured us with his promises in the first place. I despised him for his arrogance—an arrogance at odds with the world because it is what it is—

1. On May 5, 1990, that is, barely five weeks away.

for running off in pursuit of this idea or that, of essential, philosophical ideas, instead of holding one's own in the everyday world. All his qualities, some of which I admired, others merely respected—his deliberate meticulousness, his honesty, his doubts and self-inflicted agony at being unable to write even a few normal sentences—all that suddenly seemed childish and despicable because he let himself defeat himself, because he was not willing to do battle with himself, because, to put it succinctly, he acted irresponsibly.

"And what are *we* supposed to do?" Jörg asked as calmly and amiably as a radio moderator.

Georg—I don't know what else he expected—seemed to be in torment at having to say anything more than the remarks he had evidently prepared.

"We've failed," he repeated, "we didn't take our job seriously enough."

Jörg wanted to know what job it was he meant. Flaring up and gazing at me for the first time, Georg replied that that was surely clear to each of us.

I told him to answer Jörg's question, after all we'd all burned our bridges behind us.[1]

"The world lies open before us," Georg said. "Let's not forget that!"

Jörg had leaned back and kept pressing his pencil with the tip of one finger, as if playing Pik-Up Stiks. Marion followed Georg's lead and said that, yes, she was in full agreement with him, but chose to draw another conclusion—that from now on we should do everything different and better.

At which we all fell silent.

There was the sound of footsteps outside, but Jörg and Georg didn't stir. I heard a resigned laugh from Ilona, who had been told that we were not to be disturbed. Then the baron entered, our most recent issue in hand. Had we been waiting long for him? He apologized and took off his coat. Ilona brought some fresh water for the wolf.

Georg virtually turned to stone. Jörg requested that Barrista leave us alone—the future of the paper was on the line here. Then the only sound to be heard was the wolf lapping water, and then, as if the animal were bothered by the silence, even that stopped.

1. Although perhaps a perfectly acceptable idiom in English, T. has mixed his German idioms here: "burned our ships" and "destroyed our bridges."

"Most regrettable," was Barrista's initial remark. He should have been informed before now. Scheduled for today was the first discussion of preparations for His Highness's visit, a summary of which lay in triplicate before us. He had the welcoming statement with him and a letter for us written in the hereditary prince's own hand. Most regrettable, but under such circumstances he had no choice but to arm himself with patience, most regrettable as well because the number of letters in reply to his ad had far exceeded all expectation, which meant nothing less than that our little newspaper was indeed being read by, was of uncommon interest to, businesspeople.

Her face drained of blood, Ilona was standing beside the stove. "But you're not really going to do that, right?" Her pleading eyes wandered from one of us to the other. "I don't even have a contract yet . . ." She sobbed.

It would be helpful to be immediately informed of our decision, the baron continued coolly, since the prince's visit dared not in any way be put in jeopardy. He led Ilona out, the wolf trotting behind them. The door was left ajar, so that Barrista's attempts to console her were still audible—and sounded like the same English singsong I had heard on the first evening we met.

"We're going ahead," Jörg said, turning to Marion. And then to me: "Right, Enrico, we're going ahead? No matter what, we're going to keep going!"

Then Jörg turned to Georg and asked him—warily, as if inquiring of a patient—how long he was willing to grant us the right to stay in his home, whether Georg was agreeable to providing us asylum until early or mid-May, presuming we couldn't find a space before then, whether Georg—Jörg kept addressing him by name more often than was necessary—could keep the rent at its current level, and whether Georg had any suggestions of how we should deal with the telephone bill. "But of course, but of course"—it came from Georg in a stream. Jörg proposed we keep Georg on salary until the end of July, paid in D-marks, and asked if that would cover the transitional period.

But of course, that was very generous, Georg said, but it wasn't necessary. Jörg thought it was, and asked if we could count on Georg until the end of the month. But of course, but of course! Jörg proposed that we publish the hog farm article.

I found it a bit much when Georg and Jörg extended hands across the table and Georg then held out his hand to Marion and me as well. Eyes glistening, he departed. Hardly a moment later, Ilona was standing before us. Fred appeared just behind her.

"Have a seat," Jörg said. In those three words, in his simple "Have a seat," were the ease and authority that proved Jörg the born boss. At last he could speak as he wanted.

A couple of sentences later and Ilona jumped up from her chair, clapping her hands. Fred could no longer suppress his smile. They didn't need a lot of explanations. The disaster was not a disaster. It was just that no one had dared think like this before.

Three articles, Ilona exclaimed, holding up three fingers, three little articles was all that Georg had managed to produce over all these weeks—three! Fred growled that he knew enough businesspeople we could get advertising from if we really wanted.

Suddenly the baron was standing at the threshold again. And what decision had been made? From his very first sentence he fixed his eyes on me, as if I and no one else were responsible for all this. He did truly hope he would be spared such childishness in the future. He was accustomed to being able to rely on his business partners. There was no point in agreeing to a plan that no one was going to follow through on. As Jörg attempted to raise an objection, Barrista didn't even look his way. Only after I said that he need not fear any further annoyances of this sort, nor any delays, did he seem satisfied.

That was precisely what he wished to hear. The baron promised that for his part he would not disappoint me, and from his attaché case he extracted four packages, which he now distributed, remarking that we all had children who would enjoy an early Easter bunny.[1] He disregarded all our thanks and testily went on to say that he had no intention of keeping us from our work, but he didn't want to depart our office while still in our debt. As a small demonstration of support for the paper—and in the hope of his ad being effectively placed—he wished to pay in full, in D-marks, which he hoped would be agreeable.

No sooner had he completed this sentence than the telephone rang—which until then had remained miraculously silent. We could hear voices coming from the vestibule. In three shakes of a lamb's tail we were all

---

1. There are things about this narrative that arouse suspicion. How, for example, could four such packages have been stuffed into one slim attaché case?

busy, and when I looked around again for the baron, he had vanished. The exact sum lay before me on the table.[1]

When I got back from my rounds in the countryside that afternoon, Marion was at her typewriter. "There you are!" she cried in delight. From now on she would like to write Georg's articles, and by doing so ease my workload.

At which point I made the mistake of suggesting we address each other by our first names. Her face froze, her eyes bounced about in all directions. "Why not," she finally said, extending a hand. "Marion."

"Enrico," I said, and then fell silent. Thank God the telephone rang. "Our special friend," she whispered, and held the receiver out to me.

I had never experienced the baron so beside himself. They had canceled his room at the Wenzel, and he didn't want to get upset again, but just wanted to inquire if I perhaps knew where he could spend the night, after that he had other quarters, just the one night. I invited him to sleep at our place.

By the time the baron rang the bell at nine thirty every bit of eager anticipation had vanished. Robert and I had raided the grocery shortly before seven. Robert was really looking forward to the baron and his wolf and remembered to get the pickles that the baron had found so tasty the last time, plus dog bones. We made potato salad as if it were Christmas. Michaela had a performance, Hacks's *Schöne Helena*, which has officially been taken out of the repertoire, but because it's an ensemble favorite—there's a role for every idiot—they're still cranking it out a few last times.

We began eating around nine, so that the deviled eggs decorated with little swirls of anchovy paste were already gone, and obvious inroads had been made on the platter of cold cuts and the potato salad—only the two little suns cut from apple slices, which Robert had arranged on saucers, were still shining, though a bit more dimly.

If it had been up to Robert, I would have had to go on forever telling stories about Georg and "Herr von Barrista."

When the bouquet and, behind it, Barrista himself finally did appear—bouquet is hardly the right term for such a burst of jungle

1. Apparently Barrista had paid on a 1:1 East-mark, D-mark basis.

flora—all our expectations revived in one fell swoop. Our vases were all too small, the whole apartment was transformed into a dollhouse.

The baron didn't torture Robert on the rack for very long and handed him the new *Bravo* and—to Robert's jubilation—a baseball cap, whose two intertwined letters I at first took to be two knucklebones.[1]

When Robert asked about the wolf, Barrista put him to a little test of his courage by handing him the car keys. He could go ahead and free Astrid all on his own.

"If you need money," the baron said as soon as we were alone, "do not scruple to ask me. I can only advise you to buy in now!"

What do you suppose he meant? Up to that point I hadn't even admitted to myself what he now spoke of openly. Yes, I did hope to take Georg's place at Jörg's side as an equal partner. I asked what it would cost me. The amount, he said, was not the problem, almost any sum could be justified. I'd have to find out whether Georg was actually prepared to give up his share.[2] Should Georg demand twenty thousand or more— that was twenty thousand D-marks, by the way—he suggested that I ask for time to think it over first, which tended to hold the rush of speculation in check. The Schröders, that is Jörg and Marion, didn't have that sum in ready cash themselves. Twenty thousand D-marks, however, were mine to use at any time, and he was certain I'd be able to pay him back the entire amount by autumn, with the rate of interest equal to the rate of inflation. "Do it, and if only for your boy," he concluded when we heard Robert at the door. Astrid trotted in.

Barrista isn't the sort of man you respond to with a hug. But I feel as if my wishes and longings are in better hands with him than in my own, as if he is constantly shaking me out of a kind of daze and asking: Why are you sitting at the children's table? Come over here, join me, join the adults.

The baron thanked Robert, addressing him, however, with the formal pronoun of one adult to another, and had nothing but effusive praise for the handsomely set table. I told him that it was quite all right to still use the informal pronoun with Robert. If that was the case, the baron said turning to him, he would be happy to do so, but then he had to insist that Robert call him Clemens and use the informal pro-

---

1. T. means a New York Yankees baseball cap, whose logo is an interlinked N and Y.
2. Jörg and Georg were fifty-fifty co-owners of the company according to civil code.

noun too. Turnabout was fair play. It would be on those terms or not at all.

The next chance I got I whispered to him that neither Georg nor Jörg had said anything about money, but he responded with a smile and said under his breath that now wasn't the time to talk about this.[1] Then he dug in with the same gusto he had shown on his first visit, just nodded with his mouth full when I offered to warm up what was left of the sausages, and went on chatting about pop music with Robert. He pulled a couple of CDs from his attaché case and smiled because, unlike me, Robert knew how to hold them so that the plastic box opened easily.[2]

In the baron's presence Robert seemed incredibly grown-up. He even took to heart all the things Michaela was always preaching to him—he sat up so straight in his chair he looked almost ridiculous.

Robert inquired about where the baron lived. "Here and there," was the answer. Since his divorce his things were stored at his mother's, and he lived in furnished rooms all over the republic. By "republic" he meant the Federal Republic of West Germany. His son was fourteen years old,[3] and what was more, his name was Robert too. He even looked a little like our Robert. He extracted an envelope of photos from his attaché case. He was right.

Robert's questions became increasingly more specific—where did he spend Christmas, where did he go on vacation, what were his hobbies? And each time the baron responded with angelic patience and candor.

He once again declared how, except for himself, he knew no one who interpreted the job of a business consultant the way he did, that is, who invested in speculative projects by being paid his fee in shares of them—because he had no problem sharing the risk for his own decisions—provided his advice was followed. "Actually," the baron said, without taking his eyes off Robert, "it's a matter of trust. And since far too many people nowadays no longer even trust the word of a gentleman, I have to deprive them of a bit of their tidy profit." He hastily chewed a pickle and then continued, "Thus far everyone who has paid me with shares has regretted doing so. They could have had it all at less cost, far less."

---

1. It is inexplicable why they are so secretive around Robert.
2. CDs were hardly known in the East at that point.
3. In his letter of March 15, 1990, he mentions that Barrista has two children.

And after yet another pickle, he provided his summary: "I make money out of ideas in order to have money for my ideas."

What did that mean, making money out of ideas? Could the baron divulge one of those ideas to him?

"And who can assure me," the baron replied, "that you won't take it and earn a pile of money and I'm left out in the cold?"

"Because I promise I won't," Robert said, as if perfectly accustomed to carrying on such conversations.

"I read each weekly issue very carefully," Barrista began. In the latest he had found two articles that instantly gave him an idea. Could Robert guess which articles those had been—he had sold the same paper, after all. Robert looked at me, I shrugged. The baron meant the committee that was supposed to provide new street names by June. "Well? Any lights go on?"

Robert blushed.

"What's the first thing a businessman does when he arrives in Altenburg?"

"He goes to his hotel," I said.

"Wrong! Utterly wrong! How does he know here his hotel is?"

"He stops and asks someone."

The baron covered his eyes with one hand. "And what if it's one o'clock in the morning?" he asked. "A businessman," Barrista cried in triumph, "drives to the nearest gas station and buys himself—a map of the town!"

We vied with each other to inform the baron that gas stations are closed here at night. With a single gesture he brought us to silence. "I swear to you," he said, and it sounded in fact as if he were swearing an oath, "that within a year there will be maps at gas stations here at one in the morning. Our maps of the city!"

The baron pulled out a note card and began scribbling. "Before we award a printing contract, we need to have calculations of costs and profits in our pocket." Robert stared at him as if hypnotized. The entire project would be financed by the ads bordering the map.

Deducting all costs, that would leave a profit of approximately three thousand marks. We nodded approval. And that was excluding the sales revenues. And who in Altenburg wouldn't want a map with the new street names? And why just in Altenburg? Why not Meuselwitz, Schmölln, Lucka, Gössnitz? And who said that there should be just one map for Altenburg? Those three thousand marks had suddenly become thirty thousand, sixty thousand. "Let's say," the baron concluded, "we're talking about clear profit—that will amount to between forty and eighty thousand, forty to eighty thousand D-marks. Just takes a little organization. Gentlemen, money is lying in the streets of Altenburg. And this idea is my gift to you." And with that he handed Robert pencil and note card and leaned back.

The performance was over. We didn't know what to do—clap, say "Thank you," ask questions?

But the big bang still awaited us. Caught up in the mood, I thought I had to present my own brilliant idea and proposed that the same people who approached shops and firms for ads in the map should canvass for advertising in the paper as well. Robert nodded.

I could see a goo of potatoes and sausage in the baron's half-open mouth.

"What?" he asked, chewing more quickly. "You don't have a sales force?" I shook my head.

"No agents in the field, no canvassers, or whatever it is you call them here?"

"No," I protested.

"You . . ." he began, hurrying now to swallow, "you sit in your editorial offices and wait for people to come to you?"

I replied in the affirmative.

"And Frau Schorba?"

"She's the exception," I said.

The baron burst into terrible laughter—and swallowed the wrong way.

I can't describe the entire evening for you. But it ended strangely. For it suddenly occurred to Barrista to say that he had been able to keep his hotel room after all. This was followed by an abrupt departure.

We walked with him to his car, a red Saratoga. As he said good-bye he put on a cap, one identical to the one he had given Robert. As he drove off a taxi turned down our street, and Michaela climbed out of it.

At first she was taken aback, then she went into a tirade about how it was way past Robert's bedtime. She felt his forehead—he actually did have a slight temperature. We transplanted the jungle bouquet to our biggest stoneware pot. It's now standing on the living-room floor and the fragrance is enough to befuddle you.

I thought about the maps and a sales force, slept fitfully, and awoke as frazzled as if the night had cost me as much energy as the day before. But just the thought of Robert picked me up again.

My plan was to greet Georg warmly and ask him straight out to sell me his share. I planned to offer him ten thousand D-marks for starters.

Michaela had a headache and stayed in bed. I promised I'd be back as soon as I could.

When I entered the office, I abandoned all hope. Georg, Jörg, and Marion were sitting cozily together drinking tea. It sounds absurd, but I had come too late. I had missed my chance by about half an hour.

Their friendliness, or better, chumminess was a cruel blow. I was given a cup of tea and a large piece of Marion's cake. The fact that today of all days was her birthday seemed to seal my fate.

But then everything turned out differently.

One of Georg's boys suddenly let out a howl in the garden, and Georg went to see what was wrong.

From across the table Jörg remarked that everything had been cleared up, that I didn't have to worry about a thing. Georg wanted a nice clean break, that was all. And now it was up to me whether I wanted to take on Georg's share and from here on out put my head on the block with him, Jörg, and share full responsibility. He didn't want to place that burden on Marion, the paper shouldn't be their family enterprise. I didn't have to decide right off, but it would be a load off his mind if I could find my way to saying yes.

I drank my tea sip by sip and waited until I thought I could reply with a firm voice.

It's two in the morning, and I hope I'm tired enough now to finally get some sleep.

Your E.

Wednesday, April 4, 1990

Dear Nicoletta,

I have no idea whether or not my letters ever reach you, not to mention whether you read them. But as long as none is returned or you don't expressly ask me to spare you my story, I'd like to continue to write them.

I didn't hear anything from Geronimo for a long time. At the start of his junior year, he had moved to Naumberg, to a preparatory seminary there, whose three-year course was not officially recognized, so that he would de facto graduate without a diploma. Now and then he sent greetings my way in letters that he wrote to a few girls in our class.

Astoundingly enough, at the start of my junior year I was accepted into the school choir and by November—hidden among the baritones—had already taken part in a performance of Brahms's *German Requiem*. This isn't the place to describe either our music teacher or what rehearsals with him were like, although those hours as a singer—even a very mediocre one[1]—are the only classes I can recall without chagrin.

It was in the choir that I also first saw Franziska, a ninth grader, the daughter of ***,[2] whom everyone knew, and not just in Dresden—a man able to do, yes, allowed to do anything he pleased. Her existence was known to everyone in the school.

Franziska sang soprano, wore jeans and tight-fitting sweaters, and had smooth black hair. The decal on her shoulder bag was no less exciting than she herself: "Make love, not war!" During rehearsal I always took a seat on the aisle so that I was as close as possible to the sopranos seated on a slant across from us. It was months before Franziska returned my greeting. When out of the clear blue sky she asked me if I didn't want to join her class for their dance lessons—there was a surplus of girls—I saw my dreams already fulfilled. But nothing ever came of the promised dance lessons, and she turned me down all the many times I invited her somewhere. Nonetheless I lived in the certainty that I would one day win Franziska over.

I tried my hand at writing poetry and had moderate success in contests called "Young Poets Wanted" that were part of the "Poets' Movement of Free German Youth," a term that strikes me much funnier now than it did at the time. We were to write "friendly" poetry—that was one of the maxims I recall being inculcated with by a friendly, indeed downright jolly, older man who had, it was said, succeeded in writing a perfect poem about a Bulgarian jackass, although I never came across it.

---

1. T. did not have a bad voice, but he couldn't carry a tune on his own. Every attempt at a round fell apart when it was time for him to enter. He always needed someone singing in his ear.

2. Respect for rights of privacy preclude mention of his name.

I was not considered a great talent or a precocious wunderkind—terms that, if not used often, were not uncommon either—but was sufficiently stuck on myself that I was firmly convinced my day would come.

Vera was leading a bohemian life, or so my mother and grandfather called it. She delivered noon meals for People's Solidarity, for which she was paid two hundred marks a month, plus insurance and a meal for herself—and a person could live on that. Since Vera smoked like a chimney and was forever in need of money, she also worked as a model at the Art Academy—which soon developed into a career of sorts.

From the late '70s to the mid-'80s there were a good many paintings and sketches by Dresden artists that showed a woman with a broad cat-like head and auburn hair, frequently nude and looking lost, but sometimes also as a carnival queen. Vera is not a beauty, but she didn't have a GDR face. I can't explain to you just what a GDR face is, but you recognized one at once.[1] Vera soon had enough connections and money to be able to dress elegantly. Sometimes she was even taken for a visitor from the West.

She lived in Dresden Neustadt, in the garret of a rear-house that lacked a front-house. Since only her apartment had a bell and the other gates and doors were locked at eight o'clock, if you arrived in the evening or at night you had to somehow make your presence known. Vera's neighbors took revenge the next morning by ringing her bell or pounding on her door on some pretext or other. Or pilfered her underwear from the clothesline. Our conversations often took place in the dark, because one of her admirers was raising hell out on the street and, once he'd drunk enough courage, would try to scale the fence.

Two tiny rooms opened off a long hallway with a little cabinet and sideboard that served as a kitchen.

In the back room Vera would perform for me her repertoire for passing the drama school's entrance exam. "Pirate Jenny" was always included. I loved those performances in that tiny room, but feared the moment when she fell silent—should I break into tears or applause?

Of course I find it difficult to speak of Vera without already seeing

1. In creating the category of a German Democratic Republic face, T. evidently was unaware of just how problematic the notion of a national and/or state physiognomy really is.

premonitions of what happened later. Though we rarely met if she "had somebody," we were inseparable in the days and weeks between such affairs. She introduced me to what was called "the scene." I was always greeted with twofold joy: first as a brother who you were nice to in order to please her, and second because I was living proof that Vera was free game again.

I never knew when Vera would invite me in or send me on my way. I would often break off with her, but still stopped by to pick up bowls that had contained food my mother dropped off now and then.

Whenever Vera reemerged—she would usually be waiting for me outside school—she would reproach me, wanting to know why I hadn't shown my face for so long.

Vera lived a life that I wanted to live too as soon as I could—a nonstop series of exhibitions, readings, parties, performances, and night prowls. My clothes would likewise reek of ateliers, I would write whatever I wanted, until the day when I'd become too dangerous for the honchos of the GDR, and be deported, to the West, where my books had already been published and where Franziska and I would enjoy life together, making love, writing, and traveling.

But first I had to survive school. I wondered if it would be worth it to say something abrasive and so provide myself with material. An event worth writing about was sorely needed! Should I write on the black-board, maybe a "Swords Into Plowshares!"

In January 1980, panic broke out as the result of "Karl and Rosa Live!" being painted in red on the wall beside the main entrance. All I got to see was a gray cloth draped over the inscription, as if some memorial plaque were about to be unveiled. Everyone was in the crosshairs—especially those who were thought to be truly convinced. (You do understand what I mean by "convinced"? Our "Reds," the ones who believed in the GDR.)

The only thing that prevented me from confessing to the deed was fear that the real perpetrator might own up. But no one, male or female, hinted at being the offender. At least I heard nothing about it. The inscription was swiftly removed, although its traces now achieved the status of "the handwriting on the wall." Some thought they could make it out at the upper left of the entrance, others believed the four words were distributed across the whole wall, and ended not in an exclamation mark, but a hammer and sickle. Just gazing at the wall was held to be an act of resistance. Small gatherings repeatedly formed as if by chance before it. I never saw anything.

I mention this wall episode because I intended to make my memory of it the embryo of a novel years later.

In hope of being provocative I tacked a poem to the bulletin board—resulting in serious consequences for one of the school's wunderkinder. Myslewski ripped off the page along with the thumbtacks and called me to account in front of the whole class. He had walked right into my trap. That same poem was scheduled to be published in a student anthology.[1] Couldn't I have said what was on my mind somewhat more simply? he asked, and then to universal laughter sent the tattered paper sailing down onto my desk.

The publication of Ehrenburg's memoirs in the GDR offered the opportunity to raise questions about Stalinist work camps. The camps, I was told, were the outgrowth of the cult of personality, a phase that had long since been put behind us and was condemned by the Communist Party of the Soviet Union as early as 1956.

I searched in vain for something I could do or leave undone that would really have a payoff.

My hope was the army!

Ever since my first appearance before the draft board—after that first experience of being questioned by men in uniform—I knew where I could find what I was looking for.

Once inside District Military Headquarters I felt immediately inspired, ideas came to me all on their own. No other place possessed such poetry, such ineluctability. I think I compared the banner of the Army Athletic Club with my underpants—banners were intended to cover a vacant spot on the wall, but in fact revealed instead just how barren that wall was—it was the same with my underpants and my body. Or something like that. I jotted down a whole sequence of such comparisons right there on the spot. Uniforms made suffering plausible. This was no longer just pubescent hypersensitivity, or a shirking of duty that carried no risk à la Neustadt or Loschwitz,[2] this was a cold war, this was theater on a global scale.

1. Publication evidently never occurred.
2. Neustadt and Loschwitz are two neighborhoods in Dresden inhabited by a relatively high percentage of artists.

The high point of my appearance before the draft board was a certain interview. "Several highly placed individuals," the officer behind the desk said, "have great plans for you. Great plans!" He recommended a three-year tour of duty, which would be of advantage to my further development.

In his eyes my exhilaration was simply arrogance, and when I turned him down, he threatened, rather clumsily, to deny me my diploma or matriculation. He was more successful at gloomy descriptions of the everyday life of soldiers who were a disappointment to a government of workers and peasants. Much to my satisfaction I noticed the spit thickening at the corners of his mouth, his rapidly fluttering eyelids, the reddish blue tinge of his complexion, most intense around the nostrils, and watched as the ballpoint pen in his right hand practiced Morse code against the desktop. Trying hard to provide a literary fullness to my ideas, I saw myself standing at attention in my underwear, shivering in the chilly room, but undaunted.

Believe me—after my first draft board appearance, I looked forward to the army.

An intermezzo at the end of my junior year might also be worth mentioning. It was about four months after the Karl and Rosa episode, when without warning, right in the middle of class, the door handle clanked and the vice principal called out my last and first names. I stood up, she waved me toward her. I knew right away: this was not about my mother's being in an accident or some other private catastrophe.

I followed her. From behind closed doors came the grumble of classes in session. Up the stairs, past a mural of the eleventh of Marx's Feuerbach theses, according to which philosophers had just had different interpretations of the world, but the main thing was to change it. I concentrated on the play of our vice principal's calf muscles. I exchanged a mute greeting with the secretary in the principal's reception room. I would later describe the odor as a blend of cigarettes, floor wax, and plywood—but I probably didn't notice a thing. I tried to gain control over my agitation by focusing on the secretary's sandals.

Geronimo had had to deal only with the principal. Two more men were waiting for me. They sat side by side at a table turned lengthwise to abut the principal's desk. They took their time putting out their cigarettes. When they looked up, I greeted them as well.

I wasn't disappointed by their appearance. The older one at least, with his rheumy eyes and black hair combed straight back, matched my expectations. The other one seemed more friendly, the jock buddy on your team. The director sat there like an umpire, his palms pressed together. He looked exhausted and perplexed. Rheumy Eyes began in a disciplinary tone of voice, saying that they were here for a very serious matter. I already had hopes that they would let me remain standing, like a prisoner, when Rheumy Eyes briefly extended his forefinger, which was his way of saying, Sit down.

In my mind I was running through my poems. Which one had made them prick up their ears, which one did they think was the most dangerous? Jock Buddy was resting his hands on the file, it was imposing. How had they got hold of them? What I wanted to say was: "Yes, you're speaking with the author, but I've already thrown that poem out"—because of faulty rhythms and rhymes. Only recently I had run across Mayakovsky's *A Drop of Tar*, a slim volume put out by Insel, in which he describes the construction of his poems—highly recommended reading. Mayakovsky, who would take his own life, writes a poem upbraiding Yessenin for committing suicide. Yes, I planned to use Mayakovsky to lead our Checka agents around by the nose.

The bell rang for a change of class, then rang again for class to begin, and I still didn't understand the point of their questions about my family, especially about relatives in the West. Yes, we were planning to fly to Budapest. If they wanted to chat—please, I had time. This was getting me out of chemistry and Russian both. Jock Buddy and I were now engaged in a smiling contest. When he asked for his next cup of coffee, he also ordered a glass of seltzer for me and offered me a cigarette—then immediately pretended he had forgotten I was just a student.

I was expecting a nasty turn of events at any moment. I was curious how they would segue into my poems. My first district poetry seminar had begun with the question, who among those attending were of the opinion that literature must be oppositional.

It had all happened so fast that time.[1] Now I finally had the chance to correct my mistake. True literature is by its very nature oppositional.

1. T. constantly let opportunities to take action pass him by. Particularly when one assumes that these letters are his attempt at a critical self-accounting, it is amazing that he never condemns his own temporizing.

When the bell rang for the last class of the day, Jock Buddy asked why my mother was planning, together with me, with the Enrico Türmer sitting here now in this room, to leave the German Democratic Republic by illegal means. "We merely want to know why. We have more than enough proof that this is the case."

Rage and shame throttled me, I fought back the tears. So that's what they thought was a direct hit. Rheumy Eyes and Jock Buddy fired their barrage of questions, bang, bang, bang, bang. I got to hear things I had said during class breaks, disparaging remarks about the antifascist protection barrier; Vera was quoted and described as an element hostile to the state; Geronimo was granted the honor of being mentioned several times. Over and over, Geronimo! It was like some curse. Which is why it took me longer than I would have liked to regain command of a firm voice. I don't think that I did in fact stand up, but when I recall that day I can only see myself standing to deliver my speech. We both spoke at the same time. Not in my wildest dreams had I ever thought of leaving this country. For me nothing could be worse than having to abandon it. This was my spot, these were my roots—my family, my school, my home was here. What would I do in the West?

I babbled away like a windup toy, and at some point they fell silent. "I want," I said, "to become a writer, and as a writer I have no choice but to work where I know my way around, where people live who share my experiences. A person such as myself would never leave a country in which literature is of the utmost importance." Did they get my threat at all? "What would I do in the West?" I repeated, fully aware that I had succeeded in sounding convincing—except for a missing a word or two: What would I do in the West *now*? was the real question, or *at this point*. But the more I kept on talking, the more I realized that I was slowly running out—if not of rage—then at least of arguments.

I defended Vera, an exceptional talent, who found herself thwarted in her development and self-realization, Vera, who merely offered her candid opinion, which they ought to be happy to hear.

I added several remarks about the social role of literature, before I asked finally asked them what justification they had for this false charge of wanting to flee the republic. And then I heard myself calling their suspicions shameless—shameless, yes, shameless! I couldn't have put it any better. They had to know that there was no rebuke more beloved by the people's pedagogues than: "I'm ashamed for you! I'm ashamed for you all!"[1]

"We're asking the questions here," Jock Buddy interrupted, smiling yet again. I assumed that his smile came from the fact that he was quoting a well-known phrase, a joke for insiders.

Rheumy Eyes wanted to know why my mother claimed that our trip to Budapest was one awarded her for professional excellence, and whether perhaps she was, without my knowledge, planning to flee the republic. Both of them noticed how I hesitated before I replied. Then we all fell silent, until Jock Buddy gave the principal a nod.

I washed my face in the restroom—my eyes were red from tears—and leaving school, headed straight for the Café Toscana.

As for the Toscana, suffice it to say that I transposed every café scene I ever read to that particular oasis beside the Blue Wonder Bridge (so that even today I could show you the table where young Törless once sat). I populated the café with famous colleagues. Sometimes they called out my name and waved me over. Sometimes they whispered among themselves, uncertain whether the marvelous verses being passed from hand to hand had in fact come from the pen of the young fellow sitting there solitary and pallid over his absinthe. Sometimes I was all by myself. The waitresses probably thought I was a Holy Cross choirboy, one of whose greatest pleasures was to have breakfast there after morning rehearsal. I seldom had to wait for a seat.

That day I was greeted downright rapturously by my famous colleagues. They congratulated me on the courageous speech I had given. Both their reception and the *ragoût fin* did me good. I immediately ordered seconds.

Gradually the scene in the principal's office acquired some good points. After all, I had my first official interrogation behind me. That was as significant as a hundred-page manuscript. Besides which, these guys now knew that they were dealing with a future writer. From now on my response to any questions would be a whispered "Stasi" and silence. Along with my *ragoût fin* I relished the rumors that would soon envelop the whole school, arouse Franziska's admiration, and ultimately find their way to Geronimo.

1. What the latter has to do with the former remains T.'s secret.

Vera—she was living with Nadja at the time—tended to me as if I were someone who had been severely injured and walked me home that evening.

My mother not only had a three-and-a-half-hour interrogation behind her, she had also had two gentlemen escort her back to our apartment. The two had insisted on seeing the application of my request, which the school had approved, to be released from classes. There was nothing in it about an award for professional excellence. All the same we were puzzled—my mother had in fact been considering using the phrase to avoid making people envious. Were we being bugged? Were there mics behind the wallpaper? The solution was perfectly banal. The only officer candidate in our class had recently spent the night with us because our apartment was close to the airport. We two represented our class on a committee providing the hoopla for a visiting foreign nabob (whose plane never landed). Evidently the vigilance of my schoolchum had set off the false alarm.

The next day, after each bing-bong that preceded every announcement on the loudspeaker, I expected to hear our names called out. My expectations were in vain.

It was only much later that I realized the real appeal of this involuntary session had lain in the mistake made by State Security. At the time I was almost ashamed of having been interrogated on false suspicions—which is why I never made literary use of the incident.

With warmest greetings,

Your Enrico

PS: Georg has quit. I'm taking over his share of our enterprise. Not one nasty word has been said, general relief on all sides. We're looking for new quarters.

Thursday, April 5, '90

Dear Jo,

Yesterday Jörg presented me as his associate; he spoke in serious tones with unusually long pauses, lending even more weight to his sentences, which always sound as if they're ready to be set in print. Although everything he said was already known, no one dared disrupt the ritual, not with so much as a look of boredom. Marion sat erect, nodding at me as if to say: Courage, Enrico, courage! Ilona pressed her bony knees together and kept smoothing the hem of her plaid miniskirt. She and Fred are evidently especially receptive to orations of this sort and waged a contest to see who could look more dignified. Kurt, Fred's assistant and deliveryman, as well as our film developer and ad hoc photographer—he's a member of a photography club—sat there inert, arms crossed. I've never heard Kurt speak a single complete sentence. Whenever we meet he raises his hand in greeting and answers every question with "Fine" or "Could be better." For him every job is alike. If you were to ask him to wash windows, he'd immediately find himself a bucket, rag, and newspapers and would not stop until every window sparkled. The Wismut mine had let him go, which left him with just his job as a night porter at the hospital. I don't know if or when he ever sleeps.

We had also asked Pringel, one of our freelancers, to join us. I got to know him in Leipzig, where he put together the house journal, *Air Research Technologies*—he's an impeccable proofreader. Because he's stocky and overweight he can't keep his legs crossed for any length of time, although he seems to think that's important. So he's constantly changing legs, which gives him a strange fidgety look. Pringel's beard keeps growing wilder with each passing day, like a hedge framing a child's face.

Jörg spoke at length about the responsibilities and risks we'll both be sharing. He called on everyone to show discretion in terms of content and numbers, especially now, because next week we'll be leading with the announcement of the hereditary prince's visit.

Jörg will represent us in public, I'll work on in-house issues, and we'll share editorial duties.

Then it was my turn to say a few words. No sooner had I finished than Fred asked just what if anything would be different? He was upset because Jörg doesn't want him to sit in on editorial meetings—but has asked Ilona to.

Although I didn't have to answer any questions, I was glad when the meeting ended.

The baron has invited Jörg, Marion, and us to join him at the Wenzel next week. He pleaded fervently with me not to hide my wife away again this time.

We talked a good while as we sat in his new car—I'm to keep his old one until I can afford to buy my own.[1] He had to admit that he didn't know the rules of the game in the East, but the longer he thought about the fact that half the firm had been as good as foisted off on me, the more he was inclined to look for some attached strings that were dangling so close to our nose we couldn't see them. I told him what I knew—that neither Jörg nor Georg had needed his own ten thousand marks and both had already returned the money to their mothers. Steen's twenty thousand D-marks were news to the baron. The more details I told him, the less believable the whole thing seemed to him.

But be that as it may, he finally said, from now on at any rate I wouldn't be sleeping so soundly. He didn't want to have to reproach himself later, which was why he needed to make clear to me, even at this moment of my greatest happiness, that according to civil code co-owners in a company were fully exposed. "You're liable down to your wife's last blouse, to your son's last pair of pants." He swore he wasn't implying anything, but I should be prepared for the tricks and treachery of this new world. Sometimes just a roofing tile or a banana peel can lead to a firm's ruin. His motto was: "the limited liability corporation, a GmbH!" He traced the letters on the fogged-up windshield and went on with his lesson. Then he rummaged in the glove compartment and, as a farewell gift, handed me a paperback published by dtv. From long use it opens to the law covering limited liability.

Hugs,

Your Enrico

Sunday, April 8, '90

Dear Nicoletta,

I awoke a little while ago with a strange sense of joy. It was in antici-pation of something, and do you know of what? Of now, of this moment, when I can write to you. It's as if you have just sat down beside me. And through you what I tell you takes on its own special color. I share my memories with you and you alone. To whom else should I tell

---

1. A somewhat too offhanded mention of a truly remarkable offer.

these things?[1] And each time I do, I find myself just this side of writing you real love letters. It takes every ounce of will not to. You entered my life, and yet before I could even stretch out my arms to you, you were taken from me again. Without you I feel incomplete, like an amputee.[2] And I'm afraid that you will have forgotten it all when we meet again [. . .] and won't even recognize me. To keep from becoming a stranger to you, I shall go on writing.

In October 1980—I was in the twelfth grade—I received a telegram. Geronimo asked if he could spend the night at our place that coming Saturday, and noted his time of arrival. It's not as if I had expected a visit from Geronimo, but I wasn't surprised either.

Geronimo had definitely grown, he was clearly taller than I, his hair fell down over his shoulders and was so greasy it glistened, so that my mother asked if it was raining.

When we sat down to coffee, he polished off our weekend supply of rolls and scraped the last bit of honey from the jar. My mother covered her faux pas with a steady barrage of questions. Each began with "Johann," as if she were calling on him in class.

After he had eaten his fill, we retreated to my room, about which he had no comment, not a single syllable, in fact he didn't even seem to notice the splendor of my books and pictures (the latter on loan from Vera). I asked who he planned to visit in Dresden—no one except me. Was there a concert or a play he wanted to attend—not that he knew. He answered every question with monosyllables. If I fell silent, he remained mute too. I didn't know what to do with him. My question about where he intended to study theology[3] arose from the same awkwardness as the rest of my inquiries.

I assumed he was fed up with my queries and that that was the reason he was staring at me so angrily. And then Geronimo began his monologue. The sentences were declarative, but their intonation was that of

1. In view of T.'s immense correspondence, this statement may seem surprising. And yet both Johann and V. T. were too much a part of his memories, which is evidently why only Nicoletta Hansen was considered as the addressee for his description of "the path that led him astray." Cf. note 2, p. 95.

2. T. felt like an "amputee" once before, when he was describing to Johann Ziehlke what it was like to lose his car. Cf. the letter of March 13, 1990.

3. Upon completing preparatory seminary, Johann Ziehlke had only one choice: to study theology at a church college, since admission to a university required a high school diploma.

questions, as if he expected to be contradicted. Life wasn't worth anything if death was the final station. "Without eternity," he said, "our life is meaningless."

Geronimo went on and on and seemed somehow furious with me. What was he getting at? I saw only his desperation, which culminated in his assertion that it didn't matter to him if he went on sitting in his chair or threw himself out the window. I realized that for him God and the meaning of life were still one and the same thing.

My shrugs only increased his rage. He pressed his lips together and stared at me as if my silence were the same silence into which he used to maneuver me three years before. What did he want from me? So I did exactly what I had been prepared to do.

I opened my desk drawer and took my treasure from its hideaway. I was scarcely still capable of listening to Geronimo. My fingertips tapped the pages into place. I barely cast him a glance as I said that this stuff was what held me above water. I handed my work to him, to my important reader—and slipped out into the kitchen.

When I returned to my room with two glasses, Geronimo was sitting there just as before. Finally he raised his head. He wouldn't have had to say a single word, and certainly not a string of adjectives, all he had to do was to look at me like that, shaking his head in disbelief. It wasn't a success—it was a triumph!

It wasn't Vera and her entourage who made a poet of me, it was Geronimo. I believed him. He said things that it would be ridiculous to repeat today, but at the time were tantamount to my consecration—and his subjugation. That he was able to offer me such praise surely came from the fact that he himself had lost his footing.

The whole evening Geronimo talked about nothing except my poems, as if it were up to him to convince me how extraordinary they were. And I made every effort to reciprocate his pathos as best I could. I could tell him now just how overwhelming my response to him had been at one time, how much I had longed for him to be my friend.

There is a kind of openness that finds every trace of distance to be a blemish. After Sunday breakfast, my mother asked me if Johann had been crying.

We talked and talked without letup, but neither was there any letup in my fear—that with one false word, one nod given too quickly, our euphoria would be transformed into a will-o'-the-wisp. As the conductor flung the door closed behind him, I felt almost as if I had been redeemed, as if only now was his praise irrevocable.

Although that weekend might be regarded as the date of the true founding of our friendship, out of tact I also never reminded Geronimo of that evening.

When I got back home I sat down at my typewriter and began my first letter to him. "Dear Johann," I typed, left one line blank, and placed my fingers on the keyboard the way I had been taught in typing class. "Darling Johann," I said softly. "My darling Johann."[1]

Trusting that you'll continue to listen to me, I send warmest greetings,

Your Enrico T.

Tuesday, April 10, '90

Dear Jo,

The weekend was a nightmare! Now that the panic is over, even I can see that I looked somewhat ridiculous. But first the good news: We've found a new—admittedly ramshackle, if not to say dilapidated—domicile for our headquarters. It's a miracle! After even Fred's connections as a hometown lad proved futile and except for innkeeper Gallus—whose job it is to keep his guests in good spirits—no one even dared try to keep our hopes up, it was once again the baron who helped out. I'm gradually getting used to it.

When, he declared, would we finally understand what a newspaper is for: ads and local news! He would, needless to say, put at our disposal all replies he had received to his real estate ads. Unfortunately only one was worth our consideration. It sounded to us like music of the spheres. The baron came just short of apologizing for having rented a splendid villa for himself without having first offered it to us.

Once we heard his proposal, it took us barely half an hour to find our way to Moskauer Strasse 47,[2] which runs between the Weiber Market and Jüden Gasse. As we waited for the owner, we were like children

---

1. Such candor when dealing with N. H. is surprising.
2. Due to its dilapidated state the building was torn down three years ago.

waiting to open their gifts—and got a nasty surprise. Who showed up? Piatkowski! Him and a long drink of water.

Piatkowski was panting as if he had had to drag the long drink of water the whole way all by himself. Even after Piatkowski and the baron shook hands we still didn't want to believe that this was the person we had been waiting for.

Supple with the joy of enterprise, the baron gave his hips a roll and asked Piatkowski to lead the way. The first issue was whether the building pleased his clients, and then we'd see what we would see. The long drink of water shouted that he and Herr Piatkowski had already come to an agreement. We were to keep that in mind, please.

The long drink of water had a trained voice that carried very well. One after the other the heads of a father, mother, and daughter appeared in the display window of the private hardware store located on the ground floor. They watched the proceedings without returning my greeting. Passersby slowed their steps.

The baron paid no attention to anyone—neither to Fred's babbling about urgency and being a local, nor to the other fellow's booming voice. He gave Piatkowski a smile.

Unable to shake us off, the long drink of water stuck close to Piatkowski's side, amiably and politely bending his ear, but he was the first to slip into the darkness that now opened up behind one panel of the wooden door. His voice echoed as he praised the ancient plaster. "Fantastic!" he exclaimed. "Fantastic!" His footsteps faded, but then quickly returned. "What's wrong?" he asked Piatkowski. "Aren't you coming in?"

The baron had come to a halt in front of Piatkowski and stared at him before admonishing us: "Keep your eyes peeled. If you see any shortcomings, we'll ask for the rent to be reduced."

The building is nothing but shortcomings. The long drink of water, however, found it all fascinating, enchanting, and "an exciting opportunity": the smithy in the rear courtyard, which along with roof tiles, dust, and cat shit contains an anvil on a massive wooden base; the half-timbering—absolutely worth keeping!—and then there was the plaster, over and over, and at every mention it aged a couple of hundred years.

Piatkowski stood leaning against the newel, sucking on hard candy. The building had belonged to his in-laws, there had been a greengrocer here at one point, with first-rate connections to the farmers of Altenburg as well as of the more distant reaches of Saxony. They themselves,

Piatkowski and his wife, had never earned a penny from it. There had been nothing but squabbles about the rent. And now this dump belonged to all four siblings, so there wasn't anything left to speak of. The hardware store downstairs, and up in the garret a married couple, refugees back then, from Silesia—but the town had been full of them. "Ah," the long drink of water said, "Silesia," and buttoned up his coat.

The stairway is drafty and dark as a chimney, the light switch doesn't work. On the second floor, two doors lead off a small vestibule to rooms looking out on the street. The one on the right, the smaller of the two, is twice as large as our editorial office. The door on the left opens onto an almost ballroom-size space with high windows and a door to another room almost as large.

"With windows like these you might as well just move out onto the street!" The baron stuck a fingertip into his mouth and then held it up to a windowpane, as if trying to determine the wind direction. "A pretty kettle of fish you've got here," he chided Piatkowski, who took a deep breath and nodded twice.

"But I'll take it! As is! With the shop downstairs. Agreed, Herr Piatkowski? Agreed?" The long drink of water gesticulated wildly.

"Have a look at the rest," Piatkowski replied, and then warned Fred, who had shouldered open a warped door, "It gets a bit risky, leave that to me."

We entered a long windowless hallway. To the left a wallpapered door opens onto the vestibule, so that you can move in a circle. Along the right are some tiny rooms—which Fred declared to be storage space.

Suddenly it turned bright again. The hallway ends in a room with windows facing a courtyard, and beyond it the rear walls of buildings lining the market.

Piatkowski remained in the doorway. The little room that I would have liked to move into then and there has been declared off-limits by the police—both the floor and the exterior wall are in danger of collapse. We all had a look before beating a dark retreat.

"Dear Herr Piatkowski, you actually want rent for that? What if my life insurance company were to hear about it!" The baron called back his wolf, who was sniffing in nooks and crannies. Even the long drink of water fell silent this time.

"Rubble!" the baron declared. "Quite simply rubble."

The rent they had received up till now had barely paid the chimney sweep. And they'd put every penny into a new roof, Piatkowski said by way of apology.

"And now you want more rent? Who should I tell that to?"

The long drink of water shouted, "I'll take it!"

"I'm really very sorry," Piatkowski repeated.

"Are you even listening? I'll take it!"

"Let's go on upstairs," Piatkowski proposed. We waited till we had lined up in our accustomed sequence, but this time the long drink of water backed off. He wasn't about to play this game. He would rent it for a year, and that was that. He was sure they'd come to an agreement about price.

"Whereas I," the baron said, "am unwilling to buy a pig in a poke." He insisted on being led upstairs.

"But of course, but of course," Piatkowski said, trying to mollify him. And that was why the long drink of water entered both rooms well behind the rest of us. Each of these rooms was likewise entered via a vestibule.

"How much do you want for this?" the baron asked, tugging and chewing at the hairs of his mustache. "It might work for the summer."

"Now listen here . . ." the long drink of water broke in. He evidently no longer knew whom to address.

"What are you willing to offer?" Piatkowski asked.

"Not much, right?" The baron looked at me and then at Jörg. "Three hundred at most, 250 East-marks?" Jörg nodded, I nodded, Fred and Ilona thought that this was way too much, while Kurt wandered from window to window, digging his thumbnail into the putty and then blowing off the flaking paint.

"A thousand," the long drink of water shouted in relief, "one thousand West-marks! Agreed?"

That was out of the question, the baron replied angrily, it would be the ruin of the market here, offering a thousand for a dump like this, totally off the mark, it was immoral, a man couldn't do that, truly he couldn't. If that were to set the pace . . . For a moment the long drink of water looked exasperated, but then triumphed over his response and said, "It's a market economy."

"Yes," Piatkowski said, 250 would be about right, he really didn't want to ask for more than that, he wasn't a moneygrubber and the place needed some serious investment—250 East-marks, that was all right with him, but always in advance, on the first.

The baron held a hand out to him. "Starting May first," he said. "May?" Piatkowski asked, but then shook hands.

The long drink of water gave a shrill laugh. "Herr Piatkowski! Herr Piatkowski? A thousand West-marks, agreed?"

"Yes," Piatkowski said. He had understood him, calling the long drink of water by his long and melodious name, but surely he must realize that this was among locals, and just in general, it's how we were used to doing things around here.

"Yes," Fred said, "we're locals!" Kurt nodded, one thumbnail cleaning the other.

The long drink of water gave a snort, stepped up to the baron, extended him a hand like a knife to his stomach, and bellowed, "Congratulations, really, my congratulations!" Since the baron was pressing his attaché case against himself with both hands, the long drink of water made do with some vigorous motions of his head, turned around, and vanished like a shade into the gloom of the vestibule. Piatkowski handed us the keys, and we said our good-byes.

Fred immediately started planning the renovation. If we gave him and Kurt a free hand, it would be completely taken care of within two weeks, completely. Jörg asked me to keep working on my article on Piatkowski, who was still deputy chairman of the Christian Democrats, even if he was our landlord now. He had promised Marion.

The baron is proud of his achievement. As soon as he has his new stationery he'll send us his bill as the agent, one month's rent—standard is three—his first earnings in the East.

The old married couple in the attic have yet to let us know if they are happy with their new co-renters. The hardware store people don't seem to care one way or the other.

Furniture is no problem—Helping Hand is selling off the inventory of the Stasi villa cheap. And there'll be more than enough parking spaces. We just have to clean up the area at the upper end of Jüden Gasse.[1]

And now about the weekend. I wanted to check in on Fred and Kurt,

1. Overgrown lots that had been left unused after several buildings were torn down in 1988–89.

who have been renovating since Friday, and on Saturday I drove over to the new building with several boxes of cookies and a bag of coffee. Ilona had mobilized her husband and children. They were ripping off wallpaper as if there were nothing they'd rather be doing. Kurt was plastering holes in the walls with stoic equanimity. Pringel was happy that I could see him in his mechanic's jumpsuit. Fred was already painting the office. Next to the shashlik and Ilona's cream torte my cookies would have looked pitiful, so I just left the coffee.

Jörg, Marion, and I had worked till midnight on Friday, and the twelve pages for Monday were as good as finished. I don't know myself why I drove back to the office—maybe the others' enthusiasm was infectious. As always I first went through the mail, slitting one envelope after the other with Ilona's Egyptian letter opener, stamped readers' letters, inquiries, manuscripts as "received," and sorted subscription forms and small ads. Like some bonus, the last envelope was embossed with a coat-of-arms on the back.

I didn't even suspect anything when I saw the list of names on the letterhead. I read the "in Re," the salutation, moved on to the name of our newspaper, and the all-too-familiar generalization: "swinish business" . . . read ever more quickly, skimming sentences until I drew up short at the number 20,000 followed by the symbol DM, plus the words "twenty thousand" spelled out in parenthesis. This was soon followed by a "forty thousand" in numbers and words and, after a skipped line, a "Best Regards" and a signature with two big loops that tied up the name like the ribbon on a present.

I reread it from the top and, after a moment, a third time. A law firm was suing us for libel on behalf of their clients and threatened that if we were to make public such assertions yet again (that is, part two of our article on the hog farm), a fine of forty thousand D-marks would be assessed.

When I got to the door I had to go back, because I still had Ilona's letter opener in my hand. I drove to Jörg's place. No one answered. When I tried again a half hour later, a neighbor woman told me that they and the girls would be in Gotha until tomorrow, visiting grandma and grandpa. No one at the Wenzel knew when Barrista would be back, but he had booked his room for another week.

Why for just one week? And why had Georg thrown in the towel on account of that article? It seemed to me that everyone but me had seen this turn of affairs coming. I envied Jörg and Marion for their ignorant bliss, for an evening with their parents and children. In the crazy hope that I would see the baron's car standing at the door, I headed for the new building—but then drove on past. I spotted Ilona at the window. I felt like crying.

If they had at least written *marks* and not *D-marks*!

Luckily Anna, the author of the article, was at home.

"Our further existence," I said, "is in your hands."

While she read the lawyers' letter, I took a deep breath for the first time. When she said she would swear that she had reported everything exactly as it was told to her, and that her people were reliable, absolutely reliable, I found myself feeling almost cheerful. She fulfilled my deepest wish by emphatically repeating "absolutely, absolutely reliable." With tears in her eyes she promised to reconfirm everything—I needn't worry.

No sooner was I back in the car than my angst welled up again.

When I woke up Sunday morning at four, I realized I still had that damned letter in my pocket, that the goddamn thing had spent the night here with me, so to speak.

It took every bit of energy not to drive to the Wenzel right then—or at six, or seven, or eight o'clock. I had set my goal at ten o'clock, or nine thirty . . .[1]

Herr von Barrista had left the hotel shortly after nine . . . Was there anything else they could do for me?

I shook my head, I was fighting back tears. I looked for the baron in the line of people waiting to buy a *Bild* tabloid at the train station. I reconnoitered the neighboring streets. I returned to the Wenzel. I wrote the baron a few quick lines, fervently begging him to stop by the office. The file with the mail was still lying on the desk. I folded the letter up and shoved it in. When Georg appeared to say that Franka wanted to know if I would be staying through the noonday meal, I declined the invitation. In a burst of chivalry, I told myself that he no longer had anything to do with it—spare him the worry.

Yielding to sudden inspiration, I drove to the building where—as the baron had pointed out to me—Manuela, the blond waitress, lives. She's now working at Referees' Retreat. But no one answered the door.

[1]. The previous letter was written on Sunday morning. The discrepancy between the "strange sense of joy" mentioned in it and the "nightmare" described here remains unexplained.

Around seven I returned home. I could hear music even from outside the door. When I entered Astrid the wolf was lying under the mirror console. She didn't even raise her head. The baron had presented Robert with a CD player plus speakers, which they were trying to place to best effect. In their baseball caps they looked like professional installers. Michaela had a performance.

"And where were you?" the baron asked. He had missed me at the opening of the exhibition at the Lindenau Museum. So many local VIPs! It's called working your contacts.

"And? Are they right?" he asked after I had poured out my heart to him—and then calmed me down at once. Anyone who sent something like that in the mail was not to be taken seriously in the first place. But shouldn't we respond all the same? I asked.

"Yes," he said, "by ripping up that piece of trash and forgetting it. Who's to say you ever even got it?" And might there not be some other solution?

"If you like," he said, "I'll take care of it." That's exactly what I wanted to hear.

"But that always costs money, a letterhead like that unfortunately costs one hell of a lot of real money."

I asked him about part two, whether we should print it or not. "Of course," he said, "if it's good. Otherwise don't."

So now we have our little scandal issue, because Jörg's article about a teacher named Offermann is on page three. If we go under, it will be with flying colors.

Hugs, E.

Maundy Thursday, April 12, '90

Verotchka,[1]

I have to calm Mamus down every couple of days. Even with a hundred dead, the chance something has happened to you isn't even one in a thousand. Mamus will be here for Easter.

Once the telephone is connected in our new offices, we won't have to

1. This letter was sent to V. T. by fax.

worry about imposing.[1] It's strange, but I find it difficult to leave the old one behind. It's been with me for so many hours, filled with so many hopes. The dial, the spiral cord, even the receiver, they all belong to your voice, your breath, to everything that you and I have said.

Verotchka, it won't be long and I shall lay the world at your feet. At least some little piece of it. Your friend, the baron, has dropped a couple of hints, and I've responded accordingly—it's quite possible that we, you and I, will soon be going on a trip. I don't want to let the cat out of the bag yet, it sounds crazy and absurd, but I've learned to believe things for that very reason. You'll see, it'll all work out!

I'm so grateful to you for remembering Robert. He even wears the jacket in the apartment, it hangs on his bedpost at night.

Michaela attributes his "unimaginative" desire for money to my influence. What else is Robert supposed to wish for? He knows that within a few months he'll be able to fulfill entirely different wishes.

A couple of days ago, Michaela admitted that she has been carrying around a letter from Robert's father. She recognized his handwriting on the envelope.

I met him just once, that is to say, I saw him at the theater when he came to pick up *his* Christmas pyramid and *his* old candelabra. At the time it was beyond me how Michaela could have fallen for a man like him. The incarnation of the wannabe artist—gray ponytail, flashy ring, three-day beard. He was forever going on about Pablo or Rainer or Hanna,[2] and if someone asked him about it, he took offense in the name of his gods. Robert would wait until ten or eleven at night in the theater canteen,[3] until Michaela had removed her makeup. His father never had any time for him, because he was hot on the trail of another one of his inspirations or chasing some high school girl. All the same Robert was very attached to him.

But now Robert didn't even want to read the letter. He cursed his father and cried. But at some point he'll make the trip to see him. And I'll have to let him, if not in fact encourage him.

1. Imposing on Georg.
2. Picasso, Fassbinder, Schygulla.
3. He is referring to the theater in Rudolstadt.

Last night Michaela joined me at the Wenzel. We just now got home.

On the way there she claimed that by now half the town is making fun of Barrista, and that I should protect Robert from him. She'd put it euphemistically and called my nobleman a pushy, funny duck who's so ambitious that he can hardly walk in those silly boots of his.

I've learned from Nicoletta (short, brunette, with cornflower blue eyes, and unflattering but expensive glasses, she knows everything, can do anything, and does it, but basically is more helpless than a child, always afraid she'll miss out on something, and thankful just to get any "job"; she's hoping that with the help of the Lindenau Museum she can pursue a career in art history)[1]—from Nicoletta I've learned that he must have a skeleton in his closet, at least he's not allowed to do business on his own and works through a whole network of straw men. Did you know anything about that? But this flaw only adds to his attraction, at least for poetic souls—as best as I can read them—especially for Johann. He downright lusts to hear about mysterious, inscrutable types who have a finger in every pie, and are successful at it, whether in business or with the ladies [. . .] And when I describe Barrista's limp, Johann regards it as somehow diabolical and talks about his "dark luster."

Even Michaela couldn't hide the fact that her tirade against Barrista was really just the reverse side of her curiosity—that she couldn't wait to be introduced to him. And so I found it quite amusing to watch how quickly Barrista won her over.

Before he kissed her hand (and later on he would rave about her hands), before she was seated at the place of honor at our table—yes, more or less even as she was making her entry into the restaurant—the two of them were already playing their game. He likewise knows how to work an audience, without ever casting it a glance.

The baron handed us what he called the "bill of fare," on which he had had the hotel print in gold lettering: "In honor of the rebirth of the *Altenburg Weekly* and in honor of Michaela Fürst and Marion Schröder." Inside was a list of six courses, on the left in French, on the right in a German translation—that makes an impression.

Wasn't this laying it on just a bit thick, Michaela asked brusquely, only to immediately announce how happy she had been to accept his invitation. But first she wanted to make sure she didn't forget to thank him for

---

1. The inaccuracy of this characterization of N. H. says a great deal about T.

the splendid flowers, which in their own way were as seductive as the names of these mystifying dishes.

Marion jumped in to say that she had not yet expressed her thanks for the largest cyclamen in all of Altenburg.

"When it comes to flowers," Michaela resumed, "no one can hold a candle to Herr von Barrista." I was strangely touched to hear his name coming from her lips. From then on everything was really quite clear.

During the main courses he entertained us with travelogues. In the fall he always flew to the U.S., to the East Coast for lobster. He described the inns, the little harbors, the various landscapes and the play of light, pumpkins in the fields, red foliage . . . His narrative was as vivid as it was lively, and without interpolated questions it flowed along like non-stop dinner music, wrapping itself around me as I basked in my dreams of you.

When we got up from the table, the baron laid a hand on my shoulder—the restaurant had long since closed, tables were being set for breakfast—and asked if we would like to finish off this extraordinary evening with a nightcap. The bar wasn't worth much, but he had done some upgrading over the past few weeks. It would make a happy man of him if he could put a cocktail shaker to good use for us. "Why not?" Michaela responded like a shot out of a pistol.

"Well, that's an answer!" the baron said in triumph. An arm linked mine, and I found myself in the bar at a table that was just being cleared.

The baron dedicated the next minutes to me with something very like fervor. More than the words themselves, I recall the pleasant, almost tender lilt of their melody. Yes, he literally wooed me. And I realized: He isn't nearly as old as he seems, he's much younger!

When I woke up, Michaela and the baron were snorting and giggling. Except for a couple of waitresses and a man as thin as a rail bent over empty glasses at a neighboring table, we were alone.

"We were just talking about the theater," he said, as if I had just returned from a brief trip to the restroom. With one hand on my knee, he leaned over to me. I could smell his unusual perfume. It was five a.m.—which for me is relatively late.[1]

He pried us into his car. Michaela chattered away, giggling to herself. As we rode along I tried to support her head from behind—it kept slipping off the headrest whenever we took a curve.

1. By his own admission, T. usually awoke around four in morning.

As we got out, she sank into my arms. I felt like her footman.

No sooner were we in the apartment than nausea brought her to. She was so weak I had to brace her forehead above the toilet bowl.

"Are you jealous?" she asked, and apparently thought she ought to gaze especially meaningfully into my eyes. I begged her not to kneel on her dress and tried to help her out of her coat. She reached into her coat pocket and held up an envelope. "That's how much my name is worth," she cried, "one thousand dee ems!" She was to receive the sum monthly as manager of Fürst & Fürst Real Estate.

When we were counting out the money later and I asked her if she knew what she was getting herself into, Michaela said that she trusted *me,* after all *I* had taken her with me, he's *my* friend, that was the *only* reason she had agreed—only to add a little later: "He's so ugly! Don't you think he's incredibly ugly?"

Do you think he's ugly?

Kisses,

Your Heinrich

[The following handwritten lines are on a separate page and undated. Since the preceding letter was written early in the morning, immediately after their return from the Wenzel, one can presume this should likewise be dated April 12th. According to V. T., they both arrived by fax.]

Michaela had a miscarriage this morning. She immediately went to the hospital, I didn't learn about it until several hours later. Maybe it would have been better if I never had—but of course that's nonsense. I feel it's my fault for dragging her with me to the Wenzel. I can't understand how Michaela hadn't noticed anything—surely she must have known! It can only have happened in Offenburg, nowhere else.

Michaela didn't even want to be comforted, she's very cool and collected. In a show of tenderness, the hospital put her in a room with three women who had just had abortions, there were no other beds available.

In a certain sense we're both grateful that we didn't have to face that decision. Which is why we don't talk about it. Robert seems to be the one who's saddest.

Verotchka, my dear sister!

H.

Dear Jo,

Friday the thirteenth. I'm sitting here in my bathrobe, drinking coffee, and enjoying the quiet. I can't remember what I wrote to you in my last letter.[1]

On Wednesday the baron invited us to dinner yet again. There were several things to celebrate—our new building, my new position, Barrista's real estate firm.

No sooner had we arrived than he spotted Michaela and couldn't keep his eyes off her after that. I really believe he was surprised to suddenly see me right behind her.

Marion, who made a special trip to the hairdresser, looked more severe in short hair. She was wearing a lot of makeup and a muted red dress that pinched her under the arms. Jörg also seemed out of place in a gray suit that was a little too large on him.

Barrista, who was in the best of moods, cleared the long side of the table just for Michaela and asked Jörg to move down a seat, and then seated himself in his spot. He placed me next to Marion, who was already showering Michaela with compliments. The far side of the table was left empty.

There were always two or three waiters tending to our needs, young fellows who marched through the dining room with shouldered trays and, as they served up plates at breathtaking speed, removed the domed silver covers with a coordinated grand gesture as if on command. One of them would then solemnly announce the name of the dish.

Twice, without any consideration shown to other guests, the lights were turned off. The first time flames danced above the shoulders of our waiters, the second time the spray of sparklers glittered, followed by noisy minifireworks at the table. It couldn't have been more spectacular. Michaela applauded like a child each time.

We would barely take one sip of wine and the baron would refill our glasses. He was pleased with himself and the world and led the conversation with a sure hand on the reins.

He revealed to us a few of his habits. He sleeps till nine, likes to take long walks out of fondness for the wolf, spends several hours in the city

---

1. T.'s last letter to Johann was dated three days previous.

archives, and then rewards himself with an hour in the museum. Granted, whenever he and the hereditary prince had talked about his visit, the prince had insisted that he, the baron, seek out the museum, but had never been able to give the baron a true conception of what he had missed in life until now—nothing less than the key to happiness! We really should have our ears tweaked. Why had we not taken him by the hand on that very first day and led him to the museum, for it would have spared him many a gloomy hour of helpless brooding over the fate of the town. "What you have here," he said, "is a Louvre *en miniature*, don't you know that?" And segued at once to his Madonna again, which is slowly becoming an obsession with him.

As if to spare us further reproach, Jörg began to talk about Nietzsche's father, who had been a teacher at the castle. Jörg didn't get very far, however, before the baron interrupted him. Out of the blue he offered to write an article for our local pages. From the attaché case so familiar to us all he extracted a couple of photographs that he first showed to Michaela and Marion. He wouldn't have had to say another word. Marion tried to shy away, Michaela stared at me, as if comparing the picture with me. The baron explained in a chatty voice that they were taken in February '41. On Altenburg's Market Square—the savings bank and the steam-driven Winkler Wurst Factory could be made out in the background—a woman's hair was being lopped off before an assembled horde. Another photo showed her seated on a horse-drawn wagon, surrounded by a crowd of about two to three hundred spectators, maybe more. In the second picture she still had a headscarf on, and her chin was resting on a sign: I HAVE BEEN EXPELLED FROM THE PEOPLE'S COMMUNITY. A third photo showed her and an older man, with a hat and glasses, who was cutting her hair, after having first bound a traditional white cloth around her shoulders. The fourth also showed him "hard at work." In the fifth her head had been shaved bare. The sixth picture was of her walking through the town. She was accused of having had intimate relations with a Pole; her husband was a soldier.

What he'd like to find out, the baron said, was where she had lived, whether there were still relatives. Photo in hand, he had visited the spot today where it had taken place.

It shouldn't be difficult to find out the name of the barber or the circumstantial details of these—yes, you only had to look at the happy faces—these revels. What did we think? Shouldn't we search for witnesses and question the townsfolk? If the photograph were enlarged, people could be recognized more easily. Promising to write an article, he gathered up his pictures again and carefully stowed them away.

"Local news with a twist," Michaela said, raising her glass to the baron. She drank a lot, in fact.

Suddenly the baron leaned across the table. "Look there," he whispered, pointing his head in the direction of the entrance. I didn't know who he meant, since there were several parties standing there looking around for a table. A tall gaunt woman with an angular face and black hair made a beeline for our table. The man preceding her barely came up to her breasts. "Caesar and Cleopatra," the baron said sotto voce. There really was something Egyptian about the woman's hairdo. In the next moment the short man grabbed the back of one of the empty chairs at our table and was about to launch his question with a smile, when Marion and Michaela erupted into laughter. I couldn't contain myself, either.

"I'm sorry," the baron exclaimed. "We're still expecting more guests." The mismatched pair stood there as if searching for some explanation for our bad manners. Jörg, who had held out the longest, was now leaning forward, bracing himself against the table with one hand and covering his eyes with the other. His shoulders were bobbing. Marion and Michaela took turns chortling. I pressed the back of my hand to my mouth.

"I'm so very sorry," the baron repeated.

"Well, enjoy your evening," the short man replied, less angry than confused, which set Michaela into a new round of laughter, and the rest of us with her. My laughter was so out of control that the harder I struggled against it the more violently I shook. I have no idea what had got hold of us. There was absolutely no reason for us to carry on like that.

The baron tried several times to make some remark, but was so helpless against the demon that had seized us that he testily excused himself and left the table. As soon as he was just a few steps away, we fell silent. We stared at one another, each waiting for the other—and nothing happened.

I felt wretched, compromised. We just sat there speechless—excruciating doesn't come close to describing it. It was as if the baron had annulled all words, gathering them up like playing cards from the table. And we had no choice but to wait for his return, for him to deal them again.

In those few minutes we seemed to destroy everything that held us together. The silence devoured everything we had ever felt for one another, it wolfed down respect, dignity, trust, affection, love. Had someone compelled us to disband at that moment, it would have been forever.

All of a sudden the baron reappeared. As he was about to resume his seat, Michaela said, "We've calmed down, do forgive us." He took her hand and kissed it.

But now, just when the opportunity presented itself for us to forget the matter, the next catastrophe followed immediately on its heels.

Michaela suddenly raised her arm as if to signal a waiter, which was an instant alarm for the baron. "Something you need?"

I turned around. Standing in the path of the advancing phalanx of waiters were Wolfgang the Hulk, his wife, and Jan Steen. The three stepped aside, but as their eyes followed the waiters, they discovered us.

Wolfgang and his wife came over to greet us. The baron, to whom Michaela was about to introduce the pair, did not even put down his knife and fork, and turned away from her to speak to the waiter.

In order to salvage whatever could be salvaged, I joined Wolfgang as he walked back to Steen. In that same moment a new dish was solemnly unveiled. Steen asked who the silly ass was that we were sitting with, and insisted we join him at his table. There were several things he wanted to talk over.

I begged his pardon, asking him to understand our situation—whereupon in midsentence Steen lost all interest in me, sat down, and picked up a menu. The baron, on the other hand, chided us, muttering something about the quality of the cuisine losing every bit of subtlety once it had turned cold.

Whether by chance or on purpose, the courses now followed one another without the least pause—until the lights were doused again. For Steen that was the last straw. He, along with Wolfgang and his wife, departed then and there, without so much as a glance our way.

Although we all made every effort and, much to the baron's delight, ordered seconds of the crème brûlée, the incident spoiled the mood until the very end.

The next morning, however, I awoke fully refreshed and without a trace of cobwebs in my head.

Hugs, Your E.[1]

---

1. There is no explanation for why T. fails to mention Michaela's miscarriage.

Dear Nicoletta,

With each new day I still hope to hear news of you. From the start I suspected that I would have to wait a good while for letters from you. But as long as you allow me to write you, I shall not complain and will proceed with my confession.[1]

During the four months between graduation and reporting for duty I didn't look for a job the way everyone else did. I had a job. My mother or Vera gave me what little money I needed for books, theater tickets, and train trips to Naumburg or Berlin.

As if Vera knew that she would soon have her passport taken away and be placed under a so-called Berlin embargo,[2] she was constantly underway—to the Baltic, to the Harz Mountains, to Mecklenburg—and sent me postcards and letters so that I could follow her journeys on a map. While in Berlin she scribbled a few walls full with her friends' poetry, learned how to throw pottery, and, allegedly, smoked marijuana.

Vera's absence brought a certain calm into my life. I set it as my goal to write five or six hours a day. But, unlike other precocious wunderkinder, I did not write poetry that apostrophized the Elbe, Dresden, women with long hair, or the copper hammers above the roofs of Budapest.[3] That was the last thing on my mind. I wrote about the army!

Constrained by orders, licked into shape by drill and maneuver, I would acquire an instantly recognizable style. And wasn't the West waiting for smuggled messages and coded rappings from behind the barracks walls of the East, just as they had waited for the tales of Solzhenitsyn's gulag?

The scene I was able to work on was the morning of my induction—those minutes between waking up and getting out of bed, to be followed by the descent into hell.

Most likely you'll think I'm exaggerating when I claim that my thoughts had always revolved around this farewell. The army was the epitome of leaving home. Kindergarten, school, afterschool clubs, and

---

1. This is the first time that T. uses the word "confession," but from this point on he almost always uses the term for these chronicles.
2. According to V. T., she was never subjected to a "Berlin embargo."
3. Apparently an allusion to poems by "precocious wunderkinder."

vacation camps had been unpleasant, but nothing in comparison to the horrible farewell to which they were mere precursors.

We had grown up, after all, in the shadow of the endless Russian barracks that ran from Klotzsche all the way into the heart of the city. Soldiers marching in columns to their training area at Heller and the songs they sung by night behind barracks walls formed the background for grisly fairy tales. Those eighteen months in the National People's Army had always seemed to me a black crossbar bolted across the entrance to real life.

My plan was to write about a sensitive young man's despair on being inducted, illustrated with memories of a dread of the army that went as far back as early childhood. There was no evading, no escaping the totalitarian force that would soon watch his every step. It would all conclude with my hero sitting, despondent and pale, in the kitchen over a cup of coffee, while his mother—yet another German mother forced to surrender her son—silently waited on him, her face turned aside so that he wouldn't see her tears.

To refresh your memory let me add: In the autumn of '81, Poland was on the verge of being placed under martial law. I had learned from a neighbor drafted a year before that his regiment had been armed with live ammunition since summer. Even the regimental commander, a colonel, had taken to wearing his field uniform, and the officers had adopted a previously unknown cordiality. He himself had been assigned to putting up additional information signs for reservists who were to be moved up into place.

This was grist for my mill, it lent wings to my imagination. I was afraid I would arrive too late, but all the same would gladly have put off induction day, because I was enjoying my life just as it was.

At the end of October, about ten days before my induction, something totally unexpected happened.

Geronimo wanted to see me one last time before I was consigned to barracks, as he put it. We had been seeing each other once a month. We had taken long hikes and bike tours to Schulpforta and Röcken.[1]

1. Schulpforta—among the famous students of the boarding school there were Klopstock, Fichte, Ranke, and Nietzsche. Röcken—Friedrich Nietzsche's birthplace; the philosopher's childhood home, the church where he was baptized, and his grave are located there.

The tension that I had felt at our first reunion still existed, however. I both longed for Geronimo and feared our meetings. I felt really at ease only when writing him letters.

He had asked that I not meet him at the train station this time, I was to wait for him at home. When the doorbell finally rang, it wasn't him who was standing there—but Franziska. I believed it was a miracle! Franziska had found out my address and had come to see me. Thank God I floundered so long for something to say, because Geronimo now stepped forward.

Although this suddenly explained everything, I was less dismayed than I was incredulous. I had never regarded Geronimo as a being who would be of any interest to women. And now, who but Franziska!

Despite all the displays of affection between them, I initially thought it was a joke. Was she using Geronimo? Didn't she belong to me instead, especially now that she could compare the two of us? Her presence in my room, her unhoped-for existence in the midst of the same world where I had dreamed of her, left no place for Geronimo.

At first, as they say, I only had eyes for her. And yet however unwilling I was to accept Geronimo as the vanishing point toward which her every move, her every word was directed, I ultimately couldn't avoid looking at him. And that changed everything!

Geronimo's smile was so full of bliss, his face so totally enraptured, that he reminded me of a sheep.

Have you ever felt the degrading desire to hurl yourself like the devil between two lovers?

"Johann!" I said like a doctor speaking to an unconscious man. "Johann!"

I wanted to slap him, rip his glasses off and smash them, pound my fist into his face, and he would just go on smiling his stupid smile, making sloppy kissing noises, and letting himself be smothered with hugs. Make love not war! "Johann!" He didn't even hear me now! I sat crouched there beside them, the forlorn outsider in my own room.

When he asked whether he and Franziska could spend the night here with us, it didn't bother me at all to refuse, and without offering them any reason, either. I proposed he sleep on an air mattress, just for him alone, beside my bed.

They stayed for supper and held hands even while they were eating. My mother insisted on hearing every detail of how they first met. And the two of them, caught up in an insufferable need to tell their story, didn't want to talk about anything else either.

Why was no one bothered by my silence, by the way I stared at my plate, a man turned to stone? They had already banned me from their society. It wasn't just the brutal egoism of lovers—no, they were all rehearsing life without me.

At least I could tell myself how lucky I was that my mother didn't invite them to stay the night. I can't remember a word of what was said as they left.

Johann had lured me into a trap, he had betrayed me. And I lay there whimpering his name into my pillow.

The next morning I found an envelope on the breakfast table. "Is it a novel?" my mother asked later. That was Johann's second betrayal. He hadn't said one word about the fact that he had begun writing too. Was Johann secretly at war with me?

That was on Sunday. If this were a soccer match, the announcer would say: The following is being shown uncut.

Monday had more bad news for me in its pocket.

In compliance with the induction committee's instructions, I had had a chest X-ray taken—not by an army doctor, but in the Friedrichstadt Hospital, where my mother worked. The results arrived in Monday's mail. I didn't even want to think of trying to decipher all that Latin and laid the envelope on my mother's kitchen chair, so she didn't discover it until we sat down for supper. Have you ever seen a familiar face reveal, from one moment to the next, the skull beneath it?

"It can't be!" she whispered.

"What can't be?" was all that I managed. Then I felt dizzy. A minute later I asked from the kitchen floor how many years I had left.

"Four or five," she said, rammed her feet into her street shoes, and called out: "But it can't be. This just can't be!" And pulled the apartment door closed behind her.

The cold floor felt good. I looked up at the ceiling lamp where dirt had collected in its glass bowl, at the hot-water tank with its solitary blue flame. It did good to fix my eyes on things that had never changed my whole life long. Four years! I had to turn my head to see the window. I gave the chipped corner of the windowsill a smile. Four years! There was my ineluctability for me. I had time for one book, maybe two. Wasn't the proximity of death the prerequisite for any and all creative work? Didn't everyone try to fake that proximity one way or the other? Four years! I pressed the sentence to me as if it were a promise, an agreement between God and me.

Almost an hour passed before my mother returned. She had ridden her bike to various phone booths, but it had been too late to reach anyone in the X-ray department. She smiled and wiped a handkerchief over her still-reddened face. The results were wrong, she said—a mistake, utter nonsense, otherwise I would barely have made it up the stairs.

"Did you hear me, Enrico? It's our chance. There's no army in the world that would take you with those results. The dear Lord himself wants it this way," she cried with joy.

I had never heard her use that expression. It wasn't just that her "dear Lord" annoyed me, all I wanted was to be left alone, alone with the things of this world that in an instant had become mine, all of them beautiful, all important.

The more euphoric her words—"You just bewail your fate a little, play the role"—the angrier I got. "Either I'm a conscientious objector, or I go like everyone else has to."

An hour later I was walking along the Elbe, which lay under a blanket of fog. "For all flesh is as grass," the Brahms *Requiem* boomed in my ear, "and all the glory of man as the flower of grass." How should I describe the state I was in? True, I was still the Old Adam who felt superior to Geronimo, and this was an experience that would set me apart from all other people. But beyond that, I was surprised, no, I was bowled over by the startling consolation that, whether dead or alive, I would remain on this earth. To die and rot did not mean to melt into nothingness, but rather, no matter what, to continue to be here, to continue in this world. The thought, insinuating itself as if in my sleep, calmed me. I don't mean to say that as I walked along I overcame my fear of death, and yet it felt very much like that. Every beautiful thing was suddenly beautiful, every ugly thing ugly, every good thing good. For a short while I escaped my own personal madness—and would no longer have to do anything! Every compulsion, every plan, every need to test my powers fell away from me.

On Tuesday I rode to the hospital with my mother and had a new X-ray taken. When I returned home, I wrote Geronimo. It was my last will and testament, a farewell in so many different ways. Every sentence was the main sentence. I wished him luck, I wished Franziska luck. I would have preferred to tell him all this face-to-face—I was ill, I was deathly ill, but I accepted my fate, I would bear it as the lot assigned me, move forward along my path step by step. I was impressed with myself. I made no mention of his manuscript.

I had to call my mother at noon on Wednesday, at which point I learned that the enlargement of my heart was not pathological, just the opposite, I had an athlete's heart. And in that moment my lucidity and insight vanished. Yes, I was angry at having lost so much time with all this ruckus, and could feel the old pettiness creeping back into my pores. But for a few moments I had experienced a strange clarity. And every word I write about it here is merely a pale reflection.

Wednesday, April 18, '90

Since I had been writing about my induction almost every day for over two months, November 4th was as intimate as a pen pal whose long-awaited visit I looked forward to with curiosity. Granted, there was hardly any time to compare my preconceptions with reality.

As expected, I slept poorly. My mother's behavior, however, bore only a distant resemblance to my previous description. We poured a lot of milk into our coffee so that we could drink it more quickly, and were silent. I was annoyed that she wanted to push me out the door much too early, and only as we said our good-byes were her eyes a little moist.

"Tomorrow," I quoted from my manuscript, "it won't seem half as bad." (In my novel the first day wasn't supposed to be bad, only all the days that followed.) My mother hugged me and gave me a farewell kiss on the brow, which made a very strong impression on me. I decided there and then to include this gesture in my departure scene.

The route that took me to the large Mitropa Hall, where we were supposed to assemble and which was at the far rear of Neustadt Station, reminded me of the evenings spent waiting for my grandparents to return from the West.

Suddenly I was aware of the hulking presence before me of our neighbor Herr Kaspareck. Evidently he was the officer in charge here and was patrolling among the chairs. He kept kicking at all the black bags that had to be removed from his path. Despite our civvies we were already prisoners.

I was astonished to see a pistol at Kaspareck's belt. Years before he had chased after me because we had been playing soccer outside his windows on a Sunday. Now he could take his revenge.

I assigned to Herr Kaspareck the role of the Herald of Evil. He hadn't greeted me, he had stumbled over the stretched-out legs of an inductee who had fallen asleep, and Kaspareck's well-placed blow to the calves had almost pitched the fellow from his chair.

Every observation here would be of use, material for improving on my first draft.

A patrol unit, whose white patent-leather belts and straps reminded me of the harness on circus horses—a comparison that came to mind by way of *Animal Farm*—dragged a drunk past, a man in despair, sobbing his wife's name. Or was he calling for his mother? Like dogs returning a stick, they dropped him between two chairs. He lay there whimpering. Two members of the patrol lifted him up by the shoulders, about even with their hips—were they trying to see his face?—tugged him a little more to the right and then, counting inaudibly to three, dumped him again. Their aim was good. His front teeth were knocked out on the edge of a chair. They immediately pulled him up from the floor and inspected their work. One of them shouted that they'd evidently netted a little Dracula. The other four grinned. The silence in the Mitropa Hall was impenetrable. In the same way that by stretching out their legs after Kaspareck's attack, the inductees had made him stalk his way through the room like a stork through underbrush, so now their silence closed in around these traitors and came close to suffocating them.

These kind of scenes formed in my mind all on their own, as if I had finally found the beanpole on which my fantasy could entwine itself and grow. But as I'm sure you know: our inventions are never brutal and nasty enough, exaggeration makes its home in reality, and somewhere—of that much I was and still am certain—this or some similar scene had occurred.

As you can see, I felt from the start that I'd come to the right place. Here was the perfect dose of callousness and inevitability that had been lacking until then.

Watched over like convicts, we climbed the stairs to the train platform, and I listened closely to the orders, which needed to be decoded according to tone, pitch, and intensity.

Our cars were shunted several times back and forth across the Marien

Bridge. The Canaletto panorama with the Hofkirche and the Brühlsche Terrace[1] was the last thing I wanted to see at that point.

Naturally I would have preferred an escort of uniformed men, plus a phalanx of plainclothes men barricading me as I climbed aboard a train for West Berlin—where, surrounded by photographers and cameramen, I would then begin my new life. But that triumph presumed that here and now I had to fall in, buzz cut and all. Before I could display my treasures, I would have to enter the underworld and have a look around.

When we finally pulled out and passed through Radebeul—my mother and father had wandered those vineyards together, and later Vera and I, and once Geronimo and I, had strolled there too—I was for a few moments the dissident writer who was being exiled by his government, who would never be allowed to return to his hometown, who would be consoled by a speech given in his honor by Heinrich Böll[2] or Willy Brandt. I gazed from the window and formulated the first sentences of my acceptance speech, an indictment that would leave no comrade unaware of what a huge mistake it had been to banish me.

Now began a veritably endless circuitous trip. A farm boy from Upper Lusatia treated our compartment to home-butchered sausage, because he was afraid—thanks to some remark by a noncom—that he would soon be relieved of his provisions. He himself ate liverwurst, neat. He became a hero when he pulled underwear out of his bag and peeled it away to reveal a bottle of high-proof whiskey.

My new comrades made fun of the Brandenburg landscape, which had always been my Arcadia, called it a sand and pine desert. In late afternoon we arrived—sober and a little more familiar with one another—in Oranienburg, which lies to the north of what was then West Berlin.

On the way from the train station to our barracks I was annoyed that no one turned around to watch us pass.

As if on command, a hundred feet suddenly kicked at piles of leaves by the side of the road, scuffled around in them, sent leaves spiraling and drifting ahead, scooped them against the heels of the man in front, over

---

1. Bernardo Bellotto, (called Canaletto), 1721–80, painted many views of the city of Dresden. T. evidently means the famous painting *Dresden From the Right Bank of the Elbe Below the Augustus Bridge* (1748).

2. Heinrich Böll had given a speech in praise of Reiner Kunze on the occasion of his being awarded the Büchner Prize in 1977, the same year in which he left the GDR.

the shoes of the man beside, scattered them in all directions. No command, no barked order told us to stop. The rebellion didn't end until there were no more piles of leaves. The yowls of those with six and more months already behind them were silly by comparison. They flung windows open and roared the number of days they still had left, as if in this country service in the army could ever come to an end, as if they didn't know that at any moment they could always be stuck in a uniform again and imprisoned in a barrack. With a boom the gate slammed shut behind us . . .

At the rear of the base, between a frame structure and the House of Culture, you could see the building that marked what had once been the entrance to Sachsenhausen concentration camp.

I later wrote a long passage about how we stood there with our bags in the drizzle while we watched one company after another march into the mess hall for supper, about how we were vaccinated, made to fill out questionnaires and to wait until we were soaked to the skin. It was almost nine o'clock, an hour before lights out, before I was sent along with some others to a building that abutted the camp watchtower.

Although we had to stand for another hour in the entry as if at a pillory, the sparkling clean red floors and freshly painted walls had a calming effect on me. I wanted to get out of my wet clothes and, yes, I was looking forward to a dry uniform! The room assigned me came equipped with just two bunk beds—but looked comfortable. Pasted on the top bunk on the right was a slip of paper with the typewritten words: Private Türmer.

My only fear was that I wouldn't be able to make a mental note of everything I saw, heard, and smelled. I couldn't let any of it be lost.

At the sound of the wake-up whistle the next morning I jumped out of bed as if about to leave on an expedition. Morning gymnastics and breakfast were canceled for us late arrivals. Instead they threw at our feet a piece of canvas that could be buttoned up into a sack. With it in hand we shuffled through supply rooms. A steel helmet, a new and an old pair of boots, three uniforms (standard, dress, field), protective gear, gas mask, gym shoes, tracksuit—I accepted it all like a miner being outfitted. I was going down into the pit to uncover hidden treasures.

At the midday meal, as I was hungrily wolfing down my Königsberger meatballs, a big stocky fellow farther down the long table stood up and shouted that the only reason he could stomach this slop was that this was the first food he'd been fed here. Tomorrow he was going to dump this slop over the head of the sergeant at the end of the table.

I pressed my last bit of potato into the gravy—and was thrilled. My first character had just revealed himself to me, a combination of Thersites and Ajax.[1] I wasn't going to let him out of my sight.

That afternoon as we were packing up our own stuff, I inserted among the damp clothes a greeting to my mother and an envelope addressed to Geronimo. Inside it were three pages of jotted notes, with a 1 at the top, then a slash, followed by a page number. I asked him to collect and save these rough sketches. I started on 2 immediately afterward.

My mother still talks today about the moment when she opened the package and found my clothes inside—"as if you had died."

Enough for today. As always warmest greetings from
Your Enrico T.

Friday, April 20, '90

Verotchka,[2]

So that we don't waste our telephone time: Roland was here. He's on a lecture tour of the East. The Party of Democratic Socialism is allowing him to appear only in small towns. But what he loves to talk about most is you, as if you had left for the West because of him.

If I understood Roland correctly, he's soon going to have to look around for a new job. Not even universities have any use for his theories now. He of course put it differently: just when for the very first time we're going to need to give serious thought to socialism/communism, they're going to terminate his position. I asked him who he meant by we. The oppressed and disenfranchised, people dying of hunger and thirst, people who've been driven from their homes, who've been raped and have no roof over their heads, he replied without a hint of irony.

Then he laid into the New Forum for having acted so irresponsibly, for being so naive and childish, as if they had never heard of capitalism.

1. Figures in Homer's *Iliad*.
2. This letter was sent to V. T. by fax.

And now we can sit back and watch it all get smashed, everything that distinguished it "over against capitalism."

It's pointless to argue with him, I knew that beforehand. He has a knack for constantly maneuvering you into corners where you start justifying yourself all on your own. For him I was somebody from the New Forum, which, whether it intended to or not, had sold out the GDR to capitalists.

He wasn't interested in our paper. At least there used to be nothing in our newspapers, he said; nowadays they're just full of nonsense. In the very next sentence he claimed I wouldn't publish anything about his lecture—"presumably for reasons of space." When I asked him why he would accuse me of that, he mocked me, saying he could see my article already before him. I was speechless. And Roland's reaction: he'd always admired reactionaries, the way they fall silent the moment something doesn't suit them, they trust in the way things are, in the power of factuality, so why argue? I asked him whether he now regarded me as a reactionary. He laughed—I'd always been one! Unlike the people from the Party of Democratic Socialism, he has no guilty feelings and sees himself as totally above it all. That's what annoyed me most.

He would probably only be satisfied if I printed his lecture in full, starting on the front page—anything else is censorship. But how do you write about someone who uses the concept of democracy, bourgeois democracy, so cleverly that even a child would have to believe it's something suspicious, yes, despicable.

Roland claimed that his final triumphant *volte*—in which he praised Schalck-Golodkowski as the last internationalist, who was keeping Communist publishing houses and Party headquarters alive in the West, and concluded by calling November 9th the victory of counterrevolution—was an embarrassment to the cadres of the old Socialist Unity Party. They were afraid his lecture would become known to a wider public.

The Soviet Union, the socialist states, he went on, had been the only power in the world that had kept capitalism in check. We, in the East, had been the guarantors that capitalism in the West had worn a human face. But that was all over now. I would see. I would remember what he'd said when the state and its citizens were nothing, and the economy and consumerism were everything, when we'd all have to pay for kindergartens and universities, yes, probably have to pay to die.

Roland doesn't shy away from any exaggeration. Actually what he'd like is to return to the situation in which it was impossible to know anything about capitalism.

Ilona's husband, a former comrade, returned from Bayreuth floating on cloud nine because he'd been able quickly and without any fuss to find trousers that fit him, so that Ilona won't once again have to shorten the cuffs. The comforting reassurance that his body is evidently not abnormal made a convert out of him. You can regard that as ridiculous, and I didn't risk telling Roland about it either, but I understand Ilona's husband. I believe he's found happiness, a happiness that Roland can only scorn as a sign of bedazzlement and corruptibility.

Isn't it a crime to say: You're not allowed to see the Mediterranean— or only when you're old and gray and can't work anymore? Ah, enough of all this! I'm sounding like Michaela, who's forever getting high on the fantasy of running into her former teachers and professors and confronting them. As if she hadn't learned in the theater by now just how pointless that is—pointless, because you can't demand shame and contrition.

But of course I also admire Roland. If only for his vitality, the way he loves to talk, to argue, for his extravagance (and by that I don't mean just his belts, the swing in his hips, and that silk scarf). He's a brilliant logician, unafraid of consequences. Yes, I admire him for his courage, but it's a pernicious logic, not to say lethal.

I told him about how Mamus was arrested and what happened in Dresden last fall. Even while I spoke I was annoyed with myself for using her arrest as an argument, because it suddenly made me sound so self-serving. At least he didn't try to invent justifications for it or go so far as to cast it in doubt. He expressed his disgust, but then couldn't refrain from suggesting that I ask you about Shatila and Badra,[1] and then asked me about what happened in Greece or Spain, in Argentina and Uruguay.[2] And there they were again: Victor Jara's hacked-off hands.[3]

1. Refugee camps near Beirut. In 1982, after the invasion by the Israeli army, massacres of Palestinian refugees were carried out by the Christian militias.
2. Countries that had had military dictatorships.
3. The putsch by Chilean General Pinochet on September 11, 1973, led to mass arrests. Many of those arrested were tortured and murdered; about three thousand died. The singer and songwriter Victor Jara's hands were crushed, but not hacked off, before he was shot.

Why doesn't he want to live in a world that is halfway decent, why must it always be struggle, suffering, dying? You, my dear Heinrich—I hear you say—you yourself should know the answer to that better than anyone. Because for people like Roland it's not about living in a pleasant world, but about remaining productive. And for that they accept the rest as part of the bargain: revolution, chaos, death. That's why Roland has to view November 9th as a work of counterrevolution. How could he go on writing otherwise? Well, let them all put their Budyonny caps[1] back on. You'd think there could be no end to the desperation of people like Roland, because history has hurled them back a hundred years, because their whole proletarian hoopla, all those millions of victims that they bore like an indictment on their banners, will now become as meaningless as those other millions of victims who were slain in the name of their own false gods. But that's not the case. His eyes shine more brightly than ever. Are they fools? Maniacs? No matter what happens in the world—they hold on tight to their divine mission. I'm sorry, I'm repeating myself. Roland and his comrades are simply tiresome. In fact it gives me great satisfaction to see their tap turned off just like that and to watch them have to start looking for work like everyone else. We send greetings to the comrades of the German Communist Party for the last time! But let's not waste so much anger, so much energy and emotion on them. They interpret everything that has to do with them—even if you spit at their feet—as a badge of their importance. Roland is completely right to view me as a reactionary. Isn't it marvelous to hold tight to factuality, to fall silent, to smile?

How much does he actually know about us?

Love, Your H.

PS: Strangely enough, he got along famously with your friend Barrista. Barrista calls Lenin and Luxemburg terrorists, for Roland they're revolutionaries. But in terms of their "analysis" Roland and Barrista were in agreement and blamed all the evils of the world on German reactionaries, who always first create for themselves whatever it is they then take up arms against.

---

1. Budyonny—a general in the cavalry of the Red Army during the Russian Civil War. Isaac Babel—famous for his short-story collection, *Red Cavalry*—served under Budyonny.

With Roland, however, I'm not certain if he wouldn't line us all up and shoot us if he were told to do it in the name of the revolution. There's probably no danger of that in Barrista's case.

PS II: I had a dream about Mamus. She's at a spa for her health and I'm supposed to renovate the apartment. Nothing's been done in preparation; she didn't even take the pictures down. I look everywhere for brushes, buckets, paint. To no avail. But in the cellar I find Neudel's painting equipment, which he had given me to wash out the last time around, but now the paint in the can is hard as stone, there's a round brush stuck in it for good. When I try to push the wall unit toward the middle of the room, the Georgian vase falls off. But Mamus snatches it with one hand, as if she were doing the beer-coaster trick. She wants to know what I think I'm doing. At that moment I realize I've made a mistake. The woman who told me to do the renovation wasn't Mamus at all. Just look around, Mamus says, pointing with a very grand gesture at the walls. They are in fact white, freshly painted white. And outside—she points to the window—there's a blanket of snow. It glistens so dazzlingly that the building across the street is invisible. Mamus tells me to stand in front of the mirror so that I can finally see what I look like now.

Saturday, April 21, '90

Dear Nicoletta,

I sometimes think I'm way too fainthearted. But then I think of how you cautioned the taxi driver to drive less recklessly. I took pleasure in your every gesture. Sometimes I clap my hand to my brow as if I might still find your hand there, when you were checking to see if I was feverish. And I see your other hand hastily buttoning up your coat. And that's supposed to have been six weeks ago now?

Within the first few days in the army it was clear: Hell looks different. I was glad to know that, but also disappointed. There were lots of whistles and shouts ordering us around, we were cursed and ridiculed, but it was all just a big show. Besides, as part of the pack your hide gets tougher. Of course, it wasn't pleasant to run in protective gear and a gas mask or do push-ups in a puddle. All the same I put on weight at first, because as trainees to drive an armored personnel carrier (APC) we had almost nothing but political instruction at the start. Except for the room corporals, who were our driving instructors, we were all newcomers, which helped keep stunts by those who had already served six months or more to a minimum. Even when you had room duty, there was still time to read and write.

We were sworn in at the Sachsenhausen Concentration Camp Memorial, where, so we were instructed, antifascists of some eighteen countries had been murdered. During the ceremony we faced the obelisk with eighteen red triangles at its tip—created, it would seem, to help us count off our eighteen-month stint.

I tried to capture as much of daily life as possible. Military jargon, every *terminus technicus*, fascinated me. I was the only one who kept his brochures on "Being a Soldier," which appeared monthly, each time in a new color. I often took down conversations in shorthand—dialogue was my weak point.

In early December we had six days of home leave, the so-called rest and recreation we were supposed to get every six months. Vera and I borrowed a Škoda and toured almost every castle, fortress, and church between Meissen and Görlitz, then sat for hours smoking and drinking gin and tonic (if it could be had) in cafés filled with older women.

Instead of being horrified at the sight of her son in uniform, my mother thought I was "a hoot." My description of general conditions and the daily routine had reassured her. She could see how well nourished I was.

Vera, however, wept when it was time to say good-bye. I had forbidden her to accompany me to the train station, I didn't want her to see me in uniform.

But why couldn't we—or at least hardly any of us newcomers—sleep until six each morning? I would lie awake for a good while, listening to footsteps in the hall, to the clatter of the metal grill at the entrance, and held the illuminated dial of my watch up to my eye, as if afraid of oversleeping. The seconds before the wake-up whistle were counted down by beeps from a radio turned up loud.

Once outside, doing calisthenics in the dark—followed by a run that turned into an incredible farting contest—I soon forgot my restlessness.

If an alert had been declared, the morning wait was worse. Officers in full uniform and smelling of aftershave blocked our access to the toilet, while noncoms drove us out of our quarters. Nothing but shouting, clanging, rattling on all sides, as if a huge hunting party were being organized. We ran outside and then along the road in front of the barracks, as far as regimental staff headquarters, then back again, where we finally had to fall in and undergo an endless inspection of our equipment.

On December 13th,[1] however, an alert roused us out of our sleep. This time the whole regiment was throbbing. The noncoms, who couldn't get into their clothes any faster than we could, didn't want to believe what had happened and hesitated before opening the weapons store. Only after companies from the floors above us fell in did we get ourselves ready—bringing the chaos on the regimental streets to its zenith. I breathed in the exhaust from tanks that came clanking along the concrete slab road. Spotlights everywhere, an unrelenting din, columns of vehicles. I boarded our APC as if it were a cold-started ark. I felt neither fear nor opposition, nothing that could have prevented me from taking part in this decampment. On the contrary: even those of us at the bottom of the totem pole couldn't help viewing the alert as a grand spectacle. We crouched beneath closed hatches, peering out through the embrasures and hoping that we could move out without officers.[2] They were the chickenshits this time.

No sooner had we left the base than we turned off the highway. For two hours we followed country roads and woodland lanes. We kept banging our helmets against the vehicle roof. Some guys didn't know what else to do, so they pissed into their mess kit.

As it began to turn light, we climbed out and camouflaged our vehicles. We were standing at the edge of a clearing. The staff sergeant on the APC in front of us was fumbling with the antenna of a black Stern recorder, attempting to adjust it. Since this evidently didn't work, he grabbed the apparatus in both arms and spun in a circle like a dancer. We didn't learn anything from him. Gunther, a pale towheaded Saxon, who for a waiter moved with a peculiarly wooden gait and grimaced with zeal

1. On Dec. 13, 1981, the Polish military, under the leadership of General Jaruzelski, declared martial law throughout Poland and banned the independent labor union, Solidarność. T. evidently assumed that N. H. would recognize the significance of "December 13th."

2. Unless on duty, officers slept at home and first had to make their way to the base.

during every drill, held his "Micki" radio up to his ear and immediately began spouting off in a whiny falsetto. What a piece of shit, and now of all times. Hadn't he always said that they'd do better to work instead of rocking the boat, that got you nowhere, nowhere, everybody knew that, but now here we were getting mixed up in their shit. Then came the words "Polacks" and "lazy Polacks."

I realized that what I had wished for had now come true. Every hour on the hour Gunther stomped off into the woods. The first snowfall hadn't melted—a Christmas landscape with evergreens and animal tracks. Ten minutes later he would return cursing. Instead of the latest news from Radio Free Berlin, however, he treated us to cock-and-bull stories about what all he had experienced with the Poles. When the noon meal turned out to be roulades and red cabbage, with canned peach halves for dessert, there was no longer any doubt about the seriousness of the situation. Word was that the corporal had brought boxes of ammunition with him. Our convoy leader was the first one to pass around a picture of his wife. When it came my turn, I produced Vera's photograph.

As night came on it turned bitter cold. Our APC was a cave of ice. We tried to keep warm by passing around hot tea—of which there was plenty—and doing knee bends. A few men sparred with each other. The hands on my watch had evidently frozen. At one point we tried lying down, packed man to man, on the ground in the woods, but that didn't last long. I kept fingering my pants leg pocket, checking for my notebook—my amulet.

The order to remount, which came shortly after midnight, was a lifesaver. The main thing was that the engines actually started. We'd been underway for about ten minutes when our lieutenant ordered me to get out and threw two flags down to me, which I was to use to guide our APC. I ran along a wall ahead of the APC. My feet were like stumps; I could hear their plunk, plunk, plunk against the concrete slabs. Amazingly enough I kept my balance. We passed a large gate—and it was only then that I recognized our barracks.

The strangest thing about this alert was the silence after our return. I didn't hear any noise coming from the companies in the floors above us either. Men just set a stool down out in the hall and cleaned their weapon, noncoms did the same, and officers vanished without a sound. People made tea in their quarters, shuffled along in their underwear and down-at-the-heel gym shoes, and took their Kalashnikovs back to the weapons store, sort of like returning a spade to its shed.

That night I heard a cricket chirp. At first I thought I was hallucinating or that it was radio static. Maybe silence had lured the cricket from its lair by the furnace in the cellar and it had now taken up residence under our locker.

I've never read a single one of the over two hundred army letters I wrote to Geronimo. Whether they could help me describe those days for you better than I've been able to do so far is neither here nor there. It seems more important for me to observe that my memories of those weeks are wrapped in vagueness.

Just as martial law in Poland provided a *post festum* reason—beyond just personal irritability—for my restlessness before the wake-up whistle, I consider what happened to me at Christmas to be further proof that my frame of mind over the previous week and a half had been more than a mere mood.

On December 14th, the day after the big alert, my idyllic world fell apart. I slept above Knut, our driver and room corporal, a conspicuously short, but powerful, man, a weightlifter in one of the lightweight categories. His girlfriend had jilted him shortly after his induction, which did not, however, prevent him from constantly raving about her. Knut neither wrote nor received letters; once a month there was a package from his mother.

It was ten thirty, and so the beginning of quiet time. Gunter and Matthias, a bowlegged amiable fish-head,[1] were talking about what you could eat, or just in general, what you would have to do to get ill very quickly and land in the infirmary. Not that I would have made any use of their knowledge, but their conversation sounded very helpful. Dialogue was, as I've said, my weak point. I kept notes. The light was still on and Knut wasn't in the room. Writing in bed meant that the next morning, in the same three minutes we had to get dressed and go to the john, I would have to cram the pages in an envelope, address and stamp it, and then hope we would pass by a mailbox during our morning run, so that I could dash to one side, slip the secret message out of my workout jacket, and send it on its way.

Knut loved to slap at door handles and give doors a kick so that they

---

1. Pejorative Saxon slang for people who live on the Baltic coast.

would fly open and bang against the wall. It was annoying, but who was going to stop him. Knut played the major again this time, looked at me over the top of his glasses, and switched the light out. I hadn't expected anything else, finished my sentence blind, and caught a whiff of Knut's beery breath as he undressed. He tossed back and forth, the bunk frame shook and squeaked, followed by quiet, as if he had found his sleeping position. I was just signing off when I was bounced in the air, once, twice. If somebody kicks a mattress from below with both feet, the guy on top is as helpless as a beetle on its back. I held tight to the frame.

When things had quieted down, I leaned down out of bed and offered some curse or other—and he kicked again. This time I lost my balance. I wasn't hurt, it was almost like a landing off the parallel bars, softened as well by my blanket, which had slipped off first. I aimed an angry kick at Knut.

We stood there screaming at each other in the dark. He landed a couple of his blows. When the light went on, he was holding his side too. I had committed sacrilege. I knew I had.

As I went to fold up my letter the next morning, a page was missing. Even though I soon ceased to attribute any importance to the loss, I found myself feeling odd somehow. Everything about me, the sweat in my armpits and between my legs, the odor of my socks or the stain on my uniform, all of it suddenly seemed precious because it was part of me. I wanted to hide myself in my body, I was about to wrap myself in my cocoon.

In the last letter from my mother that had got through—a stop had been put on mail before Christmas—she seemed transformed. Even though I had written nothing to her about the alert, she felt guilty and was tormented by self-accusations. If she hadn't interfered I would, she felt sure, have filed as a conscientious objector, and in the light of December 13th, that could no longer be regarded as a stupid move or a matter of false heroics, but maybe the only way to save oneself. She had read all of Arnold Zweig's novels, and yet she no longer understood herself. She had evidently forgotten our argument about the X-ray.

And now I will attempt to describe an event that I've kept absolutely silent about until now. Not even Vera knows about it.

On Christmas Eve, of all days—we had had to spend the whole day cleaning—I was feeling better again. Half of those with more than six months' service were on leave, Knut had stayed in hope of spending New

Year's at home. He claimed his mattress kicks were meant to toughen me up, or just for fun. It was my own fault if I didn't get the joke. I had decided I wanted to rework chapter one and planned to read Steinbeck's *Grapes of Wrath,* which I had bought in the regimental bookstore.

After supper a couple soldiers sang Christmas carols out in the hall. I stayed in my room and wrote Geronimo about how strange it felt to be all alone, if only for a few minutes. I felt as if I were playing hooky somehow, that's how odd solitude had come to seem.

A few minutes later the door was flung open, and I had to shake off a sense of being caught red-handed. It looked as if half the company had come for a visit. My first impulse was to stand up, but I thought better of it. A kick to my stool brought me to my feet. Knut demanded I report in, he ordered me to get dressed in regulation uniform and report in to Pit, the only DC left in our company. (DC means discharge candidate—that is, the only man left who was in the last six months of his eighteen-month stint.) I could see men out in the hall rubbernecking and jumping up and down. I asked what he wanted.

Then someone grabbed me from behind, pressing my arms against my body. I was totally helpless. I thought that by not defending myself I might maintain what little dignity is left in such a situation. I was hoisted up several times, but remained on my feet. My locker was open wide. Knut flung my boots at my knees. He bellowed. I was let go of.

I put on my strap and belt and saluted, saluted slowly, with a smile. Knut demanded a confession, that I plead guilty. The guy who had grabbed hold of me—my Ajax-Thersites—pushed me from behind. When I turned around he yelled at me to look straight ahead. But all that quickly proved irrelevant once I saw a page of my handwriting in Knut's hand. Even before Gunther and Matthias stepped forward, it was clear to me what was going on here.

Cursing me and my lousy penmanship, Knut haltingly read aloud what I had jotted down that evening. After each sentence he asked: "Did you say that?"—"Yes, I said that," either Gunter or Matthias would reply. "Yes, I said that." The jabs in the side, the knuckles to the head, the shoves—I could have endured it all, if each of them had not been accompanied by that one word: Spy! Everyone said it, "Spy! A spy!" Knut didn't leave out a single sentence. The whole production was working only too well. "Yes, I said that!" Knut had become a magician. He pulled the strings. Even those with whom I was on good terms, with whom I had even made fun of Knut, were yelling, "Spy! Spy!" And they waited for something to finally happen.

Did they really think that's what a spy's report looked like? Only I could answer that question, Knut shouted. All he wanted to hear was why and for whom I had written all this. Someone else slapped my head.

Because I'm a writer, because I'm working on a book about the army. Why didn't I admit it?

"Louder!" Knut shouted. "I wanted to give my friend a true impression of army life," I repeated—every word a thrust of the knife. I had given up, I played along, I wasn't even going to try to convince them. In a certain sense I even admired Knut. Raking a spy over the coals—a scene I would love to have invented myself.

Pit, who showered with a hose in the washroom every day and then came prancing down the hall with wet hair slicked back, a ruddy face, the hose over his shoulder—this same Pit crowed: What was the point of discussion, it was clear as day—a spy!

But Knut wasn't finished. What sort of friend was that who I was writing to, the same sort of friend maybe as the girlfriend I had tried to palm off on them?

Someone grabbed hold of me again. Gunther and Matthias should be the first to "give it to him." My Ajax-Thersites helped them out of their quandary by throwing me to the floor. I fell on my back. "Get his balls!" somebody shouted. I felt nothing.

I'll spare you what happened next. You and me. The whole time I was amazed at how they did it just right, that they instinctively knew how to utterly humiliate someone. Maybe their aim was also so good because they were acting in good conscience, because nobody could have anything against punishing a spy. That is, there was one person, but I didn't learn about that until later.

Knut's one mistake was that he went too far. My chastisement lasted too long. And along with a renewed awareness of pain, my rage returned as well—and a euphoric sense of freedom. I had nothing left to lose!

Shortly thereafter I was ordered to potato-peeling duty. There I sat on an upturned crate in the tiled storeroom of the kitchen complex, peeling away and listening to what my fellow ostracized soldiers had to say. At that point I would have instantly agreed to spend the next sixteen months peeling potatoes twelve hours a day. I was assigned one penalty duty after the other. All the same, I was happy not to have to spend my free time with my company.

Since I had almost no time left to write, I jotted my notes sitting on the toilet—hurried catchwords, punctuation reduced to dashes. It was Geronimo who congratulated me for starting the new year with a unique, unmistakable style. Strangely enough, I no longer woke up before the wake-up whistle.

My silence precluded any attempt to approach me. I ignored apologies. I didn't even deign a word of reply to the noncom who confided to me that certain people hadn't notified me in the kitchen when my mother had come for a visit—he named the guilty parties and offered to be a witness on my behalf. The only part of the cake my mother left behind that found its way to me was a shopping net and an empty spring-form pan.

In a certain sense it was a comfortable role for me: I no longer had to show consideration for anyone. I ignored Knut's orders. On the same day that he tossed all my underwear out of my locker, his blanket ended up on the floor. I was prepared for anything, including a long guerilla war.

Monday, April 23, '90

It was at the end of March, on a Sunday, that Nikolai entered our room, and my life. Nikolai had the most striking physiognomy in our entire company. The tip of his long narrow nose pointed straight down, so that his face was reminiscent of a ram's. His father was an Armenian; his mother, a Berliner, who later married a German. Nikolai was a very good runner, was one of the fastest on the obstacle course, and wanted to stay on in our company as a driving instructor. His uniform fit as if tailor-made. You always thought he was on duty because even in the evening and on weekends he ran around dressed as per regulation. When he halted in front of me, removed his cap, and asked if he could sit down, I assumed he was about to announce that he was an emissary on an important mission.

His request, he admitted, was a little unusual, but he would pay well: two packs of Club cigarettes. In return I was to write a birthday letter, three or four pages, not for him, but for Ulf Salwitzky. His wife's birthday was coming up, but Salwitzky hadn't been able to put a single word to paper. I could probably ask for more, but he, Nikolai, figured two packs was about right for starters.

I was pleased by the businesslike nature of the proposal, although I really didn't need the reimbursement. Vera was modeling again and making enough money to supplement my army pay (110 marks) whenever necessary.[1]

"All you need is your pen," Nikolai said, and got up. A "junior"—that is, in his second six-month stint—Ulf Salwitzky was waiting for me in the club room with a writing tablet and some photos lying in front of him.

Nikolai sat down two tables away, pulled a bundle of colored pencils from his pants leg pocket, and began to sketch. Frau Salwitzky had a strikingly small upper lip. Her dimples showed when she smiled.

As if I had been doing this all my life, I sat down across from him and asked him to tell me about her. Salwitzky sniffed and shrugged. "We've been married," he said, "for two years now."

What did she like best, I asked, ready to take notes.

"First from behind, panties pulled down, in the kitchen or in the bathroom, the bed's not her thing," Salwitzky said, sitting as still as if he were getting a haircut. I was to start in, he wanted to see if I was any good. He didn't think it was right to have to talk to me about it. What was there to understand, he snapped, he wanted me to describe a fuck, from behind, no fancy stuff.

"And what's her name?" I asked. Before I started I had him describe their one-bedroom apartment for me.

I had half an hour, and then I was to read it to him. Ulf Salwitzky bent forward and added a few remarks of his own—"ass slapping, include ass slapping!" for example. The whole time he rocked his head back and forth. It turned out he knew what worked. He liked the way Kerstin didn't even have time to put the bouquet in a vase, so that the bouquet became a prop, at first disruptive, but then adding unexpected spice to things. Salwitzky filled me in about the next position. Nikolai wanted to know if I was planning to do it "with bouquet" too.

After an hour I gave Salwitzky my pages to copy. Nikolai's sketch showed drops of sweat flying off Kerstin's bobbing breasts. Her whole body was surrounded by sound waves—one, two, or three curves, depending on the intensity of the motion. Salwitzky wasn't prettified

1. Evidently T. considered her support a matter of course.

either, but the realism with which Nikolai had drawn his compressed lips or the way the body tapered to the shoulders only made the scene more believable. Only in the last sketch did Salwitzky's face take on a Gojko Mitić radiance.[1]

Ulf Salwitzky stacked five packs of Clubs on the table and departed without a word. Nikolai gave me a nod, put his cap on, and left two packs behind.

I now learned what it means to become famous overnight, even though I was overshadowed by Nikolai. Like a ballad-monger Salwitzky had moved from room to room, showing everyone the sketches and reading my letter. We had our next job that afternoon, and by evening we were booked for the rest of the week.

Nikolai was the star and I was his assistant. Nikolai met with our clients, arranged the terms, and made appointments. And each time he would ask for my assistance and offer me the same cordial thanks for helping him out.

With equal pride and bewilderment Ulf Salwitzky handed us his wife's letter, which concluded with her holding her husband's penis in her hand.

As discharge day for the oldest class grew closer and closer, we had more and more to do. Nikolai in particular was working to the point of exhaustion. And it goes without saying that we were freed from other duties. Knut had to stand sentry instead of me.

Once discharge day was behind us, Nikolai and I were given day leave. He had arranged it for us and informed me no one else would be on "furlough," as he called it, which meant the pubs wouldn't be too overcrowded. For me it was all uncharted territory.

We strode side by side not saying a word. The walk into town was endless. It was an odd situation; I felt as if I were at his mercy. Yes, I was annoyed at Nikolai's presumptuous way of taking charge of things.

He invited to pay for my dinner at a pub called Gambrinus, and ordered steaks smothered in onions and cheese, a specialty of the house. I insisted on a beer.

Nikolai tried to get a conversation going. First he talked about our prices and then about how we didn't need to accept every job. Then he

---

1. Gojko Mitić was famous for his roles as an Indian chief in GDR films. For a long time he was considered the epitome of male beauty. T. is assuming that N. H. knows who he was.

spoke about his own plans. After discharge he wanted to go to Armenia, to see his father, who was an artist. "That's what I want too," he said.

"What?" I asked.

"To be an artist," he replied—and looked like a wise sheep.

"And I want to be a writer!" I grinned as if I had cracked a joke.

"I know," he said, raising his chin. "You should have said that much earlier on."

"That wouldn't have helped," I replied, and was angry because by saying it I was admitting he had guessed my thoughts and quite possibly had understood the whole situation at the time.

"I was waiting for you to open your mouth. Knut is the spy."

"Why Knut?" I asked.

"Everyone knew about it, days ahead, don't you see—it happened by prearrangement. If you really had been a spy, you would have been rescued. But evidently it suited the higher-ups . . ." Nikolai looked around, as if searching for a waiter.

"But what do you mean you were waiting?" I asked. He moved the glass he had been about to drink from away from his lips, raised it, and said, "I would have confirmed your account, would have said that we'd talked about it before and that you had told me about writing a story . . ." His upper lip twitched. "I felt sorry for you," he went on, "but given how stupidly you acted—a person could almost believe you wanted it that way." He didn't respond to my laugh. Then he gazed at me—arrogant, sad, wise, prepared for any deed, and ready to meet his fate. Compared to him, Geronimo was a crude child.

Our food arrived, and Nikolai began to talk about other things. He wasn't going to be a driver, but was taking over the job of poster painter, which had just opened up, with his own workshop and the whole shebang. He invited me to visit him the next day, or whenever I wanted, to visit him in his studio. But my decision had already been made: I was not going to tolerate him in my presence anymore.

Enrico

Dear Jo,

We've moved, and I'm living on the high seas! The floor covering they nailed over the planks was a remnant out of Fred's treasure trove, and its waves roll higher and higher each day and have turned the oil radiator into a boat that dances up and down whenever I move it around the desk from my feet to my back. That's the price for my medieval view.

Our would-be visitors often find themselves before a locked house door, because the old couple above us—they've allegedly lived together unmarried for forty years now—can't be convinced not to lock up whenever they leave or enter the building. She in particular, Frau Käfer—everyone calls her Käferchen[1]—is a busy little key beaver. Ilona has developed a knack—even in the middle of a conversation and with the windows closed—for hearing someone rattling the door. Whoever does finally risk the stairs up to our office finds himself in a bright reception room—with plants everywhere, which are supposed to distract attention from the shabby Stasi furniture.

Fred has had signs painted on the doors, SALES OFFICE, for example, and written up a list of rules for each room. In my room, I am to note the following: "No more than two people at a time! No jumping, no stomping! Oil radiator, maximum level 2! Upon leaving: turn off lights, unplug all plugs! Close windows!" His final instruction: "No smoking!"—to which he added a handwritten "at least try"—"Danger of fire!"

Yesterday when I joined Fred in a visit to speak with the man from the hardware store—we have to install a new circuit in my room—and asked him to show us the back rooms, they saw my request as the transparent pretext of a spy. "We ain't got nothin' to hide," the boss exclaimed, "if you want to . . . please . . . do whatever you want . . ." And dashed ahead of us. My courtesy didn't help counter his suspicion. Just the opposite. Each of my questions seemed highly open to misunderstanding, even to me. Finally, as we were leaving the storeroom, his wife blocked the way. There were tears in her eyes as she announced that she wanted "to get some things straight here," because I probably didn't know how long they had been running this store, how difficult it had been to put all this together, to build up a business and keep it going. "It didn't do no good! He's ruined his health, his health!" Her husband accompanied each word

---

1. Translator's note: Käferchen means "little beetle," or better perhaps, "little bug."

with a sound like a muted tuba. Toward the end of her aria of desperation he chimed in for a duet, which consisted of nothing more than: "We can't do nothin' about it, nothin'! Can't do nothin'!"

"And now you can leave!" his wife said, halting in front of me. Her tears had dried. I invited her to visit our office, told her about the paper— "Yes," she responded, and it sounded bitter, "we know your paper!"— and offered to run an ad for them free of charge. "Why should we do that?" he asked. "Ev'rybody round here knows us, why would we ever wanna do that?" The daughter, a beanpole of a woman, didn't even return our good-bye, and instead snorted incredibly loud into her handkerchief as we left the store.

The day before yesterday I had just found the right headline for an article ("The Captains Abandon Ship First") when Ilona announced three journalists from Giessen. We had spent election Sunday with two of them. Rejoicing in reunion, they raised their arms as if they were going to embrace me. Right behind them came their managing director, whom I'd watched compose page proofs. His air was earnest and reserved. I led them through the newsroom as far as my door, but they climbed with me up to where Jörg, Marion, and Pringel share two large rooms. Once again the guests from Giessen found it all very "exciting," as if they were expecting some dramatic turn of events at any moment. I asked them about their own article on the election. They acted amazed and were inconsolable that it hadn't found its way to us. As we sat drinking coffee we lied about our circulation numbers, basked in their admiration—for Jörg's article and our scandal issue—and listened to remarks about the "strong ad market" that was developing here. After a half hour they departed, with a promise to send the article.

Around six o'clock the managing director reappeared and halted in the middle of the room. I was on the telephone, sitting in Ilona's chair and waiting for the baron, who had promised to stop by with his lawyer and a surprise. "You were lucky," I said, "that the front door was open."

It might well be, he said, that luck was on our side, we were lucky that he had gone to the trouble of looking in on us again. He took a seat in the chair set aside for ad clients.

He wanted to speak with me quite candidly, and hoped we knew how much that meant and would recognize our moment of opportunity. His newspaper had decided to launch a daily in Altenburg—latest printing technology, professional journalism—the jacket section (that is, everything except local stuff) would be managed from Giessen. We should, however, give consideration to the idea of a cooperative effort, which would mean that they would buy us out, but certainly it was within the realm of possibility that "one of you might take over as manager here . . ."

I interrupted him and walked upstairs. I spoke very calmly, which is why Jörg didn't react at all at first. "No," I said, "I'm not crazy. He is sitting downstairs waiting."

The managing director had to repeat the whole thing, which obviously didn't improve his mood. Just so we knew the lay of the land, he couldn't give us any time to mull it over. At nine on the dot the next morning, there would be a meeting to arrive at a decision based on what he took away from here this evening.

Jörg exploded. With Georg he had been cool and methodical, but now he was out of control.

"Of course we can do this," the man from Giessen cooed, and you could tell just how at ease he felt by the way he stretched out his legs and crossed his ankles. What did he, Jörg, expect? A couple of rooms, electricity, telephone—we knew how it's done. If things had been done by standard operating procedure, it wouldn't be us sitting in this palace here now anyway, but very different people—and the managing director pointed at himself. Even if one had allowed the locals a head start, that didn't mean that one intended to leave things that way forever.

Jörg, who for some inexplicable reason was holding his beret in his hands and flailing it about, attempted a laugh. "And who'll be doing the writing?"

That was up to us. At any rate they had enough pros—"young, ambitious, well-trained people"—who were just waiting for a chance to prove themselves. And there was no lack of local talent either. In response to a tiny ad in the Leipzig paper—the tininess dwindled to next to nothing between his thumb and forefinger—over thirty applications had been sent in, from which they had already invited seven people for a first interview. He didn't expect any headaches there. And his young friends, who—and we should have no doubt of it—always spoke about us everywhere they went with the greatest respect and admiration, had long since been hard at work preparing the first issues. "They've already taken up residence."

Jörg blinked and said nothing. While waiting to have a panic attack, I asked why they needed us at all. The managing director pouted his lips and hung his head.

He recognized what we had achieved, he began—whenever he starts to speak, his tongue separates from the roof of his mouth with a smack—he had great respect for young people who wanted to do something for themselves and society, who rolled up their sleeves and set to work with real commitment. We were the new force that people could and indeed must depend on, because although a lot could be done from the outside, not everything could. That was a head start he was happy to credit us with. He was the first to recognize our effort on behalf of democracy and a free-market economy. By the harsh light of day, however, we lacked professionalism—and where was that supposed to come from in a dictatorship. But we could learn it, step by step, he knew he could count on our good intentions. In short, it was a question of empathy and fairness. We ought to look at it this way: we would continue to write whatever came into our heads, and with the concentrated force of their experience and capital, of their connections and tricks—yes, he was speaking frankly here, tricks were part of business, haha—they would come to our assistance and do battle with the *Leipziger Volkszeitung,* that old Party rag. And with cooperation and real effort on all sides something truly new would arise as a symbol, yes, a model for the entire country.

With each new sentence he had grown taller in his chair and was now swinging a hairy fist like a prophet. "A model for the entire country!" he repeated.

On our own, he continued, we had no chance against the big concerns, who would show up here sooner or later. To that extent they, the Giesseners, were a regular stroke of luck for us, even if we couldn't see it that way yet. And smiling blissfully, he added, "Once the big boys come riding in here, no one"—and here he stubbed a finger across the table—"will ask you anything!" Now his finger began to wag back and forth like a tardy metronome. "No one will ask you!" he repeated, leaning back as if exhausted by this last statement.

Maybe I remained as calm as I did because that was the only role left me, maybe too because I sensed something wasn't right here. The managing director's inability to find a plausible sitting position sufficed for me as the basis for initial suspicion. His gestures looked fake.

"And why," I asked, "do you really need us?"

"Not bad, not bad," he said with an especially loud smack. "Okay, fine, let's show our cards." He played something like leapfrog with his chair, which had got hung up on the carpet. "What I've told you is true, every bit of it. We're coming, one way or the other. The crucial factor, however, is as always—time. Every week that we can get the jump on the *LVZ* with five pages on Altenburg brings us subscribers that we won't get later, or at least at too high a price. We have to be quick."

His hairy fingers played a tremolo on the tabletop. "Just put the two papers side by side, which would you automatically pick up? And what if state lines are redrawn and Altenburg is moved from Saxony to Thuringia? Which will happen, as sure as God made little green apples. Who'll want his newspaper out of Leipzig, who cares about Saxony!"

"And where are you going to have it printed?" Jörg asked in a monotone.

"I was in Gera," he said, his voice taking on an affable, shoptalk tone. "They're equipped with photo offset, and they're licking their fingers already at the business we could bring them. But only on our conditions. Otherwise we'll just have it all flown in from Giessen. That means the paper won't be here till seven. When does it get here now?" he asked. "At eleven, twelve, two?"

"And what about us?" I asked. "How much are we worth to you?"

"Enrico!" Jörg erupted, and fell silent.

A smile enlivened the managing director's face, but one so treacherous that I didn't even notice the Matchbox car until it was touching my hand.

"One of these for each of you at the front door here," he said. I shoved the little BMW on toward Jörg, who waved it off with his hand as if shooing a fly. "And twenty thousand up front, in cash, within a week, D-marks, twenty thousand, ten apiece."

He could pocket his shiny glass beads, Jörg said, and then stared at me. "This really is incredible, isn't it? Utterly incredible."

What I really wanted to do—candor demands candor—was to tell our guest from Giessen a fairy tale. About how the same arguments that he had presented so impressively had already induced us to look around for a strong partner, one with a presence throughout Thuringia and with a printing press in the region at his disposal. But Jörg's outrage didn't allow me any leeway to bluff.

A shift in the scenario was announced by someone banging on the front door, while in the same moment the vestibule door was flung open and the baron's voice rang out in English, "Anybody home?"—a question that always sets him laughing, although no one else can figure out what is so funny.

The office door handle jiggled uselessly several times before the door slowly swung open. All that was visible of the baron were legs and boots, the rest was a box.

In a radiant mood, the baron cordially greeted the managing director and then was convulsed with laughter, because Käferchen, whom he had just met on the stairs, had locked the others out. Jörg ran downstairs.

I helped the baron carry the box into the next room. He asked if he could leave some things with us for a few days, until his office was ready.

The managing director had got to his feet, magically drawn by the icon on the box, an apple with a bite taken out. Meanwhile Jörg had come back upstairs, together with two men also laden with heavy freight.

The one, Andy, an American who spoke as good as no German, the other our lawyer, Bodo von Recklewitz-Münzner.

We have von Recklewitz to thank that we can now sleep peacefully in regard to the Pipping Window affair. Recklewitz's face—with a pointy nose that juts out at an angle—actually does have something aristocratic about it. His smile resembles the baron's—he likewise tugs up just the left half of his mouth. Andy, a tall, broad-shouldered, blue-eyed, reddish blond, laughs a lot, and loud. His eyes are constantly checking out the baron, who translates things for him now and then. *"Wie geht's?"* Andy said, squeezing my hand and seeming to explore my eyes. The managing director said, "How do you do?" in English, and asked me in a low voice, "You're retooling?" I nodded.

Jörg must have said something on the stairs, because, rubbing his hands, von Recklewitz stepped over to the managing director as if asking for the time of day, "So you're planning to steal our daily bread?"

And Jörg, grateful for the opening to complain, tattle-taled, "Either with us or against us. That's what you said, isn't it?"

"It's not all that simple," the managing director noted in his defense, and pulled out a business card. While he recounted the history of our friendship, Andy and the baron were busy in the next room removing gadgets from their boxes.

"And what becomes of our investment?" Recklewitz barked, thrusting his nose in my direction. He was magnificent.[1]

The baron asked us to join him. "This is the best," he enthused, "there's no better . . . Are you in the business?" And after he too had received one of the Giesseners' cards, he exclaimed, "Then you'll confirm as much, won't you?" And the managing director immediately confirmed it. They themselves were considering installing a couple of Apples—it "probably made sense," at least in a few departments. And gradually the managing director once again became the same eager visitor he had been in February when he had bent over our page proofs. He grabbed hold of the box as Andy slipped the screen out. He gathered up the Styrofoam, kept close watch on every cable connection, and eyed our plugs as worriedly as Andy did.

The baron had even remembered to bring extension cords and a junction box. Only Recklewitz wanted to move on; he was hungry. We trooped upstairs with him, where Kurt offered him something from his lunchbox. Recklewitz thanked him, but refused with some irritation. He had heard so much about the local mutz roast (he too pronounced it wrong) that he'd rather hold back for now. Kurt flipped the top slice of bread back, pointed to a thick layer of country liverwurst, and then took a bite himself.

If you should ever happen to meet Bodo von Recklewitz-Münzner, you'll see that he lives up to his name. At first he's all Herr von Recklewitz, hurling commands out across the moat surrounding his castle. Yes, you can see from his eyes and temples that it gives him a headache if someone takes a seat beside him instead of waiting at a distance of several yards to be waved closer. Once he has got used to withdrawing his gaze from the far horizon and has overcome the inner resistance that each new contact with the world provokes in him, Herr von Recklewitz gradually becomes—in every utterance, in every explanation and observation—more and more the obliging Herr Münzner, who is to be at our side with word and deed from here on out. We were to pay him six hundred marks a month and in return can engage his services at any time and in any cause—only travel expenses are extra. Such an arrangement has always worked well for him, he says, and even better for his clients. We should not, however, make the serious mistake of confusing the law with justice. His business is the law, seeing to it that the law is on our side.

1. Barrista's entourage evidently had considerable practice at scenes like this.

And suddenly, once the contract had been signed, our old school-chum Bodo was all left-sided smiles, and now he was going to join us for a good meal.

"And now downstairs fast as we can," he cried, "they won't be able to get out on their own." Bodo von Recklewitz-Münzner expected fabulous things of our local cuisine.

I invited the managing director to join us. "Believe me," he said, clasping my right hand in both of his, "if I didn't have this meeting tomorrow morning, I would. Yes, I would, and I would invite you, all of you here, to dinner on me."

We accompanied him to his car, a real BMW, the model of which I was carrying in my pants pocket as the corpus delicti. "Beautiful car," I exclaimed as the managing director let the window down with a hum. He leaned back and stuck his head out as if checking to see if we were all still there. As he drove off he stretched his arm up over the roof and waved his tremolo hand, revealing, like yet another promise, a gold bracelet.

"The son of a bitch!" cried Jörg, who had lowered his arm even before Recklewitz had. "That son of a bitch!"

"Be glad," the baron laughed, "you ended up with someone like that. And be proud. No sooner are you on the market than they're courting you. What more do you want?"

"Sits there the whole time with a toy like that in his jacket, waiting to pounce. Damn him!" Jörg shouted.

The baron said nothing, as if first making sure Jörg had in fact spoken his piece, and then he said: "Rebuild the wall, but you better hurry!"

We should be grateful to this managing director, yes, truly grateful. He had uncovered our weaknesses. "Your strengths and weaknesses," the baron added. He blamed himself for not having been harder on us in the past. Because as was now evident it was rather unlikely that we would be granted any more time to learn without pain. "If there even is such a thing—learning without pain."

He asked Jörg to tell him one thing the managing director had said that was incorrect. We were going to have to change, change very rapidly, otherwise we didn't have a chance. "And at the least," he said, "rethink your page size and the quality of the printing. You need room for ads, and no one is going to pay you D-marks for such fuzzy photos."

They were still arguing as we sat in the Ratskeller. The tone remained friendly, but implacable. "You don't want to be a daily? Then you're going to have to come up with a different concept."

Each time I was about to jump in to help Jörg, he had already lost the argument. That was probably why Recklewitz kept jutting his nose at me. What did I think? he asked. I couldn't come up with anything. And I was annoyed at Jörg for carrying on so childishly that they must have thought we had forgotten to read the rules of the game.

"Enrico!" Jörg cried. "Don't let them knock the wind out of you like this!" And then Jörg rehearsed his sad account once more. Of course no one knows what will happen after July 1st,[1] of course the East isn't the West, of course we sold close to a thousand more copies of our last issue, of course it all depends on us, on what we want and on our hard work, of course we're not just any newspaper. Plus if Jörg's people get elected, then we're more likely than the others to get things directly from the horse's mouth. But will that be enough?

After that no one could think of anything innocuous to break the silence. Fortunately the food arrived. We raised glasses and I no longer understood what was really supposed to be so terrible about the baron's vision or what made Jörg just keep shaking his head. If Jörg continued to balk, the baron had said (leaving it up to us to decide how serious he was), he himself would start up a free paper financed by ads. You couldn't leave money lying in the streets. Besides it would be fun, it was always fun to make money. And in this case if you went at it right, right from the start, it would be child's play. Hadn't the managing director said they did photo offset in Gera? Well then, bring on as many Giesseners as you wanted. But it would prove fatal for the *Weekly*. "If you don't react now," he said, aiming his deep-sea glasses at me, "you're finished."

"No," Jörg said, he wasn't going to fall into that trap. He wasn't going to let us waste our energies. We were going to lay into the oars.

"Then row away," exclaimed Recklewitz, who, because the mutz roast had run out, was busy dissecting an enormous ham hock and wanted to talk about more pleasant things, soccer for example, although he had to know the baron thinks sports are ridiculous.

This morning at nine on the dot Andy appeared in the office. He sat down at the computer and three minutes later handed me a finished ad: a

1. Monetary union with the Federal Republic was scheduled to begin July 1, 1990.

full half page! In white on black, nothing more than, "Andy's Coming!" He asked for a discount, which I of course gave him. I did better with my English than I had expected, but then I didn't have a choice.

All the same I wasn't sure if I now understood him correctly, although I was sure twenty meant *zwanzig* and twenty thousand was *zwanzig-tausend*. I once again tapped the computer, screen, and printer: "Altogether twenty thousand?"

"Yeees," Andy cried, kept on saying "yeees!" I asked if that might not be something for us too. "Yeees, absolutely."

It's all so easy. We spent seven and a half for the VW bus, fifteen hundred on the camera. Our assets include the fifteen hundred[1] from the ad for videos that the baron pulled in for us, plus a few other hundred D-marks in income, comes to thirteen thousand plus a few hundred. We need another six thousand and change in D-marks.

I've already written Steen and called Gera about setting up an appointment. We're not going to go under that fast.

Your E.

PS: Michaela just told me that some woman tried to kill Lafontaine with a knife or dagger. Michaela thinks that will improve his and the Social Democrats' chances with the voters.

Saturday, April 28, '90

Dear Nicoletta,

My transfer into a company of new arrivals meant that, even though I was the youngest, I was promoted to the rank of room corporal,[2] who is assigned the best bed (bottom bunk, at the window) and newest locker, who gets his meals brought to him every morning and evening, and whose word has greater weight than that of a noncom.

The commissioned letters had more or less run their course. And I didn't have much else to do. Now and then we rode cross-country in our APCs, which was a welcome change. I enjoyed the ride—but wouldn't admit it to myself. Even setting up field camp and going on short maneu-

---

1. T. initially gave the sum as twelve hundred, cf. his letter of March 28, 1990.
2. T. was now in the second six months of his eighteen-month service.

vers had ceased to be frightening, plus the summer of '82 was extraordinarily warm.

When I wanted to write, I retreated to Nikolai's painting studio,[1] where the same banners lay draped over laundry racks for weeks on end. Each morning Nikolai would give the pots of paint a quick stir with a brush and then retreat into his studio, a small room with windows that overlooked the drill field and that he had turned into an incredibly cozy spot. He even had a record player and a scruffy leather sofa. The few guys who were allowed inside mostly served as his models.

You'll scarcely believe my naïveté,[2] but in fact I couldn't figure out why all the guys who modeled for him were very boyish and often looked almost identical.

Inspired by Baudelaire's prose poems, which Nikolai read to me from an Insel edition, I wrote one or two sketches every day. These idyllic hours were interrupted only by the 7th of October parade, rehearsals for which were an idiotic, stomach-turning grind. But that's not a topic for here.

As winter once again approached—I was now a DC—I was afraid time might be running out.

There was a good chance that much of what I had assumed would happen as a matter of course and had intended to experience would never find a place on my agenda before the end of April. I had taken it for granted that sooner or later I would see the inside of the brig. I almost managed it once without its being any of my doing. When the radio in our room, for which I as corporal was responsible, was checked out by a battalion officer, the red tuning line didn't vanish beneath one of the paper strips you had to glue on to mark East-bloc stations. They threatened me with three-day arrest, but that was the end of it. Everyone, even the officers, listened to New German Wave, and the FM reception on West Berlin's RIAS, SFB, and AFN was top-notch.

I was working on a story about sentry duty, and urgently needed more observed details. When I learned that my company would be assigned double duty[3] on the three days before Christmas, I did every-

1. This is a surprising statement inasmuch as at the end of his previous letter to N. H., T. had claimed that he was "not going to tolerate" Nikolai in his presence anymore.
2. Understandably enough, T. wanted to conceal his homoerotic relationship with Nikolai, but was also evidently unable to do without Nikolai in his cast of characters.
3. Forty-eight-hour sentry duty.

thing I could to be included. But as one of three drivers in their third six-month stint, there was little chance of that. My only help was to play Good Samaritan. In an act of hypocritical sacrifice I gave a heartbroken paterfamilias my leave pass and took over sentry duty for him. To keep the gratitude of the man, who was on the verge of tears, within limits I demanded several bottles of vodka in return, which he smuggled into the barracks at risk of life and limb.

Such intentionally arranged incidents are seldom worth the investment,[1] but this time it appeared as if my hopes would be fulfilled. Just when I had been relieved of duty at the end of the snowy second night—Christmas Eve—the police patrol brought in a stinking, roaring drunk sailor. They were holding him by his arms and legs and swinging him back and forth like a sack. They had a lot to do yet, so they unloaded him in the guardhouse and went back out on the hunt.

The sailor lived in Oranienburg and had been nabbed at his front door. He could no longer stand on his own, and would choke now and then on his gurgled curses and insults. He finally managed to make it to his knees, but then lurched over on one side again and raised one arm. He wanted us to let him go. Even in his pleas you could hear some of the disdain that he as a sailor had for men in gray. He claimed he hadn't been trying to get to his girl, but to his mother, he didn't want to fuck, but just to be home for Christmas, even "grunts" ought to understand that. He fumbled at his watch, pulled it off—it was ours if we let him go.

As a noncom and I attempted to get him back on his feet, he readily assisted us in the belief that we would bring him to the gate, and went on praising his Glasshütter watch, which had never let him down.

We moved quickly to consign him to the brig and agreed with him that the MPs were mangy dogs and jack-offs. The footprints left in the snow by his street shoes looked downright ladylike in comparison to those of our boots. He looked up as if he had only now realized where we were taking him. I grabbed him tighter. Whether because of that or because he saw the corporal stripes on my shoulder strap[2]—he took his rage out on me. He gave me a kick, the tip of his shoe met my shin. As if

1. T. knew whereof he spoke. His letters to Nicoletta read like a settlement of accounts with a life made up of "intentionally arranged incidents." At the same time the question necessarily arises as to whether his letters to Nicoletta are not also "an intentionally arranged incident."

2. Corporal stripes are incomprehensible as a reason.

out of reflex I struck back, his nose started to bleed. He had pulled free and whaled into me now, banging at me in a fury with bloody fists. I somehow got a grip on him, clinching him from behind. He booted and kicked, until I didn't know what else to do but to pick him up and fling him into the snow. Help arrived from the guardhouse. On all fours now, the sailor spun around inside the circle of his tormentors searching for me.

Four of us got the better of him, wrenched his arms behind him, tugged his head back by the hair—after he started spitting—and shoved him forward. He went limp, which is why we had to drag him down the stairs to be booked. And so I had finally made it into one of those cells I had wanted to occupy myself. The next evening, Christmas night, I sat in Nikolai's studio, drank mulled wine, ate stollen, and listened to the "Christmas Oratorio." Nikolai gave me Malaparte's *The Skin,* a well-thumbed Western pocketbook.

I was already living in the euphoric state of a returnee when we were sent on maneuvers in the middle of April, barely two weeks before my discharge on the 28th. We crossed the Elbe and burrowed our way into a pine forest.

The last night we were waiting for our orders to return to base, sleeping in our APCs. As soon as it got chilly inside, the driver turned on the motor. That was forbidden, but our officers evidently chose not to notice.

After the second or third time I fell asleep. A pain in my shoulder woke me up. Udo, a noncom, was literally kneeling on me in order to get at the crank that opened the louvers on the hood of the APC—the only way to cool the motor. The thermostat indicator was out of sight, well beyond the red zone. The motor was on the verge of locking at any moment. An incident like that could be punished as sabotage, and you ended in the military prison at Schwedt. Udo's chin lingered above my shoulder, we stared at the thermostat. I could smell his sleepy breath and awaited my fate. Out of stupidity, off to Schwedt—that would be unbearable!

When the indicator began to move I felt Udo's hand at the nape of my neck, he was squeezing with every ounce of his strength. Then he opened the hatch and climbed out. I waited until I could turn the motor off and followed him. I thought he was standing somewhere nearby, having a smoke. But I couldn't find him. It was still dark and perfectly still when I started my walk. From one moment to the next there was noth-ing to remind me of an army. No sentries, no barbed wire, no spotlights, only soft earth and silence. The vehicles were as unreal as the trees, enchanted reptiles murmuring in their sleep.

The farther I went the more excited I was. I don't know how long I walked. I stopped at the edge of a field, dropped my trousers, and squat-ted. What all I discharged from myself was simply stupendous. It seemed to me as if I were not simply emptying out what I had stuffed myself with over the past few days, but was also ridding myself of every oppres-sion, fear, and torment I had ever had to swallow. With my naked butt hovering above the forest floor by the first light of dawn, I was the happi-est, freest human being that I could imagine. I saw my sun rising with the dawn. It was all behind me, I was returning from hell, and the comple-tion of my book was only a matter of time. These minutes were now the yardstick of my happiness.

That very evening I began to try to describe the experience. And despite all the later changes, all the material I threw out or rearranged, I was determined I would end my book with this unexpected moment of happiness and dawn.

Late in the afternoon of the day I was discharged, I walked away from the streetcar stop, black bag in hand, only to run directly into my mother. She set down her shopping bag of empty bottles and threw her arms around my neck and would not let go even after I begged her to.

Sunday, April 29, 1990

I had returned, but I had brought a problem home with me. Nikolai had invited me to spend a weekend with him in Saxon Switzerland. I had no idea how I would survive those two days with him.[1]

When Nikolai came to pick me up—standing there in the stairwell of our building, leaning against the railing, in a white half-unbuttoned shirt, faded jeans, and sunglasses pushed up into his hair—I followed him like someone wading into the water although he knows he can't swim. To describe my hours with him would be a story all its own. I felt guilty for

---

1. V. T. and Johann Ziehlke are in agreement that in the first few days after their dis-charge, T. and Nikolai were a couple.

having nourished his hopes. He wasn't used to having to woo someone. As soon as he met with resistance, he turned domineering. That night we almost scuffled. We had spread out our sleeping bags on a projecting rock. The drop-off was only a few yards away. It was so dark I couldn't even make out his face. I could guess its expression only from his voice. I could deal with his arrogance, his accusations, his mockery and scorn, yes, even his disdain. What appalled me, however, was his self-hatred. I covered my ears—that's how unbearable what I had to listen to was. I couldn't console him, either. That whole night I kept my eye on him. He didn't fall asleep until it began to grow light. I didn't have to do much packing. Yes, I simply ran away. I never saw Nikolai again.

For eighteen months I had longed to return. But where and what had I returned to? To a world that didn't interest me, in which there was nothing for me, nothing worth writing about. In the army every well-used minute was an unexpected gift, every day of survival a victory.

Instead of bearing witness to having made it through hell, I felt as if I had been driven from paradise. My world was turned upside down. And one thing led to another.

Vera's boyfriend at the time was a disgusting human being. Daniel, as I learned later, was also fleecing her financially.[1] I tried to figure out if he was a writer or painter or if he did anything at all. Ostensibly he was a home health attendant, but he never went to work and lived off (besides Vera) what Dutch or French renters paid him for his apartment in Berlin. Daniel found Dresden unbearably provincial. He wasn't going to stay a minute longer once Vera's Berlin embargo was lifted. Vera admired Daniel because he could throw around words like "rhizome" and "anti-Oedipal" and had books from the West that he lent to no one. When he spoke the name "Foucault" it was as if he held his breath for a moment to listen for the echo of his own fanfare. To Vera, however, Daniel was the measure of all things.

At the beginning I couldn't resist him, either. The first time you met him his smile was like bait tossed your way. And by the second meeting you had the sense you had disappointed him, because the eyes behind his nickel-rimmed glasses were purely inner directed—today, I'd just call them dull. Everything I said about what I thought was good and right he would turn into its rhetorical opposite. If you offered any opposition,

---

1. T. feared any and all competition in this regard as well.

you were making yourself an accomplice of those in power, but if you attempted to lend support, that was a particularly perfidious way of trying to control someone. Inside half an hour Daniel would manage to brand me—in Vera's presence—as a complete idiot. How was I supposed to write contemporary prose without having read Foucault, Deleuze, Lacan, Derrida, and all the rest of them? I didn't need to waste my time on Adorno, and as for the whole Frankfurt school, I could just forget it.

As she brought me to the door, Vera tried to comfort me. Daniel wasn't blaming me for being ignorant of his authors, it was just that I should read them before attempting to write.

The last straw was Vera's promise to show me some texts about the army that one of her admirers had written and that she judged "not bad." I was alarmed precisely because Vera didn't take the guy seriously otherwise—she made fun of his jealousy and those puppy-dog eyes that followed her everywhere. And above all I was disconcerted because somebody was poaching in my reserve.[1]

Once I got my own notes back from Geronimo, who had kept them in meticulous order, they bored me. The pounds of stuff I now crammed into my desk drawer were junk. Just as I had once collected seashells at the Baltic shore and then insisted I had to take every single one home with me—where after a few weeks, with my permission, they ended up in the trash—I might just as well have tied up the bundle and taken it to the ragman.

Of course my letters—well, they weren't real letters, but notes and sketches—paraded almost every one of my 541 days in the barracks before my eyes. But to what purpose? Where were the stories I had hoped to be able to net from these pages the way fat carp are taken from the ponds of Moritzburg Castle each autumn? All my fervor seemed so childish, so vain and pointless, that there was nothing for it but to admit Daniel and Vera were right. It was my plunge into hell.

Suddenly I was just anybody. I felt abandoned, forsaken. If I couldn't write, my life was worthless.

Geronimo, who was studying theology in Naumburg, was helping Franziska study for her finals and playing in a band. Together we had argued with some Christian Democrats at the Church Congress in Dres-

---

1. T. leaves unmentioned the fact that he knew the person in question from his school-days: to wit, the publisher of these letters. I would have loved to know T.'s opinion of my texts, but he never again refers to them here.

den and had called Councilor of the Consistory Stolpe a political wet blanket. But otherwise we didn't have much to say to each other. I was jealous of him because of Franziska and because he was a welcome guest in that large hillside villa in Weisser Hirsch, where he drank tea with her parents on the terrace while he gazed out over the whole city.

To top it all off, I was told by the Army District Command[1] that I had been discharged as a noncommissioned officer in the reserves, an ignominy that was too late to protest and that I had no choice but to keep to myself.

My salvation was Aunt Camilla, who for the past two years had sent me one hundred D-marks at Christmas and another fifty D-marks at Easter, so that I suddenly had three hundred D-marks, to which my mother added what was left of her own gift; she also paid for my train ticket to Budapest and for two consignments of bed linens. I stayed ten days and lived like a prince.

If this were a biography, one long chapter would be titled "Katalin." Katalin was the niece of Frau Nádori and was studying English and German in Szeged. She was preparing for her exams. Every morning we sat in Frau Nádori's kitchen and smoked her cigarettes until Katalin was banished to the living room, where she had to study Heinz Mettke's Middle High German grammar. Each afternoon we would meet somewhere at four o'clock. Katalin was engaged and held fast to that role. After an evening at the opera, however, she visited me in my room. I pulled my sleeping bag from the bed and laid it on the old hardwood floor, directly in front of a white armoire that Frau Nádori always claimed was "genuine rococo." Katalin now opened this genuine rococo armoire and made up a bed for us from the linens hoarded in it. She just wanted to lie beside me, she said, slipped off her nightgown, and warmed my hands between her thighs. At some point we both fell briefly asleep, but when we awoke it was all quite simple and lovely and unforgettable.

I owe something else to those days in June—a book, one that I could just as easily have found in our own living room. But that copy was wrapped in such a dreadful jacket that I had never laid a hand on it.[2]

---

1. The Army District Command was where one's identification papers were returned, after having been held there for the duration of one's military service.

2. The edition he means was probably that of the Verlag Kultur und Fortschritt [Culture and Progress Publishers] (Berlin, 1964), on the cover of which is a saber-brandishing, mustachioed cavalryman.

In Budapest I received it from the hands of the same antiquarian book dealer who had wrapped several small blue volumes of Nietzsche in plain brown paper for me.

I read the first story while I was still in the shop—and suddenly knew what I wanted. Stories exactly like this, except for today—in the here and now—a new *Red Cavalry*. I had found a new god. "Isaac Babel," the lady had whispered, staring at the ceiling and elegantly spiraling her small liver-spotted hand in tiny ascending circles. Vera and David might be right a hundred times over, I was right about Babel.

Katalin noticed that something extraordinary had happened to me. And I could sense that she liked how I spoke, how I couldn't help reading her passages aloud, and how my enthusiasm was evidently blind to the fact that she wanted to kiss me, in broad daylight, even though the silvery head of her aunt might appear in the door at any moment.

Your Enrico T.

Tuesday, May 1, '90

Dear Nicoletta,

At the end of August my existence as a full-time writer was salvaged. I was off to Jena to study.

I'm almost ashamed to follow such a precise chronology. But each entry would be impossible to understand without the previous one. I promise you, however, I'll move on now more quickly.

Had it not been for my scribbling, for my wretched calling, I might have made a good student. But instead I was continually driven by the question: How far am I still from completing my army book so that I can publish it in the West at the magical age of twenty-five?

I won't write about my studies as such, although they defined my days and I was even afraid I might be asked to leave the university. There were nine of us students, five archaeologists and four philologists. I told you that day that the only faculty for classical studies was in Jena, and students were accepted only every two years. Of course that leads to arrogance, although God knows there was no reason for it.

Do you still recall the peace marches and decisions to expand the arms race in 1983? There were demonstrations in Jena—illegal and official ones, sometimes both at the same time. The unofficial signs and banners were carried by workers—and quickly smashed by Stasi agents. I watched demonstrators hold up what was left of their signs, until they were either arrested or vanished into the forest of GDR flags being waved by schoolchildren.

Together with a few other students I joined the contingent of theologians, who weren't attacked despite the fact that their slogans weren't welcome either.

Presumably all I would have had to do was bend down and pick up the remains of a sign and that would have been the end of my university studies.

That I didn't do it was not due solely to the promise of continued studies. I was also afraid. Not everyone survived his arrest.[1] Every Sunday morning a vehicle fully manned by uniformed personnel would park near Cosmonaut Square. Their lurking just around the corner had its effect on the mood of the town. Anyone entering Thomas Mann Bookstore or simply strolling across the square might be instantly transformed into a demonstrator or a Stasi catchpole.

The "personal conversations" I had known in high school (there were attempts at something similar even in the army) had their continuation at the university level. It was presumed that every male student would declare in writing that he was willing to become an officer in the reserves. After my initial refusal—my reasons for which were not all that easy to explain—I was invited to a conversation with the eminence grise of the faculty, Professor Samthoven (it was said that the "v" had once been an "f"),[2] an archaeologist—a meticulously well-groomed man, if not a downright dandy. He was as proud of his thick, perfectly trimmed beard as he was of his little feet and slender, well-manicured hands. During seminars he smoked cigarillos (we were allowed to smoke as well) and used a riding crop as his pointer. He had the reputation of being a Casanova. At any rate he had no inhibitions about showing preference for the prettier female students, especially if they had long hair. Ever

---

1. Matthias Domaschk of Jena was arrested on April 10, 1981, and the following morning was handed over to the district office of the Ministry for State Security in Gera. On April 12th, Matthias Domaschk died in the ministry's pretrial detention facility in Gera under circumstances still unexplained today. The Ministry for State Security reported that he had hanged himself with his own shirt.

2. An elegant new spelling. One presumes it was also meant to invoke echoes of Beethoven.

since I had outlined the pattern of a sonnet on the blackboard (he placed "utmost value" on general knowledge) and, as a novice, had had modest success describing early geometric vases, he overrated me far too much.

He asked me to take a seat and treated me almost paternally—made tea and shoved an ashtray my way. We had both crossed our legs and were now gazing down at very different-size shoes, both jiggling gently and almost touching toes. He stroked the corners of his mouth with thumb and middle finger, pressed his lips tight, and began to speak. It should come as no surprise that I had been invited to this conversation. But before those paid to do so talked with me—by that he didn't mean Stasi agents, but colleagues who owed their positions only secondarily to any expert knowledge—he himself wanted to have the pleasure of chatting with me, simply to make certain that I had also thought the entire matter through before making my final decision. He poured me some tea.

Except for him, he noted, probably no one else here knew I was a noncommissioned officer . . . I was about to contradict him, to explain—he knew very well what I intended to say, but begged to be allowed to finish. He himself saw that there could be some small shame connected with being a noncom. But not perhaps in the way I might think, quite the contrary. All states, whether East or West, recruited their officers from the elite. That was the case everywhere, except with us. Poles, Russians, Czechs—they weren't even asked.

It would sadden him to see me ruin my professional chances, my life, by such a refusal—particularly, and here I surely would agree with him, since I had come up with no cogent reason for it, nor in all probability would I—only to end up being psychologically humiliated by these people. "For why, my dear Herr Türmer, should a noncom be frightened of becoming a full-fledged officer? If you argue the issue on principle, then you will also have to recant the very oath you swore. Or am I overlooking some other possibility?" He raised the shallow white cup to his lips and sipped.

All that was demanded of us, he continued, was a profession of allegiance, a symbolic yes. He again put the cup to his lips and gazed out over the rim. "Georgian tea, brought it back from Tbilisi. You'll be traveling there soon, I presume."

He would be quite satisfied if I merely ran the matter over in my mind one more time. There was no need for us to discuss the imperfections of socialism as it existed in reality, our two standpoints were probably not as far apart as some might imagine. He, however, always asked himself one question: What other society had in so short a time managed to conquer hunger, whether in Russia or China or Cuba? As long as tens of thousands died daily of starvation and curable diseases one must put the question just that way. "What was Allende's first decree? A half liter of milk for every child. Allende was a physician, he knew what needs to be done."

Samthoven struck a match and took a drag on his cigarillo.

Ultimately—and this was the only reason for him to tell me this, for him to take this time from his schedule—it was a matter of providing our state with its elite. "Don't be so stupid as to forfeit your education!" he exclaimed, holding up the fingers between which his cigarillo glowed. I shouldn't let myself be trapped in the net of the very people who had done our country greater harm than the class enemy. If I understood that, then we were both on the same side. He couldn't say more, nor did he wish to. Instead of continuing to play the hero I would do better to join the Party. "The necessary reforms can come only from within the Party. You'll live to see it."

He would personally smooth the way for me.

These last words were spoken with a certain testiness, as if it annoyed him to have to say such things at all. We sat there in silence for a while, our feet still jiggling. Then he extended his small dry hand and said his good-bye.

My lungs were burning from chain-smoking. I came to a halt in front of the Haeckel Phyletic Museum. I wanted to forget his odious offer, I needed some distraction, I needed fresh air.

As I walked past the post office in the direction of West Station, however, I soon turned off to the right to avoid rush-hour traffic. My path led me up the steep hill, and I walked aimlessly through streets lined with middle-class houses and villas with gardens. From the multipaneled window of a sandstone villa hung a red and white banner that read VIVAT POLSKA! There were several of these in town. It meant that this was the home of someone who had filled out his application—who wanted out, wanted to go to the West.

I kept on walking. It was windy, but not cold. I was sweating. At one point I thought I had lost my bearings.

What can I say. I was standing halfway up the slope and suddenly knew what my army book would look like. As if guided by a magic hand, the *Vivat Polska!* and the graffiti on the wall of Holy Cross School merged with my army experiences. And I had the vague suspicion that I somehow owed the intellectual thread binding them to Samthoven.

An hour and a half later I was sitting in a pub, the Hauser, answering questions posed by the clique of four who were in their third year of studies.

I mimicked the elegant way Samthoven crossed his legs, observed the back of my outstretched hand with that same blatant self-infatuation, stroked my imaginary beard, perched a saucer at my chin and sipped, splaying my pinkie, repeating his comments about Tbilisi, and then tried to imitate his rhetorical periods, which were so lengthy that you could have laid wagers on whether they would end with the right verb form. If it was possible to lay Samthoven bare, then I did it.

The clique boomed with laughter. I relished the way our table had become the center of attention in the dark room. Edith, the owner, a woman somewhere on the far side of fifty and dressed in a white smock, waved her hand at newcomers looking for a seat to wait at the door, as if they were disrupting a performance.

I have never been a finer entertainer than I was that evening. Samthoven's invitation to join the Party was its crowning pirouette.

Samthoven might have thought that I had held my tongue out of courtesy, just as these people believed I knew what I wanted. At the end of my performance I had no choice but to respond with a yes to their presumption that I would stick to my refusal to be an officer in the reserves.

A little later Edith sat down at our table and asked for a cigarette. The last round of beer was on the house. The evening had reached its climax. Time for the final curtain.

On the way home it felt like I had a plump wallet in my breast pocket—it was my book, whose fulcrum or pivoting point was to be the slogan *Vivat Polska!* painted in white on a dark wall somewhere in the basement furnace room of the barracks. One soldier after another would be summoned. Both the interrogation itself and the interval during which each man waited for his own name to be called would give me the opportunity for character studies and descriptions of the brutality of everyday life in the barracks. Who had put it there? No sooner do they have a suspect than the graffiti appears on another wall: *Vivat Polska!*

Soon there's a third one, a fourth, and now it's ten—even in the snow on the drill field, the inscription: *Vivat Polska!* And all the while—and that was to be the linchpin of the whole story—it is the Stasi that started it all as a provocation, a way to interrogate people and lure them into denouncing each other. And now this vile trick has turned on them and is out of control.

I only had to start, I could already sense the ecstasy that would bring it all together.

Your Enrico T.

Saturday, May 5, '90

Dear Nicoletta,

In retrospect the affair with Nadja is transparent. At the time I was amazed that a woman like her would throw herself into my arms. Nadja was Vera's first great love. Early in '81 her mother had married a gay Swiss man, and they all left the country that same May.

Vera recovered only very slowly. Even now we avoid mentioning Nadja. Nadja's real name was Sabine, but because of Vera's enthusiasm for Breton it wasn't long before everyone was calling her Nadja.

During the few visits I was permitted back then, Vera had treated me and Nadja like children, called us whelps and quickly sent me on my way every time. All I knew about Nadja was that married specimens of my gender—the word "man" never passed Vera's lips in those days—had camped out at her door, leading to occasional brawls over a sixteen-year-old girl.

At three o'clock in the afternoon on March 23, 1985, I again ran into Nadja on the landing below Vera's apartment. At first I didn't recognize her, because she was wearing a hat and sobbing. She was dressed as always. But her new dialect disconcerted me.

Vera had slammed the door in her face. But Nadja was stubborn and had been trying to talk with Vera. And then I showed up. As if I had fallen out of a clear blue sky, there I suddenly stood before her . . . I can't tell you how often we told each other the story in the months that followed. She had known at once: He's the one! I want him!

I had a date with Vera, but I couldn't bring myself to leave Nadja just standing there. Nadja asked if I would accompany her on a walk to see her old school, and told me about how often she had tried to get back to Dresden. We then walked to Rosengarten and the Elbe, which we followed until we crossed the Blue Wonder Bridge—without Nadja's flow of words stopping for a second or her uncoupling her arm from mine. It was already dusk as we made our way back across the Elbe meadows.

My role was reduced to that of the listener, while she talked about money, work, her university studies, and her apartment in Salzburg, where she had landed the year before. She liked Austria better than Switzerland. Nadja didn't seem to me all that content with her life, but my question of why she hadn't changed jobs or her major was answered with a curt toss of the head and an almost irate "Why should I?"

Perhaps our meeting would have ended with that, but the sunset and the silhouette of the old city toward which we were now walking lent our silence greater meaning.

Nadja knew a waiter in the café Secundo Genitur on the Brühlsche Terrace, so we had a table all to ourselves. Nadja asked if I was still writing. I told her about my army book, but said nothing about having to report for the army base in Seeligenstädt two days later. Even after discharge, every male student in the GDR had to serve an additional five weeks.

I brought Nadja to a streetcar stop—she was staying with a girlfriend in Dresden-Laubegast. We said our farewells, precisely because we both could rely on a nose for dramatic possibilities. After all, there weren't that many afternoon trains to Munich.

Beneath the arch of the train station roof and against the dazzling sunlight streaming in from outside, Nadja was just a silhouette with hat. When she came running toward me in her dark brown tailored suit, threw her arms around my neck, and whispered, "I knew it, I just knew it," I was certain I loved her. How else could I explain the humiliation that I felt in saying good-bye—the humiliation of not being able to board the train with her—and that brought tears to my eyes.

My mother greeted me with a scolding. I had missed my appointment with a neighbor lady to have my hair cut. She now took scissors in hand herself, shaved the back of my neck, and plopped my packed bag at my feet.

The train to Jena was overcrowded. Which was fine by me. I didn't want to read, I didn't want peace and quiet. All I wanted was already inside me. I finally had time to develop[1] the scenes with Nadja and dis-cover new details.

When Nadja whispered in my ear, she had tugged at the lobe. I could feel her breath, the tips of her fingers on the nape of my neck, on my cheeks. I could feel the strength in her arm, I could feel her breasts, her lips.

The last thing Nadja heard from my lips was, "Have a good trip!" I felt my face burning for the shame of it. And Nadja? What had she said? We were holding hands, I ran alongside the train as it pulled away. The faster I ran the more rollicking her laughter, the farther she leaned out, until she pulled back in fright, as if the end of the platform were some unex-pected stroke of fate. The fright was still reflected in her face until all I could see of her was her swirling hair. And finally, the moment came when I turned around and walked back along the empty platform.

I don't recall if we were loaded onto trucks or transported by train from Jena to Seeligenstädt, nor who was in command and divided us into com-panies. All that emerges from the fog are the explosions of laughter that greeted each newcomer to a drunken bash that lasted till dawn—as if shorn heads were an original costume. I drank from every bottle offered me.

My memories first begin with a gesture, a motion of the right hand, that opens a belt buckle and grabs it by the last punch hole as it falls, while the left doffs the cap. I executed this gesture with so little thought it frightened me, as if someone were mimicking me.

This horde of buzz-cut, uniformed men bewildered me. All it took was a certain way of walking or a twitch of the mouth and I would find myself greeting someone I presumed I knew from Oranienburg. On day two I was certain it was Nikolai I saw walking directly toward me. By the time I realized my mistake I had already called out his name. Faces I was actually familiar with, however, were the ones I didn't recognize. Anton, my friend and fellow student, stumbled around so blindly and apatheti-cally under his helmet that it was days before we discovered each other.

The instant I had a few free minutes, I would stretch out on my bed as if it were the only spot where I could think of Nadja.

1. A note paper-clipped to this carbon copy contains the following quoted observation: "What one perceives in the presence of one's beloved is only a negative that must first be developed when one returns home and can use the darkroom of one's own interior, the entrance to which is 'nailed shut' as long as one can see the other person." Thus far no source for this quote has been determined.

Within a few hours it was clear to me that I had been mistaken, that there was nothing for me here in Seeligenstädt. What was going on around me neither belonged in my army book nor needed to be shared in a letter. This studious submissiveness of men of above-average intelligence was abysmally shameful.[1] And I was one of them.

My group, students from Jena and Ilmenau who were sports majors, fired one another up as they ran the obstacle course and once we were off duty tried to teach me how to take the scaling wall in one assault. They liked to play room check, showed one another how to "do a package" (folding underwear), were jealous if other men were issued more blank ammo to waste, and for pedagogic purposes liked to step on the heels of the man ahead of them on the drill field. There was no sand thrown in the gears here, no drunkenness or disorderly conduct, no reporting late or grousing. In Seeligenstädt there was no longer any need for orders— one nod, and the pack of hounds heeled.

Seeligenstädt didn't match my experiences in basic training—or those I had hoped to have here. The opposing fronts had disappeared.

I shriveled, something crumpled inside me. I kept my mouth shut during political instruction and was glad to hang my helmet from my belt during marching drills—a noncom privilege.

Nadja's letters reached me two and a half weeks later by way of my mother. Nadja had also telephoned her.

When the alarm whistle sounded the next morning—a good many slept in their sports gear in order to appear punctually out in the hall— I just lay there and fell in only after someone ripped my blanket off.

Instead of joining the morning workout I slunk over to the regimental dentist, complained about pain under a filling—and was actually sent on to Ronneburg. The dentist there didn't even make me wait, just stamped the referral and wished me a nice day. Suddenly school was canceled, and my gait was as light as if a cast had just been removed from my foot. I rummaged through a bookstore, lay in the grass beside an old cemetery wall, and enjoyed the perfect quiet. When the clock struck twelve, I went in search of a meal, drank some beer, and then took another sunbath.

It was almost three o'clock when I stepped into a phone booth and for the first time heard the ringtone of Nadja's phone, a velvety deep hum

---

1. The five weeks of reserve training were graded as if they were regular coursework. Anyone who did not "pass" was dismissed from the university.

that would become so familiar in the coming months. There was no answer.

Just short of five o'clock, before boarding the bus with a bundle of books under my arm, I tried a last time. Again with no success.

Caught up in the triumph of having managed a free day, I wrote my first letter. I printed AUSTRIA and SALZBURG on the envelope in capital letters, as if they were the slogan that would guarantee me immunity.

The next morning I fell in again. Thus far I had been able to avoid issuing orders, but this time I couldn't get out of a "target objective."[1] I reported pails of unidentified grub in the advance units, heavy friendly fire from goulash cannons that fell short of their mark, and ordered retreat. I know, that's pretty wretched too, but at the time I basked in the laughter it earned me. The lieutenant, a student from Ilmenau,[2] ordered retreat and had me repeat my target objective.

My second, and third, attempts were greeted with laughter. But then they all, without exception, wanted me to give some real orders. The other groups were waiting to move out. Now they had me where they wanted me. The humiliation was worse than having to march past a reviewing stand on the 1st of May. That afternoon I found a pass on my bed.

I rounded up some change and by eight o'clock was camped out in a functioning telephone booth.

It was after ten before Nadja finally answered. I had assumed she knew of my whereabouts from my mother and could picture my circumstances during these weeks. But she seemed happy just to hear from me and rattled off the names of friends who wanted to meet me. She asked for a picture of me, and letters, lots of letters.

I had to explain to her where I was and what I was doing here, and the longer I spoke the more palpable her silence became, a silence that forced me to reveal more and more of my daily life. I was hoping the connection had gone bad, when Nadja snapped at me, "Why would you go to a camp like that?"

Instead of answering, I began to tell her about my target objectives and how I had put my group practically into stitches and had been work-

1. A description of the enemy on the basis of certain predetermined criteria.
2. Officers were usually not from one's own university or technical school.

ing on some new scenarios . . . "Don't make such a fool of yourself," Nadja shouted.

In that moment I turned very calm. The battle was over, I had lost, all the rest no longer mattered to me.

"It's not worth it," I then heard Nadja say. She knew a lovely bed-and-breakfast in Prague—when would I be able to come, she longed so much to see me . . .

My army book had become my blind spot. I didn't know when I would ever be able to work on it. At the end of a day's duties I played chess—when I didn't just lie on my bed. Since I usually lost, I was everyone's favorite partner.

At the end of our five weeks, on the next-to-last day, we had political instruction one final time. I don't remember the exact question or my answer either, which evoked no response whatever. The topic was probably the global arms race.

At the start of the last hour—there was to be a test—previous grades were announced. With a D—in the first seminar, my silence had been rewarded with a B—I was the worst in the class.

No sooner had the lieutenant, an introverted computer science student, announced the results than a "storm of indignation" burst, derisive laughter and lots of catcalls. Gorbachev had been in power for a few weeks.

During the pause I was summoned by an officer, a colonel, who taught plastics in civilian life, who knew me by my first name, used the familiar pronoun, and did everything he could to "appeal to my conscience." I was told I shouldn't ruin my career for the sake of a few stupid remarks. He called me naive, accused me of a "running-your-head-into-the-wall" attitude. I should make compromises and so on. I replied like some simpleton that I was merely expressing my opinion, just as was always expected of us.

"It isn't worth it, Enrico," he shouted, "it really isn't." Resignation now dragged his voice down to a low, trust-inspiring register. I let him talk and gazed at the thin smile of a Honecker portrait against a blue background. And from one moment to the next I no longer felt like a castaway, but was once again the captain of my ship, the only honest man still standing, who was not going to let himself be infected with this general depravity.

I answered the poor lieutenant's question about where I had been—I was late getting back to the seminar room—with a smart-aleck "Where do you suppose?" which I regarded as a strong gambit.

Within the hour I might very well be dismissed from the university. This sad sack of a lieutenant, this tool of fate, didn't know himself which end was up—at least the red splotches on his neck seemed to indicate as much—but was able, strangely enough, to hold to his guidelines. And so inside of a few minutes he would have me on his conscience for the rest of his life.

I let question after question go by without volunteering an answer. But while I lay in resolute ambush, something happened that you might call either touching or dreadful: my chess partner from several desks away passed along a note with the "right answer." One after the other they stood up and answered; some were given two, even three tries.

When I finally raised my arm, all the other arms dropped. They were directing the poor lieutenant's attention to me. But it wasn't me who was called on, it was my neighbor.

Before I could raise my arm again, I heard my last name, and a drumroll inside my head. I asked the poor lieutenant to repeat the question.

I answered hesitantly, as if struggling with myself, wrestling for the truth, this time I added the adjectives "stupid" and "inhuman." I hope, I concluded, that I've expressed myself clearly this time. From both the silence in the room and the look on the lieutenant's face I assumed that that was that.

Everyone had "passed" the test. The lieutenant announced this at the end of the hour almost casually and left the room without another word. They celebrated me as the victor, wildly clapping me on the shoulder and back. The fact that I stood there turned to stone was taken as baffled happiness. "I never believed," the jock from the bunk below me confessed solemnly, taking me in from head to toe, "that you belonged to the firm."[1]

On the evening of a day that began with a whistle to wake up and calisthenics, I found myself in Prague, a beautiful woman from Salzburg in my embrace.

I had spotted Nadja on the milk train as it pulled in (as I recall it was coming from Linz), and was standing directly in front of her as she set her foot on the platform. She pushed me away, dropped her plastic bags

---

1. The firm was a synonym for the State Security.

and suitcase, and threw her arms around my neck. As if playing peek-a-boo, from over her shoulder I watched the other passengers detrain.

"Let me have a look at you," Nadja exclaimed, as if she had finally thought of the right thing to say. She was wearing the same brown suit she had on when we had said our good-byes in Dresden. Suddenly she pressed her lips to mine, thrusting her tongue deep.

We took a taxi to the bed-and-breakfast, which was in Vinohrady, a neighborhood of villas. It was all a little dilapidated, but neither the rotting fence nor the rust-eaten garden gate with mailboxes dangling from its chicken wire could diminish the elegance of the house. Walking between tulip beds and fruit trees, their fragrance heavy in the air, we approached the front door, where Frau Zoubková awaited us. She was holding Dora—a bitch both black as hell and somehow weary of life—by her collar. Frau Zoubková's felt slippers made it appear that she shuffled around in them all day just so she could polish the linoleum. Most of the time she moved along close to the wall, and would wait until one of her guests left the kitchen table and made a beeline for the door, only to follow after and erase the trail.

Frau Zoubková occupied the two top floors, living in two rooms adjoining the kitchen on the second, and renting out rooms on the third, each designated with a symbol on the door: sun, stars, moon.

Do I even need to mention that we were given the sun room? The high windows faced south, where we saw, if not the city itself, the suggestion of it just beyond white treetops. The splash of a fountain and the chirping of birds were the only sounds.

I didn't even know the names of some of the fruit that we rinsed off late that evening—under Dora's mournful gaze. More astonishing still: grapes at the end of April—sort of like Christmas cookies at Easter. Nadja liked such comparisons. She gave me a sample of each fruit, and I had to say what it tasted like and reminded me of. Meanwhile I watched Nadja's hands redden under the cold water as they peeled and sliced and constantly shoved things into my mouth, until I couldn't chew and speak at the same time, which set her laughing, and the more she laughed the more nimble her fingers became, the more lively the play of tendons on the backs of her hands . . . Suddenly I firmly grasped her forearm—not to make Nadja stop, but because it was all so unbelievably beautiful.

I licked the drops from the palm of her hand, let my tongue wander a second time, starting at the wrist and following her lifeline just to make sure I had found them all, and I thought the dry sweetness tasted like grapefruit. Scraps of fruit waved like little pennants from Nadja's fingernails—green, red, white. She shoved fingertip after fingertip into my mouth, brushing them against my teeth. Like a blind woman, she groped across my face, up and down my nose, tracing my eyebrows and lips, while I opened her blouse and pushed up her T-shirt.

We froze when we heard the creak of the wooden stairs, listened—water was spilling onto the tile floor. The sink was running over! Nadja turned the tap off, plunged her hands into the water, scooped the peelings out of the drain, turned slowly around to me, raised her arms, and stretched, as if to show me her breasts. I was just about to kiss her when I felt drops falling on my head. Nadja was still holding the peels in her hands. Dora, the hound of hell, lapped water from the floor.

We went to work like half-naked strangers, tidying up, rinsing off, packing our things, then waited for each other outside the bathroom before climbing those endless wooden stairs up to our room.

I saw Nadja's silhouette against the window. She still had her panties on. It sounded like a confession when she whispered in my ear that she was having her period and we couldn't do it today . . . I didn't understand why that should stand in the way, why one thing excluded the other, but was likewise—I must admit—relieved.

I learned soon enough how unnecessary my scruples were. Nadja had a gift for making me feel like the inventor of all these unfamiliar caresses.

Then, it was toward morning, there came a moment when I feared I had spoiled all our happiness. Nadja's head had returned to my shoulder, and automatically I said "Thanks"—everything she had done seemed so incredible. But the instant I uttered it, I felt her stiffen, and I knew how wrong, how stupid I had been. Her face appeared above me, she propped her head on one hand, stared at me, smiled, and wanted to know what number she was for me. I hesitated. "Out with it," she said. I raised my left hand and spread my thumb and forefinger.

Nadja said I couldn't fool her. First she made fun of me, then suddenly accused me of not having waited for her. When I refused to tell her about Katalin, she even turned angry.

At breakfast Dora plopped down between our chairs. Frau Zoubková gave us knowing nods. If we had left any traces in the kitchen they were long since wiped away.

Like somnambulists Nadja and I found the city's loveliest spots, took the train up to Petřín Hill, got out halfway up, walked through the spin-drift of blossoming cherry trees, and lay down in the grass.

Near the Moldau, just a few hundred yards from the Charles Bridge, we inadvertently stepped through the arch of a portal and found our-selves in an enchanted park, at the far end of which were wide stairs lead-ing up to a terrace of brown sandstone, where a copper beech stood. I was about to touch its leaves—from a distance I had thought they were withered—when we heard something rustling behind us. We spun around and saw two peacocks, both fanning their tails simultaneously.

When I brought Nadja to her train, all that was left of her baggage was one suitcase, and we barely spoke. We crossed the train station with-out a word. On the platform where her train was due any moment, Nadja remarked that next time I would have to tell her about my manu-script, she wanted to know all about it, since after all it would be her job to smuggle it into the West. If there was one thing still lacking in my hap-piness, it was those very words.

Back in Jena, the first sentence I wrote to Nadja took on a tone that set me on my way without any larger concept, without my even really having to think about it. As I folded the pages I was already formulating the first lines of letter number two.

I wrote Nadja every day, on a typewriter now, and was amazed that my everyday life was not at all as unliterary as I had thought.

Once I had received her first reply—the pale blue envelopes came rolling in every four or five days—in which she labeled my letter "won-derful prose," I began to lay carbon paper between my pages.

I had started too late to cram for a three-subject exam looming up ahead: the literature, art, and history of Rome, plus the languages, and tests on eighteenth-century German drama and political economics (or was it dialectical materialism?). That left me no time for *Vivat Polska!*, not unless I interrupted the flow of my letters—and if I had put off telling Nadja about my daily life until later, the tone would have been ruined. And so the only work I did on my novel was to report to Nadja how well I was progressing on it. At regular intervals I noted the conclusion of a chapter.

That's funny, don't you think? You can see, can't you, that, given everything you know about me, my behavior was totally untypical? Why, particularly at that time in my life, did I toss my manuscript in the cor-ner? Yes, love, you'll say, yes love was to blame. Yes, I did love Nadja. But even love has to fit in with all the rest somehow.

I no longer know which letter it was, but after only a few days I was already convinced that I was writing an epistolary novel. And it was powerful! If my letters found their way to Nadja—or so my calculation—the work would essentially write itself.[1]

I found myself once again in a situation much like the one in Oranienburg. Everything I saw and did became literary material. Without my intending it, each letter unfolded as a kind of narrative. I was surprised how widely disparate events suddenly wove themselves together as if they were part of some plan of composition. The moment I took the lid off my Rheinmetall, I drifted into storytelling. I barely had to make any corrections, because I was able to enhance my experiences without a second thought, almost automatically. If you know where the roulette ball is going to land, of course you bet on the right number.

I loved Nadja, I loved Jena, I loved my life, and everyone could see how love had changed me. Only Vera had nothing to say.

Nadja and I met in Prague, Brno, or Bratislava every two or three weeks, sometimes for only a few hours. We had invented a secret code for our telephone calls, only to get trapped in it ourselves. For our third meeting—in the middle of my exams—I waited in Bratislava for Nadja, who was spending the week in Vienna, where her mother had moved by that time. Her train was supposed to arrive shortly after mine. When notice was posted that it would be an hour late, I took a taxi, asked the driver to recommend a hotel, paid for the night in advance—the two hundred marks were equal to my entire monthly stipendium.[2] When I returned to the station, the train was now announced as two hours late. That abbreviation for Vienna South Station, which stubbornly stayed posted even while all the other names of cities changed, became my curse that night. Ever since, I also know that *nástupiště* means "platform" and *příjezdy vlaků* is "arrival of trains." I nursed a hopeless lust for revenge and worked up a nasty critique of the station's murals—a commentary that I hoped would make me look brilliant in Nadja's eyes— where Sputnik was skewering the dove of peace high above the heads of

1. The analogy between the situation described here and that in which T. now found himself as a letter writer is certainly self-evident. Both women "fit in with all the rest" and into his "calculation" as well.

2. As a rule each student received two hundred marks per month, with which one could just eke out an existence without assistance from home or taking a part-time job.

all peace-loving peoples. After two hours I felt nothing but an intense hatred and asked for nothing more than that the three sinister figures slinking away at the left side of the mural would turn around and empty their submachine guns on all those socialist faces gazing happily into the future, mow them all down, from the blond steelworker to the granny clad in black. After five hours I begged a cruel Olympus to have mercy on me on last. We had been robbed of five hours, a quarter of our time, a lost evening, half the night.

Finally, sometime after midnight, the train from Vienna pulled in, but without Nadja. There were still tears in my eyes as I begged the hotel for my money back. They took pity on me. I grabbed my bag and boarded the next train for Brno. Between two and three in the morning I searched the station there for Nadja. Alarmed by the notion that she might have been detained at the border but would arrive on the next train, I leapt on a train heading back to Bratislava. I was lucky no one checked my ticket. From Bratislava I called her mother, who, although I had roused her out of her sleep, said, "Ah, my boy," in a deep voice and gave me the number of the Hotel Jakub in Brno.

The people at the Hotel Jakub knew all about our story. A waitress preceded us into the breakfast room and with the gesture of a magician who has just pulled off a trick, garnered loud applause for the happy ending of our crazy trip.[1] Wasn't that the stuff novels are made of? With the help of Nadja's few schillings, we played the Western couple. Every waitress, every museum guard was drawn into our tale, made a confidant— we found our audience in every passerby, in every person who sat down at our table.

Once, it was in Prague, Nadja made me feel very unsure of myself.

I would have stepped on the yarmulke if Nadja hadn't bent down for it in time. She fastened it to my hair with a hairpin—she kept such utensils stowed in her purse. I think Nadja was curious about what I'd look like in a yarmulke. And since we were only a few steps away from a synagogue that we intended to visit, I kept the skullcap on.

Back on the street, I forgot to remove it. After we'd taken a few steps—Nadja had linked arms with me—a man spoke to us. He asked

---

1. "I still recall that 'Maria Theresia' meant Bratislava and 'go to work' meant Brno, but I've forgotten how the mistake happened and whether it was Enrico's or my fault." —Sabine Kraft in a letter to the editor.

where the synagogue was and stared at my yarmulke. I almost tipped it as if it were a hat.

Why had he addressed us in German, Nadja asked him. Her pronunciation was somewhat like Frau Zoubková's, except it had a more cutting tone. Why had he thought we would understand German, or that we would prefer to speak it.

He nodded. With a will-o'-the-wisp look in his eyes and trembling lips, he searched for an apology. Nadja, still linked arm in arm with me, took a half-step forward and directed an open palm toward the synagogue. *"Geradeaus!"* she rasped. He gave another nod, smiled suddenly as if redeemed somehow, and exclaimed, "Shalom!"

Nadja pulled me on ahead. I was waiting for some reaction on her part, perhaps even a laugh. The longer she kept silent, the more uneasy I grew. When I looked at her, we both came to a halt. Nadja was a stranger, sad and proud; yes, almost haughty.

She didn't want me to take off the yarmulke, said it looked good on me. The next day we were talking about her mother, and Nadja said there had also been Jews in her family. I don't know if that's true. The yarmulke is still lying here among our caps and scarves.

I had given scarcely a thought to my exams. I believed in my good luck and passed each one, if just barely. The panel obliged me by honoring my term papers.

The longest time that Nadja and I spent together was eight or nine days in August.

We had rented a room from a Slovakian woman in the Jizerské Mountains. A picture of John F. Kennedy in a silver frame hung in the stairwell.

Nadja was apparently determined to clarify our relationship. On our first hike up to the TV tower at Liberec, she asked me how I viewed our future. I said I wanted to finish my book (on which I hadn't worked for months). Then, if that was truly her wish, I could apply for an exit visa. Those four syllables lasted forever. They crumbled in my mouth like a moldy piece of candy. Nadja asked whether that was truly what I wanted. Yes, I said. She said that she would marry me. I said that would be the simplest way.

We hiked through the dying forest,[1] and it was too late before we real-

1. Power plants in the "three-country triangle" of the GDR, Czechoslovakia, and Poland had badly damaged the flora and fauna of these low mountains.

ized we had been misled by a faded signpost, which had indicated the remaining distance to be nine instead of nineteen kilometers.

By the time we reached the restaurant at the TV tower, my throat was so dry it took me two attempts to order a *pivo*.[1]

According to our landlady's map a narrow-gauge train would take us back to the village, but no one in Liberec knew anything about a narrow-gauge train. We had no choice but to march over the ridge in the dusk. I'll never forget those minutes on the barren summit. As darkness crept up the slopes, our path was illuminated as if on a stage by the light of the setting sun. The air was clear, the horizon infinitely distant in all directions. Our footsteps were the only sound. When Nadja suddenly hugged me, I could feel the hasty beat of her heart. We held each other tight and gazed out across the highlands, like emigrants about to wander into the landscape.

Then came three days of rain, and when the fourth day also dawned gloomy, we headed back to Dresden. Frau Krátká closed the front door behind us without a word.

In order for you to understand Nadja and me, there's something I have to disclose, something that increasingly disturbed me. Although outwardly the perfect couple, we never really became one.

At first there was always the one reason: Nadja's fear of getting pregnant, and she didn't want to take the pill. Then I would forget condoms again, or we were simply too exhausted from our escapades. I won't trouble you with any of what were for me unpleasant details. For a good while now, as soon as the door was shut behind us, we would be overcome with an inexplicable shyness.

For a long time we never mentioned Vera. I had not seen my sister since the day I turned around at Vera's door to join Nadja. Which meant I could reply to Nadja's questions with just a shrug. But Nadja would not let go. I became jealous of Vera. In addition, Nadja hinted that she had knowledge of matters that Vera and I had sworn to keep secret.[2]

I tried to develop clear plans for a future shared with Nadja. I would tough it out in Salzburg as a cabdriver, and write during whatever time was left me. As soon as my book was published, Nadja wouldn't have to work anymore and could concentrate entirely on her studies. And on

1. Beer.
2. Apparently an allusion by T. to an imaginary quasi-incestuous relationship with V. T. This fantasy later takes on outright delusional dimensions.

weekends we'd find things to do—hiking, strolling the town, or traveling to Munich, Vienna, or Italy.

I immersed myself in this new chapter and was aware of how, at the end of each of my monologues, my eyes glistened. Nadja said little, a silence all the more stubborn, the more suggestions I heaped before her.

I was afraid that she was as relieved as I when it finally came time to leave for the station. But no sooner had we boarded the streetcar than I was overcome with a great sadness and a terrible dread of losing Nadja. I told her that I would give anything to repeat the past few days, even if it meant not changing one single experience. She hugged me, and we held each other tight just as we had on the mountaintop.

Until then I had had no trouble returning to correspondence after one of our meetings—on the contrary. This time I was thrown into despair. I ripped page after page out of the typewriter and finally lay down on my bed with no idea of where to go from here. When I woke up I was certain that I had lost Nadja during the night.

From now on I merely tried to keep writing letters as long as I possibly could. Instead of looking forward to her replies, I feared them. I gave up phoning her almost entirely when, in response to my question of whether she had received my letters and what she had been doing of late, Nadja replied: Plugging away, just plugging away.

"What can I do?" I replied. I would do anything I could.

We were too short of money to be able to see each other. My bankbook showed zeros. I had used up Aunt Camilla's D-mark subsidies, asking Vera for help was out of the question. Nadja didn't have time to write letters. I accepted that, and in time everything else as well. When the semester started, I once again had loads and loads of material for letters.

During my last call to Salzburg, Nadja suddenly sounded the way she used to when just her whispering my name was like an unbelievably tender caress. "I love you," I shouted into the phone. "I love you too," she cried, and laughed. I invoked our love one more time and could hear Nadja sending me kisses over the phone. Then the call ended because I had run out of change.

My epistolary novel was going to end with that punch line—unless at some point I could come up with a better ending.

Love,

Your Enrico T.

Dear Jo!

I'll say it just once: If you want to study the confusions and complications of provincial life, if you want work and a steady income, let's talk.[1] As a columnist, you'll be paid two thousand a month after taxes—after July, two thousand D-marks—and we'll also find a decent place for you (and your family?) to live. We're going to need new people in any case. The only question is when we'll make our decisions. We could start printing in Gera tomorrow. It would be a third cheaper, on better paper, with needle-sharp photos. We can vary size by fours[2]—we'd have no limit on the amount of advertising, and we wouldn't have to break up pages already set or postpone articles. Next thing to paradise! If only we could master the computer. Andy wanted eighteen thousand for everything, including software. We're to be his showcase and are to give him a couple of free ads. He'll get his money for the pasting machine and layout tables in July. (Even though I think we'll make it through July 1st quite well, I sometimes wonder what would have happened if we had exchanged our twenty thousand back then for East-marks, which very soon now could end up amounting to sixty or seventy thousand D-marks, maybe even more.)[3]

The *Leipziger Volkszeitung* is a sad bunch. Nobody there even thought it necessary to show up at the Auerhahn on Sunday, even though all the bigwigs—except from the Party of Democratic Socialism, of course—gathered there to wait for results to come in.[4] They greeted us as kings, because they know that we know that the whole lot of them weren't exactly the spearhead of the revolution. That's one of Jörg's favorite topics. At the end of December he nominated Karmeka, who's our new

1. What lay behind this offer was the outcome of local elections held on May 6, 1990. Johann had campaigned as a candidate of Alliance 90, but had failed to be elected to the city council.

2. He means that the page count can be increased or decreased in increments of four.

3. On March 29th, the executive board of the German Bundesbank had recommended an exchange rate of 2:1, arguing that the GDR economy could not support a conversion at 1:1. The new head of government in the GDR, de Maizière, was afraid that cutting wages in half would result in "intolerable social tensions," and advocated a 1:1 rate for salaries and pensions. On July 1st savings up to four thousand marks (and up to six thousand marks for citizens over sixty) were to be exchanged at 1:1, anything beyond that at 2:1. Since the exchange rate at the end of January had been 5:1 or even higher, T. is engaging in one of his typical speculations.

4. For the local elections of May 6, 1990.

mayor, to be chair of the opposition Round Table although he was still a nobody—and that marked the start of Karmeka's rise. Jörg probably expects too much to come of contacts with his "pupil" (as he calls him a bit too often), but certainly the connection doesn't work against us. It isn't clear yet who the new district councilor (the title reminds you somehow of junkers and the kaiser, doesn't it?), but he'll likewise be a Christian Democrat. If we're lucky, it'll end up being one of Fred's buddies. Even today, three days later, there's still not one line about it in the *LVZ*. We have Karmeka headlined on the front page, with interview and photo. And the Altenburgers will learn the rest of what's going on from us first too. No wonder people like the managing director think they'll have an easy time of it here.

On Sunday I had a long talk with Marion and Jörg. I told them about Barrista's city maps, bonus gifts for new subscribers, and his "acquisitions brigade." As for a computer, he literally had to carry one up to our office himself.

After two hours I had Marion to the point where she at least agreed to contract Barrista as a consultant. I had suggested a thousand a month, and that would have been a ludicrously low fee as it is. But the five hundred they agreed to is really little more than an embarrassing gesture.

When we made our offer, he thanked us, but appeared more surprised than pleased. What was it we expected of him? Jörg wanted to run his own ideas past him, Marion talked about organizing the workload, and I said that he should help us choose and train our sales reps—and have a look at our books, because none of us here understands the first thing about accounting.

The baron listened to us for a while, then stood up quite suddenly, and stepped behind his chair, as if it were a lectern. "Would I be correct in stating," he said, his voice languid, his eyelids heavy, "that you have evidently not yet answered, indeed not even asked the fundamental question that needs to be resolved at the start of every business endeavor." Barrista tensed his body and took a deep breath. "Do you or don't you want to get rich?" He looked from one to the other and then added, "I admire anyone who decides he does not. That deserves my greatest respect. I merely need to know the terrain we've chosen to meet upon." He interrupted me brusquely when I burst into laughter.

"It's a more serious matter than you think. Take your time. Don't choose too hastily! It implies far far more than you may perhaps expect."

When Barrista gets excited, you can hear his accent. He sat down again and promised that, whatever our decision, we could count on his good counsel, he merely wanted to know what course we planned for our ship. Then he aimed his glasses at me. I saw the trace of a smile at the left corner of his mouth. "And you aren't going to contradict me?" he asked. "Why don't you refute me with my own example? It's a weird thing about exceptions . . ." He was evidently alluding to our first meeting, when he had lectured me about exceptions. "One can and should make them, one must, however, know that they are exceptions. I allow myself but two—His Highness and you! But I would advise you for now not to make any exceptions, they are for advanced students at best, and even then I'd be very, very careful."

Marion and Jörg didn't understand him at all. In their eyes the baron is an eccentric businessman trying to comfort himself for the loss of his idyllic family. I, however, have discovered in him a logician and philosopher. We, in turn, are for him a stroke of good luck, a kind of tabula rasa when compared to his own mind full of self-evidencies.

Everyone now has to tell him the function of his or her job, be it in sales, ad acquisition, accounting, the structure of actual newspaper production, etc. Sometimes we don't even understand his questions. What does *original* printing price mean? How many *deals* have we *struck*? How high is our *discount for direct bank transferals*? What's our discount percentage for write-offs? etc. When he looks from one of us to the other in that sad, helpless way, we know we've been throwing money away again.

It's easy to regard him as a ridiculous character—which Michaela and her theater dunderheads evidently love to do.

The longer I think it over, the more difficult it is for me to answer his questions—questions I would have never thought to ask and would have impatiently dismissed as childish. What arouses my enthusiasm most, however, is that he would support us with the same attentiveness, the same expenditure of energy, and the same dedication were we to answer each of them with a no. In that case, too, he would pose the same Socratic questions and prepare more diagrams, just with different coordinates.

Of course we can see how sales are slumping and ad income is rising, and it's no secret that either we'll have to expand the amount of space or raise our rates or—at the risk of going under—come up with some new idea. But all that assumes a different power of persuasion when you're looking at two curves: income from sales and from ads, lines that from week to week keep moving—or better, actually striving—closer and closer until you think you can predict where and when they'll cross. Adding the two curves together, on the other hand, gives you the relationship to printing and salary costs. And suddenly we're talking totally differently about how we can ensure our survival. In the weeks ahead we're going to have to increase our profits, because we need a buffer to get through the period after July 1st. What functioned well before may just be spinning wheels afterward. And at least ever since the baron's diagram, we know that our negotiations with the printer will decide our future existence. But the worst thing is that afterward you ask yourself how you could have ever seen it any other way.

Ah, Jo, forgive me. All this is going to bore you something awful. And my new knowledge isn't exactly a fount of originality. If only you could experience Barrista! In his presence even the most serious matters seem easy—it's all so playful, literally playful.

We had him at our place again last Monday (after he had been invited to Jörg and Marion's several times and even joined them on a weekend excursion to Saale—which, to be honest, annoyed me a bit). He doesn't enjoy living in a "hotel-room crypt" and eating nothing but restaurant food. If it were up to Robert and me, he'd be sitting with us at our table much more often.

Each time he visits, his flowers turn our living room into a hothouse. Even withered, the jungle bouquet attracted attention when Michaela threw it in the trash.

In contrast, Michaela was detached if not to say impassive as she took in the baron's report about how his real estate business was progressing. She remained remarkably unruffled when she learned that she would be earning considerably more than the amount guaranteed her, and had not one appreciative word for the baron's achievements.

Robert was grouchy because he wanted us to play Monopoly with him, which, true to character, his good father (and yes, there is such a person again) had sent him as a gift. The baron assured him that he would love to play, but please not Monopoly—that was the dullest game there is, and leads only to confusion. If a single day of his life as a businessman were as stupid and boring as Monopoly, he would look for another job right away. Robert's pouting lower lip would have moved a heart of stone. But, the baron went on, he would love to play something else. Evidently Robert's request suited his purposes. At one point he had let slip a few hints about his cultic research, as he called it. (In May '45 the only Altenburg reliquary, containing the hand of St. Boniface, had vanished, presumably into the baggage of an American soldier when his army withdrew from town.) Barrista doesn't believe his activities are ripe for sharing. Although he squanders half his time on the matter.[1]

His reaction was truly euphoric when Robert held out a boxed game of roulette. "Where do you get something like this?" And was what was inside really what the box claimed it was? The contents amused him. "Sweet flannel," he giggled as he unrolled the plastic layout with its boxes and fields, smoothing it several times. "Sweet velvet!" The jetons sent him into raptures, the little bowl with its numbered wheel turned him into a downright buffoon. "For Lilliputians!"

In the blink of an eye he had calculated the total value of the jetons and determined how many of each sort there were. Michaela cleared the table, but didn't even have time to change tablecloths. The baron had already arranged everything; while he distributed the jetons, he urged Michaela to finally sit down with us, all the while switching back and forth between French and German. "Come on, play, do sit down, it's your turn!" he cried, and began by placing a ten on the right row and the first dozen—hardly a gutsy beginning, I thought. I risked twice as much on three wagers: on red, odds, and the zero. Michaela strewed half her jetons across the numbered fields, Robert placed a hundred on black. It wasn't until the baron stretched out his arm and described an oval with the palm of his hand above the field, while whispering, *"Rien ne va plus,"* that we realized the ball was whirling. A moment later it took a few bounces back and forth, and the baron announced the results in French, then added (what we all could see), "Fifteen, black." He slid the croupier's rake across the wrinkled plastic playing field—Michaela and the baron had lost everything. Robert was given another hundred; I got a twenty,

---

1. T. surely knows more than he admits here, cf. his article in the *Altenburg Weekly*, no. 13; the most extensive and well-researched study on the history of the Altenburg hand reliquary has been done by Hans Dörpfeldt, published unfortunately in an obscure periodical, *Heidelberger Studien zur katholischen Dogmatik* [Heidelberg studies on Catholic dogmatics], no. 66, p. 55ff.; cf. P. Schnabel, *Die Heimkehr des Patrons* [The patron returns home], in *Altenburger Pfade in die Vergangenheit* [Altenburg paths into the past], no. 1, p. 7ff.; suitable as an introduction to the topic, especially for young readers, is *Arbeiten und Beten mit Bonifatius* [Work and prayer with Boniface] (Altenburg, 2004), 12th edition.

but had lost forty. Barrista smiled and doubled his bet. By the second round I was already bored, the same state I thought I could observe as well in the generous way Michaela scattered the rest of her jetons. Robert risked another hundred, this time on red; my bet was the same as before, except this time instead of the zero, I slid a twenty next to Robert's hundred. The baron repeated the same conjuring motion with his arm, the ball jangled—eleven, red. One of the baron's fingers touched the eleven, restoring Michaela's capital to its original state.

But it wasn't long before Michaela was the first to have lost everything, which had evidently been her intention. With a run of incredible good luck, Robert followed every spin of the ball. After each loss the baron doubled his bet, risking forty, eighty, a hundred sixty—and finally won. His perseverance had paid off.

And yet joyful enthusiasm had turned into crabbed intensity. He engaged in no conversation, answered no questions, just stared at the layout, and hastily tossed the ball. He was like a machine. Whereas Robert was the real player and hero. He lost as much as he won, but he still had his winnings left from the first round. I raised my bets because I was tried of the endless, dreary up and down—and was the next one to go bankrupt. The baron kept on doubling his bet until he won. I had never before seen him so inattentive, yes almost impolite. It didn't so much as occur to him that only we men were sitting there and Michaela was washing dishes in the kitchen.

He didn't emerge from under the ice until he leaned back, presented his jetons, and said, "I'm getting out now." "You did notice, didn't you?" he asked, finally reanimated, and then added with childlike pride, "Toward the end it was all wins for me."

"Unlucky in love, lucky at cards," I said. The baron gave me such a piercing look that I was on the verge of apologizing for my tactlessness.

"No," he said with a smile. "Probability. Maximal probability. Chance is only a question of the framework, the marked-off field, and, of course, of time. The more money you have, however, the less chance can make a mess of things. Just as in real life."

He knew every gambling den between Wiesbaden and Las Vegas. It was only superficially a question of winning and losing or of whether you were a hopeless gambler or an upright fellow. It involved more, much more than that, maybe everything. He had learned what it means to hand yourself over root and branch to fate and wait to see if it touched you. Instead of an apple Eve should have offered her husband a handful of jetons.

I admitted that I hadn't found our game all that charged with fate.

I shouldn't make myself look ridiculous, he said—this here was less than child's play, this was nothing, nothing at all—what had I expected? I was baffled, indeed frightened by the vehemence with which he thrust his hand under the plastic layout and flung it from him. It flopped to the center of the table, fell back, and ended up dangling from the edge of the table in front of him. A few jetons fell to the floor, which put him into a rage. He grabbed the plastic again between thumb and forefinger and held it up in disgust as if it were the filthy handkerchief of a foe.

That wasn't meant as a reproach, he said, already in a gentler mood, as we emerged from under the table with the jetons we'd garnered. But for him this game was something almost sacred, a ritual, yes, yes, a cleansing and sacrificial ritual—he meant that in earnest. He repeated it verbatim again to Michaela, who had returned to the room because, as she later said, she assumed there was an argument.

What I needed was to experience the real game sometime, he remarked with studied casualness. And when he said "real" he meant just that, a weekend in Monte Carlo, what did I think of that, he'd take care of all the details. "Agreed?"

"Monte Carlo is not as far away as you think," he said. Along with other lovely lessons I could learn there, there would be the concomitant and pleasant effect of an improvement in my financial status, because since it was my first time, and especially if I followed his instructions— "there are always rules and regulations"—I would be certain, absolutely certain, to win! We ought to consider sometime why it was that casinos set betting limits. That was the key to understanding. That was worth thinking about.

The baron hinted at something like this weeks ago, but I had just taken it for small talk. Apparently with him there is no such thing as small talk.

Hugs from your Enrico

PS: Just one question: Although he fully understands our situation, Anton Larschen refuses to wait any longer in regard to his memoirs and is behaving like an ornery brat. Jörg and I have read them, and want to publish them, but it requires lots of work by an editor. May I send you the manuscript? You'll be paid, of course, can sign off as editor, and a preface and afterword would be very welcome too.

Tuesday, May 8, '90

Dear Nicoletta,

It isn't just the spring weather that is making it hard for me to continue my report and tell you about December—at the end of November Nadja and I had separated for good.

Upon returning to Jena I felt paralyzed and lonely rather than relieved. I had heard scarcely anything from Vera since March, the number of letters that Johann and I had exchanged during the year could be counted on one hand. I hadn't even really congratulated him on the birth of his daughter Gesine.

On Monday I overslept, missing my Latin translation seminar, tried to no avail to prepare for my Greek class that evening—when I looked up a word, I'd already forgotten it by the time my eyes returned to the text—didn't wake until noon on Tuesday, and barely made it to the bathroom and back. At least it occurred to me to report in sick.

Our language teacher, a gifted translator of Horace,[1] let me know that—signed medical excuse or no—he didn't believe me. The indifference with which even Samthoven had been treating me for several weeks attested to my being hardly so much as a mediocre student now.

My weariness grew from day to day. The one thing I could manage each morning was to open one of the little doors on the Advent calendar my mother had sent me—a ritual that we maintain to this day.

At the start of Christmas break I took the train to Dresden and crawled into bed. When my mother was at home I hardly left her side.

We were expecting Vera for early-afternoon dinner on the 24th. To my surprise my mother set the table for four.

Roland was at least ten years older than Vera and a good two inches shorter. His delicate nose didn't match his thick lips. The skin on his head glistened under his sparse black hair. He wore peculiar glasses, square

---

1. T. apparently had in mind *Horace: Works in One Volume*, Manfred Simon, ed. and trans. (Berlin, 1972).

and rimless, and spoke a pleasant dialect that I took for southern Thuringian. It was striking how interested he was in everything, even the label on the bottle of soda. As he listened he would nod and keep repeating, "Okay, okay, okay," as if every sentence required his approval.

When Roland mentioned his comrades in "Torino," where he had spent Christmas the previous year, several things became clear to me. All the same I asked how he had made it to Turin. "In my car," he replied, and went on chewing contentedly. I said that I'd likewise love to have a car that you could drive all the way to Turin—Salzburg would do for me.

Roland was unimpressed, and lectured me instead on how people here have far too many illusions about the West. Travel wasn't all it was cracked up to be—and anyway you needed money for it; and after two or three weeks, the drudgery started all over again. And so on and so forth.

"But after all, a person has to see the Mediterranean!" Ah, Nicoletta, if only I had known those words back then. I stood up and went to my room. But picturing how the story of Nadja would now be bandied about, I regretted my departure.

A little later there was a knock on my door. I let Roland in. He held out his pack of Revals. Standing side by side, we smoked the Western cigarettes at the open window. I don't know if he took only deep drags or started to say something several times, but before he could get a word out, Vera appeared, ran her hand through my hair, and pulled him away. The cigarettes tasted awful.

That evening Roland was given more than his share of gifts. He himself hadn't bothered, at least not for Mother and me. Vera was wearing a pantsuit that he had brought back for her, and she thrust her chin forward for us to smell the perfume on her neck. Then Aunt Camilla's parcel was set on the table. Vera and I began at once to search for currency. As if by agreement and with a fervor worse than that of the worst customs agents, together we ripped wrapping paper from cans of pineapple and packages of coffee, tore off gold stars and ribbons, and paid no attention to what fell to the floor. When Roland turned away from us in disgust, I went at it with special gusto. I discovered the first hundred-D-mark bill in the packet of Fa soap, the second under the plastic tray in the Sprengel praline box. The third remained unaccounted for until Mother found it among the tattered wrapping paper.

The next day—granted, he did drive Mother to work at half past five in the morning—Roland made himself at home. He ran around in his underwear, smoked, ransacked the pantry, finished off the whole bowl of potato salad—standing—drank the Murfatlar[1] straight from the bottle, and never stopped scratching his hairy chest.

A decal with a white dove of peace against a blue background adorned the rear windshield of his Renault, and he and Vera used it for jaunts to Meissen, Moritzburg, and Pillnitz, and to the theater, too, along with Roland's comrades, who were staying at Vera's.

She and I hardly spoke. Roland was her revenge for Nadja.[2] From my mother I learned that the two of them had already decided to get married. At the dinner table I asked them where they would be living. "What a stupid question!" Vera said. Roland, however, admitted that he would prefer to settle in the East. But a move like that would be like stabbing his comrades in the back.

Roland talked constantly about the ban against leftists in the civil service, he had once been threatened with it himself. He asked me if I could give him something to read, something I had written, of course, or read it aloud, then and there, that same evening. He also asked if there was a "red-light district" in Dresden. I knew the term "infrared treatment" as a synonym for GDR propaganda and other expressions like "red cloister" for particularly hard-nosed schools, Red assholes, and a few others. I thought Roland meant some kind of governmental area.[3]

Mother dubbed Roland a fine man, because his outspokenness would cause him trouble everywhere, with both sides. I, however, found him tiring and pretentious. I regarded his presence as the reason for my chronic exhaustion.

New Year's Eve was dreadful, the trip back was dismal.

I had locked the Nadja letters in a drawer. *Vivat Polska!* had become a stranger to me. If I was going to continue it, I would have to do what I had thus far avoided, that is, read what I had already written.

No, it wasn't a debacle, not even a disappointment. Of course I saw how unfinished, how in need of correction the manuscript was—with no regrets I excised whole paragraphs and pages. A few details, moreover,

1. A sweet Romanian white wine.
2. T. was evidently still of this opinion in May 1990.
3. It is rather unlikely that Roland, who according to V. T. was relatively well informed about conditions in the GDR, would have asked such a question. Perhaps here as well T. is sacrificing truth for the sake of a punch line.

some of the descriptions and metaphors seemed to me so close to perfect I was afraid I had pilfered them from Babel or Mailer.

All the same, on that Sunday afternoon—cold, sunny, no snow—I was overcome with a doubt that stained everything, made it all unpalatable. I no longer believed me!

Hadn't I once considered taking the blame for the "Karl and Rosa Live!" graffiti? Why then shouldn't one of my characters come up with the idea of claiming *Vivat Polska!* as his own work? There were plenty of reasons to. And what, beg your pardon, was really so bad about the inscription itself? Couldn't anyone with some notion of the story of good soldier Schweik twist the meaning around enough to take the air out of the cheeks of Stasi interrogation specialists?

You can see, Nicoletta, that I've once again arrived at just such a point.[1] It's like when an adult talks about the worries and fears of a child. Because you're probably asking why I didn't rejoice in these new ideas and use them. That's precisely what would have done the whole project good and actually and finally made it interesting.

And yet, even if my own sense of life was not all that tragic, literature at least had to be. And that meant suffering. The greater the suffering, the better the literature. Don't laugh! I didn't know any better. Our role, the East's role, was one either of suffering and resistance or of going along, *tertium non datur*. My heroic epic was tilting toward farce; and in the next instant it had become impossible.

My suspicion was that my own falsely led life had ruined my writing. Why didn't I have the strength simply to brush my doodlings from the desk and set to work instead on Kaegi's grammar?[2] Why didn't I bring this to a fitting end? Because I didn't have the strength to live without writing, without the illusion of a calling?

Since I wasn't going to change myself, I would have to wait for the world to change.

I looked for some way out and, logically enough, I found it: I had to go further back, back to the time before my Fall, when suffering had still been suffering and God still God.

So, of course you've already guessed what comes next. Almost immediately I saw before me in seductive clarity a novella about a student who

1. When had he ever previously arrived "at just such a point"?
2. A standard textbook.

is on the verge of being broken by the system of the GDR. In fact all I had to do was write about what I had experienced, and make sure I gave it an appropriate ending, some surprising twist, something different from what had happened to me, a finale presentable to a wider public.

In my mind the tone of voice hovered somewhere between *Young Törless* and *Tonio Kröger*. The plot was quickly sketched out. Suddenly I felt free and adventuresome, as if now that my work was as certain as certain can be—its completion looked to be a matter of weeks—I could participate in other people's lives as well.

Dear Nicoletta, it's three in the morning. I'm waking up earlier and earlier. Yesterday, on the way to the office, I thought about what I should describe to you next. Suddenly there was Anton before my eyes. And in the next moment it was clear to me that Anton and his meeting with Johann ought to be part of the letter I had with me ready to drop in the mail.[1]

Of course it wouldn't contribute much to our cause and would add confusion to my narrative if I were to report about every encounter and acquaintanceship that had some significance for me in one way or another. And yet Anton deserves a few lines, so that the picture you have of my life isn't a frozen, one-sided view.

I don't know whether I can call years of living alongside Anton a friendship or not. Our daily proximity to one another did, however, create an almost intimate familiarity that now and then counterbalanced all the partialities and secrets that Anton shared with others. Our seminar clique was always called "Anton's bunch." He was the only man I knew who placed exceptional importance on clothing and hairstyles and could talk about fashion for hours. David Bowie—whose music he considered merely average—was his idol. And from a distance at least Anton actually looked like him. On those special occasions when students were expected to wear their Free German Youth shirt, Anton would appear in a black suit, white shirt, and black tie, so that at first a good many professors thought he had just returned from a funeral and left him alone. When Anton burst into laughter, tossing back his blond locks and reveal-

---

1. By now at least it should be apparent how preoccupied T. was with questions of composition when writing these letters.

ing gaps behind his eyeteeth, he always reminded me of a whinnying horse.

Anton was a man to be envied. He had a very beautiful and warm-hearted wife and a little boy. All the same Anton fell in love with a new woman every couple of weeks. He spent almost all his evenings at the Rose, the student club.

I found Anton's seminar work and translations disappointing. It's no exaggeration to say that I never heard Anton express an original thought. He reacted to criticism with defiance and even tears, and despite his stubborn resistance to wearing a blue shirt, he folded immediately when pressed to become an officer in the reserves.

Anton had never dreamed of applying for an exit visa. He was perfectly aware that his appearance and choice of majors wouldn't be nearly as unusual as they were in the East.

When Johann visited me in Jena after Nadja and I had split up—we hadn't spoken with one another for an eternity—suddenly there was Anton standing at my door, wanting to pick up the letter from his latest sweetheart, which had been sent to my address. Anton paid no attention to either me or Johann, ripped open the envelope, withdrew to a corner, read, whinnying loudly a couple of times, and immediately set to work on his reply. Johann made fun of Anton's behavior, whereas I had long since grown used to it. All of a sudden Anton asked if he could read us something, but first finished the last few lines of his letter, then sat there pondering for a moment while we waited for his presentation.

Anton read in a monotone, occasionally repeating a sentence, only to correct it on the spot. Anton's story was about the Good Lord, about how God created man.

After a few sentences Johann and I listened spellbound. What amazed me was not so much the plot as the turns of phrase and details. I recall that there was an angel who comes floating past God singing, "Thou who seest all things . . ." But God in fact doesn't see everything. Finally God puts his hands to work all on their own, so that he doesn't have to take his eyes off the earth. And like children playing hide-and-seek he keeps asking his hands, "Ready yet?" He wants to be surprised. Suddenly something from very nearby plummets to the earth, God fears the worst. And now his hands appear before him, muddied with clay but without any sign of mankind. After a thunderstorm God sends his hands away,

"Do as you will, I know you no longer!" And yet without God there is no completion, which is why his hands become discontented and weary and finally kneel down and do penance the whole day long. Which is why it seems to us that God is still resting and that the seventh day still goes on and on.

Johann wiggled his toes in his woolen socks and sought out my eyes. I looked up at Anton like a teacher gazing at his prize pupil and tried to hide my bafflement as best I could.

"A stroke of genius!" Johann exclaimed.

The real shock, however, was that, after asking for an envelope and stamps, Anton now folded up the pages as if he attached no real importance to their preservation.[1]

I said we needed to celebrate his accomplishment—and invited Anton to share our dinner. At first I didn't mind fading into the background. I was the host and my job was to take care of the two of them, who quickly took a liking to each other. What did annoy me was the way they accepted my waiting on them as a matter of course. While Anton ran through his repertoire of views and Johann, inasmuch as he was still under the sway of the story, was prepared to consider them or at least not dismiss them outright (Anton was a great fan of Klaus Mann and Erich Kästner), they began to eat and drink while I was still running back and forth like a waiter between the kitchen and the front room. A glance, a smile—and I would have been placated. Anton had moved on to his preferences in music, and Johann was trying to figure out what sort of music King Crimson played. They didn't even notice when I raised my wineglass—theirs were already empty again.

After the meal, when Anton got up to go and Johann asked what his plans were, Anton invited him to come along to the Rose. They didn't return until way after midnight, slept half the next day, and sat around in the kitchen after having first raided my fridge. It was Anton who accompanied Johann to the train station.[2]

On Monday Anton told me he thought we had both known Rilke's

1. It should be remembered that, as he did with the majority of his letters, T. made a carbon copy of these pages.

2. The assumption that there was a homoerotic relationship between Johann and T. sheds relatively clear light on this enigmatic situation. The following remark from the copy, rendered illegible in the original, also indicates as much: "Just as with Vera before him, I had no choice but to interpret this as Johann's payback for my love affair with Nadja."

"Tales of the Good Lord." It had been a little unfair of me to saddle him the whole time with my visitor. Did I want to take a walk with him by way of reimbursement? I received a letter from Johann in which he expressed his regrets that we had had so little time for each other over the weekend.

A couple of days later Vera wrote to tell me she had applied for an exit visa and had separated from Roland.

Enough, then, of my confusions for this round,

Your Enrico T.

Wednesday, May 9, '90

Dear Jo,

What should we have done, in your opinion? Where else could we have got that many desks and chairs from one day to the next? And it was Helping Hand that got our *obolus*. Should it all have been demolished and burned? In Jörg's eyes they're trophies. During the occupation of Stasi headquarters,[1] Michaela pilfered a silver Matchbox-size APC to prove she'd actually been "inside."

Yesterday morning Ilona greeted me with sobs. Where had I been? She was close to pummeling me with her fists. She had wanted to come and get me, but she couldn't leave the office unstaffed—and that's what she had told Herr von Barrista too. He had called and hauled her over the coals three times.

It was a beautiful morning, warm and with lots of birds chirping away. I had bought breakfast rolls on Market Square. I asked Ilona to make us a pot of coffee, sat down at the telephone, and mulled over what it was Barrista might want.

The day before yesterday we were in Giessen. The publisher of the newspaper, who's not much older than I, received Jörg and me as warmly as you could imagine. We assumed it was a bluff, since not one word was said about the reason for our visit. When Jörg openly addressed the issue and repeated the managing director's threats, the publisher let loose with a peal of laughter. He knew nothing about that. He was so sorry, yes,

---

1. On Dec. 6, 1989, representatives of the civil rights movement had, as was the case in many other towns as well, occupied the local offices of State Security.

really, it wasn't his fault, or at most only to the extent that he had asked the managing director to extend an invitation for us to meet with him sometime, that was all—perhaps the fellow had thought that was the only way to rouse us to a visit. He couldn't make any sense of it otherwise. All he had wanted was to learn a little about Altenburg firsthand. After that he gave us a tour of the whole enterprise and invited us to a little festive lunch in a Chinese restaurant, at the end of which he asked the waiter for the receipt.[1]

When Ilona, still stony with fright, arrived with the coffee, I put some life back into her face by telling her about the baron's proposal for a trip to Monte Carlo. It wasn't until Ilona pointed to the telephone and reproachfully exclaimed, "And you ain't got nothin' to say about that, huh?" that I noticed the silence. And it wasn't just the telephone. There weren't any visitors either. I picked up the receiver and heard the dial tone.

Ilona watered plants, I sharpened pencils. When she sat back down with her hands in her lap and stared at her shoes, I told her she needed to find something to do.

She said she'd been here till ten the night before trying to get caught up, she couldn't get anything done during the day. "This is spooky," she cried, and started crying again. "Really spooky!" And then Ilona, who is constantly and for no good reason the victim of exaggerated fears, asked, "You don't suppose something's happened—an atom bomb?"

I sent her to the market so she could convince herself this was not the case. After she left, I sat there alone, waiting; I would have been happy for any call, any visitor.

When the phone finally rang, I flinched. I answered and right away I knew from the baron's "Well, how's it going?" that the world was in shipshape order. "Guess what I've got for you?" I would have loved to have shouted, "It doesn't matter what you've got for us!" and wasn't the least surprised when the door opened and Jörg and Marion entered.

"We got it!" the baron said in triumph, and for a moment I enjoyed my own ignorance. "Sixty thousand, Türmer! For sixty thousand." I still

1. T. evidently thought he was being reduced to a "deduction." It is said of him that later on he would make a point of crumpling up the bill after a business lunch and tossing it into the ashtray. (As reported by Johann Ziehlke.)

didn't understand. "The shopkeeper downstairs almost had it in his pocket. Your building."

"You're a—genius!" I cried. I almost said "genie"—but decided to change the second syllable. "A genius!" I repeated, just to show him that I knew it was a word that ended in an s. Ever since we moved in here we've been trying to figure out how to become a publishing house with all the bells and whistles. And suddenly it's all within our reach!

While we were in Giessen, Piatkowski—who was reelected, by the way, although he had been far down on his party's list—had telephoned the baron. The baron had immediately paid him a call "with a little bouquet" for Madame Piatkowski. It turned out, however, that only one fifth belonged to her; her older brother, however, had two fifths, and the two other sisters the rest. He had hoped to take care of the whole thing by telephone, but in order to have any chance whatever, he had had to travel all the way to a village just south of Bonn, where the rest of the clan was already assembled.

He was almost too slow in realizing that it was less a matter of the brother than of his wife, and of the youngest sister's husband, who both had instantly whiffed big money. Whereupon he had made it clear to them that the shopkeeper wouldn't be able to get a D-mark loan in a hundred years—they'd have a long wait. And then he had played the "time card," as he called it, and claimed he needed their agreement then and there, otherwise his clients would have to follow through on another option. They had dispersed around ten that night. Shortly after midnight he had forced Recklewitz—still in his pajamas and robe, he lives somewhere nearby over yonder—to draw up the necessary contracts. He himself had had trouble so early in the morning freeing up liquid assets even for just the small change he needed to have for a stuffed briefcase all set to present to the family.

The baron was very apologetic for not having had me at his side. The three siblings plus spouses had been so befuddled after one glance into the briefcase that they had assented on the spot. Of course he lacked our consent, but had felt there was no real risk there, since even in the worst case, he could easily resell it anywhere for sixty thousand. Since they more or less already had the money in their hands, he was not at all worried that they might spit the bait back out. The appointment with the notary was for three that afternoon. And as if all that were not enough, the baron had booked a half-page ad for our future issues, no termination date specified. A friend of his will be opening a travel agency in Altenburg shortly and, what's more, she'll be showing people what real publicity should look like . . .

The baron succeeds at everything! There was no response whatever to his article about the woman whose head had been shorn in public in 1941. But the baron had been able to discover the descendants of the hapless hairdresser who at the time had considered it an honor to do the deed. These descendants own a beauty salon right next to the Rathaus. And? Do you see where I'm going with this? And now the baron does indeed have his shop on Market Square. And Andy's lease takes effect on June 1st.

After our noon meal I was about to go through the received mail file with Ilona, but was puzzled by her strange gestures when I asked her about what had come in so far. In the corner behind me stood Frau Schorba from Lucka. Like some oratorio soloist, she was clad in a dark dress that fell straight down from her bosom to just above the tips of her shoes. At first Frau Schorba didn't budge, as if trying to maintain her stelalike appearance. She then followed me mutely down the hall, where I now set a chair beside my desk, sliding it as close to the wall as possible.[1] We said nothing, as if we didn't know what to talk about outside of our usual ritual. Her face, which has always been something of a mask, now suddenly betrayed her agitation, her every thought. "Nice of you to stop by," I said, trying to relieve the tension trapped within her silence from getting the upper hand. Frau Schorba didn't look up. I waited.

"Can you take me? Can you give me a job? Please! And don't ask why." She grasped my hands. "You must never, never ask me why. You must promise me that."

Frau Schorba's hands were ice cold. She had edged to the front of her chair and was bent so far forward that I was afraid that in the next moment she would sink to her knees. I asked her to sit back up.

"You must!" she whispered, still presenting me the shaved nape of her neck. "You must! Please, please!"

It wasn't until I warned her that someone might come in at any moment that she straightened up and pulled a handkerchief from her sleeve. Shortly thereafter Jörg stepped in, letter in hand.

---

1. T. was probably afraid that Frau Schorba would be too heavy for a room declared off-limits by the police.

I introduced Frau Schorba and asked her to wait in the reception room. Both Jörg and I found the purchase of our building quickly helped console us in regard to Steen's letter, in which he informed us that due to internal restructuring of his firm he would unfortunately not have any time free to meet with us over the next few weeks. This also meant, he wrote, that we would not be able to depend on an extension of his ad.

I told Jörg what I knew about Frau Schorba and asked him if he could include her in the host of job applicants—since we'll truly be in urgent need of reinforcements.

Then I accompanied Frau Schorba downstairs. When I asked what sort of salary she had in mind, she gave a few joyful shrugs. She would take whatever we could offer her.

Hugs, Your E.

PS: You, of course, would receive the same salary I do.

Thursday, May 10, '90

Dear Nicoletta,

I always picture you reading my letters standing—standing or walking. No sooner have you fished the latest dispatch from your mailbox than you clutch your purse and newspaper under your arm, open the envelope with your car key, unfold both pages, and start to read without giving a thought to anything else. You don't even notice how your feet carry you up the stairs, from one step to the next, how you open your door, set down your purse and newspaper, or simply let them fall to the floor. It's not all that important which lines bring a smile or a frown to your face. The only important thing is your undivided attention. It's only on the second reading that you make yourself comfortable on the couch or in an armchair. As for anyone who might be watching you read— wouldn't he envy the writer of that letter and wish he were in his shoes?

It is dreams like these that are to blame for my continued efforts.

In the middle of June '87, barely a year and a half after Vera filed her application for an exit visa, I received a telegram. "Leaving today. Neustadt Station," followed by departure time and as usual, "Greetings, Vera."

The telegram arrived around eleven. I normally would have left my place by ten at the latest. And since it was Tuesday I would have been in the library, except that when I got up the tap didn't work, no matter how I played with it. A note in the building entryway promised running water by ten thirty. I had lain down again and didn't wake up until the pipes began to spit and grumble, flooding the sink with a jet of rusty brown water. And if, as I was leaving the building, I hadn't seen the messenger— who was scanning the doorbell register with his glasses pushed back up on his forehead—and asked him who he was looking for . . . yes, a miracle that I got the telegram in time.

It was one of my few train trips without something to read or work on. Although I stared out the window the whole time, I never even took notice of the valleys of the Saale or the Weinböhla.

I walked from Neustadt Station to Vera's apartment. The windows were closed, no one answered the door. I left a note and took a streetcar to my mother's place. No one there either. Finally, an hour later, they arrived together.

Vera had spent the whole day running from office to office; for the first time in her life Mother had called in sick and now dragged in two suitcases full of new shoes, underwear, and bed linens. She couldn't understand why Vera wanted to leave with just a little traveling bag. And if it hadn't been for photographs and my father's handkerchief collection, she wouldn't even have needed that.

"What am I supposed to do with all this?" my mother cried, dogging Vera's footsteps until she locked herself in the bathroom and we all three stood around shouting. Mother was the first to start sobbing.

As I write to you about all this, it seems to me as if this were the first time I've ever recalled those hours.[1]

Vera moved through each room one last time, opening every drawer, as if she wanted to print it all on her memory. She'd really prefer to go to the station by herself, she said. Shaking her head, she watched Mother butter one sandwich after the other, as if we were going on a family outing. We walked to the streetcar stop together.

Mother had bought a pack of Duetts and was chain-smoking. We rode to the Platz der Einheit. Vera and I had taken a few steps in the direction of Neutstadt Station, when Mother called her back. "Vera! I

---

1. This letter is among the most illegible, due primarily to cross-outs and insertions, especially in the final third.

can't do it!" Mother was still standing in the same spot where we had got off the streetcar. Vera ran back, set down her bag, and I watched as—for the first time, or so it seemed to me—she hugged my mother. I could also see my mother caressing Vera's cheeks. Then I noticed people turning around to look at them.

Vera said nothing, cast a glance into her compact mirror, and linked her arm in mine. I took her travel bag. Someone might have thought she was bringing me to the train.

Neither outside the entrance nor inside the station did I notice anything unusual. It was a few days before the start of school vacation, and there were long lines at the ticket booths. We slowly climbed the stairs. I was afraid that some of Vera's girlfriends—and boyfriends—would arrive and we wouldn't be alone.

We walked along the platform. People were standing shoulder to shoulder in little groups. Bottles of wine and bubbly were being passed around. Almost every group had children, each with a backpack and some stuffed animal to clutch. To me it looked as if all these white-splattered jeans outfits had reassembled at their point of origin.

Under an open sky, at the end of the platform now, Vera unpacked her sandwiches.

"The Stasi asked about you," she said, without looking at me.[1] I exclaimed much too loudly, "What?" Yes, I think I crowed that "What?" like a fourteen-year-old whose voice is cracking.

"That's how it is," she said, "if someone's a little more interesting than the rest." She used her thumb to lift the top of a sandwich and remarked that even after thirty years, it still hadn't registered with Mother that she didn't like blood sausage.

"Those idiots," I said.

"Why idiots?" Vera asked, tossing a pigeon some bread.

"What else would you call them," I said. Vera smiled—and fed pigeons, as if that had been the point of our coming here. The blood sausage hung like a tongue from between the slices of bread and finally landed at her feet.

1. From this point on T. insinuates—evidently intentionally—a suspicion. It is as if no letter can fail to mention some connection between Vera and State Security. And yet nothing in his presentation, either to this point or afterward, points to any such relationship. An unbiased reader will be unable to share T.'s qualms on the basis of remarks made here by V. T.

"Maybe they are idiots," Vera said, "but they do exist and nothing is going to change that soon."

The train pulled in with no announcement on the loudspeakers. While the others stormed their cars, Vera distributed the rest of the bread. "But it's possible to talk with these idiots," she said. "Do you have anything else to say in that regard?"

I felt a need to sit down or, better yet, lie down. I almost said, "That's for you to decide." Instead of asking Vera the reason for her comments, I said nothing, which was perhaps the worst thing to do. I stared at the black platform and at the pigeons battling for bread as they hopped over each other, beating their wings. From the corner of my eye I could see Vera successfully unsnap her purse with her pinkie and pull out a brown-and-white-checked handkerchief, one of the perfectly ironed huge ones that had belonged to our father and always smelled of the drawer they were kept in. She calmly wiped her hands. Appetites whetted by the bread, the pigeons waddled around pecking at anything, even cigarette butts.

Suddenly Vera was holding the yellow imitation-leather silverware pouch that I had had to make in shop class, my gift to her at her Youth Consecration ceremony. "Here," she said, "this is what's left of my fortune." The pouch was stuffed with currency.

Vera had halted in front of a car door. She kissed me first on the cheek, then on the lips. I handed her her traveling bag, and she climbed aboard—she was the last, I think.

The people in the aisle pressed against the windows to let her by. I accompanied Vera from window to window. I saw Vera light a cigarette right below the NO SMOKING sign. She held up the pack, Mother's Duetts. Then the doors closed, which unleashed a new battle for places at the windows.

Whenever our eyes met, Vera smiled.

Without any announcement or whistle, the train suddenly lurched and began to pull out. The outcry along the platform was deafening. Anyone who could reached for a hand extended from a window. Even Vera allowed herself to be caught up in the hysteria. I saw her hand in the upper corner of the window, as if she wanted to give me the last half of her cigarette. She pressed her lips tight and shook her head, until I could see her no more.

Far too many people ran after the train in order to hold the hand they were grasping for a few more seconds. As idiotic as I found it all, what a grand spectacle it was when all those hands let go simultaneously.

From the end of the platform a wave of faces reddened from crying washed toward me. One woman threw her arms around my neck and was then tugged away. The last car thundered past, and in the next second each of us was all by himself—low voices, just an occasional sob. We left the platform one by one, as if observing some previous agreement.

I walked along the Elbe, following the shore upriver as far as the Blue Wonder Bridge, and headed up the slope, all the way to the grand villa with its circular flower beds.

Franziska opened the door as if she were expecting me. Her greeting was as warm, even fervent, as I used to dream it would be. From the cellar I could hear the music of Johann's band, just a couple of bars that kept breaking off at the same spot. "All they ever do is argue," Franziska said. I said nothing yet, because I could hear singing now. I understood hardly anything, and the singer—it wasn't Johann's voice—soon fell silent again as well. How I suddenly detested this riff-raff, these church mice who never took a risk. What difference did it make what faith you sanctimoniously pretended to believe, or where you pretended it? Would Johann have been permitted to study theology if he had admitted he was an unbeliever? My revulsion surprised even me. Instead of bidding her an immediate good-bye, I followed her upstairs. The light went out on the landing of the stairs leading to their attic apartment. Franziska came back down to grope for the switch, or so I thought. By the glow of the streetlamp I could still see Franziska shove her glasses up into her hair, felt her press against me—and we kissed.

We barely budged the whole time, but the hardwood floor under our feet creaked now and then. Of course I had noticed Franziska had had a little to drink. But it wasn't clear to me that she was completely drunk until she suddenly slumped and I was unable to keep her from slipping to the floor. I tried to sit her down on a step, and she almost fell off. Franziska held me tight. "It's true, isn't it," she whispered, "you do love me, don't you?" I said I did.[1]

The light went on, Johann was saying good-bye to his buddies.

1. The next three lines are blacked out in both original and copy.

I soundlessly freed myself partway from Franziska and pulled her glasses back down on her nose. But neither my presence nor Franziska's condition seemed to surprise Johann.

"He loves me," Franziska said, "he loves me!" But since she was glancing back and forth, now at Johann, now at me, it wasn't clear whom she meant.

I waited in the kitchen while Johann attempted to put Franziska to bed. When he reappeared in the kitchen, all he wanted was a bucket, into which he ran some water, and then vanished back to her bedroom.

"She'll be all right," he said later, after he had drunk a glass of tap water and sat down beside me. He looked bone tired.

"I just brought Vera to the train," I said. "She sends her good wishes." I don't know why I invented that. But Johann was happy to hear it.

In sequence I told him about the telegram, my trip home, about my mother and her suitcases and how she had called Vera back to her. I regretted that Franziska wasn't at the table with us, since, or so it seemed to me, it was a great story. I had just got to the part about the pigeons when Johann leapt up and took off for the bedroom. As if in some film take, I watched him go and saw how the kitchen door swung farther and farther ajar.

And suddenly it happened—a feeling, a yearning, a certainty: I want out! I want to go to the West!

Maybe it was only my admission of a wish long latent within me. I sat there and enjoyed the clarity that comes with being governed by one single emotion. Yes, I too now loved the West with my whole heart—a love that flooded over me and coursed through me and that embraced Vera and all those people sitting on that train with her.

When Johann returned, we quickly said our good-byes—it was well after midnight. I ran the whole way to Klotzsche.

I was too exhausted to deal with considerations that would have led me any further. I wanted nothing more than to carry home with me this one decision, whose perfection would relieve me[1] of every uncertainty.[2]

Your Enrico T.

---

1. Crossed out: if only for this one night.
2. Crossed out: and all my problems.

Dear Jo,

I'm sitting on the balcony of our room in the Hôtel de Paris, wrapped in a white bathrobe, gazing out at the casino and a swatch of sea to the left and right. I'm sick as a dog. My exhaustion is like a crying jag, but no sooner do I close my eyes than I'm dizzy. Writing is a good distraction. Vera hardly slept, despite earplugs. She's out strolling through the hotel now and, if she manages to strike up a casual acquaintance, will probably end up in the pool. Vera is far more suited to this life. She'll not be return-ing to Beirut all that soon. The latest bloodbath, although it took place on the "other side," was the straw that broke the camel's back.[2]

I've been asking myself the whole time why Barrista took the risk, why he pressed five thousand D-marks into my hand, paid for the flight and a hotel room, and in return demanded only that I not leave the roulette table until I had either lost my stake or doubled it. I'm gradually beginning to figure out what he had in mind.

Just taking off all by myself, boarding the flight alone, was something new for me. The flight, the Alps, the Mediterranean, Nice, palm trees, then Vera—as if I had landed in a Belmondo movie, as if the West still existed! Vera looks the same as always. She had flown via Damascus and Athens to Paris on Thursday, but arrived here just before me. She can fit what few things she has into two suitcases.

Barrista had recommended we take the helicopter. Like blasé secret agents we ducked under the earsplitting rotors, the doors were closed behind us, and we lifted off a moment later. Is there any better metaphor for our new life than being hauled up into the air? We flew out over the water; the sailboats below were like a herd of wild beasts. Suddenly Monaco in the noonday sun. The sublime view, however, was visible only over a buzz-cut conk.[3] Once we landed, Barrista's Hôtel de Paris was

1. T. is mistaken here. Sunday was the 13th.

2. V. T. lived in West Beirut during her three months there. On April 18, 1990, a school bus got caught in an exchange of fire between rival Christian militias. Fifteen children lost their lives.

3. Saxon slang for "head," "skull."

a magic charm that was rewarded with respect. While the buzzed head climbed into a taxi, someone opened for us the doors of a vehicle that Vera claims was a Bentley.

Palm trees, yachts, blue sky—just as I had imagined it. Following the route of the Grand Prix, we floated up to the hotel. The carpet in the entrance lent my gait a feathery spring. All the same I felt like a tourist at a castle. Vera, on the other hand, passed out currency in all directions as if it were an old habit of hers.

I gave our names to an elderly gentleman who stood up to greet us with a smile and was immediately certain that there would be no reservation for us.

"*Bienvenue, Madame Türmer, bienvenue, Monsieur Türmer*"—and like a bride and groom we sank into armchairs opposite him. Mirrors set in the wainscoting and patricianly dimmed by time reflected only our faces.

John, yes, his name was John, recommended we reserve a table for the Grill that evening. We agreed, without any notion of what we were getting into. I passed on Barrista's good wishes—"Makes no difference who you run into there, they all know me"—whereupon John spread his arms and bowed, as if only now had he recognized us. The crown at the top of this page of stationery is warranted if solely on the basis of his demeanor and tone of voice. John accompanied us to the "belle chamber" and explained how the telephone and remote control, light switches and refrigerator function. He was outraged by a full ashtray left on the balcony.

I couldn't find it in my heart to dispose of a gentleman like John with a tip—though Vera assures me that was a mistake. She had not only given away all her francs, she didn't have any cash whatever left.

After our luggage arrived—I hadn't touched it since Nice—we went across to the Café de Paris for "lunch," as Barrista would call it. Just that hour and a half on the café's terrace would have made the trip worth it. But I have more important things to write about.

Before falling onto our king-size bed for a siesta, we bought me a bow tie and a pair of sunglasses.

When I woke up it was twenty till eight. I instantly panicked. The very idea of risking all that Western money seemed ludicrous. I didn't calm down until I was under the shower. I put on fresh clothes as if suiting up in armor. These were the socks I would wear, and these the undershorts. Every button I buttoned became a token of security. Except that the top button wouldn't close.

That bit of bare skin called everything else into question. It's more than likely that I don't own a single shirt whose collar button I *can* button.

While Vera got herself ready in the bathroom, I put on my bow tie—and behold, a miracle! *Le nœud papillon* hid the blemish, was my seal of approval, so to speak.

An hour later I was confident I had discovered why I was here. This wasn't about the casino, this was a totally different game. Here, in the Grill, on the ninth floor, vis-à-vis the castle of the Grimaldis—this was where we had to pull it off, to hold our own.

Doesn't it require courage to pass in review before a phalanx of waiters, each repeating with the most cordial of smiles, *"Bonsoir, madame. Bonsoir, monsieur."* Doesn't it take bravery to fall blindly back onto a chair without reaching for it, in utter trust of a waiter's dexterity? And what is valor if not a tranquil smile when confronted by such a menu? Although I admit I did warn Vera, whose menu contained no prices, about the Iranian caviar. At that point I couldn't have brought myself to order an appetizer that cost over a thousand francs. On the other hand I repressed my thirst for beer and demanded the wine list. While I searched for a red wine under four hundred francs, Vera discovered that the footstool between us at the corner of the table was an ideal spot for her purse.

Our curiosity annoyed the waiters' hypersensitive organs of perception. Just a fleeting glance or a careless gesture brought them bounding over, to no purpose of course, since our glasses were appropriately full, the ashtrays empty, both raisin and olive bread in plentiful supply, and they had only just now crumbed the tablecloth.

Isn't there some form of meditation by which you cleanse your soul with a sequence of the most exquisite dishes? Rich people live healthy lives, Vera says.

At this point I thought that I might pull a fast one on the baron and be able to cheat him. Because the eighteen hundred francs that I gladly placed on the silver tray could not be taken away from us, either by him or the casino.

How naive of me! As if there were any emotion, any thought that was not included in the baron's calculations. The more abundant, the more contradictory my own responses might be, the more successful his lessons proved to be. Presumably if Barrista had this letter in hand, he would first point out by way of critique that I've already mentioned prices three times.

Unfortunately Vera and I messed up at the end. My paying in cash had itself caused bewilderment, but our departure proved so abrupt that our personal waiters, who had intended to pull our chairs back, just raised their hands in reproachful disappointment.

Once in the casino we soon found ourselves standing at the first roulette table. I would have liked to have gone to work right away, but had not yet bought my jetons. I asked Vera what number she guessed would be next, and chose "eighteen" for myself. There was no reason to pick eighteen. It isn't one of my favorite numbers. "Eighteen," I repeated— and didn't understand what the croupier announced in French. Vera looked at me in shock. Eighteen.

How was I supposed to interpret this oracle: "This is your lucky day!" or "That was your one and only chance!"?

Instead of the six thousand francs I had planned to bet today, I exchanged only fifty-five hundred with the cashier—and smiled at my own faintheartedness.

A guard at the entrance to the rear rooms made us hesitant. But we showed our gold hotel cards, waited for him to bow, and crossed the invisible border to the *salon privé*.

Two places at Table 7 were open. The board promised an above-average variety. To win all you had to do was muster a little consistency. The red field lay directly before us.

I passed on the first few rounds, trying to get a feel for the game. Then I placed a hundred on the lower third[1]—it had not appeared for four times in a row. I lost and doubled my bet. Perhaps the most beautiful jetons are the greenish mother-of-pearl hundreds. The others at the table, all older gentlemen, bet on numbers. I won. A pink five hundred, an orange two hundred, and a green hundred were added to my bet; I was ahead five hundred francs after three turns of the wheel. "It's working," I whispered.

Vera played the thirds, the rows, the red, the odds. She didn't always

---

1. T. means dozen. Correct terminology, as we shall soon see, would have spared him a moment of panic.

keep good track—the ball landed on fifteen and seven twice. The thirds alternated in an almost regular sequence.

Suddenly Vera wanted to leave; 20 percent profit was more than enough for her. I said that I couldn't develop a method, a system, if she kept betting such sums simply at random. Maybe, she conjectured, my real task was to find my own rules. I had made a promise, I said testily. After that I lost four times in a row.

One glance at our cash on hand, and my courage failed me. Instead of doubling my sixteen hundred, I risked only a thousand—and lost. I bet fifteen hundred. It was already my last chance. So, I thought, that's how fast it all went.

Vera stood up. We said our good-byes while the ball was still spinning in its bowl. I watched Vera go, she turned around, I waved, heard the ball bouncing, then its last *click*—the announced winner had several syllables. All I recall is that it was in the right third—victory! Victory! I was back in the running.

From that point on I played my apple green hundreds with childlike abandon, happy at last to be able to do or not do whatever I pleased. Success proved me right. My winnings grew steadily and always in the same way: as soon as a given third had not appeared four times in a row, I entered the fray: one hundred, two hundred, four hundred—and at the latest won with eight hundred.

I didn't care if other people were speculating on the same third I was. Except that when a bet was larger than mine, I feared some alien gravity might spoil my luck.

Currency was constantly being changed into jetons. Anyone who left the table, left with nothing. I, on the other hand, had the feeling I was doing good work.

The only other player I admired was wearing neither tie nor bow tie and chewed the whole time on the stump of a cigarillo. I don't know how big his stake was to begin with. After a half hour, however, there they lay before him: two big white ten thousands, those Lipizzaners among the jetons. I wanted so much to give him a nod of approval, but his eyes were relentlessly fixed on the green felt.

His counterpart was a freckled, unshaven gentleman, who sat at one corner and, tilting his head like a grade-school boy, jotted down each number in a plaid notebook. He calculated and calculated and looked up only to place one of his nominal bets—which he promptly lost.

The only person working harder than I was a delicate Frenchman, who was playing two tables at once and evidently trusted my choice of thirds. Our fate hung from the same thread—which for him, however, was no reason to return my smile. I soon realized how alone a person is, even in success.

I got too cocky twice and lost four lemon fifties on red, and lost again with an orange two hundred on *passe*. Have I already told you that at every spin I defended myself with a pink mother-of-pearl twenty on the zero? There wasn't one zero, however, the whole evening. (The chambermaid doesn't know if she should chase me off the balcony or not. She opened the door so that I can hear her vacuuming.)

Taking a cue from the man with the cigarillo, I awarded the croupiers an occasional lemon- or apple-colored chip. Shortly before one o'clock I totaled up the books: I had ten thousand francs in my pocket—winnings of forty-five hundred, plus a motley collection of other chips that came to twelve hundred, which suddenly meant nothing to me. I bet on red—and won, let the apples and lemons lie there, pocketed a blue mother-of-pearl thousand and all my oranges.

I had already whispered my *bonsoir* and started moving toward the cashier, when I noticed the cleavage on two women at the next table, and changed course.

I bent deep over both the ladies—and placed all my oranges on red. Seconds later I took another look down into the décolletage and raked in my winnings.

The cashier was cross-eyed, but that was the only irregularity. I strode out, bounding down the casino stairs and then up the stairway leading to the Hôtel de Paris, shouted, "Yes! I won!" and left it to Vera to sort out the bills on the bedspread. All in all, winnings of almost seven thousand francs.

It was when I woke up that I felt the angst. I know how silly it is to talk about angst. The fact that even if I had lost, I would have lost nothing, didn't help. It was my own big mouth that was at fault. Without giving it a second thought, I had accepted the baron's offer. But now I no longer comprehended where I had found the courage to bet a fifteen hundred francs. It seemed absurd ever to want to risk that much again.

Vera was not happy with me. Under a springtime sun, we trotted out into the bay and then up to the Grimaldis' castle, missed the changing of the guard, did a circuit in the cathedral, and finally landed at the oceanographic museum. From its rooftop terrace we could watch the sailboats. But none of it proved a distraction. I tried thinking about soccer.

I dozed on the bed till seven, and had no idea how I would play it. I was convinced that I wouldn't be successful again if I followed the same method. All the same, after a shower I put on the same outfit as the evening before, even the same socks. Vera, on the other hand, looked more elegant than ever—she had a new hairdo too. Neither she nor I had thought of a dinner reservation.

After being turned away at the Louis XV, I suggested we eat in the casino. Vera shook her head in revulsion. The front desk implied there was some hope of getting us into the Grill's Churchill Room.

Bonsoir, bonsoir, bonsoir, bonsoir. We strode past the phalanx of waiters again, crossed the huge dining room, and in the end had a pick of any table in the empty Churchill Room. I didn't understand why the waiters apologized for putting us there. To me it seemed more of an honor. Only after we sat down did I notice the large photograph of Churchill. His gaze was directed straight at me.

We recognized half the waiters, the stool for Vera's purse was put in place, my menu was in English.

(With a heavy heart I've been forced to vacate the balcony and the room. Now I'm sitting over tea and zwieback in the hotel café, an insufferable piano plinking in the background. At least there's not someone constantly taking your picture here.)

We went right into the routine, immediately chose our bread (olive), knew which butter was salted. I quickly selected a red wine; by now three hundred francs seemed a bargain. The waiter who had taken our order personally supervised the serving of the first course. And not just that. As if the cream in the middle of my empty soup bowl were the entire appetizer he wished us *"Bon appétit!,"* hesitated mischievously, and only then elegantly poured the mushroom soup around the cream.

I tasted Vera's risotto—and for a few minutes I didn't think about the casino. The next transitional course was on the house. By then I was full.

Where had these knots in my stomach come from? During the entrée I concentrated on the fish, but just picked at it and left the rest untouched. The cheese cart wasn't even allowed to approach us. This was followed—once again on the house and with the compliments of the chef—by filled crepes.

I was feeling sick to my stomach. I chose a calvados from the liqueur cart. It went down gently, gradually started to burn—and my nausea exploded. Our chief waiter helped me double-time it through the restaurant—don't look at the tables!—to the restroom. I went to my knees before the toilet bowl and gagged a few times. In the corner lay some scraps of packaging, from a shirt maybe. I overcame my resistance, and stuck a finger down my throat. All I managed was a harmless belch.

My crepes had been sent back to the kitchen to be kept warm. Their return marked the return of my nausea. The waiters didn't catch up with us until just before we reached the elevator—with my change on a silver tray.

Back in the room I turned on the television, locked all the doors, and planted myself on the toilet, hanging my head over the bidet. Twenty minutes later, mission unaccomplished, I crept into bed.

Shortly before one, Vera was forced to watch me dress again. As I stepped into my shoes, I broke out in a sweat. Vera retied my bow tie for me, spat three times over my left shoulder, and sent me on my way.

I exchanged six thousand francs, showed my gold card, and proceeded to Table 7, where the freckled, still unshaven gentleman was sitting at the corner, staring at his notebook, and calculating, head atilt.

The other players were standing. But I needed a chair.

Propping my elbows on the ledge, I was just about to stack my jetons when my gaze drifted across the table—for a moment I had to close my eyes. The sign above the croupier's head still announced a minimum bet of fifty francs. But what was being raked in at that moment were two greenish white candy bars, each worth a hundred thousand, two violets at fifty thousand apiece, and countless Lipizzaners. My nausea was all that prevented me from bursting into laughter. Why had I let my fears torment me all day?

Totally liberated, I now began to play, working both my third plus red and odds, and smoking—although the dryness in my mouth told me my stomach wasn't going to permit me all the time in the world. I employed my oranges only in little towers, and wasn't niggardly with my blue thousands either. When I won, the jetons were too big to be distributed as gratuities. I ignored the zero entirely.

The combination of concentration and nausea apparently predestined me for an exegesis of the board. I was soon moving to the rhythm that concealed a world hung in the balance. A pink five hundred on the lower third—I won. That third had been neglected so long that the ball was not going to move elsewhere right away. I stayed with it—and won. And now enough energy had collected for a bounce that hurdled the middle third, and so back up top—I won. I smiled because any child would know what must come now. A pink on the middle third—and of course I won.

Side bets lost on red, odds, and *passe* reduced my winnings, but not my confidence. One pink on the upper third, and I owned another blue. By the next round I had doubled my six thousand francs—but that didn't phase me much. I now wanted twelve thousand!

Believe me, my friend, in the same moment that the thought crossed my mind, I realized my mistake. I knew that the wish would be my downfall. But I went on playing.

I lost a pink on the middle third twice in a row. My nausea was now tinged with a sadness unlike any I'd ever known—sadness in expectation of my next win. And I did win, and once again had as much as I had had three spins before.

Nevertheless I let my pink chip lie—I could come up with nothing more clever. Suddenly a light went on: blue on red—and against my better judgment I held back. It landed on black and the first third.

No sadness now. I was in any case still four thousand to the good. No reason to be down in the dumps. I remained faithful to pink on the middle third. Or should I risk a blue? But I held back again—and lost.

I no longer felt anything, except the need to throw up. I had lost all my pinks, reached for a blue—and lost.

Something inside me rose up in protest at this injustice—blind rage! I wanted my blue back. It belonged to me. All I had to do was make a grab for the jetons and run!

I was sure I was going to have to vomit under the table any moment. But first there was something I had to do—an act of self-respect, the restoration of my honor.

Six blues in my breast pocket. The board showed the following sequence: red, black, black, red, black, black, red, black, black—everything on red? Six blues between my fingertips. I had to do it, I demanded it of myself. I was not going to be a pussyfooter.

The ball rolled—no! Not on red, not on odds, not on *passe*—stay with the second third! I was the only one to build my little blue tower there.

As the cry of *"Rien ne va plus!"* descended over the table like a bell jar, I glanced at the ceiling for the first time, and in the far corner saw a three-foot-high mural, *Le matin*. What did *le matin* mean? My eyes wandered to the right, across the empty tables in the restaurant and out into the darkness. Don't think of victory, I admonished myself, resign yourself, you did the right thing.

There were several clicks, the ball bounced—I looked down, in the next moment came the announcement. I didn't understand the croupier, but I saw it, the thirteen, I looked at it again, and then again, thirteen. Which third was the thirteen in? Thirty-six divided by three, twelve, twelve, twelve. I didn't shout. On the contrary—as if I'd been standing the whole time, I felt as if I had finally sat down.

Freckles was staring at his notebook. The table was raked, no one had won—except me! Only me! I silently made fun of Freckles—go ahead and analyze, while I play. And when I've won yet again, you can mull it over and analyze what I've done some more. And on and on, to the end of our days!

My blue tower fell apart between the croupier's fingers, all six jetons, I counted along with him—and received at last, along with two more blues, my Lipizzaner!

I would never have dared to dream of that white rectangle. If there is anything I regret it is only that I possessed my Lipizzaner for no more than two minutes. That's all the time I needed to scrape up my little pile and head for the cashier without so much as a farewell.

I was too weak to wipe the sweat from my brow. Out in the lobby, somebody shouted something at me, a whole group of people burst into laughter. I was pale, my feet moved me with exaggerated precision toward my goal—I was seen as the epitome of the loser.

When I entered our room, Vera was holding her hand to her eyes, from the TV came screams. I disappeared into the bathroom, gagged and retched and fought for air—nothing.

I don't know how I'll survive the flight back. My third cup of tea is on its way. I'm still tortured by the idea that I could have failed at the crucial moment and not have bet all my winnings.[1] If I had lost my nerve, I'd no longer be able to look at myself in the mirror. As you can see, I have stopped asking questions and have begun to understand.

Vera asked me to say hello for her. She's insisting we be on our way.

Your Enrico

---

1. The agreement with Barrista was that he would risk everything, not just his interim winnings. Judged on that basis, T. did fail.

PS: As we walked out to get our taxi, John was sitting at the front desk again. He bowed, I extended my hand and slipped him a hundred in farewell. I saw immediately that I had not committed a faux pas.

Vera and I went our separate ways in Frankfurt am Main. She boarded a train for Berlin, I took the one for Leipzig. As soon as Vera has broken up her apartment in Berlin she's coming to Altenburg for a few weeks. I gave her my winnings, and that was a great relief in the end.

Wednesday, May 16, '90

Dear Nicoletta,

It really is strange. Now that I'm coming to the point in my narrative where I first met Michaela, we're about to separate. Not one angry word has been spoken, that's all well behind us. Robert says that he and I will still be together, that of course we're a family—him, me, Michaela, and my mother—no matter what happens. "We are and always will be a family," I promised.

Unlucky in love, lucky at cards. I did in fact win a few thousand, so there's nothing standing in the way anymore of an excursion to Bamberg or Italy.[1] So much for my present life.

If it hadn't been for Anton I would never have ended up in the theater or in Altenburg, would never have met Michaela and Robert, would never have become a newspaper man—and we two would probably have just walked on past each other.

Anton wanted to become a dramaturge and move to Berlin. He pursued both goals with such unqualified zeal that he was willing to sacrifice everything else. Anton explained to me what all a "dramaturge" has to do. He wasn't really looking for work as such, but for a comfortable position that would leave him plenty of time for his escapades.

In January '87, six months before Vera's departure, I sent applications to every theater in the country; there were circa forty (and if you didn't

---

1. In his letter to Johann, T. had just boasted of having handed Vera his winnings.

find a job yourself, you ran the risk of the university assigning you to some library, museum, or publishing house).[1] Four theaters invited me for an interview: Potsdam, Stendhal, Zeitz, and Altenburg. Not long thereafter I found a letter from Anton in my cubbyhole, which began very formally—so I took it for a joke. A few lines later, however, and I couldn't believe my eyes. Since he, Anton, was leaving the entire country to me, he hoped I would in turn have the good grace to waive any claims to Berlin and Potsdam.

Vera raved about Altenburg's Lindenau Museum and about how Gerhard Altenbourg lived there—and furze-faced Hilbig[2] likewise came from Meuselwitz, a town just a few miles away. Besides which, the town had survived the war practically unscathed.

And so I traveled to Altenburg, and after only ten minutes the general manager (a long-haired man in his late thirties, who wore his shirt open halfway to his navel) informed me that I would be hired—providing I passed my internship—turning my first walk through town into a tour of the arena where my real life was to begin.

It was snowing. The approach to the castle lay in spotless white before me. I had a headache from all the excitement and because of my spare pair of glasses, which had a different prescription from my regular pair (Vera had them on her conscience). Snowflakes big as postage stamps were falling faster and faster with every step I took. When I turned around and looked down as if through a veil to the theater below me and to the town rising off to the west, I could scarcely see my own footprints.

After a circuit of the castle courtyard (this was before the fire), I walked to the park, whose paths were now discernable only because they lay between rows of benches. At the foot of the hill, but removed into the distance by the drifting snow, stood the Lindenau Museum. All I knew about it were illustrations of its vases from antiquity. I don't need to describe to you what happens when, having climbed the stairs and stridden across the octagon, you enter that suite of rooms hung with Italian paintings. I knew almost nothing about the Sienese, and very little

1. The university was required to find a job for each of its graduates.
2. Wolfgang Hilbig, born in Meuselwitz in 1943, was allowed to publish only one thin volume of poems and short stories in the GDR, *Stimme, Stimme* [Voice, voice] (Leipzig, 1985); since 1979 his books have been published by S. Fischer in Frankfurt am Main.

about the Florentines,[1] and yet I felt I had arrived. Perhaps you're thinking that I'm just mouthing your words.[2] But just as some people suffer when they must do without the Elbe or the sea, I would never be able to move to a place if I knew there wasn't such a treasure somewhere nearby.

The great collections in Dresden, Prague, Łódź, Budapest, or Leningrad lack a certain serenity. Here, however, you are alone with each painting. Even the guards remain hidden and you are reminded of them at most by a distant creaking of floorboards. I was already in Italy here. It was here that I understood that the best of the Renaissance comes from the pre-Renaissance. Here I could let pass in review the two hundred years so decisive not only for Italian art, but also for the intellectual spirit of all of Europe.[3]

To this day the same paintings that I took into my heart that afternoon have remained my favorites. Of course the three Guido da Sienas, *Man of Sorrow* by Lorenzetti, the *Madonna* by Lippo Memmi, the *Adoration* by Taddeo di Bartolo, the crucifixions by Giovanni di Paoli, everything by him really and by Lorenzo Monaco, and of course Masaccio; but I'm almost even fonder of Fra Angelico's *St. Francis' Trial by Fire*, with its skeptical sultan on his throne, but also his saints, plus the *St. Jerome* by Lippi, Botticelli's stern *St. Katherine*, Signorelli's artistic torturers, the Madonnas in his *Internment*, the *Annunciation* by Barnaba da Moden, Puccinelli's *Madonna* with its angels and saints, and the joy of the one to whom the baby Jesus has turned his face.

As I left the museum a bluish red patch of late-afternoon sky shone bright above me.

Three weeks later I passed through the theater's portals with a nod of my head, managed to catch the grated door before it closed behind a dancer in her warm-up outfit—and froze at the sound of a shrill "Halt!" The gatekeeper had jumped up and was pressing her forehead to the

---

1. The collection consists of 180 early Italian paintings on wood panels.

2. Something she might very well have suspected. T. was only fleetingly familiar with the museum and regarded exhibition openings there primarily as an opportunity for nurturing social contacts—both Johann Ziehlke and V. T. agree this was the case. Moreover this passage about the museum interrupts, for no good reason, the description of his theater experiences.

3. T. is quoting the same passage from the introduction to the museum's catalog that was already mentioned by C. von Barrista, cf. the letter of March 28, 1990. The panels referred to in the next paragraph are found in the same sequence in the registry of the collection.

pane of her booth. Called to account as to who I was and where I was headed, I finally answered with "Hoffmann! *Undine!*"

"Step back! All the way back!" My shoulder bag and I were blocking the way for others. I was told to explain why I had tried to "break into" the theater. When I asked her to call the general manager, she laughed, grabbed the telephone receiver, and took her eye off me only long enough to jab a finger into the dial. With each new arrival she again asked me to give my name. I was forced to shout "Enrico Türmer" several times, and to repeat it a little louder, "if you please," to spell the two words—so that every newcomer had learned the name of this stupid young fellow at the gate before I even got inside the theater. "Do *you* know a Türmer, Enrico maybe?"—or in her dialect: Dürmer, Ähnreegoh. That indefinite article before my name obliterated me.

I begged her to inform the chief dramaturge. The outraged gatekeeper laid the receiver down, put a finger to the cradle, and pressed hard. She was well aware of what she had to do, she didn't need instructions. Besides which, people there would have no more idea of who I was than she did.

"He don't even know where he wants to go," she shouted into the receiver once more as two ballerinas came tripping by, "that's what got me so riled, that's the problem," to which I could only keep on replying, "Hoffmann, Hoffmann!"

"Nobody knows you here," she declared, and set down the receiver. Giving me another once-over, she leaned back in exhaustion and started to thumb through whatever it was that had been lying before her the whole time. It was unclear whether she was going to pursue my case or had already filed me away for good.

"Wait!" she cried out, still turning pages, but as she reached for the receiver again a woman in a white blouse emerged out of the darkness of the stairwell, bounded down the last three steps, and cast me such a friendly glance that I was afraid she had mistaken me for someone else.

"I know who you are," she said with a smile, linked her arm under mine, and guided me in the direction of the gatekeeper.

"May I introduce you, Frau"—here she inserted the gatekeeper's name—"to Herr Türmer, our new dramaturge . . ." This time it took the gatekeeper two tries to get up out of her chair; she extended a hand through the oval hatch in the pane and exclaimed, "Why didn't he say so right off!" And with that we strode through the portal.

The woman in the white blouse ushered me through a labyrinth of hallways and stairs. Every few feet the odor changed. We passed the ballet room, a canteen, skirted a baroque sandstone stairwell, and stood there in the dark. I heard a key and followed her into a room where light barely seeped through the curtains. The odor was of midday meals.

On the way back we stopped in front of white french doors and listened. Suddenly my guide pressed down the door handle and shoved me inside, just as a piano struck up again.

Who was I, what did I want, who had sent me? . . . My good fairy had vanished, the director, hardly any older than I and with a haircut that highlighted the back of his head, had interrupted the rehearsal and was paging quickly through the piano reduction.

I gave my name, I repeated my name. I was informed by the director, who went right on paging through the score, that one did not attend a rehearsal uninvited, nor did one interrupt it. One needed to request permission in advance from at least the director, if not the entire ensemble. "In advance!" he repeated and finally stopped turning pages. Had I done that? No, I replied, I had not. It was too late for any excuses for my misconduct. A gentleman kneeling on the floor expressed in a bass voice his outrage at such a disregard for his person. How long was he supposed to keep crawling around, didn't we people have eyes in our heads. He said "people," but he had looked only at me.

Over the next five weeks, during which I was allowed to audit Tim Hartmann's production of *Undine,* there was little I could do to improve the situation I had got myself into when making my entrance. I made it worse by using formal modes of address. Tim Hartmann took it as an insult that I did not call him Tim like everyone else. Just opening the door to the canteen was awful, leaving the counter with my tray of bockwurst and coffee was awful, taking a seat at an empty table was awful, joining other people at a table was awful. What's more, I smelled like the kitchen, which was directly under my room.

Every so often the assistant director, a tall, beautiful woman from Berlin, took pity on me. When she stood before me, I realized what might have saved me: something to do.

Although I did like sitting in on rehearsals. At first I thought I needed to say something that would prove my theatrical credentials. I amazed myself at what all occurred to me. At the end of the first week I handed Tim Hartmann a list of suggestions. I hoped in this way to commend myself as a worthy partner in the conversation. At the start of the next week of rehearsals the assistant director asked me to refrain from taking notes from now on.

When there was no evening rehearsal I attended performances, where I sat in one of the first rows with program in hand and tried to memorize the faces of the cast. As if my future depended on it, I devoted great energy, indeed passion, to learning names. Which was why the last week of *Undine* rehearsals was especially important, because I could now coordinate names and functions even for people who never appeared onstage, but whom I knew by sight. I found it easy to learn names and equally difficult to correct my mistakes. For example I thought the lighting director was the man in charge of painting sets, and took the director of the set workshop for the lighting director.

I considered my audit to have concluded on a conciliatory note when I was assigned to write the press release, which Tim Hartmann then handed out at dress rehearsal, all the while repeating *"à la bonne heure."* At the premiere I was even allowed to spit three times over the left shoulder of Undine herself, who had ignored me longer than anyone else.

Tim Hartmann's production was no thundering success, but the audience applauded until he appeared onstage in a black suit, bowed, and rocked his head back and forth in the hope that everyone would notice his brand-new stub of a ponytail.

At the cast party I was given lots of hugs. I expected a speech from the general manager, a few words about the production and the singers' fine performances. And I hoped he would also remember his promise to me.

He congratulated Tim Hartmann, shook hands all around the table, and also responded to a few bons mots with a laugh that was almost indistinguishable from a cough. But he refused to sit down and join us. His entourage, recruited mainly from stage actors, but especially from the ballet, were waiting for him two tables down.

I drank and chain-smoked and for the first time felt at home in the canteen. The assistant director introduced me to Antonio, a young Chilean from Berlin. Antonio asked what I thought of the production, which he himself termed a "yawn." Antonio told me to sit down beside him, and pulled a chair over for me to join the "Jonas" table—he called the general manager by his first name. How easy it all was. Antonio offered me some vodka. Everybody at the table was drinking vodka.

In claiming that marriage and fidelity were unnatural, pointless, and ridiculous, Jonas managed to antagonize most of the women, which didn't prevent him from plowing right ahead. He kept brushing strands of hair from his face while shifting his gaze from one person to the next. As our eyes met I automatically noddèd as if I agreed with him. I was angry at myself for doing it, and all the more so since the actress Claudia Marcks loudly contradicted him, even laughed in his face—which he took half as an offense, half as confirmation of this theory about women.

I admired Claudia Marcks. I had never been able to strike up a conversation with her, I hadn't even managed to work my way into her vicinity. Everything about her was beautiful and desirable, I especially loved her hands. They led a life of their own, which no one except me seemed to noticed. Suddenly I wanted nothing more than to feel the touch of those hands—today, tomorrow, whenever—and then to kiss them. And I was strangely convinced that that hour was no longer all that distant.

I asked Jonah whether he himself believed the stuff he was spouting.

He stared at me with reddened eyes. "Why don't you just go get laid!" he shouted. "Why don't you just . . ." Jonas repeated the sentence two, three times, four times, until the whole canteen had fallen silent.

Instead of laughing in his face as Claudia Márcks had done, I thought of Nadja. And now I heard myself saying, "Why should I do that?"

Everyone joined in the laughter. Even Claudia Marcks and Antonio. Antonio said he admired the people who were pure intellect, people like me. It was hell.

Sometime long after midnight the assistant director asked if she and Antonio could spend the night in my quarters, the bed in the guest room was nice and wide, after all, and they had missed their train. Neither of the two slept a single minute.

Lying at the edge of a bed and having to listen to those two beside me seemed to me the perfect metaphor of my life as an outsider. Jonas had humiliated me before everyone, and tomorrow Antonio would tell him about this night. Wasn't the reason I hadn't defended myself that I was afraid of losing my position, my job as dramaturge? How life takes its revenge on you, I thought, when you want something else from it. My life was that of a storyteller. And for telling stories a man needs distance and a cold eye. How could I have forgotten that.[1]

---

1. T. evidently failed to notice that he was describing himself here as the quintessential observer, the voyeur.

In the middle of June, a few days after Vera's departure, I was back again in Altenburg. One more unpleasant experience—and what else was I supposed to expect from the theater?—and my desire to follow Vera would have been all the stronger.

The chief dramaturge handed me a small bright orange book, for which I had to give her a receipt. From bottom to top I read: Bibliothek Suhrkamp/Fräulein Julie/August Strindberg. I wouldn't be staying in the guest room this time, but in the Wenzel. Flieder, the director, had not yet arrived.

That evening in the hotel I opened Vera's imitation-leather silverware pouch, sorted the bills, laying them out in separate rows on the floor. At three thousand marks, more than my stipend for a whole year, I stopped counting.

From the bed I watched as the bills were caught up in a draft from the open window and began overlapping as if trying to couple, and finally I just closed my eyes and listened to their rustling. When I woke up the bills were strewn about the room, in one corner they had formed a little pile of leaves.

I showered, sat down at a breakfast setting in the restaurant, and, as the clock struck ten, headed off for the Lindenau Museum. After that I took a walk through town, circled the Great Pond, looked for the house of Gerhard Altenbourg, and had my noonday meal at the Ratskeller. Then I lay down in the park and read. In the evening I went to the movies. That was more or less how I spent the whole week.

My favorite pastime was to sit in the garden café beside the Great Pond and imagine I was with Vera somewhere on the Landwehr Canal in West Berlin, recovering from the interviews I had had to deal with all day.

That Friday I traveled to Dresden to see my mother. Despite my having announced my arrival, she wasn't waiting for me at the station, nor was she at home. Nothing in the apartment indicated a welcome—no note, no stew in the refrigerator, my bed hadn't even been made up.

When Mother arrived—after all, I ought to know she worked late sometimes—we spoke only about Vera. Vera should have left a lot sooner, Mother said, her path had been blocked from the start, she had been robbed of valuable years. I said that Vera had enjoyed her life and had learned more about the theater and read more books than I had at the university. How could I say that! That had all just been makeshift.

Vera belonged in a drama school, they should have accepted her at the Deutsches Theater in Berlin. I hadn't any idea of just how desperate Vera had been at times.

For supper Mother placed an unwrapped camembert on the table, I opened a tin of fish, the bread was stale. I felt miserable. This shabbiness toward both herself and me was something new.

I arrived late for Monday's rehearsal discussion. It was a bad omen that Flieder likewise had a ponytail, even if it was just bound-up remnants of his wreath of hair and hung gray and scraggly over his collar. As was to be expected he didn't turn to look at me when, after first knocking, I opened the door and took a seat at the table. As was also to be expected he had me repeat my name. Imagine my terror when I saw Claudia Marcks sitting at the table. She hadn't been listed as a cast member.

"So this is our Enrico," Flieder said, "Enrico will be helping us with everything here. At least I hope so. Good thing you're here, Enrico." No one laughed.

The only others at the table besides Claudia Marcks were Petrescu (Kristin, cook, thirty-five years old) and Max (Jean, servant, thirty years old). I also got a wave from Flieder's young female assistant, a long drink of water with short hair, who was also the set designer and was perched on the arm of a chair off to one side, sipping at her Karo.

What followed was more like a seminar than a rehearsal. And I wasn't prepared. It was just for me, or so it seemed, that Flieder went on at length about the book that he had left at the front gate for me, along with a note inside. As he paced back and forth, giggling every now and then, he began to look more and more like a faun or a satyr. His assistant repeated and augmented his comments, talked about behavioral research, squinting each time she took a drag on her cigarette.

At the noon break, Claudia Marcks took a seat beside me. "Do you know each other?" Flieder asked.

"Yes," I said. Claudia Marcks looked at me. "Where from?"

"*Undine,* the premier, the cast party, at this very same table."

"Oh, please, no," she cried. "I was so sloshed, so sloshed, oh please, I'm sorry." And as if by way of apology she laid a hand on my forearm and asked almost anxiously if we had drunk to our friendship that night.

"Sad to say, no," I replied, "but I would have been happy to."

"Just call me Michaela," she whispered. "Okay?"

"Happy to, Michaela," I said, repeated my first name for her, and gazed at her gorgeous hand, still lying on my forearm.

Your Enrico T.

Thursday, May 17, '90

Dear Nicoletta,

Before I tell you any more about Michaela, I need to insert something that happened in the summer of 1987, but that I didn't mention to anyone, since it didn't seem worth mentioning. And how was I supposed to understand it anyway?

Maybe in fact there is something in us beyond our conscious and unconscious mind, something akin to the sixth sense animals have that lets them register an earthquake or storm, long before we do. Should I call it instinct, or the power of premonition? Or simply a heightened sensitivity?

In August I had gone to Waldau for two weeks so that I could finally do some more work on my novella. One night I awoke and thought I heard a shot reverberating through the house, through the whole woods.

If it hadn't been for the creaking of the bed I would have thought I was deaf. I snapped my fingers. Not a rustle, not a breeze, not a bird. I had broken into a sweat and knew that I wouldn't go back to sleep.

Naked as a jaybird, I stepped out the door. Everything seemed frozen in place. With each little noise I made, silence closed in all the tighter. The more intensely I listened, the more impenetrable the hush, until finally I thought I could feel it above my head like some giant black block of stone.

I tried several times to take a deep breath, but my lungs felt only half full of the air I sucked down into them, as if I were several thousand meters above sea level. It didn't help to sit down either. I felt a rippling, swirling sensation around my heart. I was amazed I didn't panic. At least I could distinguish between the deep black of the trunks of the firs and the grayish darkness between them. I was on the verge of saying a prayer or humming a tune just to escape the silence, the hush. Suddenly it seemed incredible that I should be sitting all alone at night in a stock-still woods—the only restive thing in a mute world. I thought I might be dreaming or losing my mind. My own laughter gave me a fright.

And like some stroke of grace a fly joined me. It whirled around my head, and suddenly I could see an illustration from a physics text before my eyes: an electron orbiting the nucleus of an atom.[1]

The fly landed on my left shoulder—I flinched and then held my breath. Had I scared it away? The fly dared not abandon me, it had to stay, the only living creature standing guard with me, my sole companion. When I felt it stir, I again held my breath and relished its touch as if it were a caress. Have you ever let a fly crawl over your shoulders and back? In the midst of my fear that sooner or later the fly could forsake me, for the first time in my life the idea crossed my mind that the world, just as it is, might end up lost to me.

It was not fear of nuclear war, of the end of the world. It was the fear that everything from which I took my bearings could be lost; the structure of the world to which I had adapted the permutations of my thoughts and emotions, might vanish from one day to the next, leaving nothing more than a great emptiness behind. Just as I had feared I would be inducted into the army too late, so now I feared that before I could fire my gun all the real game would be slain and only mice and rats would be left for me.

It was an absurd thought, but no less absurd than sitting naked in the woods, happy and grateful for the companionship of a fly.

Only the fly and the pain just above my heart seemed to exist, the sole realities at my disposal, the one thing that prevented my thoughts and emotions from evaporating into weightlessness.

On those spots where my sweat hadn't dried I sensed a draft, and I felt chilled. With empty brain, with empty heart, yielding to my fate, I crept back to bed.

When I awoke, it was warm and flies, a whole swarm, were buzzing above me.

I presume that by now you think I am indeed crazy or at least more than a bit odd. But viewed from the present, that nocturnal experience is one of the few episodes that I can look back upon with sympathy for the person I was at the time.

But to return to Altenburg, to which I traveled in early September '88, before starting my last year of studies.

---

1. Here as well T. is fantasizing. For if in fact it was as dark as he describes, he could scarcely have experienced a fly "whirling" around him.

Flieder's rehearsals of *Julie* deserve a chapter of their own. Read the Strindberg play again yourself and pay attention to the breaks, to the steady flow of staying—going—staying—going. In a certain sense it was so much about me that it was eerie.

No less eerie was the realization of how closely related directing and writing are. From Flieder I learned that the purpose of dialogue is not to communicate something, but rather to clarify the relationships among the characters. That it doesn't matter what the characters are talking about as long as you know what you want to say. That there is hell to pay if you neglect even one of the relationships, that not one item, not a single step in the choreography can be ignored.

Is there anything more beautiful than a plausible character? If I were able to attain Flieder's level in my own writing, my novella would be a masterpiece. But then why, I anxiously asked myself, isn't Flieder a *famous* director?

But what would Flieder's rehearsals have been without Michaela! I was allowed to gaze at Michaela, to observe and study her, and no one, including her, could reproach me for it. One of my tasks was to devour her with my eyes. I dreamed that Michaela and I were a couple. This fantasy collided, to be sure, with my desire to leave the country as soon as I could. But I kept postponing taking the step—out of concern for my mother, only because it seemed better to first get my degree, because I hadn't heard from Vera since her departure. And I had put on blinders to the fact that day after day Michaela arrived and departed with Max (our Jean). From her first marriage she had a son who sometimes waited for her in the canteen, where he painted or played cards with the kitchen staff.

After a rehearsal at the beginning of my second week, as always I gave Michaela a good-bye hug—and our cheeks touched. I was about to stand up straight again, but she held me tight—for an eternity, or so it seemed to me. And then as always Michaela climbed into the Wartburg with Max. I took that long hug to be part of the ragtag intimacy typical of the theater. The next evening, however, the same farewell repeated itself. This time I likewise held Michaela until she couldn't stand tiptoe any longer. After Wednesday's rehearsal we ran into each other in the entry to the canteen, or better, we ran *toward* each other. I still had my notepad in one hand. It would be too much to claim that the way she moved told me everything, but it would be no exaggeration to say that we virtually flew into each other's arms—we were lucky not to have stumbled on the rippled linoleum.

"Do you know how to drive?" was the first thing Michaela whispered in my ear. She asked me to wait, stepped into the canteen, and returned with the keys to the Wartburg. It belonged to her, or actually to her mother, but neither of them had a driver's license.

I drove Michaela home that evening for the first time. The light was on in Robert's room. She called back to tell me what time to pick up her the next day, and ran off. The heels of her shoes echoed in the horseshoe of the new apartment building—and for whatever reason it filled me with pride. I stood at the open driver's door, one elbow propped on the roof—it was as if I had won first prize in a raffle.

The next morning she asked me if I was a free man, whether the difference of seven years—she had found that out somehow—mattered, and whether I realized that she would always have to take Robert into consideration. Before I could answer, she gave me a kiss, and then Max rapped on the windshield.

I waited by the car for Michaela after rehearsal. When she finally appeared I could tell she wanted to leave with me. She said that I had on the shirt she loved to see me wear. I turned the ignition on, she slipped her left hand under my collar, I drove off, and we both stared straight ahead as if into heavy fog.

We scurried past the front desk; I had intentionally not left my room key with them. In the elevator Michaela said she felt like a fraud for having been taking the pill all this time. Robert wouldn't be home before four thirty, so we had a little time. She pulled an alarm clock from her purse, and set it.

Once in the room, Michaela pulled down the blinds and drew the curtains. She extricated herself when I started to unbutton her blouse. She wouldn't even let me watch her undress and called me out of the bathroom only after she was lying in bed with the covers up to her neck. At first I thought it was a game, but Michaela had very definite notions of what all I was and was not allowed to do.

Before evening rehearsal began, Flieder said he had done some rescheduling and needed only Max and Petrescu. Michaela and I drove to the hotel, and once again I waited in the bathroom until she called me. I asked her why she was embarrassed in front of me. I'd learn that soon enough—or maybe not—Michaela said, holding a hand over my mouth before I could ask the question I was on the verge of asking.

Later on we fell asleep and didn't wake up until after midnight. In sheer panic Michaela could barely dress, but insisted that I turn my face to the wall.

The light was on in Robert's room. I waited and listened again to the echo of Michaela's footfall.

During the days left before semester began, we saw each other only at rehearsals. It was now Max who was again driving her between home and the theater.

A few weeks later Michaela revealed to me the reasons for her puzzling ritual. "It has to do with Robert," she said, "with his birth." I didn't understand. "A C-section," she said, and stared at me almost in fright, only then to suddenly bark at me, "It left a scar, a big, ugly scar." I said that was no news to me, but only now had I made the connection.

"Well everybody doesn't have to see it!" she cried angrily.

You're probably asking yourself why I'm telling you all this? What does our love story have to do with my confession?[1] Just be patient.

Robert fought me all the way. Plus he hated everything that had to do with the theater. And I had to admit Robert annoyed me. I wasn't used to taking anyone else into consideration. I wanted to read, write, attend the theater and exhibitions, see movies. And that's what Michaela wanted too. But I'm getting ahead of myself. In those first weeks the very idea of my spending the night at Michaela's was out of the question. And in case I tried, Robert threatened to run away from home. The first time I paid an official visit, he locked himself in his room and wailed so loud that after ten minutes Michaela asked me to leave. There were times when I traveled to Altenburg to see Michaela for just half an hour. And even then Robert was the center of attention.

My first overnight came at the end of November, and that was because Robert had thrown my shoes out the window and they had to be dried on the radiator.

And it wasn't just that Robert was a mischief-maker, he was a blemish on Michaela. I was in no way on Robert's side, but at times I wished he would win out. Because I had had a different idea of a love affair.[2] What was more, I didn't want to stay here, here in Altenburg, here in this country. At least that's what I wrote to Vera.

---

1. One cannot avoid the impression that T. was reveling in a certain nostalgia during the period of separation from Michaela.

2. It would be interesting to learn what T. imagined a love affair was supposed to be.

When Michaela glowingly announced that Robert had agreed to travel with her and me to Dresden—he wanted to meet my mother too—I couldn't have been more conflicted.

My mother had baked and cooked, our beds—Robert had my room all to himself—were decorated with chocolate animals and licorice sticks, the kind I hadn't seen for years. The towels were new and soft, and each of us was given a pair of slippers. Robert had apparently expected nothing less. While we sat drinking coffee he roamed the apartment, knocked over a vase, and peeked in every cupboard and drawer. Mother wasn't upset and helped calm Michaela down. They competed at chain-smoking, and Mother gave her the pair of shoes she had bought six months before, on the day Vera left. Every few minutes Robert presented us with another one of his discoveries. He found not only my old teddy bear and children's books, but also my first cartridge pen, the cap of which revealed distinct teeth marks and that had been such a trusty friend that it was as if I had laid it aside only a moment before. Finally Robert dragged over my grandfather's compass set—the compasses resting in shimmering blue velvet. Robert asked if he could keep it. To my horror my mother said yes. But Michaela's "No!" was so determined that I didn't have to intervene. Then it was time for photo albums, and that evening Robert cracked every egg we had in a skillet and called the result an omelet.

Shortly before we left the next day Robert insisted on playing badminton with me in the courtyard. Yes, only with me. On the way back he fell asleep, so that Michaela could snuggle up against me. It was then that it first struck me: I have a family—a family. And I didn't know if it was a dream come true or if I was caught in a trap.[1]

Saturday, May 19, '90

Dear Nicoletta,

It may perhaps amaze you when I say that the next eighteen months—from the day of our weekend together in Dresden until May '89—was a happy time. The internal conflict that I described still existed, but it wasn't hard to live with. I kept postponing applying for an exit visa—no,

---

1. Presumably T. has once again forgotten the complimentary close that had already been reduced to a rather mechanical "Your Enrico T." in his preceding letters.

I was saving it as a kind of reward that I would first have to earn. The longer I stuck it out in the GDR, the more I would ultimately have to show for myself in the West. Besides which I regarded family life as a new experience. It was a marvelous feeling to watch Michaela shave her legs, and it felt like the proof of intimacy to hang our laundry on the clothesline or to take it down.

The strain between Robert and me remained. I met with Robert's approval only sporadically, for instance when I succeeded in holding the spout from our laundry spin-drier directly over the bucket. To do that I had to throw myself on top of the machine. My mother on the other hand was accepted without qualification, which was why we made frequent trips to Dresden.

My studies came to a lusterless end. A few months before my oral exams I came very close to being dismissed from the university without my intending it, because I had tacked a page of "concrete poetry" on the bulletin board.[1] As liberal as it sometimes seemed, the university had never really become so.

After defending my thesis, my last task as a student, we—Michaela, Anton, and I—went to District Military Headquarters. I had to cancel— or to put it more correctly, change—my address. Michaela listened while I was told that as a driver I had a good chance of being called up again after two years. (Which would be now.)

That threat charged both my school novella and my army book with new energy.

The premiere of Miss Julie that September[2] was a flop. When Michaela led Flieder onstage there were a few bravos, but three quarters of the audience was already waiting for their coats. We coerced four curtain calls. Smiling up into the empty balconies, Michaela curtsied each time like an opera diva. In Berlin this Julie would have been as celebrated as Danton's Death or Macbeth had been.[3]

It was not until we were driving home after the cast party that Michaela burst into rage. She had been stuck in Altenburg way too long,

1. Cf. Appendix, "May."

2. T. means September 1988. Because of construction work that began without warning in the fall of '87, the theater was closed for almost an entire season. The company did not resume production until September '88.

3. Legendary productions directed by Alexander Lang at the Deutsches Theater and by Heiner Müller at the Volksbühne.

and all the talk about how the theater here was a stepping-stone had never been true. "I can't take this Podunk any longer!" she shouted. Her despair reached the point that she declared she was ready to join the Party if that was what it took to get a role in Berlin. Half her friends at the Gorki or the Berliner Ensemble were comrades—none of them someone you would ever have guessed was.

"And what about *West* Berlin," I asked as we turned down our street. "In an instant!" Michaela cried, and stared at me with eyes open wide. "In an instant," she repeated.

When we got home she handed me a package—her premiere gift. It contained several smaller packages, which I had to open one after the other until I got to the last one wrapped in gold paper—a pack of Club cigarettes, but filled with peppermints. A note slipped inside read, "Smoking is dangerous for expectant mothers and fathers." We hadn't yet managed it, but we were trying to give up smoking.

Miss Julie had five or six performances. In Michaela's eyes the fact that her *Julie* wasn't on the season's consignment list[1] was pure censorship. There were a few scattered reviews, the local paper's was scathing.

When I began working full-time as a dramaturge I was assigned a one-and-a-half room apartment in the home of eighty-eight-year-old Emilie Paulini.

We two shared a chemical toilet, halfway up the stairs, and a kitchen whose sink was my ersatz bathtub. The cellar, however, was filled with briquettes. I needed this refuge because Robert's television habits, plus a cassette recorder that never stopped playing, literally drove me off. I had moved in with just a table and a chair—deeply disappointing Emilie Paulini. She was afraid, you see, of being alone "when it comes time to die." To fall asleep some night and never wake up, that's what she hoped for. But there should be someone close by. In my honor she wore a wig, usually perched like a lopsided beret. At regular intervals she would wave me into her parlor, invite me to have a seat, and then hand me a framed, brown-foxed photograph of a beautiful young woman. Did I have any idea who that was? She would then giggle, thrust her bewigged head forward like a turtle, and ask very loudly, "Well?" I would glance back and

1. East German term for "subscription series."

forth between her and the photo and finally say, "But of course, Frau Paulini, that's you!" Emilie Paulini would screech, fling her arms into the air, and jump up to fetch me a piece of pastry from the kitchen.

Emilie Paulini didn't like Michaela because she was a "theater person"; besides which, she was to blame for my not living at her place.

Her daughter Ruth came to visit on Wednesdays and picked her up every Sunday for dinner. Ruth spoke very fast and, rather than pausing between sentences, let out a long high-pitched "aaah" or "nooo" that fell slowly on its column of air. In the kitchen she told me ("Herr Türmer, what all I could tell you, Herr Türmer, aaah, but there's not enough time—nooo—so much, so much") about how, while fleeing in April '45, they had "fallen into the hands of the Russians" in Freital near Dresden. Her mother had always sent her away and told her to sing. "Whenever the Russians came, I would be sent out to sing. Aaah! Those are stories, Herr Türmer, stories . . . aaah! Even though our mommy was no longer young, but that didn't help. Stories! Aaah, Herr Türmer. She arrived here pregnant, at age forty-three, pregnant! Nooo, and with no husband, just imagine it!"[1] Ruth dabbed at one corner of her eye with a lace handkerchief she always kept at the ready.

I couldn't figure out the point of the singing, but since Emilie Paulini never left us alone for long, I didn't get around to asking Ruth about it until some time later. "Aaah, Herr Türmer, it's really very simple. It eased her mind. She at least knew I wasn't being molested. Aaah, nooo, stories!"

It was Michaela who initially suggested I turn the tales of the two Paulinis into a play, a monologue. For her as an actor it would of course be better to have Ruth narrate the whole thing, but a mother-daughter piece was also a possibility. If I could get them both to tell their stories, the piece would write itself.[2]

I now began spending an occasional night at Emilie Paulini's. The idea that I could have at my disposal materials dealing with war, flight, looting, and rape—perhaps even with Jews and the SS—lent me a sense of strange superiority.

I began modestly by keeping track of Emilie Paulini's routine: when

1. During World War II only the industrial plants on the periphery of Altenburg were bombed, which was why the city had taken in a disproportionate number of refugees.

2. This turn of phrase, which T. has used before (cf. the letter of May 5, 1990), can also be found in a slight variation on the next page. It is thus quite probable that T. has put these words into Michaela's mouth.

she went to the toilet or to the kitchen, what she had Ruth buy for her, which noonday meals that People's Solidarity brought her she liked and which stood in the kitchen until the next day. Her television habits were all too audible. I was sometimes awakened in the night by Emilie Paulini's mumblings, which were indecipherable despite a very thin wall. I had to give up trying to slink up to her door because at the first creak of floorboards she would fall silent.

I never missed a Wednesday evening. Just as I had hoped I was always invited into her room, which I knew only by dim twilight, because Emilie Paulini skimped on electricity. The older any object that I could make out with Argus eyes, the more I expressed my admiration for it, in hopes of rousing the Paulinis to conversation. But there were no "prewar goods."[1] I was hoping for photographs, but was shown no others than the ones that stood framed on the sideboard.

I asked about Czechs, Jews, the outbreak of war. Nothing, and certainly nothing gruesome, occurred to her. By this time I was sure Emilie Paulini had realized there was some purpose behind my curiosity. She said of her husband, "They fought to the bitter end!" and burst into high laughter. I learned more in the kitchen. But Ruth's aaah's and nooo's were so loud that Emilie Paulini would immediately come scurrying in from her room. Her husband had been a member of the Special Field Force, a bandog, and had been reported missing in action. Not so much as a picture of him was left. Long before her marriage and while still underage, Emilie Paulini had given birth to a son. He had grown up in an orphanage, volunteered to join the navy, been badly wounded in Norway, and in the end had died in an air raid on Bremen. Ruth had spoken about him with her mother only once. There had to be letters from him somewhere. But there was no point in asking her mother, Ruth said. The two of them couldn't even talk about Hans, the Russian boy—but then Ruth didn't want to talk about her half brother either.

I used index cards marked with felt pens. Black for household habits, red for Emilie Paulini's stories, green for Ruth's, blue for objects that arrested my interest. I hoped that at some point, by arranging themselves all on their own, so to speak, my notes would spin out my tale. Michaela read a whole stack of books about the end of World War II and swamped me with suggestions.

---

1. T. surely ought to have expected as much from a refugee family like the Paulinis.

I had never had so much time to write as I did at the theater—we were required to be on the premises only from ten till two, and for that I got paid! And what's more, my gross salary of nine hundred marks left me a take-home pay of seven hundred, which could only be called a princely sum.

I was in charge of the annual Christmas fairy tale, a reworking of Andersen's *Snow Queen*, in which I even appeared onstage a few times as a wise raven. I waited in vain for a director the likes of Flieder.

The best productions were still those of Moritz Paulsen, who earned his living with fashion shows and who demanded extensive lighting rehearsals of two to three days. What won me over to Moritz Paulsen was his decision to turn a so-called *glasnost* play into a revue, the high point of which was a series of short scenes that interrupted the plot, each beginning with a shouted phrase he'd coined: "The Party flamingo!" All the actors stopped and, smiling radiantly, gazed up at an imaginary Party flamingo evidently winging its way across the stage sky. We figured we had a good chance of being closed down after the premiere. But except for an angry outburst by Jonas, the general manager—nobody was going to understand the point we were trying to make—there were only feeble protests. A teacher who had attended a performance with his class criticized us for stabbing pedagogues in the back instead of using our art to raise Party consciousness. Letters of that ilk, which we posted as trophies, remained few and far between.

You might say we were a happy family during the second Christmas we spent together. The presence of both grandmothers calmed Robert down. He spoke when spoken to and didn't walk away when I sat down beside him to watch television.

And then, the morning of the second day of Christmas, I suddenly knew how my novella would end. I couldn't understand why it had taken me almost three years to see it.

It must have had to do with the general mood, a mood influenced by what we were reading at the time. Michaela was busy with Eco's *Name of the Rose,* and I had given Robert *Tim Thaler, or Don't Sell Your Smile* as a present. Laughter was in the air, and all of a sudden Titus, the hero of my novella, could smile. Titus was no longer going to let himself be blackmailed. His suffering was replaced with irony. He had become an adult.

I was going to begin all over again, right from page one, but this time with a sure voice. Titus's smile bathed the novella in a cheerful light and freed it from the sour tragedy of puberty.[1]

As the new year began I set to work. I couldn't write as fast as the ideas bombarded me. And because I was now spending a good deal of time in my refuge—our Herr Türmer is always friendly and in a good mood—Emilie Paulini was a happy woman as well.

These days everyone believes that with the local elections[2] that spring they heard the tolling of the system's death knell. Viewed after the fact, that seems plausible.

Whereas at the university there had been major discussions about what time a student should appear at his polling place—that is, no later than fifteen minutes after it opened—no one at the theater paid any attention to elections. After Ceauşescu was awarded the Order of Karl Marx,[3] Jonas himself had threatened to quit the Party.

Election Sunday was May weather at its finest. We got out our bikes and set out for an excursion. I can't begin to give you any notion of the terror that used to accompany me on the way to my polling place. Or of how you always tried to conceal from yourself—just as everyone else was doing, and each well aware that he was—that your path led to the ballot box. Standing in line at the polls was like standing in a pillory.

We picnicked beside a lake near Frohburg and didn't start back until well into the afternoon, when hardly any voters were still out and about. We had just stretched out when the doorbell rang. Robert answered. I thought it was his friend Falk. A woman and a man wanted to speak with us, Robert said. We got dressed again.

I felt up for a fight! I would take care of the matter with a few explicit words.

1. At least on the basis of the version printed here (*Titus Holm: A Dresden Novella*), I cannot second T.'s judgment regarding the quality of his novella.

2. The last local elections in the GDR, held on May 7, 1989, marked the first time that fraud was ever proved, because in many precincts the counting of votes was observed by civil rights groups. The official tally showed 98.77 percent of votes cast went to the "candidates of the National Front."

3. In January 1988.

The woman was around fifty and was bouncing up and down on our landing as if on a diving board. Her bright red lipstick held an old smile in place. He was in his mid-thirties, had scraggly yolk yellow hair, and wore a black leather jacket. In order to prop his left elbow casually on the railing he had to lean ridiculously to one side. A ballpoint pen was thrust up out of his fist. He was holding a satchel in his right hand.

He spoke, she observed our game of Q-and-A.

No, I said, we had no intention of heading for the polling place before six o'clock, no, our reason had nothing to do with local politics, no, we didn't know the people on the ballot, they didn't interest us, we had a very different notion of what an election is.

I worked hard telling myself not to smile. But first Michaela and then the yolk-haired fellow himself began to grin. And even the woman tried to no avail to prevent her bright red lips from breaking into a smile. By now his elbow had slipped off the railing.

Did they need any other information, Michaela asked in such a friendly voice that it sounded as if she were offering them a glass of water. No, he said, they had no further questions. They were grateful for our being so candid with them, and they could now inform the polling place that the volunteer staff wouldn't have to stay on and that the mobile ballot box needn't stop by at our place.

"Well then, your visit hasn't been completely in vain," I said. And Michaela added, "So at least you can enjoy the rest of your Sunday."— "Ah, wish we could," Herr Yolk-Yellow exclaimed, laughing and rapping his satchel with his pen. We came close to extending our hands in farewell.

Michaela had to calm down Robert, who had been listening and was afraid he would be called out of class at school because of us. He was crying, threw himself on his bed and shouted, "Why can't you be like everybody else?" When the doorbell rang again, he cringed. This time it was his friend Falk.

I'm not sure I can make you understand. But the wretchedness of one side made the wretchedness of the other all the more obvious. From that day on I was overcome with a sense of absolute futility. Wasn't it absurd to sit down to work on my novella again? Wasn't it a kind of unintentional parody? Just as in the scene on the landing, everything took on an undertone that provoked laughter. Every accentuation ended up vacuous, every gesture, every protest was superfluous. And my cool observer's eye seemed equally incongruous. It was the most ridiculous thing of all, the purest kitsch.[1]

I sat down at my Rhinemetall and hammered away. I didn't comprehend what I was writing. But I did suspect that it no longer had anything to do with literature.

It was a kind of farewell; I was driving myself out of paradise. Or maybe I should say, was driving it out of myself—sacrificing my individuality, my own distinctive voice, to the extent that I had ever had one.

I thought what I was doing was a necessary infliction of self-punishment. And by doing so, I was castigating all the others, the whole country, the whole system. What I was fabricating here was crap, but I, this nation, this society deserved nothing but crap. Maybe, I thought, this was a little like what Duchamp had felt in declaring his urinal to be a work of art. Just as he was perhaps tortured by the certainty that he could never again pick up a brush, never step up to his easel or smell the paints on his palette— that's what this eruption felt like to me. It was a brutal exorcism I felt forced to perform. With each sentence of my election story, of my primitive fecal orgy, I was moving farther and farther away from Arcadia.[2]

I was outraged not by the revolting and disgusting facts, but by the realization that these revolting and disgusting facts could no longer be communicated in any traditional way, as if every attempt to tell the truth and to call lies "lies" made distinguishing among them all the more difficult.

For me the massacre on Tiananmen Square in Peking[3] was above all a signal that the world would remain just as it was. That it would roll along like this for an eternity. I had not expected anything else, or had I? I couldn't understand why such horrible news left me with a sense of relief.

During the summer theater break we loaded a tent into the car and drove to Bulgaria. In Achtopol on the Black Sea—where Robert burst into tears when he saw a dolphin stranded on the beach—I was struck with the idea of using Nikolai Ostrowski's *How Steel Is Tempered*[4] as the basis for a truly caustic work.

1. T. has failed to provide any basis for such statements. Why should cool observation be purest kitsch?

2. Cf. the story "Voting," in the appendix.

3. June 4, 1989.

4. Required reading in school. A novel about a member of the youth organization Komsomol who became a Hero of the Soviet Union during the Russian Civil War.

What all had actually happened that summer didn't become clear to me until the start of the new season. We in dramaturgy laid bets as to who would be returning to work and who had already exited. Max, our Jean, and his family had traveled to Hungary. He was generally viewed as the favorite for clearing out. Max returned too late to attend the opening general meeting and couldn't understand why he was greeted so effusively in the lobby. It was a strange mixture of joy and disappointment— yes, maybe there was even a little disdain involved too, as if people had expected more of him.

At the same time Michaela and I had been having arguments, or better, disagreements. Although Michaela had now turned thirty-five, we wanted a child of our own.[1] It used to be, she said, that it was a relief to see the blood, but nowadays she just got more depressed every time. Each new menstruation ended up as a reproach to me. Michaela insisted I get a checkup. I found that humiliating, but to have argued the point would only have made things worse. The checkup was exactly how I'd pictured it. I stood there in a toilet cubicle reeking of disinfectants and suddenly didn't even know what woman I was supposed to be fantasizing about. A week later I handed Michaela my certificate. "Funny," she said, and that was her only comment about the matter.

Your Enrico T.

Monday, May 21, '90

Dear Jo,

Gale warnings were sounded here early this morning. Waiting at the door were Black and Blond, two policemen I recognized. I asked if they wanted to search our apartment.[2] "Last night," they said without any change of facial expression, "someone broke into your newspaper."

1. In the GDR women in their early thirties were considered almost too old to be bearing children.
2. "Black and Blond" will be introduced later. At this point all that needs to be noted is that this had to do with "the two men in the white Lada" that T. thought he had seen at the accident on March 7th (cf. the letter of March 9, 1990). The reason behind T.'s question must have been just as incomprehensible to Johann Ziehlke. The explanation is revealed in letters to N. H. that follow.

Black and Blond weren't authorized to give me any further information, including an answer to the most crucial question: Were the computers still there?

I would have loved to hug and kiss that big screen. I turned on one machine after the other as if inquiring after their health, and stood there happy amid the humming. Everything else, I thought, is secondary. The metal cabinet in my office had been broken open, Ilona's box containing last Friday's cash take was missing—not more than three hundred marks. In Fred and Kurt's office the petty cash had been plundered. It all looked more like a prank by some kids. Black and Blond took their leave.

We should be glad they found something, the detective said. Upstairs they had pulled drawers out and left Jörg's, Marion's, and Pringel's manuscripts strewn across the floor.

I asked about Käferchen and her husband. The detective didn't understand my question—we already knew each other from the police page, a squat fellow with a handshake like a vice and eyes like portholes.

We groped our way up the dark stairwell. The detective kept stumbling on the uneven and badly worn stairs. I searched for the doorbell by the flame of his lighter. The door was unlocked, but could be pressed open only a crack. He held the light up to the door frame. "Crowbar," he said. The lock itself dangled loose. I called out Käferchen's name, two, three times. In reply came—my blood froze!—I have to put it this way: an inhuman howl. Even the detective winced.

I didn't recognize the old man's voice at first. I shouted my name. The old man bellowed. "Butchers! Oooh youuu fouuul butchers!" The old man cursed us as bandits too.

With the help of two more cops we managed to get the door open, shoving the wardrobe to one side. The old man came at us with an ax, the lighter went out. All the same, the two cops managed to grab hold of him. I heard the ax sliding down the stairs.

The old man gave off an awful stench. He kept rasping his gruesome "Butchers!" in an almost toneless voice and threatened to wring our necks.

Frau Schorba pushed me into the computer room and offered me one of her green tranquilizers. She had arrived at seven o'clock and had reacted perfectly as per guidelines—back in Lucka she had been given instructions on how to handle a break-in.

Through the window I could see the flashing blue light. Shortly afterward I heard the old man's voice as he and Käferchen were brought downstairs.

We set out on a tour with the team of detectives. Each of us had to say what was missing or damaged at their workstation. At first I thought I had come off scot-free. But then I could hardly believe it: the photograph of Robert, Michaela, and me had vanished. It had been lying among my papers. The burglars had dealt with Ilona's framed family portrait by tossing it to the floor and stomping on the glass. Then they had dumped the contents of her "opera bag" over it. Surely I knew, she sobbed, what that meant. She was talking about the mirror. Ilona is superstitious. It's seven years of bad luck, I explained to her, only if you break the mirror yourself. She shook her head, no, no, that's not how it is.

The burglars had got in through the hardware store's only window to the courtyard. The cash register had been emptied and was still open. Evidently they had been looking just for money—the only other thing missing was a mixer. There were crowbar scars in our space as well. Hardly neat work, the shorter detective said disparagingly. I couldn't keep my eyes off his hands. He had more strength in two fingers than I did in my whole arm. Although the cup was hot, he held it like a mug, but with his pinkie sticking out. He is the older of the two, but evidently ranks lower. He always lets his partner through the door first. Even when I offered him coffee, he waited for his partner to say yes. His boss seems unsure of himself, is always quick to agree with us or laugh at some remark, while not a muscle stirs in Shorty's face. He nodded, however, when his boss suggested it didn't take much imagination to picture what they had done to the two old folks. Käferchen, he said, had been lying there wrapped in a sheet, whimpering. "It's a disaster uptop"; Shorty said, "Everything busted to smithereens." The grandfather clock had been knocked over, the blanket shredded. How those oldsters had managed to push that wardrobe in front of the door is still a mystery.

The two detectives were just about to take their leave when Jörg arrived. They extended their hands to him too. But instead of shaking hands, he took a step back. Shorty said something to the effect that we had set up cozy offices here in this old ramshackle place—a harmless remark, it seemed to me.

He'd do better to refrain from such comments, Jörg responded with an icy stare, then shrouded himself in silence until they had left.

He was not going to put up with such insinuations, he exploded. And why had I let somebody like that sit down at a desk? I said that I had often sat at a desk with those two and that I'd had no other choice, because otherwise I would have had to stand to fill out a report they were filing solely on our behalf.

Jörg thought the remark had insinuated something about our office furniture. He had met these same two guys during the occupation of Stasi headquarters and had assumed they were both Stasi themselves. The whole bunch had been on a first-name basis. Only gradually had he realized that he was talking with a prosecutor and police detectives, and that the ones who kept their mouths closed belonged to the Stasi. "I mean," he corrected himself, "officially belonged." And it was in fact ironfisted Shorty who had accused him, Jörg, of being aggressive. Jörg was not about to let himself be calmed down.

Marion leads him around by her apron strings. Last week he admitted to me that ever since the day Piatkowski visited our offices, he's been trying to write an article about him.[1] "Winners Can Be Insufferable" is to be the headline. But the moment he sees that headline in front of him, he goes totally blank. No sentence, no phrase that he doesn't immediately strike. He feels like a fly banging against a windowpane, over and over—even though the article is a matter of self-respect for him, of self-respect and independence.

Then we shouldn't have agreed to buy the building, I said. Yes, Jörg replied, it wasn't appropriate, and he hadn't actually agreed to it. What was that supposed to mean, I asked. He couldn't say really, and it wasn't intended as criticism of me—he'd been happy about it himself, as I could see at the time, and he wasn't trying to offer excuses by blaming the baron. "But it isn't right, it isn't right."

"The voters elected Piatkowski," I said. "He's justified in claiming that at any rate."

He understood that, he rejoined. But he can't bear it when someone like Piatkowski floats right back up to the top, that really cheapens everything else. Doesn't it? He just wanted to pose the question—at least that, a question.

"What are we supposed to do with people like those detectives? 'Send

---

1. In his letter of April 10, 1990, T. wrote that Jörg had asked him to "keep working on his article on Piatkowski." It was therefore originally T.'s assignment to write the article.

the Stasi to the mines' only works in socialism,"[1] I said. I helped him tidy things up.

Jörg is a man full of scruples. After we published our scandal issue he was afraid that Meurer, the school director, whom he had attacked in his article, might become suicidal. Which is why he was happy when he spotted him on the street. Meurer, however, doesn't know what Jörg actually looks like. People here in town really are afraid of Jörg. I likewise profit from his reputation.

I had to force myself to sit down at my own desk and get back to work. I would have loved to have asked the Catholic priest—he had accompanied the baron to "entrust" us with an article about the Altenburg hand reliquary—to move from room to room with his censer, cleansing everything with the proper ritual. Ilona once again burst into tears when the priest spoke a few comforting words to her. From hour to hour she was getting more and more wrought up over something that she herself couldn't actually say what it was. Frau Schorba was filling in for Ilona after having sent her back to the kitchen, where I could hear her sobbing. Astrid the wolf loped from room to room sniffing excitedly, as if following a trail. I drove Ilona home. We drank some more coffee in her kitchen. She couldn't stop talking about herself—for example, about how at age eighteen, after only a few months of marriage, she had been ready to throw herself in front of a train.

When I got back, Kurt—who normally doesn't say a word—asked if I'd had a nice time at Ilona's and gave me a nod, a thoroughly approving nod.

I first noticed Kurt wearing one of the bombastic watches that the baron had brought a whole boxful of. They say an authentic original costs hundreds if not thousands of dollars, but the baron gets them for just nine marks apiece. They're intended as an incentive for new sub-scribers. Anyone who subscribes to the *Altenburg Weekly* prior to July 1st and pays 45.90 marks in advance gets a watch—while the supply lasts.

The problem is we need to provide ourselves with a little buffer so we can get past July. If just a thousand people respond to the offer that would come to 45,900 marks, minus nine thousand for the watches.

By evening the locksmith had got all the doors more or less back to normal. We had him repair the old folks' door at the same time.

Hugs, Your Enrico

---

1. One of the most popular chants at the Monday demonstrations in Leipzig.

PS: I spent two hours running the figures yesterday and put together a paper with my ten theses that I want to hand out tomorrow. We have to act. If we just keep on going as we have up till now, we're done for. Marion—who reproaches me for having accepted an ad from South Africa[1]—thinks that polishing doorknobs to get ads is demeaning, yes, humanly degrading for anyone, especially women. It borders on prostitution. I of all people should be able to sense the discrepancy between what is of importance to us—which is why we put out a newspaper at all—and what it is I'm planning. When I said nothing, she kept at it: Could I imagine that kind of door-to-door promoter on a stage or in a novel as anything but a wretched character. I don't know if she noticed her mistake[2] as she said it or if she now fell silent because Manuela[3] had appeared in the door, beaming.

Ascension Day, May 24, '90

Dear Nicoletta,

I do so hope that my ruminations about my need to write aren't boring you. But my weal and woe depended on my writing. For if writing was a blunder, then I was a blunder.

By writing one reassures oneself of the world—it's a platitude, but I filled it with life. As long as there are blasphemers, we needn't worry about God. In my case that meant: as long as I succeeded in raging with a pure heart, something out there must exist—big game, monstrosities, socialism as it really exists, the Other, or whatever you want to call it.

You can see what thin ice I was already moving across. Security was reduced to *a pure heart*. Call it, if you like, a sense of style, or a regard for what was appropriate.

Michaela found my grotesque brain children amusing, but didn't take them all that seriously and continued to torment me with suggestions for my Paulini piece. Geronimo never mentioned them. Vera, on the other

---

1. The help-wanted ad for a South African paper factory appeared on p. 1.

2. Johann Ziehlke reports that T. often called Leopold Bloom, the central figure in *Ulysses* by James Joyce, the "patron saint of the advertising business." In T.'s opinion, then, Marion's "mistake" lay in not immediately being reminded of Leopold Bloom, who was anything but a "wretched character."

3. Manuela, "the blond waitress," who by this time had become a sales rep.

hand, sent me a congratulatory telegram. She thought that precisely by abandoning my self, my ego, I would find my way to a unique position. I had, she said, discovered a shortcut on the road to fame and eternity. I'm afraid she still believes that. Just early last January she assured me that I am a player in an "immortal game." My art, and it alone, was worth living and suffering for—she had long since staked her own life on just that, on her brother's talent.[1]

Despair alternated with euphoria. Eureka! I cried jubilantly, convinced that I had developed and radicalized my method. (Sitting on the john I discovered too late that there was no toilet paper and reached for a newspaper close at hand. As I departed, I noticed that one article had been torn on an angle and was missing its conclusion. What was left was a series of lines, each shorter than the previous and concluding in mutilated words that yielded a throttled stammer I found touching. The penultimate line ended with a "hear," the last line with a "t." I would never have been able consciously to achieve so convincing a linguistic disintegration of persons, things, and ideas as had inadvertently emerged here. When I typed it out, maintaining the same length of lines, what I finally pulled from my typewriter was a page that looked like a poem.) But no sooner did I have my effort in hand than I sank back into melancholy. What would such reductionism get me?

That was two days before the Hungarians opened their borders.[2] Until that point I had ignored the Hungarian vacationers as best I could. I don't know what I had expected, maybe a compromise that would allow them to return, but never that the borders would be opened. A permanent gap in the wall was unimaginable. Michaela said we had to toast the event. And so Robert drank his first glass of wine to the health of the Hungarians. "Maybe," Michaela said, "something will come of West Berlin after all."

I didn't correct her, because her failure to understand seemed too fundamental to me.

Norbert Maria Richter, the director of Nestroy's *Freedom in Gotham*, was trying at the time to have me replaced as dramaturge. Our differences were, he said, unbridgeable.

---

1. According to V. T., a very exaggerated version of a letter that has not survived.

2. On September 11, 1989, Hungary opened its border to Austria. By the end of the day approximately ten thousand citizens of the GDR had fled to the West.

As far back as June, Norbert Maria Richter had wanted to turn the play into a kind *Knights of the Roundtable,*[1] a farce about a betrayed revolution, about revolutionaries turned nabobs, about history and how they prettify it by remembering lies. And all of it with lots of glitter and show.

And now, in September, Norbert Maria Richter thought he could see in the piece the spirit of revolution.

Precisely because it was this Norbert Maria Richter who told me about the founding of the New Forum—calling it "a significant step in the direction of democratizing our society"—I wanted nothing to do with it.

Nevertheless that same day Ramona, one of my colleagues, laid a couple of filled-out applications for membership in the New Forum on my desk. Michaela had promised her to take them along to a contact address in Halle.

I had no choice; I likewise had to fill out a form with my name and address. I knew what a stupid move it was, what childishness. Now I was playing "opposition" too. And sooner or later I would be shown this same form during an interrogation.

Michaela, on the other hand, wasn't acting like someone risking her own existence and the future happiness of her child, but more like someone who had finally found the right role in the right theater.

The last Monday in September, the day on which we were supposed to drive to Halle, I couldn't find the applications in my pocket. I ransacked my desk at the theater—but didn't dare let my colleagues notice what I was up to. The idea that in my negligence I might have put Michaela and the others in jeopardy was unbearable.

I drove home, I could barely speak. "Gone," I panted, "the applications are gone."

Michaela had taken them out of my pocket to write down the addresses of the others.

As we drove along we saw several police cars, but even the highly unlikely possibility that we—Robert was with us—could have been waved out of the car and searched had lost all its terror.

Michaela was glad to make the acquaintance of someone named Bohley, evidently a relative of Bärbel Bohley.[2] Except for a functioning

---

1. Play by Christoph Hein (1944–). Johann Nepomuk Nestroy (1801–1869), Austrian playwright, *Freiheit in Krähwinkel* [Freedom in Gotham] (1849).
2. Painter, cofounder of the New Forum, one of the best-known civil rights advocates.

doorbell and a nameplate on the mailbox, nothing suggested that the house was still occupied. The whole block looked as if it had been designated for demolition. Michaela was disappointed. We decided to come back later and drove to the center of town. We ran up and down the market square and ordered the most expensive ice-cream concoctions at a milk bar. We tried to describe for Robert what Feininger's painting of the cathedral looks like; we extended our walk to the Moritzburg and then down to the Saale River. Michaela didn't want to visit the Albert Ebert[1] house or buy shoes, although she saw some she liked. She didn't want to appear on the Bohley doorstep with a shopping parcel.[2]

We had no luck this time either. Application forms in hand, Michaela hesitated, looking first at me, then at Robert, and back to me, as if wanting to give us a final chance to stop her from doing something stupid. Or was her point to consecrate the moment in some way, because from now on nothing would be as it had been before? The slips of paper vanished soundlessly into the mailbox.

We hardly talked to one another in the car. On the highway from Leipzig to Borna I felt as if I had finally put something behind me for good. I hadn't weaseled out, I had signed—and I wouldn't deny it or take it back—and had sacrificed half a day doing it. I felt as if this justified me to go ahead calmly with my work. Even in the midst of that lunar landscape, even in Espenhain, the gentleness of that autumn was palpable. I thought of the smoke of burning potato plants after the harvest, of hiking the Saubach Valley near Dresden, all the way to the mill with its giant waterwheel, of country roads littered with windfall fruit, leaving you drunk on the scent of overripe apples and plums, on air quivering with wasps. I thought of the first home games at Dynamo Stadium, of the Königstein Fortress and the taste of bockwurst and herbed cider. My Dresden novella reminded me of some favorite book I hadn't read for a long, long time.

The next day it was Jonas, our general manager, who told me—as if he had just accidentally happened to have been there—about Leipzig. There had been ten thousand people, ten thousand demonstrators! I would gladly have believed his fairy tale that they were all applicants[3]—but ten thousand was too many, far too many.

1. Albert Ebert (1906–1976), a master of small-format paintings and graphic works.
2. They could have stored their purchases in the car.
3. Applicants for exit visas to leave the GDR.

Michaela told me that cameras had been set up on the roof of the Leipzig post office. She repeated everything Max had told her as if to say, "And what were *you* doing while this was going on? Where were *you*?"[1]

What I found so ridiculous about the demonstration was its "workaday" quality. One conscientiously does one's job, then it's off to demonstrate, but not for too long, because one wishes to report punctually and with renewed energy for work the next morning.

On Wednesday Michaela bought a new radio.

Norbert Maria Richter had scheduled an evening rehearsal for the next Monday. Michaela took this to be an alibi, a pro forma announcement. To judge from Norbert Maria Richter's behavior and the way he had reacted to Max's descriptions, the crew could only assume he would be the first to take off for Leipzig. Norbert Maria Richter, however, had no such intention whatever. Michaela called him a shifty bastard. Anything anyone wished to say, Norbert Maria Richter remarked, could best be said onstage. The latitude of the stage was a privilege to be used for the benefit of the audience—a responsibility that must be respected and not cavalierly misused.

Those who would play at rebellion, Petrescu allegedly interposed in best Stanislavsky tradition, could and ought not shirk from studying it. It would be a betrayal of one's duty as an honest actor not to make full use of this opportunity. Otherwise some lovely day *we*, the people of the theater, would find ourselves being instructed by the *audience* as to what rebellion and revolution look like. Norbert Maria Richter spoke of being considerate of those who thought differently about the matter and of how necessary it was at precisely this juncture to maintain discipline and, by good work, demonstrate one's irreproachability.

Michaela declared she would report in sick. As we listened to the news about the refugees in the Prague embassy, we fell silent, and Michaela made a gesture whose message was: There, you can hear for yourself, we have to go to Leipzig!

Monday noon Michaela appeared in the dramaturgy office. She just wanted to tell us that no one was going to Leipzig. There she stood, Miss Eberhard Ultra, our revolutionary in chief, in her leg and ankle warmers, a scarf flung over her shoulder. "It's all so absurd," she said, "I'm so ashamed."

1. They had driven through Leipzig on the way from Halle back to Altenburg.

"Then I'll go alone," I said, as if that were the only possible reply.

Of course I had no real desire to. But to have missed the whole thing would have been reprehensible. If there was ever going to be a second demonstration, then it would be on that Monday, the last one before October 7th.[1]

No sooner had I said it than Michaela decided she didn't want me to go. She kept going on about Krenz, about how he had just got back from China—and everybody knew what that meant.[2]

They couldn't just take aim and mow down ten thousand people, I replied, at least not in Leipzig, and they couldn't arrest them all either. I concluded by telling her I'd leave the car somewhere near Bavaria Station—and handed her the second set of keys.

We said good-bye, and Michaela actually appeared then on the balcony and waved as I drove off.

The sunlight was dazzling, late-summer warmth lay like a heavenly blessing over the day. The landscape in the rearview mirror was the paradise to which—after this final ordeal, filled with countless observations and sensations—I would be returning.

By four o'clock I was in the German Library, where I ordered up a couple of books on Nestroy and found an empty desk in the reading room. The lamp didn't work, but that didn't bother me; on the contrary, I was content just to be able to sit here in this asylum, aboard this ark.

Before me lay the script of *Freedom in Gotham*. When I pushed my sleeve up past my watch, my cold fingers felt like the touch of a stranger.

I figured I would be revealing my intentions if I were to leave at five on the dot. So I had hung on for a few more minutes, asked about the books I'd ordered, and then went to the restroom. Who knew when I'd have another opportunity.

After parking the car near Bavaria Station and stashing my Polish leather briefcase in the trunk, I slung an empty bag around my wrist as if I were going shopping.

At a pedestrian stoplight I ran into Patrick, Norbert Maria Richter's assistant director. "Playing hooky?" The question just slipped out. He

1. The fortieth anniversary of the founding of the GDR.
2. At the end of September, Egon Krenz, chairman of the National Defense Council of the GDR and Erich Honecker's crown prince, had visited China and congratulated our Chinese comrades on having "restored order and security by deploying armed force."

replied like a student caught in the act and avoided my gaze. He introduced the woman beside him as his fiancée, Ellen.

We were walking past the Gewandhaus when I heard the first
chanted slogans. I couldn't make them out. *"Stasi raus!"* Patrick repeated
like someone forced to quote something embarrassing. He couldn't have
said it more softly.

Ellen was free only until seven o'clock. She had a piano lesson in
Connewitz[1] at eight. The two of them discussed whether—and if so,
when—streetcars would be running again. Even if she had to go on foot,
Patrick said, a quarter till eight would work, otherwise she'd miss the
best part. I figured it was inappropriate to ask what he thought the "best
part" was.

I checked out everyone close by, from head to toe. Like an overeager
dog, I let my eyes wander from one to the next, because now—it was a
little before six, in the vicinity of St. Nicholas Church—there could be no
one who was actually here to shop or simply on his way home from
work.

Although close to the Krochhaus now, I saw no indication of anything
overwhelming, although the chanting of slogans never stopped.

On the square in front of St. Nicholas people were standing shoulder
to shoulder. Unable to move ahead, we craned our necks. That was quite
enough for me. Ellen, however, was able to twist and wriggle her way
through the crowd. People yielded to her as if she were a waitress. She
would have made it even farther if Patrick hadn't run into an acquaintance. Without exchanging names, we shook hands.

I stood on my tiptoes. I don't even know anymore how I came to recognize the group shouting those outrageous words. Was there more
light there? Were their arms raised? I can no longer match the image I
still have today with what I saw that day on the square in front of St.
Nicholas. All of it—the people, the twilight, the warm air, the underground current that flowed from that group—seems like a dream or a
vision to me now.

Instead of registering each detail, each vibration, I felt less and less.
All the same I was convinced I was experiencing a historical moment.
Even if the partylike mood were to vanish in the next moment—the
square would be easy to block off—this nevertheless would have been

---

·1. A neighborhood in Leipzig.

the biggest protest since 1953. People would soon recall October 2nd in much the same way they remembered June 17th.

As the crowd pressed tighter together in the twilight, the chants spread more quickly.

I was prepared to acknowledge and admire as our alpha animals those at the epicenter who invented and struck up chants. But did they truly believe they could change things?

The call of "Sanction New Forum" was a little work of metrical art, whose last three syllables pounded like a fist against a door. It touched me in some unique way, as if those squawkers were fighting for me, for legalizing my membership. The chorus's chants bounced off the facades. It took people on the periphery a while to notice that those at the center had fallen silent or struck up a new slogan. "Sanction New Forum!" Patrick's friend bellowed directly beside us. I admit—I felt embarrassed. Although *he* had done his part, I could not bring myself to utter something like that.

In the same moment they shouted their first "Let's move out!" I thought I heard the trample of boots—it was just a flock of pigeons taking off from a roof. I would have loved to move out—the people nearest me had already taken up the chant—but we were stuck in the middle of it all. And in the next moment Ellen and Patrick had vanished without a trace.

Inside the pedestrian zone there was almost no way to tell where the demonstration ended and everyday life began. It was equally unclear in what direction the demonstration was going to move.

Hoping to find Patrick and Ellen again, I pressed up against a display window. And only then did it finally hit me: this is a demonstration, people are demonstrating here. I only needed to take a couple of steps forward and then keep putting one foot in front of the other. So it's that easy to take part in an illegal demonstration, I thought.

I can no longer say how we made it to the train station, whether we had veered off before we got to the opera or not until Ring Strasse itself. Later images are superimposed on earlier ones. I can still see us with buildings on either side, in front of display windows, making us look like a second demonstration waiting to merge with the main column. A banner that when folded up was no bigger than a switchyard flag was passed along over our heads. "Travel Visa to Pisa." I saw this as a clever way to smudge the fingerprints left on the sticks. Just as it was my turn to reach out my arm and grab one end of it, the cry of "Gorby, Gorby" swept over us in chorus. I looked at my feet and hoped that that one would soon be over.

I had to talk myself into walking out onto the streetcar tracks. All trams had been halted. One driver had crossed his arms and with a blank expression was staring directly down at me. "Join with us!"[1] was the next chant. People in the lighted car pressed their foreheads to the window-panes, watching us as if we were characters in some boring movie. "Join with us!" It's hardly likely you would recognize the song—we'd had to sing it in music class—and the refrain goes, "So left, two, three, so left, two three / Find your place, good comrades / Join with us in the Work-ers' Front / Cause you're a working man too!" That's where it had come from, this "Join with us!" of theirs. Banal, isn't it?[2]

Then came the cordon of special-alert police. I showed you the spot where they blocked the street. I instinctively moved toward the side. To me it looked like an all-too-obvious "step-into-our-trap." The crowd marched straight ahead, pushing its front rows practically into the arms of the cordon. And all of a sudden—just like in the square in front of St. Nicholas Church, which they never should have let us leave—the whole scene could be taken in with one sweeping glance. They were sure to correct their mistake now.

On a high curb to my left stood a frail elderly woman with arms crooked at the elbows, half ballerina, half supplicant. The reason for her pose became clear to me only after I noticed she was holding leashes, at the ends of which two poodles were leaping about excitedly.

Written in lights above a new building that worked like an exten-sion of the blockade was the announcement: *"Bienvenue,"* "Welcome," *"Dobro poshalovat"*—greetings from another time when there were more pleasant things to do than stand in the street with thousands of others, shouting slogans until you were hoarse and waiting for backup units of the special alert police. There were hardly any lights in the windows. Were the people inside standing behind drawn curtains, sitting at their evening meal, or in front of a television? I envied them. The Astoria, the train station—their lighted billboards worked like the backdrop to some

---

1. Other demonstrators claim that the slogan was, "March with us!"

2. It is possible that this slogan came from the demonstrations of '68. "Don't just stand there, make a fuss, come on friend, join with us!" (Suggestion by N. H.)

familiar play against which a new sketch was being rehearsed between performances.

To this day I still don't actually know why we just stood there, why we didn't move around the cordon or set off in a totally different direction. Weren't we demonstrators just asking the powers of the state to encircle us? Or had our little stroll first found its meaning in this row of uniformed men?

I had seen and heard enough. I took my first steps in the direction of freedom, when at my back the cry went up, "Shame on you! Shame on you!" The third "Shame on you!"—yes, I was ashamed of such a childish chant—was earsplitting and drove the poodles crazy. They barked and got tangled up in their leashes. Suddenly one jumped at me, I could feel its claws through my pants. The woman didn't react. She even let the leash out as I pulled back, and brazenly stared me in the face. Her mustache was especially thick at the corners of her mouth. The woman turned away only as the "Shame on you!" began to ebb. She had a limp, the poodles obediently followed her—by some miracle their leashes had untangled themselves.

If I was going to stay, at least I wanted to see something, and so I tried to press as far to the front as I could. People were helpful, calling out to those ahead by name or tapping them on the shoulder. I moved very slowly, trying not to upset anyone, especially after a man, almost still a boy, cringed and fell silent in the middle of his chant.

When I finally saw the cordon of uniformed men linked arm in arm directly before me—as far as I could tell they were unarmed—I couldn't understand why we had let them stop us. They were ciphers compared to us. The faces under their billed caps lay in shadows. It was difficult to make out any expression.

In the narrow corridor that separated demonstrators and police three young women were running back and forth—or better, pubescent girls. Two of them blew a bubble, both at once, then smacked away at their gum with open mouths and laughed defiantly—they wanted everyone to see what fun they were having. In their white-splattered jeans they came across as both vulgar and charming. Why were they being allowed to carry on like that? And apart from me they appeared to be the only ones not joining in the chants.

Then the girls came to a halt in an almost classic contrapposto, hands on hips or an arm thrown around a girlfriend's shoulder, and pretended to strike up a chat with someone they knew in the cordon.

I missed the crucial move. You'll say I'm fantasizing, but I did hear the silence that announced the deed. It was like a great pause, the kind we know from nature, that moment when day and night collide and all creation falls silent for a few heartbeats. The silence caused me to look around—people were looking up, something was whirling above our heads—the cap fell with a *smack!* as its bill struck the asphalt, tipped over, and lay there upside down not five feet from me. Before I could decipher the name on it, one of the girls grabbed the cap and flung it over her shoulder high into the air again.

Her face was like a miniature portrait, hung at the far end of the world, but in perfect focus. I saw it all at once: the cap rotating on its axis, the head of a black-haired lad, the motion of the girl, and the witnesses frozen in place. What bewildered me most was the bare head, the black hair plastered to it, the forehead with white welts[1] cut across it.

And now the second girl fished with one hand for the cap of a tall fellow and instantly tossed it into the air. Her other hand was casually thrust into her jeans pocket. This time the cap landed behind me. I picked it up. "Jürgen Salwitzky"[2] was printed on the slip of paper under a plastic strip. The first cheers came now from the rear. Jürgen Salwitzky—he too with welts across his forehead—watched his cap go flying again. Before I could give it back to him, it had been wrenched from my hand like booty to which I was not entitled.

The jubilation that greeted each flying cap competed with cries of "No violence!" I couldn't understand what the uniformed men were waiting for. What still had to happen?

The third girl twirled a billed cap around and around on her head.

Jürgen Salwitzky and his two bareheaded comrades now looked like the prisoners of the men in caps to their right and left.

The chants of "No violence!" had died away. The demonstrators wanted to see more caps, and a few brave souls snapped up a trophy. It was easy game. With their arms linked the only thing the uniformed men could do was throw their heads back and stare at the bandit's hand with a mixture of rage and fear.

But people had grown used to all this. Which was why it came as a

1. He means the imprint left by the cap.
2. The name in this passage appears to be T.'s invention. He uses it both in his letter about his army days (April 23, 1990) and in his story "Hundred-year Summer." Surely no coincidence.

relief when a young fellow climbed up on something and gave a brief speech. We shouldn't let ourselves be provoked, but go home now, and return next Monday, each of us bringing a friend, a colleague, a neighbor along. We had achieved a victory today, a victory that we could be proud of. The applause was sparse.

He waited, as if he intended to resume his speech or answer questions, but since nothing occurred either to him or anyone else, he vanished again into the crowd.

How easily I could have taken on that same role. But I would have said something quite different. My speech of indictment and rebellion had been lying at the ready inside me for years. A little courage, a bit of climbing skill, would have sufficed to accomplish something historical at such a moment.

I was among the first to leave, and saw how small the world of the demonstrators was, how few strides it took to return to familiar scenery, to the old play of which we had grown so fond.[1]

I got home shortly after nine. Robert had been waiting for Michaela, not me. At any rate his door closed again before I had caught sight of him. Michaela could hardly conceal her disappointment at my report, which ended up pallid and monosyllabic, as if I had been the one who played hooky. She may well have secretly doubted I had even been in Leipzig.

As I lay in bed I couldn't help thinking about what we had been taught in school, about how the workers in the GDR didn't need to strike or demonstrate, because anyone who took to the streets in a socialist state was ultimately demonstrating against himself. That turn of phrase was a perfect description of my situation. As a writer, that was exactly what I was doing. I was demonstrating for the end of my material, my theme. I don't think I need to explain that any further to you. What was I, as a writer, going to do without a wall?

Fondly as always,

Your Enrico

1. Whether intentionally or not, T. says nothing about the fact that the confrontation between the demonstrators and the police that day came to a head and ended in violence. For a more precise account of what occurred later, cf. Martin Jankowski, *Rabet oder Das Verschwinden einer Himmelsrichtung* [Rabet, or the disappearance of a point of the compass], p. 155ff., including, among other things, why and under what circumstances the chant of "We are the people" was first taken up at this same demonstration.

Dear Nicoletta,

At the time I found it difficult to talk about those hours I had spent in Leipzig, but what was already in the past was no longer of interest to anyone else either. Michaela, who barely tolerated someone in the hall when she was sitting on the toilet, now began to leave the door ajar so she could still listen to the radio. We bought another radio when the border to Czechoslovakia was sealed.[1] I had been expecting the trap to snap shut, but not before October 7th. Michaela was triumphant—the bankruptcy could not become more obvious, the opposing fronts more clearly marked. Her greatest disdain was for those who only now gave vent to their criticism and outrage.

It wasn't easy to find words to counter Michaela's euphoria. Without the windbreak of October 7th, I said, people could never have pushed things this far. The demonstrators had had a nose for the few days when they could count on easy treatment. The upcoming anniversary was the only possible explanation for such restraint. But now, earlier than I had expected, the game of cat and mouse had begun. Step by step, bit by bit, the end was drawing near.

I asked Michaela to hold back. Within ten days at the latest we'd be living under martial law. Or did she perhaps believe they would be impressed by our slogans and abdicate voluntarily? Why else did she suppose they had their State Security, their police, special forces, army?

My arguments seemed to me so cogent that ultimately it wasn't just Michaela who was daunted by them, I was afraid myself.

And yet, my dear Nicoletta, that is at best only half the truth. These letters will not have been in vain only if you believe me when I say that above all else I felt a sense of relief, even a certain cheerfulness.

I would like nothing better than to break off my confession at this point. But my descent has not yet come to an end.

I had hardly anything to do at the theater and so I often sat in on the Nestroy rehearsals. Michaela was playing, as I noted before, Frau Eberhard Ultra. Ultimately it was no longer a role. Day by day she was playing herself more and more.

A description of those rehearsals would more than suffice to characterize the period. It would serve as a kind of chronicle, even without

---

1. Oct. 3, 1989.

ingredients like demonstrations and police deployments: from the initial discussions of May and June, when Norbert Maria Richter had still regarded the piece as a kind of lampoon of functionaries and their revolutionary blather, to the excitement of early September, when the concept was to stage the idea that revolution is possible, on into October, when the production grew triter and triter with each passing day, because the street was always a good two steps ahead of the stage, until the point when—but I don't want to get ahead of myself.

Michaela couldn't be talked out of traveling to Berlin that Saturday,[1] just as she did every year, for Thea's birthday. I thought it was absurd for us to be separated on the very weekend when the die would be cast. She couldn't turn Thea down, and they needed to stay in contact, especially now. Besides which, I was invited too. Even though she really didn't want me to come along. Robert and I took her to the train on Saturday. She leaned out the window and waved, as if saying good-bye for weeks. Then I delivered Robert to Michaela's mother in Torgau, where he was to spend the night.

On the way back I was able to gas up in Borna without a long wait. Once home, however, being all alone felt like unhappiness weighing down on me. I drove to the autobahn on-ramp, from there it was only sixty-five miles to Dresden.

Do you remember the trains carrying the refugees from the Prague embassy? I heard on the news that there had been scenes of tumult at the Dresden Central Station. Everyone who wanted out had tried to get to those trains.

I had last spoken with my mother on Wednesday, and it had sounded as if she was too frightened or cautious to talk about any of it on the clinic telephone.

On October 7th, however, it was all about Berlin and Gorbachev and what would happen on Monday in Leipzig. While I drove I listened to early music, some famous Neapolitan whose name I didn't really try to remember, but even Bach reworked some of his stuff.[2] Listening to the arias and duets a sense of calm came over me for the first time in months, as if these chords were setting the world and me as well back on a familiar track. But that mood didn't last long.

1. Saturday, Oct. 7th.
2. It is possible that T. means the *Stabat Mater* by Giovanni Battista Pergolesi (1710–36).

After ringing my mother's bell and waiting a while, I unlocked the door. As I pulled back the curtain separating the small vestibule from the hallway I smelled the odor of my childhood. The cup in the sink was half filled with water, no traces of lipstick on the rim. Bread crumbs were floating on the plate under it, a dark substance had dried on the knife, liverwurst or plum butter. The pot scrubber was full of grains of rice and stank just a bit.

I walked to the telephone booth and called the clinic. A nurse I didn't know answered. Judging by the voice, she had to be very young. Frau Türmer wasn't available at the moment. I asked how long the operation would last. She couldn't say. I asked her to tell my mother that I would see her at the clinic. At first I thought the nurse had hung up, but then I learned my mother wasn't on duty this weekend, and so wasn't even at the clinic.

I called Geronimo. His line was busy. I called Thea. One of her little girls picked up the receiver, but before I could say a word, she shouted, "Nobody home!" and hung up. Geronimo was still on the phone. I walked to the little round bastion in the park with its monument to Theodor Körner, and then tried a third time, again with no luck.

When I got back home lights were on in the living room. I stormed up the stairs, unlocked the door, gave a shout, ran to the living room, where I stood for a while listening to the tick of the wall clock and finally turned off the light. I walked from room to room, made a second round, turned on the heat, and finally sat down in the kitchen. I wasn't hungry, but didn't know what else to do at the moment than to fix myself something to eat. The bread was stale, and what few things I found in the refrigerator I put back after standing there holding each one in my hand for a while. With my tea I ate one section after the other of some West chocolate I'd found in the butter compartment.

You will ask why I expect you to read such trivia. Of course none of these details are important, but the early music, the familiar four walls, and my mother's absence had turned me into a child again. I drove off to see Francisca and Geronimo.

There was no mention of Dresden in the news on the car radio, at least nothing from which you could draw any conclusion about what was happening at the moment. On the far side of Dr. Kurt Fischer Platz[1]

---

1. Now Olbricht Platz.

I could see streetcars a quarter mile ahead backed up as far as the Platz der Einheit.[1]

I turned around and took Dr. Kurt Fischer Allee to Bautzner Strasse,[2] meaning directly past State Security, decorated with "anniversary lights." But except for one patrol car that turned just ahead of me, I saw no uniformed personnel.

In order not to awaken Gesine, I threw gravel at a window, over and over, until I heard footsteps in the darkened stairwell. Geronimo appeared at the little pane in the door, opened up, and gave me a hug. But that was his one little burst of joy. "What's up?"

Just so I wasn't to be surprised, he whispered on the stairs, he had a visitor.

Geronimo preceded me, the kitchen was empty. He opened the pantry. "It's Enrico," he said, and held the door open as if he were presenting me with his Golem. Nothing happened for a few moments. I sat down—and stood right back up again. Because he had to duck to get through the doorway, what I first saw was just a white turban, a bandaged head. And out came Mario, Mario Gädtke, the reddest Red in our class, who had left for the army as if setting out for summer camp. The left half of his face was swollen. We shook hands. "Nice coincidence," he said, "here we are all together again." Mario sat down on the sofa and pulled a stationery notepad from under his sweater. I waited for an explanation, including why he had vanished into the pantry at the sound of gravel against the window.

"He's just been released," Geronimo said. Mario pursed his lips, the same way he always had.

"Released from where?"

Mario sat there smiling to himself.

"The special alert police," Geronimo answered for him. They had nabbed him the evening before and hadn't sent him home until two hours ago.

"He brought that with him," Geronimo said, pointing to the bandage. Mario raised his head. I asked about Franziska.

"She's in no danger," Mario said, and smiled again.

"She's working on a conference for the Hygiene Museum—'Bicen-

1. Now Albert Platz.
2. Now Stauffenberg Allee.

tennial of the French Revolution,' " Geronimo explained. In such situations only one of them left the house, the other stayed with Gesine. He was about to go on, but Mario had begun to read—so loud that Geronimo got up and closed the kitchen door.

Mario's report is reprinted in Geronimo's book,[1] naturally with some changes to what I heard that day. In his foreword Geronimo describes how he had barely recognized Mario—he was so badly battered and wearing that head bandage. Mario had drunk one glass of water after another before he was capable of uttering a word. At that moment, Geronimo writes—that is before he learned anything from Mario—the thought crossed his mind for the first time that all this would need to be documented. Then comes a lot of stuff about forgetting and preserving, about guilt and justice and atonement and forgiveness. One gets the impression, moreover, that Mario had come to him because Geronimo was just the man one turns to in an emergency, a rocky refuge in a tempest-tossed sea.

In his description of the evening Geronimo omits my visit. And in fact I said hardly anything. But as you'll see it would nevertheless have been appropriate to have mentioned me, if only in a minor role.

What Mario read to us sounded at first like an accident report already officially on file, a statement of grievances addressed to whomever. First the date, time (8:15 p.m.), and the statement that he had gone to the Central Station in, he emphasized, "a totally sober state," plus an enumeration of his "personal effects": ID, wallet, cigarettes, matches, house key, handkerchief. This list made its way unaltered into the printed version. There it reads: "My goal was personally to witness what truth there was or was not to the reports of friends, neighbors, and colleagues. Near the Central Station and along Prager Strasse several thousand people had gathered. Prager Strasse and especially the area adjoining the Rundkino had been cordoned off by security forces. Several areas had obviously been declared off-limits. A canine unit was posted directly in front of the movie theater. There was no untoward rowdiness that I could see. As nearly as I could ascertain the security forces were made up of units of the special alert police, the transportation police, as well as the National People's Army. One could hear chants coming from in front of the movie

1. Johann Ziehlke, *Dresden Demonstrators* (Radebeul, 1990), pp. 9–23; cf. also Eckhard Bahr, *Sieben Tage im Oktober* [Seven days in October] (Leipzig, 1990), pp. 80–88.

theater, about where the music instrument shop is: 'Father, no billy club! Brother, no billy club!,' 'We're here to stay!,' 'Nonviolence!' "

I asked if it shouldn't be "No violence!" but Mario insisted it was "Nonviolence!" Missing in the book is his commentary on "We're here to stay!" He had thought it necessary to explain that the slogan was meant to set them off from people wanting to leave the GDR and was in no way meant as resistance to a police order to vacate the area.

"A passerby took a picture of the barricade in front of the Exquisite Clothing Shop. In response 2 uniformed men approached him; the passerby attempted to flee, but appeared quickly to resign himself to being grabbed. He was roughly pulled behind the barricade, his camera ripped from his hands. It all happened in double-time. The security forces now advanced, clearing Prager Strasse. Anyone who didn't run fast enough ahead of them was ruthlessly apprehended. Before each successive phase of their advance, they rhythmically rapped their truncheons against their shields, first slowly, then faster and faster, until they broke into a running charge. This obviously raised the level of fear and dismay among those fleeing before them."

As I recall the passage about the sound the truncheons made, it was considerably longer. There were comparisons. In one of them Mario confused Roman legionnaires with gladiators. Whenever he fell silent he would tug his pursed lips to one side.

"Around 10:30 p.m. units of the army took up positions in the street along the front of the Central Station, roughly where the bus station is. Tightly linking arms, they spread out the full width of the street. There were approximately 10 to 15 rows, one behind the other. To a loud unison, 'Left, 2, 3, 4,' they set out at a quick pace, marching down the street in the direction of the Zeitkino. At this point, however, only a smaller group of citizens were gathered in front of the Central Station, where the situation could be described as relatively calm, whereas chanted slogans were coming from the direction of Leningrader Strasse."

Something happened now that I hadn't in the least expected. Mario smiled and shoved the pages across the table to Geronimo. I at once saw what I should have noticed all along: it was Geronimo's handwriting, not Mario's, which I had always envied for its even flow, the way it filled paper like an engraving.

Mario leaned back on the sofa. Geronimo arranged the pages to suit him.

"As a witness to the truth of my testimony," Mario dictated, "I can mention my former classmate Johann Ziehlke, whom I met by chance on Prager Strasse. Do you have any objection?" Geronimo shook his head as he wrote. Mario spread his arms along the back of the sofa and, laying his head against the wall and gazing at the ceiling, continued to dictate. I also recall this passage differently and think I can spot the omissions.

"Nevertheless the uniformed men continued their relentless march and to no obvious purpose cleared the street before the Central Station (including the intersection). Behind them came an army vehicle called a Ural. Objects trailing smoke came flying from it and rained down on the crowd. I quickly realized this was tear gas. For about 10 to 15 minutes I couldn't see much of anything, my eyes burned terribly, the stuff attacks mucus membranes—despite the fact that I immediately covered my face with a handkerchief. At that moment I realized that upon arrival earlier in the evening I had noticed the uniformed forces were equipped with gas-mask bags, but had paid the matter little notice until now. A short time later more men in uniform moved up from Prager Strasse, so that they had now encircled the large lawn across from the bus station. I had in fact previously moved to this open spot because only a very few citizens stood scattered across it."

Did you catch it? During the minutes that Mario saw nothing or hardly anything, the scene goes blank. But that's not how it was. Plus it was precisely at this point that the report lost its semiofficial tone. He and Geronimo had linked arms because they were afraid of being "collected like ladybugs with wings stuck together." There were two, three humorously grotesque sentences in which he described the two of them running around blindly—there was mention of drunken chickens and the stench of rotten eggs. Suddenly Geronimo's arm slipped out of his, he groped for him, shouted his name, and finally decided they were safely out of the tear-gas cloud. In the end he assumed Geronimo had remained behind, had turned back to look for him.

Geronimo hadn't even looked up when Mario removed his arms from the back of the sofa, stared at him, and said, "You'd vanished from the face of the earth." I thought Geronimo was just finishing up the paragraph before offering his explanation. But instead Mario resumed his previous position, put his head to the wall, and went on dictating.

"Very quickly, however, I realized that the uniformed men, banging away on their shields with their truncheons, were still advancing. Coming now from the direction of the bus station as well, they were moving down the street in a broad phalanx—there was no escape. Three or four youngsters tried to slip away to one side. A uniformed man made a dash for one of them and, lunging at full speed, purposely and brutally upended him. Then he began to whale away mercilessly with his truncheon, even though the fellow wasn't even trying to defend himself. Another uniformed man hastened to lend a hand. Together they dragged their bundle back out of the way." Mario described the actions of the uniformed personnel, the ebb and flow. Finally it was his turn. "Storm troopers started hunting and snatching up the last citizens still standing scattered about, dragging them inside their closed circle after first working them over. I heard someone shout: 'There's one!' I didn't notice that 3 soldiers were rushing me until it was too late. I turned around, looked around—no one else nearby. I realized—they're after me. I took off. But because of that pause in my train of thought they were faster at getting at me than I was at getting away. So I just stood there, raised my arms, and shouted: 'I'll come voluntarily, I won't put up a fight.' Two uniformed men grabbed me, one put a head hold on me and squeezed very hard. The other pulled my right arm painfully up behind my back. They slugged me in the back 4 or 5 times and bellowed: 'Shut your filthy mouth! Not one word, or you won't be talking for days.' They dragged me into the circle. 'Don't go easy on him. Or else I'll help out!' another soldier yelled. I was thrown to the pavement, with a booted kick in the back for good measure. Other citizens were already lying there, maybe 10 people. Somebody roared: 'Face to the ground, arms spread above your head, legs spread, ass down!' A man in uniform gave my rear end a kick and shouted: 'Lower, flatter!' I was able to read my watch. It was 12:25. The cold ground was slowly penetrating my clothing, I was freezing. Trucks (W50s) pulled up after a while. We were now frisked, all the while forced to hold the position I've described. To our right another soldier flung 2 bottles, one after the other, to the pavement. Some of the splinters flew dangerously near our heads. Soon, starting on the far right, they began dragging us one by one to our feet."

Mario had spoken in a monotone until now, lowering his voice only at the end of each sentence. Given the already extraordinary situation, I wondered why neither ever looked at the other. As Mario described the tortures he was put through his voice grew more lively. Sometimes, as with the kick to his rear end, he even burst into laughter. Geronimo, on the other hand, bent farther down over his paper like a poor student. I remember Mario's account, especially what comes now, as far less clumsy than it reads here:

"We were led to the truck and forced to climb in. That earned me more blows. 4 citizens were placed next to me. Swinging their truncheons 2 men in uniform sat down across from us. A soldier outside roared: 'You'll get yours, you filthy bastards!' During the trip we weren't allowed to look out the rear window and were ordered to hold our position. The trip lasted about 15 minutes and took a lot of curves. The 2 guards banged their truncheons against their bench as a threat. The truck halted. We were told to jump out. This was to be done in sequence, one by one. But on the other hand it didn't go fast enough for our uniformed guards, they helped with a shove. We were on a military base. It was raining. We 5 were told to line up, hands clasped behind our heads, legs spread. I don't know how long we stood there. Then we had to run up some stairs into a building, hands still behind our heads. We entered a room. Each of us had to stand with his forehead against the wall, legs spread wide but not touching the wall, hands behind our heads. We were frisked a second time. Each time, the uniformed men used the opportunity to make it even more painful to have your forehead bear your entire weight. Pockets emptied. After that each of us had to step up to the table and identify ourselves. Then we went into a larger room (the Officers Club?) with hardwood floors. Position: legs spread, face to the wall, hands behind the head. The room was filling up. I was able to glance at my watch again. It was 1:45 a.m. (Oct. 7th, 'Republic Day'). We were guarded by 2 men. From somewhere in the background one of them gave us our instructions: 'You are in a militarily secured location. Attempt to flee and you will be shot.' "

Mario gradually began to show some theatrical qualities when doing quotes. He seemed especially taken by the word "shot," which he repeated several times. From here on I had the impression he was speaking more and more to me.

"During this period of standing we were frequently maltreated and humiliated. The man standing to my left had his legs pulled out from under him, he fell flat on his face on the hardwood floor. Any movement was repaid with blows by a truncheon. A fourteen-year-old young man requested that his parents please be informed, and added that he had kidney problems and had to take medication. For that he was beaten and led away. When you could no longer stand, you had to kneel down on the backs of your hands until they swelled up. I had to listen to things like: 'They're all ringleaders, we'll be giving them a good hard look.' And: 'His won't be the first skull I've cracked, or the last.' We were called 'Nazi swine' and heard threats like 'Now it's time to play Chile.' Around 5 a.m.—my watch had been broken during a beating—we were regrouped several times. The large window was opened. It was drafty. I no longer had any feeling in my arms and legs. I fainted at one point. That was when they bandaged my head, but it wasn't long before I had to return to my row. After another regrouping my row was shoved into another room. There was a bucket of tea. One of us then had to crawl around on his knees and clean up the mess on the floor. Then we were given bread and lard. Then regrouped again. Finally we stood for a long time in a hallway, near the kitchen. Another identification check. Then we were called out one by one. My name was included, too, my real name. Until then they had just called me the Indian. 'What, y'mean to say we got Indians here too?' A police lieutenant in civvies, lent for the occasion from the criminal division, did the questioning. Then it was back down to the room. As before, 1 or 2 guards stood in the doorway. They were charged with making sure no one slept. Whoever showed a sign, even the slightest sign, of dropping off, was hauled to his feet and freshened up, which meant special treatment out in the hallway. 'Tired? Well then, wake up!' They made sure we could hear them going about their business out there. Those who received special treatment came back with no blood left in their hands and for several minutes couldn't even hold on to a mug of tea. One well-dressed gray-haired man sat inert on his chair, staring apathetically straight ahead. One side of another man's face had been badly beaten, it was swollen and bloodied. An older man very plainly dressed had hands that looked like pulp. At the end of my interrogation I signed a statement. A woman in uniform, a captain, gave me my ID back, handed me a notification of disciplinary proceedings that I had to acknowledge with my signature, and asked if all my personal effects had been returned. After being advised to cut a wide path around the Central Station, I was released at 6:30 p.m."

Toward the end here—there is no reason to keep it from you—I have departed from the printed version and relied more on my own memory. But even with my changes there is no way of capturing the eeriness of it all, which grew sentence by sentence, almost word by word. Mario was sweating. Toward the end he started and concluded almost every sentence with a burst of laughter. He downed what was now a cold cup of tea in one gulp.

Geronimo stared wearily into space. Mario insisted we break this up. I don't know why I didn't stay behind with Geronimo and wait at least until Franziska returned. We hadn't exchanged two sentences with each other. I led the way down the stairs, and heard Geronimo lock the apartment door behind us.

Mario asked for a ride to the center of town. Just when I thought he had fallen asleep, his eyes flew open and he asked whether I still wrote poems.

At an intersection between Fučík Platz[1] and the Kupferstich-Kabinett we caught up with the demonstration. I stopped and let Mario out. Our good-byes were brief. As chance would have it, someone took a photograph, and so that's how I ended up in Geronimo's book. Except I'm the only one who knows that. In the photograph at the top of page forty-five, I'm the driver standing beside the open door of his Wartburg.

I had just waved to Mario, who had called something back to me over the tops of other people's heads—my eyes were following his white turban—when I heard my name spoken behind me. I turned around and there he was, coming toward me on raven legs, shoulders raised, smile askew, his hand extended. His feet looked like they were still stuck inside his father's work shoes. I shook Hendrik's hand. "I'm looking for my mother," I said. We should get together sometime, he said. I asked whether he wanted a ride home. He no longer lived in Klotzsche, he said. Shortly thereafter I lost sight of him too.

As always when I was home alone, I lay down on my mother's bed and soon fell asleep with her nightgown tucked under the pillow.[2]

Your Enrico

1. Now Strassburger Platz.
2. A somewhat remarkable confession in a letter to a woman who was to become his fiancée.

Dear Jo,

If you were a local politician you'd be calling every day to announce you'll be mailing us a letter—or maybe will just drop it off yourself—in a last desperate attempt to get on the list of candidates for a five-minute audience with the hereditary prince. Thanks to two pages on "His Highness," our latest issue sold better than our scandal sheet.

The *first* resolution of the *first* meeting of the *first* freely elected people's deputies in a little less than sixty years was an invitation to the hereditary prince—Barrista had more or less made the matter conditional on a unanimous vote, since "His Highness" did not want his wish realized in the face of any opposition or reservations. Even our members from the Party of Democratic Socialism thrust their arms high. They were all grateful that they could begin their work with an act so pregnant with symbolism. First they praised us—the visit carries the epithet "organized by the *Altenburg Weekly*"—and then themselves for attempting to revive a tradition eminently important for the city and region after its having been suppressed and suspended during the decades of socialist dictatorship. At the local dance school they're already practicing curtsies.

A couple of black sheep are trying to sidle up to the hereditary prince behind our backs. Half of them want to touch him up—which, according to the baron, the prince wouldn't even regard as brazen impudence.

The baron has bought two large apartment houses, one adjacent to the other. On the north side, facing the street, they are black with soot. And his enthusiasm likewise remained a riddle as we stood in the stairwell. The high ceilings with their ornamental plaster and antique doors made the deal more plausible. Every apartment has two wooden balconies, one of which is to be converted into a winter garden. And the view! To the south it's a direct shot to the castle and—on clear days—to the crest of the Ore Mountains. The facade of the castle glistens like a snow-capped peak in the twilight. In the distance, a dark blue streak. And as if that weren't enough, down below is a meadow filled with fruit trees and ending in a rocky drop-off ten or twelve foot deep, which marks the beginning of the backyards of properties down in the valley. Renovation of his favorite bit of real estate will be done around the clock, since he pays in cash.

Even though I think I'm hardly pampering myself, in comparison to others I live an almost contemplative life. Andy not only wants to open a second shop, he's also taken it into his head to open a car dealership just for 4×4s—something you won't find anywhere around here thus far. Even when I drive home at midnight, the lights are still on in Cornelia's travel agency. You can book with her now too, and not have to pay until July. People stand in line outside from morning till evening. Her husband, Massimo, wants to open up a pharmacy in the polyclinic, which is why he commutes back and forth two or three times a week between Fulda and Altenburg. Recklewitz-Münzner is recruiting partners here, offering continuing education classes, and buying up one piece of property after the other for himself and others. Together with his friend Nelson he's reconnoitering for places to put gas stations. Olimpia, Andy's young wife, who speaks every language on the globe, is doing research for Jewish organizations at the land registry office. And Proharsky, the Ukrainian, has gone into debt collecting on behalf of his whole family, and thus for us too. Need I even mention that all these threads come together at Fürst & Fürst Real Estate?

I gave the baron a copy of my calculations for a free paper financed by ads, and assumed it would evoke no more than a smile. He gave it a once-over, said it was perfect, handed it back, asked, as he riffled through his attaché case, what I thought of the reunification of Yemen[1]— about which I hadn't heard a thing, was clueless as to the point of his question—and pulled out his own figures, which, he suggested, reached conclusions similar to mine. The only entries I had forgotten were the interest on credit and the rent.

The baron invited me to accompany him to visit Dr. Karmeka, our new mayor. He guaranteed it would be interesting, since he planned to make him a proposal—and I should watch the mayor closely as he made it—that could prove crucial for the future of the town.

Karmeka, who's actually a dentist and switched to politics because of a bad back, has fired as many members of the city administration as he could. Only the "antechamber" has survived. Along with two secretaries there's a personal assistant, Herr Fliegner, a pallid, frail young man who was busy sorting papers on Karmeka's desk and didn't even look up as we entered.

Karmeka, as everyone knows, receives all his visitors with the same

1. On May 22, 1990, the Democratic People's Republic of Yemen (South Yemen) united with the Arab Republic of Yemen (North Yemen).

ritual—no sooner have you taken a seat than he pulls out a pack of cigarettes (he smokes Juwels, an old GDR brand) and, holding it and his lighter up, asks, "Do you mind?"

In lieu of a reply the baron handed him a shiny brown leather etui. "A little something." Karmeka (the accent is on the first syllable) froze, laid his own toys to one side, extracted a cigar, and sniffed as he drew it under his nose. With our permission, he proposed as he slid the case back to Barrista, he would smoke this delicacy come evening, in peace and quiet, which during work was almost out of the question—for although our presence was of course most welcome and ought not be considered work in any real sense . . . then he took a puff on his cigarette and forgot to end his sentence.

The baron led off with a complaint about the flood of petitions that had followed the announcement of His Highness's visit. He himself had been forced to devote a great deal of time to them, since it was not something one could ask of the hereditary prince. Further lamentations of much the same sort followed. The vertical crease that began in the middle of each of Karmeka's cheeks, ran past the corners of his mouth, and ended at his chin, began to twitch every now and then.

Things had in fact gotten so bad, the baron exclaimed, that our valued friends from the *Altenburg Weekly* were being subjected to something close to extortion to get them to publish His Highness's home address. He mentioned this vexation only so that one might have a very clear picture of what all the visit would demand we be prepared for.

In response to Barrista's palaver Karmeka's gestures grew increasingly guarded and limp. He cautiously extended both arms to accept the schedule for the visit—a suggestion, merely a suggestion—contained in a folder of the same fine leather as the cigar case. And the instant his fingertips touched the leather, he was seized with a coughing fit that caused him to draw his arms up and hunch over as if he were being beaten, until he rotated to one side and finally, still bent over, stood up and turned his back to us.

The baron was relentless. "His Highness will not be arriving empty-handed," he exclaimed, but since he was trying to drown out Karmeka's coughs it sounded more like a reprimand than a promise. His face fiery red, his head tucked as he fought for air, Karmeka stared at us wide-eyed. He hadn't understood what the baron had said about the hand reliquary. The solemn ceremony itself had not merely been a subject of discussion with the church, but indeed enthusiastic preparations—for the procession, for the transfer of the object—were already underway. "Can you—please . . . I didn't . . . I mean—repeat that?" Karmeka managed to gasp.

"We're bringing Boniface home!" the baron shouted, and with a smile handed the folder back to an exhausted Karmeka.

"Just a moment!" I heard a voice above me say. Fliegner had stepped between us and Karmeka with a glass of water. Fliegner shielded him so deftly that we couldn't even see him take a drink. "Ten minutes," Fliegner said, addressing Karmeka, and stepped soundlessly back.

"Please," Karmeka said, now obviously recovered, "where did we leave off?"

The baron handed him the folder with the schedule one more time. Karmeka laid it down in front of him and gazed again at the baron.

"And now an offer," the baron said. "I have an offer to make to the city." And with a glance at Fliegner he added, "And I expect the greatest discretion." Karmeka just kept smiling steadfastly at him. The baron appeared to be considering whether he should even continue the conversation. There was the sound of papers being reshuffled on the desk.

"A three-figure sum in millions, currently invested abroad in dollars, will become available this year," the baron said. He was considering parking the lion's share of it here, yes, here in Altenburg, and of course in D-marks, with the proviso that the city come to an understanding with the local savings and loan and offer him—given the size of the sum and its investment over several years—terms appropriate to such a transaction. "Altenburg is dear to my heart," the baron concluded.

Karmeka's attention was now directed inward, his tongue probed a molar. As he attempted to stub out his cigarette, it broke and lay still fuming in the ashtray. Fliegner had once again stepped soundlessly behind Karmeka and now bent down to whisper something in his ear.

"How can I reach you?" Karmeka asked. The baron pointed to me and bowed, as if thanking me for my services ahead of time. His smile flickered and died.

Karmeka, who was the first to stand up, grasped the baron's elbow, as if to help him to his feet. "I shall enjoy your cigar this evening in my garden." His eyes sparkled with cordiality. "See you soon," he said. Turning to me, he whispered, "Keep up the good work!"

In the reception room Fliegner caught up with us to return the cigar case. We departed without an exchange of greetings. We crossed the main hall of the Rathaus in silence.

"Incredible," the baron sighed as we stepped out under a blue sky. "Have you ever seen the like? Of that shyster? Plays the village idiot and the next moment gives us the cold shoulder." The baron groaned. "Now that's a humbug, that's a bamboozler!"

I had never seen the baron so peeved.

"You need to send a shot across his bow, otherwise he won't know whom he's dealing with here. 'Keep up the good work!' How dare he! Did you notice that proboscis as he sniffed my cigar? But no, no luxuries, these Protestants can't handle those."

I would have liked to inform the baron that Karmeka is a Catholic, but there was no holding him back. " 'City Hall Turns Down Three Hundred Million!' " The baron punched the headline word for word in the air. "A shot across the bow, a nasty one!"

At our portal he blocked my path. "Do you know how much I hate that? How I hate to be kept waiting?"

"But what had you expected?"

"I hate it, hate it, hate it!" he shouted.

But then, when Frau Schorba opened from inside, the mere sight of her sufficed to make a total gentleman of him. Astrid the wolf came trotting up behind her. Frau Schorba takes care of her during the day. The dog lies under her desk, waits to be fed and taken for her midday walk, and to be played with. She never tires of fetching her green ball. In the afternoon Georg's boys or Robert take her for a walk. These walks are a regular fountain of youth for her. Of an evening the baron stops by to pick her up.

The baron's concern for our welfare did not prevent him from making a less than decorous attempt to steal Frau Schorba from us. But she swore she would never forget the trust I had placed in her, not for all the money in world.

She visits Käferchen and the old man at the hospital every day. Käferchen has pneumonia or something even worse; she talks as if she's delirious with fever and babbles on about not knowing where she's supposed to go now. Frau Schorba tries to talk the old man out of his craziness and hopes she may actually be able to speak my name in his presence soon. Leaving aside her warm heart and her gifts as a secretary, she would make an ideal advertising rep or a good bookkeeper. She's the most inconspicuous student during computer classes, never interrupts with some silliness, never inattentive.

Andy began our first class two weeks ago by clipping on a little name tag and pulling a telescope ballpoint out to full length. It was as if he were talking to a hundred people. Each answer to his incisive questions was exuberantly affirmed with a *"Rishtick, zerr goot!"*

In Andy's eyes we're all equal, all pupils, and everyone has to take his or her turn in front of the screen—sort of like being called to the blackboard. Pringel is head of the class, has always done his homework, is always eager to give an answer, his childlike face beaming. Jörg has much the same, if not a better grasp of the material, but is calmer, not quite such a grind.

I feel a lot like a paterfamilias,[1] who would rather ask for something to be repeated and assume the role of the slow learner so that everyone moves with the class toward our common goal. Marion is inhibited. Some criticism early on in front of the whole class ruined any interest she had, so that willy-nilly she's at about the same level as Ilona, who never even gave it a try, but enjoys the cooperative spirit of the class collective and sees all criticism and scolding as a kind of special attention. She sits ramrod straight on the edge of her chair so that, whether her answer is right or wrong, she can plop back again with a happy groan— "I'll never catch on, never, huh?"—luring Andy's gaze to the hem of her skirt almost every time.

We're paying Andy a hundred marks an hour—doing a friend a favor, as the baron says, although neither Jörg nor I see it that way. But he did manage after three sessions to get us to the point where we could print out a perfect newspaper page, spread out over two standard letter pages. *Quod erat demonstrandum.*

We then cut and pasted and stood around gazing at it as if it were the baby Jesus in his manger.

Hugs, Your E.

---

1. This patriarchal attitude is said to have been typical of T. in his later enterprises as well.

Dear Nicoletta,

As long as I was still having dreams that I could remember in the morning, they stood in direct contrast to how I felt. If I was miserable, my brain spun out the most cheerful images. Days that I took to be good ones were often followed by horrible nights.

Early on the morning of October 8th—I was still in Dresden—the doorbell wrenched me out of my paradise. It was my habit to leave the key in the lock. Which explained why my mother couldn't get in. I unlocked the door—but there was nobody there. I got dressed, went downstairs in my bare feet, found the front door ajar, looked out, nothing. Even today I would swear I heard the doorbell.

Back in bed I tried to find my way back into my dream, back to a table where Vera and I were peeling apples and cutting them in the shape of little boats and then dipping them in honey. But that was only the backdrop. The true joy lay hidden within a world whose logic fell apart on awakening. And yet what was left of it in the other so-called real world was a sense of warmth so palpable that I could actually console myself with it.

I woke the second time to the ringing of Sunday church bells. I found a glass of honey and toasted some stale bread. I went for a hike in the Dresden Heath—I hadn't walked most of its paths since my schooldays—and then around one o'clock drove by way of the Platz der Einheit and Pirnaischer Platz to the Central Station. What the radio and Mario had reported, including any trace of a demonstration the evening before, had vanished like a ghost. A half hour later—I had stopped at Café am Altmarkt, one of Vera's favorite spots—it looked as if something was brewing on Theater Platz. The Dimitroff Bridge[1] had already been closed off. After keeping an eye out for Mario's turban for a while, I drove home via the Marien Bridge. I wrote my mother a note saying I was sorry we hadn't been able to go on our outing to Moritzburg. After reading it I almost tore it up again, but then decided I was happy to have put anything to paper.

I never went over sixty on the autobahn, obeyed all other posted speed limits, listened to music, and for fractions of seconds thought I actually had seen Vera the night before.

1. Now the Augustus Bridge.

Robert was waiting for me in Torgau. With a plastic bag in each hand, he ran ahead of me to the car. One contained some pastry, the other a pot secured in several layers of cellophane bags and canning-jar rubbers—stuffed peppers, Robert said, all of it for me. Why for me, I asked. "For all of us," Robert said, "but especially for you."

He asked what I had done. Just as I later told Michaela, I said that my friend Johann had sent a telegram asking me to come see him. And so I had driven to Dresden. He asked about my mother, and I said she hadn't been at home. We drove to the train station.

Michaela got off the train directly in front of me. I could tell from the way she diligently avoided looking at me, from the way she kept brushing her hair behind her ear, and only then finally greeted me, that she was deep into a role, her new Berlin role, which she was now going to perform for us. Robert came running up to her, his backpack bobbing up and down, and even before giving her a hug asked if she wasn't feeling well—because Michaela's role now included looking exhausted, even as she summoned what little energy she had left so that we wouldn't notice her weariness.

The only thing I talked about in the car—and she has held it against me ever since—was the stuffed peppers and the pastry. Months later Michaela accused me of having left her in the lurch and of behaving like a total idiot. Even though she ignored every one of Robert's questions and just kept repeating that Thea sent her love and said we should definitely come along the next time.

I saw nothing disconcerting in the fact that immediately after we got home she withdrew to the bathroom. I put the pot on the stove, set the table in the living room, Robert spooned the sour cream into a little bowl and lit the candles. And just for us he put *Friday Night in San Francisco* on the record player. He called Michaela to come join us several times. After I turned the volume down, we could hear her sobbing.

She finally appeared trailing a streamer of toilet paper, as if she needed a whole roll to dry her tears and blow her nose. She opened the balcony window—the odor of food was making her sick to her stomach—collapsed onto the sofa, and pulled Robert to her. She gazed out over his head into some remote distance where she evidently saw what she had been keeping from us.

Before the birthday party was to begin that evening, Thea, Michaela, and Karin (another actor) had spent a couple of hours in Thea's favorite pub on Stargarder Strasse, not far from Gethsemane Church. They had stayed there until seven o'clock, and Thea had talked about her guest appearances in the West—successful productions that nothing here could compare to. And the audience had been much more spontaneous and open, too. Tipsy not so much from beer as from her stories, they had stepped out onto the street only to be confronted by a phalanx of uniformed, helmeted men armed with shields and truncheons. They turned around, but there was no way to get through in that direction either— Schönhauser Allee had been blocked off at the same point. They walked back and asked the helmeted men to let them pass, they really needed to get home. Thea even showed her ID and said it was her birthday. There was no response. They tried again on the other side of the street. The uniformed men there had neither shields nor helmets.

At this point in her narrative Michaela blew her nose. The toilet paper rustled on the coconut-fiber mat.

They figured, Michaela continued, you could talk to the ones without helmets. Thea spoke to several of them, each time mentioning her birthday and the children and guests waiting for her at home. When she got no reply she raised her voice. She hadn't realized that it was now forbidden to return to your home—that would be just like this government, they might as well arrest her on the spot. Thea had just turned back around to Karin and her, Michaela, when three men in civvies stormed through the cordon and pounced on her from behind. One of them had stepped between her and Thea, which was why she, Michaela, couldn't say exactly what happened to Thea in those few seconds. Thea had screamed, probably in pain. They both could see Thea holding up her ID as she was led away. Then she had vanished behind a truck. They picked up Thea's purse, gathered up the spilled contents, and discussed what they should do now. They tried to describe for each other what the three Stasi guys had looked like, but had to admit that they could never identify them in a lineup. Five minutes later they saw Thea being thrown into a truck by two cops. She and Karin could swear to that.

They fled back into the pub and called Thomas, Thea's husband. Karin began to weep hysterically and had to stretch out on the bench of the corner table reserved for regulars. They could hear screams coming from the street, and new people kept dashing inside, many with scrapes, bruises, and bloody noses. They were all afraid the uniformed brigade might storm the pub. She, Michaela, had almost wished they would, since just waiting was the worst thing of all.

When they got back to Thea's apartment around half past midnight, all the birthday party guests were still sitting there. Thomas had first yelled at Michaela and Karin, as if they were to blame for Thea's disappearance. More than ten guests had spent the night in the apartment—on the floor, in armchairs, sleep was out of the question in any case. Thomas spent the entire night making phone calls. He also drove to the police academy in Rummelsburg, but no one would let him in. They waited the whole day and left the apartment only to take the children to a playground.

Talking had helped Michaela calm down somewhat, but only to the extent that she could now be all the more vehement in her self-accusations. Thea had called to them as she was arrested. She, Michaela, had even tried to hold on to Thea, but had been pushed back by the cordon of uniformed men. Michaela broke into tears again now. One of the policemen—or whatever that uniform of his was—had asked her if she wanted to end up there too. "End up there," those had been his words, and it had been clear that "there" was some horrible place. But now she could only ask herself why she had been so horrified, why she hadn't joined Thea as she ought to have. "No!" Michaela cried, rejecting all our attempts to comfort her, it had been her duty to follow her and not to have let that "there" frighten her. She could understand Thomas's reaction—of course he was right to reproach her. "I let it happen! I abandoned her!"

Robert sat there totally helpless at her side. Then Michaela stood up and announced she was going to the telephone booth to call Thomas. Besides, she could use the fresh air.

Robert and I ate alone. As we were washing up, he told me how his homeroom teacher, Herr Milde, had said we ought never shed a tear for those who turned their backs on our republic (a well-worn phrase in the newspapers at the time), but that his friend Falk had responded that he was sorry that Doreen, his deskmate who had emigrated with her parents a few days before, was no longer here. At first Herr Milde hadn't reacted at all, but then had admonished him to raise his hand if he wanted to say something. Falk had then raised his hand, but wasn't called on. Herr Milde had said it would be easy for a boy like him to find a prettier girlfriend than Doreen. Robert asked me if he should have raised his hand too.

"Bad news," Michaela said. It seemed to me as if at some basic level she was proud of the fact. Karin had stayed with Thea's children,

Thomas had written up a report on Thea's arrest and read it aloud in Gethsemane Church before posting it there. Karin had signed as a witness and had given her address. Karin had promised Michaela that she would add her, that is, our address to it as well. "All hell must have broken loose there," Michaela said.

We were at the theater by a little before ten the next morning. There was a press of people in the dramaturgy office, a long, low room directly under the roof.

Michaela at once grabbed for the telephone receiver, clamped it to her ear, and put a finger to her other ear while she talked.

Most people seemed to have ended up there out of pure boredom. They inspected our little library, paged through old programs, and spoke about productions and colleagues, as if this were what the occasion required. Each time the door opened, conversations faltered for a moment.

Amanda from props appeared and shortly after her our stage manager, Olaf. Norbert Maria Richter hadn't arrived yet. Amanda lit a cigarette and asked what we planned to do. "I'm not planning anything," I said.

Some were discussing a resolution that came from the Dresden Theater and was to be read from the stage there, others talked about blood banks and hospital wards cleared for patients. Word of it was in fact circulating in Leipzig, Patrick confirmed—Ellen had called him at the theater just to tell him about it. Amanda showed us an article from the *Volkszeitung*. "Working People Demand: Hostility Toward the State Should No Longer be Tolerated!" read the headline. A cadre that went by the name of Geifert felt inconvenienced by certain unprincipled elements disrupting their well-earned rest after a day's work. The conclusion: they were ready and able to defend and protect the work of their own hands and to effectively put an end to these disruptions once and for all. "With weapons in hand if need be." I read the article aloud and passed the newspaper around. Amanda held her cigarette butt under the tap and laid it alongside others next to the soap. She smiled.

"Today will decide everything," I heard Michaela suddenly declare. "If we fail today, then we will have failed for good." Her eyes wandered from one person to the next. "If we ourselves don't take to the streets today, we'll be betraying every person who's been arrested and tortured." This was followed by her report of what Thea had just told her.

Michaela took time to give her speech, rarely raised her voice, and let everyone sense that she was struggling to be factual and understood that she had to hold her emotions in check—this was, after all, her best friend. She sounded a lot like a television reporter when she mentioned a girl who had been forced to strip and then chased naked along the hall to the laughter of the police. Thea had been spared that bit of martyrdom. But she could still feel the blow to her head—she had lain unconscious in the truck for several minutes. But even worse was the pain in her back, her whole right side was one single bruise. They had been beaten at every turn, even when they were standing facing the wall with their hands behind their heads. And some of the younger guys had frisked them over and over again.

After thirty-eight hours without food or sleep they had been released. Yesterday evening someone had thrown the switch for all the streetlights in the area around Gethsemane Church and then uniformed men had started whaling away—to the sound of church bells ringing out a tocsin.

"If we don't act today," Michaela said, giving her coat collar a tug, "we'll have squandered our chances for a long time, maybe forever."

All of us were discomfited by Michaela's speech. Which is why news that Norbert Maria Richter had arrived broke things up rather abruptly.

Had it been me and not Thea—of that I was absolutely convinced—Michaela would hardly have been inspired to make such a speech. Once again Thea had been one step ahead of her. *That's* what Michaela found unbearable! Her famous friend was to blame for Michaela's conviction that she would lose face if she didn't risk her own neck.

My dear Nicoletta, I know how petty I must sound to you. Perhaps I still have too little distance on the whole affair. But in this case it's not just my opinion at the time that I'm sharing with you.

There was no cure for Michaela's madness.[1] I knew she would be going to Leipzig. I knew better than to pin any hopes on Norbert Maria Richter or Jonas. Robert remained my sole argument, but then Thea had certainly shown no consideration for her family either.

At noon in the canteen everyone had stories about gyms and emergency rooms that had been cleared to take in patients. Jonas, who had held his tongue until now, said with a knowing smile that he would not advise anyone to travel to Leipzig today.

---

1. It's remarkable that in May 1990, T. can still call Michaela's brave conduct "madness."

When we met after rehearsal—a real rehearsal had, of course, been out of the question—we drove to see Aunt Trockel. If she did not hear from us before ten o'clock, she was to look after Robert. After that we went to the Konsum Market—the shelves were incredibly well stocked, but the only thing I recall now are jars of pickles, oodles of them suddenly seemed available—likewise ultrapasturized milk and ketchup. Our refrigerator ended up as crammed full as if it were Christmas time. Michaela laid two hundred marks on the kitchen table, plus our hoard of twenty-pfennig pieces for the telephone, the rest of our pocket change, and my mother's number at the clinic. I also jotted down Geronimo's number. It wasn't until he saw the currency that Robert began to grasp how different this afternoon was from all others. He wanted to come along. I was for it, Michaela against it. She talked with him in his room. When she came back out, I could see she had been crying. We took off around four o'clock. No one at the theater had taken Michaela up on her offer of a comfortable ride.

Just beyond Espenheim we were waved off the road—traffic control. All I would have had to have done was leave my ID at home or put a turn signal out of commission and that would probably have been the end of trip. We were sent on our way with good wishes. Before I got back in the car I surveyed the scrawny trees and shrubs that lined the rest area—and in that moment there was something idyllic about it all. It was relatively warm. It seemed to me as if I had not given a thought to writing for years.

Shortly before Leipzig, Michaela started to put on her makeup. We could do some window-shopping, she said, we had plenty of time, and laid a hand on my thigh as if to buck me up.

What happened then is quickly told:

We parked in front of the Dimitroff Museum. In a side street directly across from us were the special-forces trucks. Tea was being ladled from big buckets for men in uniform. They didn't appear to be armed. We crossed the street and walked up to within ten yards of them. Those few who noticed us quickly looked away.

Passing the New Rathaus, we came to St. Thomas Church. We acted a little like tourists who've been given a free hour before their bus departs. We walked around the church and stood awhile in front of the Johann Sebastian Bach monument. Michaela was drawn to the bookstore across the street. In situations like this, she said, it was especially wonderful to be surrounded by books. I fell into old habits, but before I had scanned even the first few feet of a bookshelf, I knew I wouldn't buy anything. I no longer saw any point in even picking up a book.[1]

We must have been fairly near the Opera when we ran into a whole convoy of those troop carriers. We walked on by—and it almost felt like we were reviewing them. A couple of uniformed men were trudging back and forth, eyes focused on their equipment. They also had dogs and water cannons.

We halted in front of the Gewandhaus. From its steps you have a view of the entire square.[2]

My dear Nicoletta, you may perhaps assume that we had some serious discussions during these hours, conversations about the future and Robert, or that at least we promised each other to relish every moment of our lives from now on and to love one another. But no, nothing of the kind.

What made the scene so unreal was that I had never seen the state massed in such threatening force before. Each time a column of troop carriers turned onto the Ring from the direction of the Grassi Museum, they were greeted with honking cars and shrill whistles. But when the trucks had moved past, it was once again a lovely October evening with people smiling at one another, browsing in bookstores, and waiting for streetcars.

I explained to Michaela—I was carrying her purchases—from what direction the demonstrators would be coming, that was if they were granted access all the way to the main square. Once they got this far, there would be no stopping them. We had found an almost perfect spot. From here we could flee or join in or simply stay where we were. Who was going to prohibit someone from standing in front of the Gewandhaus with a bag of books under his arm?

Suddenly noise started coming at us from all directions. From loudspeakers came an appeal for nonviolence,[3] and at the same time I could

---

1. And here as well, one would like to know: Why?

2. The entrance to the Gewandhaus is at ground level; there are no steps.

3. An appeal made by the "Leipzig Six" (the secretaries of the district leadership of the Socialist Unity Party, Kurt Meyer, Jochen Pommert, Roland Wötzel; the conductor Kurt Masur; the theologian Peter Zimmermann; and the cabaret artist Bernd-Lutz Lange): "We all need a free exchange of opinions about the continued direction of socialism in our country." The appeal, which was read by Masur, ended with: "Our urgent plea is that you act with prudence so that peaceful dialogue can be possible."

hear chants, some close, some farther away. And all at once there it was, the demonstration. From one second to the next Opern Platz was filled with people, as if they had just cast off their magic caps. We were now part of the demonstration. It's too late now, I thought. Michaela was kneading my hand. I was about to tell her she no longer needed to be afraid, when she pulled me away with her. Michaela was trying to make her way to a man with a mustache and bald head that made him look like a seal. They hugged. He was wearing West-style glasses and pretended not to notice me. For at least thirty seconds I waited behind Michaela and gazed at him over her shoulder. At some point she said, "This is Enrico, he's in the theater too." I asked what *he* did. To which Michaela exclaimed, "This is ***!" *** gave a quick nod as if deep in thought, then turned his seal eyes back to Michaela. And now we three were walking together in the direction of the post office. I wedged myself in beside Michaela and crooked my right arm for her to link onto. But she did nothing of the sort, just kept her eyes glued on the seal. I didn't even know where she knew him from. "Crazy," the seal kept saying, "crazy!"

If it hadn't been for me, I think they would have flung their arms around each other several more times. Michaela told him about Thea. Was this what the director who could make Michaela's dreams come true looked like?

I found it unbearable that this day would be eradicably bound up with this man. From now on he would be latched on to our memories like a tick. Comrade Seal had now switched from "crazy" to "not good." Every one of Michaela's sentences was blessed with this "not good, not good." She seemed goaded on by it. Suddenly he pointed up at a camera and said, "What if those were machine guns!" Someone else had begun to wave at the camera, and now everyone around me was waving up at it. We halted for the pedestrian stoplight.

I'm sure you've seen the dim televised version. Did you notice how slowly people put one foot in front of the other, the considerable distance they kept from one another? The only demonstrations I knew were those from May Day, where you stood and stood until your leg fell asleep, shuffled a couple of yards forward, waited, only to be driven ahead at double-time so that there was never a gap in the parade before the reviewing stands. But here you strolled across the square in pairs, in threes, in little groups, making sure you didn't crowd up on anyone else. The stoplight turned green. But we just stood there and waited. A man asked, "We can go on the next green, right?" And so when the little green man flashed again, we finally stepped out into the street.

We turned left, in the direction of the Central Station. People in cars that weren't going anywhere now sat as if frozen in place, fear in their fixed stares. There was not a squad car, not even a policeman in sight—except for one policeman who stood legs astraddle in a side street, as if he wanted for once to get a good look at the demonstration for himself. After two or three hundred yards we turned around to look. As you perhaps recall the street falls away from the station at a slight slope. Michaela burst with joy and hugged me, the seal shouted, "Crazy, crazy!" The whole city seemed to be one huge demonstration.

All of a sudden the seal bellowed, "Join with us! Join with us!" At the second shout he raised his arm and chanted it with a balled-up fist as if threatening the people in a restaurant who had come to the window and were waving. "Join with us!" he roared, and Michaela chimed in the third or fourth time. Then they switched to "Gorby, Gorby!" It was awful. The two of them were making such a racket that conversations died away and people had no choice but to pick up the chant.

Michaela turned to me as if to say, "See, this is how it's done!"

Whenever the seal paused, Michaela would tell more about Thea. Without complaint she accepted his interrupting her midsentence to break into the "International."

We walked beneath the pedestrian bridge, thronged with people, and found ourselves at the vast open intersection on the other side, which was now completely empty. It was fun to be able to walk in the middle of the street. But at that same moment I saw helmets and shields, maybe three hundred yards ahead. We halted. The seal enlightened us by explaining that this was the "Round Corner," the State Security building.

As we had at the pedestrian stoplight, we waited for people to move up behind us, for the demonstrating crowd to grow denser. It was at this intersection that for the first time I heard the chant "We are the people" (*Wir sind das Volk,* which in local Saxon sounded something like: *Meer zinn das Foulg*), which at the time I took to be an answer to the letter to the editor submitted by the Geifert cadre.[1]

At the Round Corner—not a single window was lit—I now realized how small the cluster of uniformed men huddled shield to shield at the

1. T. heard the slogan a week after it was first chanted.

entrance really was. To my eyes these hoplites looked like horses shying and prancing in place.[1] In an attempt to calm them down, a row of demonstrators had formed opposite the shielded forces. Joining hands they watched as other demonstrators set lighted candles on the pavement at their feet.

Suddenly the seal vanished from our side and forged his way into the human chain opposite the men in uniform. As he did he glanced now left, now right, as if making sure all the others would bow simultaneously with him for the final applause. Instead of moving on and leaving him standing there, Michaela stepped in front of him. Caught up in the thrill of his new role, however, he now ignored her.

Michaela and I trudged in silence past St. Thomas Church, until we arrived at the New Rathaus.

I was amazed by the jubilation all around us. To me it felt more like we had ended up in nowhere. So what now? Another wide turn and back to the Gewandhaus?

Michaela wanted to stay. I kept walking straight ahead toward our car. She had no choice but to follow me. What did I have against ***, she cried, and why in the world was my nose out of joint? She had never told me anything about him, I said. There wasn't anything to tell, she said, they had met only once in the canteen of the Berliner Ensemble, Thea had introduced them to each other. I said I didn't believe her . . . I just didn't want to admit, she interrupted, that this was perfectly normal for theater people, that they were all one big family and a greeting like that didn't mean anything at all. Maybe so, I said; she had, in any case, acted as if I didn't exist.

We didn't speak the whole ride back.

When I unlocked the door, I at first assumed Aunt Trockel had arrived, but it was my mother who was having supper with Robert. I expected her to upbraid us for our foolishness and having left Robert all alone. But that didn't seem to bother her. She had just wanted to look in on us, she said and, cocking her head to one side, listened now to Michaela as if this were all about her latest premiere. But when I went to fetch the key, Aunt Trockel wanted a full report. I owed it to her, after all, she had already packed her things. It sounded like a reproach, as if she had been robbed of a trip, of an adventure.

Your Enrico T.

1. A description easily identified as an exaggeration.

Dear Jo,

I promised you a job, and I'm going to keep my promise, for purely selfish reasons. But I need a couple of days yet, maybe even a week or two, to have a clear picture of it all. I don't know what's been going on behind my back for the last few days. Out of the blue, things have taken the nastiest possible turn for the worse. The atmosphere has changed so completely that I can hardly breathe.

I start each morning with the best intentions, but then, with every unreturned greeting, every evaded eye contact, every comment just left hanging in the air, I find myself turning more and more into the shifty character people take me for.

Maybe I should have gone at things with a little more tact. But I don't like that kind of finagling. Maybe I should have waited, biding my time just with Jörg. But he knew exactly how to prevent that. He and Marion love to play the happy, inseparable couple.

I had asked them what they thought of my worksheet, of my calculations for a free paper financed by ads. Jörg's jaw literally dropped when he looked up at me. "It's easy to put stuff on paper," he said. Marion had buried herself in her work as I stepped in. He hadn't given up a career as an engineer, Jörg said, to run some fish wrap.

You need to know, Jo, that I don't want to do a free paper for its own sake, but as a backup, a moneymaking machine, to relieve the *Weekly* of its burden of ads—but without our losing our advertisers. We have to make the most of our resources, use the structure at hand, just as we did with the city maps or want to do with trips for subscribers, which I'm working on with Cornelia. What I said to Jörg was, "We really both want the same thing!"

"Every respectable newspaper has a chance," he replied, "if it concentrates on the essentials." As soon as we started printing in Gera, the paper would be able to take on enough ads without neglecting content. And with that we'd have everything we needed.

I tried to make it clear to him that the one didn't exclude the other, that we would have to occupy positions before other people could lay claim to them. I'm with Barrista on that—he bends down to pick up coins he finds on the street.

I could set up a free paper on my own, Jörg said, since what I had written up to this point was more suited for that sort of thing anyway. Marion laughed, but didn't look up—as if she had just read something funny.

I swallowed that too. It was our duty, I said, to make use of any and every possibility in our attempt to protect the newspaper—not only in our own interest, but in our employees' interest too. I didn't want anything more than his simple approval to give it a try. "And if it goes bottom up, what then?" he asked.

In that same moment Marion turned around and told Jörg she really couldn't understand why he was even discussing this with me. He and she didn't want to do it, and that was surely reason enough. "And if he doesn't like it, he can give us back his share."[1]

Ah, Jo, I stood there like a stupid little boy. Jörg at least had looked at me when uttering such monstrous things, whereas Marion didn't think that was even necessary.

I didn't need to worry about our employees, Jörg said. None of them wanted to work for a free paper. I could ask them myself. And then he made a comment about Frau Schorba, my best friend, "my bosom buddy," with an exaggerated accent on the second word. She had chased the new mayor away on her very first day here—which, by the way, was a generally known fact, but something that I had kept from him for whatever deeply regrettable and inexplicable reason. And one could only be thankful she was here strictly on probation.

I asked him to think it over one more time, because I planned to bring the topic up again at our next editorial meeting on Wednesday.

He hoped I wouldn't do that, he said, turning his back on me. Maybe it was simple cowardice that prevented me from demanding a decision then and there. At any rate, yesterday morning (what a long time ago that was!) memories of the conversation seemed more like a bad dream that would be forgotten the next day—that's how much I trusted my arguments.

They, however, had read my amiability as weakness. Ilona, whom I treated to a new "opera bag" a few days ago, was too busy to look up and return my greeting. Jörg muttered something in passing, Marion ignored me entirely, Fred was leaning against the doorframe and talking about something with Ilona (suddenly they get along, suddenly she had time), which so preoccupied him that he just gave me the kind of nod he would

---

1. Jörg Schröder vigorously disputes T.'s description of this event—and of those that follow. They had neither said anything derogatory about T.'s articles, nor, as T. would later repeatedly claim, had they asked him flat out to give back his share. They had merely reminded T. that his share of the newspaper had been given to him gratis. And he should keep that in mind, in case he no longer wished to work together with them.

give any customer. Even Kurt scurried quickly by and ducked into his office. Pringel was always on his way somewhere. Only Astrid the wolf came bounding happily toward me the way she does every morning. But ever since Ilona sprained her ankle stepping on Astrid's ball, she mistrusts even that greeting. Frau Schorba presented me the booty collected by our sales reps, but without devoting so much as a syllable to the whole brouhaha. She smiled, business was going incredibly well.

To think that I would seek refuge with Georg, my old boss, of all people! I met him on Market Square, at the fish-sandwich stand. Although we had moved out of his place only two months before, I would scarcely have recognized him; his gait, his body language is so different. Not a trace of the old stiff knight on his steed. He moves downright supplely on those long legs now. The deep creases between his eyebrows and across his forehead have likewise vanished. In greeting me he almost gave me a hug. Did I want to have a cup of coffee or tea at his place? Yes I did, if only just to keep from having to go straight back to the office.

The garden gate is now overgrown with roses. But imagine my amazement when I entered our old editorial office and recognized the same screen we use, and the same Apple next to it too. His printer is a little smaller than ours.

The baron had proposed two books, and paid for a thousand copies of each in advance. The book about the hereditary prince will be the first, then a book about the Jews in Altenburg and environs and their deportation. Just on his own, Georg said, he had enough ideas to last for years. Although the barometer and the clock and the postal scales—everything really—were still in their same old places, I felt as if I were in a totally different room. It was the same out in the garden, which is green now and bursting with flowers and almost impenetrable along the edges.

Franka embraced me as if I had just returned from a long journey. When I saw the big table set for coffee and the three boys waiting for us along with their grandparents, Georg admitted it was his birthday.

And so I spent a cheerful hour in the company of his family. Georg told about an extraordinary encounter. Late one evening recently—it was raining cats and dogs—their doorbell had rung. Before him stood a short woman drenched to the bone, her hair plastered to her head. She stepped inside and asked if she might spend the night—her car had broken down and there wasn't a room to be had at the Wenzel for all the money in the world. Just as he was about to ask why she had chosen to ring their doorbell, he recognized her: the newspaper czarina from Offenburg. Franka and Georg spent the night on air mattresses so that their guest could have a real bed to sleep in. The next morning, however, the czarina sat at the kitchen breakfast table pale and with circles under her eyes, claiming she hadn't slept a wink—the bed was a disaster.

Wearing some of Franka's clothes, which were too large for her, she was soon on her way. A trace of her fragrance still hung in the bathroom, or so he claimed. "A real millionaire," Franka said in conclusion.

Later I climbed the slope with Georg. As we shielded our eyes from the sun with our hands to gaze out over the city—all the way to the pyramids—I told him my troubles.

"You guys have got to do it, just as you've said, it's the only way, otherwise you don't stand a chance," Georg concurred. I had expected reticence and scruples, if not outright opposition. But now I spoke like a man set free.

If only Jörg had been there! Up there on the hill I could have persuaded him. Never before had even I myself so clearly understood the necessity for a free paper.

According to Georg it's already a done deal that the major presses will be divvying up the Party newspapers among themselves—but dividing them up according to the old state boundaries. Since Altenburg would now be assigned to Thuringia, we'd be the only one to straddle the old lines; and in no time we'd be making deliveries from Ronneburg to Rochlitz, from Meerane to the gates of Leipzig. We wouldn't just be holding the region together, we would be a little empire with Altenburg at its center.

We indulged ourselves in predictions about the size of the printing— I figured 100 to 120,000—and it came to me that the baron had been wrong. It's of no importance whatever whether you want to be rich or not. No matter how many possibilities you think you're choosing from, the crucial point is to make one single decision—the one that guarantees your survival. Yes, in the end there is always just the right decision, and the wrong one. And ultimately it's far better to do something yourself than to write about what others have done.[1]

On the way back I applied for the official seal of our *Sunday Bulletin*.

---

1. This idea, which will increasingly take up more room in his thoughts, already stands in contradiction to T.'s assurance to Johann that his sole purpose is to save the *Weekly*.

Back in the office, Frau Schorba greeted me with bad news. Käf-erchen has died, the old man is plotting revenge. When he gets back, there'll be no one to protect me from him, because the police can't take him into preventive custody, and he can't be locked up in a psychiatric ward either, not unless he has caused harm of some sort. At least Marion will have something to be happy about.

The one hour each morning when Frau Schorba coaches me on the computer makes me feel like I'm inhaling air for the whole day. If I make no progress, she says, "Yes, just like this," as if in the next moment I would have stumbled on the solution myself. Only her upper lip betrays her impatience by creeping back and forth like a pink caterpillar over the firm line of her lower lip. The first ad I laid out by myself was Cornelia's "Italian Weeks for Soccer Fans." We cut the World Cup logo out of the *Leipziger Volkszeitung,* and simply pasted it in.

While I waited for Fred, my mind went limp at the thought of the afternoon's upcoming argument. Fred's reports of his country rounds lay before me. I compared numbers for the last two weeks listed on page one. Here one copy fewer, there three. In the best case, stagnation. But his totals showed an increase of thirty newspapers sold.

Of the ten reports that I had checked by the time Fred arrived late for our meeting, two were correct. I underscored the mistakes in his math with a red marker and exclamation points. Oddly enough, however, the errors more or less balanced out.

When he arrived Manuela, our secret weapon, happened to be in my office—she brings in more ads than our three other reps combined. Legs crossed, hands folded across his belly, Fred rolled his eyes to signal how pointless he found my putting up with Manuela's chitchat. When he started shaking his head too, I handed him his lists without comment. If I didn't know him, I said, I'd have to think he was cheating on us. I then sent Manuela on her way, asking her to have Ilona report to my office.

"Can you explain this?" I asked Fred after a long pause. "Can you tell me how you came up with these numbers?"

He had always turned the money in, never held a penny back, and Ilona had given him receipts.

"And you never," I asked, putting the pages back in numerical order, "noticed any discrepancies?"

Fred shrugged. I said nothing. Fred asked if he could leave now. "No," I said, "we'll wait for Ilona."

That sentence was the last one for a long while, until Fred volunteered to fetch Ilona himself.

"Good heavens!" she said when I spread the reports out for her.

"And you always took his money and wrote receipts?"

"I wrapped the coins and took it all to the bank, what else?" she said as if expecting praise. She didn't seem to be in the least aware what this had to do with her.

"But didn't check the figures?"

She had received the money and taken it to the bank, she repeated.

They competed at sniffing in outrage when I said they should put everything aside and recheck the reports. We would need numbers by afternoon. "Maybe," I said in conclusion, "we've been broke for a long time."

When things got underway shortly after five, the mood was excruciating. Ilona and Fred sat directly across from me, talking about something that kept them in stitches. They had had other things to do than to recheck figures, they announced. I was the comptroller, after all, that was really my job.

Pringel sat off to himself and stared at the blank sheet of paper in front of him. He already knew what awaited him, I was the only one still in dark. Kurt was missing, the sales reps hadn't been invited. Only Jörg seemed his old cordial self.

His first question called Ilona and Fred to account: Why hadn't they followed my instructions and studied the totals? They were completely flummoxed.

Frau Schorba gave the figures for the advertising receipts. We no longer had any need of a free paper, Jörg said, we already were one. Starting with the last week in June the Weekly would be printed in Gera, with four or eight additional pages. That would make room for more articles, which would be considerably more likely to increase the number of copies sold than this flood of advertising we were drowning in. And with that Jörg's survey of the future came to an end. He presented his new lead article, which the Commission Against Corruption and Abuse of Office had delivered free of charge—they're having to elect their third chairman, since the first two are themselves both under suspicion of corruption.

Then Jörg pulled out a sheet of paper and said, "We need to talk about this, Gotthold, you have to deal with this now." Pringel's childlike face shrank even smaller. Jörg explained the contents of the letter, signed by more than thirty employees of Air Research Technologies. In it they accused Pringel of being a "Red scribbler." "What is a Red scribbler doing on the staff of your newspaper?" They had enclosed an article Pringel had written for their house journal in October '89.

Jörg began to quote from it, and after citing phrases like "with the full force of the law," "a threat to the health and welfare of our children," broke off with an "and so forth and so on."

When Pringel looked up he was hardly recognizable. His lips were quivering. He tried to smile, his glance skittered across the room.

He couldn't really understand, Jörg said, why this letter came as such a surprise. But above all he wanted to ask why Pringel hadn't shown his cards to us to begin with. In his mind that was the real offense. Pringel nodded. By October no one had had to write stuff like that anymore, Fred muttered, squelching Pringel's own answer after he had just taken a deep breath.

It had been right after the riots in Dresden, Pringel finally stammered. But the text had been shoved in front of him, he had had no choice but to publish it, it hadn't been his article at all, but he had had to sign off on it—as the accountable editor he had to put his name to it. His eyes wandered wildly. "What was I supposed to do?"

"Show us the article," Marion said, which set Pringel stammering again—but it hadn't been his article.

I asked him what he had been afraid of. Of course I meant in terms of the situation last autumn. But he misunderstood me.

"That you wouldn't let me go on writing," he said. Working for a newspaper had never been such fun before, so fulfilling. He was so happy to show up every morning . . .

What was the point of torturing him any longer? He agreed that for now his name would no longer appear in the paper. Pringel is an amiable fellow, and intelligent. You only need to tell him what you want, and the next morning you've got it. His little stories about various firms are a big hit at Gallus. Hausmann furniture has been placing half a page a week with us ever since.

Were there any questions, Jörg wanted to know.

Yes, I said, we hadn't yet discussed the most important topic.

This was an editorial meeting, he interrupted, any discussion of fundamentals would have to be between the two of us. He wished I would finally get that into my head. Besides which, the matter was already settled.

As far as I was concerned, I replied, the matter was not settled, and the others should at least have a chance to hear my arguments. But "the others" had already stood up. Even Frau Schorba was reaching for her handbag. Only Pringel had remained in his seat. The two of us had evidently forfeited any power to influence decisions. But then I felt Astrid the wolf's muzzle against my knee. She was looking up at me with her one good eye. Sure, you can make fun of me, but I'm certain that the wolf understood my situation precisely. I am going to have no other choice than to double my bet. I believe in winning.

Hugs, Your E.

PS: Maybe it would be better to publish Anton Larschen's memoirs with Georg. I think Georg would be pleased, and the book would have a real publisher.

Sunday, June 3, '90

Dear Nicoletta,

I hadn't actually been all that surprised that my mother had shown up at our place on October 9th. But after Robert was in bed, she said, "I've got something to tell you two." And after a short pause: "I was arrested."

My mother's report was far less detailed than Mario's. She had also been arrested on Friday evening, that is, on the 6th, in front of the Dresden Central Station. She had wanted to verify with her own eyes what she had heard in the clinic and on the radio. But no sooner had she stepped off the streetcar—that is, well before she was able to get any sort of sense of demonstrators and uniformed personnel—than she was grabbed and thrown into a truck. They had beaten and cursed her. After her release on Sunday morning, she had taken a streetcar to Laubegast, to see Gunda Lapin, a painter and friend of hers. She had recuperated there until Monday morning. She had then had herself examined at the polyclinic and placed on medical leave for a week. If she were still locked up, she said, no one would know where she was.

Listening to her was pure agony. Michaela fought back her tears and tried to clasp Mother's hands in hers. That seemed wrong to me, because it was like a restraint on my mother, and I was glad when Michaela left to call Thea from a phone booth. Being left alone with Mother, however, was even less bearable. I turned on the television. But neither she nor I watched. We cleared the table without saying a word, and didn't break our silence as we made up her bed. Mother went to the bathroom, and I could hear her gargle and spit into the basin. I sat in front of the television—I had turned it back off—and gazed at my silhouette on the dark screen. I kept taking deeper breaths, until the rise and fall of my shoulders was clearly visible in the reflection too.

Suddenly my mother was standing before me in her underwear and asked me to rub her with lotion. Her back was covered with bruises, they had even struck her on the thighs and calves. She braced herself against the table and bent forward. There was a slight odor of sweat. In prescribing such things, she said, few doctors actually thought about the fact that old people are usually alone and can't rub themselves down. We exchanged good-night kisses. My mother hadn't turned the bathroom light off or screwed the top back on the toothpaste. Her towel lay on the toilet lid.

Michaela asked what that odor was, and then said that Thomas had just rubbed Thea down with liniment too. The word had a cozy sound, as if we'd put everything behind us now.

By Tuesday there was no longer any way to prevent the Dresden resolution from being read from the stage. Except for Beate Sebastian, who was unwilling to take part in such an action unless the Party gave its approval, the whole house was for it.

As for as the resolution itself, I didn't share the others' enthusiasm. When I proposed we write our own, I was told that the orchestra, most of the singers, and the corps de ballet had already agreed to it and that we couldn't start all over again now.

The whole tone was taken from the ritual of criticism and self-criticism. There's a worried functionary hiding behind every line, I said. Michaela shook her head, no, I was mistaken. We went through it line by line, and even I was surprised at how with just the slightest pressure on the lever, the pseudorevolutionary rhetoric gave way. For instance, this sentence: "A national leadership that does not speak with their people is not credible."

"Don't you hear the whimpering of some disillusioned lickspittle?" I asked. "Who says I'd ever want to speak with that bunch? Why call them our national leadership when they came to power by fraudulent elections? And what does that mean: with *their* people? Why don't they quote Brecht: 'They should dissolve *their* people and elect another . . .' "

Michaela admitted that those lines could be deleted, but that the formulation "a people forced to be speechless will turn to violent action" was not just courageous, but true as well in the present situation. Why, I asked, didn't they write: "A people imprisoned for twenty-eight years and treated as property of the state, punished and bullied for the slightest contradiction, has finally taken over the street! Down with a band of criminals who beat defenseless people, mock and torture them."

Michaela didn't reply. "Why," I asked, "don't they simply say: Tear down the wall, throw out the Socialist Unity Party, establish human rights, take to the streets, be brave, don't let them bully you anymore."

"That's going too far," Michaela said, "that calls everything into question."

"Of course," I shouted, "it calls everything into question! Leipzig calls everything into question, what happened to my mother, to Thea, calls everything into question. We have to call everything into question." Why was she willing to put up with the same old crap from the pens of apparatchiks? " 'It is our duty,' " I quoted scornfully, " 'to demand that the leadership of our country and Party restore their trust in the population.' Isn't that disgusting? To conclude with that? Doesn't that mean, please don't beat us, we're really in favor of socialism? That's more wretched than wanting some prince to take us by the hand? You know what that Dresden crowd is like."

"Then why," Michaela asked, "don't *you* say it?"

"I will say it," I replied. "You can depend on it!"

I have to add that we weren't alone. We were standing beside the little round table in the dramaturgy office and had those who were sitting at it or leaning against their desks for an audience. Ever since her performance of the day before and our return from Leipzig, Michaela had become the Bärbel Bohley of the theater and I her husband, whose mother had been beaten, no, tortured by the police. One by one the others had all fallen silent. We had spoken the last sentences as if onstage.

Under their attentive eyes, Michaela walked over to my desk to get her purse. "There is a difference," she said, returning to her first position, "whether something is said in the theater or on the street. There is no anonymity in the theater—"

"Which simply means," I broke in, "that the street needs to enlighten the theater. God knows, not a single person arrested was anonymous. They all had to present their IDs!"

In her eyes, she said, it would be an achievement for the theater to arrive at a point where the resolution could be read at all. With that Michaela left the dramaturgy office. From my vantage point at the window I saw her walk to the bus stop. Yet another *Gotham* rehearsal had been canceled.

My arguments were so irrefutable that I found myself in a state of euphoria. I had given my aversion free rein and, by following it as if it were a divining rod, had discovered a logic that worked. Do you understand me? Suddenly I had cogent reasons why I did not want to be a part of it all.

My new outlook provided me, I thought, a line of defense that no one would breach all that soon and that allowed me to observe these theatrical follies with a derisive smile. Of course people said I was right, but they took Michaela's side and talked about small steps, cunning, patience.

At two o'clock on the dot I drove home. Mother had prepared a meal. She had filled Robert in on what had happened to her. He enjoyed the "extended family" and the "Sunday dinner." "The longer I think about it," Mother said, "the more clearly I realize they all belong behind bars, not just their bullyboys and officers, but all of them, Modrow, Berghofer, Honecker, Mielke, Hager, the whole rotten pack. And if they didn't know anything about it, so much the worse." Michaela didn't look up. Had I arrived earlier, she probably would have thought I had coached my mother. For coffee we drove to Kohren-Sahlis. There was poppy-seed cake and whipped cream. Mother ordered seconds and said she'd earned it. Then I drove Michaela to the theater. The *Gypsy Princess* matinee for retirees had begun at three o'clock.

While the performance went on up front, backstage the battle over the resolution had flared up again.

The orchestra and corps de ballet had voted yes, as had the soloists, with one exception, but the chorus was divided. The gypsy princess herself could not be persuaded to read the resolution. Kleindienst, the conductor, likewise refused. Finally we had a volunteer, Oliver Jambo, our gay heldentenor—I mention this only because Jambo celebrated being our gay heldentenor with every step he took. He would consider it an honor to read the letter. And with that I drove home.

That evening Michaela told us that the whole thing had fallen apart because of Jonas. He had sat in the smoking corner, smiling. He asked everyone who made the mistake of wandering past to put a hold on "this gesture." He was asking for just one day. They should wait one day more. He had spoken to Michaela as well. It was difficult even for her to hold her own against him. One day, he kept saying over and over, just one day. When asked how that would change anything, he cited the meeting of the politburo.

At this point in Michaela's narrative I couldn't help laughing. Yes, she said, she found it shameful too, but in the end there had been nothing she could do. The singers were suddenly in favor of a one-day postponement. But the orchestra hadn't been informed, so they had waited in the wings. Finally Kleindienst called them onstage to receive, or so he said, their well-deserved applause. The musicians had left in such a rage that they probably couldn't be counted on from now on.

Wednesday, however, was to be Michaela's big day. Mother, Robert, and I took our seats for the performance of *Emilia Galotti*. Michaela wasn't at her best. At the point where Emilia starts to tell her story, she forgot her lines.

At intermission I ducked out to go to the dramaturgy office. All the lights were on in the general manager's office. The technical director, the office manager—she was also a Party secretary, and is currently the general manager—were sitting with three or four others whose voices I didn't recognize.

I kept hearing footsteps and the sound of a door opening and closing. All the same I was surprised at how many people had gathered. On the lowest tread of the little set of steps that led to the stage stood Jambo, lost in thought and playing with the cord of his glasses. A woman's voice whispered, "The general manager!"

I hadn't even noticed him. He was sitting at the table, his head resting on his crossed arms as if he were asleep, his shoulders jerking. At first I thought there had been an accident, that someone was dead.

There was a crackle in the loudspeaker, and Olaf, the stage manager, called the actor playing Odoardo onstage. He left the loudspeaker on, so that we could now follow the performance. "Is no one here? Good, I shall be colder still," snarled the loudspeaker.

"Didn't you hear it on the radio?" Jonas asked in the middle of the line, "He who obeys no law, is equal in power to him who knows none."[1]

---

1. In the original: "He who obeys no law is one in power with him who has no law."

Jonas's eyes, veiled with tears, moved around the room, crawling from one person to the next in search of mercy. "Didn't you hear it on the radio? Don't you pay attention anymore? Can you think only in one direction?" He shook his head. "So you don't know," he shouted, "you don't know about the most important change in decades. Haven't any of you heard the politburo's announcement this evening?"

"Hah!" Jambo exclaimed. "Is the wall gone?"

Jonas bellowed, his voice exploded into the room. Michaela claimed later that you could even hear him through the steel-plated door. His head turned such a livid red that I expected to see him collapse onto his desk, eyes staring wide, mouth hanging open.

The cord had got tangled on the bridge of Oliver Jambo's glasses, so that it looked as if he were shaking a thermometer down. "Could you repeat that?" he asked in a low voice.

Instead of hurling himself at Jambo as I expected, Jonas began to preach. His entire statement was so silly that I don't remember any of it except two sentences, which he repeated several times: "There won't be any Chinese solution," and "The politburo wants an honest face-to-face dialogue with the nation."

The applause at the final curtain was now coming over the loudspeaker. Jonas kept on talking. He was starting in again with his "face-to-face" when, a little short of breath, Michaela's voice could be heard from the loudspeaker: "Okay, here we go!" "Ladies!" Jambo said, holding the steel-plated door open. I was the last to follow. When I turned around once more, I saw Jonas standing there with one arm raised, pointing vacantly.[1]

Michaela stepped forward and began. One couple stood up and dashed for the exit. In the dim light cast over the audience I could see Mother and Robert, both sitting up ramrod straight and listening as if Emilia Galotti had risen from the dead to take her revenge on Marinelli. Her tone of voice when she said, "We're stepping out of our roles here," was the same with which she had said, "But all such deeds are from times past!"

I felt uncomfortable just standing there, reduced to a physical presence.[2]

---

1. T. is presumably using this gesture to denounce Jonas as a "Lenin monument."

2. It is difficult to discover any logic in T.'s actions. Previously in this same letter he claimed he had now found reasons "why I don't want to be part of it all."

The audience applauded, most of them stood up, including Mother and Robert. I saw Michaela reflexively want to bow in response to applause. She was just barely able to control herself, but now spread her arms, as if to say, All of us here agree, and then stepped back. People continued to applaud as if waiting for something, a song or a postlude. Some of those onstage followed Michaela's example and extended their arms to applaud the audience. Instead of an orderly exit, a few of us began to wander offstage one by one. The last ones to leave, including Emilia Galotti, looked as if they were in fact fleeing. The audience, 124 purchased tickets, kept on clapping as if to force an encore.

When we arrived at the theater the following day, an emissary of the Library on the Environment was waiting for us at the door. "The whole city is talking about what you did," he said with an earnest nod, and invited us to Martin Luther Church that evening so that we could inform others about our declaration. Since I had never heard about a Library on the Environment in Altenburg, I thought at first he had come from Berlin.

The invitation extended to us was for a "prayer service."

At the noon break Michaela took up residence in the canteen and received her due homage, even from the orchestra and chorus. Nothing like this had ever happened to her, not even after a premiere. Michaela announced who would read the resolution that evening, since she intended to appear at the church.

Martin Luther Church, that neo-Gothic forefinger rising at the far end of Market Square, was jam-packed. I followed Michaela down the center aisle to the front, where the emissary greeted us. It had been ages since I had been inside a church!

"Ghastly, truly ghastly," a woman with short hair and a long, thin scar across her right eyebrow kept repeating. "Truly, truly ghastly!" She was referring to Bodin, the pastor of the church, who had demanded that instead of presenting bombastic speeches they should hold a thanksgiving service. God needed to be thanked for the politburo's declaration, which was an attempt at reconciliation. There were, moreover, strong elements of his congregation who would have no sympathy whatever for such proceedings. If she and her friends did not understand that, he had no choice but to yield to those members of the congregation and close his church's doors to a crowd of rowdies.

Somehow I sympathized with Pastor Bodin, an elderly, totally bald man, who had seated himself in his clerical robes against one wall and now appeared to be deep in thought or prayer.

Michaela and I were greeted by several people. The founder of the Altenburg New Forum (every town had its own New Forum) fought for air as he told us how that same morning he had found the lug nuts loosened on his Trabant. A gaunt long-haired fellow with an inscrutable Chinese smile was holding a rolled-up banner in his arms like a giant doll. There was a steady flow of young women who introduced themselves as members or chairpersons of environmental and peace groups.

Women were likewise in the majority among the people thronging the aisles and balconies. "Something has got to happen today!" the woman with the scar said, and planted herself in front of us.

"What's supposed to happen?" I asked.

"Why, a demonstration," she exclaimed. "We've got to get things started here! Somebody's got to speak up today for once."

The long-haired fellow came over and interrupted her to say, "If someone is going to speak, it ought to be a person no one here really knows." Strangely enough at that moment that seemed plausible to me. I realized too late that by nodding I had got myself into a precarious situation. The fellow from the New Forum returned to repeat his lug-nut story and said he was already asking far too much of his family. Michaela didn't budge. "Can't you do it?" the woman with the scar asked, gazing at me. I was trapped.

"And what am I supposed to say?" I asked. "Super," she cried, "that's really super!" The fellow with long hair bent down over me and patted my shoulder. "Fine, Enrico, very fine!" I was so discombobulated that I asked how he knew my name.[1] In the same moment the church orchestra struck up. The bass player, who had given the downbeat, nodded like one of those plastic dachshunds that for a while you saw in every rear windshield.

After the first few bars I regretted the whole thing, after the first stanza I was desperate. Had I not very wisely kept my distance from such people until now? I could understand Pastor Bodin better and better as he sat there breathing heavily. His pouting lower lip dangled like a trembling reddish blue nozzle through which far too many words had flowed.

While someone from the civil rights movement was speaking, I was passed a note: "Get ready, you're up soon. Thanks."

Michaela, who had been greeted with lots of applause at the start,

---

1. Crossed out: "We were just introduced."

made the mistake of reading the Dresden Resolution with the same flair she had at the theater. I could hear Emilia Galotti. She herself was aware how from one line to the next she was losing energy and how ultimately all that was left was an artificial theatrical pose. Toward the end she spoke faster—a deadly sin for an actor.

"I wasn't good," she whispered. I took her cold hand, held it tight for a while. "Doesn't matter," I said as the bass player gave his downbeat nod to that rotten orchestra.

Hundreds, thousands of times I had imagined giving a revolutionary speech, as if my life had been aimed toward this moment, this wish, this dream, which I was now damned to turn into reality.

Clutching the little note in my left hand, holding fast to the pulpit with my right,[1] I fought back the urge to laugh.

I looked up. Not a cough, not a cleared throat, not a shuffled foot. And into this perfect silence I said, "My name is Enrico Türmer. For a year and a half now I have been living with my wife and son at 104 Georg-Schumann Strasse. I work in the theater and am a member of no party."

I looked out over the heads of the people and down the center aisle, and began:

"We have made mistakes, we confess we have, we indict ourselves.

"We tied on our pioneer neckerchiefs and sang the song about the dove of peace, while tanks drove through Budapest.

"We wept and laid our hands in our laps as we were being walled in.

"We said nothing while Soviet tanks crushed the Prague Spring.

"We paid our solidarity dues while workers were being shot and killed in Gdansk."

The breathless silence lent my words a strength that had nothing to do with me, these were no longer my words.

"On May Day we demonstrated in honor of our unending loyalty to the Soviet Union while its troops murdered people in Afghanistan.

"We cracked jokes about lazy Polacks while the Poles were fighting for free labor unions, and we swore an oath to our flag as the National People's Army took up its position along the Oder and Neisse.

"In the midst of the graveyard silence that has reigned over Tiananmen Square for months, we still hear Honecker and Krenz clapping their approval."

1. It was merely a lectern, not a pulpit.

I could feel the words whirling about me, felt them rip me from the spot, felt myself being swept away with them.

"We put on our finest clothes when we went to vote.

"We learned to talk about our country without using the word 'wall.'

"We let ourselves be draped along the curb like living garlands.

"We went to our Youth Consecration and swore loyalty to the state.

"We practiced throwing grenades and shooting air guns while the best of our writers, actors, and musicians were forced to leave the country.

"We congratulated one another on our brand-new apartments while the old centers of our towns were being razed.

"We counted our Olympic gold medals, but the dentist didn't know where he would get material to fill our teeth.

"We hung flags from our windows, although in Prague and Budapest we were ashamed to be recognized as citizens of the GDR. We rose from our seats for the national anthem, although we would have preferred to sink into the ground."

I cast my eyes into the distance.

"We do not want to burden ourselves with guilt any longer. Our patience is at an end. We will let them see us, on the streets, in the marketplaces, in churches and theaters, in the Rathaus, in front of the buildings of local government and the State Security's villas. We have nothing to hide, we will show our faces. There is no reason for us to keep silent, we will speak our names. The time for begging is past. The wall must go, State Security must go, the Socialist Unity Party must go! Bring on free elections, a free media, bring on democracy! We need no one's permission. We will now take to the streets! This is our country!"

The silence burst open. The whole room was in an uproar—stomps, applause, whistles. If it doesn't sound too absurd, I stared out into the clamor, clutching the pulpit, dizzy from my own words. People were crowding out the doors. "Super," the woman with the scar shouted, "really super!" Michaela had crossed her arms, clutching her elbows with her hands. Later she said the pastor had pushed me aside to get to the microphone. But the organ had drowned him out.

The closer we got to the exit the more clearly we could hear the chants.

The demonstration moved past the police station, past the Rathaus, on across Market Square, and turned left at the far end onto Sporen

Strasse. We formed the rear guard. Suddenly someone opened the police-station door, two uniformed men raced toward us, and asked where we were headed. How should we know, the long-haired fellow shouted as he started to unroll his banner (FREE ELECTIONS!). The woman with the scar described our probable route for them: past State Security and the District Council and then up the hill to District Administration. They should probably block Zeitzer Strasse and Puschkin Strasse.

As we crossed Ebert Strasse, we heard a concert of whistles that could only be directed at the Stasi villa. "Let's hope they don't do anything stupid! Let's hope, let's hope," Michaela whispered.

That night around one thirty, I heard car doors slamming directly below our window, I listened for footsteps, thought I could already hear the doorbell. But then nothing more happened. And that was almost more unnerving.

Your Enrico T.

Pentecost Monday, June 4, '90

Verotchka,

now I really must write you a letter:[1] Mamus was here for two days.

The first evening Michaela invited us over.

Suddenly it was all just like old times, each of us sitting in his chair, and if our friend Barrista hadn't been running around in his slippers we might have taken him for a guest. Mamus acted as if nothing had happened and ignored the new constellation. Robert is her grandchild and Michaela her daughter-in-law, and now as luck would have it the baron has been added to the mix. Mamus agreed with everything he said and praised Herr von Barrista's objectivity several times. He kept going on about Dresden and how much he had enjoyed the tour by streetcar and her warm hospitality. That was three weeks ago.[2]

It was news to Mamus that Michaela has given notice at the theater. "But why?" she exclaimed. Michaela just went on eating, as if she hadn't heard the question. And instead her baron began to hold forth for her. First he talked about the state of the world and declared our current

1. Usually the two telephoned each other.
2. At the time T. and V. T. were in Monte Carlo.

situation to be flat out the best this old earth has ever known—strong democracies without rivals and technological progress that increasingly relieves man of his burdens and allows him the freedom to pursue his true calling. Now that the iron curtain has fallen, what lies before us, or so the baron said, is an era of action and deeds, while contemplation and brooding belong to the past. Things change now more in one week than they used to over the course of years, which means that art, be it in the East or the West, is a losing proposition. Life's experiences are not to be found in the theater nowadays, but in commerce, in the marketplace. The changes we see daily are not only more exciting than Shakespeare, but also can no longer be grasped through Shakespeare.

He was basically saying nothing all that different from what I had heard him articulate last January. At times he used the very same words. But now Michaela was nodding with egregious eagerness, and Mamus seconded the baron and kept repeating that we needed to see things with businesslike objectivity now.

After the meal our friend Barrista passed around something in a little box with a glass lid. It didn't look at all promising, some sort of desiccated stuff in a kind of mousetrap. Have you guessed? It gave our poor Mamus such a fright that she flinched and pressed her back to her chair—a couple of Boniface's knuckles.

Our farewells were also "businesslike," although each of us felt embarrassed. Robert came with us to the car. (Our friend Barrista has such a bad conscience that not only has he transferred the car's title to me, he's also paying the insurance.)

As I drove I told Mamus about the new apartment, described to her the view to the castle and the spaciousness of our rooms. I mentioned it in the hope that it would make the bleak room where she would be spending the night with me more bearable.[1] Besides which, it seemed to me it was better to talk with her than to leave her wrapped in silence.

"I'm not moving in alone," I suddenly said—it just slipped out. Mamus didn't react. Only when we came to a stop did she announce the results of her ruminations: "Vera!"

"Yes," I said, "Vera." I asked Mamus if she wanted to take a walk with

---

1. T. never mentioned in his letters to Johann and N. H. that he had moved out of the apartment with Michaela and Robert and was now subletting a room from Cornelia and Massimo until the building C. von Barrista had bought was fully renovated.

me, because besides the two air mattresses there was only one chair in the room. She shook her head. I was truly alarmed at how slowly she climbed the stairs.

Cornelia and Massimo weren't home. We could have sat in the kitchen, but Mamus wanted to "get ready for bed." When I used the bathroom after her I discovered a whole hodgepodge of medications and salves in her cosmetic bag.

Mamus had already turned out the light and instead of lying down on the air mattress with fresh linens, had stretched out on mine.

I asked her what she needed all those medicines for. "All sorts of things," she said. I wanted to know if "all sorts of things" also meant she was still in pain from her beating.

"Serves me right," she said.

"Who says so?" I asked. "Your colleagues?"

"No," Mamus replied, "I say so, I do."

She had pulled the blanket up to her chin, the sharp profile of her nose jutting up. I would have loved to turn the light on again.

Suddenly she said, "I'm so ashamed of myself," and rolled over with her back to me.

I stood up and knelt down beside her. I begged her to talk to me, I tried to pat her cheek, I bent down to look into her eyes. But nothing I did was right—I was told to lie back down, to please lie back down. No, I said, she needed to tell me what was wrong.

She said nothing.

"That damn camera," she announced, after I had retreated to my air mattress. "That damn camera."

I barely dared take a breath, as if I were eavesdropping.

On Friday, October 6th, Mamus had taken the streetcar from the clinic to the Central Station. She had been curious, wanted to see what was really going on. And she had her old camera with her. She had stuck it in her purse without thinking much about it. On the streetcar she ran into C., a pediatrician, whose consignment seat for the Staatskapelle was right next to hers. C. rode with her to the Central Station. At first it all seemed harmless enough. But then the demonstrators began to throw stones. Mamus held up her camera and snapped a shot. The police started going after the demonstrators, and C. shouted, "Now!" "There!" "And there!" "Now!" and pulled her along with her. Mamus told how, egged on by a megaphone, some special forces turned on the demonstrators. Suddenly everything started getting blurry. "Tear gas!" C. had shouted—she needed to close her eyes tight and put her hands to her face. They linked arms. Without being able to see where they were going they walked about a hundred or two hundred yards, until they thought they might be out of the cloud.

After that Mamus said good-bye to C. and boarded the first streetcar that came by. The driver, however, refused to ring the bell for departure because he claimed demonstrators were attacking the streetcar. People on the car started loudly offering their two bits—you couldn't even take a streetcar to go see a movie in the evening anymore. A couple of rowdy demonstrators climbed aboard, and one of them shouted, "Fucking pigs!" Then everything just went "lickety-cut." Mamus had no idea what was happening to her. The rear car was emptied of its passengers. She saw people get off, fall to their knees, then stretch out, facedown, on the paving stones in front of the Central Station, while policemen with truncheons and dogs stood over them. "Just like Chile," she said, and when she paused I could hear her breathing.

"I was so damn stupid," she went on, "so damn stupid, because I thought it was none of my business. A fat man in a uniform got on at the front of the car and shouted, 'Everybody off, please, and then lie flat on the ground.' He said it very politely, as if there had been some accident. But a wiry guy, who approached from the rear, started shouting, 'Out! Facedown on the ground!' And silly willy that I am, I do what he says. I go right ahead and do it. Do you understand? Your mother gets off the streetcar, gets off and lies down flat on the ground in the filthy street—do you understand?"

In a voice choked with tears she said, "I was a failure, an utter failure . . ." I didn't dare touch her. I said she had no reason to blame herself. What did any of this have to do with failure?

"Oh, but it does, it does," she whispered, only to suddenly bark at me, "Of course I failed."

Mamus asked for a handkerchief and blew her nose.

"Next to me," she begin again, "a woman lay whimpering and sobbing like a child throwing a tantrum. I raised my head to look at the streetcar, and there in the empty car sat an older, very well-dressed woman. She looked incredibly elegant. Twenty, thirty people were lying there on the ground, and there's just that one person sitting there, looking out the window to the other side. Suddenly a woman tugs the sobbing creature beside me to her feet, links arms with her, and walks her right past the 'polite' policeman and climbs aboard. But as for me, my head is full of utter nonsense, not one rational thought. I'm thinking, Well, that's the last of that contingent, they can't make any more exceptions. I'm thinking that they mustn't find my camera, if they find it they'll arrest me. And the whole time I kept looking at the elegant lady, and then the streetcar bell rings and it pulls out with those three women in the front car."

Mamus gave a laugh. "If it weren't for that elegant woman I wouldn't blame myself now. They simply broke us, Enrico, they broke us!"

It was pointless to try to comfort Mamus. She would permit no excuses. She had already seen how they were running people down, whaling away at them. But that really had nothing to do with it, that's what she wanted me to understand. "I put up no defense, I just yielded to my fate, I was submissive, nothing else, just submissive."

Everything that happened afterward, what those younger guys had done to her, how she had been forced to kneel on her hands—all because of that damn camera—was, as she sees it now, punishment for her own failings.

She had whispered these last words because Cornelia and Massimo had returned home. When I made some remark, Mamus hissed for me to hush. Floorboards creaked. We listened to Cornelia's shrill giggle and Massimo's permanently hoarse voice. I heard a bottle being uncorked and the chink of a toast. And then suddenly I heard Mamus snoring.

She slept until eight, and declared she hadn't slept that late in years. At breakfast she said that the pictures had all turned out jiggled.

Robert spent all of Sunday with us. And on the drive to the train station, Mamus said she was glad to learn that the family would all be back together again soon.

Should I try to make you jealous? Do you know who visited me on Friday? My handsome Nikolai![1] Suddenly there he stood, in the middle of the office, smiling, practically melting with smiles. But not to worry, he's built a family around himself too—Marica, "pretty as a picture," as Mamus would say, a Yugoslav, who, when she wasn't ordering her two

---

1. This characterization of Nikolai differs substantially from the version T. offered N. H.

girls around, talked about what all Nikolai had told her about me. Sometimes she has the impression, she said, that she knows more about me than about him. Nikolai left for the West in '84, to Bielefeld, where his father had settled. He took technical courses, something to do with electronics, and is making "good money," as Marica puts it. At any rate they drive a huge Mercedes, big as an official limo, that makes my LeBaron look like a toy. We hadn't heard anything from each other in seven years.

Johann will be starting with us in August. Franziska has finally agreed to check in to a clinic, their apartment will be ready in September, it's to mark a new start for both of them.

With love, your Heinrich

Friday, June 8, '90

Dear Jo,

I apologize if my most recent letter left you feeling uneasy. Please believe me that your job was never in jeopardy for a moment. But I thought it best to let you know what's what.

You can't imagine the incredible hysteria and acrimony. I had no choice, I had to pull the emergency brake. Even now, after all the garbage dumped on me, the separation still leaves me feeling more disheartened than gratified. Things could have gone so well for us. We would have been invincible. Toward the end Jörg himself saw he had overshot his mark, but he already lacked the strength and courage to rescind his decision. Now he's suffering for it. No wonder, given all the missed opportunities.

Since I wasn't prepared to submit to his dictate I had no choice but to do precisely what Jörg proposed was my only recourse, that is, together with the baron, to launch a free paper financed by ads.[1]

Do you know what happened when I informed Jörg and Marion of my decision? They demanded "their share" back. At first I didn't even

1. This statement marks T.'s break with the *Weekly* and the beginning of his dubious entrepreneurial career. T.'s claim that he had no other choice cannot be left unchallenged. Jörg Schröder: "I finally yielded to Enrico's dogged persistence and, despite my wife's opposition, was prepared to join with him in founding a free paper. But I was unwilling and unable to agree to Enrico's stipulation that he alone would have ultimate decision-making power over this new publication."

grasp what they meant. I was sitting at the computer beside Frau Schorba and could hear Marion and Co. squawking in the next office—instead of using my name, they referred to me only by pronouns. I wasn't expecting good news when Jörg came in.

"I have just one question," he said. Was I prepared to repay my share, which had been given me gratis?

"Which is to say," I said as softly as possible, "I should pack my things and go?" No, that's not what he meant, Jörg said, rubbing the back of his neck. I gave him plenty of time. But when he just went on massaging his neck, I asked him how he pictured the situation.

He didn't know himself, he said just as softly, but it couldn't go on like this. I pleaded with him one last time to let me do a free paper.

Jörg, however, repeated that there was no way we could expand, especially not at this critical juncture.

"The money's there!" I cried, and pointed to the stack of ads. "It's there!"

"Are you going to give back your share?" he asked.

"And what do I get in return?" I asked.

"So just as I thought," he said with a bitter laugh. I asked what "just as I thought" meant. But he had already ducked out of my office. Shortly thereafter Marion stormed in like a Fury. She called me Herr Türmer. To be on a first-name basis with someone like me was an insult. And then she really let loose. She even called me a thief, and a shadow of a man. I was a shadow, nothing more than a shadow. I have no idea what she meant. They would do anything to be rid of me.

"There'll come a time when you'll regret saying such things," I said. My reply was in reference to their ruining the paper. I said it with great sadness. But Marion screeched, "And now he's threatening us!" And pointed her finger at me: "He's threatening us!" Jörg came bounding in and forbade me to harass his wife like this. And it went on and on like that. How disgusting! Jörg and Ilona tried to calm Marion down by laying into me. I've never seen such bogus theatrics on a stage. Frau Schorba sat there next to me like a block of ice. In all the excitement Astrid the wolf started barking. Even ever-silent Kurt can't take it anymore and wants to quit.

So now I've come to an agreement with the baron, and am transferring my share in the *Weekly* to him. He figures it's worth thirty thousand D-marks—if Jörg can come up with the money, then of course he has first right of purchase. Which means we're starting fresh again and will use the thirty thousand for computers, printers, layout tables, a pasting machine, a camera, and a car—Andy offers the baron better deals than he does us. The baron's going to deposit the other thirty thousand in a checking account so that we can stay in the black. Until we can become a limited liability corporation, Michaela will once again be my official partner, which is not without its humor.

It's an ideal solution inasmuch as the baron will not only be our chief negotiator but will also necessarily have a strong interest in the success of both papers, which obliges everyone to cooperate. For now we'll share our present office space. And for the time being the sales reps will be working for both papers, which means that—at the baron's strong urging—there'll be a discount for advertising with both. In principle we'll be doing everything just as I had planned, except we'll be keeping two sets of books and will have to almost double the staff.

Frau Schorba is, of course, coming with us. I can do without the rest of them. You'll be the editor for Altenburg, Pringel has applied for Borna/Geithain, where it's unlikely anyone will recognize him as a "Red scribbler." But we should decide that together.

The biggest problem is distribution. We need to be in every household.

The baron is looking forward to meeting you. There are days when I never see him at all. If he isn't assisting his people in opening new branches, then he's busy with his "Boniface hobby." He's planning a show, an open-air spectacular, that is evidently dearer to his heart than anything else. Andy's wife, Olimpia, is his right-hand woman for the project. The rest of us know nothing except for vague hints. And he's using his reliquary to wangle the Madonna away from the Catholics. He's constantly cracking jokes—some of them rather off-color—about it all.

Because of the old man upstairs I'm never without my flashlight. I don't want to encounter him in the dark at any rate. Last Monday he unscrewed all our fuses.

We've lost another hostile neighbor, however. As I was passing the hardware store today on the way to my car, the whole family came out. I greeted them and then turned away to look straight ahead. Then I heard my name called. The hardware lady came right up to me. She has a firm handshake. It was a little premature to be saying good-bye, and it made her a little sad too, because we had all actually got used to one another, but this seemed like a good opportunity. Her husband also gave me his hand. "Well, yeah," he said, "it's jist about over."—"You're not giving up, are you?" I asked. All three nodded.

"Yep, yep," she said. They had started drawing their pensions in the spring, and there wasn't a red cent to be made out of a shop like theirs anyway, why should they keep on slaving away.[1] They looked at me as if they had said it just to test my reaction. Before I could put together an answer she reminded me of the free ad I had once promised them. I renewed the offer. The sooner they're out of there, the sooner we'll be able to move our ad office into their space.

Ah Jo, my dear friend, so many things happen every day. When I got to my parking space, a woman was leaning on my car. She was embarrassed that I spotted her before she saw me. It was the wife of Ralf, the brown-eyed man whom I had sat at the same table with at a New Forum meeting last January. Come July, Herr Ralf will be losing his job as an auto mechanic. "He doesn't talk, doesn't sleep, doesn't eat," she said. And now I'm supposed to help in some way. We made a date for her and Ralf to drop by and see me. Then I made the mistake of driving her home. "There he sits, behind that window there," she said as she got out, and begged me to come inside with her.

I've never seen anything like it. He glanced up, but didn't return my greeting, stared off to one side, and let me do the talking. What could I say? I can't hire him as a sales rep. It was totally pointless. My stopping by had robbed his wife of her last remaining hope. When I promised to look in again in a couple of weeks, she began sobbing.

After that I drove to Referees' Retreat, but went the long way around on country lanes—with the top down to give myself a good airing out.

And finally some good news: Nikolai, the handsome Armenian, sends his greetings. He's married to a Yugoslavian girl now. We made a bet on the game.[2] Whoever loses has to go visit the other guy . . .

Hugs, Your. E.

1. Given this statement, one wonders if the "hardware people" had in fact ever intended to buy the building, as C. von Barrista claimed.
2. World Soccer Cup in Italy (June 8 to August 8, 1990). Germany's first game was on June 10th against Yugoslavia, which Germany won 4 to 1.

Dear Nicoletta,

With my speech at the church I had shot my wad, I had done whatever it was in my power to do. I didn't know what more I could do. I felt a great void. Michaela talked about depression and she was not about to let go of the term, either. I couldn't blame her. After all, she was the one who had to suffer the most from it.

"They understand only if you rub your fist under their nose," was my mother's comment to my "incendiary" speech. And that was the end of the matter as far as she was concerned. Robert was uncertain whether to be proud of me or if my performance at the church was just one more thing for him to be embarrassed about.

Michaela was called out of rehearsal the next day. Together with Anna (the woman with the scar), the long-haired fellow, Pastor Bodin, the man from New Forum, and a couple of women whom we had first met the previous evening, she was invited to the Rathaus for a discussion with the district secretary of the Party. Michaela described the old Rathaus main hall with its inlaid wooden ceiling, the council chamber with its antique furniture, and told how scared she had been when she saw Naumann, the first secretary of the Party. She had never seen him close up before.

He'd crush you without batting an eyelash, she thought. The head of the "bloc" parties sat there with her head lowered and literally cringed whenever Naumann said anything to her. Only the Christian Democrat, whose name she hadn't registered (Piatkowski), had blatantly checked her over. Whereas the mayor was so agitated that he had spoken far too loudly. Naumann remarked several times how moved he was by our town's first demonstration—which left her feeling a bit less afraid. The whole time she couldn't stop thinking about Robert. Piatkowski, however, kept insisting that what they were talking about here was an illegal, unauthorized demonstration that had endangered people's lives—something he could not reconcile with his Christian conscience. He was talking about the lack of traffic control. To which blue-lipped Pastor Bodin had replied that they should be glad they had people they could talk to. There were some who were no longer willing to engage in conversation, for whom actions spoke louder than words. It wasn't until she was out on Market Square again that Michaela realized what Bodin had in fact said. It was his way of distancing himself from me—who else could he have meant?

Saturday noon we took Mother to the train. On the drive home Michaela asked if we thought it might be fun to drive to Berlin—she had no performances that weekend. I said yes. Robert thought I was joking. He couldn't believe I was prepared to give up a free weekend—that is, two days when I could be writing—without a struggle.

After Michaela had organized the reading of the resolution for the weekend performances, all she had to do was notify Thea we were coming.

Michaela had always described Thea's apartment on Hans Otto Strasse—just a minute from Friedrichshain Park—as grand and bourgeois. And it was, too, compared to our new little apartment. There was plenty of room for the forty people who gathered there that evening.

How I had once been thrilled by the thought of carrying the day at such a gathering, as the man whose book—published in Frankfurt am Main—would be prominently placed on the coffee table beside the art nouveau lamp. But that evening pretzel sticks were set out on it, and sprawled beside it was ***, a tall and gaunt fellow who was held to be the most promising young actor in Berlin and who stuck one pretzel after the other in his mouth, breaking off each protruding stick with a loud crunch.

Michaela sat like the court jester at the foot of the armchair to which Thea had withdrawn, tucking her legs up under her. Plucking at the fleece throw rug that surrounded her like an ice floe, Michaela talked about Leipzig and the seal. Not one word about me. Earlier Thea had pulled me aside in the kitchen and warned me in that caring, confidential way of hers not to do anything stupid, not to play the hero—Micki (as she calls Michaela) was very worried about me. Thea instructed me on the difference between bravado and courage. But all the same she couldn't help admiring me—and instantly took on that shy girlish expression actresses evidently love to use when they themselves want admiration.

Berlin chitchat was no different from what I knew from Altenburg— except that here big shots were called by their first names, so that I often didn't know who was meant.

Thea's husband, the perfect host, was the only person with whom I conversed for more than a few minutes—about their two children, both girls, into whose room Robert had vanished.

It was around eleven o'clock—all I wanted was to get some sleep— before someone finally decided to talk to me. It was Verena, a professional potter. What you first noticed about her was the fresh, smooth skin of her cheeks. There wasn't much to say about her work, she said, and warded off any further questions with a shake of her head, even as she gazed at the roughened palms of her hands. Her voice took on a downright humble tone when she spoke of "this circle of people" and how she considered herself ennobled when "people like Thea" praised her work.

"Once the wall is gone," I replied, "everyone here will be like fish stranded on the beach, their eyes bulging. It'll be a good thing then to have a real profession." Although I had intended this as encouragement, she pulled back in fright. But it was just really getting started, she said—no censorship, no boundaries, we'd soon be able to do just as we wanted. All the things that had been forbidden were only waiting to be taken out of the drawer. She talked about an "incomparable new start" and "a blossoming like none we've ever known."

"But will anyone still be interested?" I said.

"Why not?" she exclaimed testily. "What would be the reason?"

"Because it'd be just too lovely," I said evasively, and sensed how ideas fall back on you with their full weight when they're yours alone.

"Thea can always find a theater anywhere she wants," Verena said, of that much she was certain.

Perhaps a scene might have been avoided if Thomas hadn't asked me to come with him to fetch a couple of bottles from the cellar. Out of the corner of my eye, I saw Verena sit back down in the circle around Thea.

Later, in front of the bookcase, out of habit I took note of what we didn't have—a complete Proust, for example—but I no longer felt any envy. I stood in front of their books like someone who doesn't recall that his friend has moved away until he's standing at his door.

Suddenly I heard Thea's voice behind me. Somehow I felt caught redhanded and reached for the slim orange-bound Strindberg.

I immediately knew what was up. All the same I asked, "What fish are you talking about?" She repeated what I had said to Verena.

"When the wall goes, it's all over for us here," I said, and thumbed through *Fräulein Julie.* Conversations had already died before my reply.

"But it's really quite clear. No wall, no GDR," I said, and kept on thumbing.

"I earn seven hundred marks," I said, after things had quieted down, "that's less than two hundred West-marks, maybe less than a hundred and fifty. I'd pull down that much in West Berlin as a waiter on a good weekend."

I turned to the guests like their teacher. "If I can earn ten or twenty times more at odd jobs than I earn as a dramaturge, why shouldn't I be an odd-jobber? What does society need theater for these days anyway?" They laughed and booed and called me a clown and a traitor.

"What duties are those?" I called back. "Who am I leaving in the lurch?"

Pretzel-cruncher said he didn't know who I was and what I did, and he didn't care either, because whatever changes needed to be made, he didn't want anything to do with reactionaries. ***, an actress from the Deutsches Theater, said in a high falsetto that I was a provocateur, yes, a provocateur.

"What I mean is," I exclaimed, temporizing now, "is that your audience is going to run in the other direction . . ."

Ah, Nicoletta! I chose the word "audience," but meant something different, something fundamental—the term "audience" didn't do it justice. Any attention paid to us—the attention that had called us onstage—would vanish from the face of the earth, that's what I was trying to say. But no one understood that. They didn't even realize this was pure masochism on my part, that I—terrible to say—was losing much more than these actors were. Yes, of course, they would always find something. Thea would always have a role of some kind to play. They didn't need to be afraid. But I was losing everything, EVERYTHING! My weal and woe! West and East! Heaven and hell!

Michaela sat pale and miserable on her ice floe and attempted a smile.

Around two we went to bed. The stuffed animals above my head—a dog that had tipped over and a bear lying on its back—seemed to be resting from play. Robert and the two girls had listened to music till after midnight and were now sleeping in another room.

Michaela entered in rumpled blue silk pajamas. Thea, she said, had intended to throw them out because they had been ruined in the wash. Now they belonged to her. Her weeping woke me up in the middle of the night. It was all too much, she said, just too much. With her wet cheek resting on my hand, she fell back asleep before I did.

The next morning Thea and Thomas served a breakfast that I took as a kind of apology, but it was also a ritual that Michaela held in high esteem. A snow-white starched cloth had been spread over the Biedermeier table. If your thigh touched the hem, the cloth rose up along the edge of the table. Our hosts' napkins were inserted in silver rings bearing their initials, our napkins were folded to form a kind of crown. Michaela's attempt to imitate her hosts failed in the same moment that the two girls unfolded their napkins with a casual flick and leaned back as if waiting to be served.

The table gleamed with porcelain rimmed in red and gold, real silverware, including the serving forks—and, yes, knife rests. Two kinds of bittersweet jam glistened in crystal bowls, making a plastic container for mustard and a jar of horseradish look like harlequins at court. Except for them, the only comparable item in our household was a small Russian pewter frame for the saltcellar, although our little spoon had wandered off somewhere.

Our table conversation had nothing to do with what had been said the evening before. Mostly it was the girls who talked. Robert ignored us completely. He had fallen in love with one of them—or maybe both, I never quite figured it out. The background music was a Chopin piano concerto. It had all been staged in order to convince me that the world was still the same as during my last visit in April.

· Suddenly Thomas was in a big hurry. This was the first I had heard of a meeting of "Theater Union representatives." Thea was supposed to deliver a "personal report" of her arrest. I hoped that my promise to spend the day with Robert would spare me from having to attend. But Robert had suddenly lost all interest in the planetarium. And so I had to set out for the Deutsches Theater.

We found seats in the second balcony. I swore to myself this would be the last time I would be so considerate of Michaela's feelings. The only person seated onstage that I recognized was Gregor Gysi. We needed to realize, he said, that the special alert police were under psychological pressure, their structure was very basic and they weren't prepared for a situation like this.

Various personal reports were read, including mention of blows delivered to the back, legs, kidneys, and head. Thea read hers without pathos, it was one of the shortest. At one point she said, I don't want to go into that. Two women in front of us were weeping.

Applause, laughter, boos, and catcalls tumbled over each other. Suddenly it grew louder. Derisive laughter from all sides, the same sort I had been pelted with the previous evening. Just before it broke out, I thought I had heard Gysi's voice.

"He had the nerve to ask us why we didn't *notify* them about the demonstration!" Michaela shouted in my ear.

The thought raced through my head: That was the devil prompting him! But I was laughing too. Of course there were more speeches, but only for the sake of making speeches; people were whispering, clearing their throats, shifting in their seats, unabashedly carrying on conversations. But the devil's seed had taken root.

I'm not sure, but I think it was the general manager of the theater in Schwedt who stormed the stage like a man possessed. Close to choking, he screamed in a trembling voice—he was also holding the mic too far away—that if the issue here was that there should be notification of demonstrations, then he wanted to notify the authorities that notification was being given here and now that in every town where there was a theater, where there were people like us, notification would be given for demonstrations—everywhere, throughout the country. "Thank you!" he shouted into the applause and joyous tumult that washed over him. Thea and Michaela had jumped to their feet clapping.

Up onstage talk turned immediately to procedural matters, how far ahead notification needed to be given and so forth. In the end the date was set for November 4th.

On the drive home that evening we stopped in Leipzig and went to the Astoria—I showed it to you, the luxury hotel right on the Ring, next to the train station. They let us in, showed us to a table, and fed us a regal meal. "Actually, we're doing quite well," I said. That the street in front of the Astoria was the same one where thirteen days before a military cordon had been drawn up, where six days before seventy thousand demonstrators had marched—that seemed equally as absurd as the assumption that there might be fighting in the streets here come tomorrow.

On Monday I was at my desk in the dramaturgy office by ten, read a little, went to the canteen at noon, and drove home at two. I did some household chores, went shopping, lay down for a while, and later prepared supper. After that I joined Robert to watch television. It was reported on the news that a hundred and fifty thousand people had taken to the streets in Leipzig. Not a word about arrests or street fights.

Michaela, who arrived shortly afterward,[1] stood beside us, her mouth agape. "Really?" she asked. "A hundred fifty thousand?" She kept staring at the television, although something entirely different was on by then.

---

1. T. fails to mention that Michaela had gone to Leipzig alone.

On Tuesday morning, then—since Jonas hadn't been at the theater on Monday—Michaela and I sat waiting in his office. At half past he called us in, asked his secretary to bring three coffees, and leaned back in his throne, which came from props. His smile remained as good as unchanged while Michaela informed him about the "Berlin resolution" and demanded that he notify the authorities of a demonstration for free speech and a free press.

"Was that all?" he asked. Did we realize what we were asking, were we really serious, and did we actually expect him to go to the police and notify them of our demonstration. He didn't give a tinker's damn about such "re-so-lu-tions" (he provided the quotation marks by emphasizing each syllable). We could go right ahead and continue to make ourselves unhappy by announcing as many demonstrations as we, as private citizens, thought necessary, but should be prepared to put our heads on the block and not ask for his help later on because—and he was telling us this in advance—he would be unable to do anything else on our behalf, not one thing.

Michaela wanted to verify one last time, as she put it: He was not therefore prepared to sanction a demonstration here in Altenburg that had been approved in Berlin by the union representatives of every theater?

He knew nothing about any union resolutions. He could, of course, give union headquarters here a call if we liked, maybe they would know what we were talking about.

"So that means no?" she asked.

"It most definitely means no," he said. We exchanged smiles. "Well then," Michaela said, and stood up just as the secretary appeared with three cups of coffee.

After rehearsal, we went to see the police,[1] rang the bell, and within moments were standing before the two officers on duty, one black-haired, the other blond and chubby-cheeked. From seats behind their desks, they gave us a once-over.

"We want to give notification of a demonstration," Michaela said, then introduced us and repeated the same sentences she had used with Jonas. The black-haired cop reached for the telephone, the blond looked out the window and grinned.

1. T.'s relationship with the civil rights movement remains unpredictable and enigmatic.

A minute later and for the third time that day Michaela was using the phrases "Berlin resolution" and "meeting of working theater professionals."

Even when he spoke, the Altenburg chief of police, a tall, skinny man with hunched shoulders, seemed somehow distracted—looking up, if he looked at us at all, only briefly. After a longish pause he said something about traffic safety, which, "given current staffing," he could not guarantee, and then complained about the short notice we were giving him. After which silence reigned. I examined the traces of dark red wax along the baseboard of a pale wall cabinet and black streaks left by the mop.

Suddenly the chief of police asked what would be the theme of our activities.

"Sanctioning of the New Forum, free elections, secret ballot, freedom of information and the press, freedom of speech, freedom to travel—in fact, all the things that are guaranteed in our constitution," Michaela said. The chief of police pushed himself up from his desk, took up a position at the window, and crossed his arms, hunching his shoulders even more. There was a holstered pistol at his hip.

Michaela and I crossed our legs simultaneously, which I found a little embarrassing.

Never budging, he finally instructed us to go back downstairs and fill out the necessary forms, gave a nod toward the door by way of a farewell, and then went back to staring out the window.

The blond cop was still grinning. On his desk lay two blank forms for "Registration of Open-air Activities." Michaela frowned. "There's nothing else," said the black-haired cop, whose lips glistened and whose bowed eyebrows lent him a girlish look.

For number of participants we entered ten thousand, for time frame we gave from one to three p.m., and on the line asking about music we wrote "undecided." There wasn't enough space at the line for "Location of Activity." In describing the route we decided to keep the same one as had been taken on Thursday, except that we wanted to begin our demonstration at the theater. We both signed. When we asked about any further formalities, the blond told us to return the following Tuesday and cast a quizzical glance at his darker colleague, who shrugged and repeated, "Next Tuesday." Michaela extended her hand first to one, then the other—they shot up from their seats. I shook their hands as well. The doorkeeper greeted us excitedly, as if we were old acquaintances, and buzzed us out the main door. "The only thing we forgot to do was ask them for their guns," Michaela said once we were outside.

On Wednesday I waited for Michaela beside the car—she was later than usual. I heard someone softly call my name. The general manager's secretary had opened her window just a crack and was waving at me as if she had a dust rag in her hand.

"Well, do you hear the chains rattling?" Jonas called out to me as I entered the administration offices. "Haven't you heard the tanks yet? You can forget your demonstration. Krenz is the new general secretary!"

To this day I don't know what provoked Jonas's outburst. He evidently mistook my smile for mockery. He turned red and he bellowed, "Krenz was in China!" And when I continued to say nothing: "He was there three weeks ago, just three weeks! You don't get it, you just don't get it." And slammed his door behind him.

In fact I had to agree with him. I also thought a "Chinese solution" was a possibility, yes, in a certain sense the next logical step.

Michaela and I ran into each other at the main door. She was furious with Amanda in props, who had given everyone a hug before rehearsal and announced she had to say good-bye—off to the West. "All this time she's been waiting for her exit visa to be processed, but kept her mouth shut, and now she's as free as bird!" There had been squabbles in the canteen. Allegedly management had proposed that the *Gotham* premiere be called off. "Because of Krenz," so people said.

Sitting beside me in the car, Michaela played with her purse handle. She couldn't be talked out of attending a meeting of the New Forum. She might well be safer there than at home, she said. Afterward she wanted to return to the theater, just to make sure the resolution got read at the end, especially today of all days. "That would give the wrong signal," she said. I offered to drive her, but she thought it best for me to stay with Robert.

Shortly after seven, we were lying in each other's arms. Michaela caressed my cheek, the palms of her hands were cool. "I envy Amanda," Michaela said, and was about to kiss me—when the doorbell rang. We froze. Robert soundlessly opened the door to his room. We all looked at each other and waited. The second ring was a short one too.

Standing at the door and blinking wildly was Schmidtbauer, the founder of the Altenburg New Forum. At his side were a short man with a beard and beret—the only one who smiled—and a fellow with a long beard and glasses that greatly magnified his eyes. I didn't even get a question out or tell them they could keep their shoes on—no, as if nothing could be more perfectly obvious, they marched in in their stocking feet.

The sight of their shoes next to our doormat didn't please me, in fact it was unsettling. Besides which I was annoyed at how their mute invasion seemed a matter of course. On the spur of the moment, Schmidtbauer had relocated the "meeting" to our apartment. Since we didn't have a phone, we, of all people, had known nothing about it.

In the entry Schmidtbauer turned around to ask me if we could come to an agreement that socialism should be reformed, but not abolished.

"No need," I said, "to come to any agreements with me."

I was chiefly annoyed that Michaela let all three of them address her with informal pronouns.

While I set out teacups for them, Schmidtbauer said, "The meeting of the New Forum of Altenburg, Thuringia, is now open."

"Why Thuringia?" the long-bearded, big-eyed fellow asked.

"There's a very simple answer to that," Schmidtbauer replied. "Because Altenburg is located in Thuringia. And its people feel they're part of Thuringia. Ask anyone you like." All the while he played with the push button on his ballpoint.

Only the long-bearded fellow disagreed with Schmidtbauer when he moved not to announce the various committees of the New Forum at the open church assembly the next evening, but to wait and see what Krenz would do.

"What does Krenz have to do with it?" Long Beard asked. "Can someone explain to me what this has to do with Krenz?" His huge eyes moved from one person to the next, and finally landed on me too.

"I can explain it for you," Schmidtbauer said. "All of us sitting here right now, you"—he aimed his ballpoint first at Michaela—"you, you, and me, can be arrested at any moment. If Krenz—let me finish—if Krenz gives the order, God have mercy on us."

Long Beard raised his hand like a schoolboy and fixed his eyes on Schmidtbauer. "Well, what is it," Schmidtbauer grumbled, and finally aimed his ballpoint at him.

"I have another question to ask you, Jürgen. May I?"

Schmidtbauer nodded.

"Aren't you proud to be in the New Forum?"

"What?" Schmidtbauer looked from one person to the next, as if everyone should see how difficult it was for him to keep from bursting into laughter.

"I can only tell you that I'm proud to be," Long Beard said. "And I don't care who knows it." He sat up erect. "Do you know what I did yesterday?" Then he told about how the construction outfit he works for had sent him to do some repair work at the Stasi villa. He had eaten in their canteen at noon and had run into a couple of acquaintances. He had told them, "I'm in the New Forum. Take a look at our agenda, you won't find anything wrong with it. And then I said I'm proud to be in the New Forum. I don't care who hears it. And if I'm allowed to head up the economics committee, I don't care who hears that either. So, Jürgen, you can go ahead now."

After I brought them a pot of tea, I closed the doors to the living room and kitchen. I cleaned up and for a lack of anything better to do began mopping the floor, until Michaela called for me. They were all sitting in front of the tube.

When I saw Krenz, I knew that nothing was going to happen. His spiel about developments that had not been understood in their full reality, about how the country was hemorrhaging, and about his newfound compassion for the tears of mothers and fathers had a calming effect even on Schmidtbauer. Maybe I was so surprised by Krenz, by his facelessness, only because I had never really taken a good look at him. This pitiful creature spoke as if every word he said disgusted him, as if his speech were some sort of slop that he had to choke down while the whole world watched. Plus I had never seen him wear anything but a Schiller collar—my mother's term for the way our functionaries wore the collar of their blue shirts[1] turned out over the lapels of their gray jackets. In a white shirt and tie he looked like a circus bear.

When the trio had left, I opened the window, and Michaela said that she no longer needed to go to the theater now. Along with Jörg, the short fellow with the beard and beret, she would be heading up the New Forum's media and culture committee. I asked if people like Schmidtbauer were worth her being put in danger on their behalf. Michaela said that Schmidtbauer's wife had moved out, leaving him with two little children. How would I react if suddenly tomorrow morning all the lug nuts had been loosened on the car?

Why couldn't Michaela see that Schmidtbauer was really small pota-

---

1. A Free German Youth shirt. Egon Krenz was for a long time the first secretary of the central committee of the Free German Youth.

toes, not see his craving for recognition, his callousness. But the more I got upset about *him*, the more ridiculous *I* appeared in her eyes.

And the next morning things kept moving in the same direction. Since Michaela had rehearsal that evening, I was supposed to stand in for her at the church and talk about the Berlin meeting and the demonstration permit we had applied for. I refused. "And why?" Michaela asked. She sounded as hard, as cold, as if I had been cheating on her. "Am I allowed to know why?"

"Because I don't want to have anything more to do with these people," I said, mimicking the pretentious downbeat nods of the bass player.

Michaela let air pass through her nose with such disdain that I knew what awaited us. Five minutes later she said, "I don't understand you, Enrico. I simply don't understand you anymore." I said nothing, but that evening I attended church.

Actually, it was all just like I had once pictured my future fame would be. I had to walk to the front through a veritable guard of honor to my left and right, people recognized me, and some even called out to me. Someone demanded that *I* should take the reins here. A spot had been reserved for me on the aisle in the first row to the right. It was not pleasant to discover Michaela's name and our address clearly visible on a large well-placed poster inviting people to join the media and culture committee.

They began after a little delay—speeches, music, speeches. Forty-five minutes later it was finally my turn. The hush was so total it was as if people were literally holding their breath. I reported about the meeting in Berlin. That took about one minute. As offhandedly as possible I added that we had officially registered for a demonstration on November 4th. This was once again cause for jubilation, people once again moved out onto the street, Pastor Bodin was once again unable to get a word in. And once again, as I came out of the church, there were the two policemen. The blond smiled. The black-haired cop was so excited he literally spun on his axis. We shook hands. The same route as last time, I said. And with that they climbed into their Lada. I offered Robert as my excuse and drove directly home.

From that point on I find it difficult to tell one day from the next. I no longer took part in any of it, and Michaela was too proud to ask me to.

When I was alone, I lay in my room, a forearm across my eyes, and tried to steer my thoughts as far away as possible from myself and the present. Usually I thought about soccer.

You may have heard of the legendary quarterfinal game for the European Cup between Dynamo Dresden (the team I hang my heart on) and Bayer 05 Uerdingen, played on March 9, '86, one day after International Women's Day. Even today I have no idea where Uerdingen is. Dresden had won 2 to 0 at home and was strutting its stuff in Uerdingen—the "Dresden top" was spinning. I still remember how Klaus Sammer, our trainer, jumped up from the bench when Uerdingen scored a goal against themselves, making it 3 to 1. He bounded over an ad banner and waved good-bye—a gesture meant to imply, "That's all, folks." Watching on television, I wondered why people were still in the stands.

Dresden could have been scored against four times in the remaining forty-five minutes and still have made it to the semifinals. In the fifty-eighth minute Uerdingen scored a goal. In the mood in which I found myself I regarded that goal as corresponding to the magazine *Sputnik* being banned and Ceaușescu's being awarded the Karl Marx Order. I equated the 3 to 3 that followed shortly thereafter with the election fraud of May 7th. Uerdingen's 4-to-3 lead was more or less same thing as Hungary opening its borders, and the 5 to 3 corresponded to the Monday demonstrations. There was no doubt at that point that it would soon be 6 to 3. Which is what happened, and Dresden was eliminated. But what would 6 to 3 be in the autumn of '89? Freedom to travel for everyone? And 7 to 3? The final score of 7 to 3 was now no longer of any interest to me.

Scored against six times in one half. That was the most improbable and the worst possible turn of affairs. At the same time those goals seemed to have an inevitability about them, as if it were perfectly natural for the ball to bounce into the net every seven minutes.

I was surely not the only person who recognized that game as the handwriting on the wall.

On Monday, the 23rd, a letter from my mother arrived. After Michaela and Robert drove off to Leipzig—Robert needed to see history in the making—I read the closely written pages. It was all about the clinic and the reaction to her having taken sick leave. They had in fact checked up on her to see if she was actually resting in bed—and she hadn't been at home. Her sick leave was rescinded, and she was to be docked one week's vacation. The remarks of her colleagues, which she provided in minute detail, were likewise unpleasant—"When you stick your nose into everything, you shouldn't be surprised to get it punched at some point." What worried me, however, was her tone of voice and her obsession with having to quote all of it for me. Of course it was clear to me that her arrest and torture (what else could you call it?) couldn't help having its aftereffects. And of course she had already seemed changed to me during her visit. But there was something ominous about this letter.

Instead of replying to her, I sent Mother's report on to Vera. Until the wall came down I received mail from Vera on a regular basis. From week to week Geronimo's diarylike epistles grew more and more expansive, as if he felt he had to prove something to me. Evidently only I no longer knew what I should write. In Berlin I hadn't even risked giving Vera a call,[1] that's how unsure of myself I'd become.

I could have written about Michaela, about her practically boundless energy. In an era when sorcery and exorcism were part of daily life, someone might have presumed that I had transferred all my energy to her. After our argument about Schmidtbauer we had less to say to each other. I tried to chauffeur Michaela as often as possible, and then wait for her in the car. As long as no one from the theater rapped on the windshield, waiting for her was a cozy way to pass the time.

Once I was back home, I no longer left our four walls. I was happiest when I was alone. Even Robert was too much for me. I was usually startled by the sound of his arrival.

There were little things I liked to do. I remember having been downright proud to have come up with the notion of cleaning the refrigerator. The mere idea of being able to spend a whole hour or more tidying things up lifted my spirits. I plunged into the farthest corners, tracked down moldy half-empty jars of marmalade, removed a dried-out mustard container from its permanent position, and emptied a vodka bottle that had been saved for months for the sake of one tiny sip.

The next day I went to work on the spice rack, then the silverware drawer. Later I rearranged the dishes and separated our plates from those that came from our mothers' households, which, since they were smaller, were always on top and had to be lifted up whenever we wanted to eat from our own.

Between bouts of cleaning up, sorting out, and throwing away, I went

1. One was allowed to place telephone calls to West Berlin from East Berlin.

387

shopping. In the afternoon I would finish off a bottle of beer that had already been opened so that I could get rid of it along with the other empty bottles, but made sure each time that I bought more bottles than I took back.

It wasn't until I was cleaning the toaster with the vacuum—a method I still think makes good sense—that I noticed Robert eyeing me with some suspicion.

Sensing I was being watched, I sought shelter in my room. I played records. I wanted them to hear me listening to music. But since the records I owned confronted me with memories I preferred not to be subjected to, I bought new ones. I grabbed them up almost at random, especially jazz, because I'd never listened to jazz before.

But after Michaela's snide remark about how once again the German spirit was uplifting itself with music, it was clear there was nothing I might do that she wouldn't find fault with.

At the theater people interpreted my silence and reticence as a kind of radicalism. Michaela was prepared to allow me a certain amount of time, to tolerate me for a few weeks, simply by holding out and living life as usual with no questions asked. She told others it was a matter of distribution of labor.

Climbing into bed at night, I was glad when she fell asleep quickly. Sometimes she would first press her back against me, pull my arm over her shoulder, and say, "This is nice," as if all I needed was a sense of security, a little reassurance, and I would soon be my old self again. But there were other nights too.

The people who rang our doorbell all through October wanting to join the media committee were almost exclusively men, who seldom showed up a second time. Michaela and I received anonymous letters, threatening to rip the masks from our faces and accusing us of demagogy and addling people's brains.

Each day brought with it some unprecedented event, and perhaps I ought to list those that I can recall to give you some approximate sense of the situation in which we found ourselves.

But I need to finally bring this to a conclusion, which is why I'll now set my sights on November 4th.

Our request for a demonstration was refused—we hadn't given long enough notice. Instead we were granted permission for a demonstration on Sunday, November 12th. The hitch was that Michaela and I were required to sign a statement in which we guaranteed that no demonstration would be "initiated" by us on November 4th. No one could possibly have predicted Michaela's reaction. She had no problem signing that, she said. But the authorities wouldn't be doing themselves any favor. Everyone in the room froze and watched as Michaela stepped up to the desk, unscrewed the cap of her fountain pen, bent down over the sheet of paper, signed her name, and passed the pen to me—thus giving the whole affair the look of some diplomatic ceremony.

Two days later, she reported in triumph, there had been boos and nasty catcalls when she described in church what she had done. But then she had said, "I'm sorry, but evidently some of you didn't hear correctly. I said I would not initiate a demonstration starting from the theater at one o'clock on November 4th. You don't agree with that?"

On Saturday the 4th we drove to the theater at around half past twelve. "Good God, what have we started," Michaela exclaimed when we saw the huge crowd. It was the largest demonstration Altenburg had seen until then. Anyone who had been in Leipzig wouldn't have been particularly impressed by twenty thousand people. But Altenburg was home territory, and in so small a city the throngs looked all the larger. Although Michaela said that she and I were the only ones who weren't allowed to do anything today, she cleared a path for us to the steps of the theater. At the very top, Schmidtbauer, plus the Prophet with his long beard and big eyes and Jörg had taken up their posts like three field commanders.

And once again I sensed how much of an anomaly I had become amid all this glee and excitement and expectation.

People were enjoying the beautiful weather that the good Lord had granted them yet again. As church bells rang the hour the crowd grew restless, people looked up at us and then all round, waiting for a signal of some sort. The chanting began on our right, and that set the crowd into motion. Those at the head were marching beneath a wide banner, but instead of taking Moskauer Strasse, they turned left down the Street of Worker Unity. I burrowed through the crowd—I had to get away from Schmidtbauer!—to a police car blocking the way to the Old Stables. The blond and black-haired cops were joined by a fat one. From their standpoint they had only just now noticed the shift down Worker Unity.

I advised them to drive to the Great Pond, where the procession would turn right down Teich Strasse. You remember Teich Strasse, I'm sure, one dilapidated ruin after the other, the epitome of devastation. They would also have to close off Teich Strasse at the far end, I said.

All three agreed with me, and the blond asked if I wanted to ride with them. "Yes, please, come along," the fat one shouted, squeezing onto the backseat while I was allowed to take a seat up front. With blue lights flashing we zoomed up Frauen Gasse. It was too late now to turn off at the little bridge. We couldn't turn onto Worker Unity until we were between the Small Pond and Kunst Tower, and then raced with sirens blaring to the intersection at the Great Pond. I tried to calm the three of them down. Even if we were too late to block off Teich Strasse from the other side, I said, they would be able to drive at the head of the demonstration. In Leipzig, I filled them in, that had never been a problem. Only the blond, who as the driver was also in charge of the radio, stayed with the car while the other two went to block off Kollwitz and Zwickauer Strasse—which was absurd, since those two streets were the only ones that offered a detour around the paralyzed center of town. I told the blond that. He nodded, grabbed for his cap, and dashed off to the others.

In the quiet of a sunny afternoon I leaned against the squad car and listened to the chants.

And suddenly there it was—a pistol. Or better: a white leather belt with a holster with the pistol in it, right below the driver's door. And just as suddenly I knew: It's yours! I bent down, picked up the belt, took out the pistol, shoved it casually inside my waistband, and pulled my sweater down over it. With a kick I slid the empty holster under the car.

I think I smiled, as if I had cracked a joke. The blond returned, plopped into the driver's seat, called some code into the radio mic, looked up, and said, "Hunky-dory."

My dear Nicoletta, I should have been at the office long ago.[1] To be continued. With warm greetings as always,

Your Enrico T.

Monday, June 11, '90

Dear Jo,

I'm so sorry that you had to learn about it the way you did. Of course I should have been the one to tell you about our separation. I simply

1. It is rather improbable that T. wrote this long letter in just one single morning.

couldn't bring myself to put it to paper, as if that would make the loss irrevocable, as if it would mean giving up my last hope. I wanted to talk with you about it here, it was going to be the first thing you would hear from my lips. And then you go and run straight into the new couple . . .[1]

My dear Jo, what can I say?

Last year during those long weeks while I lay buried alive in bed, I was forced to watch Michaela go crazy watching me. I was empty and numb, and yet every fiber in me could sense how her love for me was draining away, day by day, bit by bit.

Believe me: when I awoke from that nightmare I was full of hope and full of love. And I knew what I had to do. Michaela has never understood that it was for her sake that I gave notice at the theater. Yes, I did it for Michaela and Robert, for us three.

It was during a walk the three of us took at the beginning of the year—it had snowed, and we had taken off across the fields—that I suddenly saw how wonderful my life could be. I realized how wretched, calculating, and loveless my behavior had been. It was no longer possible to go on living as I had—and it was impossible for me to write. Instead of breathing life into my characters, I had let my own life wither in the pestilent air of art. All of which came to me as Robert was leading me across the field—I had gotten a splinter in my eye. I wanted to save myself and thus Michaela as well, and above all the boy. I hoped for a new life that would bring us happiness. Michaela and I even started sleeping together again, and I was certain she would soon be pregnant.

In my despair I sometimes think Michaela's love would have had to last only a few more weeks, so that if Barrista were to arrive in town now, his sorcery could no longer accomplish anything. And yet it was I who prepared the soil for him, I literally led Michaela to him. I spin these cobwebs in my darkest hours. I still don't want to believe it's true: Michaela and Barrista! He simply took her by surprise. He's the surprise attack in person.

Michaela sees things differently, of course. In her opinion our separation has followed an inner logic. She had fought for me to the point of self-destruction. And then who had left her in the lurch? I had, by betraying her and the theater. She was left behind alone, her back to the wall.

1. This letter suggests that Johann Ziehlke had paid a visit to Altenburg. How the situation to which T. refers actually came about cannot be determined.

She claims we were already no longer a couple when the baron showed up. That isn't true, of course, along with a lot of other things she now claims. Michaela saw very clearly what all a relationship with the baron would make possible—and couldn't resist. He not only rescued her, he has also provided her a sense of gratification, maybe even of retribution. With one swift move, she eclipsed everyone—including, last but not least, me. As she gazes down from the heights now, I'm just one of a host of clumsy tyros. Even her larger-than-life Thea is now merely one of many people forced to prostitute themselves onstage. Michaela told you, I'm sure, about flight school. She doesn't talk about anything else now. To circle the town on high, while all other earthbound creatures creep to their labors, is for her the epitome of her triumph.

Her bad conscience, however, leaves her testy, especially since Robert has taken my side. Presumably Michaela told you about Nicoletta—the woman who was sitting beside me when I had the car accident last March. Michaela read some letters I wrote her[1]—and of course found nothing improper in them. But she has managed to magnify into grounds for separation her conviction that I confided things to a "woman who's a total stranger" that I had "held back" from her. Ah, Jo, I actually wish her accusations were true, because it would probably make it easier for me to deal with the separation. It's so absurd. I don't even know if Nicoletta has a boyfriend, or if she lives alone or with someone or even what she thinks of my epistles, which I write early in the morning when I can't sleep. Nicoletta is the ideal person—at least the Nicoletta I imagine when I'm writing—for me to tell about the past. By picturing her, I can understand what has happened to us.

Nicoletta didn't believe me when I told her that I had voluntarily left the theater to put together a provincial newspaper. Her ideas about writers and artists are similar to those my mother entertains—even though she now sees the world with "businesslike objectivity." Besides which, Nicoletta has read ten times more Marx and Lenin than all of us put together. She's not like Roland, Vera's old admirer, but she still goes on and on about exploitation and capitalism, even concepts like "aggressive imperialism" or "the military-industrial complex" (allegedly a term first used by former U.S. president Eisenhower) flow from her lips with no problem.

---

1. Presumably Michaela found some of the carbon copies T. had made of his letters to N. H.

I suffered irredeemable loss of status in her eyes when I began "working in tandem" with Barrista. To her Barrista is unadulterated evil. I am not going to try to convince her otherwise, but I have every intention of making clear to her why I have chosen this life. And someone can only understand that if they know how we used to live.

I'm really not talking about love. I'm not in any condition yet for that either.

Besides which—and up until now it wasn't even a possibility—I want love between equals, between people who act on the same assumptions. I want love without quirks and contortions. I want an alarm clock ringing in the morning and supper at the same time every evening, I want vacations and Sunday outings. I want a family. Yes, I long for a bourgeois life, for order, both within me and around me. Nicoletta would probably run for cover if I confessed that to her.

Did you read the article about the Lindenau Museum in our next-to-last issue? Nicoletta is behind all those plans. What's more, she has her heart set on reconstructing Guido de Siena's altar at the Lindenau—she's already been to Eindhoven, where one panel is—the others are at the Louvre, in Princeton, and of course in Siena. The Dutch have evidently already agreed—a reconstruction would be a sensation![1]

As soon as my apartment is ready to be moved into, Vera is coming to Altenburg for a few weeks or months.

She has separated from Nicola, or he from her, which she would never admit—Vera's vanity, her feminine vanity, is too easily wounded for that. Which makes it so difficult for me to console her. But she still can look very chic. No one would believe she lives out of two suitcases. Beirut turned out to be a bit too much of an adventure for her. Nicola's mother's constant chatter about kidnappings left her terribly anxious, the power keeps going out, generators make a deafening racket and pollute the air. There's no such thing as a "green" movement there. The sea is a sewer, and cars speed through the streets at sixty miles per hour, brake hard, then speed away again—for fear of snipers. Compared to West Beirut, West Berlin is as expansive as a prairie. The only thing that worked to her advantage was that she was baptized. That's accepted. But please, no atheism!

1. This project was not realized until 2001—to international acclaim. Cf. *Claritas: The Main Altar of the Cathedral of Siena after 1260: The Reconstruction*, Lindenau-Museum (Altenburg, 2001).

Nicola thinks he's about to make some big money. His oracle is a glazier: if people are buying window glass, there's hope for peace. So people are sure to buy up everything he has in stock.

She definitely doesn't want to go back to Dresden, and she no longer has a job in Berlin—in her beautiful West Berlin. She's giving up her apartment and closing out Nicola's shop, dumping everything at a loss. And if her luck runs out she may even end up with debts to pay. So you'll be seeing each other here.

Give yourself and Franziska a couple of weeks to get acclimatized. As far as the business goes, the baron takes a very down-to-earth view of things. Don't let it bother you. I've already written you about my first meeting with him. Pringel and Frau Schorba have no reservations whatever, and as far as our *élèves*[1] are concerned, you're a celebrity already. They'll probably fight over who gets to initiate you in the arcana of layout. Jörg is jealous of you because of the book. He and Marion really didn't expect to see someone like you at my side.

Anton Larschen, who was on the verge of turning into an evil spirit, is back to extracting fine items from his backpack. Your suggested changes are "correct from start to finish." Frau Schorba will be typing the text into the computer this weekend.

Let me worry about the business end of things. Time is on our side. We'll pay for your driving classes, and you no longer need to get on a waiting list. Come autumn, then, *you'll* be driving the LeBaron.

You'll be able to move into your new place by September at the latest, since the construction firm has to shell out for every day of overrun past August 31st—it's in the contract. The rent will be modest. Did I tell you that the plans are not just for a snazzy tub in the bathroom, but a real small-size whirlpool?

Just picture a late-summer afternoon, the scent of apples drifting up from below, everything up top smells a little new yet, the castle rises up before you, behind it hills and, in the distance, mountains. You'll have enough money, no worries about the future, and each of us can peacefully pursue whatever he wants. And next year we'll all go to Italy or fly to the U.S. for lobster.

Give Franziska a kiss for me,

Your Enrico

1. Female employees recently hired by T.

Dear Jo,

I've thrown myself into work—I really don't have a choice, either. The situation is sorting itself out faster than I would have thought possible. Hardly a week has passed and already our newspaper is taking shape in the midst of all the mayhem.

And we are undergoing a transformation too. Whether it's Frau Schorba or her husband, who's our distribution manager, or Evi and Mona, our *élèves* at the computer, even our bruised Pringel—we all are not just working faster and more focused, downright impatient to tackle each new task, but we're also more cordial and open—we have nothing to hide, nothing to lose! This is what the daily routine should always look like. Yes, this is how things should stay.

Officially Herr Schorba is still working for Wismut. But he's been put on leave and is just waiting for termination papers and a final settlement. As a mining engineer he's a good organizer. I enjoy watching someone attack problems with intelligence and prudence. He has papered a whole wall with maps. By his calculation we should do a printing of 120,000. Schorba assigns clearly defined tasks and supervises rigorously. When I asked Kurt how he pictured his post-July world, he replied, "Why, here with you." Fred, on the other hand, is completely overwhelmed. Every day, almost every hour he has to patch up his distribution network because vendors go out of business or are selling fewer and fewer copies, so that it's no longer worth the drive.

Plus we're calculating on the basis of ten or even a hundred times larger accounts. Jörg and Marion are kids playing store. My dear Jo, it's the start of a new life! Our articles have, if at all, raised some dust now and then, but it always settles quickly. But now we're really going to set some things in motion. Our ads are the motor. We're going to be changing the world. Just imagine our publishing house, and the passage we'll build to connect with Market Square. And above all: Who else is going to pull it off—a free paper, and in every household? Jörg reminds me of the eternal loser sitting at the roulette table, studying and analyzing the numbers, and when he does bet, he loses again. But we're going to win at this game. Because we have probability and time on our side. And the more money we have, the less chance chance has to muck things up. Just let Jörg go on studying and analyzing and writing about it; in the meantime we're playing a new game for him to study and analyze. How lucky we are to start all over again with a clear head.[1]

I was only too happy to accede to the baron's request that, after all the uproar and confusion involved in our project, we go back and recheck every detail from start to finish. Amid the muddle of trying to accomplish everything all at one time, we're likely to lose the thread. I had assumed it would be a working dinner, but he saw me as giving my report in the mundane space of our editorial office. Suddenly I knew what needed to be done: every single person in the office had to be assigned his or her role and make an appearance onstage. And I was the director.

For four days I did almost nothing else but talk with everyone. Nothing was to be accepted without question.

Fred and Ilona, who were happy to be spared such "gimmicks" at first, are now feeling neglected. Ilona looks like a cross-eyed magpie every time I assign a task to Frau Schorba. Besides which, the "Rolex affair" is about to drive her crazy. People come into the office and slam the "piece of junk" on her desk—either it's stopped running or the new subscriber has figured out it's not a real Rolex. Some of them refuse to leave until they get their money back. And then Ilona's explanation that the ad never mentioned a Rolex, but simply read, "You will receive this watch . . ." really drives them up the wall. Ilona's only port in the storm is the wolf she's always disparaged; since the commotion usually wakes Astrid up, she often yawns—and shows her fangs. Her white blind eye likewise instills respect in hoodwinked subscribers. Thank God that nuisance isn't our problem. We don't have to woo subscribers. Isn't that a marvelous emancipation from our readers?

Yesterday was the big conference. I had asked Frau Schorba to set the room up a bit, by which I meant clearing the table and making sure there were enough chairs.

But for my people this meeting was a kind of special celebration. They had covered the long table with sheets of newsprint and set out candles on saucers. Each place had two plastic cups. They had bought mineral water and wine, plus loads of pretzel sticks. The room was, of course, too bright for candles.

Pringel and Schorba were wearing the same gray suit, and both had

---

1. Crossed out: "and complete authority."

on dark shirts and both were sporting reddish blue ties. You might have thought it was the office uniform. Kurt, on the other hand, was clad in Bermuda shorts and a yellow short-sleeved shirt. Sitting silently off to one side, his elbows on his knees, he was openly and calmly ogling the women. Manuela, who has had the wart on her chin removed, was showing off one of her skirts split up one side, and her décolletage is getting more and more daring. Evi and Frau Schorba had been to the beauty parlor and their permanents made them look the same age, like those supernumerary spinsters who used to attend Youth Consecration ceremonies. Mona had merely put on some lipstick. For the first time I noticed that she's quite beautiful.

All the chairs were on one side of the table, as if it wasn't us but the baron who was to be put to the test.

When he came swooping in ten minutes late, he crossed the room in double time, chucked his attaché case on the visitor's table, grabbed the telephone receiver, and dialed.

Deathly silence reigned as he spoke his full name. He was so perfect at reporting the accident it sounded as if he were reading from a Red Cross brochure. "Yes, I'll wait," he said, looking around at us for the first time. "Right outside your door," he whispered.

I don't know why none of us made a move. Only after the baron had hung up did we follow him out.

The baron, who had maneuvered the crazy old man to a stable position on his side, knelt down beside him and called out, "Herr Hausmann, help is on the way!" The old man groaned, blinked, and seemed to be checking us all out, including me, but with no visible reaction that I could notice. His hands were smeared with blood. The baron kept calling out, "Herr Hausmann, Herr Hausmann!"—it was the first time I'd ever heard the old man's name—and told him to try to stay awake. After the baron had rejected a glass of water for the old man, there was nothing more we could do other than keep pushing the button for the light timer. The baron later helped heave the old man onto the stretcher, who then closed his eyes as if he didn't want to watch while he was being jockeyed down the steep staircase. Astrid the wolf barked at him as he was carried out.

As cold-blooded as it may sound, the accident had eased the tension and awkwardness. Without a trace of irony, the baron thanked us for the lovely setup of the room. Within moments he had succeeded in making himself the center of attention. And so the next few hours simply flew by.

The baron promised everyone—"and when I say 'everyone,' I mean each and every one of you"—a thousand D-marks if our city-map project succeeds. We just have to be the first.

Evi and Mona now knew that when it came to advertising there was not a better, more modern, more efficient workplace in the world than theirs. They might well be the very first secretaries in East Germany to be already working on an Apple Macintosh.

He called Herr Schorba and Kurt the backbone of the enterprise. Distribution would grow in importance from week to week. Were they aware that their work would prove crucial for the success or failure of such a medium-size company?

He dubbed Pringel the salt in the soup, Frau Schorba the heart of the enterprise, and Manuela the diva and star of our troupe. Because without her and her colleagues, no matter how good our product, how hard we worked, we would simply have nothing whatever to do. (He didn't mention that her earnings will turn out to be a serious problem. Manuela has moved her mother in with her, and since that means she no longer has to worry about the children she's scouring the countryside day and night; I'm afraid that she'll soon be able to live solely from her contracts.)[1]

A time like what we all—"all of us sitting here right now"—would be experiencing over the coming months and years was not likely to come again soon. "One hundred twenty thousand copies!"—we should let those words melt in our mouths. And that was only the beginning. "Do you know what a concentration of power this is? From the Battle of the Nations Monument to the foothills of the Ore Mountains, from the fortress churches at Geithain to the pyramids at Ronneberg—that's your territory. That's you!" His gaze shifted continually from one of us to the next.

"And you need to keep in mind that you are the only ones who are going up against the big boys in the business. This newspaper, you—you who have gathered here today—are defying international conglomerates. You're sailing out in a nutshell to do battle with a whole armada.

---

1. The reference is to one-year contracts for weekly, fortnightly, or monthly placement of ads.

Whether you want to or not, you are defending something that makes this world worth living in."

Like a sorcerer the baron held us spellbound in his gaze. And if a pair of eyes did wander off and lose themselves in the room, then it was only to make certain that all this was not a dream.

Our enterprise is going to have to grow in the near future. We'll need more new staff. And yet each of us has had the good luck to be in on the ground floor, and each of us will soon be in charge of a smaller or larger division. That's an enormous responsibility. Because if one of us fails, we'll all feel the consequences.[1] He admonished me to be hard and uncompromising when it comes to sloppy work and to make no exceptions, always to keep a firm grip on the wheel.

It was only after we broke up that we thought about the old man again. There were a few splotches of his blood on the hardwood floor. Which was why each of us took a giant step, as if he were still lying there.

Hugs,
Your Enrico

Dear Jo,

I forgot to take this letter with me this morning. I can now tell you the outcome. The relationship has now been clearly defined. We set up an appointment with a notary public. I sat across from Jörg and Michaela—she represented the baron.

I can talk with Jörg. If only it weren't for Marion! Just as dirt always collects in the same corner, I find some new hatred written on her face each morning [. . .] Besides which, she has lost weight till she's just skin and bones. Her belt is all that holds her trousers up. She looks right through me, and if I don't get out of her way, she jostles me. If I let her provoke me, we'd come to blows every day. Of late she's been claiming that the articles I write are intended to block out as much space as possible so that really essential things won't get published. My "machinations," my "shameful behavior," are the essential thing. Marion has

---

1. This paragraph seems to suggest that these are T.'s own words, but he is in fact only repeating more of the baron's speech.

even come up with the theory that journalists should be elected by the voters.

How quickly the worm has turned! So now you can go right ahead and plan your move to Altenburg.

Hugs, Your Enrico

Verotchka,

I've tried a hundred times now, but can't get through. Where are you hiding?

We have nothing to blame ourselves for.[1] Not on Michaela's account. I always guessed it was the case, but now I know for sure. The affair with Barrista didn't happen just by chance. Michaela planned it all, in cold blood.

No, it's not just my imagination. I'm talking about her miscarriage. It was all so unreal, in this world, but not of this world. I've never forgotten, of course not—but how to talk about it?

I was at Michaela's today, I needed to speak with Barrista (his stupid Rolex scheme has become a curse!), I thought he would be at home. Michaela didn't hear the doorbell. I rapped on the window of my old room. It's now her "studio," her "exercise studio."

There she was, standing in front of me in her underwear and red sneakers, covered with sweat, and told me how she'd "lost four and a half pounds, four and a half pounds in two days." I watched her get back on her treadmill, dumbbells in hand. "Another five hundred meters," she panted.

I waited in the kitchen. How strange things can seem in so short a time. Mounds of zwieback, diet crackers, and low-fat milk. I didn't notice the freezer at first glance. Its gleaming whiteness made everything else look grungy.

Michaela patted her stomach and said she wasn't tucking it in, the fat was gone—I had to admit it, didn't I? She talked about willpower and how much you can accomplish just by training once a day. She kept talking about her tummy while she puttered around half naked. And then I

---

1. The meaning of this sentence remains inexplicable.

said, "Actually it's kind of sad that your tummy's so flat." Verotchka, don't misunderstand me, you and I, we could have taken the baby, I would have wanted it. At first I thought Michaela hadn't got what I was talking about or didn't want to. But then she looked at me and called me a dreamer and egotistical and some other things too. Suddenly she said, "You'll believe anything"—and was startled by her own words. I asked what she meant by that. She didn't reply. Even she couldn't find a way to talk herself out of it that fast. YOU'LL BELIEVE ANYTHING!

At the time I had hauled the head nurse over the coals—how could she allow it, what a brutal thing to do, to put a "miscarriage" in the same ward with the "abortions" . . . The hallway would have been better, I said, yes, the hallway, that would have been more humane. No one said a word, not even the nurses. YOU'LL BELIEVE ANYTHING!

I told Michaela to swear it had been a miscarriage, and she swore it. But it was a lie. A lie, perjury. I couldn't take anymore, I left, without a good-bye.

That's all, Verotchka. We would have taken it, wouldn't we?

Your Heinrich

Thursday, June 21, '90

Ah, Nicoletta,

It seems to me as if untold riches await me, await us at the end of this month. Everything will be, must be, very, very wonderful. Please don't be angry that I haven't written for so long, there's been so much to do here. What I really want to ask is: How are you? What are you up to? Would you have an hour to spare if I came to Bamberg? I would love to talk with you in the present, instead of always writing about the past. But it looks as if I have no choice.

And so back to Altenburg and the pistol under my sweater.

During the whole demonstration I was completely calm and detached. If someone had noticed I would have shown them my booty, pretended it was a joke, and handed it over at the next best opportunity. Michaela kept me at her side by linking her arm in mine and was busy the whole time responding to greetings, whether she knew the people or not. She whispered to me which of our neighbors she had spotted, and now and then called my attention to someone. Sometimes we tried to guess where we knew them from—a salesgirl, a post-office clerk, and Robert's grade-school teacher was in the crowd too. A couple of times people greeted us, and then after just a few words crowned our serendipitous camaraderie with a hug.

There was the usual barrage of whistles and chants in front of the Stasi villa. Once we arrived at Market Square, the whole thing threatened to peter out, but then a voice caught people's ears—it sounded as if it were used to bellowing. The man had climbed up on a bench and was hurling his tirades of hatred to the crowd. The adjectives he assigned to the Socialist Unity Party got nastier and nastier: rotten, prostituted, fucked-up. He thrust a fist heavenward at every stressed syllable. After six or seven sentences he couldn't come up with anything else, and so started over again, so that his brief oration began to turn into a kind of refrain. Above all his demand that all these fucked-up functionaries be sent to the coal mines was greeted each time with cheers. But then, just as I thought he would call for us to storm the Rathaus, he let it go at that, shouted, "We'll be back! We'll be back!" and climbed down from the bench. I've told you once before about this revolutionary orator. He was the guy who offered to write a letter to the editor demanding that Wieland Förster's sculpture be demolished.[1]

As we drove home Michaela was euphoric. But it was only when we turned on the television that the day became a real triumph. A live report of the demonstration in Berlin was on. She had never watched television with such a good conscience, Michaela said, because ultimately we too had made our contribution. And she kept on watching the entire afternoon, slowly moving ever closer to the screen, hoping to catch a glimpse of Thea.

But as for me, from one moment to the next my mood turned so wretched that I would have loved to break into sobs and confess everything in the hope that Michaela would take pity on me and remove that pistol from my life. I was convinced that at any second they would arrive to search our apartment. I gave fate its chance by going to the kitchen after first laying the pistol on the sofa and leaving the door ajar. And in fact Michaela did call my name, but only because the pretzel-cruncher from Thea's gathering was on. He gave the appearance of profound

---

1. Cf. the letter of Feb. 27, 1990. The "revolutionary orator" also appears in the letter to Johann Ziehlke dated Jan. 18, 1990, as the "loudmouth" at the meeting of the New Forum.

thoughtfulness and concern, all the while moving his small head from side to side as if he wanted people to remember his face from all angles. I stretched out my arm, aimed over my forefinger, and pushed down with my raised thumb—"Bang!" Michaela laughed.

I put the pistol in the cupboard with my manuscript files and sat down next to Michaela. My wooziness appeared to have passed. When the live report was over, all the news broadcasts, both East and West, included clips of the speeches. That gave me the opportunity to pursue the question that all my thoughts were whirling around: Who was it that I was supposed to shoot?

At first I thought any of the speechmakers would do. Then I chose my victims on the basis of sympathy and antipathy. In the end I realized how pointless it was to make the forces of opposition my target. That narrowed my choice down to Schabowski and Markus Wolf, and so I decided on Wolf, because that would result in the mobilization of Stasi troops. Every time Wolf lowered the hand that clutched a sheet of paper and the chorus of whistles and boos swelled louder, I pulled the trigger, sometimes from out of the crowd, sometimes from the rear. I came close to creeping into the screen, trying to find the best standpoint, and could feel the pistol fly upward, recoiling against my right wrist as I fired the shot. I realized how difficult it would be to escape without anyone recognizing me. And there might be sharpshooters posted somewhere too. Far and wide, not a policeman in sight. Suddenly it came to me: I don't want to remain unrecognized. Why shouldn't I own up to my deed?

At the next repeat of the clip I am already on the podium, just two steps behind Wolf, and as the concert of whistles reaches its high point, I shout, "Comrade General!" Wolf glances my way, I take aim and say, "You're gone!" As he turns around his eyes reflect incredulity to the point of doltishness. "You're gone!" I shout once more, and point the barrel toward the stairs. For several seconds no one moves. Then, in a monstrous failure to grasp his situation, Wolf reaches inside his coat—the Napoleonic gesture, or so I think. We stare at each other as if turned to stone. Wolf grows smaller and smaller. The motion with which he pulls out his gun scurries before my eyes like a shadow. Then the shot rings out, and the hot cartridge bounces across the podium.

I see the little silver pistol in Wolf's right hand, its barrel aimed down and away, and I'm still wondering how much lighter, more modern, and accurate it may be, when he falls full length right in front of me, his pistol skidding past the tip of my shoe and vanishing under a loudspeaker.

I use the moment to look out at the crowd, where the whistles are ebbing away. I leave the podium unmolested. I have to walk a long way before I spot the first squad car. Relieved and happy, I hand over my weapon, because I have now done what it was in my power to do.

The whole time she watched, Michaela had been jotting down notes and working on the first draft of her speech for the following Sunday. Once in bed, she fell asleep immediately.

Around half past midnight I got up, went to my room, and sat down at the foot of the couch. As if my task were to awaken a beast and release it from its cage, I was afraid to open the cupboard door.

The weapon had been well taken care of and the clip was full. All the standard procedures came back completely naturally.[1] Even removing the ammunition proved to be no problem. Bracing my left hand against my hip, I took a breath, raised the weapon above the target, and slowly lowered it along the window frame until the bottom edge of the window handle was in line with the front and rear sights at the precise moment your breath rests between exhale and inhale and your finger presses the trigger. The first shot yanked my hand way off target. And on my next tries it was the especially hard action that gave me problems and drew the weapon off its ideal position. It would barely have been possible to hit a target more than twenty feet away. I practiced for a while, then stuffed the bullets into a matchbox[2] and wrapped the gun in the undershirt I had tossed over the back of the chair as I had undressed. I washed my hands several times, but they still smelled of smoky gun oil, as if I had emptied the whole clip.

After a few hours' sleep I woke up in a fright because, just as a month before in Dresden, I thought I heard the doorbell ring. I assumed a squad car would pull up in front of our building at any moment. Shortly after seven the doorbell did ring. Michaela ducked into Robert's room. I answered.

Emilie Paulini's daughter Ruth stared at me in a dulled daze. I asked her in. "She's dead, Herr Türmer," she said. "She's dead now."

1. T.'s expertise came from the fact that from age eleven to fourteen he trained for the Olympic rapid-fire pistol competition at the District Training Center in Dresden. Cf. the letter to N. H. of March 13, 1990.

2. Consulted policemen declare it would have been impossible to "stuff" all the bullets into a matchbox.

I again invited her in. "She had waited for you to come see her, Herr Türmer, ah, she waited and waited." Ruth took two steps into the entry-way and then stopped.

Michaela greeted her with equal amounts of relief and annoyance. But Ruth ignored her outstretched hand and words of sympathy. Ruth's gaze was fixed on me. "Why didn't you stop by?" she whined. "Aaah, Herr Türmer! How our mommy waited for you."

I said that there had been so much going on this autumn. We had scarcely been home at all in the last few weeks, Michaela said in my defense. "Aaah, Herr Türmer!" Ruth exclaimed. "Why didn't you stop by just once for an hour or so? Nooo!" As if by way of punishment, my question as to when her mother had died was left unanswered.

"You will be coming to the funeral," Ruth commanded. She gave the date, turned around, opened the door, and vanished without a good-bye.

Once Ruth had departed the scene, my fears returned. I spent the whole day interrogating myself. In the same way that we can get caught up in imagining our own funeral, I began making a detailed and water-tight inventory of what I had done over the last three days or tried to recall exactly when I had gone to bed two weeks before.

Then I again found myself being tried as Markus Wolf's assassin. As a result of my deed, tanks had rolled across Alexander Platz, and now they were in every town, side by side with the Russians, martial law had been declared. I was to be found guilty in a show trial. Like Dimitrov[1] I pre-sented my own defense before the eyes of the world.

That evening I drove to the theater and hid the pistol in props, where no one was now in charge. I thrust the bullets into the soil of a flowerpot on the desk of one of my colleagues.

I drove with Michaela and Robert to Leipzig that Monday. It was to be my dress rehearsal. But there was no longer a single uniformed man in sight. After marching around the Ring, the demonstrators quickly dis-persed. Everyone wanted to get home in time to watch themselves on the news.

On Tuesday I was called into the general manager's office. And who was sitting there—just as I had expected? Two policeman, one blond, one

---

1. Georgi Dimitrov (1882–1949), leader of the Bulgarian Communist Party, after 1946 prime minister of the People's Republic of Bulgaria. In 1933 he defended himself in a trial related to the burning of the Reichstag, with the result that he had to be released.

black-haired. Jonas said he was merely putting his office at our disposal, nothing more.

Of course I was the obvious suspect. "Why should I want to steal a pistol?" I planned to reply with as much amusement as possible. They had put on deeply serious faces, they looked tired. Their chitchat about a "partnership for safety" for the demonstration on the 12th could only be a pretense. Although far more people had volunteered to help keep order than they could possibly use, they still couldn't banish their reservations. They made statements like, "That's a presumption we can't make," or "The comrades need to know what is going to happen." I said nothing because I didn't want to encourage a harmless conversation out of which would burst the surprise of the real question. Finally there we sat, helplessly staring in silence at the general manager's empty throne.

Later that day something happened that actually did take me by surprise. Constantly revolving around death and corpses, my thoughts evidently obeyed an old reflex—suddenly an idea lay before me, the idea for a story, in the science-fiction genre. In the society I was going to describe, hardened criminals were imprisoned for life on a well-guarded island, the Island of Mortals, where they truly lacked for nothing, not even amusements. All the same—and this is their real punishment—they are doomed to die a "natural death." As the result of gene manipulations or brain transplants, everyone else can count on living, if not for eternity, for one or two thousand years.

The rest of the story followed from the premise. A man condemned to normal mortality—his youth gene had been removed, and he was aging from day to day—escapes from the Island of Mortals and strikes terror in the heart of the capital. Because he really has nothing to lose, people consider him to be without any scruples. In the minds of those living "eternally," it's all the same to him whether he's shot or dies a natural death after twenty or forty years.

Suddenly I was back at my desk. I worked on describing daily reports in the media aimed at inflaming the public to feel fanatically disgusted by mortality. Anyone who no longer enjoys eternal life—so the upshot of such stories—is a priori a ruthless man.

My hero talks about his fear of death and how creepy the thought of death is, because he's so alien to everyone else. I kept finding new starting points from which I could circle the moment of death, the inconsolability that is part of experiencing something all alone.[1]

What spurred me on was the hope of returning to the German Library. I could see myself plowing through all the relevant medical journals. Weren't the body and death the last topics still open to me?

When she returned home late from dress rehearsal, Michaela was surprised to find me at my desk. She smiled and went straight to bed.

On Wednesday Robert woke me very early. He was standing in the middle of the room, shouting something. The first thing I saw was Michaela's calves. Michaela was running. And then I heard it—way too loud—the radio.

Robert's voice, the garish light of the lamp, the weather report—suddenly I felt unending shame in having yielded to the temptation to write. Now I understood what Robert was shouting.

The fall of the wall felt like stern but just punishment for my regression. I pulled the covers up over my head.

"Nobody will be coming to our demonstration now," Michaela grumbled. Later I thought I heard her heels clacking on the sidewalk. Alone now, I was overcome with the sense of being personally responsible for the fall of the wall, because I had hesitated, because I had never managed to simply pull the trigger. I had never been in the vicinity of an actual deed. So this was the 6 to 3, the inconceivable fifth goal scored in the second half, the end, the knockout punch.

Michaela returned almost cheerful. She had phoned her mother, had got her out of bed, and said how strange it made her feel to tell someone about IT, about how odd the moment was, because the other person was blindly continuing to live in the old world.

At the dress rehearsal—and this is the only memory I have of it—I said in the presence of both Jonas and Norbert Maria Richter that I would advise against a premiere. Jonas agreed with me, but left it up to Norbert Maria Richter whether his production should open.

Whereupon Michaela called me a traitor. "I'm living with a traitor!" I was obviously trying to pick a fight, evidently all I wanted to do was destroy, everything, willfully destroy everything—family, work, everything.

Michaela and I said scarcely a word to each other until Sunday, and

1. The literary level of this story casts a telling light on T.'s literary ambitions.

then only to discuss the demonstration. I asked her to plan at most two minutes for my speech on Market Square. She asked what I was going to talk about. "The future," I said, a remark that in regard to myself sounded absurd, since I no longer saw any future whatever.

Only half as many people came to the demonstration as on November 4th. In front of the Stasi villa and Party headquarters there was the usual music of catcalls, but no one halted. There were traffic wardens everywhere—Michaela had distributed white armbands, was wearing one herself, and had offered both Robert and me one. I saw the fat policeman from the previous Sunday again—Blond and Black, however, didn't show.

As the procession turned onto Market Square, I saw red flags and GDR flags being held high in front of the speaker's platform by a group of a hundred or two hundred people, almost all of them women. They were also carrying old banners and signs: THE GDR—MY FATHERLAND or SOCIALISM AND FREEDOM.

A short, mustached man kept circling this bunch and shouting, "Keep together, keep together!" although not one of them had stirred from the spot. Surrounded now, the Red bunch was being pelted with a seemingly never-ending chorus of "Shame on you!" In response they waved their flags.

Standing on the speaker's platform I could see the angry, but also frightened look in these women's eyes. One of them, way at the front, was resting her head on her neighbor's shoulder and sobbing. It may sound rather strange to you, my dear Nicoletta, but I can honestly say that these women were the first people I had ever met who championed the cause of the GDR of their own free will.

I had put together a note card with a list of my points. I didn't want Michaela to think I was taking the matter too lightly.

While giving my short speech, I gazed steadily at those women. I spoke to them like a doctor trying to explain to his patients what therapeutic measures need to be taken. Basically I said what I had said in Berlin three weeks before when Thea had confronted me.

I was the only person that day to offer a few remarks about money. "In West Berlin the exchange rate for the D-mark to the East-mark is one to seven." That's what I claimed, I didn't know exactly what it was, but Vera had mentioned it once. Plus I invented a minimum wage of eleven D-marks an hour and said anyone could figure out how many days a man would have to work in the West to earn what he earned here in a month. "For most of us," I said, "it probably wouldn't take two whole days." This earned me some applause. But the woman whose shoulder had supported her weeping friend's head shouted that money isn't everything.

"We have only two alternatives: either we close the wall again, or we introduce a market economy here too, otherwise no one will stay." I had to repeat my conclusion over the enraged howls of the Red bunch. They hurled curses you might have heard shouted at strikebreakers at the beginning of the century. "Capitalist lackey" was among them, and "reactionary" and "counterrevolutionary." Someone—alluding evidently to my white armband—called out that I belonged in the White Army. The women had the upper hand until the large crowd whipped itself up again to a "Shame on you!" and drowned them out.

The sooner we understand, I shouted, that there is only an either-or, the better it will be for all of us. "Or do you want to go to Paris as beggars?" Unable to read my next point, I stepped back from the mike and turned to one side—with the result that the applause for my last statement continued to grow. As backup music to my departure, the women had struck up the "International," and no sooner had I reached the pavement than their singing could be heard above the applause. At first there were some whistles; then, however, the majority of the crowd likewise began to sing the "International," just as I had heard people do in Leipzig.

I planted myself on one of the concrete flower boxes and hoped the whole circus would be over soon.

You probably can't suppress a suspicion that what I'm trying to do here is to put myself in the best light after the fact, to paint myself as the only person who knew so early on what lay down the road ahead.

But that's not the case. Just as in a game of chess, I was merely trying to calculate a few moves in advance. I certainly didn't see reunification coming, although even then there were a few already demanding it. And as I've said, I had no concept of any future. With the fall of the wall, my personal future had dissolved into nothingness. Had I not had to climb the orator's pulpit for Michaela's sake, such pronouncements would never have passed my lips. Of course I could have said something different, too. But what? What else was there to say? There wasn't anything else to say.

Whenever Michaela took the podium to announce the next speaker and, as the *Leipziger Volkszeitung* put it, request that the crowd show "moderation and decorum," she seemed so free and self-assured—and earned more applause for her quick wit than most of the others had for their speeches. But now that she had managed to extract herself from the cluster of people wanting to talk with her and came over to us, she seemed depressed. She didn't deign to give me a single glance. On the drive home her mood toppled into total darkness. I took it to be stage fright before a premiere.

Once we were home and I was finally able to ask her what had happened, she said, "Nothing," and vanished into our room. She was crying.

"Is this it?" she asked when I entered. She held the envelope up. "Is this why you're the way you are?" I recognized Nadja's handwriting on the envelope. "You don't need to worry about us," Michaela said, "we'll manage all right." She blew her nose.

It was one of the few moments in my life in which my conscience was pure, ready for any kind of interrogation.

I asked Michaela to open the envelope. She shook her head. "Please," I said. "No," she said. She wouldn't subject herself to that.

I slit the envelope open with a nail file lying on her nightstand, unfolded the sheet of paper, and began to read aloud. Right at the start Nadja wrote that she was aware that I now had a family. She herself was living with Jaroslav, a Czech, and was expecting her first child at the end of February. She asked about how my manuscript was going and complained about her work.

Michaela said nothing. Even when I laid the letter down in front of her, she didn't budge. Finally she asked if she could have the stamps. Then she folded the letter back up and inserted it in its envelope.

"So then what is the reason?" She stared at me.

"For what?" I asked.

"For being the way you are."

Before I could reply the doorbell rang for all it was worth. My mother was standing there, her chin jutted forward so she could peer out from under her cap. A cyclamen rose up threateningly from her right hand, and in her left she was holding a swaying shopping net, whose contents I recognized as the familiar springform pan.

"Justice triumphs!" she cried. She spoke very loudly, carrying on like someone hard of hearing, and each of her movements was accompanied by a rattle, rasp, or jingle.

Loyally devouring his cheesecake, Robert didn't let Mother's chatter disturb him. The fall of the wall was her personal triumph, and she made fun of us for not having been in the West yet. She definitely wanted to travel to Bavaria, because the "welcome money" was highest there,[1] and together it would come to 560 D-marks, a sum that you could actually do something with.

Later, at the theater, my mother admitted how shocked she had been by the way Michaela looked. Weren't we happy because of what had happened?

Except for one woman whom nobody knew the whole first row was empty. The balcony hadn't even been opened. Of just short of sixty people in the audience, fifteen belonged to Norbert's entourage and about thirty were friends and family of the actors, just like us.

At first the audience fell into old habits and applauded every punch line. But this enthusiasm soon faded, as if they finally realized what had happened over the last few days.

After intermission several people did not return to their seats, and the play simply sickened and died. Since there was no reaction to the punch lines now, the actors rushed their lines all the more.

At the end Norbert Maria Richter barely managed to get a bow in.

Tuesday I was called to the general manager's office again.

Jonas and Frau Sluminksi were both sitting at his desk, as if they were doing homework together. They both stood up at the same time, extended a hand without saying a word, and we all sat down. Jonas looked at a letter in front of him. His hair fell down into his face. "I'm leaving," he said. And then, raising his head and flipping his hair back, he added, "I've resigned."

He enjoyed my surprise. Happiness glistened in Sluminski's eyes. Had it been because of *Gotham*, I asked. He shook his head, and Sluminski rocked hers slightly too.

"What's left here for me to do?" he said, gazing at me with his perennially moist eyes as if actually expecting some sort of answer.

"Yes," I said. "I've asked myself that question."

Instead of wishing him good luck, extending my hand, getting up from my chair, and leaving, I just sat there. I was sorry to see him go, I said. But I could well understand his decision.

He knew, he said, that people talked behind his back and how they

1. In Bavaria the "welcome money" was normally set at 140 DM, rather than the usual 100 DM.

would lambaste him now, but he had no regrets. If he could see even the slightest chance of being able to accomplish anything meaningful here, he would stay. But that was out of the question now. I nodded. And then he said that Sluminski would be running the business end of things for now—and she looked up and noted that she would welcome any and all support. I nodded again. "Or would you like to do it?" Jonas asked, grinning his old grin. "Would you?" I shook my head, and then we shook hands again.

As I entered the canteen Jonas's departure was already being celebrated as a victory. I sat off to one side like someone from the old regime, happy to be left in peace.

"Jonas is leaving," I told Michaela, who hadn't been at the theater. And because she looked at me as if she wasn't about to have her leg pulled, I added, "He told me himself."

I had no explanation for her as to why I of all people had been singled out for special consideration. Michaela presumed one of Jonas's tricks lay behind it, some really nasty machination. When I didn't reply she asked if I was actually so vain as to think he had done it out of personal concern. I shrugged. "No, no, my dear," she said, "there's strategy and tactics behind it. Did someone just happen to drop by and see you two together?"

I said no, but did mention Sluminski. At the sound of her name Michaela jumped to her feet. "What was she doing there?" she exclaimed.

Even as I repeated Jonas's words, a vein swelled at Michaela's temple. "She'll be running things for now? Her? The Party secretary?"

"Only the business side," I said.

"And you?" she shouted. "What did you say?"

I tried to recall my words. "You didn't say anything," she shouted before I could even answer. "Nothing, not one thing." Michaela stared at me, her head was starting to tremble, she was about to say something else, but then fell silent, as if she didn't dare say what she was thinking, and left the room.

Somehow I had lost the capacity for emotions that Michaela experienced on such a grand scale. I had become numb, mute, devoid of emotion. I no longer felt my wounds.

When at the end of the week and without an inkling that anything was up, I called Mother, the first thing she said was, "Did you know about this? Did you?"

"Know what?" I asked. And when she didn't reply, I said, "What am I supposed to have known?" Instead of answering, my mother hung up.

I called her back. I knew she would *never* be able to survive it. I had no hope at all, but she answered.

"Mother!" I exclaimed. I don't think I've probably ever sounded so pleading.

"Actor my foot! Vera works in a *fabric* shop. She's a *sales clerk*! And *you* knew that! Right?"

I was just happy to hear *that* accusation.[1]

"You wanted to believe it," I shouted. "Didn't it ever bother you that Vera never sent any reviews?"

My mother said she'd always thought the Stasi had removed them from the envelope.

Finally she said, "I demand only one thing: not to be deceived by my children. That's something I cannot handle, Enrico, not in my own family. How can you even expect me to take it?" Then she hung up.

I walked home. On the way I thought about Emilie Paulini again for the first time, and how she had presumably been buried at some point over the last few days.

Your

Enrico T.

Thursday, June 28, '90

Dear Nicoletta,

Why have you remained so present to me, Nicoletta, so much so that it sometimes makes me shudder? How many times have I painted your portrait in my mind—it's so vivid in my memory. As if in a fever I evoke your presence with an unhealthy craving. I'm frighteningly good at it, but when I find myself alone again, my own company seems intolerable. And then I write you a letter.

Two weeks after the wall was opened there was no one left who hadn't been in the West except us. All the kids in Robert's class had seen

---

1. This scene remains inexplicable unless one recalls the farewell scene on the occasion of Vera's departure. In his letter to N. H. of May 10, 1990, T. insinuated that there was some connection between V. T. and State Security. He had thought his mother was alluding to that.

Batman. Michaela found some excuse every time. "The West isn't going anywhere," she said, and she had tons and tons of work to do, by which she meant the meetings she attended at least once a day, sometimes holding them at home. It was her idea to publish a newsletter in which all of New Forum's working committees would have an opportunity to place items. In Michaela's eyes that meant publicizing injustices and abuses—the Sluminski case, for instance—because no one else was going to do it.

When the chief dramaturge assigned me the task of delivering several cartons of libretti to Henschel Verlag in Berlin, I agreed mainly because I was worried about Vera. I could guess what the opening of the wall meant for her. Her lies, big and small, would blow up in her face.[1]

When I invited Robert to come along, he hugged me for the first time. And now Michaela wanted to go to Berlin too.

First, however, my self-control was to be tested.

In November you still needed a stamp in your papers to cross the border. Robert accompanied me to the provisional office set up by the police in the one-story building behind the Konsum Market. (Michaela had refused to appear as a supplicant before these people ever again.)

Since the place looked dead, I assumed the door was locked and was just trying to jiggle at it when it flew open in my hand. There was the odor of a noonday meal. The room we entered through folding doors was as dark as a church. Except that just above some desks that had been shoved together, a lamp had been hung, and beneath it sat the uniformed personnel, all of them hunched over as if trying to hide their faces. The counters and the door to the kitchen were barricaded with stacked tables and chairs.

Uncertain from which side I ought to approach, I chose a circuitous route. I kept at least one person's back in front of me and glanced down into a drawer full of stamps and inkpads, keys and seals. A metal lunch box shimmered beside a briefcase, there were two apple cores in the wastebasket. For a second I was afraid I'd walked into a trap. The blond didn't recognize me, or at least pretended he didn't. He raised his arm, his hand opened up, I gave him my papers.

It was like remembering a dream. In the same moment the two other uniformed men looked up from their work, and by the light of the lamp

1. T.'s suspicions proved to be totally unfounded.

I could tell that it was the black-haired cop and the fat cop. The trio that I had joined in their squad car on November 4th was now complete.

I didn't seriously consider trying to flee. But I did glance toward the door as if I expected someone to be standing there blocking our retreat. I called Robert over to me.

"Have *you* been over yet?" I asked, looking at the blond as he inspected my accordion-fold passport to the last page,[1] as if every stamp from every border crossing held great interest for him. The blond then added his stamp and folded it all back up again. Robert said later that I paid a fee, even got a receipt, but I don't recall it. With the same gesture with which he took my pass, the blond handed it back. Just as he had ignored my thank-you, he now ignored my question. I headed for the exit, Robert kept close to my side.[2]

The next day we made our libretti delivery in Berlin and then had our noon meal in a pub near Henschel Verlag. We had driven our old route, instead of the one I had pictured in my mind: turning off in the direction of West Berlin just after the three-lane asphalt stretch near Michendorf. Berlin, by which I mean the eastern half of the city, was nothing more than an antechamber where you waited before striding into the great hall. I was amazed that the waitress and counterman were still working here in the East, as if the wall were still there. After we had eaten, we drove down Friedrich Strasse in the direction of Checkpoint Charlie. This was Robert's wish. While we were waiting to be passed through— there were only a few cars ahead of us—I realized for the first time the meaning of the word "checkpoint." The syllables check-point-charlie had been just a sound, a noise, a bubble-gum bubble that bursts just as the bells of the Spassky Tower ring[3] out into the moment of greatest silence. I asked Robert if he knew what the word "checkpoint" meant. He did. Michaela said I shouldn't play high school teacher. Pass, glance, pass, thanks—and through. No thumbing to find the stamp, nothing. Michaela said the real checkpoint had to still be up ahead. I turned right. I had no idea where I was driving. We had wanted to go to West Berlin, and here we were in West Berlin. Do you understand? West Berlin

1. Cf. the prose piece "Voting" in the appendix.
2. This passage seems too carefully constructed, which makes it rather difficult to believe. Presumably a "tall tale."
3. The main tower of the Kremlin in Moscow, also called the "Savior Tower."

meant arriving there, meant being in the West, not just driving around aimlessly.

An hour later and we ran ashore at the lower end of the Kurfürstendamm, where I found a parking place to squeeze into and a bank where we collected our "welcome money." Then we walked up and down the Ku'damm, lost our bearings in the adjacent streets, and landed on another major thoroughfare with lots of stores. With Michaela in the lead we entered a bookstore where several stacks of a novel[1] by Umberto Eco were sprouting from the floor. I had to laugh when I saw those oversize wheeled shopping baskets outside a supermarket.[2] They instantly roused a desire in me to hoard supplies, so that I wouldn't have to leave the house for days.

Later we found ourselves in a department store in which it was way too warm and, with coats draped over our arms, we moved from floor to floor as if looking for some particular item. When Michaela suddenly got the idea to buy Robert a jacket for his Youth Consecration,[3] we went our separate ways for forty-five minutes. She handed me two fifty D-mark bills and shoved Robert ahead of her to the escalator.

I watched them go, but I had no real desire to spend three quarters of an hour alone. I thought: You're free, freer than you've ever been before in your life.[4] I was in the middle of West Berlin and could do or not do whatever I felt like.

I was most interested in the kitchen utensils and housewares—coffee machines, pots, tableware, and corkscrews, but there were also gadgets whose purpose I would have liked to inquire about. I definitely wanted to buy something for myself. Just for me. Suddenly I had an idea I couldn't shake—if I didn't spend the money now, it would be lost for good. At any

1. *Foucault's Pendulum* (Munich, Vienna, 1989).

2. The grocery stores in the GDR usually had handbaskets, but no shopping carts.

3. Youth Consecration is a rite of initiation intended to mark the transition from youth to adulthood. It is a nonecclesiastical alternative to confirmation in the Protestant church or the sacrament of confirmation for Roman Catholics. Its origins lie in the nineteenth century. In the GDR it was officially promoted by a decree of the Soviet government in 1953. It is rather surprising that E. T. and his life partner observe this ritual without any pressure from the state, although such behavior is still quite common today in the eastern states of the Federal Republic.

4. A similar statement can be found in T.'s letter to V. T. of Feb. 6, 1990: "The realization that for two hours I would now be freer than I had never been in my whole life robbed me of my will."

rate, with much wringing of the hands, I searched for some perfect object. One moment I thought I had made a decision, the next I lost my confidence. I needed a Chinese teapot, I needed a windbreaker. I was already at the cash register with a Walkman when, tormented by regret, I stood there just shaking my head as if I didn't speak German, left the Walkman on the counter, and fled. If Michaela and Robert had been on time I would have greeted them empty-handed. But then, lured by a clutch of people, I began to rummage through a square box full of gloves. Large or small, they were all the same price. At first I tried thrusting my hand down into unexplored regions and trolled along the bottom, but all I brought to the surface was junk, children's mittens or singles, one of them a black leather glove that fit perfectly. I kept it on and searched for its mate, but in vain. Finally I conquered my aversion and considered those that other people had tossed back. It was difficult to try them on because each pair was sewn together at the wrist. Once you had pulled off the trick, however, you stood there manacled. I decided on a dark blue pair lined in a red and green plaid, and, properly handcuffed, walked over to the cash register.

"I thought you don't like gloves," Michaela said. "Because I didn't have any," I said. Robert was carrying a plastic shopping bag so cleverly crafted that rain couldn't get into it. Michaela confessed that she had only one D-mark left, but at least we no longer needed to worry about a suit for Robert to wear at his Youth Consecration.

I treated us to currywurst at a food cart. That improved the general mood.

After that I dialed Vera's number. It was the first time I had ever used a push-button phone and I felt like I was in a movie. I kicked the phonebooth door open again and asked where exactly we were. Michaela ran off to look for a street sign.

Vera had an answering machine. Her voice had a hard, stiff sound, as if the only calls she got were from total strangers. I was sure she would pick up the receiver as soon as she recognized my voice. I said, "Hello!" a couple of times and that we would love to have coffee at her place. I called the shop, and the male voice—presumably Nicola's—on the answering machine said in German that I was to leave a message after the beep, after which I heard what I presumed was the same message in Arabic and French.

The woman at the food cart explained how to get to Wedding.

It was already dark by the time we found Malplaquet Strasse. At first I couldn't locate Vera's name on the doorbell register because the name was reversed as Barakat-Türmer.

"They live in the rear building," Michaela said, a fact that I likewise found disappointing. When I heard footsteps behind the main door I assumed it was Vera. All we saw of the short woman in an ankle-length robe was her face—she didn't bother to give us a glance—and she now retreated like a windup doll. The rather shabby corridor was crammed with prams and bikes, the main door sprayed with graffiti, the lighting dim.

We had to climb to the fifth floor. There was no one at home, but there was something special about just seeing her door and her doormat.

On the back of the receipt for Robert's suit I wrote, "Greetings from your Altenburgers." I folded the receipt and stuck it in the crack of the door.

Michaela asked if I would invite her and Robert to see *Batman*.

I let them out in front of a movie theater near the Zoo Station and drove off to find a parking place. I got lost several times during the endless odyssey. I didn't really care about the movie, but I panicked at the idea of missing the beginning and I was afraid they would wait for me. Every parking space proved too small. I was lucky nothing happened when I drove through a red light at a pedestrian crossing. Finally I hit it right just as someone pulled out. I parked with my right rear tire up on the curb. The cold air did me good. The exhaust in West Berlin really did smell like a pungent perfume.

I was surprised when the woman at the ticket boot told me I was just in time.

Michaela and Robert were sitting near the entrance. Given the plush armchairs I at first thought we were in a private box. But then the lights went on, and Michaela burst into laughter as a vendor appeared beside us selling the same ice cream we had just seen advertised. I couldn't get my head around the notion that we were allowed to eat ice cream while sitting in such plush seats, and in the dark besides. Calculated on the basis of what money I had left, one movie ticket plus ice cream cost as much as my gloves.

After the movie Robert was as happy as could be, and Michaela seemed to be too. From the map the woman in the ticket booth had given Michaela free of charge we saw how easy it was to reach the autobahn. Michaela played navigator. Robert had turned on his cassette recorder and, to the accompaniment of Milli Vanilli and Tanita Tikaram, gave us a detailed plot summary of the film, as if we hadn't just seen it. When he was done he demanded we all list our favorite scenes. Five minutes later we were at the autobahn. With the lights of the Funkturm rising up in the background, I merged into traffic. After a couple of hundred yards I changed to the middle lane.

Michaela shouted for me to be careful and not to drive so fast—this was absolute madness. "What do you mean?" I exclaimed. "What else can I do?" I wanted to hit the brakes and slow down but I didn't dare risk it. Next to us, in front of us, behind us—we were racing along with them, faster than I had ever driven in my life, a pack of wild dogs, with us in the middle. I tried leaving more space in front of me, but immediately a car would shoot in from another lane and just make things worse. I had no choice, I had to drive like everybody else. But since everyone was driving at that speed, it couldn't be all that dangerous, or at least not as bad as we feared. I gradually calmed down.

At the airport exit I realized we weren't headed south but north. Michaela was also aware of our mistake. Trying to find a more comfortable position, she stretched out her legs. Robert had fallen silent and, propping his elbows on the backs of our seats, stared straight ahead.

We sped along through wide curves and tunnels—a little like a roller-coaster ride. Instead of driving on to Hamburg I followed the sign for the last exit before the border and turned around. We had an even longer stretch of asphalt autobahn before us now. The music on the radio was seldom interrupted.

During the trip back I kept thinking about the sea, I pictured ships crossing the ocean and I made a list of harbors: Hamburg, Hong Kong, Valparaiso, New York, Helsinki, Vancouver, Genoa, Barcelona, Leningrad, Istanbul, Melbourne, Alexandria, Odessa, Singapore, Auckland, Marseille, Rio de Janeiro, Cape Town, Aden, Bombay, Rotterdam, Venice. I saw these giants of the ocean anchored beside garland-trimmed seawalls. The radio reception had grown worse and worse, but there was one AM station that held a signal—music and words sounded equally magical and distant. I saw terraced cafés above a town, with day-trippers and lanterns and fireworks. I was already traveling in some foreign region of the world. Just as Jim, the slave in *Huckleberry Finn*, believes he can see the lights of Cairo and the pyramids in the distance, I wouldn't have been surprised if suddenly a road sign had announced St. Louis or New Orleans.[1]

I no longer know what I saw as I steered the car through Leipzig. The first thing I can recall is a gesture of Michaela's hand that passed directly from the light switch to my forehead as we stood in the entry hall. "You have a fever," she said, and showed me the sweat on her fingertips.

"I'm ill," I replied.

"No need to shout," she said.

"I'm ill," I repeated, and immediately whispered it again, as if I dared not forget it.

"I'm ill" was the expression I'd been looking for in vain over the past several weeks. I quickly washed my hands and face, undressed, and took to my bed, from where, with ample time and no disruptions, I would finally be able to marvel at all the ships and cities of the world.

The next day I awoke alone in the apartment. I had the feeling it would take hours before I had assembled enough willpower to spread a sheet over the couch in my room as well as transfer my pillow and blanket from the bedroom. I knew that this would be the last chore I would accomplish for a long time, and closed my eyes.

And with that I've really said it all. Because it's impossible to describe my condition. Words don't come close.

My dear Nicoletta, looking back on it now, I am writing to you from terra firma. Anyone who can tell about his own adventures didn't perish with them—a certainty that in fact stands everything on its head. Besides which, the logic of dreams is hidden from the eyes of those who are wide awake, just as sunlight obliterates an image on film.

If I had lost the *sensibilità* one needs for this world—in lesson 14, Signore Raffalt[2] says that a corresponding word does not exist in German, only to translate it boldly one sentence later with *Resonanzfähigkeit*—it was not because I had become numb, callous, and apathetic, but simply because I was a broken man. There was no me left.

Do you understand, Nicoletta? Everything that had defined me since

1. T. is in error here. Jim and Huck Finn were on the lookout for Cairo, Illinois, the town at the confluence of the Mississippi and Ohio rivers.

2. Reinhard Raffalt, *Eine Reise nach Neapel e parlare italiano* [A trip to Naples e parlare italiano] (Munich, 1957). During these weeks T. apparently first studied Italian—which, so it is said, he later spoke fluently—with the help of this old, if steadily reprinted, introduction to the language.

that first Arcadian summer, everything that had interested me, had kept me alert and alive, had now been rendered immaterial by the last few weeks and months.

The vast emptiness that had taken my place corresponded exactly to the overwhelming endlessness of time in which it floated. I was amazed at what an infinity lay hidden in each day. No, it wasn't that simple. I lay in bed, getting up only when I had to go to the toilet and sipping at the tea Michaela placed beside the bed every morning and evening. I dozed off and woke up, dozed off and woke up, and wondered what was keeping Robert, why he hadn't come home from school yet. But it wasn't just him, Michaela kept arriving later and later. It seemed to me that the longer I waited, the greater the probability, yes, inevitability of some kind of trouble, maybe even an accident of some sort. When I finally brought myself to fetch my watch from my desk, it had stopped at half past nine. But my touching it had started it up again. Later—it was still light outside—I managed to make it to the kitchen. The clock above the door read twenty till eleven, the same as my watch. I lay there in bed, filled with amazement at what had become of minutes and hours, at what monsters they had turned into. I sneered at the thought of what all I could have accomplished in a single morning. I could have easily written one story per day, taken care of household chores as well, watched a little television, and read. Now that all that was of no concern to me, I had a godlike dominion over time. Not even eleven o'clock yet! Imagine that you've just had a long dream, a very long dream, one that unfolds into further dreams. When you wake up you're certain the alarm will ring at any moment, when in fact not ten minutes have passed, and all the lights in the building across the street are still on.

I counted the seconds it took for me to take a breath in order to get some sense of what a minute, what five minutes meant. As soon as I laid my watch aside, I was convinced that I could break every diving record. Another experiment, one that I had often performed as a child in the hope of speeding up time, proved less successful: with the help of a magnifying glass (Robert has one for his stamp collection) I watched the minute hand. Yes, I saw it move, but that was no help.

At some point pain paid me a visit. I have to put it that way, the toothache seemed like a guest in my void. I was grateful. Closing my eyes, I tried to discover where it would settle in, for at first it darted about like a will-o'-the-wisp, bounding upward, plunging downward, now on the right, now on the left. But then it found its spot, lower left. To help you understand I probably have to express it this way: I clung to this pain. Or better, it has to be put like this: *I* was the pain. Outside it, there was nothing. And so it was only natural for me to try to nurse it. I watched it constantly, the way a child watches a hamster on that first day, and gave myself over to time beyond all measure. The greater the pain, the smaller the void. It first had to take total possession of me, and only then, as the capstone of my torment, did I want to see the dentist. I kept losing myself in the details of an agonizing session in the dentist's chair.

Like someone who fears he has been robbed as he slept and starts hastily patting his pockets, I explored my pain each time I awoke. And was always relieved to find it in its proper spot. And not only that, it spread, creeping and pommeling[1] its way along my jaw, until it slammed into the back of my head. For me it was a kind of guarantee, the only reliable unit of measurement.

I went to seed. The odor that hit me when I lifted my covers, the long fingernails, the fuzzy coating on my teeth—I perceived it all simply as a defect in my environment, like a burned-out lightbulb when you don't have a replacement in the house. When my stubble had grown so long it stopped being prickly, I forgot my body entirely. That was, of course, in part due to my fatigue, a permanent exhaustion in which dream and reality often remained indistinguishable. I continued my survey of distant cities and ships. It didn't matter whether I kept my eyes open or closed, I wandered aimlessly around those same cities, without ever actually making an appearance myself.

To Michaela and Robert it looked like uninterrupted sleep. When Michaela brought me my tea each morning, she put her hand to my brow. She made every effort, cooked rice pudding, and asked Aunt Trockel to make me her applesauce. I didn't want any of it, I wanted peace and quiet, but let it all roll over me as if it were a way of thanking Michaela for having Dr. Weiss sign off on my sick leave first for one, then for a second week.

When the time was up, I dragged myself to the polyclinic. It was St. Nicholas Day, December 6th, the very same day on which Michaela and Jörg and a few others occupied the Stasi villa, after first printing and distributing a flyer at noon that called for the demonstration to assemble at

---

1. The more common, and correct, spelling is: "pummeling."

the theater at six o'clock. Michaela appeared finally to have incorporated all the energy I lacked. In the half hour she spent at home that afternoon, she used my absence to toss my bed linens into the washing machine, but didn't have time to put on fresh. When I got back with a renewal of my sick leave, this time for two weeks at a shot, I found my sickbed had been dismantled—a smack in the face that made me feel as if I had been thrown out. I did without new sheets, rummaged in the wardrobe till I found my old down sleeping bag, unrolled it on the couch, crept into it still in my underwear, and pulled the hood up over my head.

That evening Michaela was out of control. I couldn't remember her ever having entered my room without knocking first. Suddenly there she stood before me—I had heard her key ring and her voice before I opened my eyes. It wasn't just that she was talking too fast. Every sentence demanded three or four more sentences of explanation that drew still more sentences in their wake, so that she barely had a chance to catch her breath or swallow and so kept on talking faster and faster. But the real demand upon me was her presumption that I would get up, get dressed, and return with her to the demonstration.

Even if I had not been ill, she surely must have known how little I cared about any of it, yes, how it made no difference to me whatever whether those at the head of the demonstration chanted "Germany, united fatherland" or "We are one people" and whether some Jörg or Hans-Jürgen had or hadn't attempted "to bring a halt to that."

With each of her statements I realized anew how incapable I was of taking any part in this life, how pointless every effort seemed.

My response to Michaela's question about what the doctor had said rekindled her anger. At some point she compared me to a caterpillar, a fat caterpillar—which, given the sleeping bag, was not exactly original. I understood it as an announcement that from now on she wouldn't be taking care of me. What was annoying was the covert charge that I was faking it. The accuracy of this conjecture was revealed the next day when Robert asked me to help him with his homework. The worst thing was his nagging me to drive him here, there, and everywhere. Michaela seemed actually to be egging him on to do things she had once forbidden for pedagogical reasons. As if she had completely forgotten my condition, she in fact tormented me with wishes of her own over the next several days.

Living together with the two of them became more and more of a torture. I ruled out the idea of returning to the theater. Vera had ducked out of sight, but the mail brought rambling letters from Geronimo almost daily—which after a while I no longer bothered to open. At the time I still knew nothing of the difficulties my mother was struggling with. She offered the absolutely foolish assertion that Vera was to blame for my breakdown. Michaela, on the other hand, took the miseries of the world upon her shoulders on an hourly basis, including feeling responsible for my deterioration, until finally she would once again lose all patience with me. I stubbornly defended my sleeping bag against her onslaught, but did allow her to tuck a clean sheet on my couch.

As I've said, my condition at the time is alien even to me now. I'm reporting to you like someone who repeats hearsay for better or for worse.

Then it happened. It simply happened. Have you ever collected your kitchen garbage in a paper bag? And when you pick it up the next day, all the crap plops right through it. The horror of it suddenly hit me.

But what does that mean![1] I had suddenly realized what had happened to me and what a state I was in.

Ah, Nicoletta, the total disappearance of Herr Türmer is almost incomprehensible. You can, of course, also attribute it to the loss of my writing, or more accurately, the loss of the West, the loss of our Beyond, the death of the benevolent gods . . . And with that, if you recall, the circle of my observations has closed on itself.

On the other hand, perhaps my descriptions have, or so I hope, laid a foundation that will make what is yet to come comprehensible.

But enough for today.

Yours,

Enrico Türmer

Sunday, July 1, 1990

Dear Jo,

I can move in the day after tomorrow, that is, if the baron has no objections. I've ordered a new mattress—thanks to Monte Carlo, the best of the best.[2] All the rest in due time.

---

1. Crossed out: "All that was left was exertion and agony. Every self-evident reality was erased, not to mention every joy or desire; utter trivialities demanded a decision, from whether to open the window to whether I needed to go to the john."

2. By way of refreshing the memory, his letter to Johann Ziehlke of May 14, 1990, ends with the statement: "I gave her [Vera] my winnings, and that was a great relief in the end."

Vera will be coming by train, with her predictable two suitcases.

The new family has flown to the Baltic, to Denmark, which makes a lot of things easier. No one knows just how the baron gets permission for his aviation stunts or how he has managed to get around the Russians.[1] It wouldn't surprise me if he's soon flying a MiG-29. D-marks will get you anything. The baron is already making grand plans for the day the Russians have departed for good. Discount fares from Altenburg-Nobitz to London and Paris! I wouldn't put anything past him.

As I was getting out of my car on Friday, I thought I saw seagulls— seagulls here in town. But it was only paper, whirling scraps of paper of all kinds coming toward me along the sidewalk and out in the street. I stopped for a moment and watched the pages as they skittered over the parking lot, fluttered down the slope, pirouetted across car roofs, and finally landed along the brick wall or in the chain-link fence. I even stepped on one and wondered if it was worth bending down for the paper clip. I kept on walking—only to turn on my heels a moment later and start chasing these white birds like a desperate child. Marion's shrill voice from the window had wrenched me out of my trance. Evi, Mona, and Frau Schorba came dashing and screaming out our front door.

Frau Schorba attempted to snatch up the pages drifting along the street. She shrieked at regular intervals whenever the one she was chasing escaped her grasp at the last second. Meanwhile Ilona and Fred had joined the pursuit, and like the drivers in a hunt we were now combing the parking lot. We were able to glean the lion's share of the flyaway ad forms from along the wall and fence. Evi climbed up and over the fence to pluck Rüdiger Bajohr Finance Agency and Noëlle's Bookshop from the bushes. Mona crept under every car and fetched Copy Service from under my front wheel.

Ilona and Fred checked along Jüden Gasse and on Market Square, while the rest of us hurried to assist Frau Schorba. She had changed tactics, and now trotted along behind the pages and then slammed her heel on the pavement with a cry of "Bastard!" It took at most two or three "Bastards!" and the ad was saved. Cars that had been forced to pull over had turned on their warning signals.

Fred proudly displayed his muddy pants, and, apparently happy to have lost a heel, Ilona hobbled along pretentiously. We learned from

1. The town of Nobitz, near Altenburg, was home to a large Soviet military air base.

Pringel—whom we probably have to thank for the fact that the computer came through unscathed—that Jörg had already loaded Marion into their car and driven off.

She, Marion, had stormed into the computer room and, without saying a word, made a grab at the pile of ads and flung them out the window. Then, as wind from the Baltic scattered the forms, she had once again cursed everyone as shadows. I asked them all to treat the matter with discretion. I would encourage Jörg to get Marion to a psychiatrist. No sooner do we have one lunatic out of the house—the old man had to be put in a nursing home—than we're threatened by a second one.

Yesterday Marion even came at me with a knife. It was a perfectly innocuous situation. Because Schorba was out of the office, Fred was answering some questions two of our new deliverymen had asked. Marion had accidentally overheard him, and began laying into Fred right in front of them. Her screeches fetched Jörg and me to the scene.

Since Jörg refused to do anything about Marion's outburst, I let myself be drawn into it with a few words—enough was enough, and would she please leave us alone. As I turned toward the deliverymen I realized their eyes were wide with terror.

Marion was holding Fred's knife clamped in both hands, the blade and the pupils of her eyes directed menacingly at me. Her face was contorted, as if an attack of madness had suddenly obliterated her familiar features [. . .]

"Just try to drive me out of this office," she shouted ominously. "You evidently think I wouldn't dare?" Marion's mouth wrenched into a skewed smile as I backed away.

"No," I said, "I don't think there's much of anything you wouldn't do."

"Then we understand each other," she announced with satisfaction, lowered the knife, and turned to leave. We all stood there frozen in place. As she departed Marion shouted a cheerful "Hi there!" to Schorba—who was just back in the office—a greeting that he happily returned. But Schorba now stared at us as if we were a gathering of ghosts.

I've learned from Fred that the Weekly's printing is now under ten thousand, despite Jörg's histrionic headlines: "Poison in Our Groundwater?" or last week's "Mass Graves in Altenburg?" He no longer knows what to write. While the celebratory mood is increasing day by day, Jörg hunkers down in his office, growing ever paler and smaller. The baron has given him a free hand. The only question is for how long yet. Have I told you about Ralf?[1] I've hired his wife as a sales rep, he and his daughter will be delivering our Sunday issue in North Altenburg—not bad extra pocket money.

I've been spending my evenings at Referees' Retreat. Each time the Germans score a goal, Friedrich, the bald owner, shoots off fireworks and pours a round on the house. A shame we're not playing today.

Hugs,

Your Enrico

[This letter was never sent.]

Tuesday, July 3, '90

Verotchka,

Yesterday Michaela showed up at the office to bring Barrista his thick pocket calendar. It was the first time I've ever seen her kiss him. She was wearing her fancy red sneakers. She couldn't look me straight in the eye.

Later I happened to hear Mona and Evi talking about Michaela. Their suspicion that Barrista would move in on "one of the prettier ones" has now been confirmed. A little later Robert called and asked when I'd be free. We made a date for lunch.

I would barely have recognized him. Not because of the new outfit— he's wearing sneakers now too, plus a jacket with heavily padded shoulders. His hair is a lot shorter. Maybe I have been a little inattentive of late—Robert has turned into a young man. He gave me a hug all the same.

I let everything lie just as it was and left with him. Outside we ran into Pringel, who had been doing research for his report on Day Zero and the introduction of our new money. (Johann will have to work hard to hold his own against Pringel.)

On Market Square I took a place in line at the fruit stand. It went fast, since most of the others apparently just wanted to view the wares. I felt like a gate-crasher, like the guy who's at the buffet table before it's even open. I asked for four kiwis, which I was allowed to select for myself—

1. T. could easily have determined this himself, since he kept carbon copies of all his letters.

and at the same moment recognized our old friend, the D-MARK ONLY fruit vendor who had helped Robert sell his first newspapers. Our last meeting seemed so long ago now, he was like a figure out of a fairy tale. His greeting was friendly, but his mood was gloomy. He hadn't done a hundred marks' worth of business yet. He wouldn't even make the cost of his fee to set up his booth. The prospects were bleak, hopeless. While bystanders watched, I impetuously began grabbing at random, as if I had to buy any piece of fruit I touched. I paid with a ten-mark bill and held out the palm of my hand, where he deposited the change. Robert was given a free banana, which he immediately deposited in my pocket out of embarrassment.

The whole town was like an exposition that had just opened its gates, and we strolled through it like visitors. My sack of fruit was duly noted in the same way that I eyed every filled shopping net, every even half-full plastic bag. The air above Market Square seemed to flicker with expectation and nervousness.

The Ratskeller was completely empty. It wouldn't have taken much and I would have used the open door as our excuse for having barged in, but then the waitress told us to take a seat anywhere we wanted and handed us each a menu.

Robert and I had scarcely spoken. He had trotted alongside me lost in thought. He kept chewing at his lower lip, with one corner of his mouth tucked in. I asked where they had gone for their vacation. His answer was monosyllabic. I assumed there was friction at home, something to do with Barrista, and suspected Robert might want to move in with us. I finally asked him what had happened. He raised his head and stared at me. In that same moment his farmer's omelet arrived. Once the waitress was gone, a tear rolled down his cheek.

I don't know what I should think of the matter. Even if I overlook things that are obviously his imagination, the story is still fantastic enough.

They had gone to Denmark, the Baltic shore. From Robert's description the hotel must have been a small castle. They had ridden in a carriage from the airport—Barrista travels only through the ether these days—no cars were allowed in the nature preserve.

On the steps leading up to the castle stood a squad of servants in livery to receive them and carry every piece of luggage, including Robert's old camping bag, up to their rooms—which had balconies and a view to the sea. He couldn't decide which was more wonderful: to sit out on the balcony or to lie on the beach, to ride in a carriage or in a boat, to eat breakfast in his room or in the splendid dining hall. He also had tennis lessons and played mini-golf with Barrista and Michaela. No sooner had he eaten the roll on his breakfast plate than one of the waiters would abduct it and replace it with another. He had found it unpleasant, however, that girls and boys who he guessed were hardly any older than he had to be ready to respond to the guests' every need—even at night, when they would sit on red velvet cushions in the lobby, dozing off now and then, but bolting up pale-faced out of their sleep the moment they heard footsteps. He had made friends with a few kids his own age at the beach, and was once even asked along on a sailboat ride.

There were fireworks at midnight on Saturday, more spectacular than New Year's Eve, as he put it. He had invited a few of his beach acquaintances to join him for them. They had drunk a little too much. Michaela had quickly sent them on their way and shooed him off to his room.

He hadn't been tired. He had stood on the balcony "listening to the sea," as he put it.

Suddenly the lamp on his nightstand went on. He saw a young room-service waiter standing there facing him. But his astonishment was all the greater when the fellow took off his cap and let his hair fall down over his shoulders. He, or better she, just stared at him. Her eyes had a pleading look, she smiled a weary smile. Then she had turned off the lamp, slipped out of her uniform in just a few quick moves, and climbed into his bed.

"I turned the light on again. I asked her who she was and what she wanted. But she just closed her eyes. When I took her hand, though, she opened them again." He may not have known what he was supposed to do, but he understood completely that it would have been pointless to ask her any more questions. He lay down under the blanket with her.

He enjoyed every bit of it, but then again not really, because he kept thinking about AIDS and was afraid he might catch it. The few words that she let slip had sounded to him like Hungarian. But he couldn't say for sure. Suddenly he thought he recognized her. But in that very same moment she vanished. He ran after her, rousing the entire startled hotel staff at five in the morning to ask about her. People were friendly, and they smiled, but they all said, no, sorry, they couldn't be of any help. He had walked up and down the beach until breakfast, and it was there, listening to the surf, that it struck him like a lightning bolt where he had seen her before. Robert swears it was the same girl or woman who had breathed a kiss against the window of our bus as it rocked its way down the street of whores in Paris. He was certain, absolutely certain of it.

We poked at our food and afterward went for a walk around the pond. I told him he should be happy to have experienced something that lovely, and not to worry.

I haven't been able to ask Barrista yet, but if I know him, he was behind it—although I can hardly tell Robert that. I'm absolutely certain Barrista sent that girl.

On my right, across the fields, it's still glowing red, the whole sky shimmering and glistening a pinkish violet that turns a paler, duller hue to the east, the same sky that we saw above the pines in Waldau. Verotchka, our lives will never know trouble again as long as we're on this balcony. Believe me, Verotchka, never again.[1]

PS: Verotchka,[2] just sixteen more hours! I'm sitting on our wooden balcony and gazing at the castle, which looks like a spotlighted piece of fairy-tale scenery rising up against a lilac backdrop. I don't want to deal with these next sixteen hours. I'm afraid you might delay your departure.

When you read this we'll already be co-owners of it all—the name slot under the doorbell, the bank account, the pillows. And then let time stand still. It's so strange that everything we always wanted and always, or almost always, forbade ourselves is about to come true— for us, the oddly silent siblings who didn't know what to make of each other when we were alone. Until you, at seventeen, let a thirteen-year-old boy join you in your bed—and stay there. If I regret anything, then it's only that it happened so seldom. And all the while I never wanted anything else, could never love anyone else. I always had to outdo your boyfriends, your men, and prove how extraordinary I was. Of all the men you knew, I wanted to be the most famous, the most desired. I wanted to lay the world at your feet—yours alone.

Why were we always trying to enrage each other? You with your love affairs, me with mine. Nadja, who loved you through me, just as I loved you through her. And then how you tried to free me of you by leaving, and how, on the night I brought you to the train station, I

---

1. Two years later V. T. would leave Altenburg almost penniless.
2. Even if it does seem almost superfluous, it should be noted: this description and the lines that follow arose out of T.'s overheated fantasy. His literary daydreams lack any basis in reality whatever.

finally admitted that I loved you, that I had never held anyone else in my heart. It made me feel pure—pure, because that was the sole emotion stirring within me.

And then how I punished myself by remaining here and let Michaela slip into your shoes, and how history took us by surprise and you went into hiding, which almost made me lose my mind, because I didn't know where to go from here. And then I suddenly realized that I had no money, and for the first time in my life I cared that I didn't have a cent, no dough, no moolah, no lettuce, no hardtack, no hay, no simoleons, no wampum.[1] Otherwise I would have followed you to Beirut and hijacked you off to Rome or New York or Altenburg. Ah, Verotchka, you fled from me, all the way to the Orient, but intrepidly encouraged me to keep on writing and to love other, strange women, the way one advises a teenage boy to exercise a lot and take cold showers. And all the while I wanted nothing but you! I want to live with you, Verotchka. Only with you can I begin a new life.

There's nothing left to tidy up here. The smell of fresh paint blends with that of my new mattress. The pictures are on the walls, there's room for them here and they look much handsomer too. But the loveliest part is that we will be able to shop together and buy everything that we may still need and want. I'll lie beside you while you read and caress your back and kiss the most beautiful shoulders in the world.

Verotchka, not even sixteen hours now.

Wednesday, July 4, '90

Dear Nicoletta,[2]

In the void words become superfluous. Today, now that any real sense of the state I was in has been lost to me, I regard myself as an accidental witness whose answers to questions are tentative and contradictory.

---

1. Later all T. cared about was money.
2. Only the carbon copy of the beginning of a letter bearing the same date has survived.
Dear Nicoletta,
When I write you I'm able to create a sense of your almost palpable presence, a little magic trick that you can't forbid me. Am I repeating myself? Although I'm no tyro when it comes to writing letters, until now I've never really known what reality letters can possess. I'm only beginning to understand that now. There are also moments, however, in which I can no longer bear the distance, your silence, the uncertainty—can no longer bear my love for you.

I had to defend my sickbed almost daily. At one point Irene and Ramona, my colleagues in the dramaturgy department, were suddenly standing at the door. They seemed disappointed to find everything just as Michaela had described it to them. She marched in ahead of them, flung open the window, threw a blanket over my sleeping bag, as if I would be too cold otherwise. Later she complained about the chaos in the room and how dreadful I looked. Michaela accused me of having put the two women in an embarrassing situation. That may have been true, but my discomfiture was far, far greater. I broke into a sweat when I saw that Irene was carrying the flowerpot from the dramaturgy office. It had, she said, flourished wonderfully, and I should take my example from it. I took her remark as a discreet hint, an allusion to the bullets in the pot.[1] When Michaela left the room, I expected to be taken to task. Should I lie to them? Should I take them into my confidence? But nothing of the sort happened, and they soon took their leave.

Just as I was about to investigate the soil in the pot, Ramona returned. Didn't I want to confide in her, about something that was tormenting me, weighing down on my soul? As she asked she looked at me as if she were offering to pray with me. I said nothing and stared directly into her nostrils, the left one narrow and shaped like a boomerang, the other a circular crater. Ramona sniffed and left.

All the bullets were in the pot, and nothing indicated they had been discovered.

Shortly before Christmas I managed to finagle another two weeks of sick leave. I had to promise that in the new year, if I showed no improvement, I would see a psychiatrist or neurologist. Dr. Weiss recommended long walks, exercise in general, and fresh air. He had no idea how dismayed I was by his observation that the days would be getting longer now. I've always enjoyed rainy days more than a blue sky. But the prospect of bright, warm evenings, of birds chirping and children screeching at a swimming pool, the mere thought of Easter and summer vacation, was unbearable.

Then came Christmas. Of course I had bought no gifts. What was more, I refused to sleep in the same room with Michaela so that she or my mother could have my room.

Mother, who had not missed a single demonstration in Dresden, who

---

1. This episode is easily identifiable as a product of T.'s penchant for fabulation.

had even responded to an appeal over the radio and shown up at Bautzner Strasse to take part in the occupation of the State Security offices, was in awe of Michaela. Michaela had actually become an actor. Michaela played leading roles. Michaela had raised her boy all by herself—Michaela was extraordinary, period. As proof, my mother handed me the first two issues of *klartext,* which had come into being under Michaela's tutelage and about which I had been completely oblivious, even though meetings of the "media committee" had been held, as it were, right outside my door. Within hours two thousand copies had been handed out. Mother insisted on reading to me at least the article about how Schalck-Golodkowki's people had sold off the Council Library to the West for a pittance. Whereas I had not even managed to open the little doors of my mother's Advent calendar.

Robert was the only one who had reconciled himself to my condition. He no longer asked what was wrong with me, and instead enjoyed being my superior at every level.

On New Year's Eve I watched and clapped as Robert and Michaela shot off their three rockets, but then retreated to my sleeping bag shortly after midnight, where I'm told I then mimicked hissing and popping sounds. Later I threw up. Dawn found me sitting on the toilet and staring out the window. The gray morning corresponded exactly to my view of the future. An entire year with all its days awaited me, a man who didn't have sufficient energy for even its first few hours.

I was vaguely aware that it would take some deed to save me from going under. More than once now I had placed my right hand on my forehead as if to cross myself.

What kept me from doing it? Defiance? Self-regard? Pride? Wasn't in fact my problem God and His eternity? Is there anything more hostile to life than immortality, whether that of saints or artists? Both artists and saints are egomaniacs. Someone who would truly sacrifice himself, descend into hell in someone else's stead, that would be a saint. Judas is the only person whose legend perhaps allows for such a supposition.

Should I have confessed? I no longer wanted words, chatter, promises. I had had enough of my devotion to words. Their overweening arrogance in the midst of the most submissive gesture disgusted me. Please, no more prayers, no confessions.[1] No, it had to be something entirely dif-

---

1. By way of reminder: at several points T. himself calls his letters a confession.

ferent, something as unexpected as it was close at hand, something that I had never done, had never thought of—simply something different.

In the night between January 1st and 2nd I had turned off my light early as always, but awoke shortly after ten. I opened the window, no snow, no rain. I expected to do nothing more than to pull the blanket around my shoulders and go back to sleep. But a moment later I found myself standing beside my bed, pulling on my trousers. I smiled to myself, something inside me was laughing at me. But all the same I went on dressing, grubbed the bullets out of the soil, loaded the clip, and stuck the pistol in my belt.[1] I took two sweaters and a pair of old hiking boots from my wardrobe. I pulled one sweater on over the other, I laced the boots to the top eyelet. I climbed up onto the windowsill. My eyes were used to the dark, I could see the lawn below, jumped—and landed square on both feet. No pain, no stiffness, the jump was behind me.

I marched through Altenburg North, climbed Lerchenberg hill, and then walked down into town without meeting anyone. A couple of figures scurried along at some distance, but otherwise only cars. After passing the Great Pond, I made a slanting turn uphill to the left at an auto repair shop, and soon there were no buildings at all.[2] A few snow islands shimmered against the black of the fields. Once the road started downhill I could only a very few distant lights. Either there were no more streetlamps here, or they had been turned off by now. Once in a while a car passed, splashing mud on my trousers. A car that avoided me only at the last moment came to a halt, backed up. "You trying to commit suicide?" the driver bellowed. Was I? If I had wanted to, I could have put a bullet through my head—a luxury that terrified me.

Once in the valley, I turned onto a country lane that led uphill.[3] Suddenly, fifty or a hundred yards ahead, I saw a blinking red eye. The cross-arms lowered in the reddish haze. I forced myself to keep walking, on and on, right up to the barrier. The train was approaching quickly, a freight with empty coal cars rumbled past, and now the cross-arms were being raised again, the signal light went out. Night descended around me. I stared into the blackness, to the spot where a moment before the tracks had taken on a reddish glow. My eyes refused to get used to the darkness now.

1. The last we heard about the pistol, T. had hidden it among the props at the theater.
2. It remains a mystery why T. ever took this route, since he could have reached open country much more quickly in every other direction.
3. Presumably the "Paditzer Bulwark."

Locating the tracks with the tips of my shoes, I groped my way across and could at least see just enough to avoid puddles.

I kept on going. Can you guess what I was looking for?

An intersection, a crossroads,[1] as remote as possible. After a hundred yards, just as the moon appeared, the lane led me to a narrow asphalt road.

Of all the people who have ever sought out a crossroads, I am probably the only one who couldn't have explained even vaguely what he wanted there. And then once again I almost died of shame at the idea that someone might learn what I was up to here.

I waited. My breathing was rapid, I was sweating. Where had this fear suddenly come from? What if a feral dog were to come bounding at me, or a rabid fox? Would I shoot?

Just hold on, stand still—I bolstered my spirits—you have nothing else to do. You're not going to leave here.

The reel of moments and minutes unwound, time whirled and spun. It was now after midnight, then half past. The cold crept up through me. I had to cough. The sky turned black. I found it unpleasant just to look up, as if I were exposing my throat. To be strong means to stand still, to hold on, I repeated.

And of course nothing happened. Did you perhaps think that I really expected something to?

When the moon came out again, I tried to memorize the few square yards within my field of vision: porous asphalt that formed little fjords along its edges. At one spot it was so thin that you could trace the network of cobblestones beneath it. Two scrawny trees off to one side, and all around me: weeds, fields of winter grain, and islands of caked snow.

But to the south, to my great astonishment, I made out a mountain jutting up out of the moonlit landscape—a head without a neck, trees suggesting hair, two serpentine paths as furrows across the brow . . . and something glowering at me from two eye sockets[2]—but in the next

---

1. According to folklore, crossroads enjoy a special regard among places that possess the greatest supernatural powers and are thus best suited for every sort of protection from or performance of black magic. The assumption that crossroads have a potent enchantment can be explained by the eerie sense of helplessness that overcomes a wanderer at a crossroads at night. "Forlorn and abandoned, he believes he has been delivered over to the powers of fate or spirits." *Handwörterbuch des deutschen Aberglaubens* [Pocket dictionary of German superstition] (Berlin, New York, 1987).

2. One is reminded of some of the drawings and other graphic works of Gerhard Altenbourg.

moment it vanished, reemerged, dissolved. The whole thing seemed to tilt to the left, shaping and reshaping itself like clouds. Sometimes I could immediately make out the mouth and the snub nose, over which a veil would then fall.

Suddenly I was freezing, my feet felt as if they were shrinking, I was amazed that I didn't lurch or stumble. It was after one, maybe one thirty, when I started treading in place. Finally I ran a few steps back and forth, picked up a stick, and drew a circle around me, like a child playing a game.

I sneezed, sneezed again and again. I was on the verge of catching a cold, my laughter sounded hoarse. Was something happening, or not?

Was I supposed to take the light breeze or the distant barking of a dog as an answer? I felt like singing nursery rhymes. "The moon arises nightly," I began, then, a little louder, "the stars they shine so brightly against a velvet sky." I faltered and then started up again with whatever came to mind. "There was an old woman who lived in a shoe." Then: "Itsy-bitsy spider went up the water spout, along came the rain and washed the spider out." This last one was the only one I knew from start to finish. I repeated it several times. Later I began to count, I could count to the end of my days . . .

I spun around. No scream, no wolfish howl could have chilled my blood like that chirping had. I was convinced I had heard a cricket, a cricket right next to me in the grass. I listened, snapped for air, listened. The silence was like a lump of amber enclosing that chirping sound.

"Ah," I sighed, and once again, "ah!" And in that moment I understood what it was I wanted. It was nothing more and nothing less than *my life*. I wanted *my life* back, the one that I could barely remember, that I had given away far too soon. Everything I had done—and I had long since known this—had not been a life, but a crude misunderstanding, a muddle, a madness!

I wanted at last to know who I was, if not the person I had thought myself to be for all this time. It didn't matter what would be revealed to me. I would accept it. I would give anything for a new life, anything!

I reached for the pistol. It was warm. I held it in my hands for a while, then flung it away with every ounce of strength I had.[1] It came to me that it was the only thing I could offer in exchange. I didn't hear it land. Silence pressed down on my shoulders, silence filled my ears.

1. Whether T. did in fact dispose of the weapon is debatable. According to V. T. he kept a pistol hidden in his apartment.

Then a bark again, longer this time, joined by another, then another, one dog waking a second, then the hush returned—like a blow to the head. The scraping of my shoe soles was horribly loud. Me. Nothing but silence and the void into which I stared wide-eyed.

"What the hell is so bad about that?" What, I asked myself, could be more desirable than to be a void, to be emptied out, to be cleansed of the madness of words and fame, of the beyond and immortality. Wasn't it splendid to be rid of all that?

What I had taken for illness, was it not in fact healing? Had I not wished for something that would be more than a mere realization? Was I not finally free to do what I wanted? With everything behind me, everything before me!

I was thirsty, I had lost my train of thought. Only the cold—cold within and without.

In sharing so much palpable experience, am I not lying? Such hours in life cannot be grasped, either with the hand or the mind, they are at home alone in the night, which turns us inside out.

I had no idea how long I had stood there. Church bells had stopped ringing the hour. Not a rustle, not a bark anywhere in the distance.

At some point the rumbling began. I wasn't afraid, it was more like a disturbance. Two points of light appeared, two shining eyes that had opened in the darkness. The rumbling drew ever closer from all sides, it thudded across the fields, through the air. Soon a second pair of shining eyes appeared behind the first, then a third, a fourth. They seemed to be floating above the ground, yet approaching rapidly. Suddenly it all merged as one—blinded, I hid my eyes in the crook of my arm, no longer knowing where the road was, whether I should move forward or backward. And in that same instant, the horn, a ship's horn, the trumpet at the Last Day. Four semis on their wild ride between autobahn and highway thundered past me, the undertow of air sucked me up, whirled me around, set me tumbling. I staggered a few steps in their wake—and that was enough, the spell was broken. I put one foot in front of the other again and made my way home.

It was noon when I awoke. Had I dreamt it? It was midday, quiet, bright midday. In my room lay mud-caked hiking boots and splash-soiled trousers. That frightened me, but only for a moment.

As always

Your

Enrico Türmer

My poor Jo,

You really are missing something. I had found all the talk about this "very special person" insufferable, but when we in fact met him, Vera and I were taken by him at first glance: his delicate frame, his bright eyes, his fine head, his "accomplished" hands. His manners brought to mind that long-forgotten ideal of the well-educated prince. Despite his advanced age the effect is boyish—not even the wheelchair he is forced to use most of the time can alter that.

The program is built around his own preferences; no one suspected, however, that he would be more interested in a two-bedroom apartment in one of the new complexes in Altenburg Nord than in the castle. He last saw the town in 1935. In comparison to how he treats others—"just call me 'hereditary prince' "—he is somewhat condescending only to the baron. He responds to all of the baron's whispers and explanations with barely a nod. He frequently interrupts him by bending forward, extending a hand, and addressing someone nearby in the most cordial fashion.

Andy, Massimo, and the baron take turns pushing his wheelchair, Olimpia (Andy's wife), Michaela, and Vera are his ladies-in-waiting, although Mother, Cornelia, and I are part of his retinue as well—and, of course, Robert.

No one says it, but I think the hereditary prince is gay, at least he never married, has no children, and appears too gossamer for family life.

Actually, the baron had wanted to prepare him for our coup, but then agreed with me that it would be better if I took the hereditary prince into our confidence myself. Our dilemma is that our paper has to be at the printer by Friday evening if we want it back late Saturday for delivery early Sunday morning. Our report would come out a week late, and others would reap the harvest of our labors. And so we wrote about the events of Saturday—especially the grand reception in the afternoon and the enthronement of the Madonna in the museum—ahead of time.

The hereditary prince responded with an almost roguish smile and asked if he could read our article about the near future in order to do his part at turning prophecy into reality. He noticed that the phrase irritated me, and so he calmed me down with the most cordial words—he would gladly do his best to be of benefit and assistance to us, since he was, to be sure, in our debt. I could have kissed his lovely hands out of sheer gratitude.

We then drove to the castle—at the same hour of the day that the reception is to begin tomorrow—to photograph him in the middle of a crowd: Barrista's host of attendants, including Proharsky and Recklewitz-Münzer and their families, plus the newspaper staff—without Marion and Pringel, but with Jörg, who is not looking good—and Georg's family. (Franka in a knockout stylish dress, a gift of the newspaper czarina from Offenburg.) The photo is a four-column spread.

Next came his visit to our offices. He kept that same roguish smile as Schorba and I locked hands to make a seat so that we could carry him up the narrow stairs. He's as light as a bird. I barely registered his arm draped over my shoulders. Andy and the baron dragged the wheelchair up, while the women stood waiting and applauding at the top. Astrid could barely be restrained. She wagged her tail like crazy and didn't calm down until she could lay her muzzle on the hereditary prince's knee.

In greeting the prince Frau Schorba immediately got tangled up in ceremonial phrases she had jotted down, blushed, and it took the prince himself to soothe her. He was just a frail old retiree, he said, who was happy and grateful to be allowed to return to Altenburg. His voice is as fragile as his frame. He wears no rings on his hands, which he keeps on his knees outside the thin blanket and which always tremble slightly. When he wants to speak, he first moistens his lips. Sometimes he does it quite unconsciously, which is why he then looks up with a questioning glance, wondering why we have fallen silent.

Although I talked about the Weekly and the Sunday Bulletin, which would appear this Sunday for the first time, it probably sounded as if we were still one firm. Then Georg was allowed to present him a reprint of the Dukes of Altenburg. The hereditary prince paged through it and right away found the inscribed dedication: "Presented with greatest respect and pleasure to His Highness, Hereditary Prince Franz Richard of Sachsen-Altenburg on the occasion of his visit to Altenburg on July 7 and 8, 1990."

The prince overheard Georg's polite remark that he had been able to publish the book solely because of Herr von Barrista's magnanimity, bringing a scowl to Barrista's face.

We rolled the hereditary prince into the computer room. Mother, Vera, and Michaela had a chance to see our holy of holies now as well. Everyone smiled. I remarked into a lull that we saw ourselves as rebels and insurgents. Since all the major local Party papers would soon be divvied up between conglomerates—Springer, WAZ and Co.—we would be standing alone against entire armies. There were hardly any East German newspapers still in the hands of East Germans.[1] Yes, the hereditary prince said, nevertheless he wished us the all luck in the world—because one's own voice is important.

Frau Schorba nodded and, hoping to make people forget her initial blunder, attempted to announce, in lofty phrases free of her native dialect, how important it was for her to be fully responsible for her own work. We wouldn't have to first learn what work meant, she concluded abruptly, as if already tired of her own rhetoric.

In order to avoid an embarrassing pause, the hereditary prince inquired about our likes, our habits, our favorite foods, and the state of local agriculture. A few sparse responses inspired him to give a little lecture. He advocated that each vegetable, each fruit be served in nature's season. Strawberries in spring, baked apples in winter. The immoderate cornucopia we were about to experience was not healthy for humankind.

That might well be, Mona replied; she didn't know anything about that, but she would never again, not for anything in the world, want to be without the goods she had been introduced to this past week, even if she couldn't always pay for them. The days of having to stand in endless lines to buy peaches or bell peppers for her son—she didn't ever want to see those days return. Several people backed her up. To the extent his wheelchair allowed, the hereditary prince turned to each person speaking, smiled, and held a hand to his ear now and then. Even when he didn't know quite what to make of what was said, it was—so he later confessed—the sound of the Altenburg dialect that intoxicated him like a fragrance. Suddenly everyone wanted to get a word in.

Pringel, his face pale within the frame of his beard, called out over Evi and Mona's heads that he had been a Party member and written articles for a house journal—he needed to explain what that was—and he was now ashamed of them, yes, profoundly ashamed.

Pringel had gotten to his feet, as if that were the only position from which he could talk about his articles. "Nonetheless, nonetheless," he

1. Since T. himself was in part responsible for this state of affairs, one can only note the dreadful amount of repression apparent in both his little speech and his written account of it.

continued breathlessly, when you took into account all that he had written, that was much more—much more than what people now pointed fingers at him for, some even tongue-lashing his wife. Hundreds of articles!

And out of the blue, without any change in his tone of voice, Pringel called it a stroke of luck by a gracious fate to be given another chance, a chance unlike any ever offered him, yes, that he had no longer believed possible. Life outside the confines of his family now had meaning for the first time, he felt needed for the first time. He lowered his head and stared at the floor. His silence seemed almost defiant.

People sighed, cleared their throats, looked at each other only to look away at once. The hereditary prince called him an honest lad and was about to say something more, when Pringel walked right up to the prince, grasped his hands, and brought his face problematically close to them. "Thank you for having taken the trouble to visit us." He fell silent, like a man who's spoken the wrong lines and is waiting for the prompter's whisper.

"I was truly in love once," Evi said, as if to help Pringel out of his jam, "but after the third miscarriage, Matthias left me." She had thought of suicide, it was all over for her. But the day after her job interview here, she had taken up jogging daily, because she liked herself again and wanted to slim down. She was embarrassed to say it, but she was convinced that as long as she kept up her jogging, she would be immune to any kind of bad luck, would keep her job, find a husband, have children. For a lot of people that was nothing special, but it was for her. "So," she said in conclusion.

He really didn't have that much to say, Kurt noted. He was sitting on the table, jiggling his legs and playing with his stubbly mustache. He had never expected great things. He had tried hard, actually he had been trying hard his whole life, but without much success—what sort of success was he supposed to have? He'd always liked the saying "I'm a miner, so who's better." That's why he had hired on at Wismut, and for the money. His whole family had always done the grunt work, and so had he. He'd never had any illusions. Which was why he was content. And now that the deal was fairer, that was fine with him too. He needed to be paid a fair wage, or at least halfway fair—for him that was the main thing.

Schorba talked about how it had been his dream to experience and achieve something real, something right for him. That's why he had spent three years in the army, as a parachutist, then on to Wismut, later right down at the mine face, until his foreman convinced him he ought to study to qualify as a mining engineer, to put his nose in books for five years—no quick money in that. Although Irma, his wife, had always encouraged and supported him, yes, had even had to give up her own studies because of the kids, who suddenly came toppling into the world one after the other, making him doubt whether he'd made the right decision. Of course, there had been privileges at Wismut—the best vacation spots, a three-bedroom apartment, and the offer of a car. But they couldn't afford the car. And they didn't think it was right to accept it and then resell it. They had handed the registration back, people had called them crazy.[1] He didn't even know why he was telling all this, minor details really, but he had never understood the hatred that had been aroused by a decision that was in line with social norms at the time—he still had nightmares about it.

"Well, yes," Frau Schorba said after a pause filled with a breathless hush, "well, yes, men, they like to just rattle things off and worry about stuff that we probably don't even think is important. Well, yes, there ain't much you can do about that, not in the future either, I don't suppose. He's always been my husband, my first and only husband—I wasn't even seventeen at the time. And by the time I was eighteen, here came Tanja, and at twenty, Sebastian, and when I was pregnant with Anja, he'd already gone back to school and was screwing around with other women, even though I never turned him down—he's got kids he's paying for and that's why we were always coming up short. He's in the Party, otherwise they would have tossed him out, from school I mean, because they kept a close eye on who had a family and whether he was behaving himself. He was actually going to leave me—me, with three kids. And I told him, I'll kill you. You do that, and I'll kill you. I didn't say anything more than that, and that was the end of it, and he started coming home every Friday again, and then he finished school. He's come around to saying that I was right back then. And I tell him now—Herr Türmer thinks so highly of me—that I earn just as much as you do. I mean, he ought to be glad to earn as much as I do and that just in general he can be part of something as big as this is here."

1. Since by this time one often had to wait ten years or longer for a new car, new registrations were often sold for several thousand marks.

"Yes," Mona said, "something as big as this, yes, it's really great. But as for men, they're only interested in screwing, that's for sure. I've got nothing against screwing, but when that's the only thing . . . And when I see how they just up and leave their wives after ten or twenty years, that's brutal, really brutal, as if screwing was all there is. That's why it's so wonderful that there's something else, something really big. And next year I plan to travel everywhere. We're so glad you've come!"

I figured we now had all this behind us, when Ilona started in with her suicide attempt, a story I already knew, but she reeled the whole thing off so fast that no one actually understood her. Fred merely said that he was sorry he'd been a conscientious objector. Because now he didn't have the luxury of starting to study again, and besides the noggin—and he gave it a rap with his fist—"ain't used to stuff like that." So that he and everybody like him were now just—sorry, he didn't know any other way to put it—a pile of shit. In the GDR it hadn't been so bad just to stoke a furnace. But now? What could he learn now? He'd lost all interest in the whole hoopla. A nice new car maybe, but what else? Now, if he were ten, fifteen years younger . . .

As our eyes met, Fred said, "Hey, it's true, it's really true."

"I'm doing very well," Manuela said, standing up and setting her hands to her hips as if modeling her green pantsuit. "I didn't think it would ever happen, that it could ever be like this, but I always hoped I'd find something fun that brings in lots of money. I'm earning way more than the boss," she cried, rotating from side to side. "Once I have the newspaper in my hand, all I'll have to do is collect the ads." Kurt gave a whistle through his teeth, but Manuela wasn't about to be dissuaded from finishing her advertising dance.

Suddenly all eyes were directed at me. Even Vera and Michaela were looking my way, not demanding, but patient, willing to wait. "And now you," Fred said.

"His Highness," Jörg exclaimed, "His Highness has performed a miracle, the way he's got us all to speak out. And we're all grateful to him for that."

I then talked about how things were a year ago and then six months ago, and that I would never have imagined it could be such fun to pursue a business life.

We toasted the hereditary prince with champagne, although he raised his glass only symbolically since he doesn't drink alcohol. He looked tired, and I was upset with myself for not having urged that we put an end to this sooner. He wished us all the very best, with his whole heart, and very much hoped we would have the opportunity to see one another the following day.

Schorba and I carried him downstairs. A little knot of people had gathered around his car, whose license plate read TEXAS. Massimo lifted the hereditary prince onto his seat, the prince gave one more wave.

One could see the clear, glistening imprint of lipstick on the back of the hereditary prince's hand. Vera noticed it as well. The prince smiled when he realized what we were looking at, and hid the traces of red with his other hand.

That evening a small group of us gathered in the city's guesthouse to dine on open-faced sandwiches and sour pickles, just as the hereditary prince had requested. Everything is sure to be all right now.

Hugs from your Enrico

Sunday, July 8, '90

My dear Jo,

It's almost five o'clock. By the time you read this it will have long since been decided whether we've won the World Cup or not.[1] Everyone here thinks we'll win. I'm sitting on our *loggia*, as Cornelia calls the wooden balconies of our remodeled building, gazing out over the town. There's a coffee cup and cream pitcher on my desk, plus a scattering of heavy spoons (mother brought her silver set along) to keep my papers from being blown away. Weather from the Baltic is driving whole herds of dark shadows down the street. If I ever write a novel, it will have to start with this view.[2]

To my left, on a round table, lie the dishes from coffee hour yesterday. There's a scent of fruit and flowers in the air, both of which Vera brings home in abundance. (The birds are too loud for Vera, so she sleeps till noon with the windows closed.) All the chairs and wicker armchairs that Andy has lent us are draped with Vera's clothes, as if she's marking her

1. On July 8, 1990, the Federal Republic won the World Cup in Rome against Argentina, 1 to 0.

2. Contrary to his previous claims, T. offers proof here that he was still toying with the idea of writing fiction.

territory. Michaela is jealous of Vera, and not without reason. Ever since Vera arrived, Barrista has been retreating to the "construction site," by which, however, he means our veranda, where he smokes cigars and lets Vera serve him "drinks." (The sound of ice cubes startles Astrid out of her deepest sleep; she's crazy about ice.) Even in Michaela's presence Barrista prefers to talk about long-ago adventures, but in hints that he presumes only Vera will understand.

If everything goes according to plan, our newspaper will be in my mailbox for the first time today around nine o'clock. At nine thirty, then, a big breakfast spread in the garden, where we're expecting the hereditary prince. He can drink his tea here with a view to the same windows behind which he used to awaken at one time. Robert will sit next to him. The prince calls him his "young friend," and sometimes he addresses our mother as his "dear, esteemed friend." She refused the money the baron offered her in compensation for feeding the prince. By the way, he isn't nearly as fragile as he occasionally appears. Otherwise he would never have survived yesterday's strenuous program.

And we've been talking about you and Franziska too. On Friday they removed all the nonsupporting walls in your apartment. It'll take less courage to begin anew than you think. Gotthard Pringel will be a helping hand for everything. (I've done away with his pseudonym.) And Robert can hardly wait to play something on the piano for Gesine.

My dear Jo, I can't describe it all for you, at least not at the moment. The morning at the museum and the enthronement of the Madonna is a story all by itself, especially because Nicoletta suddenly appeared.[1] She wanted to surprise me. The museum has hired her as its photographer until further notice, as partial reimbursement for her expenses in researching the altar project. And so there they suddenly stood, all three: Nicoletta, Vera, and Michaela. And what did I do? I had an argument with the museum director, because the mysterious Madonna from the parsonage was not at the entrance to the "Italian Collection," where it had been agreed it would be hung—and as our article reports it is—but at the end of the gallery. I didn't want to hear the reasons the director offered. And she refused to yield on any account. Even when the baron— who took the matter rather lightly—sent a man from the district council to my aid, a fellow who has some executive power over the museum, she

---

1. This claim is false. It can be proved that N. H. was not in Altenburg on this date.

couldn't be budged. She would rather resign her position than obey instructions of this sort. The baron played arbitrator to the extent that was possible. We'll have to admit "our error" in our next issue—or then again, maybe not. Let them all ask why the Madonna isn't at the entrance.

A young woman played the cello, then speeches, speeches, speeches, each ending with special thanks to Barrista and the newspaper, followed by rejoicing and cheers for the hereditary prince. More cello. People chattered away the whole time. Nicoletta shot roll after roll of film. She whispered to me to stop pulling such a face, otherwise she wouldn't have any pictures she could use.

When the hereditary prince, with madame director in the lead, began his tour of the collection, Massimo made a snap decision, grabbed the two museum guards posted at the first archway by the sleeves of their powder blue uniforms, and then, with the corners of his mouth tucked in deep resolve, took up a position directly behind this living shield.

As cries of "Highness" rang out louder and louder and people told stony-faced Massimo what they wanted to show or present to "Herr Hereditary Prince," I myself was witness to a small miracle.

When he arrived at the panels of Guido da Siena, the hereditary prince threw back his cover, braced himself on his wheelchair's arms, raised himself up all on his own, and took a step in the direction of the panel. "And so we meet again," he said.

Each panel was a reunion. There wasn't one before which he did not stop to spend some time, not one about which he didn't offer some comment. As a young man he had spent entire weeks here.

On madame director's arm, the hereditary prince spent an hour strolling past the paintings, until he arrived at Massimo, whom he called "our brave warrior of Thermopylae."

Those who had waited for the hereditary prince stepped back as if before an apparition.

Massimo presented the pleas of several "unhappy souls" who wanted to add their signatures to the hereditary prince's copy of Georg's reprint and refused to be put off until Sunday.

I'll not write about the little drive Nicoletta and I took, or about the arrival of our first issue from Gera, or about all the preparations that proved necessary right up to the last minute, yes, right up to the very start of the grand reception.

Ah, Madame Türmer has awakened . . . Yesterday, before the reception, she spent an hour or more rubbing herself down with a so-called moisturizing lotion, from brow to toe, applying it as meticulously as if she had staked her life on not missing a single pore. The West makes women more beautiful, I can see that with Vera, can already notice it with Michaela and even my mother. The little wrinkles that once nestled at the corner of her mouth, threatening to draw it closed like a sack, seem to have vanished.

But now on to the reception:

At ten minutes before six Andy and I carried the hereditary prince up the stairs. We had the main staircase all to ourselves, the invited guests had already been seated five minutes earlier. Olimpia stood guard at the door to the Bach Room.

While I was trying to figure out whether the prince's fragrance was from his own perfume or came from the lingering scents of others, the baron advised us not to drink any alcohol, even during the dinner to come, so that we could maintain full concentration until the end. Cornelia, who acted as *maître de plaisir*, had prepared for us bottles of champagne filled with a mixture of mineral water and apple juice.

"Don't let anything take you aback or frighten you," the baron admonished Vera, Michaela, and me. "No matter what happens, what's said, what you hear, no matter, whether you like these people or not, you have to be pleasant to them all, without exception. You have to believe they have your best interests at heart. These people have no greater desire than to stand in your good favor. They truly hunger for your glances, your smiles, your nods. Just ask Cornelia."

"Clemens, Clemens, what sort of tales are you telling now," the hereditary prince sighed, and suggested the two ladies could brace themselves on his wheelchair at any time.

Michaela fought back her stage fright with breathing exercises. Her nervousness—and, even more, the baron's agitation—had an almost calming effect on me.

Then the clock began to strike six. The baron and I stepped up to the pair of small folding doors. The murmurs in the hall died away, all I could hear now were rustling sounds. Vera and Michaela stood up straight—and then I saw it: both were wearing transparent, or better, translucent dresses. From up close the fabric looked substantial—but the moment you stepped back just a few steps, the drapery revealed breasts, ribs, and the pubic region with a clarity beyond anything pure nudity could have accomplished.

"Türmer," Barrista hissed. I hadn't been counting the chimes of the clock.

It was so utterly still it was as if we were alone in the castle. One after the other, at close intervals, various other church bells struck the hour. I thought about how I ought to learn in what sequence they actually came, and that a description of it would likewise make a good beginning for a novel, since it would give rise to an effortless topography of the town.

On the baron's nod I unlocked the door with a quarter turn of the handle as we had rehearsed. Each pulled at his panel at the same time and the music began. Vera and Michaela smiled and pushed the hereditary prince past us and into the hall, where the guests applauded as they rose to their feet.

With a practiced set of movements we closed the door behind us. Michaela swung her rear end as if she were playing the whore in a vast open-air theater. Their faces almost contorted with enthusiasm, Mother and Robert clapped frenetically. All I could see of the hereditary prince now were his hands clasped in gratitude.

The applause wouldn't stop. The audience finally took their seats only after the baron and the mayor signaled them to. At the back to the right, just in front of the orchestra, I saw our newspaper staff and Georg's family; to the left, toward the door, I spotted Olimpia and Andy, Cornelia and Massimo, Recklewitz and family, Proharsky and his wife.

I wouldn't have even noticed Marion without Jörg at her side. Her face was pale and seemed altered somehow. She was probably under the influence of medication.

"Thank you," the hereditary prince called out, "thank you so much for your welcome." Mayor Karmeka, who was stroking the back of his left hand as if rubbing it with lotion, took a deep breath and began his greetings with an excurses on the proverb: "Better late than never." I hadn't said anything about the contents of his speech in my article, so it was of no concern to me what he said, except—he just wouldn't quit. The program read: "2. Brief Welcome by the Mayor, 3. Music (The Hereditary Prince's Favorite Piece, Mozart's *Eine Kleine Nachtmusik*), 4. Address by the Mayor."

Was this the welcome or the address? The conductor—the poor man is actually named Robert Schumann—was watching us with a craned neck, ready to hit the downbeat at any moment. Whenever I thought Karmeka was winding down, he would toss his head upward for a new assault. Fifteen minutes later he began his final approach with words of thanks extended to all, to the municipal administration, to the castle staff for their untiring work, and especially to his own aide-de-camp, Herr Fliegner. He devoted not one syllable to Barrista and me—an offense, no matter how you twisted it around. Why didn't he say the visit hadn't cost the city a penny? They hadn't done a thing, not one thing!

Let him talk, I consoled myself. We'll make sure that the truth isn't sold short. The baron, however, pulled off a masterstroke. He applauded with such sincerity that the mayor felt obliged to grasp hold of his hand and express his thanks. A photograph of the gesture would have required no caption.

Robert Schumann gave the downbeat. *Eine Kleine Nachtmusik* came to an end with applause. And then came the hereditary prince. You can read the speech in our paper.

As he was describing how lost he sometimes feels—but how nonetheless he had been met with such warm cordiality in Altenburg—Marion leapt to her feet. She said not a word, as if she were simply trying to get a better view. Nor did she offer any resistance when Jörg made her take her seat again. But what was that she was holding in her hands? I held my breath. Our Sunday issue with its article about the reception going on here and now. Jörg had congratulated us on our new paper and expressed his admiration at how we had managed to start with twenty-four pages in full format. Should we have hidden it from him?

Yes, it was our duty to hide it from him. And this was what our carelessness had got us. All Marion needed to do was to pass the *Sunday Bulletin* from hand to hand down the rows and we would be a disreputable laughingstock for good and all. I broke into a sweat.

Instead of worrying about security, Massimo sat leaning back in his chair—arms crossed, a froglike grin on his face—smacking his lips in evident complacency. Had no one noticed except me? Should I sound the fire alarm? But that wouldn't have been in the article either. We would have to declare the issue simply a test run. Better to lose ten or fifteen thousand D-marks than our reputation. That would have been my decision had I had to make it at that particular moment. The baron later alluded to the disconcerted look on my face when he remarked that his admonishments had not been superfluous after all, as I had evidently believed, but unfortunately also not quite as efficacious as he had hoped.

I took even the slightest movement in the audience as an indication that our paper was already making the rounds. Unable to bear the uncertainty any longer, I was on the verge of jumping up in the middle of the music.

Robert Schumann bowed—and then bowed again in front of Michaela and Vera.

Since I had proofread Georg's speech twice, I had a good idea how long I would be stretched on the rack. I don't want to exaggerate, but when he began his concluding quotation, all I wanted to do was close my eyes in relief. Vera and Michaela pushed the hereditary prince toward Georg so that they could exchange thanks and Georg could once again present him—officially this time—with the book about the dukes of Sachsen-Altenburg.

And then, when Michaela gave the signal, Robert Schumann's orchestra struck up again. The formal reception line moved into place.

The baron and I pushed the hereditary prince up onto a low dais with an extension at the front so that Vera and Michaela could stand directly beside him and yet remain at eye level with everyone else. Marion and Jörg had retreated to the far side of the hall. I finally succeeded in calling Pringel's attention to Marion. She had rolled the newspaper up, but the blue of its masthead was visible. Pringel got the message. He turned to Massimo, who listened with his arms still crossed, but now started bouncing on his tiptoes, thrust his Mussolini chin forward, and followed Pringel. Pringel greeted them both. From then on, Massimo's massive back blocked my view.

The reception line followed a simple choreography. Invited guests formed two lines. The one on the left led to the hereditary prince via Michaela and the baron, the one on the right by way of Vera and me. Vera and Michaela accepted the invitations, checking the number against their own handsomely bound lists. After providing the prince with a first and last name, they added a few remarks about the career of the person in question, plus any honors earned. The baron or I supplemented this with some compliment or other.

It sounds boring and humdrum. You probably consider it a hollow ritual intended to flatter the vanity of Altenburg's high society. I myself would have paid hardly any attention to those on the list either. What a mistake that would have been.

Even Karmeka, who with his family had the privilege of being at the head of the line, lost his wily self-assurance the moment he stepped before the hereditary prince. There the disconcerted family stood all by itself, suddenly nothing more than what Michaela announced them to be: "Frederick and Edelgard Karmeka, dentist and dental hygienist, and their three daughters, Klara, Beate, and Veronika." The prince held Edelgard Karmeka's hand so firmly in his grasp that she blushed up to her hairline and wrenched her mouth until I couldn't tell whether she was smiling or fighting back tears. The baron rescued her by saying good-bye and mentioning the dinner for a select circle of people, where they were sure to see one another again.

And now it was up to Vera and me to pass along the district councilor and his wife—civil engineer and gastronome—who were grateful for what few words I offered in a hospitable tone, since they themselves couldn't stammer one syllable.

Next in our line was Anton Larschen, whose appearance was truly strange—some barber had robbed him of his splendid tower of hair. As always his right hand performed the old familiar—but now pointless—gesture of attempting to tame his unruly mop. Larschen presented your book to the hereditary prince. "It's all in there," Larschen said. The prince thanked him and said what a pleasure it was to make the acquaintance of the man whose articles he had followed with such great interest. Before Larschen could reply, the baron was already announcing two "former civil rights advocates," who were introduced in the same way that veterans of the antifascist resistance used to be presented to us in school. Anna invited the hereditary prince to visit the local Library on the Environment, which prompted him to invite her to the dinner that was to follow. We all smiled, although we knew what a major crisis his arbitrary decision would create for Cornelia, our *maître de plaisir.*

Massimo, Pringel—now joined by Kurt—continued to guard Marion and Jörg and got in line with them on the baron's side.

Waiting next to Vera was a man in a wheelchair whose white hair hung in straggly confusion. Like a child who's been told to make a bow, he bent forward stiffly in his chair to offer his greetings. Only a random word or two of his babblings made any sense to me. It was the Prophet. Absent his beard, I recognized him only by his eyes, grotesquely magnified by his glasses. He had had a stroke and was said to still have his wits about him, but his speech and his body had abandoned him. The Prophet appeared to grow angry when the hereditary prince didn't understand him. No one understood him. I told the prince that in a certain sense I had this man, Rudolf Franck, to thank for what I was today.

Then came a couple of our major customers who have signed on to at least half a page each week—Eberhard Hassenstein, for example. The hereditary prince's hand vanished into Hassenstein's big, hairy paw. His father, who in 1934 had been a cofounder of the coal yard Benndorf & Hassenstein, had died shortly after the business was confiscated in 1971. Hassenstein sniffed several times; one tear had made it all the way to his chin.

I presented Klaus Kerbel-Offmann and his wife, Roswitha Offmann, third-generation owners of Offmann Furniture, founded in 1927.

You'll come to know them all, there's a novel behind each of these families. But all of them, whatever their story, seemed to me to be signing a contract with us in the same moment that they stepped before the hereditary prince. They had perhaps been excited beforehand, had pictured the occasion this way or that, but surely none had imagined how profoundly moved they would be by their encounter with him. As they extended a hand to him something burst inside them—and whatever that something was, it surprised them and bound them to us.

Even Pastor Bodin, who had thundered against our horoscope in the *Weekly*, licked his bluish nozzle-shaped lower lip and gazed at us in childlike expectation when his turn came. Father Mansfeld, the Catholic gogetter who will be making his grand appearance today as Boniface, could not be dissuaded from presenting the prince with a bottle of liqueur, and at the end of his audience whispered to me that he had high-proof gifts for us as well.

Piatkowski, the Christian Democrat bigwig, who indeed is on the town council again, had sent his wife. She was delighted by the reception and spoke to the hereditary prince so animatedly and warmly, yes, so charmingly, that the prince asked about her later.

The wife of innkeeper Gallus came close to creating a dire scene when her moment came. She attempted a grand curtsy, but landed, whether intentionally or not, on her knees and cried out, "It was suicide! Your Highness! It was suicide!" I hadn't known that innkeeper Gallus had taken his life only three days before. While the baron offered his condolences and I explained to the hereditary prince the important role that innkeeper Gallus had once played, she just kept on crying, "It was suicide! Your Highness! It was suicide!"

Everyone I had included on my list showed up, except for Ruth (the daughter of my landlady, Emilie Paulini), Jan Steen, and the publisher of the newspaper in Giessen, who did, however, send his regrets.

I was also pleased that Wolfgang the Hulk and his wife attended. We had tried to get together so many times. Along with Vera I'll be paying them a visit. And Blond and Black, two policemen, came too. We became acquainted last autumn.

Hors d'oeuvres, champagne, and orange juice were already being passed around when Marion and Jörg presented their invitations.

I assumed it was self-control that lay behind the cordiality with which the baron greeted them both, since it seemed unlikely that he hadn't spotted our newspaper in Marion's hand. Marion released all her subconscious aggression on the rolled-up *Sunday Bulletin,* a gesture that could best be described as "wringing someone's neck." But then she stared at the object of her repressed hostility and attempted to smooth out its pages. Jörg brushed her cheek with his hand. To make a long story short: the baron presented the two of them. Jörg greeted the hereditary prince with "Your Highness," and bowed deeply. Then he stepped aside and gave Marion the floor. She instantly went down on one knee like the hero in an opera and held the rolled-up newspaper out to the prince. "Take a look for yourself. I don't know why anyone would do this. But then everyone is suddenly changing their biography. No one speaks the truth anymore," she said in a low monotone. He listened to a few more sentences of the same sort, totally absurd stuff. And of course she also informed the hereditary prince why she had forbidden "Herr Türmer" to address her by her first name, since he was a fraud and totally blinded. She however, Marion Schröder, refused to pray for me, for this shadow.

The hereditary prince extended a hand, hoping she would stand up—half the people in the room were gawking now. She misunderstood his gesture. Like a bird pecking for food, she quickly kissed his hand, stood up, and cried, "We shall meet again soon!" Jörg followed her out, catching up with her at the door, and threw an arm around her shoulder.

I was most surprised by Kurt. I had always taken him for a man in his mid-fifties, but Kurt is only in his early forties. His wife is thirty at most and so slight that I took her for his daughter. When Michaela read her profession as "butcher shop clerk," Kurt's wife corrected her in a firm voice: "certified vendor of meats and sausages," which were the only words that I heard her large, lovely mouth utter.

Pringel's wife, a pharmacist's assistant, handed the prince a tiny box that contained a four-leaf clover she had found in the castle courtyard. It had brought them such good luck recently, they wanted to pass it on. "Our ace reporter," the hereditary prince said, and Pringel, who had trimmed his beard short, replied, "Every, every good wish."

As we were entering the great Hall of Mirrors for dinner, I asked the baron when he had first noticed the newspaper in Marion's hand. She had had it with her when she arrived, he said. She had used the *Sunday Bulletin* as a fan, which he hoped hadn't wounded my vanity. The baron didn't understand a thing! He even suggested it would be good idea to place a stack of *Bulletins* outside the door to the Hall of Mirrors right now. I was such a scaredy-cat, he exclaimed, and asked what else I was afraid of at this point.

I've got to go.

Hugs,

Your E.

Monday, July 9, '90

Dear Nicoletta,

I've been remiss in writing, but I no longer wish to muse about my past. It's not that the World Cup has gone to my head. But isn't the joy I feel at our victory the overt expression of a much greater, more all-encompassing happiness? My wish to begin a new life at your side has never been stronger than now. But since my letters appear not to have achieved that purpose, my hopes are dwindling—for these letters are motivated by nothing else.[1]

But I must bring all this to a conclusion, just as a losing team dare not leave the field before those ninety minutes are over. And so back to the start of this year.

As I looked back in chagrin on my nocturnal crossroads adventure, I would have much preferred to have regarded it as a dream. And yet it also pleased me to have risked it. What I had thought and felt there, however, had been left behind in the night.

---

1. Even N. H. has her doubts about this, as she herself revealed in a conversation with me.

I took a bath beneath laundry hung up to dry. When I went to dress, I couldn't find any of the things I wanted. I opened the laundry basket and began rummaging in the dirty clothes, and finally just upended it. Everything I picked up belonged to me. Two towels were the dubious exception to the rule. Only then did I notice that the items hung up to dry belonged solely to Michaela and Robert.

Okay, we're even, I thought.

Michaela was out somewhere. I dined on fried herring and potatoes with Robert. "You're eating again," Michaela exclaimed when she returned home, and then announced there would be a meeting in the living room. Meaning, the space was taboo until evening.

Robert protested that he'd be missing one of his TV shows.

Michaela's media committee arrived on the dot. While they moved chairs around, clicked open their briefcases, and struck up their usual murmurs, I tidied up my room, gleaning underwear, dishes, shoes, records, record jackets, newspapers, and letters from the floor, until slowly but surely the square fiber mats beneath began to emerge. I worked fast, hoping to escape beneath my headphones before the meeting really began. I had already stretched out on my couch when I remembered I still had laundry in the washing machine. I was trapped. To get to the bathroom I had to go through the living room. I had an overwhelming aversion to appearing before strangers—before people I didn't want anything to do with, didn't even want to be spoken to by. I spent a good while wondering whether I should knock or not. Finally, out of habit, I knocked—and felt as if someone had pushed me onstage. The light was blinding, the discussion died. Everyone gawked at me as if I had emerged from the wallpaper. "Why, there you are," Michaela said. She sounded embarrassed. Sitting with propped elbows at the head of the table, she took a drag on her cigarette and blinked as she stared at me. "Don't let me interrupt," I said, closing the living-room door behind me.

Later I could recall the sudden clatter of voices. But at that moment I barely noticed, and was angry at myself for my hasty "Don't let me interrupt." I could well imagine what was going through Michaela's head as she saw her barefoot husband whoosh through the room like a ghost.

I stuffed half a load of wet laundry into the spin-drier, pressed the lid shut, and threw myself on top so that I could hold the spout over the bucket.

I took the laundry down from the clothesline and folded it as neatly as

I could. Every undershirt, ever pair of panties, every bra was familiar. I had the feeling I was saying good-bye to each piece. Then I hung up my own things.

No sooner had I opened the living-room door than two bearded men got to their feet.

"Herr Türmer," said the fellow with long legs and a short, skewed torso, "we would like to know . . ." and the other one, whom I recognized as the Prophet from his cotton-candy beard and thick glasses, broke in with his variation on the question: "We really have no idea . . . why you don't want to work with us." Silence. The third fellow, Jörg, whose beret was lying on the table, leaned back and nodded encouragement like a teacher at an oral exam. The dainty woman with a pageboy hairdo seated across from him gazed at me as if she were infatuated. Only Michaela went on reading the text in front of her.

"There's no reason, actually," I said, just to say something.

What was I waiting for? Why didn't I simply vanish into my room?

Rudolph, "the Prophet," took a step toward me, extended both hands, and clasped my right hand between them. What great good luck, he said, to have this unexpected opportunity to thank me. He had wanted to do it ever since the first time he had heard me at the church.[1] He always told his wife she should never forget what Herr Türmer had done for us. I had been months ahead of events, I had truly spoken the same clear text that they wanted *klartext* to speak, and if there was anybody in this town whom he trusted, it was me.

Although he was still grasping my hand tightly, his gaze met mine only occasionally.

I should be writing for them, he said. With my name on the masthead he would no longer worry about putting out a newspaper, my name was a "guarantee of success."

"So grab a chair and sit down here with us," Michaela said, interrupting my eulogist.

It was like a rehearsal with a cast change—everybody knows what's going on except the actor at the center of things. But soon the discussion turned to things like cost projections, printers, distribution possibilities,

---

1. It is rather remarkable that T.'s presence at this meeting of the "media committee" was met with such surprise. The Prophet and T. had, after all, encountered each other before and after T.'s speech at the church. The Prophet could have thanked him on that occasion.

copies per issue, number of pages, departmental assignments—which strangely enough relieved some of my anxiety since I had nothing to contribute and yet listening caused me no distress. It was all both as interesting and as boring as if they were explaining the rules of a parlor game.

Michaela was the only one who opposed the others' plans. "But that won't work!" she kept exclaiming.

I finally asked why they were discussing all this instead of proceeding just as before.

"Precisely," Michaela said, tossing her pencil aside, "that's what I keep asking myself. Precisely that!"

Jörg burst into laughter. And then for the first time I heard the words: *Altenburg Weekly*. Jörg didn't let anyone get a word in edgewise now. When someone tried to speak, his radio moderator's voice grew louder in anticipation of the objection or comment.

"But it won't work," Michaela shouted once more, to which he responded with another laugh and said, "But we're going to do it anyway!"

After that no one said anything, they all just stared straight ahead. Suddenly the woman with the pageboy turned her head to me with a birdlike jerk and said, "And what about you? Do you want to work with us? We'd consider it an honor."

It was our job, she continued, to win over public opinion, in fact, to actually create public opinion so that we could help sustain the transition to democracy, to steer and direct it, yes, even to provide a little control—and self-control—when necessary. "Independence is the crucial thing! And we'll see to it that the New Forum gives us that in writing." We didn't need to go into the fact that in a provincial town an effort like this would take a different form than in Berlin or Leipzig. "The wheel of history," Rudolph the Prophet interjected, "dare not be turned back." Then Georg said, "We, that is the New Forum, which will be financing us, are planning a weekly, starting in February. In seven weeks we'll be holding our first issue in our hands."

I liked the idea.

"And what you do think?" I asked Michaela. She had stubbed out her cigarette and was shifting her puffed-up cheeks back and forth as if rinsing with mouthwash.

She had joined the New Forum out of a sense of responsibility, she had helped found *klartext* out of a sense of responsibility, she had taken on the role of publisher out of a sense of responsibility. A newspaper, journalism, political activism—those were important things in a time of crisis, but interested her only in a time of crisis. What was essential for real life, however, happened in literature, in art, in the theater. Where, if not in the theater, did society's problems get bundled up together and take the shape of action? Then she turned to phrases like "the swamps of local politics" and "everyday picayune stuff."

At first they all listened, but the longer she gushed on about art, the stage, and "real life," the more restless they grew. Only the pageboy woman was still giving her her full attention. Michaela closed her sermon with the statement, "Only in art do our lives experience justice, only in art is there a language appropriate to justice."

After that all eyes refocused on me. "It would mean a great sacrifice," the woman with the pageboy said, "would truly be a sacrifice on your part."

"Marion," Jörg said a little testily, "it's a leap for us all."[1]

"That's absurd!" Michaela cried. It should be clear to me that it would mean my giving notice at the theater, it wasn't something you could do on the side.

I promised to think it over.

Michaela flared up: "You can't be serious!"

I repeated that I would think it over.

Michaela disappeared into our room.

This turn of events was a stroke of good luck for Robert. He didn't even complain about the cigarette smoke, because everyone had departed from the living room just in time for his show to start. I said good-bye to Michaela's media committee at the door.

Once Robert had gone to bed, Michaela elbowed my door open and turned around to reveal the drawer from her desk suspended like a vendor's box at her stomach. "Here, you can practice," she said, as she dumped the contents on the floor and was gone again.

A pile of papers scribbled full, the *klartext* files, as it turned out—plus bobby pins, Band-Aids, and a nail clipper.

I immediately set about sorting it all: printing costs, income from vendors, income from mailed copies, bills (paid and outstanding), printed texts, unprinted manuscripts, correspondence.

1. That is to say: "We're all taking a leap into the unknown, none of us know what lies ahead."

Standing up again at last, I surveyed my little ordered world—and then I removed my manuscript files from the cupboard, emptied the first, erased the title *Barracks Heart/Final Version,* and wrote "Printing Cost Estimates" in its place. On the pastel blue one that had read *Titus Holm,* I now wrote "Vendors' Accounts." And so on, until only one file was left without a title. I extracted my most recent attempt at prose from it and added it to the others on my desk. It was now the capstone of my collected works. And on the file itself I wrote: "Rejected Manuscripts"—and at that moment I realized how appropriate the title would have been all along. If we'd had a stove, my "Collected Works" would have gone up in flames that same evening.

But after I had turned the pile over with the written side down, it looked like any stack of blank paper. The pages were usable on *one* side—a metaphoric fact that both frightened and delighted me. The *other half* ought not to be wasted.[1]

My dear Nicoletta, I'm not quite finished yet, but that's enough for today.

This comes with greetings as warm as they are disheartened, from
Your Enrico Türmer

Tuesday, July 10, 1990

Dear Jo,

Referees' Retreat was our stadium. We celebrated on into the morning. Mother and the hereditary prince held out until just after midnight. They didn't want to miss a single moment of our Sunday, either. Everyone was there, except for the baron. He was in consultation with Jörg. I don't know what came of it. I don't want to know, either. It was unpleasant enough when Fred and Ilona interviewed with us yesterday. We don't need anyone new at this point. It's a bitter pill for them, because I was unable to recommend them to anyone in the family[2] with a clear conscience—I know them too well for that.

You and Franziska really missed something on Sunday. It will be a

1. Until this letter T. never commented on the fact that there were prose texts on the reverse side of his letters. If one is to believe T.'s logic, one must presume that he already had a correspondent like N. H. in mind. It should be expressly noted yet again that his "works" are to be found only on the reverse side of his letters to N. H.

2. Apparently this refers to the Barrista entourage.

while before I'll see another spectacle like it. Besides which, I would have been interested in your impression—last but not least, from the theologian's point of view.[1] It was truly an extraordinary, yes, a strangely preternatural event.

After breakfast in our orchard the baron invited us to board a small bus. Except for him I don't think anyone had the vaguest idea what awaited us. Michaela climbed up front into the driver's cab. Seated in the back were the hereditary prince, Robert, Mother, Vera, Astrid, and I—each in his own seat upholstered with the same velvety fabric that lined the entire vehicle. The television up front flickered—and the baron and Michaela appeared on the screen. They waved to us, then the screen went blank again. Music was coming from somewhere, Mozart, I think—we were already on our way. The vehicle smelled new and strange, filtered light came through the windows, the cool draft from the air conditioning was pleasant. We could see people halt in their tracks to stare at us. But I knew that all they could make out would be their own reflections in the black windowpanes. We roared out of town in the direction of Schmölln, past the baron's scaffolded villa, where workers scrambled about like ants. No sooner were the last buildings behind us than I drifted into a kind of half sleep. But at the same time I noticed every detail—each tree and field, each ear of grain and leaf, revealed itself with painful clarity. Even the faces of people working in the fields or waiting at a bus stop seemed to glow as they looked up and waved.

In Grosstöbnitz we turned off the highway. We picked up speed. The houses, gardens, and fields flew past, we started uphill, a steep climb that it seemed would never end. I closed my eyes again—and sank into another world, a world of sounds and melodies. I lost myself in the music, unable to tell whether it came from inside me or from outside. I felt as if I had exchanged my human existence for a different mode of being, and for the first time ever I had the premonition of a redeemed world in the midst of our own. Yes, go ahead and laugh, but there are dreams that the instant they brush our consciousness burst like a fish from the depths of the sea when it's forced to the surface.

As the door opened, I could feel how the outside temperature corresponded exactly to that in the bus.

In a tone of voice that sounded as if we had been carrying on an unin-

---

1. Johann Ziehlke presumably did not welcome this reference to his course of studies.

terrupted conversation, the baron explained that what awaited us would be real theater, if not to say theater as reality. He laughed, but in the next moment announced, in the voice of a master of ceremonies: A drama performed on the occasion of the return to Altenburg of the hand reliquary of St. Boniface, the apostle to the Germans, and in honor of the visit of the hereditary prince to the city of his birth.

I pushed the wheelchair forward, and Massimo, who along with all the others had been following us, lifted him into it. Vera laid the prince's blanket across his knees, Mother handed him binoculars, and Robert raised a parasol to prevent the hereditary prince from being blinded by the sun. Astrid never left the side of the wheelchair—the right side, let it be noted, so that she could always train her good eye on him.

And here came the district councilor and mayor. Together with their retinue, these "first freely elected officials" formed a guard of honor along both sides of the steep bumpy path, up which Massimo labored to push the wheelchair. The top of the hill was crowned with a little chapel. I had no idea where we were.

A white tent had been pitched in front of the chapel. Perhaps it would be better to call it a baldachin, because except for the four corner struts clad in triangular strips of fabric leading down to a point, there was only a roof and no walls. The sun stood at its zenith, the view was overwhelming, a downright shock. To the north of this hill fit for a commanding general—as the baron termed our nameless elevation—lay Altenburg and the flats of the brown coal mines, with Leipzig's Battle of the Nations Monument far in the distance. To the south rose the expanses of Vogtland and the Ore Mountains. To the west, the pyramids of Ronneburg were so close you felt you could reach out and touch them, and behind them the Thuringian Forest. To the east you were offered a view of lovely rolling hills.

"For the fields lay sere and not yet freshened with heavenly dew!" a stentorian voice proclaimed. To our left, not fifty yards down the slope, stood several hundred strangely garbed people. Divided into two large equal clusters, they were staring at a man in a broad-brimmed hat. Hitching up his long robe, he descended from a mound of sand that, according to a sign, was FRIESLAND and climbed another, where a sign that read ENGLAND had been planted. Basic theater for the masses. And we were the audience.

A tree was now raised with the help of a hand-driven winch.

The hereditary prince asked to be pushed as close as possible to the edge of the slope. Once the tree was standing—its equilibrium maintained by several men holding the ropes—a man stepped out in front of the troupe of players and called out: "The oak of Thor!" At that same moment a sign appeared above some heads that designated this new scene of action as GEISMAR/HESSIA. The man in the hat quickly stepped forward—it was Mansfeld, the Catholic priest—followed by three companions who had evidently learned their nervous gestures from studying bodyguards. When he pulled out an ax from under his robe, they lifted their voices in wails of lamentation. Their efforts were amateurish, but the effect was tremendous.[1]

The baron pointed toward the man in the hat. "That's Boniface," he offered in superfluous explanation, and smiled at Robert. Boniface had fallen to his knees, and as he prayed his brow touched the ax handle he held in both hands. As he rose to his feet, above the more general cries of "Woe! Woe!" I could hear howls so desperate, so shrill they gave me goose bumps.

Step by step the throng retreated before Boniface and his ax. A few seconds later, what I had taken to be splendidly simulated apprehension turned into genuine fear on the part of the actors. As Boniface struck the tree with his ax—amid utter silence—the trunk split into four pieces that, as each was tugged by a rope, fell away to the ground. The Germanic heathens burst into a wild outcry prompted less by the spectacle itself than by their fear for one of their fellow actors posted farther down the slope, who had barely missed being hit by one quarter of the tree. But since evidently no harm had come to him and he like all the others knelt down to gaze up at the cross that Boniface now held in his hands in lieu of the ax, none of us regarded it as a serious matter either.

Besides which, a chorale had been taken up. I would have sworn I also heard an orchestra. More and more heathens sank to their knees and raised pleading hands to their new God.

Before the chords of their song had died away, the narrator announced in his powerful bass voice that a church would now be built.

That was the starting gun for a race. Four teams lifted the four pieces

---

1. Beyond T.'s own article in the *Sunday Bulletin*, no. 2, and a more general summary in the *Bonifatiusbote* [Boniface messenger], no. 1, no other written accounts of this episode have been located. Eyewitnesses, however, are unanimous in reporting that the effect of the performance was indeed "tremendous."

of trunk that formed a cross on the ground and now rushed uphill as if to take a city gate. Their goal could only be the chapel behind us, which, although it had a fresh coat of paint, had not been newly plastered. The painters had left obvious traces of their work in the grass and the gravel.

Without so much as a glance our way, the converted Germanic men, women, and children panted past us. Viewed from close up, their makeup was good enough for a movie take—disheveled hair, bruised arms, feet and legs mud-caked halfway to their knees. We considered ourselves lucky not to have been overrun by this mob in their thespian frenzy. They set to work on the chapel, attaching the pieces of trunk beside the entrance and at the apse with chains that had been previously bolted there.

A searing sun blazed in the sky, but it was still pleasantly cool where we stood. The hereditary prince, who had been intently following the proceedings, dismissed with a smile any questions about how he was holding up.

Meanwhile the performers had returned to their previous positions. But whether to heighten the dramatic effect or to underscore the significance of these events, they all moved toward us now, and one woman who held a sign reading DOKKUM—PENTECOST 754 propped against her shoulder took up a position not forty feet away from us.

As Boniface approached her with several of his adherents—he was moving more slowly now and was bent low to indicate his advanced age—he was presented with a book so large that he almost lost his balance. His three disciples lovingly supported him and cast pleading glances in the direction of the narrator, who then announced, "They await the newly baptized."

The throng had split in two. On the right side, with women in the majority, a bright doxology was struck up, while on the left one could hear the supernumeraries murmuring "broccoli broccoli," a sound intended to suggest that they were the "barbarians." Boniface, who stood with his profile to us, was just straightening up in expectation of greeting the women, when gruesomely shaggy figures came storming up from the rear and with a few heavy blows slew the apostle's companions. Doxology turned into lamentation.

All eyes were directed toward Boniface, who now stood at full stature. He held up the large book to counter his attackers, who had at first shrunk back before his presence. But then the most savage of these savage fellows stepped forward—piercing the book, his sword was thrust directly into the saint's heart. In the breathless silence that followed, I heard only the wind in the grass and Astrid's whimpers. Along with the actors, we all stood frozen in place. A few white strands of the prince's hair danced in the breeze.

Boniface staggered, but still held himself erect. Slowly he sank to his knees, his eyes directed heavenward. Finally he fell forward, burying beneath him the sword-pierced book that had been unable to save him. A bleak, dissonant cry of woe rose up, with the barbarians, now transformed back into Christians, joining in.

Father Mansfeld, easily recognized under his broad-rimmed hat, was suddenly holding high the silver, jewel-bedizened hand reliquary. Whether by chance or calculation—it seemed to catch fire in the sunlight, its radiance so blinding that I had to put a hand before my eyes and turn away. And then I saw that almost everyone who had watched the spectacle with us was now kneeling. The few still standing were for the most part elderly. Her tail wagging wildly, Astrid was bounding back and forth among the faithful, probably hoping someone would pet her.

"Play along," the baron hissed at me from below. After a brief hesitation I yielded and knelt down, which to my surprise I found quite relaxing and pleasant.

The throng had now taken up a hymn and formed a procession, with the reliquary carried solemnly before it. Again and again it refracted the sun's rays, sending us its signals even after the hymn was no longer audible and we had given ourselves over to the pervading silence and gazed down on the procession as it moved across the countryside below. The book—now that I had time to think about it—had not saved Boniface's life, but in the end it had indeed proved a token of victory.[1]

Surely everything will turn out well now. We are waiting for you.

Hugs from your

Enrico

---

1. On July 8, 2002—twelve years later to the day—the rebuilt St. Boniface Church, which stands above the St. Boniface crypt, was dedicated in Altenburg. It now serves as the starting and end point of the many branches of a path laid out for Boniface pilgrims.

Dear Nicoletta,

As you can see I have a new address and am living in a three-bedroom apartment, whose smallest room is larger than my old living room. If you were to stop by over the next few days or weeks, you would find me out on my veranda with its new greenery and dreamlike view of the city and town. You would see Altenburg and yet not believe that it is Altenburg. Our building also has a large orchard enclosed by an entwining hedge right out of *Sleeping Beauty*.

So much for the present—to whose beginnings I hope to bring you with today's chapter.

Unfortunately there has been no real opportunity before now to tell you about Aunt Trockel,[1] who used to take care of Robert. She would always prepare her annual "New Year's dinner" for us. Sometimes she also played something for us on her piano.

Michaela had promised me we wouldn't stay long, and so I gave in and accompanied her on a visit to Aunt Trockel. Robert had been invited to his friend Falk's birthday party.

As we got off the bus we saw Aunt Trockel vanish behind her balcony door. Michaela picked up the pace, and now the familiar race began. At the same moment that Aunt Trockel opened her door, Michaela pushed the doorbell.

It wasn't easy to recognize Aunt Trockel's smile in her crumpled face. Over the last few months she had literally shriveled up—except for her belly, whose vault pressed against her tight-fitting dress, so that in both shape and size it looked deceptively like the last stages of pregnancy, an impression enhanced by her otherwise girlish figure. Climbing the stairs behind Aunt Trockel, I once again had a chance to admire her slender calves.

Aunt Trockel handed us hangers, folded her hands across her belly, and, as if she owed us some explanation, said she had eaten too much chocolate and this was the result. Almost all of her Bavarian "welcome money" had been spent on chocolate. Not that she didn't have anything left, but whenever her neighbors drove to Hof she would ask them to buy twenty bars for her at the Aldi supermarket and would then repay them upon being presented the sales receipt. Once those bars of choco-

---

1. T. mentioned Aunt Trockel to N. H. in his letter of May 31, 1990.

late were in her cupboard she could think of nothing else. Aunt Trockel's voice had reached an uncomfortably high pitch. I was troubled by the vehemence of the words tumbling from her.

I simply can't bring myself, Aunt Trockel continued, to wait until evening to open the first bar. On the contrary it took all her strength to save one or two squares until the evening news. Yesterday she hadn't even managed that, and had devoured two bars in one day. But she certainly couldn't say it was too much of a good thing yet.

She served the first course: fennel with shaved almonds and oranges, along with an aperitif in tiny glasses, their rims wreathed with a dusting of sugar.

As always Aunt Trockel had used up almost every ounce of her energy preparing this feast. She herself sipped at her water glass now and then, and kept up a flow of words even when she was busy in the kitchen. She never stopped long enough to give us a chance to pay her culinary arts their due until she presented the saddle of venison on a heavy tray.

And then—my plate had just been heaped with a second helping—Aunt Trockel told us about how a classmate of hers had once given her a piece of tinfoil to smell, so that she could have some idea of what chocolate was. And she, only eight years old at the time, had been grateful. "Imagine that!" Aunt Trockel exclaimed, and looked at me. Her voice growing louder and louder, she told her tale as if it concerned only me. I tried to return her gaze as often as I could, but then grew unsure of myself—as if I had overheard whatever reason it was she had given for her exclusive attention to me—and proceeded to eat more hastily. Only then did I notice that Michaela had leaned back in her chair and closed her eyes. Aunt Trockel was sitting bolt upright at the edge of her chair.

So now it was my turn, and in a low voice I listed all the things Michaela had accomplished over the last few weeks.

"You don't have to whisper," Michaela said, "but with my eyes closed I have a better picture of little Annemarie Trockel sniffing at that tinfoil."

Aunt Trockel bounced once on the edge of her chair and rewarded Michaela's hasty excuse with praise for *klartext*. Which also gave her an opportunity to tell about her sister-in-law, who had decided not to buy *klartext* because it called itself a newsletter for Thuringia, and according to her Altenburg was a Saxon town, belonged to Saxony—which she, Aunt Trockel, did of course agree with, but that could be changed, the newsletter's masthead, that is.

Michaela finally asked what she thought of the articles themselves. "Very good," Aunt Trockel replied, "really very good, critical I'd say, very critical." She took a sip of water and kept the glass in her hand.

So she liked the criticism, did she?

Yes, she did, why shouldn't she, that's how it was everywhere now. The truth was coming to light.

Both women, it seemed to me, were waiting for the saddle of venison to finally disappear from my plate.

"No!" Michaela screeched when Aunt Trockel brought in two plates with an eighth of a Black Forest cake on each. This launched Aunt Trockel into her story about the whipping cream she had ordered, which despite several assurances to the contrary had not been set aside for her, so that she had gone all the way to the manager, who finally got on the phone and found two bottles for her at the store on Stein Weg. "Two bottles!" Michaela cried. Two bottles of whipping cream was asking too much, she mustn't do it, she mustn't fatten us up like that, or herself. When Aunt Trockel set the plate down and then turned right back around again, even Michaela was taken aback by her own outburst. On each piece of cake, a maraschino cherry crowned the highest peak of whipped cream, with syruplike liqueur forming a mountain lake at its base. I was picturing Aunt Trockel leaning her head against the kitchen window, tears streaming down her face, when she appeared with an even larger piece of cake and set it down for herself. Suddenly there was a bottle of fruit brandy in front of me, and three glasses. "Oh, Aunt Trockel!" Michaela exclaimed. I poured the brandy, and we clinked glasses in a toast.

At the first stab of the fork, a purple brook burst from the dammed maraschino mountain lake and spilled through the spotless white. We ate in devout silence.

Then I did something I never failed to do when visiting Aunt Trockel; I went to the bathroom: sparkling fixtures without one water-drop stain to mar their beauty, a toilet bowl whose depths and rim were both a perfect white, a battery of combs without a single hair left behind. With childlike curiosity I always opened her mirrored medicine cabinet, which gave off the decorous odor of venom and liniment. In that bathroom it would never have occurred to me to piss standing up.

Suddenly a remarkable event from my childhood popped into my mind. But at that same moment Aunt Trockel was pounding on the door and calling out my name in an imploring voice. Eyes wide with horror, she ripped two pairs of panties from the clothesline, pressed them to her chest, and fled with her booty.

When I returned, Aunt Trockel was leaning back in her chair, hands at her sides, gazing down over her belly. Michaela already had her purse in her lap. "Have I ever told you about the most important event in my life?" I asked, and, paying no attention to Michaela's reaction, began to tell them what I had just now recalled.

I was ten or eleven years old when a neighbor boy persuaded me to spend the night with him at his grandmother's. We would be allowed to watch the Hit Parade and then a movie after that. Besides which we'd have as many banana gumdrops as we could eat. Although to my mind nothing was more horrible than spending a night with strangers without my mother and Vera, I agreed, out of cowardice and for the lack of any good excuse. After the Hit Parade and the movie were over, the banana gumdrops devoured, and I was lying there in the dark in a strange bed, surrounded by strange things and strange odors, I started weeping bitterly into my pillow. Yes, because I was homesick and full of longing and because that's what I always did in such situations, I sobbed away. After a while I was amazed to realize my crying had stopped. I immediately tried to start blubbering again, but couldn't.

"Do you know what had happened?" I asked Michaela and Aunt Trockel. Both were looking at me as if I were speaking in Chinese.

"Okay, what happened?" Michaela asked out of boredom.

"I no longer knew why I had been crying," I exclaimed. "I didn't understand myself what was supposed to be so awful about my situation."

"And that occurred to you just now?" Aunt Trockel asked.

"Yes," I said, "that came to me while I was in the bathroom."

"Well, fine," Michaela said, gave Aunt Trockel a nod, and started to get up. But then I asked for a second piece of Black Forest cake. Aunt Trockel bustled off to the kitchen, Michaela fell back into the sofa; resting her head against it, she stared at the ceiling. I refilled our glasses. Aunt Trockel came back from the kitchen giggling and in her excitement got our plates mixed up—I could tell from the traces of maraschino cherry I had left behind on mine. Aunt Trockel kept right up with me. We toasted. I was trying to do Aunt Trockel in, Michaela remarked in outrage. "How's that?" I asked. "How's that?" Aunt Trockel echoed with a giggle. "That's lethal!" Michaela cried, pointing at Aunt Trockel's plate.

"As far as I know," I said, "it presents no danger to pregnant women." Michaela went rigid. Aunt Trockel threw her head back and started laughing for all she was worth, releasing a spray of whipped cream and crumbs.

"You're both crazy," Michaela said, picking up her purse and getting to her feet.

But I didn't want to leave! At least I could see no reason whatever why leaving was any better than staying. On the contrary: I had all the time in the world! I didn't need to write anymore, or read anymore.

"Shall we finish it off?" I asked once our plates were empty. Aunt Trockel nodded. "It always tastes best fresh anyway." She picked up our plates and toddled into the kitchen.

Michaela stared at me. "You're going to stop right now, if you please!" she cried. "You've got to stop, you're going to kill her!"[1]

Instead of our plates Aunt Trockel brought in the whole cake under its transparent plastic cover with a red knob in the middle for a handle.

"Just one more drink," I said.

"Have a great time," Michaela called out as she opened the apartment door and closed it behind her before either of us could say a word.

Aunt Trockel and I ate the rest of the cake right from the platter, without plates. We tried to work at the same speed, both of us attacking our pieces from the center out.

I don't know whether you can comprehend it, but as I dived into the remains of the cake along with this potbellied, shriveled-up old woman, I felt liberated in some strange, unexpected way—liberated from all pressure, all stress, all claims on me. A peculiar calm took hold, a peace of mind that I attributed to the influence of alcohol.

I awoke a little before four o'clock out of a deep, dreamless sleep that had left me completely refreshed, taking the last trace of my previous exhaustion with it.

My "good mood" irritated Michaela. I evidently enjoyed tormenting her, she claimed. Whatever I did or said was cause for some rebuke or criticism.

And then it began to snow. It snowed all evening and through the

---

1. T. quite wisely neglected to mention to N. H. that Aunt Trockel died only a few weeks later. Cf. his letter of Feb. 6, 1990.

night and on into the next morning. From my window I could see children with sleds. Our neighbor was shoveling snow.

Over the last weeks I had paid no attention at all to the weather, but I was as delighted as a child by this white splendor. I wanted to go out in it, and so I got dressed. Robert yelled that he wanted to come along.

When Michaela, who was lying on the bed memorizing lines, saw we were ready to go, she put on her winter things too.

We were a curious trio. Robert ran on ahead, I chased after him, with Michaela at my heels. As soon as Robert was out of hearing range, she began to lay into me—why was I suddenly so interested in Robert and was I trying to estrange the boy from her. "Why are you like this? What have I ever done to you? Why are you like this?" she kept shouting.

We walked straight across the fields. The ground under the snow had not frozen everywhere, and sometimes we had to run just to keep from sinking into the muck beneath. Michaela's sermon exhausted me more than the physical exertion. I would have gladly turned back. But Robert wanted to make it to "Silver Lake."

The pond was frozen over and smooth as glass. Robert and Michaela broke into a skidding competition. Several times I thought I heard the ice breaking. I turned to go, so the two of them could be together. But when I looked around once more, a snowball struck my right eye. It wasn't just snow, as Michaela claimed, at least it hurt like hell, as if a pebble or splinter had wounded my eye. I couldn't see a thing and feared the worst.

Robert took my hand as if I needed to be led. He never let go of my hand as we crossed the field, while Michaela kept telling me to stop carrying on.

Will you believe me if I tell you that as I crossed that snow-covered field I felt utterly happy? But that's exactly how it was. Yes, I wept because my right eye hurt so bad, but I wept even more for happiness.

How can I explain it?

The pain had awakened me. I finally comprehended what I had known since that night at the crossroads and my visit with Aunt Trockel: my old life lay behind me. Or better: I could now really begin to live.

Ever since my original sin I had played the miser with time—not a moment in which I had not been a driven man who lived solely to grind more writing, more literature—my works, my fame—out of each day, each hour.[1]

I had finally freed myself from art, from literature, and thus from time as well. Suddenly I was simply just here, to live, to enjoy—I no longer had to create anything.[2]

Robert and Michaela, the snow and the air, barking dogs in the distance and sounds from the road—I took it all in as if I had just set foot on this earth, as if I found myself in the midst of the world for the very first time. Ah, Nicoletta, will you understand me?[3]

Liberated, at ease, and happy, I walked behind Robert. And when a big dog came running toward us from the village of Oberlödla and Robert and Michaela tried to hide behind me, I soon quieted the yelping mutt by scratching his neck and head until he pressed against my knee and closed his eyes.

The mangy animal escorted us all the way to the road. Robert waved a car down, and it took us to the polyclinic. Outside the entrance I ran right into my physician, Dr. Weiss. He probably assumed I had found some pretext for him to attest that I was still too ill too work. Which is why he treated me a bit condescendingly. But when I told him that, no matter what happened with my eye, I didn't want any more sick leave and he then practically forced my right eye open, it was Dr. Weiss's friendly face that I first viewed with both eyes again.

And with that I am at the end of my story. You yourself know what happened then. And now it should actually be your turn. As for me, there's nothing to stop me from a trip to Rome.

Your

Enrico Türmer

1. In comparison to the previous pages, both the careless handwriting as well as numerous cross-outs on the last page would seem to indicate that T. regarded this passage as a rough draft, which he then did not copy out again.

Crossed out: "Suddenly I was freed of the curse of having to describe the world, liberated from the bedazzlement of believing I should become a famous man, redeemed from the mad obsession of wanting to live eternally."

2. These things are not mutually exclusive.

3. Crossed out: "I had in fact felt sorry for anyone who lacked artistic talent, who had no possibility of creating fame and opening up eternity for himself. Now I pitied those who held fast to such an ambition. Did they not realize that the age of art, the age of words, had passed and the age of deeds had irrevocably begun? I at least no longer had to cast about day and night for the stuff of a novel!"

APPENDIX

THE SEVEN TEXTS collected in this appendix were found on the reverse side of twenty out of a total of thirty-three letters addressed to Nicoletta Hansen. The right half of each of these manuscript pages was left blank to leave space for corrections. This explains the smaller size of these texts in comparison to the letters they accompany. Although Türmer occasionally mentions his own works in some detail, he never comments directly on what is on the back of his letters. His letter of July 9, 1990, contains the sole reference to these texts: a rather dubious explanation of the origin of these two-sided pages. One might speculate about Türmer's motives and intentions. I have chosen merely to document the chronological connection between the "reverse pages" and the letters they accompany.

Türmer evidently considered it important that his works be read, otherwise the chronology of the letters would not match the chronology of the individual attempts at fiction. They are printed in the sequence Türmer himself chose.

I. S.

Schnitzel Hunt

. . . and lots of hellos to you all from Thalheim. Something's always going on at camp. There's never enough time to write. But it's been raining all day today. The mood here is really great. Adelheid, our group leader, always helps out, even if it's just somebody who still doesn't know how to make her bed right. She certainly has shown us how often enough. The girls from the other groups are jealous of us because of Adelheid. Although at the end of the day when we're in bed and the lights are turned out, she's nowhere to be found.

We often have chores to do, working in the kitchen or cleaning up. I get along with everybody. We've had dancing two evenings already, and tomorrow there's another dance. All the older girls are in love with Rolf, Herr Funke's assistant. He has a moped and a helmet. Herr Funke always says Rolf is his right-hand man. Rolf played the trumpet at the memorial stone in honor of all the fallen. Before that we had *subbotnik* and pulled weeds.

Yesterday we had a schnitzel hunt. Maik was on the verge of tears when he was told to step forward. Frau Borchert read his letter aloud to us. Maik doesn't want to be at camp. Frau Borchert asked him what he wanted to do at home, since everybody would be working and nobody would have time for him, and all the other kids would be at camp. We all had to laugh. Herr Funke had asked why he wanted to play at home and not here at camp. He should tell us what he doesn't like about camp. And of course he didn't know. First he writes letters like that and then doesn't say a peep and he's always just goofing off. Adelheid says Maik looks like he just might run away. Kids like Maik like to make a run for it and then the police and everybody else have to go looking for them. And of course all sorts of things can happen in the meantime and nobody's around because they all have to go looking for Maik.

Maik started to bawl. He should have thought twice about it. It was scary, because Maik had broken camp rules. Herr Funke asked him about it—but of course not a peep. Herr Funke said he had no choice if Maik wasn't going to talk. Maik had brought it on himself. But he was going to give him one more chance anyway. It was a way for Maik to prove himself, and Maik nodded and then said okay. We marched to the athletic field and fell in for roll call. As the brigade leader I always give the report of present and ready. It's so crappy when I have to be the last to report in because somebody's chattering away and just won't hush up. We had to discuss Maik. Maik swore an oath before everybody that he wouldn't run away. But he's got to make up for it, for writing letters like that! What if they had ended up in the wrong hands, Herr Funke said. Children all over the world long to go to a camp like we have here, but they have to go to work and never get to attend camp. And they don't have enough to eat, either. But we get to come here every year. Everybody was in favor of Maik having to do it. Herr Funke asked if anyone didn't agree, but we all wanted Maik to do it, and even he raised his hand, so it was unanimous. Then he took off, just like he was, in his shorts and undershirt. We all counted out loud, eight, nine, ten, bango! Bango marks the start. Maik ran off carrying the sack, up the hill into the woods. Herr Funke called out to keep in mind that he'd sworn an oath. Then Herr Funke gave a little speech and said we shouldn't disgrace ourselves. A half-hour head start was a real long time. But we had to keep practicing until we got it right. Just keep practicing, every day if we could. A schnitzel hunt is a fine thing, after all, Herr Funke said, and it helps the kitchen out too. If it were up to Herr Funke there'd be a lot more schnitzel hunts, throughout our whole republic. We formed four groups. The older boys divided into two groups. We were supposed to gather pinecones. Adelheid had put everything in a sack and closed it tight, and the boys took it along with them. Herr Funke came too, of course, and Rolf. We kept our eyes peeled here. You never know what somebody like Maik may do. What if he sneaks back around and suddenly he's here and we're all in the woods? We kept our eyes wide open and collected wood. We piled it at the kick-off circle, right at the center of the athletic field. It was a little eerie in the woods, but nobody wanted to be a scaredy-cat. Just yell, Adelheid said, if Maik shows up, just yell. Nothing's going to happen. He's a good two inches shorter than me. So yes, we just kept our eyes peeled. We collected more than enough wood. There'd be no gripes about that. And then we heard the siren. Herr Funke had taken the camp siren along. And so we knew that it had turned out okay. Then we took off, along with Adelheid and Sylvia, whose hair is so long it reaches her rear end. She's always one of the first to be asked to dance. Sylvia's the prettiest girl in camp. She has a broad belt with a golden buckle, she's going to have her parents get one for me when we go home, because her father can arrange things. Then we'll both have one. We went at least a kilometer into the woods. Adelheid showed us the poop of deer and other animals. We want to learn stuff like that over the next few days, and to identify bird calls too.

We waited by a little shed with lots of signposts. Then Herr Funke and the boys arrived with Maik. Two boys in front, two behind, and Rolf kept trying to show them how to rest the branch on their shoulder without it hurting. Herr Funke told us how really angry they had been. Maik hadn't resisted much. Even though he promised he would. Then he just sat down on a tree stump with the empty sack across his knees. Pine trees all around. Maik ran away when the boys started throwing. Didn't do any good, of course. Especially when Herr Funke is with them. He can throw from a hundred yards away, and still hit his target. They all threw at the same time. Herr Funke said it was like what used to be called an organ, like those big "steel organs" the Soviets had. Maik kept his undershirt on, so no matter where he ran he was easy to spot. They just had to aim for his undershirt. Maik didn't have any shoes on, either, but his eyes were wide open. He bumped into things a couple of times anyway. When Herr Funke realized we all wanted to be part of it, he said we had the right stuff. Herr Funke is strict, Adelheid always says, but he's fair. It's pretty rare for him not to have something to gripe about. But we did our job because we worked together with Adelheid. We stood in formation around Maik just like at morning roll call. Herr Funke said he was proud of us. Everybody had done his job.

The boys carried him up onto the porch where Herr Funke and Herr Meinhardt, the caretaker, were standing. Adelheid said Herr Meinhardt had said how great it would be to have a nice little devil like this delivered every day, that would sure make things easier for the kitchen. Then it all went real fast, because everybody wanted some. Herr Funke praised Herr Meinhardt for being so good at his job and always remembering to bring the basins to hold underneath. The boys were busy the whole time. We got the bread sliced and carried the tea bucket out to the athletic field. We used the wheelbarrow and the boys brought the frame for the spit. And Rolf got the fire going for under the spit. Herr Funke laughed at how unrecognizable Maik was now. It took a real long time before we could dig in, well after our usual bedtime. But I like sausage anyway. It tastes better than schnitzel. Herr Funke went on for a long time about how things used to be and how hard they had fought and all their sacrifices, but how they had always believed in victory no matter what. That's why we have an honor guard too. And then Herr Funke played his guitar, and Adelheid sang, and so did we. I kept thinking about that belt. If only I could have been wearing it. And then Herr Funke said: Who would like to see the head? And he pulled it out of the sack it had been in all along. Who wants to carry the head? Herr Funke asked. I grabbed Maik's head the way Herr Funke showed me, by the hair. It was really heavy, and I didn't want to get my hands dirty. I never thought Maik's head would be so heavy. Holy cow, I thought. Because it was so heavy we took turns, Sylvia and me. Sylvia is my best friend. We want to visit each other when we get home.

All the best from your Sabine, Group M 4

Hundred-year Summer

His hands in the pants pockets of his dress uniform, Salwitzky is standing between the door and the table, staring out the window. Because of the afternoon sun and the heat, the blackout drape has been drawn halfway. Vischer is sitting with his elbows on the broad windowsill, his back to the locker, a book in his left hand. It's as quiet as a day in the country. Except occasionally you can hear the shuffle of boots or the high-pitched whine of the troop carrier's flywheel. The company is out taking target practice.

"Quarter till five," Salwitzky says, pushing the bill of his cap back even farther and wiping his brow with his hand. "And?"

"Nothing," Vischer says.

"You're not watching."

"I can see if anything moves."

"If you don't keep an eye out, you can't see anything."

There's a whistle, but not from their hallway, then the scraping of stools upstairs.

"If they come back and see us here and laugh themselves silly, I'm going to raise hell."

"Go ahead," Vischer said softly, laying his open book aside. He gets up and takes a writing pad and ballpoint from the locker, sits back down. He shifts the lined paper into position.

"What're you doing now?" Salwitzky walks just far enough around the table to be able to see the grayish blue door of the officers' barracks—the handle is broken.

Vischer's head is cocked down over the page.

"What're you up to?"

Vischer glances at his book and then goes on writing.

"I asked you something."

"Dammit, Sal, you can see for yourself."

479

Salwitzky turns around. He jiggles the lock on his locker, moves his briefcase from the stool to the table, unzips it, and then zips it back up again. He airs his cap and wipes his forearm across his eyes and brow. The armpits of his light gray shirt have darkened.

"You writing an official protest?"

"Nope," Vischer says, turning the page. He crosses his legs and bends down again.

"I'll never do it again," Salwitzky says, "this sort of thing's not for me. I want to take my leave with the whole company or not at all."

"You'll get home all right."

"I don't believe it, not when I see you sitting there like that."

"Nothing's going to happen before five o'clock, you know that."

"If I don't catch the eight twenty . . ."

"You won't make it, you know."

"You're right. Shit!" Salwitzky gives his stool a kick, sending it crashing into the bed and toppling over. Salwitzky sets it upright and gives it another kick. The stool ends up just short of the door.

"This is what they call a hundred-year summer, Visch. A hundred-year summer, but not for us! We're hanging around here, and out there . . . Never be another like it!"

"Nothing you can do. Not even if you stand on your head, Sal . . ."

Salwitzky whips around. "That's just like you. Sal standing on his head, you'd go for that." Salwitzky picks the stool up and shoves it back to the table. "You'd really go for that, man oh man!"

Salwitzky throws himself onto one of the lower bunks in the middle of the room; his dress shoes are on the cross brace at the foot of the bed. "Got problems, Visch? Did she dump you?"

Vischer thumbs some more in his book.

"You can tell me, Visch. She did, didn't she?"

"Bullshit."

"It's okay, Visch, you don't have to tell me." Salwitzky presses his hands together and cracks his knuckles one after the other. "You need to get out of here more often, Visch, then you wouldn't have these problems."

Vischer goes on writing. A radio is booming in the hallway overhead. Salwitzky sings along while the tune lasts.

"No, really," he then says. "About as talkative as a screwdriver—read, write, read. Probably don't do anything different at home either." Salwitzky presses his hands against the mattress above his head.

"Out of cash? Need some?"

"No thanks."

"Really?"

"You haven't got any anyway."

"Not here, I don't need any here. But at home. Try guessing how much I've got at home. You need some? Only have to say the word."

"I don't have to do anything, Sal." Vischer leans back and reads, the ballpoint still between his fingers.

"There's plenty of stuff you'd like, I'm not that stupid."

"Peace and quite, for instance," Vischer says. They can no longer hear the radio overhead.

"For me to stand on my head. You go for that. You really do like it here, don't you?"

"What?"

"You couldn't have it better anywhere else, what with boys always standing on their heads."

"What's with 'standing on their heads'?"

"You know what I mean, you know very well. Plus your little vase of flowers and the tablecloth and all the rest of the shit."

"You mean this?" Vischer pointed to a milk bottle behind the blackout drape, with a couple of withered wildflowers still stuck in some water.

"You ooze your way up to everybody here like a grease gun. 'Can I bring something back for you? Coffee, vodka? Ring-a-ding-ding and thanks a bunch too.' It pisses me off!"

Vischer shakes his head and goes on writing.

"But you just bring the stuff back, never take a drink yourself. It's your way of paying them off."

"For what?"

"Cocks and balls."

Vischer bursts into laughter. "Head fulla shit, Sal, nothing but shit."

"Didn't you let that pansy give you a massage, I saw it myself, you stretched out here, couldn't get enough."

"You mean Rosi?"

"Moaning the whole time. Hey, I was there."

"And you stretched out on your bed, too, Sal, don't forget," says Vischer, and looks up for the first time. "Somebody was all hot to get himself a massage from Rosi."

"I had my shirt on and didn't moan and carry on."

"Undershirt pushed clear up, Sal, and remember what you said, about how somebody could sit on your ass?"

"You really like it here, Visch, just like our flamer. Rosi himself said so, because he's not the only one, the place is fulla ripe boys who stand on their heads for him, Rosi said. And you, Visch, are just like all the rest, like all of 'em."

"Shut up, Sal," Vischer says, standing up and pulling the drape back. "Just shut your mouth."

There's a flash of lightning above the officers' barracks. Vischer sits down, uses the windowsill as a table, his knees against the cold radiator, his back to Salwitzky, who goes right on talking.

[Letter of March 30, 1990]

Vischer didn't turn around again until the squeaks began. Salwitzky is holding on to the metal frame with both hands behind his head, pressing his feet against the cross brace at the other end, and thrusting so that the bed frame shakes back and forth. "Rosi, you hot little piggy," Salwitzky cries, and loses his rhythm, braces his feet against the mattress of the top bunk, and then, getting into the swing of it, kicks first against the cross brace and then the mattress. He rocks back and forth. "You hot pig!" he shouts. The springs squeak, the frame scrapes the floor. "Piggy, piggy, you hot pig!"

Suddenly a high screech—the metal poles disengage, Salwitzky shouts, holding the bed above him with his feet, shouts again. Salwitzky is an acrobat, a shouting acrobat. He can't see Vischer because his legs, the bed, the mattress are in the way. "Have you got it?"

Vischer doesn't answer. "Have you got it?" Salwitzky shouts, and, with what looks like incredible effort, sticks his head out to one side, so that he can finally see Vischer, who is supporting the top bunk now and smiling.

Salwitzky rolls to one side and stands up. Together they relink the poles at the foot of the bed. Salwitzky bends down and pinches the crease of his right pants leg, but so cautiously it looks like it hurts him to do it. Then he inspects the crease of his left pants leg. Little sweat stains dot his back and shoulders.

Vischer goes back to writing, his head cocked down close to the page. Salwitzky is standing behind him. Only the clumps of grass reveal how windy it is.

The first raindrops are so big you can see each one strike the pale gray asphalt, which is almost bluish in this light.

Salwitzky bends down across Vischer's shoulder, cranks the window handle to open one of the panels. Like snowberries, the drops hit the asphalt with a loud slap. The sound even drowns out the trampling of boots, at least until the grid of the boot scraper starts resounding with a steady, almost rhythmic rattle.

Vischer sees a hand in front of his eyes, a strange, heavy hand with fat fingers, which as they spread reveal the tips with fingernails only half grown back and which remind Vischer of worms, or worse. Tendons and veins bulge, and the scar under the wedding ring turns white. Slowly the hand sinks down onto Vischer's sheet of paper, and as the trampling of boots and the voices out in the hallway grow louder and doors bang and the asphalt turns black, the hand soundlessly crumples up the page before Vischer's eyes.

The Spy

"Don't we have to make the spy talk if the spy won't open his mouth? What you say, spy? That's logical enough. Doesn't the spy think that sounds logical?"

Edgar was pushing the floor waxer back and forth in the hallway. Inch by inch he came closer again to the pack crowded before the open door of their room. To get a better look some used the shoulders of the man in front to jump or yanked a guy back who was doing the same thing. If it wasn't a yowl or a bellow, Edgar could understand every word.

"Great idea! Okay, spy, why so tongue-tied?"

"He's not tongue-tied. If there's one thing he isn't, it's tongue-tied— that he ain't."

They were ranting on just like before. Edgar had thought it would last ten, fifteen, at most twenty minutes. Twenty minutes waxing floors is a long time, the whole hallway: from the polit officer's room and the johns past the doors of the floor leader, supply room, and weapons store, past the stairway and the orderly room, then two doors for the first squad, two for the second, two for the third, washroom, stairway, noncoms, TV room, club room.

"Did you hear what he said, spy? Why's the spy holding out?"

"He only talks to the polit officer—chooses his words well, pot of coffee, milk, sugar, Duetts, the best of the best."

"I'll bet you anything he won't open his trap, won't do it."

Edgar didn't recognize the voice. The other two had been Mehnert and Pitt—Pitt, the little pink asshole with his jokes.

"Then we'll just have to cram something in it," Mehnert says.

"Unzip his zipper," shouted the voice he didn't recognize.

Edgar had figured there'd be a lot of talk but no real action. Which was why he had had no problem continuing to speak with the spy. "Don't

484

do anything to make them suspicious," Mehnert had said. "If they get wind of it, they'll transfer him or whatever," although no one knew what Mehnert meant by "whatever." Mehnert had gone so far as to borrow money from the spy. As compensation he'd offered to see that he got a pass. The spy had given him thirty marks, but turned down the pass. "That's proof," Pitt had said. "Now that all hell's broken loose in Poland, they need all the eyes and ears around here they can get." The spy had grown more cautious. He was writing less and then only when he was alone. But just now they had caught him at it again.

Today was the ninth day. For nine days now, Edgar had known what was going to happen to the spy—to the spy in his section, third squad, second section.

"We want to hear your voice, spy, you know so many words, fancy words, real pretty spy man's words."

"I told you, spy won't answer. Spy needs help, spy needs motivation, spy needs us."

As unpleasant as the affair with the spy was, it kept you from thinking stupid stuff. At least better than the singing did. Edgar couldn't understand how anybody could volunteer to go from company to company singing Christmas carols, as if this were an old folks' home. The reserve first lieutenant, who took over the quartermaster's job at Christmas, joined up—carols in harmony. Then he had gone with them, just picked up and went, as if they were going for a beer, and the noncom on duty had left to go eat, and his second-in-command had put his fingers to the corners of his mouth and whistled, a secret whistle, so to speak. And then he'd turned the radio up loud, some station in the West, and that had gotten them all in the mood—I wanna be a polar bear, up in the cold, cold north—and they'd all walked along the shiny hallway to the door of the spy's room and waited until the song was over.

Edgar had thought that the way they were standing silently at the door had actually meant they'd come to an agreement. Discipline, Mehnert had demanded it. It had been a victory for discipline, the way the entire company gathered outside the door in silence.

"He'll start bawling, but that'll be all he'll do, you'll see."

"There'll be more to it than that. Just wait and see what all he'll try."

Edgar kept on working, with even more regular, more rhythmic strokes, he thought. Like a musician Edgar could close his eyes, concentrating just on the rustle of the brush weighed down with metal plates and on the clicking sound when he changed directions. His arms knew, his whole body knew when he needed to brake the waxer so it wouldn't bang into the wall. Whenever a corner of the brush hit, it left holes in the plaster, which trickled down and was then evenly distributed by the brush. The only thing that bothered Edgar was how he couldn't help thinking about Pitt's stupid joke about waxing and stomach muscles and screwing.

The spy's weapon was a submachine gun. Edgar would have loved to trade with him, although a machine gun was heavier. But his own grenade launcher looked like a bassoon or something. He always felt ridiculous crawling through the sand with an instrument like that on his shoulder, even if it was the only weapon that could take out a tank. So they said, at least. In the APC they sat next to each other on the bench behind the first gunner. They could stretch their legs there or change off lying on the floor. But Edgar was quartered in a different room. Otherwise it might well have been him instead of Teichmann and Bär who had to testify as his victims: Yes, I said that, yes, I said that, in a regular rhythm, so that it took Edgar three swipes with the waxer, left, right, left—yes, I said that, three times across the width of the hall, click, click, click—yes, I said that. The spy had written it all down, word for word. And Mehnert had the proof in his hand, Private Mehnert, a "junior," driver, room corporal.

Teichmann—who because of his ponderous gait and gray hair everyone assumed was from the reserves—didn't want to have anything to do with this circus. It was different with Bär, who approved of what Mehnert was doing. But Bär didn't want any blows struck either, at least that wasn't part of the plan.

"Nobody said anything about 'at ease.' Did some one say 'at ease'?"

"Hey you, hey spy, that's a question, did anyone give the order 'at ease'?"

[Letter of March 4, 1990]

They had kicked the spy's legs out from under him.

Edgar pushed the waxer up close to the first pair of boots and past some slippers, and Frank—the first gunman from his group, who always said he was the lucky one, because during an attack he wouldn't have to get out and run across an open field—offered Edgar his stool. "He wants it this way, he's provoking it," Frank exclaimed as he ran to the john.

The spy doesn't know anything about a plan, and so he's not scared. And you can always tell if someone's scared or not. They don't have to say anything. Just a glance will do. And a glance like that is the worst sort of provocation. Or a gesture of the hand. His hands aren't bound tight, although his wrists are tied even with his head to the cross brace where it joins the frame at the foot of the top bunk. Bär had moved his hands during the dry run, as if he were trying to wave or fly—at any rate it had been so funny that even Mehnert and Pitt had laughed.

That cracking sound was slapping. It was perfectly natural for all this to escalate. Kicking his feet out from under him was childish. If you hit the heel just right, the guy went sprawling. But the spy couldn't fall, he was bound to the bed. Slaps hurt.

"Stuff his mouth with the shit!"

"Swallow it, spy."

"Dicks on parade, dicks on parade!"

When the spy didn't open his mouth, they tried to force him with slaps. Mehnert wanted to rip the page in pieces, three times, not too small and not too big, the spy should have to chew a little.

Edgar had held the page, scribbled full of slanted lines, in his own hand. Mehnert had given it to anyone who wanted to see. But whoever wanted to read it would have to join in, it was as straightforward as that—straight straightforward, Bär had said. Edgar tried to imagine what it looks like when you stuff paper into somebody's mouth. Crumpled up or in a stack of little slips like a piece of pyramid cake. Edgar had once cut his tongue licking an envelope. But how did you force him to chew and swallow? And what if he spit it all out? Who would pick up the soggy pieces? Did you then start all over again? They were bellowing so loud now it was as if there weren't an officer anywhere in the whole regiment.

Edgar shoved the waxer along behind the pack of them. When he had room again, it took a while for him to get his rhythm back.

Edgar stopped humming once he noticed that it was the melody of "I Wanna Be a Polar Bear." He didn't like the song any better than he liked Pitt's joke about it. But what with all the noise, he couldn't come up with another tune. Edgar was working much too fast now, as if trying to get away from the yowling. But he didn't want to get away. He wasn't afraid. He knew the plan and he knew Mehnert's laugh—the way his mouth repeated the curves of his chin, a clownish laugh. Maybe Mehnert would laugh like that when he removed the spy's belt and pulled down his pants—laugh with pride at how his plan had been no empty promise.

487

With uniform pants all you had to do was unhook the front and pull the suspenders aside, but he'd have to take hold of his own long johns and pull them down. Or were Mehnert and Bär already rubbing the spy's butt with shoe polish? No, Mehnert would spare himself that—that was dirty work for somebody else he'd call forward, somebody who would make the others laugh. The spy wouldn't laugh, even if it tickled. Who knows what a shoe brush feels like on your naked ass and if you might not get used to it—or whether the spy's cheeks would pinch tight in reflex. And if he did laugh? He'd regret it. Or start bawling? What do you do with a bawling spy? He wouldn't bawl. The spy keeps his eyes down or looks at the ceiling. And what if he looked at the others, looked them in the eye? What would be the point? To memorize their names? To swear revenge? The whole affair was too cut-and-dried for that. If there was such a thing as hard proof, that was the case here. The spy was being served his just desserts, taught a lesson. Edgar wondered how much Mehnert was risking in deciding to do this. Mehnert had guts, he was the ringleader, he'd be the first to be punished.

Where the hallway opened onto the stairwell, Edgar gave the waxer more of a free rein. He could in fact feel his stomach muscles. The second-in-command stood up from his desk as if to make way for Edgar, and then headed to join the pack.

Why hadn't the spy yelled for some noncoms? Two of them had watched, Detchens and Freising, the good-looking Spaniard. Someone brought them a stool. But even if they were to say something, give the order to cease and desist, it wouldn't have made any difference. It would only impair their authority. And if the spy begged for them to help free him? Let him try it, just a simple "Comrade officer, help me!" That would put Freising and Detchens on the hot seat.

"Mehnert's painting his dick," the second-in-command said as he passed Edgar on the way to the john.

They were really into it now. Mehnert dabbed the tip of the spy's cock with a brush. Like an animal trainer Mehnert would get the spy's cock to rear up. And every one of them wanted to see some other guy get hard, since his was the only dick he'd ever had in his hand. Edgar forced himself to think of soccer, school, hiking trips. "I wanna be a polar bear, up in the cold, cold north, wouldn't have a single care . . ." Mehnert in the role of his life. The spy's cock would rise above right angle, like an obscene salute. Mehnert planned to hang the spy's belt over his hard-on and then count how long it would hang there, like a boxing referee. Then it would be time for photographs—of the woman the spy claimed was his girl-friend, although he never wrote to her. The spy hadn't thought about that. The only letters he gets, Mehnert said, are from his mother and some other guy.

Maybe the best thing the spy could do would be to start bawling or fight back, really fight back, screaming and spitting—whatever he could still manage. The pack suddenly closed ranks, everything got quiet, then whistles, applause.

Edgar let the waxer swing back and forth between the polit officer's door and the john. He'd have to turn around soon. Mehnert wanted to "milk the spy." But maybe the spy was so intimidated that his cock wouldn't give any milk, no matter how Mehnert went about it, with gloves or without.

Edgar tried to think of something else. But not of home.

Actually Teichmann and Bär were to blame. If they had just punched the spy out, they wouldn't have had to tie up a guy lying writhing on the floor, or blacken his ass or milk his cock.

Edgar reversed direction and saw the pack up ahead. That's our Christmas party, he thought—and the moment he saw them and thought of the Christmas party, Edgar knew that from now on there would never be a Christmas when he didn't think of this Christmas party. He realized it was like the sentence of a condemned man: he would never be able to celebrate Christmas without this pack, without Mehnert, without Pitt, without Bär and Teichmann, without the spy and the plan. Step by step, word for word, the plan was imprinted in his mind—he'd thought of it too often. The plan would stick with him just like this polar bear song and Pitt's joke about stomach muscles. Just as he would never forget the moment when all this had become clear to him—even though he hadn't joined in, wasn't even watching. All he could hear was the steady barrage of roaring laughter. Should he clamp his ears shut? There was no way he could keep the whole thing from being imprinted on his mind.

He wanted to do something else, fix his mind on other things. But he couldn't stop now, what else could he do? It was absolutely impossible to stop now.

At first he didn't realize that boots had ended up in the path of his waxer. But then it was like a herd in flight—slippers, gym shoes, socks, boots, leaping and hopping in front of the waxer, and those that didn't leap or hop got bumped. It was like a children's game, like tag. The faster he worked the more he hit. Eeny, meeny, miney, mo! I wanna be a polar bear. He gave the waxer its head. The "mo" hasn't landed on you yet, up there in the cold, cold north.

He heard shouts, but those were part of the game. And somebody punching the spy and pulling him from the bed frame—it was all in the plan. Just like kids. If they lose, they tear everything up. But he had to keep working. Here, where the pack had stood, there was still lots to do, countless heel marks in an unusual and complicated pattern.

And suddenly he saw him—the spy. The spy came out of the room. The spy didn't look upset or angry, not even sad. The spy hadn't screamed, he hadn't cried. The spy had his kit under his arm and a towel over his shoulder. He was holding tight to his pants with one hand. A couple of steps, and the spy had vanished into the washroom.

And Edgar went on working. He now realized that he had been standing still, still and erect, the waxer at his feet, the handle clamped perpendicular under his arm.

But first he had to memorize the patterns of the heel marks—at the very same moment that his waxer passed over them. It wasn't easy, but he worked hard, he could feel his stomach muscles. And at last he got his reward too. The faster he swiped back and forth with the waxer, the more clearly he could see the heel marks under the shine, locked in permanent ice.

Voting

—So twenty?

—Ten, four buttons, ten marks.

—Hey! You just said, twenty. Four buttons, twenty.

—Ten!— Michael held out his hand.

—No way, you doofus.— Rolf blinked through the smoke of his cigarette. As the ash fell it bounced off his sweater.

—Twenty.

—Ten. I've only got ten. Here.— Michael smiled and pulled a crumpled bill out of his pocket.

—Then you'd better start worryin' about how to come up with the rest. Twenty for four buttons.— Rolf flicked the butt into a flower bed and sat down on the rim of a trash can.

—And what if she's already here?— Michael checked his watch.

—You think they're waiting for *you*?— Rolf nodded in the direction of the polling place, where two photographers were standing at the entrance. A group of women emerged laughing. Two of them were holding little red flags. A man in a light-colored suit walking behind them sang: "So comrades, let us rally and the last fight let us . . ." and then fell silent when a few people turned around to look at him. The women snorted and nudged one another and walked faster.

Rolf rummaged in his sack. He pulled the red cap off a plastic bottle, filled it to the brim, and drank. He poured another and handed it to Michael.

—Smoking leaves a man thirsty.

—What's in it?— Michael gave it a cautious sip.

—Tea, what else?— Rolf grinned.

Michael sipped a second time and made a face.

—Take a gander!— Rolf whispered. A well-dressed, middle-aged couple had come to a halt not far from them. The man buckled forward as if he had a stitch in his side. The woman was trying to comfort him and caressed his shoulder briefly. The man stood up straight again. They linked arms and, taking small steps, slowly made their way to the polling place.

—Full ballot— Michael said.

—He hasn't gone for three days. I remember how it was with my old man.

—Three days?

—That's what I said!— Rolf drank straight from the bottle.—That's nothing for them. They used to hold out for a whole week.

—They didn't use to have anything to eat. That was no great feat back then.

—Bullshit! There's always been plenty right before elections, even chocolate. They really chowed down.

—My mother couldn't hold out any longer yesterday and started bawling, I mean really bawled. And my old man just kept going: You'll make it, you'll make it, you will. And when she wouldn't stop bawling, he said, okay, fine, do whatever you think is right.

Rolf whinnied.—Do whatever you think is right? . . . whatever you *think*?

—Do whatever you think is right— Michael repeated in all seriousness.

—And, did she?— Rolf coughed. He pulled out a pack of old Juwels and tapped it on the bottom until a filter popped out a little.

Michael shrugged. —Things calmed down. She crept back into bed or whatever. Do I get one?

—Moocher!— Rolf held out the pack. —I thought you didn't like the taste so early in the morning?— Rolf gave him a light.

—Look at 'em waddle.— Michael glanced over to the bus stop.

—They're used to it. They've been waddling their whole life long.

The oldsters had trouble stepping from the bus onto the sidewalk. Once they managed it, they hurried as fast as they could to the end of the waiting line.

—Why don't they order the mobile ballot box? I'd cast my vote with the mobile.

Rolf made a face. —Too revolting for me.

—Revolting, yes, but still better than a hullabaloo like this.

—Absolutely revolting.— Rolf downed the bottle in one gulp, screwed the top on, tapped the last few drops out of the red cap, and fit it back over the bottle.

—A mobile ballot box turns my stomach!— Rolf turned away to one side and let his spit drip down the trash can.

—Frau Rollman said the Free German Youth unhinged three doors, at least three.

—Three doors? They're not allowed to do that, not by law at least.

—Don't give me any bullshit, you'll see. It was an FGY initiative, from way high up.

—My grandma without a door, no way.

—Your grandma'll get a door.

—And Tina?

—Are you so dumb or do you just act like it?— Rolf let the spit splat on the sidewalk pavement between his sneakers.

—Dammit all!— Michael hid the cigarette in the palm of his hand. —Shit, they're waving, hey, they're waving us over!

—No need to piss your pants.— Rolf wiped the back of his hand across his mouth. His cigarette fell to the ground, he wrapped the bag around his wrist, and followed Michael.

—Don't fall asleep, sports fans!— Michael and Rolf broke into a run the last few yards.

—So why the loitering?— The policeman hooked his thumbs into his belt.

—Just for once we were . . .

—I didn't ask how *often*, sports fans, the question was *why*!

—I'm not feeling good— Rolf said.

—But smoking like a chimney?

—An occasional cigarette.

—So what's that?— The policeman pointed to Rolf's right hand, to the yellow stains on his index and middle fingers.

Rolf winced.

—First-time voter, huh?

—Yes— Rolf and Michael responded both at once.

—Your papers!

Rolf and Michael handed the police their passports.

—So what's with all the trips to Czechoslovakia?

—Mountain climbers— Michael quickly replied. They could hear the radio in the police car. The shotgun responded as car 17.

—The Red Mountaineers, ever heard of 'em?— The policeman thumbed back and forth in their passports.

—Kurt Schlosser, sure, know about 'em— Michael said.

—The bag.— Rolf handed it over. The policeman unscrewed the bottle and sniffed.

—Chamomile tea, why's that?

—Little sick to my stomach— Rolf said.

—So why haven't you voted yet?

—Waitin' for a buddy.

—And what's the buddy's name?

—Sebastian— Michael said. —Sebastian Keller.

—Keller, Sebastian. Okay. And where does this Keller, Sebastian, live?

—Georg-Schumann Strasse, one hundred . . .

—Don't you own a blue shirt?

—I've got it on underneath— Michael pulled at the crewneck of his sweater and tugged the blue collar out over it.

—And you?

—I'm not in the FGY.

—Not in the youth organization?

—Religious reasons.

—But elections, I mean, casting your vote, you are going to cast your vote, right?

Rolf nodded warily. —Plan to.— Rolf turned around and spat on the lawn.

—Well then, enjoy yourself, have a good one!— He handed Rolf back both passports. —And congratulations as a first-time voter!— He gave a nonchalant salute. As he opened the driver's door of his Lada, his shotgun was just saying —Over and out!

Michael and Rolf shuffled in the direction of the polling place.

—What kind of shit was that, religious reasons?— Michael whispered.

—Didn't you see how he backed off?

—And what if he checks it out?

—What's he supposed to check out?

Squad car 17 passed by them and stopped right in front of the polling place.

—Religion is always good. They're even glad if you say you're religious and then tell them you're voting anyway.

—Have you ever imagined being the only person to do it.

494

—Do what?

—Cast a vote.

—What d'you mean, the only person?

—Just picture it. You come here to do it, and nobody else shows. You're the only one to vote, just you.

—Oh man . . .

—I'd die. I'd rather die.

—Why die?

—Because it would be so embarrassing. Everybody would say that's the guy who cast his vote, and then they'd giggle and shout stuff as I walked past.

—I'd like to have your problems, I mean really.

—I'll be damned, meathead, there's Tina. There!

The crowd in front of the polling place had begun to stir. The two photographers trotted toward the curb, a second squad car pulled up, a man with a tape recorder and mike around his neck was the first to step up in front of the family, in whose midst stood a young brunette of average height in a blue blouse, a bright red ribbon in her ponytail.

Running the last little bit, Rolf and Michael arrived to hear Tina tell the man with the tape recorder —Oh, quite normal really, like always, lots of exercise, healthy diet, lots of fresh air.— As the reporter was about to ask his second question, she added with a smile— And never get to bed too late.

Everyone laughed, Tina's dark eyes sparkled.

Michael pulled off his sweater, so that he was standing there in a blue shirt now too.

—Four, there are exactly four!— Rolf said in triumph. They had to stand on tiptoe.

—Twenty, Mishi, you owe me twenty. Four buttons!

Michael gazed spellbound at Tina's blue blouse and nodded. —Okay, okay.

—As far back as kindergarten— Tina said —I always pictured just what it would be like, casting my vote for the first time. We painted pictures of it, lots of times. And once we were even allowed to use modeling clay. We've still got that one at home in the living room.

Her father and mother nodded. Tina was the spitting image of her mother, down to the eyebrows almost merging.

—My vote is my good health. My parents taught me that early on.

And I always envied my parents, how genuinely happy they were after they had cast their vote. Yes, really, they'd come home simply beaming. And I thought, I want to be able to do that too.

The faces of those waiting in line bore a look of concentration and strain, if anything was said at all it was in a low voice. The line was moving so slowly that some of them had sat down on the pavement, and didn't even stand up to edge forward.

—Is that really necessary?— a balding, skinny man asked as he emerged from the polling place. But the woman who was seated on the steps up to the entrance didn't answer. She didn't so much as look up. The volunteer election warden shook his head and walked on, greeting someone now and then and tugging at the knot of his tie. He stopped beside Michael.

—Comrade Becker!— he exclaimed.—Comrade Be . . . — An elbow struck him in the sternum. The volunteer doubled over.

—What are you making a pest of yourself for? This isn't your shindig— a young, sturdy guy in a beige anorak hissed. —Can't you see we're broadcasting?

The volunteer nodded and raised a conciliatory hand. He gave a little cough, he cleared his throat, but then stood up straight and reached for the knot of his tie.

—My favorite book is *Fate of a Man* by Mikhail Sholokhov, I found it very moving, such a hard and difficult life, and he struggles and hopes because he wants life to be beautiful. And I have to add that that Sholokhov manages in a hundred pages to capture a man's fate, where other authors write big fat books and have far less to say, yes, Sholokov.

[Letter of April 21, 1990]

I really do admire him. And Aitmatov, *Jamila,* how difficult happiness can be, yes, Aitmatov and Sholokhov.

The volunteer held his left arm up high and tapped his watch. The young guy in the beige anorak cast him a suspicious glance.

—Can it.

—Schedule. We do have a schedule.

—So do we.— The young guy in the beige anorak gave him a gloating grin.

—I think I'm well prepared. And I'm looking forward to being able to cast my vote now. And I'm also happy to be doing it together with other first-time voters.

The volunteer reached into the sleeve of his sport coat and pulled his shirt cuff down. He was watching Michael out of the corner of one eye.

—First-time voter?

Michael nodded.

—And you?

—First-timer too.

—And where's your blue shirt?

—Forgot.

The volunteer was still plucking at his sleeves. —Come along with me, we're going inside right now— he told Michael.

—Me?

—Got your passport? Police record?

—No, I mean, yes, I have my passport.

—Me too?

The volunteer gave a quick shake of his head. He removed his glasses, rubbed his eyes, and stared at Michael.

—Comb your hair, and don't fall asleep when the time comes.

The volunteer handed Michael a little white comb and stood on tiptoe.

—We, my friend and I, he's a first-timer too, we actually wanted to do it together. . . .

—Without a blue shirt? Sorry.

—And if I go get one, I live nearby . . .

The volunteer took a little hop to one side. —Comrade Becker, Wilfried, here, here I am!— He was waving both arms and running along the queue in the direction of the entrance. Michael and Rolf followed the volunteer.

—Doofus! You're such a doofus.

—I can't help it, I just asked him if . . .

—Such an asshole!

Suddenly the volunteer pulled Michael by the arm, and a moment later the bright red bow of Tina's ponytail was right in front of his nose. The collar of her blue blouse was rolled up a little. She smelled of shampoo and fresh underwear. Somebody pushed him from behind. —Doofus!—a voice shouted.

In the next instant Michael found himself pressing against Tina. He could feel her rear end, her hair, a shoulder.

—Oh, oooh.

She turned halfway to him so that he could see the dimple on her right cheek.

—Oh, beg your pardon, but . . .

Michael fumbled for his passport. When he looked up the ribbon and ponytail had vanished. There was the odor of stale air, footsteps echoed through the large tiled room, whose far wall was glass brick. The election commission behind separated desks stood up like a school class and waited. Dead center was the ballot box, a piece of standard stationery covered its opening. The banner on the wall behind it proclaimed in white letters against a red background: OUR VOTES FOR THE CANDIDATES OF THE NATIONAL FRONT!

The lights were switched on, fluorescent tubes flickered. Voices blurred the way they do in an indoor swimming pool.

A fly crawled across the back of Michael's right hand. He raised the hand, the fly vanished, only to return to the same spot a moment later. Michael slapped at it with a loud smack.

The volunteer looked up briefly and winked at Michael. Stepping forward with him were a boy and a girl, both FGY members. They were waiting for Tina. A man with yolk yellow hair and a black leather jacket shook her hand and smiled. The woman beside him had thin bright red lips that shifted in an ashen pale face. Gold-rimmed glasses dangled from her neck.

—Take your places here, my young friends. Now pull yourselves together. So, here we go now. Lots of luck.

Approaching the long table one after the other, they gave their names, handed over their passports, and quickly received them back. Tina was the last to be given her ballot.

—Hey there, my lad, no daydreaming, report over there now.

Without glancing at the names on his ballot, Michael turned around toward the voting booths. Of those missing a door, the middle one was still unoccupied.

—Look sharp, my lad, look sharp. We have to keep to our schedule here.— The volunteer clapped his hands like a gym teacher.

From his voting booth Michael was able to watch as the yolk yellow man and the woman held tight to the table while Tina climbed up on it. She stood up carefully and, without grabbing hold of any of the many hands offered her, walked to the ballot box. She laid her ballot across the top of the box, hastily unzipped her trousers, which slid down her legs. She quickly slipped her panties down, squatted over the ballot box, and began to press. With half-open eyes she stared at the damaged tile at Michael's feet, a vein bulged above her right temple, her face took on a bronze color.

The volunteer, who had turned half away, suddenly shouted: —Face toward the election commission, Tina. Toward the election commiss—!

Tina stood up in fright. Even for a fit young woman it wasn't all that easy to move across the wiggly tables. Tina corrected the position of her ballot and squatted down over the box again. Her blue blouse hid most of her rear end.

In the meantime Michael had laid his ballot across the porcelain bowl, pulled his pants and underpants down both at once, and sat. He pressed hard too. In the booth to his left he could hear a jet of urine meet the water in the bowl, grow gradually fainter, and then abruptly end without any drops to follow. To his right Michael heard a loud fart, and a groan, and then, as something heavy fell on the ballot, a crinkling sound. Closing his eyes, the volunteer gave several nods of approval.

Michael couldn't take his eyes off Tina. Her blue blouse, beneath which he could see the outline of the broad fastener on her bra, emphasized her athletic figure.

Suddenly she raised her rear end, hiked up her blouse—and something appeared between her butt cheeks, grew longer, a thin little sausage dropped, gases escaped, a restrained —Aaaahh— followed, and then another, somewhat darker, shorter, sausage.

The first-timer on Michael's right had already shoved his massive vote out in front of his booth and was frantically tearing off toilet paper. And the first-timer to his left had likewise given all the candidates her vote.

Michael got up and carefully removed his work from the bowl. The ballot had gotten a little damp at the top. In the middle, however, lay his vote, round and smooth and ending in a jaunty peak.

—Like a meringue tart, just a little browner.

As he laid it on the floor, Michael couldn't entirely suppress his smile. The rustle of toilet paper could be heard on all sides. The pattern on Tina's panties wasn't red polka dots, no, those were ladybugs. Her cheeks were flush, sweat glistened on her upper lip and forehead. The election commission was already removing the bouquets from their pails of water. Michael needed to hurry up.

Suddenly someone squeezed his arm. —One casts one's vote for an entire list of candidates, not individuals.— Michael stared in bewilderment at the volunteer.

—You see, there, there, Wilfried Becker, doesn't he get your vote? Do you have something against the Society for Sport and Technology?

—Should I . . .— Michael raised his right forefinger.

—Yes of course, do it, do it, everyone's waiting for you.

Michael tried to smear his round sausage toward the top and bottom, but it was more solid than he had thought. He spit, he spit a second time, it just barely worked. But now it looked so untidy, unaesthetic. Michael was the last to stuff his ballot into the box and now glanced down very earnestly at the Thälmann Pioneer who handed him three carnations with lots of greenery. The handshake that followed the Pioneer salute was limp and damp. Now that everyone had a carnation bouquet, the applause began.

The four first-timers were given a rousing reception outside. All the people standing in front of the polling place had turned toward them and were clapping enthusiastically.

Michael was numb somehow. —I thought they'd be mad at us.

—But why?— Tina laughed.—Why should they be mad at us?

—I just thought . . .— Michael spotted Rolf clapping wildly. Michael gave him a nod and a tortured smile. Rolf, on the other hand, seemed to be in a great mood, and gestured to him by dangling his right hand below his belt, swinging it back and forth, while his thumb and fingers kept snapping open and shut like a hungry mouth.

—Is that your buddy?— Tina asked.

—Well yes, buddy, we went to school together.

—Tell him he's a little pig, tell him I said so. A real little piggy.

—Because of the four . . .

—He wants you to pinch me in the butt. Don't you see it?

—Oh, he's just pretending.

—What a little pig. He's jealous.

—Jealous?

—Why sure. But we deserve this.

Michael counted the number of open buttons on her blouse. There were in fact four. He had lost the bet. But on the other hand he could see her cleavage, the shadow between her breasts.

Tina smiled.

—You're a little piggy too!— Her eyes were sparkling again. People just wouldn't stop applauding.

—Wave, wave!— she whispered.

Michael began to move his right hand from side to side.

—You see, Mischa, it works!— Tina exclaimed.

Michael felt uncomfortable because his fingers were sticky. But that didn't prevent him from waving. And so he kept on swaying his right hand from side to side.

May[1]

MAI

```
NELKENELKENELKENELKE
NLKENELKENELKENELE
NKENELKENELKENEE
NENELKENELKENE
NNELKENELKEE
NELKENELKE
NLKENELE
NKENEE
NENE
NE
EN
ENEN
ELNEKN
EELNEKEN
EKELNEKELN
EEKELNEKELNN
ENEKELNEKELNEN
ELNEKELNEKELNEKN
EELNEKELNEKELNEKEN
EKELNEKELNEKELNEKELN
```

1. Translator's note: This piece of concrete poetry is an example of how certain texts defy translation. The poem's subject is the carnations (German: *"Nelken"*) distributed to all citizens of the GDR on May Day and worn in the lapel or otherwise publicly displayed. The poem ends, as it began, with the letters of the word *"Nelken."* But the final five letters likewise spell *"ekeln,"* which is German for "to disgust, repulse, nauseate."

Titus Holm

A DRESDEN NOVELLA

I

Titus Holm walked across the school courtyard, his satchel in his right hand, and in his left, dangling a little lower, a gym bag that slapped against his thigh. It had turned warmer again, leaves flickered yellow and orange in the afternoon sun. He would have taken off his anorak if it hadn't been for the wind, which came at him now head on, now from the side, carrying with it the sound of choir rehearsal drifting like a defective recording through an open window. It was not until Titus passed the rusty bicycle stands and emerged through the main portal that he actually pieced together a melody.

He turned right. At the foot of the wrought-iron fence that enclosed Holy Cross School—including a boarding school for choir members—and whose tips ended in coiling flames, he could still see the traces of the wire broom he had used to rake leaves the day before. At first he had been uneasy about having to put in his hours of People's Mass Initiative here, where he could be observed from the boarding school dorm.

"Call me when it's over," Joachim had whispered at the end of last class. Titus came to a halt in front of the dorm and glanced up at Joachim's window, where the left casement was wide open. Titus would have preferred to keep on walking. He was in fact in a hurry. What was he supposed to tell him? That he had sat in the cellar for an hour facing Petersen, or was it a half hour or maybe only twenty minutes?

When Mario, who had had to precede him in the cellar with Petersen, returned to the classroom and called out, "Next, please!," Titus, who sat waiting amid all the other chairs stacked on their tables, had been too agitated to check the clock. He was the last of the boys from grade nine.

Mario had evaded Titus's questions until he finally more or less sulkily declared that he didn't want to see things like an egoist and claim his life only for himself, but to achieve something for society as well.

"What would that be?" Titus had asked. "I thought you wanted to become a doctor."

"Of course I want to be a doctor, but someplace where I'm needed." With that Mario had stuffed his gym clothes into his satchel, rolled up his right pants leg, knotted the laces of his gym shoes together, and hung them around his neck. "You really can't be . . ." Titus had started to say, when he noticed the white smock at the open door. Petersen, their homeroom teacher, shook Titus's hand as if presenting him an award. And then he called out to Mario, "Keep thinking along those lines!" Then, pointing to the stairs: "Titus, if you please."

In the basement physics lab Petersen had pressed his way past him to open the door to a small chamber that was little more than a narrow passage between two tables with some oscillographs, scarcely wider than the old swivel chair under the cellar window where Petersen had taken a seat. The stool beside the door was for Titus. "We have plenty of time," Petersen had said, carefully laying his watch to one side.

Later, when the conversation was over and Titus had already got to his feet, Petersen was suddenly holding a book in his hand. To Titus it looked like some evil magic trick.

Book in hand, Titus climbed the stairs, taking one step at a time, uncertain whether he should go on ahead or wait for Petersen, since there had been no response to his second "good-bye" either. Outside the door to the physics classroom, Titus had wedged his satchel and gym bag between his feet, as if there were no other way to push the handle. Rattling his keys, Petersen came marching up and then, after ignoring a third "good-bye" as well, vanished into the teachers' lounge.

The stale air of the physics room, its hardwood floor a dull black from too much waxing, the apple core under his seat, and the bulletin board that always hung askew—suddenly it all made him feel right at home . . .

Outside the boarding-school dorm Titus called out for Joachim, shouted just loud enough that he had to hear him. In lieu of a reply, a window on the ground floor opened. Titus repeated his call at short intervals. Despite a sense of being slighted because Joachim had not waited for him, he was glad he could now avoid his friend with a good conscience.

But in the very next moment Titus was startled to see that Joachim was one of two boys crossing the street from the public park. He ran toward them, but they halted in their tracks. Titus set down his satchel, rummaged around in it as if looking for something, and was suddenly holding Petersen's yellow book in his hand. The back cover was ribbed, a rolling landscape that came from too many moist fingertips. When Titus looked across to them again, Joachim was now headed toward him. The other boy, a book clasped under his arm, was loping toward the dorm. Titus stuffed Petersen's book behind his atlas, so that it wouldn't touch his notebooks and textbooks.

"There you are already," Joachim said, groped for and produced a cigarette and, turning abruptly to his right, bent down over the match. His tight extra-long cardigan made him look even skinnier. He blew the smoke out of one corner of his mouth.

"We've been reading his first novella," Joachim said, "want to walk a little?" Titus nodded.

"To think they printed it! It must have slipped past them somehow." Joachim pulled a couple of folded pages out from under his cardigan—checkered, letter-size sheets written full on both sides. Titus recognized the handwriting—printed letters bouncing along the squares in tight formation, plus arrows, underlinings, and fat periods.

" 'Why do they have power?' " Joachim's forefinger traced the line. " 'Because you give it to them. And they'll have power as long as you're cowards.' What do you think?"

"Who says it?" Titus looked down at the scuffed toes of Joachim's shoes.

"Ferdinand, a painter, gets a letter, on official tan letterhead, telling him he's been drafted and has to return to Germany, World War I. He doesn't want to, his wife doesn't want to. But he feels some inner compulsion . . ."

"A compulsion?" Titus asked.

"They've fled Germany, but not officially. Listen to this," Joachim said. " 'For two months he managed to go on living in the suffocating air of jingoism, but slowly the air grew too thin, and when people around him opened their mouths to speak he thought he could see the yellow of the lies staining their tongues. No matter what they said it disgusted him.' " Joachim read slowly and clearly. He kept shifting his body to protect the pages from the wind. "Great writing, isn't it?" Joachim pushed his long dark blond hair behind his ears and stuck the pages into his waistband under his cardigan.

"Yes," Titus said. " 'The yellow of the lies staining their tongues,' really good stuff."

It was always like this. Joachim talked and Titus listened, because he hadn't read the book, didn't know the composer or the Bible verse, or because names like Gandhi, Dubček, or Bahro meant nothing to him. Joachim had time to read. Joachim had time for everything that interested him. But even if Titus had read the novella, the words would have paled beside Joachim's retelling of them.

Joachim described the conversation between Ferdinand the painter and his wife, Paula, who hopes to talk him out of returning to Germany, to war, and how desperate she feels with a husband who actually sees through it all, is so weak—here Joachim hesitated—so tepid that he's unable to find anything to hold on to, and so is caught up in the maelstrom. He leaves for Zurich on the first train the next morning.

"For Zurich?" Titus stopped in his tracks. "Why for Zurich?"

"Because they're still in Switzerland!" Cigarette smoke rippled from Joachim's lips. "He goes to the consulate in Zurich with the idea that because he knows people there he can change their minds—and falls flat on his face. He arrives way too early—premature obedience."

Premature obedience, Titus thought. But he was even more taken by "Zurich." If you lived in Zurich, you didn't have any problems, at least no serious ones. It was easy to be brave in Zurich.

"We were thinking of you the whole time," Joachim said. He flicked the butt away. Titus blushed. It was his turn. He had to say something now.

"And not just thinking," Joachim added, and with a quick twist of his shoe tip, the butt vanished in the gutter. "So now you've gotten to know the cellar."

"For over an hour," Titus said.

"Among the oscillographs?"

"Yes," Titus said. He wanted to speak with the same sort of deliberation Joachim did.

"He's most comfortable in his little lair," Joachim said with a laugh. "When all is said and done, Petersen is a poor bastard."

Titus wanted to ask why Petersen was a poor bastard.

"Got some money? Want to go to the Toscana?" Joachim asked.

"Yes," Titus said, although he was supposed to meet someone and was in a hurry.

Titus knew the café only from the outside, the last building on the left before the bridge. He knew Holy Cross choirboys went to the Toscana after rehearsal when they should have been in class—for breakfast, as they put it. Titus could see himself now standing beside Joachim at the curb, directly across from the parking lot, and heard himself say, "My treat."

They walked along Hübler Strasse. They stood awhile outside the bookstore. When they got to Schiller Platz they watched the traffic cop's pantomime and let him wave them across. Instead of waiting with the others to change sides of the street, they headed for the Blue Wonder Bridge.

The wind was blowing harder now, directly in their faces. Ever since they had known each other, Titus had tried to see the world through Joachim's eyes. Everything was straightforward and compelling, and Titus's own life seemed to gain clarity whenever Joachim talked about him, just like he could suddenly understand a math problem or a tricky bit of grammar once Joachim formulated it. At the same time, however, he found it painful that he had no advice for Joachim, couldn't give him anything. Joachim didn't need him.

Titus hung up his anorak in the Toscana's coatroom, then slipped into a seat at the round window table near the door while it was still being cleared. Joachim walked over to the pastry display and came back with his ticket. Titus followed his example. He was surprised to see so many old women in hats here.

Joachim greeted the waitress, whose lacy décolletage opened onto a view of the top of her breasts. The wrinkles at her neck looked like strings cutting into her skin. He ordered two pots of coffee and gave her the pastry tickets.

"While he's in Zurich Ferdinand gets a shave and has his good suit brushed." Joachim simply picked up the story where he had left off, as if there had been no interruption. "Ferdinand buys gray gloves and a walking stick, he wants to make a good impression. He's ready now, every 'i' dotted, every 't' crossed. But then it all turns out very differently."

Joachim went on talking, tapping his cigarette on the tabletop as if to some secret rhythm. Titus was miffed that Joachim hadn't asked him anything else about the cellar and Petersen. Or was he trying to go easy on him? And what was so special about the Toscana, with its flock of bird-faced women? Why had he agreed to come here? Didn't he have a will of his own?

Joachim went on talking, leaning back now, his legs crossed, a cigarette in his right hand, his left hand resting on the table as if to show Titus the large half-moons of his fingernails and veins like you see on men's hands—worms wriggling toward his wrist.

Joachim had unbuttoned just the top buttons of his cardigan. He inhaled deep, his chest rose and fell. Titus stared at him and suddenly found himself inexplicably repulsed by this breathing, as if it were unseemly. He had never seen Joachim naked, not even from the waist up. During gym he always kept his undershirt on under his blue gym outfit. All he could remember was that Joachim's arms were freckled with moles.

[Letter of May 5, 1990]

Titus bent forward, but Joachim didn't lower his voice. Or wasn't he going to read any more of it? " 'If only people had the will,' " Johann declaimed, " 'but instead they obey. They are like schoolboys. The teacher calls on them, they stand up, trembling.' " He wasn't holding the page between his fingers, but with his whole hand, wrinkling it along the edge. Titus would have loved to interrupt him: That's my book! I ran out and bought it during recess. You borrowed it from me. I refuse to let you talk about it. I won't let you copy it out, and above all I forbid you to give it to somebody else you meet in the park, somebody I don't know.

Titus could feel things between him and Joachim coming to a head. But he had no name for it. He was powerless against it. He swallowed, and his throat hurt from his gratuitous accusations. At the same time a kind of shame left him feeling uneasy, as if they had actually had a fight. Titus barely noticed when their coffee and pastries arrived.

He wanted to pull Petersen's book from his satchel, hold it under Joachim's nose, slam it onto the plate of cheesecake he was scarfing down. He let the idea carry him away.

"He dumped this on me," he heard himself exclaim. Titus looked down at the book in his hands, *Bundeswehr, the Aggressor,* flaming red letters against a yellow background. And when Joachim responded with just a hint of a smirk, he flung it at his chest. "He dumped this on me," he shouted. "A little report on the Bundeswehr as the aggressor, and what conclusions we should draw from it. Get it? My conclusions."

Joachim was just describing how Paula tried to block Ferdinand's plan—why didn't he just shut up. Angry and frightened, Titus looked around the café in search of help. Out of here! he thought. He couldn't waste any more time here. He was supposed to meet someone. He wanted to wake up, shake off this strange state he was in. He watched a redheaded woman at the next table, the way she was laughing and at the same time biting her lower lip to contain herself. Her pale knees shimmered through her black stockings. The laces of her shoes were tied in large bows.

Titus saw her putting on those shoes that same morning, tying those large bows. Did she sometimes ask herself what all would happen before she took off her shoes again that evening? Every morning when he leaned over the bathtub to wash his neck and armpits, Titus asked himself whether he would have the courage to declare as Joachim had: I will not join the army.

Titus knew how Petersen's words would spread inside him the moment he was alone. The way a wound first begins to hurt at night, the way a fever needs a couple of hours before it takes hold, that's how those capsules of memory would open up inside him and release Petersen's words, so that like poison they would course through him and paralyze him. He would be lying in his bed again—rigid, stiff with nothing but memory and anticipation.

The woman jiggled her feet as if they had fallen asleep. The pendant on her necklace, a silver square, rested in the hollow beneath her throat. Her hair was brushed back and up at the earlobes, turning her mother-of-pearl earrings into drops dangling from her hair. Her pallor made her look seriously ill.

" 'The great truth of emotion leapt up mightily within him,' " Joachim cried, " 'and burst open the engine within his breast. Freedom towered up in blessed grandeur and shattered his obedience. Never! Never! came the shout within him, an unfamiliar voice of primal strength.' "

How could he say that he thought what Joachim was doing was right and then do the opposite himself? How could he admire Joachim's integrity and then cower and lie? Titus felt that Joachim wanted something from him, that something significant might soon become reality.

Suddenly he saw it all as his fate, as something to which he merely had to give himself over, let it carry and direct him. It lay beyond words, it was a melody deep within all other sounds, one of those moments in which a fragrance is bound forever to a particular place and season.

Joachim fell silent. Titus couldn't think of a single question. "Do you have even the vaguest notion what I'm talking about?" Joachim would respond any second now. Titus stared out the window.

"Aren't you going to eat that?" Joachim held out his empty plate, and Titus shoved his custard torte onto it.

"I have to go," Titus said.

Without looking up, Joachim set to work on the pastry. Titus wanted to turn away again, but he now realized he could watch without feeling a thing. He even tried counting the bites, and was at five when the waitress came up to them.

"For both," he said. She laid her narrow pad on the table. Titus gazed down into her décolletage, where the skin wasn't wrinkled but smooth and white and quivered just a little. Without shifting his glance he groped for his wallet. He opened it—he blushed when he saw what he should have known. The twenty-mark bill was gone. The two volumes of Stefan Zweig had cost him fourteen marks.

"Joachim," Titus queried softly. Joachim went on chewing.

"Help me, God!" Titus whispered. He first fumbled for one-mark coins, then the two half marks. Finally he just dumped his change on the table, including three twenty-pfennig pieces. The waitress bent down again. But this time she was so close to him that he could easily have kissed the tops of her breasts. She set her forefinger to each coin and shoved them one by one over the edge of the table, letting them drop into her open purse. And each time Titus saw that little quiver.

Suddenly it was too late. All he could do was spread his thighs. The waitress smiled, thanked him, and thrust her purse under her apron. Titus wanted more than anything to reach for her hand. It was happening—even though he was looking out the window at traffic thundering over the bridge. He thought his legs and feet would start jerking and that weird noises would rise up in his throat. But in fact he just sat there frozen in place, his breath inaudible. And for a moment he closed his eyes in total bliss.

His grandfather turned to check the wall clock. "Five till eleven!" he repeated in the same voice cracking with outrage. Titus knelt down at the mirror by the coatrack because a double bow was now a knot. "I was at Frau Lapin's," he called out. "I told you that."

His grandfather pulled his watch from his pocket and held it out, "Five till eleven!"

Titus stepped on the heel of one shoe to free a foot from the other. In slippers now, he followed his grandfather to the kitchen, where a teacup was set at his place. As always when his mother was on night shift, the tablecloth hung over the back of the third chair.

"She was painting my portrait," Titus said.

"Oh, that Lapin. All she does is chatter. Eleven o'clock. Does your mother know about this?"

"Yes," Titus said. His plans hadn't included an argument with his grandfather. While still out in the stairwell he had decided he wanted to set out again and wander through the night. He longed for something totally new, something he had never thought of before. His clothes were damp from the rain and he had sweated, but he just had to hold his sleeve up to his nose to take in the smell of oil paints and cigarette smoke lodged there—and for some reason that left him incredibly awake.

"Did you eat?" his grandfather asked.

Titus nodded. The windowpane rattled softly with each gust of wind. And if he couldn't wander the night, then at least he wanted to write in his diary until morning.

After his grandfather had poured tea for them both and taken four cubes of sugar for his, he sat there waiting for his tea to cool. Five, at most ten minutes was all Titus intended to sit with him—that was to be his final concession. After that no power in this world could keep him from pursuing his plans.

His grandfather's liver-spotted hands lay motionless to the right and left of his cup. When he was in a good mood, he would drum his brittle, slightly bluish fingernails to some melody running through his head, usually a march he had heard on Sunday during the one o'clock broadcast of *Merry Musicians* on Deutschlandfunk. Except for a small, shiny mole on his left nostril, his face bore hardly any irregularities. The fan of wrinkles at the outside corners of his eyes was more noticeable on the left. When he came home from the barber it took two weeks before his white brush cut grew back. Since he went for a long walk every day, his face never lost its tan, all year round.

"Anything new?" Titus asked. They both stirred their cups at the same time.

"It was suicide."

"The terrorists?"

"Yes," his grandfather said, and spooned tea into half a lemon that had already been pressed dry, squeezed it again, and rubbed it several times along the rim of his cup. Then his hands returned to the edge of the table.

"And what about you?"

"It was lovely," Titus said, "wonderful!" He was already talking like Gunda Lapin, who had exclaimed each syllable as if propelling a fly-wheel: "Won-der-ful!"

His grandfather didn't like Gunda Lapin or any other visitors, because they merely wasted his daughter's time and drank her coffee. And late one night he had surprised Gunda Lapin at the fridge, stuffing her mouth with ham and drinking beer straight out of a bottle.

Titus wanted to provide his grandfather with five minutes of company. He always had to provide his grandfather company, because he was alone all day, because he ate more slowly and liked to enjoy his tea.

"Well, shall we," said his grandfather, pushing his chair back and wincing as he stood up. "Good night, Titus, my boy."

Titus jumped to his feet. But, teacup in hand, his grandfather had already taken his first steps, so Titus followed him only as far as the kitchen door. "Good night," he said, and could hear the second syllable echoing in the bare entryway. His grandfather didn't like Titus to give him a peck on the cheek. At least, he always squinted one eye and pretended he didn't.

What Titus wanted most was to run after him. How could his grandfather desert him so suddenly? He was close to tears—yes, he would have loved to break into sobs.

Titus no longer understood himself. He wasn't sure if he had remembered the yellow book in his satchel a moment before, or whether it had come to him just as his grandfather stood up.

Titus took the tea egg out of the sink, screwed it open over the garbage pail, banged the two halves together, rinsed them out, and laid them on the dish rack to dry. At the same instant he turned off the light in the kitchen, the lamp in his grandfather's room went out—he always undressed in the dark—leaving Titus to grope for his satchel, which he had left beside the front door. He already had it in hand when he switched the light on again

[Letter of May 10, 1990]
his desk and opened the drawer where he kept his grandmother's fountain pen, unscrewed the cap, and wrote, "Friday, October 31, 1977, 11:34 p.m. till . . ."

As if counting his words, he moved the pen cautiously. Titus wanted to go on writing, pursuing his thoughts, which, if they came too quickly, would have to be jotted down in catchwords on scrap paper. He was delighted by the idea of filling these pages with his even, looping hand, until he had said all he had to say and the blue ink was used up.

Ever since he had boarded the streetcar in Laubegast and lost sight of Gunda Lapin in the dazzle of headlights, he had longed for this moment, when he would merely have to unscrew the cap of the pen and start writing—and in writing learn what had happened to him.

This evening he had understood that he must finally stop running around blind, lacking all feeling, unable to act on his own—someone merely living the life he was served up, an utterly impossible sort of life.

As he sat bent over under the light of the desk lamp, he looked up at his reflection in the windowpanes, where the room seemed as large as some great hall in a villa. The posters behind him shimmered. The only thing outside that found its way into the picture were the red lights outlining the water tower. Titus ducked so he could bring an uneven spot in the windowpane into line with one red light—which unfolded like a blossom.

His pen moved slowly. "Gunda Lapin," he wrote. He set pen to paper again. He had to fight the urge to keep from repeating the same two words, filling a whole line, an entire page with "Gunda Lapin Gunda Lapin."

He wished that everything he wanted to write was already there on the page, so that he could read what he had experienced, beginning with the walk from the streetcar down to the Elbe. With sketched map in hand, he had followed the street, Laubgaster Ufer, with its long row of old suburban homes and garden sheds. From here one could barely make out the opposite low-lying shore, which was hardly built up at all until where the first vault of the steep slope itself began. The rounded crowns of trees were barely higher than the grass, as if their trunks lay inundated and their shadows were reflections in the water. With each step he had come closer to the bend in the river and been able to gaze upriver to the ridge of the Elbe's sandstone mountains, to Lilienstein and Königstein, between which the Elbe meandered under pale blue clouds outlined against the yellowish white light.

The last house before the dockyards—indicated on his sketched map by a woman dancing on its roof and a balloon that read HERE I AM!—lay hidden behind trees and shrubs. He rang and heard a sound, halfway between a squeak and a creak, like planks once nailed together now being pried apart, and then a voice.

From the moment Gunda Lapin had opened the garden gate, she never let him out of her sight. There she stood before him—in her fleece vest, a sweater that was too long for her and that rolled up at the hem all on its own, wide trousers splattered with paint and tapering down to felt shoes—half clown, half ragman.

The path to the house meandered between acacias. It was as if light were scudding before the wind through the foliage. Gunda Lapin had proceeded him with long strides, her key ring dangling like a pail from her hand.

A shiny, well-scrubbed, wooden stairway that spiraled in a hundred-eighty-degree turn led them to the second floor, where they took another set of steep stairs. The kitchen lay to the right, not much bigger than their pantry at home. The sink lay under a dormer window, and the sunlight fell directly on a mountain of plates and cups, guarded by a kind of palisade of forks and spoons. There was nothing remarkable here, and yet he took note of the hodgepodge atop the water heater—a collection that included a Fit bottle, egg shampoo, lipstick, a green deodorant from the West, toothbrush and mug—with a precision and clarity as if he were looking for clues, though he couldn't say to what. Gunda Lapin had been the first adult he had ever visited unaccompanied by his mother. Her quarters consisted of two rooms. It was only because half the dividing wall was missing that they were able to sit across from each other, he on a footstool pulled from under a dainty desk and she on the sofa.

He had been afraid his pants might reveal traces of his accident, although before leaving the Toscana he had stuffed his underpants with toilet paper—a scrap of which he had suddenly discovered lying between his feet on the streetcar.

At the moment she was deep into Kurt Tucholsky, Gunda Lapin had said, and Franz Fühmann. He couldn't understand how anyone would voluntarily bother with textbook authors. His German teacher had said Tucholsky could have been another Heine, and Gunda Lapin had, much to his bewilderment, agreed.

Sitting here at her desk, the disappointment he had felt on entering her studio seemed absurd now—as if a house like this could ever have contained a grand hall flooded with light.

Instead he found himself in a low room with heavily draped windows and a pervasive odor that still clung to him. A carpet of splattered paint had led all the way to the paintings and frames that took up the left half of the space.

He had stepped up onto a little dais to the right of the door and sat down on a dark red settee, its back and arms threadbare, and although it had been the obvious and appropriate thing to do, it had likewise seemed both an honor and an act of presumption on his part. Gunda Lapin had spread a sheet over his legs, placed a bowl of fruit and chocolate on a low stool beside his feet, and taken up her position at an easel ten feet away— any greater distance was an impossibility.

Up to that point it had all been quite clear, with nothing more to his visit worth describing. The garden, the house, the apartment, the studio—all of it a little peculiar and alien and seductive.

And then? Gunda Lapin had stared at him squinting, as if she had discovered something unique about him. He had held up under her gaze, but hadn't dared to reach for the chocolate or take a sip of his coffee.

The easel was positioned almost horizontal before her. Which was why her brushes had been bound to small rods that she held in her hands like magic wands. Instead of a palette she used bowls in which she hastily stirred her paints. This meant, however, that she had to hold the bowl in an outstretched arm so she could dip her brush in it.

Titus saw his reflection in the windowpane, outlined by the triangle of the water tower's red lights. All these superficialities, however, were merely holding him back now, they were irrelevant, a stage set. He wanted to concentrate on the essentials. Besides, he would never forget that studio, every detail remained fixed in his mind's eye.

But why didn't he write about what actually happened? The more precisely he tried to recall it, the more blurred and inexplicable the events seemed.

"Talk to me," Gunda Lapin had said, applying the first brushstrokes to the grayish white canvas. Her lips had grown thin.

"What about?"

"What you're up to, what you're reading, what you've experienced over the last few days, what encounters were important to you."

Should he tell her about school, about Petersen, Joachim? Why did all that send him into a panic?

Gunda Lapin had let out a little groan, as if she could read his mind. The features of her face seemed as sharply defined as in a sketch. Sometimes she squinted, sometimes she peered at him wide-eyed.

"So, that's good," she had declared, "stay . . . stay just like that, very good, very, wonderful, really wonderful."

He hadn't any idea what he was doing right, what had got Gunda Lapin so excited. The more hectic her movements, the more sure of himself he had felt.

And then?

He had told her about Joachim and about Petersen. Of course Petersen had it in for him. Yesterday Petersen had asked him what PMI meant, and, incapable of collecting his own thoughts, he had grabbed on to what a schoolmate had whispered and answered with: "People's Mass Endeavor." And Petersen had said that he was no longer amazed that Titus had got an F in spelling, which he had at first found incredible, a big fat F like that, but which he now understood only too well and which left him highly dubious whether Titus should really be pursuing an academic degree, especially since he wanted to become a German teacher. But of course he was glad to hear that people were "indeavoring" to do good things in their Mass Initiative and they would all now assume that he, Titus, would be their model of an "indeavoring" citizen.

He had had to explain to Gunda Lapin what had been so dreadful about it: less the threat that he would be tossed out of high school at the end of tenth grade than how he had felt so naked and exposed. Of course he didn't want to become a German or history teacher. But he had once said it, back at the start of eighth grade, in order to increase his chances for the academic track, because boys who weren't prepared to become officers could at least become teachers.

But Gunda Lapin didn't react with real outrage until he told her about his cellar conversation, and then she called his teacher a sadist. She had struggled with her brushes as if wrestling with Petersen himself. And later she had said that a person has to build his own separate world. And you either do that as a young person or not at all. And that only the kind of thinking that determines existence is worth anything, and that you need first to find out for yourself what is prohibited and what is allowed.

Like two craftsmen they had sat down to an evening meal of deviled eggs and bread with cottage cheese and marmalade. He had been afraid she would send him home, and so had instantly agreed in relief to sit for her "nude."

[Letter of May 16, 1990]

While he had undressed she had crouched in front of the stove and fed it more briquettes, and then placed her canvas behind him and traced his outline in pencil—and later asked whether he was in love, and wouldn't let him get away with his answer. Maybe meant yes.

"Is it a girl or a boy? Or a woman?"

"Why a boy?"

"Why not?"

"Her name's Bernadette."

The first Sunday in July. He was hurrying up Schröder Strasse where it grew steeper and steeper, with each house set in a little park. He was sweating, and the paper wrapping the roses had long ago gone soggy where he held them. He at least wanted to be on time.

He had met Bernadette at Graf Dancing Academy—Bernadette, who, if she had had a choice, would never have picked him as her partner for the Graduation Ball. But just as he had, she had missed the class where students were asked to chose partners. She hadn't been allowed to turn him down with a flat no, but she had known how to nod without smiling, how to not say a single word while they danced, how to stare blankly out over his shoulder. He had had to ask her for her address twice. Bernadette Böhme, Schröder Strasse 15.

Half the yellow stones on the path leading to the house were cracked, to the left and right were large circular beds of red flowers. The view to the Elbe was blocked by fruit trees. A loud jumble of voices was coming from the open windows.

He recognized her mother right away. She had the same hair, black and smooth and parted in the middle, and wore it just like Bernadette did, falling in a last little curl at her neck without touching her shoulders. And he had first taken her brothers for girls too as they descended the stairs to greet him in the entryway, because their faces were framed by the same black hair and because they all had that same way of abruptly raising their heads to get a better look.

Her mother's friendly manner calmed him down, and having to wait helped as well. She brought him a glass of water and set it on a green coaster in the living room. When she smiled all you saw of her eyes were her lashes. He found it pleasant to sit there alone, he saw it as a vote of confidence. Of all the valuable items placed openly about the room, he was especially attracted to the dark wooden bas-reliefs of nude or semi-nude women. Gazing out the large window to the city in the distance was like looking out of an aquarium. Chaise longues were strewn about the yard, plus sun umbrellas and a grill.

Just when he started to think he was being put to some kind of test—he hadn't touched or picked up anything—her mother stepped into the room again. As if completely transfixed by the inscrutable smile of a Chinese figurine, he didn't turn to look at her. But that made the fragrance of her perfume seem all the more intense.

"Do you like him? He's made of soapstone," she said as she placed the vase of his roses on a long table. The way she opened her old-fashioned lighter and placed the cigarette dead center between her glistening lips reminded him of the way some men drink schnapps from the bottle. She cocked her head to one side to reattach an earring. Her lilac dress left her tanned shoulders bare. The skin was sprinkled deep into her décolletage with freckles. As she tilted her head in the other direction, she asked him to hold her cigarette with its red-smudged filter. At that same moment Bernadette's aunt came in. "Am I interrupting?" she asked, approaching Titus with her hand extended. And one after the other they entered the room to greet him. Even Bernadette's brothers came in to say their hellos. Martin and Marcus kept off to one side, while the adults formed a circle around him.

"Bernadette had her hair done just for you," his mother whispered to him. "Don't say anything to her about it. We rescued what there was to rescue." Out loud, however, she declared it was probably time for a few petits fours. Rising above a flat porcelain serving plate were pale pink, marzipan white, and yellow towers, which you put on your own plate along with a little paper coaster and then divided vertically with your fork. Even the children were masters of the technique. Her mother poured tea. You could choose between red and white china cups as thin as paper or larger shallow bowls decorated with women with pointy breasts and shaved heads.

Bernadette's permanent made her look like she had a bird's nest atop her head. Only her mother continued talking. The boys giggled. Without blushing, he got up and walked toward Bernadette. They shook hands, and the first thing Bernadette said as she turned slightly to one side was, "My father." He entered, taking hurried, short steps.

Titus did not recognize him. At first he looked like Bernadette's father, nothing more, and only when the great Böhme simply introduced himself as "Böhme" was Titus aware of who was standing before him—"Ah," he responded, it just slipped out of him, "Ah." And they all knew what he meant. He almost added that given the address he should have realized, or something of that sort. But he held his tongue, because nothing could have a greater effect that his "Ah."

"What did he say?" Rudolf Böhme asked, and now the two women repeated his "Ah," but without either striking the right tone, so that they both chided and corrected each other, then broke into laughter and measured Titus with glances he didn't know how to interpret. All the same, he tried to hold his own when Bernadette linked her arm in his as if she wanted to claim him for herself, and assuming that the waves of life would simply carry him along, he deserted half a petit four and his bowl of tea.

They were the last couple to arrive at the ball in the Elbe Hotel, to which no one raised an objection—on the contrary. Bernadette's girl-friends had kept two chairs free, so they could take their seats like a bridal couple. They danced with each other—and one of them always knew the right steps.

Later he made the rounds with Bernadette and introduced her to his mother and grandfather. And everyone realized who she was when he said, "Bernadette Böhme." And finally, just as his dance card required, he asked Bernadette's mother to cha-cha with him, but had no success in correcting the way she held her arm.

Bernadette and he came in third in the dance contest—the best of the beginners. But that wasn't the half of it. There was something "magnetic" about them. He meant that literally. They were the pole by which people oriented themselves. Not a word, not a gesture, not a glance that failed to provoke some sort of response from the others. Even Martin, her brother, came over to him. Titus realized by the way Martin corrected the sit of his tie that he was not younger, but quite possibly older than he. "You'll be going to Holy Cross School in September?" Martin asked. "To our school, I mean." The three of them toasted.

Sitting at his desk, Titus recalled how uneasy he had felt when Gunda Lapin pressed him to go on with his story. He had merely remarked that Martin was a Holy Cross boy—in the same grade, but in a different class—and that they had sports in common.

"And Bernadette?"

Titus had looked at Gunda Lapin as if it surprised him to hear that name on her lips.

"Bernadette is in tenth grade."

"Do you run into each other often?"

"No."

"And tomorrow?"

Had he mentioned the invitation? But how else could Gunda Lapin have known about it?

After the ball he and Bernadette said good-bye without arranging another meeting, because it was clear they would see each other over the next few days in any case. While he and his mother and grandfather waited for the streetcar, the Böhmes and their relatives drove past in their cars on their way up to Weisser Hirsch. Summer vacation began that weekend.

Since there was no Rudolf Böhme, Schröder Strasse 15, in the telephone book, he took a streetcar to see her three days later. The place was as deserted as a theater during summer break. Once or twice a week he took the same number 11 to Weisser Hirsch. He stormed the mailbox every day, but not even photographs from the ball ever arrived.

In early August the gate was at last unlocked, and he could once again breathe in the odor of the house. Martin seemed happy to see him. Titus assumed Martin would lead him to Bernadette, and once he was left alone, he expected Martin to knock on Bernadette's door. But Martin returned with nothing more than a pot of lukewarm coffee—Titus, it turned out, was Martin's guest.

Bernadette was in Hungary, with or staying with friends—he didn't quite catch which. He would have loved to see the living room and her parents. Titus drank too much coffee. He emptied one cup after the other, as did Martin, without asking for cream or sugar, without really tasting what he was drinking.

That night he couldn't sleep and had a fever. Maybe Bernadette's letter had got lost in the mail. Did she even have his address?

A couple of days before school began he was received once more by her mother.

[Letter of May 19, 1990]

"How nice to see you, Titus," she cried, and led him into the house, where he had to let her take a good look at him. Did he perhaps have time for afternoon *tea*? She sent him out to the veranda and returned with a table setting. "Bernadette will be so sorry. The girls have gone to Potsdam. Didn't she write you?"

A no would have been impolite, a betrayal of Bernadette, in fact. Besides, it eased his mind to hear her speak of "girls."

"What an attractive woman your mother is," Frau Böhme said. Titus had been on the verge of replying that his mother was almost forty, but then maybe Frau Böhme was even older—and was definitely someone his mother would have called an attractive woman.

"At thirteen, fourteen, children are on their own, it's the end of parental influence—on the contrary, the more you preach the more quickly you lose them." Frau Böhme slid her wicker chair closer to his and poured him tea. There were the same large circular beds of red flowers on this side of the house too.

"Friends are what's important, and so you see, Titus, that's why I'd like you to use your influence on Bernadette. She's doesn't exactly have it easy. But don't say a word of this to my husband, if you please. Rudolf is a problem all to himself."

Titus was dazed. Wasn't she confiding to him something that not even Rudolf Böhme was allowed to know?

Before Rudolf Böhme could step out onto the terrace, Titus stood up and walked toward him, grabbed the hand dangling like a little flag at his side, and looked into eyes closed in deep concentration.

Titus followed the Böhmes' example and scraped butter over his toast and then added dollops of *jam* from glasses that bore no labels. He tried all of them, without ever taking his eye off Rudolf Böhme, who, so it appeared, had never once really looked at him, although his thick lips had never stopped speaking at him the whole time.

Titus marshaled all his powers of attention, every ounce of them, so that he could respond to Rudolf Böhme's words, and now marched bravely ahead, like a soldier in a war of liberation who refuses to be disconcerted by explosions all around him. But at the same time Titus was completely elsewhere. He drank one cup of *tea with milk* after the other and praised each serving of *jam,* although to him it tasted bitter, not sweet at all. And was once again amazed how little was accomplished by will and reason, while pure chance, or whatever you wanted to call this twist of fate, opened doors for him like in a fairy tale.

Finally Rudolf Böhme led him through the house and showed him his collection of paintings. And Titus remarked that this was the real collection of "New Masters," not the one in the Albertinum—a statement that Rudolf Böhme repeated to his wife when the three of them sat down in the kitchen for *Hawaii toast.* Titus stayed until ten and as he rode home at last, he was carrying three books Rudolf Böhme had lent him. That night he threw up. It was his oversensitive stomach, his mother said. He evidently couldn't go see the Böhmes without getting sick.

He didn't see Bernadette again until school started. He avoided her as long as he could, since he felt like a freshman in her presence. He could spot her from afar by the way she tossed her head back and forth. She greeted him then in the cafeteria line, introduced him to a girlfriend as her partner at the Graduation Ball, and asked them both to step in line in front of her.

Each time they crossed paths at school, Bernadette seemed surprised to see him.

To Titus it was as if ever since the ball time had been running in reverse, that he was getting younger, not more mature. And everything he had dreamed of suddenly lay behind him in the fairy-tale world of the past.

He had told Gunda Lapin all about it. He talked on and on without interruption. Why had he suddenly felt certain that everything would change now? How had the change he wanted to describe come about?

"My, you're thirsty," Gunda Lapin had said. No sooner would she fill his glass than he would empty it again. But this time it was only water.

Titus stared at the open page of his diary. He read the day, the date, the time, and the name Gunda Lapin. He finished the sentence he had begun with the words "wasn't wearing a bra." He also completed the top-line entry by noting: "1:16 a.m." Then Titus closed his diary.

3

Titus had wanted to be a half hour or forty-five minutes late—that way people would ask about him as they sat around the table at Martin's birthday party and someone would hold a spot open for him. He couldn't say himself how it had turned into an hour and a half. He was sorry for wasting so much of the time he could have spent at the Böhmes' villa. And now, instead of assuming the role of the mysterious latecomer, he was kicking himself.

He still had the path's cracked yellow stones ahead of him, when Bernadette opened the front door and came out to meet him. She was wearing a sleeveless blouse. Her arms were crossed. They shook hands without saying a word. Her arm had goose bumps all the way to her shoulder.

Titus took in the smell of the house. When he tried to describe it to himself—nuts, fresh laundry, furniture polish, cigarettes, perfume, browned crust, pineapple—there were too many things to keep track of all at once.

"They're all crowded in the kitchen," Bernadette said, and handed him a hanger. A plate of cake in hand, she started up the stairs.

"No big deal," Martin said, laying Titus's present on the windowsill. "No big deal at all." They had just sat down to eat. Bernadette's mother's handshake lasted a long time. Joachim was there, and also the Holy Cross boy he had emerged from the park with the day before. Titus didn't know the three girls. There was coffee and *tea with milk,* petits fours and a homemade plum cake with whipped cream. Joachim's presence disconcerted him, as if his friend prevented him from being the person he had been here before.

Bernadette's mother soon found a spot beside Titus and inquired about his mother and grandfather, whether he had made it nicely through the first weeks in his new school. What he would have liked best was to stay in the kitchen with her.

In Martin's room they were talking about a teacher Titus didn't know, and Joachim then held a lecture on sentimentality in the music of Heinrich Schutz.

The sun was so low that its light struck the clouds from beneath and alongside, lending them a sharp, dark outline. When he finally noticed the two figures out on the lawn, they were too far away.

He recognized Bernadette only from the way she tossed her head. They were holding hands. He almost groaned aloud from the pain the sight of the couple caused him. They had walked across the lawn and were now close to the bushes lining the property on the left. Titus pressed his brow to the windowpane, but they had vanished.

He heard his name. "Like spilled syrup," he said calmly. The light was switched off, the others came to the window. Titus didn't turn around or make room for them either. To the south the sky was green, but blurred then toward the edges, where it turned lilac and then flowed into pastel and then darker blue.

"My senses were reeling," Martin sang, "it went black before my eyes, black and lilac and green." Martin turned the light on and put the Manfred Krug record on. Titus kept a lookout from the corner of one eye, but all he saw was his reflection. Martin, Joachim, and the other guy sang along, even though their voices didn't fit this kind of music. But they had found something to help pass the time until supper. Even Joachim, who normally couldn't do anything but whisper "tonic, dominant, subdominant," until a cut of the Stones or T. Rex was over, growled along in his change-of-voice tenor.

In today's German class, the second class of the day, they had discussed Gorky's *Mother* and literary heroes in general. Their German teacher had called David and Goliath literary heroes too. "As long as she doesn't mess around with the New Testament," Joachim had said during the next break, "she can collect all the literary heroes she wants." To which Titus had responded that people with character were pretty rare in the New Testament.

What had he meant by that?

"When one of the two thieves at the crucifixion suddenly converts—that doesn't sound right to me. The other one," Titus had said, "the one who goes on mocking, is a lot more natural, a much better character."

"Why?"

"He doesn't get anything out of continuing to play the heavy."

"He spits at someone who's worse off than he is."

And when Titus didn't reply, Joachim had laid into him: "The other one knows he's done wrong, but Jesus is innocent. He knows the difference. What do you think makes him better?"

But Titus hadn't had a response to that question either.

"Who told you the other one is better?"

"Nobody," Titus had answered, "nobody," and then suddenly added, "I'm supposed to give a short report on the Bundeswehr as the aggressor, on Monday."

Joachim had looked at him as if expecting something more, but then finally said, "Well just go ahead and give it, give your nice little report."

The girls were sitting huddled together on Martin's bed. The three singers appeared to be occupied with themselves and the record jacket.

The colors had faded from the sky, all that was left was a bright streak, like a crack of light before a door closes.

Why had he been so sure that he had seen Bernadette outside? It might have been her mother and father. Wasn't Bernadette in the next room, eating cake? Yes, he was now convinced he hadn't seen anything out there among the circular flower beds. That took a weight off his shoulders, left him happy.

[Letter of May 24, 1990]

He turned around. They were still singing the same song. "It was at the dance, just yesterday, I saw you in a trance . . ." Was that about him and Bernadette?

Titus sat down with the girls on the bed. He would have loved to bounce around the way they were doing, would have bounced better than any of those three. But he couldn't sing, although he did know the words. "My senses were reeling, it went black before my eyes, black and lilac and green, then I saw gulls, swans, and cranes fly by . . ."

He had never been able to express himself as an instrument of music, whereas these three, though they had surely never spoken about it with one another, did so with self-confidence and conviction. Titus tried at least to be a good audience, and applauded the trio, who showed no signs of quitting now and were so loud that they didn't hear the gong calling them to supper. Marcus, Bernadette's little brother, had made place cards, and Bernadette had turned the napkins into three-tined crowns. Rudolf Böhme lit candles and distributed the candelabra about the room, a task that complemented his short steps. Once the dogs of darkness had been driven from every corner, as Rudolf Böhme put it, he greeted everyone, closed the kitchen door himself, and took up a position behind his chair. "My dear Martin . . ." he began.

Titus smiled. He looked first at Martin and then at the others, one by one. But evidently no one except him thought a speech in honor of the birthday boy was overdoing things.

Titus now fixed his gaze with earnestness on Rudolf Böhme, who spoke with chin held high, eyelids closed, and lashes quivering as if he were dreaming, while his fingers groped along the edge of the table as if finishing the job of smoothing out the tablecloth. By candlelight the siblings revealed their resemblance to one another, and to their mother even more, as if they were all wearing the same wigs. Bernadette had glanced up at the same moment her father mentioned Titus by name.

The speech ended with laughter, because when they reached for their glasses for the toast Rudolf Böhme proposed, they found them empty, and Rudolf Böhme interrupted himself by declaring he knew something was missing.

No sooner had they begun to eat than the ketchup bottle was empty, but for some reason it kept moving around the table, a bit of utter foolishness that reached its high point when finally Rudolf Böhme looked up and innocently asked for the ketchup—and after several futile attempts remarked that evidently they were out of ketchup.

Bernadette sat leaning back in her chair, staring at the rest of her toast. She hadn't joined in the ketchup prank, which was why Titus tried not to laugh too hard.

Martin and Joachim kept on joking around with each other, bringing the rest of the table to silence. As he searched for a question he could pose to Rudolf Böhme, Titus made every effort to put down his knife and fork with as little clatter as possible. He watched Rudolf Böhme bend deep over his plate each time he removed a bite from his fork. The motions of his lips and tongue, as well as the way he gave each mouthful a long, thorough chew, suggested to Titus a kind of reverse speech, as if Rudolf Böhme were now incorporating into his body the words, sentences, and thoughts he would later write or speak.

"What are you working on at the moment, if I may inquire?" Joachim asked.

"He means you, Papa," Bernadette remarked.

"Or would you prefer not to talk about it?"

Titus used the pause to take a deep breath, in and out.

"I'm translating," Rudolf Böhme said as he continued to chew. "I'm pretending I know how. I'm working on it with your Brockmann, Boris Brockmann. He's tremendous, really tremendous, a real translator in fact. I just add the poetical touch afterward."

With the help of some melted cheese, Rudolf Böhme dabbed up the last toast crumbs.

Boris Brockmann, who would be their Latin and Greek teacher from the tenth grade on, looked like Bertolt Brecht and dressed like him too. Titus never ran into him except if he used the corridor on the top floor of the main building. Seated half on the radiator and half on the windowsill, Brockmann always seemed to be waiting for someone to greet him so he could say his own "Good morning!" with such earnestness and precise articulation that Titus actually heard the original good wish contained in the stock phrase.

"Someone should write a big book about translation," Rudolf Böhme said, "from Humboldt to today. If you take a closer look, you soon realize that ultimately translation doesn't exist. And suddenly you're caught in a trap." He meticulously wiped his lips.

"Which is why it always sounds so funny, and quite rightly so, when you ask, 'So what's the author trying to tell us?' " Rudolf Böhme laughed softly to himself, while his tongue brushed across his teeth. "Here's the original, so translate it, and everyone thinks that's just as it should be. What's the problem, if you can arrange them prettily together on the bookshelf? But what does original mean then, there's an original only because someone sits down to grapple with it, otherwise there wouldn't even be an original."

Subjective idealism, Titus thought.

"But if the original isn't the original," Martin asked, "what is it?"

"The original on the bookshelf is nothing more than printed paper," Rudolf Böhme stated. "The moment you open it and start reading, things get complicated."

"Maybe you could give them a hint of what it is you're translating," Bernadette's mother said, after having lit yet another cigarette.

"And there's the problem right off," Rudolf Böhme declared. "The *Bacchae* by Euripides, the *Bacchantes*, *The Possessed*, or *The Frenzied*—or what should I call them? Do you understand?"

"No," Martin said.

"If I say the *Bacchantes*, then I see Jordaens's painting before me, and Bacchus reminds me of Caravaggio, of a Bacchus not feeling so well— and what does that have to do with Dionysus?"

"Then choose a different word," Martin said.

"Which one?"

"Whatever's in the dictionary."

"Whatever's in the dictionary?" Rudolf Böhme asked, closing his eyes. "In the dictionary you'll find: 'bacchic: frenzied, roisterous, bewitched, possessed,' something like that."

"And what fits?"

"Yes, which of them fits?" Rudolf Böhme looked at his plate. "We had a joke in school," he began. "The ancient Greeks didn't know the most important thing of all: that they are the 'ancient Greeks.' Do you understand? Time, which turned the Greeks into the 'ancient Greeks,' keeps bringing to light new meanings the Greeks themselves, of course, knew nothing about, could never have known about, although the words came from them. I see in them something different than you do, and Mama sees something else entirely. And our friend Titus here, he would find some other facet to be of significance. Each person has his own experiences, and so he reads the same sentences very differently."

"Is that true, Titus?" Martin asked.

"Yes, that's true," Titus said in a serious voice.

"Yes, that's true," Martin aped him.

"A text is not a dead thing," Rudolf Böhme continued, "but rather it answers my questions in its own special way, or refuses to answer. There's a voice in there, an encounter, a conversation . . ."

"Wow!" Martin exclaimed. "The witching hour for the bewitched."

Bernadette's mother shook her head and angrily exhaled a puff of smoke.

"He's right, Sophie," Rudolf Böhme remarked before Bernadette's mother could say anything. "Reading is always the witching hour."

"And so what's this bewitched play about?" Titus asked.

"That would just spoil our evening," Bernadette's mother said.

"In any case it was Goethe's favorite tragedy, but it's cruel, it's gray

"And now I've lost my train of thought. Well fine," he said, and placed his forefingers at the edge of the table, flexing them outward like horns. "Dionysus takes on human form—it's important that he's welcomed in human form—and arrives in Thebes in order to bring his cult to the city of his mother, Semele. All Asia worships him by now, only Greece still knows nothing about him. Semele, one of Zeus's lovers, had given in to Hera's whispered suggestion and demanded that Zeus show himself in all his divinity. Zeus appeared as a bolt of lightning that struck and killed Semele. But her sisters, Dionysus's aunts, claim this story was merely invented by Cadmus, Semele's father and the founder of Thebes, in order to preserve the honor of his daughter, and thus of the royal house as well. In truth Zeus struck Semele down because she had bragged that she was pregnant by him. Dionysus doesn't like any of this gossip. That is why, so Dionysus says, he has turned the women of Thebes into frenzied Maenads and driven them off to a nearby heavily wooded mountain, Cithaeron. Dionysus demands the Thebans believe in him . . ."

"Which, as a god, he's allowed to do," Joachim inserted.

"If he were to reveal himself as a god, yes," Rudolf Böhme rejoined. "Pentheus is the ruler of Thebes and a cousin of Dionysus, since his mother Agave is one of Semele's sisters. Cadmus is thus the grandfather of both Pentheus and Dionysus. Pentheus is a god-, or perhaps better"— here he gave Joachim a nod—"gods-fearing man. It is only to Dionysus that he fails to offer sacrifices and prayers. Although to be fair, one should add that Pentheus knows nothing whatever about him."

Bernadette had stood up and, while Rudolf Böhme described the first commentary of the chorus, began to clear the table. Titus stacked the plate of the girl next to him on his own and pushed his chair back.

"No," Bernadette whispered, laying a hand on his shoulder. She picked up the plates and vanished into the kitchen, from where, just as in the theater, a wedge of bright light first struck the table and then went out again. Rudolf Böhme told about the scene where two old men—the blind seer, Teiresias, and Cadmus, the founder of the city, declare their intention to visit the mountains to worship Dionysus. He compared them to two retirees on their way to a disco.

Titus concentrated on his right shoulder, on the spot where Bernadette's hand had touched it. He would rather have helped Bernadette tidy up than have to listen to Rudolf Böhme. Titus could well understand why Pentheus would make fun of Teiresias and Cadmus.

He didn't start paying attention again until her mother declared, "Dionysus afflicts women with *mania,* and Pentheus wants to lock them up behind bolted doors. We should keep that in mind."

"We should keep that in mind," Rudolf Böhme agreed, and remarked on the fine differentiation that Teiresias makes between *kratos,* external force, and *dynamis,* energy and power as an inherent quality.

As he spoke Rudolf Böhme stared at the table. When he did raise his head, his eyes were closed. It was only from close up like this that you could see all the wrinkles that started at the corners of his eyes and spread down like a delicate mesh over his cheeks.

Just as when his mother used to tell him stories, Titus could see it all before him now too. The castle of Pentheus looked like Holy Cross School, Pentheus was a kind of principal or teacher, and Dionysus, or so Rudolf Böhme had claimed, was a hippie, a lady's man, an artist.

"The cult of Dionysus," Rudolf Böhme said, "isn't something that you can simply be told about, you have to become part of it, join in its rituals and abide by its rules—as with any religious faith."

Titus saw Dionysus being locked in the cellar coal bin, there is an earthquake, and the school building collapses. But Dionysus walks out into the courtyard unscathed and boasts of how he has driven Pentheus mad. In the same moment Pentheus comes running up—was it Petersen? Was it the principal? Everything has turned out just as Dionysus predicted. But Petersen doesn't want to hear any of it. He orders the school gate closed and bolted, as if he hadn't already learned how useless such commands are. Joachim points that out to him, but Petersen has had enough of this schoolboy who always wants to have the last word. *"Sophos, sophos sy!"* he shouts. "Wise, wise you are, only never where you should be wise!"

"He's hard of hearing, as my grandpa would put it," Joachim said.

"We can understand Pentheus, and yet we don't understand him either," Rudolf Böhme continued. "Everything he has learned in life so far, all his previous experiences, contradict what he is now going through. We shouldn't expect that, just like that, he can put aside the spectacles through which he has seen the world all his life. On the other hand, it's amazing how blind he is to the changed situation."

In that instant the wedge of light fell on the table again. Bernadette entered with two small bowls and set them on the table. Titus got up and went to the kitchen, following the fragrance of apples and vanilla, picked up two more bowls, and carried them out. Bernadette smiled, her lips moved as if she were about to say something. They passed close by each other twice more. When they were seated at the table again, Bernadette looked at him. Looks are all we need to read someone's mind, Titus thought, and waited for Bernadette to pick up her spoon and start eating—baked apples with vanilla sauce.

"This is marvelous," Rudolf Böhme said, pursing his lips and waving his spoon in the air as if trying to crack an egg. Titus didn't join in the general praise, that seemed silly somehow. Bernadette was silent as well. But it was a cheerful silence that cast even tragedy in its bright light.

"Where's Stefan?" Rudolf Böhme asked as he scraped at what was left in his bowl. Martin evidently hadn't heard the question. He was very intent on his dessert, Titus noted. He had to smile and wanted to let Bernadette see his smile, but at the same moment she remarked, "I'll go check," and looked right past Titus, who was now at a loss where to direct his smile. He shoveled it away, shoveled it full of pieces of apple as if filling a grave with dirt and didn't look up as Bernadette left.

"Her friend is being inducted the day after tomorrow," Rudolf Böhme whispered. "A little like the end of the world for both of them."

When Titus felt Bernadette's mother's hand on his shoulder, he could have broken into sobs. Without turning his head, he gave her the empty bowl, but his voice failed him for even a simple "thank you."

"Would anyone like a cup of *tea*?" Bernadette's mother asked, setting the pewter bowl of rock sugar directly in front of Titus.

"Let me quickly bring this to an end," Rudolf Böhme declared, "or are there seconds?"

He told about a shepherd who had been spying on the women in the mountains. But what he has to report—scenes of perfect harmony between man and nature—is not to Pentheus' liking . . .

Titus could see Stefan in his mind's eye, with his buzzed haircut and a steel helmet on his head. Titus tried to recall the loyalty oath Joachim had written out for him weeks before. He let this Stefan recite the oath, while Bernadette was forced to listen. I swear, Stefan said, faithfully and at all times to serve my fatherland, the German Democratic Republic, and when so ordered by a government of workers and peasants, to protect it against every enemy. I swear I will be prepared at any time to defend Socialism against all enemies and to lay down my life for its victorious cause. Should I ever . . . may I be subjected to the strict punishment of the law . . . and the contempt of all working people.

"The women hurl themselves at the animals, ripping sheep and cows to pieces with their bare hands, tearing them limb from limb as blood spurts and hunks of flesh dangle among the branches, as bones and hooves fly through the air . . ."

Titus enjoyed listening to this part. He didn't wince. Rudolf Böhme didn't have to show him any special consideration.

Joachim said that it had been violence that evoked the women's violence.

"Yes, of course, Pentheus hears only what he wants to hear. Besides—and he offers this as his reason—there is nothing worse than defeat at the hands of women, a disgrace to which Greece cannot be subjected. Suddenly it's no longer about Thebes but about Greece. One must admit that Nietzsche—and those who agree with him—is right in saying that Pentheus does not cut a very good figure here. On the other hand, his reaction is perfectly normal for a ruler. In any case, Dionysus, offended by such stubbornness, warns him yet again not to take up arms against a god."

"Dionysus shows patience," Joachim said.

Titus was disappointed the carnage was over already. Because that's what war was like, horrible, cruel beyond words, and this Stefan would be in the thick of it—he had sworn an oath that he would. And instead of listening to Rudolf Böhme, who was now talking about the tragedy's *peripeteia,* he watched as Bernadette, disgusted by such mealy-mouthed cowardice and blind submission, turned away from her uniformed boyfriend at last.

"Pentheus translates everything he hears into his own language. And because he believes he never receives the right answer to his questions—never realizing he is asking the wrong questions—he will perish. Or to put it succinctly: because he is not willing or able to question himself, he will meet a gruesome end," Rudolf Böhme said. And Titus would have loved to shout: Because he's a coward! Because he doesn't understand what he's doing! Because he doesn't deserve Bernadette!

"Horny old goat," Martin exclaimed.

"Yes, Pentheus is a voyeur," Rudolf Böhme said. "But now we also understand why when others speak of consecration and worship, he sees nothing but lewdness and prurience. Believing he knows himself very well, he also believes he knows what other people are like. And his playing the old goat, as you put it, is really the first and only time he escapes his own obstinacy. Suddenly he reveals qualities he has always fought against and repressed, both within himself and in the state. The horrible thing is that this is precisely what destroys him."

Even as Rudolf Böhme told about how Pentheus disguises himself in women's clothes and slinks off to Cithaeron, afflicted now by Dionysus with *lyssa*, madness, which lacks any of the ambiguity that defines *mania*, Titus realized he had to act, that only in action could he save Bernadette and himself.

" 'Were Pentheus possessed by reason, he would not don the garb of women,' Dionysus says," Rudolf Böhme continued. "And the question is whether in saying this Dionysus hasn't become absurd himself. For from now on every step is a step toward annihilation. Dionysus isn't content to slay his adversary, Pentheus must die at the hand of his own mother."

Titus felt hot, his head was burning. He tried to force himself to listen and not think of everything all at one time. But he couldn't manage it. There were too many worlds, too many dreams, too many lives. He had to make a decision.

Rudolf Böhme spoke as if he had watched with his own eyes as Dionysus bends a pine tree down and sets Pentheus in the crown, then carefully lets the trunk swing back upright. The women see him before he sees them and grab hold of the pine tree and uproot it. Pentheus rips off his women's clothes, pleads with his mother—it is I, your Pentheus, the son whom you bore, have mercy, Mother, do not slay me because of my wrongdoing, for I am your child! His mother, Agave, however, grabs him by his right hand, braces her feet against his body, and rips his shoulder out . . . After the butchery, Pentheus's head ends up in his mother's hands. She fixes it on her thyrsus in place of a pinecone and bears it in triumph into the city. Agave boasts that she was the first to strike this wild beast and to have slain it, and demands that the chorus share in the meal. The chorus refuses in revulsion. Agave pets the calf she believes she has in her hands, scratches the fuzz on its chin. Her son Pentheus, she brags, will praise her for this hunt, for this prey. "And whoever sheds no tears at this," Rudolf Böhme said, "has no tears left to shed."

When a few minutes later they got up from the table, Titus had come to his decision. He stepped over to the large living room window and gazed out at the city. *The spell of arms and voices: the white arms of roads lie*

*before him. And the voices say with them: We are your kinsmen. And the air is
thick with their company as they call to me, their kinsman, making ready to go,
shaking the wings of their exultant and terrible youth.* He had once memorized it, not perfectly but almost.

Titus wanted to talk with Joachim, just with him. Titus was afraid
that they wouldn't be undisturbed on the walk home either. But Joachim
never left Rudolf Böhme's side.

They all gathered at the entry for their coats, and Titus was the first to
say good-bye and step out the front door. He was trembling with impatience. Every second he stood there alone while Joachim kept him waiting threatened to undo his decision. But once he had shared his decision
with Joachim, there would be no turning back. Titus wanted at last to be
different, to be honest, good. He shuddered, as if the decisive moment
would not be the day after tomorrow, at the end of their last class, but
now, right now.

The wind had picked up, the sky was black. In among the trees, streetlights came on, the only light near or far. He heard Rudolf Böhme's
voice, and Martin's. The girls were looking for something. Bernadette's
mother offered to let them stay the night. The girls turned her down.
Rudolf Böhme repeated the invitation. "Come on, come on," Titus whispered. He banged his hands in the pockets of his anorak against his hips,
spun around, and bumped his shoulder harder than he had intended
against the door, which swung open. In amazement they looked at him,
like at some new arrival. Titus smiled. There it was again, the odor of the
house, that fragrance, more befuddling than ever. And as if obeying a
request, Titus stepped back inside.

4

When Titus awoke, his room, flooded with daylight, seemed strange to
him. Next to his alarm clock lay an open book of fairy tales, which he
had read to calm himself down.

In the same way that he sometimes raised his head from the pillow to
check whether his headache was still there, he now began searching for
the decision he had made yesterday. But his "no" to the army had crossed
the no-man's-land of sleep unscathed, it was already a part of him. Titus
felt so strong and certain that he would have loved simply to skip Sunday.

He started doing his push-ups, increasing his goal by two, and at
forty-four got to his feet again, panting and wide awake.

He greeted his grandfather, who was sitting at the radio and winced when Titus kissed his cheek. A place had been set for him at the kitchen table. Only some bread crumbs and the tea egg in the sink indicated that he was late. As he ate a weird feeling came over him, because every object he looked at reminded him of something. And so to his mind the white tiles above the stove—which had had to be set in the middle of the other cloud gray tiles when the position of the stovepipe was shifted—once again looked like a dog dancing on its back legs. His sister used to carry on long conversations with it. The coffee can with its Dutch winterscape, the towel calendar from three years ago with its Black Forest girls, the amoebalike spot on the ceiling—Titus saw them all that morning as if for the first time. He felt like a guest. He enjoyed the sense that things were so remote.

The sections for music, civics, Russian, and gym in his homework notebook were empty, but he figured he would need two hours for math and physics.

Titus was a bit unsettled by his rapid progress. Equations with two unknowns.

[Letter of May 31, 1990]

since it was no longer a matter of grades—as a conscientious objector he would be tossed out after tenth grade in any case—he was slowly getting his footing again. Before he went to work on the physics homework, he made his bed and picked up what was lying on the floor around it: a dictionary of foreign words and phrases, the fairy tales, his alarm clock, two postcards from Greifswald and Stralsund that his sister had sent him, the TV program from the previous week, and the *Sächsische Zeitung*—his grandfather had of late taken to passing it on to him when he was finished reading it. Titus packed his satchel, without touching Petersen's book, and took in the view of an empty desk, except for his physics book and notebook. He opened to page 144. Assignment 62 read: Summarize the life and influence of Isaac Newton. Base this on pp. 33–35 in your textbook. Further recommended reading: Vavilov, S. L., *Isaac Newton* (Berlin, 1951). Assignment 63: Explain the difference between the mass of an object and the gravity of an object.

Titus was feeling strong and clever. He would complete these tasks in nothing flat, just like Joachim. Ten minutes later he stuffed the physics book into his satchel. If he could have, he would have made a sandwich for Monday break then and there—that way he wouldn't have to open his satchel again until he was at school.

Although it was still early, Titus prepared the noonday meal, sliced the sausage into the potato soup and, just as if his mother were home, set the table in the living room, including the bottle of Maggi seasoning, which he placed on a saucer. He didn't want his grandfather to have to do anything when he returned from his walk.

He didn't have to help out around the house. His mother would never have demanded that he peel potatoes or hang up the laundry. He himself would have regarded that as child labor. He didn't know how hard kernels became rice, how raw meat was turned into something edible. Only last summer he had hung a teabag in a glass of cold water. But he would gladly have learned all that rather than have her drill him in declensions, conjugations, reducing equations, solving percentages, punctuating with commas . . . From seventh grade on he had not dared bring home a C on his report card; anything below a C was out of the question. In major subjects it had to be an A, and if he managed that, a B in some minor subject was pure laziness and thus even more unacceptable. He was not to make his abode among the dull and lazy.

Although a Sunday worthy of the name included his mother's being at home, he was glad he wouldn't see her again until everything had been decided. Because in her eyes all his efforts, all the drills, all the worry would have been in vain—the joy at an A pointless, not to mention the concern over a B or the despair over a C. Oh, Mother, he wanted to say, I'm not giving up anything, just the opposite, it's a liberation, a resurrection. I truly have no choice. I had to do it because otherwise everything else would dissolve into nothingness. If truth and falsehood, right and wrong, good and evil, are to have any meaning, then I have to say "no."

He felt as if he could really breathe easy for the first time ever. Wasn't what he was experiencing at this moment the same freedom felt by all those who had been willing to confess the name of Jesus and take up their cross? Wasn't his life just beginning? How could he have lived with himself as a mealy-mouthed coward? How unnecessary all that truckling and kowtowing was.

Titus heard the key turn in the door. He lit the candles and put on a recording of the *Brandenburg Concertos*.

"Your mother wants you to call her," his grandfather said after taking his seat and stirring some Maggi into his soup.

"Did you talk with her?"

"She wants you to call her," his grandfather said.

Titus tried to imagine how his life would be the following Sunday. He couldn't say just how the living room would be any different then from what it was now, except that his mother would be sitting at the table too. But it would be a totally different room.

After the meal Titus rode his bike to the ponds in the woods. He knew every buckle in the asphalt, could have slalomed practically blind-folded around the potholes and little bumps that were like warts left behind by repair work. The thought of that phone call grew more depressing from minute to minute.

Ever since he had started school it had never occurred to him to tell his mother about punches or curses or any sort of humiliation. Because everything that happened to him hurt her twice as much. And now he was going to have to hurt her. He had always been grateful to his mother for not treating him and his sister the way children are usually treated. After his father's death she hadn't expected them to put up with a new husband. Men were crude and expected you to wash up stripped to the waist, like in the army.

The wind tugged at him. Titus now had Klotzsche and Hellerau behind him and, turning off to the right at the end of the village street, began the climb through open country. He stood up, but that didn't help much. It was better to lie flat over the handlebars and pedal for all he was worth.

His mother had grounded him only once, but he found even that completely unacceptable. It had been so embarrassing, he had been ashamed for her. But she had felt much the same way. So first she had sent him shopping, then they had gone to the ice-cream parlor together, and after that he had been allowed to pick out a real man's wallet in a leather shop.

He thought of how he had had to drink scalded milk in kindergarten, how the skin had clung to his lip, and of how in the days before they had a television he and his sister, Annie, would ring the neighbor's doorbell every Sunday afternoon so they could watch *Professor Flimmrich*. In those days he could recognize stairwells and apartments just by their smell. Annie had roused the Beckers, a retired couple, from their midday nap so she could watch *The Snow Queen*. The Beckers had chased her off, only to call her back upstairs a few minutes later. The Beckers offered Annie and him their glittery, silvery armchair. They gave them sweetened gelatin to eat from a wooden pot. From then on he had always asked himself whether, if everything else in life went wrong, he would at least be able to sit in front of a television and eat sweetened gelatin. That idea made the world seem a much less frightening place.

There atop the low hill, with its view across miles of fields, as far as the line of the Moritzburg Forest on the horizon, Titus suddenly realized that his childhood lay behind him.

He picked up speed as he started down the slope. The trick was to take the curve to the left leading to the woodland ponds without braking. If you leaned into the turn just right, so that the asphalt along the shoulder banked in a steep curve, you could feel your body being tugged and steered by the countervailing torque and resistance. The tingle of that moment of joy lasted a long time. If you got the angle wrong, you were thrown out of the curve and dumped into the field.

(Here insert a few more daydreams about his new life and other lovely observations. And how he tries to stop thinking about Bernadette.)

Titus was startled, frightened when he heard the key quickly inserted into the apartment door, and then was startled all the more by his fright . . .

His mother, gray as an eraser.

She had never wept, not in his presence. But her eyes were glistening with tears now. Staring down at the toes of her shoes, she looked weary and thin. Her hands folded across her knees smelled of chloramine.

"Mother," he said. "You're acting as if I'm some sort of criminal."

"You're running straight into their knife, Titus," she said. "So honest and upstanding. But that doesn't change a thing, you're only hurting yourself."

He was glad to hear her say something, anything.

"Someday you'll understand," he said without looking up, and would have loved to add, "and be proud of me." And then he did in fact say it.

"I'm proud of you just as you are, Titus. I couldn't be more proud than I am now."

He still didn't look up. "What's so awful about my getting kicked out of school? Most of the others won't go on to university anyway."

He heard his grandfather's footsteps.

"You're throwing yourself away, Titus, pearls before swine."

Titus received his grandfather with a smile. "Where's your mother?"

"Right here," Titus said, and his grandfather pushed the door open wider.

"Is something wrong?"

Titus shook his head and smiled again. His mother didn't budge, but just stared at the floor until his grandfather left again.

"What are you going to tell them?"

Titus didn't respond. He had already told her. He couldn't repeat it, his words were stuck in the ruts of what had already been said. He heard the radio in the kitchen and felt like he had lived through this scene before.

"Do you think you're going to make a better person of Petersen? Or of your classmates? You'll just embarrass them, make it more difficult for them . . ."

"Am I supposed to lie?" He looked at her now.

"Who said you're supposed to lie?"

Titus sat down now.

"You're supposed to talk about the Bundeswehr, nothing more than that."

[Letter of June 9, 1990]

"But they've got it all wrong."

"What have they got wrong?"

"Aggressor and all the rest of the crap."

"How do you know that?"

"They would never attack us."

"If the Russians didn't have an army, didn't have any rockets . . . do you think the West would nobly refrain from attacking? They didn't even allow an Allende. Think about Vietnam. Just because they drive better cars and have better pantyhose doesn't automatically make them more humane."

"What are you talking about?"

"They'd cash in the whole kit and caboodle."

"I think that the West . . ."

"Would help themselves . . ."

It was as if someone had erased the despair from her face. It was like when they played chess and she let him take back a stupid move. But he didn't want to take anything back.

"You can't be the judge of that," Titus said.

"Imagine we're talking about lightbulbs or cars or anything of that sort."

"Why should I?"

"You don't know any more about those things than I do, do you?"

"He wants me to draw conclusions . . ."

"Everyone has to draw their own conclusions."

"Mama . . ."

What had become of his ideas, of the arguments he wanted to present her with. Why couldn't he convince her? Was it so easy to put him in checkmate? Joachim was right, Gunda Lapin was right, his mother was right, they were all right each in their own way—only he was wrong.

(Or better, set in a telephone booth.)

"He asked if I had settled in okay, how I was doing meeting the challenges of a new class, and then he said that this wasn't some attempt to talk me into enlisting, into hiring me as a mercenary, those days were over, thank God. That wasn't how we did things. But a government of workers and peasants that made it possible for us to get such an education surely ought to be able to demand something in return from those to whom it gave special assistance."

"He was very calm, but stern, calm and stern. He asked why I didn't want peace. I told him that of course I wanted peace. Was I prepared then to defend my homeland with a weapon in hand, or would I just stand aside and watch my family slaughtered before my eyes."

"Then I'll just become a garbage collector. I don't think I'll starve."

" 'Here on our side no one is left to make his decisions all alone,' he said."

"A short report, by Monday."

"I don't know, I really don't. He gave me a book to read . . ."

Then Titus didn't say anything for a long time. It was almost dark now.

"It will just go on like this," he said finally. "Over and over and over."

"Yes," he said then, "yes."

5

Five thirty. Titus saw the drops on the windowpane. He rolled over on his back and listened. Something had awakened him, sort of like when the cat used to jump up on his bed. Everything sounded very close—tires on asphalt, the streetcar, buses on their way up to the airport, trains out on the heath.

Titus squeezed his eyes tight. His heart was making progress, beating fasting, closer to his skin.

Six thirty, seven thirty . . . he counted on his fingers, twelve thirty . . . in seven hours it would be time, in eight hours his life would be different.

He rolled onto his side, doubled the pillow, and pressed his face into it as if he were crying. The front door clicked into its lock. Footsteps on the sidewalk. He wanted to enjoy the next seven minutes, as if it were the middle of the night, kept cutting the remaining time in half so there was always one half left. He tucked up his legs and pulled the covers higher.

Seconds before it rang, Titus reached for the alarm clock and got up. He closed the window, knelt down, and started his push-ups. He shouted the count to himself. As if an officer were standing beside him, each shout was a blow across his back. He didn't stop until forty, he was out of breath, but forced himself to keep going to the point of exhaustion. He could see his distorted face and hear himself gasping for air. At forty-seven he no longer felt the riding crop on his back, forty-eight, forty-nine . . . even after his stomach touched the floor, his arms were still supporting his shoulders. Then he lay there, awaiting his sentence.

Titus was awake now, wonderfully awake. He leapt to his feet like a sprinter from the starting block. He put water on, got the butter from the fridge, and washed at the sink. Seven hours. All he had to do was stick to his opinion. The worst part, yesterday afternoon with his mother, was behind him now. Maybe Petersen would take him to see the principal. Titus smiled while he dried himself.

At seven thirty-five he left the apartment, gym bag in hand, sprinted when he heard the streetcar coming, and leapt onto the last car just as the final bell rang.

The man beside him smelled of cigarettes, shaving lotion, alcohol, and peppermint. Titus pushed his way to the middle of the car, found an opening on the handrail to hang on to. He positioned his satchel and gym bag between his legs.

Hadn't the people around him already agreed to live out their lives with the least expenditure of energy possible, as if saving all their strength for the beyond? Had not one of these people ever received the call of God?

At the Platz der Einheit he had to get off the 7 and cross to catch the 6. At the stoplight his mother was standing directly opposite him. He didn't spot her and was startled when he heard his name spoken so close to his ear.

"Good morning, Titus," she said. They hugged.

"All you have to do is read it to them," she said, and held out the book and some sheets of paper. "Ten minutes, if you read it slowly."

He looked at the pages. The book was in a plastic bag decorated with pictures of coins.

"This is not your decision, Titus," she said. "This is how I want it, and you have to behave accordingly."

Titus looked to one side. It was as if she were grounding him.

"You're fifteen. When you're eighteen, after you've graduated, you can be as much of a conscientious objector as you want."

"Not so loud," Titus whispered. What was she thinking, ambushing him here like this?

"Promise me that!" Titus looked across to the Red Army Monument; the soldier carrying the flag had his other arm drawn back to toss a hand grenade. He was aiming directly at his mother and him.

"You have to promise me!"

"I'll try," Titus said.

"Not just try!" she cried sternly. "This has nothing to do with 'trying.' You will do what I tell you to do. Do you understand, Titus?"

"Mama," he said with a smile. He didn't understand what was happening inside him. Everything was tumbling, it was as if something had broken loose inside him—something pleasant. She had forbidden him. Just like that. Suddenly everything had returned to square one. He tried to suppress his smile, he wanted to gaze at his mother with a suffering look. He couldn't admit defeat without any resistance. He had to challenge her.

"I've made my decision," Titus said. "I'm not going to serve in the army."

"I don't object to that," she said. "Just don't say it now, but when the time comes, before you're drafted."

"Petersen wants to know now. I don't want to lie anymore."

"It isn't your decision, Titus. I want you to read this report. And that's why you're going to read it too. And if he asks you, then you say what you've said all along, eighteen months and not a day longer."

"I'm not going to read lies."

"What do you mean, lies? I've cut out all the foolishness. You tell them about the Nazi generals that they've had and still have, about the names of the bases, the old songs they still bellow, the organizations looking for revenge, and above all about the money. The big companies that profit from it. And if you want to make money selling arms, you need fear and war. Your conscience will be clear, which is true in any case, and as for this . . ." She turned around because a streetcar was pulling in.

"The eleven," he said.

"You'll see," she said.

Even in the open air Titus could smell the chloramine on her hands.

"Was it a slow night?" he asked.

"It was okay," she said. "You've made me a promise." She lifted his chin, he turned his head away. But when he looked at her, he couldn't suppress his smile any longer.

"You promise me you'll read it?"

"Yes," Titus said.

Because their routes took them in opposite directions, they stood opposite each other at the stop like total strangers—until two streetcars crossed in front of them almost simultaneously.

Sanddorn, their music teacher, slammed the door behind him, loped in great bounding strides to the piano, put down the grade book, and shouted, "Friends one and all, take your seats!"

Sanddorn raised the lid, plopped down onto the piano bench, and played a couple of bars, a variation on, "Hark, What Comes Now to Us from Afar," the same song they each had had to sing for him solo a few weeks before.

"We need men," Sanddorn cried, "more men!" And the melody wandered off into the bass voices. Sanddorn opened his grade book, thumbed through a few pages, and propped his forearms on it, so that all the class could see was his large head.

Titus liked Sanddorn, although when he had had to sing solo for him, he sent him back to his seat after the first stanza and to everyone's delight played Titus's warped version of the melody on the piano. But Sanddorn never gave anything lower than a B when you sang for him. Titus was glad the week began with a stress-free hour.

"Mario Gädtke." Sanddorn had read the name from his grade book. He only knew the names of those who sang in the school chorus by heart. Mario had stood up.

"An A in singing, and you're not in the choir?" Mario listed all the things he was involved in and why he couldn't join the choir. Titus wished Sanddorn would ask him something like that—and meantime Mario talked about the chemistry club, the brass ensemble, and judo. What Titus wouldn't have given to be in the choir. They sang the *Christmas Oratorio,* Brahms's *Requiem,* Verdi, Mozart. And they only wore their blue FGY shirts at start-of-the-year ceremonies. When Peter Ullrich was asked to come forward to sing a second time, Titus began to worry that this least dangerous of classes might turn dangerous today. But Sanddorn would never ask him, not him, to come forward again. He would be the last person Sanddorn would test a second time. And in fact Sanddorn now closed the grade book.

"*Haydn Variations!*" he cried, and quoted what Brahms had said about the symphony—that writing a symphony is a matter of life and death—and that Haydn ("How many symphonies did Haydn compose?") was a master at it, Haydn and Mozart, Haydn and Esterházy, Brahms and Haydn.

The record crackled. The music began. Titus leaned back. The motif was obvious.

While he listened to the music, he watched Sanddorn pace back and forth between the piano and the window, his eyes fixed on the floor, his right hand marking each entrance.

Sanddorn's corpulence struck Titus as a provocation—it rendered Sanddorn unacceptable for military service. On the other hand, Sanddorn knew how to carry his weight with such grace that you suspected he would make a good dancer. During breaks between classes it looked like he was promenading up and down in the hallway outside the music room—you couldn't possibly picture Sanddorn in the teachers' lounge—

all the while humming some melody, which the moment he stopped he would write out with his finger on a radiator, a windowsill, or the window itself. He returned every greeting very amiably, bowing with his entire large upper body to faculty and students alike.

Sanddorn, who had stopped by the window, raised a finger to underscore the original motif. Titus would have loved to ask Sanddorn whether he had been in the army and what advice he had to give him.

[Letter of June 21, 1990]

Titus walked to the front. He didn't want to sing, he couldn't sing, Sanddorn had to know how impossible it was for him to be put through this torture a second time. He would have accepted any black mark against him.

Sanddorn first ran the piano through an eerie rumbling prelude, only to follow it with a very spare version of the lines: "And 'cause a man is just a man he needs his grub to eat, dig in!"

"Just sing along," Sanddorn cried, "just join in!" Sanddorn started all over again, nodding to him in encouragement, and Titus sang along. He didn't even hear his classmates laughing, Sanddorn was singing so loud.

But when it came to the "So left, two three, so left, two three," Titus thought he might have to start marching around with Sanddorn, while he and Sanddorn sang, "Find your place, good comrades! Join with us in the Workers Front, 'cause you're working men too!"

The second stanza began and they marched forward together. Titus could hear himself now, he leaned on Sanddorn's voice—or it embraced his own. He knew the words, had memorized them. And Titus instantly cheered up when the "So left, two three" came round again. He sang loudly—and when Sanddorn and the piano fell silent, he sang on alone. But a moment later Sanddorn reentered, and they marched in step to stanza three.

"Wednesday, one thirty p.m., choir!" Sanddorn shouted as Titus returned to his seat. The burst of laughter was worse than ever before. Titus turned to stone, Sanddorn was toying with his most sacred feelings. Titus hated Sanddorn now, that fat reptile at the piano. It was not until Sanddorn exclaimed, "We'll make a real tenor out of him yet," that Titus began to realize what had just happened. Sanddorn entered an A in the grade book.

Titus had to hurry, the bell for the end of class had rung in the middle of the second stanza. But he took his time, because he knew he still had Joachim ahead of him. There he was waiting on the stairs beneath the mural with the eleventh Feuerbach thesis.

"My mother wants me to read it," Titus said quickly.

"What?" Joachim smile.

"About the Bundeswehr, she wrote it."

"Your mother? Your mother wrote it?"

Titus shrugged.

"Your mother is actually a very wise woman," Joachim said, sucked his lips in, and then opened them with a soft pop. "Why isn't she helping you? Why is she making it more difficult for you?" Titus greeted Frau Berlin, who was glancing back and forth between Joachim and him as if she had been eavesdropping.

"Why is she doing this?"

"For my sake," Titus said defiantly, and with two quick steps slipped in front of Joachim to avoid opposing traffic. He couldn't spot Bernadette anywhere. Only when they had reached the broad middle flight did Joachim appear again at his side.

"You don't have it easy."

"She's just afraid," Titus said without turning his head. He had always believed God was gentle and kind, but now he sensed that God could also be stern and demanding.

"There'll be others to help you," Joachim said. "Everyone I've told about your decision is in awe of you."

Titus nodded to Dr. Bartmann, who was leaning at the windowsill directly opposite the classroom door and just as they were leaving the dark middle flight had looked up from his newspaper as if expecting them. Dr. Bartmann was always smiling, except when he talked about the future of socialism—then he turned serious. Dr. Bartmann always wore only light-colored clothes, even the stripes on his shirts were somehow pallid.

"Well, sports fans," he cried. Then the bell rang, and Dr. Bartmann folded up his newspaper.

There was something nonchalant about Dr. Bartmann's "friendship." If someone offered too feeble an answer, he would content himself with mimicking it while drooping his shoulders and bending slightly at the knee, as if on the verge of collapse.

"Is there anything new in the epoch of the transition between capitalism and socialism?" Dr. Bartmann hiked up his trousers, until his belt buckle reached the point where his belly stuck out farthest. "The score, nine to nothing, a whole long day of hoping, and out of the running all the same. And what does our local paper have to say?" Just then the door opened, and Martina Bachmann entered carrying the grade book.

" 'I love discipline,' " Dr. Bartmann declared, " 'though I'm famous for not loving it.' Well, Mademoiselle Bachmann, who said that?"

She laid the grade book on the teacher's desk and without pushing her chair back squeezed into her seat.

"Yevgeny Yevtushenko!" Dr. Bartmann declared. "Haven't read it? 'Soviet Writers on Literature'?" He pulled a narrow newspaper column from his open briefcase and held it up: "Communism cannot be complete without Pushkin, without the murdered poet and without his successor who perhaps has not been born yet. Great poetry is an inalienable part of Communism. Andrei Platonov—and those to whom that name means nothing, should now take note of him."

With the flat of his hand Dr. Bartmann smoothed the column on the open grade book as if it were proof of something and reached again for the newspaper. " '. . . which hurled the Turks (including those in the stands) into the abyss of being resigned to their fate.' " And then: " 'The GDR soccer fan staring at the TV screen found himself in the extraordinary, uncomfortable situation of crossing his fingers for the Turks . . .' "

"Show me," Joachim whispered again. Titus stacked his civics book, report notebook, homework notebook, and pen holder on the desk.

" '. . . the same team that in November 1976 had robbed us in Dresden of that single point that many a fan still mourns, as if it were the cause of all the soccer woes that became a constant companion in the months following and that are the reason why we aren't in Argentina now. Even though on October 29, 1977, things didn't look so awfully bad after our team had pulled it off in Babelsberg, beating the underdog Malta by the same score of 9 to 0, which, when the Austrians managed it, had practically landed them in the realm of unique achievement. I admit . . .' "

Titus slid the notebook with his three-page report across the desk.

" '. . . and tip our caps to our teams for having masterfully passed this test of nerves. But great exceptions are in fact exceptions . . . Over the long haul, the ball doesn't roll along unpredictable paths leading to good or bad fortune. And so he who does not succeed has the duty of asking himself where he has failed or done the right thing. This question will certainly preoccupy the public and those in positions of responsibility in the days and weeks ahead. And one hopes that this will mean that as they stand before the portals of new, great, complex . . .' "

"Balance of terror," Joachim hissed through the left corner of his mouth.

" '. . . cannot yet expect this of our top teams as the second half of the season leading to the Europe Cup begins the day after tomorrow. But let us arm ourselves . . .' "

". . . It's just pure claptrap!"

" '. . . to revitalize ourselves! There's hardly much else left for us at this point.' "

Dr. Bartmann lowered the newspaper. On Wednesday Dynamo would have to defeat Liverpool by at least 4 to 0 to make up for its 5-to-1 defeat earlier in the season. "I wish," Bartmann said, turning the page, "all our problems would be discussed the way Jens Peter writes about soccer. Starting with what he has to say about the Turks . . ." Dr. Bartmann gave a laugh, ". . . the abyss of resigning themselves and such— I tipped my cap right then and, then, my ballpoint started twitching. And then he goes on to call a spade a spade."

Titus watched Joachim fill the margins with questions and exclamation points.

Dr. Bartmann often wrote to *Neues Deutschland* or the *Sächsische Zeitung*. Before the autumn break he had read them aloud a letter in which he had asked how the editors of *Neues Deutschland* could use nicknames when writing about a president of the United States. If they had to use first names—although "Carter" or "President Carter" would be quite sufficient—the correct form was James Earl, not Jimmy. For what could be the reason for using the name Jimmy for a man who represents the most aggressive circles of imperialism and threatens humanity with the most perfidious weapon ever developed, who himself calls the neutron bomb a "fair" bomb? Dr. Bartmann also explained to them why they should use the term German Democratic Republic and not simply GDR. In his class from now on he wanted to hear only the terms German Democratic Republic and FRG.

Titus saw Joachim write "nonsense" in the margin of his report.

Then it was time for the chronicle of the day.

Titus tugged at his notebook, dragging it back along with Joachim's elbow. But Titus had to write now, ten catchwords needed to be added to his notebook.

"Disclosure in New York—with the help of Western countries Israel began developing nuclear weapons over twenty years ago. A crucial role was played by Israeli agents who had acquired fissionable materials from nuclear facilities in the USA. Others involved in these transfers besides the USA included the FRG and France."

"Right," Dr. Bartmann said, "but too long."

"Greed knows no morality. More than 350 corporations in the USA, along with 500 British companies and 400 from the FRG have established offices in South Africa. A quarter of the moneys invested in South Africa comes from abroad."

"Very good. But let's have some new news."

"In Italy mass protests are steadily increasing against the plans of the USA to produce a neutron bomb. On Tuesday thousands of Rome's residents marched in the capital to protest this planned aggressive move, which in terms of world peace would . . ."

"And so on and so forth," Dr. Bartmann exclaimed.

"New wave of rent increases in the FRG. Because of rising construction costs of up to 20 percent rents had to be . . ."

"Something else, something else!"

"More bank robberies in the FRG."

"No!"

"An 8,000-ton freighter has been named in honor of Vasili Shukshin . . ."

"*Nyet, nyet, nyet.*" Dr. Bartmann accepted the impressive strikes in Italy, but rejected torture in Belfast, a new phase of rocket construction in the FRG, the temporary weapons embargo against South Africa, and the poison bomb developed by the U.S. Navy.

It wasn't until the world reaction to the Panama Canal Treaty that Dr. Bartmann nodded and turned around briefly as if checking how many seats were left until Joachim, who the last time had suggested "Record number of visitors for Stolpen Castle"—for which Dr. Bartmann had demanded he supply his reasons. And Joachim had given a brief excursus on historical consciousness and how it shouldn't always be limited to the most recent past, but requires experiences from all epochs, and Dr. Bartmann had let the visitors' record be included.

It wasn't clear who Dr. Bartmann had pointed to; at any rate Joachim said, "Andreas Baader, Gudrun Ensslin, and Jan-Carl Raspe were buried on Thursday, October 27th, in Stuttgart's Dornhalder Cemetery."

Dr. Bartmann smiled. "We covered that topic last week. Is this really so important?" Dr. Bartmann recalled that Lenin had said that the radical Left was the children's disease of communism and did great damage to the cause of the proletariat.

Instead of calling on Titus, Dr. Bartmann was now nodding at Peter Ullrich, who sat at the desk in front of them. Tears welled up in Titus's eyes. He would have loved to have broken into sobs.

Peter Ullrich talked about the underground explosions in Nevada and Great Britain's antitank rockets. It was absurd to break into tears just because Bartmann had passed him over. How could he ever make a decision if he was a wimpy crybaby?

He was afraid of what would happen during the next break, the five minutes until Russian class began. He had said what he wanted to say. If Joachim didn't understand, if he still believed he would listen to him instead of his mother . . .

"First," Dr. Bartmann dictated, "an electronic computer of the EC 1040 series was presented to Havana by Robotron Kombinat. KOSMOS 962 was launched. Second, recruitment of Egyptian scientists by the USA and the states of Western Europe has reached dangerous levels. Seventy percent of such students don't return home."

There were twenty minutes left for regular instruction.

[Letter of June 28, 1990]

Titus opened his notebook at the front and jotted down the date for the second time: Oct. 31, 1977.

Dr. Bartmann wrote 9.1.2. on the blackboard. The nature of cap. society. 9.1.2.1. The nature of cap. exploitation. Followed by two columns, capitalists on the left, the working class on the right.

From there on it was all a matter of who held up his hand. If no one did, Dr. Bartmann provided the answer himself. Joachim's shorthand was so good that he not only kept pace with Bartmann, but even got ahead of him at the end of every passage.

"The goal of capitalist production is the achievement of the highest possible surplus value, that is, profit, by intensified exploitation." A box with the words "appropriated profit," from which two arrows extended right and left. Left: personal use/luxuries; to the right: capital for buying new machinery to constantly generate more surplus value.

"At the risk of his own ruin," Dr. Bartmann declared, "every capitalist is forced to modernize production and do battle with other capitalists. This competitive struggle results in constantly intensified exploitation."

Dr. Bartmann dictated quickly, but as soon as a hand was raised, he would repeat the second half of the sentence. ". . . constantly intensified exploitation. That is the brutal law of capitalism. That brutality results in a) the continued expansion and contraction of the powers of production, b) increased exploitation and destruction of large segments of the peasantry and capitalist entrepreneurs themselves, c) a battle for markets and raw materials, open parenthesis, wars, neocolonialism, close parenthesis."

Dr. Bartmann erased the box of appropriated profit. "That leads to 9.1.2.3. The fundamental contradiction of capitalism, new line, quotation marks: The bourgeoisie has, dot, dot, dot, created more massive and colossal productive forces than all preceding generations, period, end quotation, open parenthesis, Marx, Engels, *Manifesto,* close parenthesis. And now don't write this because it's from our next class and merely for you to mull over." And then Dr. Bartmann wrote on the blackboard without comment: "The contradiction between the soc. nature of production and the priv. appropriation of cap. is the fundamental contradiction of capitalism."

He stepped to one side of the blackboard, pointed with an open hand at what he had written, and said, "This is the source of the antagonistic class dichotomy between the working class and the bourgeoisie." He shouted over the sound of the bell, "The upshot of which is the abolition of capitalist conditions of production—friends, one and all!"

The first students to look up returned the greeting mutedly, as if talking to themselves.

Dr. Bartmann jotted something in the grade book, buried the newspaper clipping in his briefcase, closing it with a click.

"I have a funny feeling," Joachim said, standing beside their desk, waiting, "a very funny feeling."

Titus packed up his things. But when he looked at Joachim he realized that their friendship had only a few hours left. Joachim would say that you can't wash your hands in innocence and that one must be prepared to leave Father and Mother.

Joachim talked as they descended the stairs, went on talking even after they had taken their seats in Russian class, so that Titus had not yet unpacked his stuff when the toxic blonde, as Joachim called Frau Berlin, appeared at the door.

The toxic blonde took her time. The longer the "hullabaloo" and "ruckus" lasted, the more relentless she would be in the hour ahead.

"Zdrastvuitye!" the toxic blonde announced, and the class responded in chorus: *Zdrastvuitye!* They stood there immobilized, no one resumed their seat. The toxic blonde gave them a wink. *"Khorosho, zadityes, poshaluista,* and who was it said you can teach a young dog new tricks. *Vot!"* And after a brief pause while she opened the grade book, she addressed them desk by desk. *"Vy gotovy? Vy gotovy? Vy gotovy?"* Each time she let her chin drop for a second, wagging her head and blinking like a simpleton. Titus had nodded as her gaze shifted in his direction. He thought she had asked him if he was ready for the lesson. But when she followed up with, *"Kto khotchet?"* he felt flushed.

"Uh-oh," Titus whispered, "we forgot about the dialogue."

Peter Ullrich and his benchmate began to reel off the memorized exchange. Joachim shrugged. Of course it was beneath his dignity to have prepared for this. A dialogue was something for students who, like Titus, had already been given a D.

The class laughed. Peter Ullrich was good in Russian; he had spent a few months in Leningrad and liked to show off his cooing pro-nunciation.

"I'll start it," Joachim whispered. And even if he started a hundred times, it wouldn't help him, Titus, one bit. Excuses didn't count unless you offered them up front.

The toxic blonde asked questions and Titus tried to take note of Peter Ullrich's answers. Peter Ullrich was awarded a *"yedinitsa,"* his third, as the toxic blonde herself remarked in surprise, but that was only befitting an officer's candidate. His benchmate likewise received a *yedinitsa*—it was her way of honoring spontaneity, the toxic blonde remarked.

Martina Bachmann at the desk in front of them raised her hand, and the toxic blonde cried, "Behold, a miracle!" Titus was grateful, because there was now a only slim chance they would be called on. Martina Bach-mann wanted to explain why she hadn't been able to prepare the lesson. "Am I supposed to swallow that?" the toxic blonde interrupted.

Titus was hoping she wouldn't allow the excuse and test Martina Bachmann anyway. But the toxic blonde turned away when two students in the second row raised their hands, to which she responded with a "You too?" But they wanted to take their turn and kept up the dialogue so long that the toxic blonde sat down on her desk, crossing her arms, smiling with satisfaction. And when they were finished, she didn't ask them any questions, gave them both an A in the grade book.

That left only his row. Titus didn't know where he should look, and felt how little the last class of the day and his report mattered, if only he could survive this hour in one piece. Then he heard a name, not his and not Joachim's. The toxic blonde had called on Mario, because she thought she would be doing her Mario a favor. Mario shook his head. "I'd rather wait till next time," he said. The toxic blonde smiled. "What a shame," she said. "It's still very easy at this point, I'll expect more the next time." She called on Sabine, and Sabine immediately began, and the Sabine sitting beside her responded, and so it went back and forth between the two Sabines. Each row had now had its victims, and Titus thought he knew what the toxic blonde would say in conclusion: Close the mouths and open the books. Of course she'd say it in Russian.

"Chto?" the toxic blonde squealed. *"Chto?"* Peter Ullrich and a few others laughed. After the next sentence by Sabine number one, Joachim laughed too. Sabine number two replied. The toxic blonde had jumped to her feet. Sabine number one was blushing and attempted a smile. *"Chto?"* the toxic blonde squealed after the next sentence as well.

By the time Titus finally realized that Sabine and Sabine had skipped a line in their memorized text and been exchanging nonsense, Sabine number two was crying. The toxic blonde damned them both to a D, but with the possibility of improving their grades the next time. Now Sabine number one likewise broke into tears.

"Let's go," the toxic blonde said, giving Joachim a nod.

Titus saw Joachim shrug and heard him say, *"Khorosho."* And then he pretended to lift something up onto his desk, reached for an invisible telephone receiver, and moved his finger in circles. He dialed, and when he was finished, leaned back. Titus felt sick to his stomach. Joachim went, "Ring ring." Titus pretended to pick up a receiver too, someone laughed. Titus waited a moment, then he said, *"Allo?"* It was in God's hands now.

"Zdes' govorit, Joachim, zdrastvuitye!"

"Zdes' govorit, Titus, zdrastvuitye." With his right hand to his ear, Titus propped his elbows on the desk and stared down at the surface.

"Fsyo khorosho?"

"Fsyo khorosho," Titus repeated.

"Ya khotchu priglasit tebya . . ." The rest was unintelligible.

"Oh, spasibo," Titus said, and then a word came to mind that he had never spoken before. *"Otlitchno!"* he boomed into the receiver. It came to his lips so perfectly naturally that he repeated it. *"Otlitchno!"*

The toxic blonde erupted in a sharp squeak.

Titus didn't understand Joachim's answer, but he hadn't heard a time of day, and so he simply asked: *"A kogda?"*

Joachim made several suggestions and ended with the question: *"Eto udobno?"*

Titus repeated the words without knowing what they meant: *"Da, eto udobno."*

Joachim went on talking. When it was Titus's turn again he simply said: *"Ponimayu. A chto ty khotchesh?"* That always worked.

"Chto ty khotchu?" Joachim asked.

"Da," Titus quickly replied.

Joachim talked about books, records, theater, and said something about soccer too, which once again evoked laughter.

"Muy idyom f teatr," Titus replied, as if it were up to him to straighten things out.

Joachim followed with another long sentence Titus didn't understand. Titus stuck to his guns: *"Muy idyom f teatr."* Joachim pretended to be upset. Evidently he didn't want to go to the theater. Titus could sense people around him getting ready to laugh.

"Kak ty khotchesh. A ja khotchu kushat tort."

Joachim had to wait a moment for the class to settle down. *"Do zvidaniya,"* Joachim said.

"Fso khorosho?"

"Fso khorosho," Joachim declared.

"Spasibo," Titus said. *"Do zvidaniya."*

They both put their imaginary receivers down at the same time. The toxic blonde said, *"Otlitchno"* and *"spasibo"* and sat back down on her desk. She pointed out two mistakes Joachim had made, praised him for the liveliness of the conversation, and said, giving Titus a wink, that with a little effort one can achieve one's ends even with somewhat limited means. She even said something about acting talent and noted Titus's poker face. As she entered the grades in the grade book her hand made the same motion twice.

What a wretched little creature he was, looking for salvation in a grade, a good grade in Russian. He had pleaded with God for that? And

Joachim, to whom he had lied, to whom he had not yet admitted that he would read the report—that same Joachim had just rescued him. Wasn't that a sign? An unexpected turn of events that he wouldn't have dreamt of in his wildest dreams? Wouldn't God, if He were on his side, have led him just as He had now? Wasn't Joachim his best model? Didn't he want to be like him?

Titus stared at the new vocabulary words they were drilling in chorus. He joined in, but they were meaningless sounds and syllables.

For a moment he dared the thought that, as a reward for his own honesty, God would favor him with abilities like Joachim's. Couldn't he decide all on his own to do what needed to be done?

"Poker face," Joachim whispered when the bell rang. Titus liked hearing the words "poker face" coming from Joachim.

and went "Ring ring." In that same moment Titus felt something icy brush up against him, curdling his blood.

"Ring ring," Joachim went for the second time. Why was he dragging him into this? Titus pretended to pick up a receiver too. *"Allo?"* He didn't know whether the class was laughing at their act or because his voice sounded so pitiful. *"Zdes' govorit Titus, zdrastvuitye."* Titus propped his elbow on the desk, pressed his knuckles to his right cheekbone. He stared at Martina Bachmann's back, at the spot where her hair almost touched the back of her chair.

"Fso khorosho?"

"Fso khorosho," Titus repeated.

"Ya khotchu priglasit tebya . . ." Titus hoped it would all be over soon.

"Spasibo," Titus replied.

Joachim strung sentence after sentence together. Pirouettes, Titus thought. The last of them a question. Titus nodded. He wanted to show: I know, it's my turn now. He had even understood the question. But he couldn't make it work that fast. He wanted to say that of course he accepted the invitation and wanted quickly to finish his homework so he could help Joachim get things ready for the party. He wanted to ask who else was invited besides him and if he should bring anything and whether Joachim had any definite wishes as to his birthday present.

Joachim said: *"Nu?"* and started over again. There was a few laughs. Titus said, *"Da."*

Joachim went on chitchatting. Titus managed one more *"Spasibo."* It made no difference whether he spoke or not. Titus could feel his own hand on his cheek, he could even see himself. Joachim whispered something, but since no one else was speaking they all heard it too. He wasn't going to repeat it. His pride wouldn't let him. Titus heard his shoe tapping the floor.

Joachim talked about books, records, theater, and even mentioned something about soccer. Titus didn't want to say anything more. She should just give him his F and leave him in peace. Her nickname shouldn't be Toxic Blonde, but Band Saw, she had a voice like a band saw. Joachim fell silent.

When the toxic blonde demanded he look her in the eye—those little eyes—he raised his head. He didn't care what was coming from her blurry mouth. "I forgot," he said, only making things worse. Compared to him Martina Bachmann was a hero.

He had had better things to do than memorize this bilge, which he would never use anyway.

Titus saw himself in the bright world where he had lingered yesterday, a world with no place for a toxic blonde.

All the same Titus was surprised when she did in fact give him an F. Why was she still picking on him? You don't kick someone when they're down, he thought. But of course she wouldn't know that. What was he supposed to apologize for? He had forgotten, and for that he'd got his F. He said not a word. The toxic blonde flung her silver ballpoint across the desk, sending it bouncing off somewhere. Someone picked the pen up and brought it forward to her. She didn't say thanks. They opened their books.

How could he have imagined he would get away with it? From one moment to the next he forgot the weekend as if it were a dream. He wouldn't be allowed to stay in school with a D in Russian on his next report card. So graduation was out of the question now. Would God give him a second chance?

It wasn't that he just hadn't studied, he had been wrestling with other problems, with essential questions. Had all that been meaningless?

He was convinced he had deserved this chastisement, as a reminder of what his real intentions were.

The Almighty, Titus thought, can use even someone like the toxic blonde as his instrument.

When the bell rang Titus was afraid the toxic blonde would ask to talk with him. But she paid him no attention. He walked across the courtyard to the other building. The fresh air did him good. He took up a position at the open window in the math room, his knee resting on the radiator. He waited for the warmth to find its way through the fabric.

Titus hoped Petersen would call on him now and not wait until the last class. Petersen began by repeating the story problems to be solved. "Write this down," he said, and let his right forefinger dive headfirst into the void. "A freight train is transporting 730 tons of brown coal briquettes in 38 cars. Some cars carry a load of 15 tons, others of 20. How many of each kind of car are there? Second . . ." Titus heard whispers, could sense the fear that Petersen might spring a pop quiz on them. Instead Petersen let his forefinger make another dive and repeated, "Second. A tank of the National People's Army has traveled 230 kilometers. There are now still 40 liters left in what had been a full tank of fuel. If it could limit its fuel usage to 15 liters per 100 kilometers, the tank would have a deployment radius of 270 kilometers. How large is its fuel tank? How much fuel was used per 100 kilometers? Third! A reconnaissance plane of the NPA . . ." Titus wrote it down. He could do these kinds of problems. Petersen had to leave the classroom for twenty minutes. Peter Ullrich was assigned to keep order.

And the quiet held even after Petersen left the room.

Joachim was done in ten minutes. Titus just in time for Petersen's return.

"I assume," Petersen exclaimed at the door, "that you've already compared solutions. Were there any difficulties?"

No one responded.

His mouth half open, Petersen looked around the room, raised his arm, and asked again, "No difficulties?" and nodded several times in approval. He looked for a good piece of chalk and wrote on the blackboard: "Equations with more than two variables."

Titus began a new page and underlined the title twice. Petersen said he wouldn't spend a lot of time on this, because anyone who knew how to solve equations—and they had just been able to test themselves on that—would have no problems with this. It was only a matter of expanding the framework for setting up the equation. The process was based on a step-by-step reduction of the number of variables one by one.

Five minutes later Petersen put equations on the blackboard and transformed the first one. Titus quickly caught on to how the equation was set up.

It wasn't long before Petersen tossed the chalk onto his desk, stepped up beside the blackboard, and shoved his glasses back into place. Anyone looking skeptically at the equations was in danger of being called to the front.

[Letter of July 4, 1990]

Evidently all it took was mastering a specific principle. Everything else proceeded from that. Titus was amazed that such a long row of numbers could be no mystery.

Petersen didn't assign any homework and ended the class before the bell. On the way to the door he stopped in his tracks. "Did you understand it all, Titus?" he asked. Petersen's fingers wriggled like marionettes beside his pen holder. Titus raised his head, said, yes, smiled, and looked back at his notebook. Petersen's sleeves had slipped down over the backs of his hands. His fingernails drummed on Titus's desktop, a quick rhythm that ended with the words: "That's fine then."

Gym class. Titus pulled on his old uniform. Martin's class arrived late in the basement dressing room. Mario and Peter Ullrich were warming up outside already. In his lumpy gym shorts, Joachim was leaning against the goalpost.

Kampen, their gym teacher, whose gray hair made him look like a snow-speckled Dean Read in *Alaska Kid,* was juggling the ball. After a three-thousand-meter run they would still have twenty minutes to play.

They were a bit late crossing to the public park. Martin and Titus were the last to run the warm-up lap. No one took the high-kick sprint and the ankle and stretching exercises as seriously as they did. Bernadette was sick, Martin said. She'd had a fever of almost 104° on Sunday.

Kampen was waiting at the bottom of the slight rise and repeated what times would earn what grades. Then the whole herd dashed off at a mad pace. Titus let Martin move ahead of him, which left him in last place for the first two hundred meters. It wasn't until they got to the oak tree where they looped around to head back down the long straightaway that they first started passing some of the others. They overtook Joachim right at the starting line. Kampen called out to Titus to stay hot on Martin's heels. "Chase him!" With short strides they took the slope without slowing down.

Titus thought how he could run forever behind Martin Böhme, in the wake of his fluttering hair with its fragrance of shampoo. Titus enjoyed the effortlessness with which they both passed the others. After three rounds they had only Peter Ullrich and Mario ahead of them. But Peter Ullrich would soon buckle like a limp pickle and Mario would give up because of his knees. On the fourth lap they passed them both, and by the fifth they were one lap ahead of Joachim.

"Chase him!" Kampen shouted. Titus was happy. He wasn't going to let himself be shaken off, he'd rather be torn to shreds. He now understood better what the article had meant when it said: Dynamo could deal with Liverpool, but only if every single player tore himself to shreds in the process. Torn to shreds, but still holding on. More and more students and teachers were lining the course now. Another two laps, another eight hundred meters. He would hold on, he'd match any tempo. They kept on passing people, shot past them like arrows. Titus knew every single meter, knew how to place his stride as he took the curves and that it took more effort to round the oak in a somewhat larger arc and still hold your pace. Titus could hear cheering, saw pennants and people bending over the barricades to call out their names. He felt the pain in his lung, but what did that have to do with him? His legs were running, there was no stopping them. Martin Böhme could run as hard as he wanted, he wouldn't get rid of Titus. As they approached Kampen for the last time, they were already heroes: Martin Böhme and him. Titus saw eyes and mouths gaping wide and almost crashed into Martin's back at the oak. Titus didn't need to breathe anymore, that only hampered him. There were backs ahead of him, more backs, he saw Kampen, saw Kampen's astonished face, and heard Bernadette call out his name—it wasn't "Martin!" that she shouted, but "Titus! Titus!"

Suddenly there were no more backs in front of him, and he flew past Kampen and kept on going because he no longer had control of his legs, because they were still running, with him, and he brought his arms down now and looked around and kept on going until finally he could walk and Kampen was beside him, holding the stopwatch under his nose, and Martin was clapping him on the back and congratulating him, Martin with his red and white face.

His breath returned, it was like being stuck with needles. Instead of a lung, he had a pipe inside him, an old water pipe, his whole mouth was rusty, he could even smell it. He wanted to stop it, stop his breathing, stop himself, but his legs kept going, now right, now left, he staggered, and Kampen shouted, "Keep walking, my lad, keep walking!" And Martin said, "Total wipeout."

Titus saw the girls heading toward him, bounding splotches of color, they crossed the street, those same voices he had heard lining the course. They stared at him. But it wasn't admiration in their eyes, it was more like dread, horror, pity, or maybe just incomprehension. Suddenly she was standing in front of him, short, pale, with restive eyes. She stuck her chin out over the collar of her training jacket, which seemed to be in her way. "Here," she said, and unfolded something, a tissue. And since he hesitated, she pressed the tissue to his brow and eyes, a touch that did him infinite good. The tissue stuck to him. He wiped the tatters off and turned around to her, but couldn't spot her among the others. He was holding the soggy clump in his hand.

Joachim made his agonized way up the slope, his elbows pressed against his ribs, his knees glued together. As he shambled along, he turned his heels out, which Titus thought looked effeminate.

Later Titus and Martin were told to choose teams. Titus started. After each had selected seven names, Titus chose Joachim. That left Peter Ullrich among the last few. Martin likewise despised Peter Ullrich, and Titus pointed to a boy with huge nostrils and eyebrows grown together. Peter Ullrich was the last, he went with Martin.

Joachim volunteered to play goalie. "Time for revenge, Martin," Kampen said, and blew his whistle.

It was a poor game. No one wanted to run any more. Joachim had sped ahead of a backward pass, which meant a corner kick, and somehow it ended up a goal. There were too many players for the size of the field and the goals were too narrow. Shortly before the final whistle the ball bounced out into the middle of the field, with no one in control of it for a few moments. Titus was the first to arrive and landed such a lucky kick with the side of his foot that the ball flew into the net. No one cheered. "A shot like a beeline," Kampen said, and whistled the end of the game.

Titus entered the room just as the bell rang, the girls were missing. Petersen called out, "Friends, one and all." On the blackboard he wrote, "Isaac Newton 1643–1727," tossed the chalk on his desk, stuck his hands in his smock pockets, rolled back and forth on his tiptoes, and repeated what was in the textbook about the founder of classical mechanics. To Titus it seemed as if he knew nothing more than what Petersen was telling them at that moment, as if Newton were the first human being that he had ever bothered to take note of. He was still dazed from his goal. How often Titus had dreamt of a shot like that—like a beeline.

When the door opened the first time and a couple of very red-faced girls entered, Petersen didn't react at all. Petersen stared in grim silence at the second bunch, watched them take their seats. The third time he erupted—he wasn't going to take this anymore, the same thing every Monday.

Martina Bachmann, who was the last to slink in, was about to offer an apology. Petersen waved her impatiently to the front of the room, "Come on, come on, come up front!" and presented her with a piece of chalk as if it were a flower. "So you may now proceed, please, proceed." Petersen sat down on an unoccupied desk up front on the left, let his legs dangle. More and more girls offered their excuses. Martina Bachmann was allowed to return to her seat.

When Titus looked up again, Petersen was writing "$F = m \cdot g$" and then "$G = m \cdot g$" on the blackboard. Titus tried to fix in his mind that mass and gravity are different values for a given body and that gravity can't be measured in the same units as mass. "The gravity of a body," Joachim said, "is the force with which it presses vertically on what lies beneath it or pulls at what it is dangling from—that is, mass times acceleration. Which means, G equals mass times nine point eighty-one meters per second per second and is measured either in Newtons or kiloponds." After first making certain that Joachim's book was closed in front of him, Petersen nodded, and then said that they would now move on to the law of inertia. He wrote a couple of equations on the board. Titus was amazed at how calm he was, as if this hour were like any other, where the worst thing that could happen before the bell rang would be a bad grade. Maybe Petersen had forgotten the whole thing by now.

"Unless force is exerted on a body, it will stay in motion," Petersen wrote on the blackboard, and drew a box around it. While Titus was wondering what that meant in his case, Petersen drew a ship, with waves and four arrows, up and down, right and left. Those were the exerted forces: weight and buoyancy, propulsion and the resistance of the water.

The greater the mass of a body, the greater its inertia. Someone giggled. Petersen called out to Peter Ullrich that he would have the chance to apply his newly acquired knowledge.

Titus didn't know if he was sick to his stomach because he was hungry or because he had eaten his sandwich too quickly just now. Or because there was something wrong with his sense of orientation, or because he was experiencing a kind of weightlessness, an emptiness in which you could depend solely on science and its laws, where opinions didn't count. His time in the three thousand meters was an objective reality, and his soccer goal; Newton was real, equations were real.

"Every body," Petersen said, tossing the chalk on the desk, "tends to keep moving ahead in a straight line as long as the sum of all forces exerted on it is zero. Come up here, there's the chalk."

Peter Ullrich kept on writing as if he hadn't noticed Petersen's pointing forefinger, but then suddenly stood up and staggered forward.

"According to the law of inertia," Peterson said, raising his voice, "the ship will move forward in a straight line. Why isn't it at rest?" And with that he left Peter Ullrich all to himself and sat back down on the unoccupied desk on the left. It was so quiet Titus could hear the others breathing.

He imagined himself standing there instead of Peter Ullrich, saw his own glance skitter across the class and fix on Petersen.

"I can't do this report." And corrected himself. "I don't want to do this report."

"Why?" Petersen barked at him.

"Because I'm a conscientious objector," Titus replied.

"What?" Petersen asked. "What does the one have to do with the other?"

"I don't know," Titus said, "I really don't know anymore, I've forgotten."

"Hot air, pure hot air!" Petersen called out to Peter Ullrich. "You've understood nothing, nothing whatever. Why isn't the ship at rest?" Petersen turned to the class. Joachim was the first to raise his hand, then Martina Bachmann.

Titus saw the vacant expression on Peter Ullrich's face as he passed Martina Bachmann and returned to his seat.

I can't go ahead with this, I can't, Titus thought, it's so pointless. And what did a lot of words like that mean anyway? Never before had he been so deeply aware of the nothingness and senselessness of such opinions and claims. It seemed to him he no longer knew what was up or down, and once he was up front, at the teacher's desk, he would be far less certain.

Petersen praised Martina Bachmann for her ability to think concretely about a world of real things. With a laugh that looked more like she was crying and with odd gestures of her shoulders she returned to her seat.

Petersen looked at his watch. "Don't worry, Titus, I haven't forgotten you," he said, and told them that they had used a general law, the basic Newtonian law to derive a special law, the law of inertia. He called this deductive reasoning. "There is, however, a fundamental difference between mathematical statements and physical laws."

[Letter of July 9, 1990]

Was Petersen alluding to him, to the conflict between statements and the law? With every word Petersen spoke, the emptiness inside Titus expanded. It was close to a miracle that the three typed pages lay within reach at the same moment Titus heard his name called. As he stood up he fumbled to check if his shirt tail was hanging out.

He still had time to make a decision. As he took his place at the front of the class he was suddenly aware of his knees. They were trembling, shaking—he had always thought that was just a turn of phrase. He paid it no further attention, because he was visible only from the waist up. Titus was amazed to discover how totally unprepared he was for this ordeal. No one would believe him. All his torments had been pointless, utterly pointless. Each moment erased the previous one. Titus sorted the three pages, he hadn't even managed that—and laid them down in front of him for fear his hands might begin to tremble.

He groped through the first sentence word by word. He exerted all his energies, but just sounds burbled up, sounds outside the human realm, gibberish that provoked giggles, laughter, and snorts. Titus was terrified, they were laughing at him. Except for Joachim and Petersen—they were glowering at him. He choked on each syllable, his tongue performed wondrous feats, but his vocal cords remained out of control. More laughter. Only now did the first sentence start to form.

Petersen bellowed. Titus didn't understand why. It wasn't him, it was the class that was laughing. What fault was that of his?

The class fell silent, went rigid, Joachim tipped his chair back. Petersen was standing in front of Titus, and Titus watched as words distorted Petersen's mouth.

From somewhere far away, like the bell now ringing in the distance, Titus felt an inkling of something that, as it grew clearer and clearer, erased all the tension from his face, revealing the trace of a smile, a very delicate smile. Gradually Titus realized why Petersen was raging like that. And with this realization came another that he had no name for, but that was bright and buoyant and drove the black shadows from his soul.

Petersen was still talking. A dribble of spit reached his chin. Titus put his arms behind his back. His body felt light and relaxed, no effort could exhaust him now. He would sing, he would sing a duet with Maestro Sanddorn. And he would model for Gunda Lapin, listen to her talk, tell her things.

Titus saw the clouds, lopsided in the wind, whitish yellow and a dark blue gray. When he recalled how his knees had shaken, he laughed out loud. He would tell Bernadette about his shaking knees, that would cheer her up. And from the way he would talk about himself and laugh, she would understand what he had come to understand just now.

Titus laid the three pages together, carefully folded them, and, as Petersen now demanded, returned to his seat.

Last Practice

It was long past midnight, but Corporal Türmer couldn't sleep. Bracing himself against the steering wheel, he stared at the thermostat of his APC. The pointer was almost at the red zone. Corporal Türmer asked himself if he would ever have the courage to be a partisan in resistance, an agent, a man rigorously opposed to all wars, who would let the motor of his APC run so hot that its cylinders locked. But each time the pointer crossed into the red, Corporal Türmer would crank open the louvers above the motor. And each time the temperature fell immediately and the pointer went back to vertical.

In the first weeks after induction Corporal Türmer—just Private Türmer back then—had upbraided himself for not finding the soldier's life all that awful. He hadn't had to put up with anything horrible. And as soon as he slid behind the steering wheel of an APC, he was actually happy. He liked driving it. He loved his vehicle, his hippopotamus, for which no road was too steep or sandy and in which he could even swim across the Elbe.

Corporal Türmer couldn't get to sleep. His hands lay folded in his lap, his right foot resting on its heel at the gas pedal, his left leg pulled up— just like always when he was waiting. Most of his year-and-a-half hitch had been spent waiting. But this was his last night of camping out on maneuvers. Tomorrow they would drive back to their regiment—back home, so to speak—and then it was less than two weeks until his discharge. He wasn't surprised that the thought made him feel melancholy. He would have liked to talk with somebody. He loved standing around with the other drivers, smoking and shooting the bull, while the company had to spread out across the fields.

Corporal Türmer stretched. The back of his seat had an indentation on the left side. Other drivers called it the "cripple seat." Corporal

Türmer had grown comfortably used to the driver's seat and over time had helped hollow out the indentation. The backrest had become his backrest, just like the hood of his vehicle was his hood. When all was said and done, he felt cozy in his APC.

Corporal Türmer could hear the breathing of his squad as they lay like one big family on the metal flooring or sat angled on the front bench or wedged on the floor under the first gunner's seat. Fast asleep in the seat beside Corporal Türmer sat noncom Thomas, his squad leader, his helmeted head resting against the wall. If the motor was ruined, it would be his responsibility and he'd be thrown into military prison at Schwedt. Because as a noncom officer, Thomas should have forbidden Corporal Türmer to let the motor run, no matter how the squad might freeze— and in mid-April the nights were still chilly, at least out in the forest. Of a morning the puddles in the ruts were covered with a thin layer of ice. And no driver let his men freeze.

The pointer was in the middle of the red zone. Corporal Türmer's ran his hands down over the steering wheel until they touched just above his lap. He rested his right hand against the center of the steering wheel and almost honked the horn. How often had he had to warn the driver ahead when he drifted off the road. He himself relied on the driver behind him to make sure he didn't drop off to sleep. Because you got hypnotized by gazing for hours at red taillights as your only point of ori- entation. He had hallucinated railroad crossings or dump heaps big as houses—and then let the hatch above him fly open, so that the cold could shake him awake, had cursed himself and slapped his face. All the same, all he wanted was to be a driver. Only drivers watched through endless nights while the others slept, lulled by the rattle and warmth of the engine. Corporal Türmer was amazed, yes, truly touched by how the others had trusted him from the start, as if it were perfectly self-evident that he would steer this dancing, rocking ship safely through the night. That was the origin of every driver's pride. They were like fathers to their families. They, the drivers, were the ones who gave the company its sense of security.

Corporal Türmer didn't have to turn around to look at them. The gentle snore was Private Sommer, the whimper was Corporal Kapaun, a whimper that absolutely refused to match his bearish body and laugh. Private Petka, who had a rumpled face that made him look like a mush- room in his helmet, sometimes laughed in his sleep. No, he would never be able to bring himself to betray them by harming the army. Not because he had sworn it, that would be ridiculous. No, Corporal Türmer was grateful because—whether you wanted to believe it or not—everything had its place in the army. Corporal Türmer had to take a piss. He cranked open the louvers above the motor. Gave the switch a slap, silencing the engine. He pulled on the new boots the staff sergeant had finagled for him. They were a little too big, but only one or two sizes. So it didn't matter.

Corporal Türmer cranked the hatch open above his head and, tucking his boots up on his seat, pushed himself up. With his butt against the edge of the hatch, he pulled his legs up and wriggled out, pressed down on the hatch with his fingertips, and closed it cautiously, slipping the precious square-cut key into his right pants-leg pocket. He groped for the running board and crouched down. He had expected a few lights, at least in the guard tent. He really wanted somebody to smoke with and talk with. And maybe even drink with.

The forest floor silently greeted Corporal Türmer, as if he had jumped down barefoot. The only sounds were the rustle of his uniform and with each step the *slupp slupp, slupp slupp* of the tops of his boots.

The cold forest air was invigorating. Odors drifted toward Corporal Türmer from all sides, rising from the soil, dropping from the branches overhead—he only had to stretch out his hand to grasp the air in all its palpable moistness.

He undid the top buttons of his padded jacket, tugged at the opening of sweater and undershirt with both hands, and let the draft of fresh air rush over his skin. Suddenly he could smell all the stuff his body had stored up inside his winter uniform—mostly cigarette smoke cured in the cold iron atmosphere of the APC, but also the odor of mess kits sticky with splotches of brown gravy and bits of potato.

Corporal Türmer looked for a guard, but found no one. All the same he didn't want to piss right here, where somebody might surprise him. Besides, it was pleasant to walk. The pines weren't too close together. Branches and twigs crackled only rarely under his feet, for the most part his boots just pressed them down into the needle-covered moss. He could see the pale spots where tree trunks had been scraped by the APC's until each vehicle had found its spot—those dozing reptiles, some of which, as if caught up in lively dreams, had left their motors running.

The restricted area was good for the forest. No foresters, no loggers here, and certainly no mushroom hunters. There was nothing here but slow growth and slow dying. Here trees sprouted, grew, lived their decades or maybe an entire century, and then perished again, striking the forest floor with a boom. They were followed by sunlight that awakened the underbrush, caused ferns and shrubs to flourish, weeds by the thousands, until the snow buried it all and a few patches of lichen and moss clinging to fallen tree trunks were the only bits of color. Everything contributed to the rot, everything worked to advance the process of life in the mold at the earth's surface, the humus of all existence. Even the silence here seemed ancient and impenetrable, and the air sated with odors that enervated every waft of wind that struck their heavy curtain.

Corporal Türmer had walked a good distance when he began to feel dizzy. Bracing a hand against a tree trunk he rested as if he had overexerted himself. He was hungry. And above all he was thirsty. Corporal Türmer breathed through his mouth. But some hidden, nameless herb refreshed him and set him back on his path, which had been cleared not by man but by the forest itself. The animals, the moods of the vegetation, would guide him, if only he understood the hints they gave him. He liked the idea of finding his way through the trees, through the night. Only in the dark did the body awaken, only then did it trust the knowledge embedded in its limbs.

Corporal Türmer drifted into an easy jog, moving his arms and shoulders like a skier in a slalom. The joy it gave him was obvious.

As the first light of dawn crept closer, dead branches in the pines stood out like snakes, some of them still coming to a point, but some split, so that their tips looked like bats or the fierce faces of gargoyles. He ran faster and faster, dodging with his head, ducking, avoiding branches like a boxer in training—some of them struck him, however, lashing him awake, driving him forward. Several times he thought he had reached a clearing, but it turned out only to be a bit of fresh growth, or a small pond. The shafts of his boots bumped rhythmically against his shins and calves, *slupp slupp, slupp slupp.* He heard birds. Just now it had been silent and dark, and he the only unsleeping creature. And now the whole forest had evidently awakened.

Corporal Türmer felt needles pricking his bowels. A few more strides and he reached a wide, seemingly endless field. He stepped out of the forest, tossed his padded jacket aside, slipped his suspenders from his shoulders, tugged his pants down, and squatted. He moaned once with pain, then came the release. He tried to recall the last time he had taken a dump. It had been a long time. Corporal Türmer enjoyed feeling himself empty out.

A few moments later, however, the process began to unsettle him. It wouldn't end, and the stench was bestial. Corporal Türmer waddled forward because the pile he created had nudged him like an animal. He looked around as if afraid his shit was following him. Wet grass brushed against his butt.

Corporal Türmer no longer understood how he could have lived such a caged, meager life, penned up with all those others. He shuddered at the idea of returning to the APC.

Even with eyes closed and trusting only his nose, he could have said what all was in that pile. The worst stench came from what he had last eaten, that once-a-month meal when old canned supplies were used up. But the goulash from two days before and the cabbage that had been combined with something that made it taste like car exhaust—it all befouled the silver gray morning. His thighs and knees hurt.

"Dammit! Dammit!" Corporal Türmer shouted. "Dammit!" He had pissed on his pants, and hadn't noticed. He stood up. He didn't even pull his pants up, but tramped on them, until he finally had them off, along with his boots and socks.

He unbuttoned his holster, took the pistol out, flung it in a wide arc, and watched as it vanished soundlessly in the high, wet grass. He didn't want to have anything more to do with the army.

He quickly stripped off all the rest. He was a little chilled, but he likewise enjoyed the way his sphincter had relaxed. Every step was now a blessing that made his gait more supple. The contrails of the jet fighters were already turning reddish, the fresher ones looked like veins in the white of your eye, others were broad and translucent, as if someone had made strokes with a brush.

All he asked for was a little something to drink and a bit of food, but even that wish wasn't of any real significance. Would he even have any wishes in the future? And what would be left as memories? A song maybe, a melody, or not even that? He accepted this—no, it didn't bother him anymore, he didn't give it so much as a thought.

Corporal Türmer scratched his belly. He looked down at himself and glumly, yes, almost disgustedly, examined his cheesy white body strewn with pimples and moles. What a strange odor human beings give off. The cows had stood up and were staring at him. It comforted him that there were living creatures nearby.

He felt an urge to stretch out in the wet grass, to cleanse and refresh his body. Corporal Türmer sank to his knees, let himself fall to one side, and in the next moment felt morning dew along his back. Directly overhead he spotted the pallid moon. Moaning with pleasure, Corporal Türmer rolled onto his belly, and then onto his back again, he scrubbed his shoulders, butt, belly, chest, and pressed his forehead against the ground.

On his back again, he stretched his left arm heavenward and loosened the band of his wristwatch—and the first ray of sunlight struck his fingertips. Corporal Türmer could sense that he was sobbing, and felt his watch fall off.

In the next instant he was on all fours, he shook himself and howled up at the pinkish disk of the moon. He bared his teeth. The cows began to low, turned around, and tried to flee. He wanted to yell something, say something, but all he could manage were growls and whimpers.

Then he froze in place. The only sound came from the cows and the very distant tolling of a village church bell. The wolf sniffed at the wristwatch, skirted the boots and pieces of uniform lying in the grass, and trotted off soundlessly, thirsty, hungry, voracious.

Acknowledgments

I WISH TO THANK THE BERLIN VERLAG, and especially my publisher, Elisabeth Ruge, together with Julia Graf and Fridolin Schley, for all their suggestions and corrections.

Special thanks as well to Silvia Bovenschen for cordial conversations and advice that accompanied the book in its initial and final stages.

I received encouragement and criticism from: Ursula Bode, Christoph Brumme, Jörg Fessmann, Ulf Fischer, Matthias Flügge, Robert Fürst, Ulrike Gärtner, Thomas Geiger, Martin Jankowski, Reinhard John, Simone Kollmorgen, Katja Lange-Müller, Carsten Ludwig, Elena Nährlich, Jutta Penndorf, Sarah Schumann, Lutz Seiler, Elisabeth Türmer, Vera Türmer, Frank Witzel, John Woods, Johann Ziehlke.

I also owe thanks to Mario Gädtke for allowing me to use his personal report, and to Jens Löffler for typesetting the book.

The Joseph Breitbach Prize made it possible for me to work without financial worries. I likewise received generous support from the Berlin Senate Office for Science, Research, and Culture; Deutsches Haus in New York; and the Kulturfonds Foundation.

Above all, however, I want to thank Natalia Bensch and Christa Schulze, to whom this book is dedicated.